The Pack

Pine View County Trilogy
Book One

Lee W. Payne

Published by Rogue Phoenix Press, LLP

ISBN: 978-1-62420-824-9

Cover: Designs by Ms G
Editor: Sherry Derr-Wille

Dedication

For my mom, Elizabeth Payne. You make my life possible. I love you.

Acknowledgments

I would like to thank my nieces Amanda Schneider-Martinez and Alyssa Schneider-Thomasson. They read the first chapter, subsequent chapters as I wrote, and encouraged me to keep writing. The Pack would not have been written without their support. I love both of you more than words can express.

I would also like to thank my friend Keith Boozer and my cousin Judith Rinker-Öhman for reading my novel and offering needed feedback. In a way, they were my first editors. They pointed out mistakes and helped make my novel better.

Katy High School holds a special place in my heart. Not because I was I good student, but because of my teachers, counselor, and vice-principal. Mrs. Joyce Davis was my Health teacher, Mrs. Carol Rogers was my Biology teacher, and Mrs. Sharon Staehli was my English teacher. These three women were my favorite teachers. Even though I failed each of their classes several times, they never gave up on me. They saw potential in me when I didn't. I'm a better person for having them in my life. Mrs. Hilda Burns was my counselor and helped me through some troubling times. Mr. Tom Shields was my vice-principal. I can't begin to count how many swats this man gave me for my constant trouble making. Mr. Ed Pepper was my high school Government teacher. I failed his class, too. That I ended up with a BS, MA, and Ph.D. in Political Science and a Full Professor of Political Science would have seemed very unlikely back in the early- to mid-80s. As tribute, all these wonderful people are characters in this novel. Sadly, Mrs. Staehli, Mrs. Burns, and Mr. Pepper have passed away. They live on in The Pack, though.

Finally, I would like to thank my editor, Ms. Sherry Deer-Wille. I'm well published in academic journals, book chapters, etc. and thought I could transfer this ability to a work of fiction. I was wrong. Sherry gave me a crash course in how to write fiction. I still have a lot to learn, but Sherry put me on the right path. I would like to thank my proofreader, Ms. Amada Armstrong. She took about a thousand edits and made The Pack readable. I would like to thank Ms. Genene Valleau for creating The Pack's cover art. I had a very specific idea of how I wanted it to look, and Genene nailed it. All three are extremely talented and I hope to work with them on the remaining books in this trilogy.

Prologue

A lazy quarter moon hovered over the Gulf of Mexico. High, thin clouds passed in front of the moon, causing its light to flicker off the calm, dark waters below. Small waves broke with milky-green foam and gently lapped at the shores of South Padre Island, Texas. At the far south end of the island, in Isla Blanca Park, a lone figure stood on the beach at the water's edge and looked out across the Gulf at the moon's reflection on the water.

Aside from the sounds of the waves and the soft rustle of wind blowing through the fronds of scattered palm trees, the sounds of partying college students engaged in many acts of debauchery filled the night air. It was Saturday, March 14, 2015, which had been the kick-off week for Spring Break in Texas. Over the next few weeks, tens of thousands of party eager college students would invade the small resort island, hoping to get drunk, get high, and get laid. This created the perfect conditions for an entrepreneurial individual—the demand for drugs had been there, someone needed to provide the supply. Alexis Jordan planned to be that someone.

Spring Break came toward the end of Alexis' second year at Stephen F. Austin State University in Nacogdoches, Texas. She pursued a Bachelor of Science degree in Business Administration. Not that she had an affinity for business, per se, but she lacked interest in anything more focused.

"The important thing," her dad would say, "is that you get a degree."

Those imprinted words shaped Alexis' plan—get a degree. She wasn't a bad student, but she didn't try to be a good student. In the spirit of 'getting a degree,' she put the least amount of effort into that outcome as possible. This resulted in Alexis being a B and C student.

By most measures, Alexis was an attractive young woman. She had long blonde hair and big blue eyes. Alexis was meticulous about health, vegetarian, not vegan, and fitness. She spent more time working out in the recreation center than she did in the library, and it showed. Attractiveness ended at her outward appearance, though.

On the inside, egotistical, vengeful, and uncaring best described Alexis. Since she had money, looks, and a deceivingly good-natured personality, usually when she wanted something from someone, girls wanted to be around her, as well as boys who wanted to be inside her. Even though Alexis didn't lack acquaintances, she was a Tri-Delt, to party with on Thursday nights at the Flashback and Frogs bars, she didn't have any real friends and that suited her just fine. Friends meant caring about someone else and she couldn't be bothered with that.

Alexis had a boyfriend, though. His name was Seth Daniels, and he was in the Theta Chi fraternity. They met at a Greek Mixer in the fall of 2014. It wasn't love at first sight, or even love after six months. He had been attractive—six feet tall, one-hundred eighty-five pounds of finely honed muscles, with dark brown hair and smoky brown eyes. Most importantly, for Alexis' standards in dateable men, he came from a wealthy, Dallas family.

At first, Alexis thought of Seth as nothing more than a living, breathing sex object. When she'd allow him to touch her, she loved making him beg, the sex was satisfactory. He came more than she did, but Alexis was used to this in lovers. She had toys to make up for his 'shortcomings' in bed. Seth also provided a way to supplement her allowance, she willingly let Seth spend money on her. No begging required there. To her surprise, she missed his company over the four-week Winter Break. Despite her predilection not to, she cared for Seth.

They would spend Spring Break apart, too. Alexis begged Seth, which was something she rarely did, to come to South Padre Island with her, but he stood fast on plans to go skiing on Powderhorn Mountain in Colorado with several of his fraternity brothers. This angered Alexis so much she almost broke up with him. She didn't, because she wasn't sure Seth would approve of her entrepreneurial Spring Break plans—he didn't complain about the money his parents 'allowed' him to have. Besides, she would make him pay for choosing a week with his frat brothers skiing, over a week with her in skimpy bikinis on the beach, by withholding sex. After all, she could go longer without sex than he could. If she found herself particularly horny before Seth suffered enough, she'd never had a problem getting boys into bed. If she were feeling vengeful, she'd have sex with one of Seth's ski-buddy frat brothers.

Bros before hos my sweet, tight ass, Alexis thought as Seth kissed her goodbye the last day of class before Spring Break started.

~ * ~

On her way from Stephen F. Austin State University to South Padre Island, Alexis stopped off at her dad's house in Houston for one night. It had been on the way, and she scored 'daughter points' for doing so. The daughter points would pay off in the future in the way of more purchasing power on her dad's credit card. Alexis had another reason for 'dropping by' and spending one night in Houston—her dad's safe.

Her dad, Alex Jordan, was a wealthy man. Not Bill Gates, billionaire rich, but he was worth around fifty million. He made his millions in real estate—rode the housing bubble through 2008 and got out just before the bubble popped. Since that time, he made his money off the misery of others by purchasing underwater, foreclosed properties for pennies on the dollar and reselling them for a nice profit.

Alexis had no compunctions with the way her dad made money. She believed in making money any way she could, short of selling her body. Her dad's millions made her life much easier, too. She drove a silver, 2013, Mercedes-Benz CLS Coupe, her high school graduation present, and had a Chase Visa with a twenty thousand dollar limit her dad paid off each month. He would complain if Alexis spent more than a couple of thousand dollars in a month—he 'allowed' her to spend five-hundred dollars a week, but he kept the limit high 'in case of an emergency.' So, Alexis didn't have a problem with over-spending, often buying jewelry, expensive clothing, and more shoes than she could count in an afternoon. As is often the case with spoiled, rich offspring, enough wasn't enough for Alexis.

Alexis knew her dad kept a 'chunk of change' in his home safe for occasions when he needed quick cash for an evaporating deal. She planned to 'borrow' what she needed, purchase drugs in Mexico, sell them for a nice profit to spring breakers, and replace the money she borrowed from her dad on the way back to Nacogdoches. She even knew the safe combination—the month, day, and year of her birthday, 08081995. It was like he wanted her to borrow the money.

After her dad fell asleep, Alexis went into his home office. She didn't need to sneak—the house was huge, and her dad was sleeping many rooms away. Once inside his office, she pushed the wood panel in the wall behind his desk that concealed the safe, it slid aside. She punched the combination into the keypad and waited. A second or two later, the safe's red light switched to green. Alexis opened it.

Chunk of change, my ass, Alexis thought as she looked at the stacks of bundled cash.

Although tempted to take as much as she could carry, she'd already agreed on an amount with her 'associate' in Brownsville, Texas. She knew she could trust the associate because she had the same arrangement with him the previous Spring Break, but on a much smaller scale—five thousand dollars. That deal netted her three thousand dollars. With the same markup, Alexis stood to net thirty thousand dollars this time.

Using her head, Alexis removed bundles of cash from the back of the safe. When she'd removed the agreed upon fifty thousand dollars, ten thousand for her associate and forty thousand for the Ecstasy, she couldn't tell, at a glance, any cash was missing. Satisfied, she started to close the safe. Just because she could, she took another five-thousand-dollar bundle—her dad would see her Spring Break spending on the credit card statement, and she didn't want him bitching at her if she splurged. He wouldn't see the extra five thousand dollars on the credit card statement, and she would replace it with her profits when she returned. At least, that had been the plan.

Alexis shut the safe and went to sleep with visions of bundled cash dancing through her dreams. In the morning, she kissed her dad goodbye, loaded her heavier by fifty-five thousand dollars bags into the back seat of her CLS Coup, and headed for South Padre Island.

As Alexis pulled into Isla Blanca Park, the clock on her dashboard read two thirty-seven a.m. She was supposed to meet Carlos Garza at two thirty and he wasn't a man who liked to be kept waiting.

Not wanting to call unwanted attention to herself but, also, not wanting to keep Carlos waiting any longer than necessary, Alexis set her cruise-control at five miles over the speed limit and merged south on to the Channel View Loop. When the Loop curved east toward the Gulf of Mexico, Alexis slowed down and looked for the horseshoe offshoot road on the right that would lead to her and Carlos' meeting spot.

After pulling into the offshoot road, Alexis parked her car next to Carlos' crappy, old Chevy pickup. He was still there. She locked her car, and headed across the sand to where Carlos was supposed to be waiting.

~ * ~

Alexis crested a high dune and spotted Carlos standing on the beach looking out at the calm Gulf waters. Alexis stopped well short of the water's edge—she'd dressed for the beach in a black bikini top, white shorts, and black sandals, but they were five-hundred-dollar Fendi Isabel sandals, and she wasn't about to get them wet.

Instead of joining Carlos at the water's edge, Alexis shouted, "Hey, Carlos. Sorry I'm late. Best laid plans and all that shit."

Carlos turned and walked toward Alexis.

When he was close enough to not shout, he said, with a heavy Mexican accent, "Jou make me wait while jou party?"

Alexis laughed. "Cut the Tex-Mex, gang-banger accent shit, Carlos. I wasn't partying. It was a long drive from Houston. I took a nap, and I overslept."

Carlos smiled and, in a perfect Texas drawl with no hint of his Mexican heritage, said, "All right, all right. Ya know, I don't like waitin'. Time is money, *amiga*."

~ * ~

Alexis considered Carlos Garza a bit of an enigma. He looked like the stereotypical gangbanger. His body was covered in tattoos, which included a tear under his left eye. Whether Carlos ever killed someone, which is what that tattoo signified in gangs, Alexis didn't know. He had a hangman's noose around his neck, pistols on his forearms, spider webs on his shoulders with nasty looking black widow spiders with human skulls for heads hanging by a thread of webbing on his biceps, a beautiful wooden cross on his back with the cross member going from shoulder to shoulder, the top going up the back of his neck, and the base going to the small of his back, and an equally beautiful depiction of a praying Virgin Mary that covered his entire chest and stomach. Those were just the tattoos Alexis had seen.

Continuing with the gang-banger theme, Carlos had a shaved head, a long, black, braided goatee that hung to the middle of his chest, and a gold upper grill that twinkled when he smiled. He always dressed in very baggy jeans that were prevented from sliding off his ass by a thick, black, leather belt with his name in silver letters on the back, tight, sleeveless, white, 'wife beater' T-shirts, beautifully engraved silver-tipped, with turquoise inlays, black, cowboy boots, and a very large, black, leather wallet that was attached to his belt by a larger than necessary, chrome-plated chain.

Although Carlos looked like a gangbanger, he chose to remain unaffiliated in the United States. To Carlos, being affiliated meant inviting unwanted attention. His contacts were in Matamoros, Mexico, which was just across the border from Brownsville, Texas, where he was born and raised.

His contact, the *Cartel del Golfo*, the Gulf Cartel or CDG for short, afforded him security and why state-side gang members left him alone. The CDG had been one of the oldest organized crime cartels in Mexico. It started by smuggling alcohol into the United States during Prohibition and shifted to drug trafficking in the 1970's. Carlos used this connection to facilitate drug trafficking in South Texas.

By all outward appearances, and his chosen profession, Carlos appeared to be a poor, uneducated thug who fell into drug trafficking because he didn't have options. This had been where the 'enigma' came into play. Alexis knew the other side of Carlos Garza. He wasn't any of those things. Carlos came from a well-to-do, well-respected, ranching family. His father served six terms in the Texas House of Representatives.

Carlos had a good education, too. He graduated from St. Joseph Academy with honors and received a Bachelor of Science degree in Criminal Justice from Texas A&M Corpus Christi. The irony of Carlos' college degree was not lost on Alexis. Not a victim of circumstance, Carlos trafficked drugs because it was profitable and because he enjoyed doing it.

~ * ~

"Speakin' of money," Carlos continued, "ya got it?"

Alexis nodded. "Yeah. Fifty thousand, like we agreed. Ten K for you and forty for the X."

Carlos stroked his goatee, he did this often. "Okay, *amiga*. This is different than last year. I could do four thousand outta my supply. The guy I found doesn't deal Ecstasy…he's a cocaine dude, but he got what ya needed. Your forty-K will get ya two thousand pills…that's twenty bucks a pop. You should be able to sell 'em for thirty-five or forty bucks a hit. That's decent profit, *chica*."

Alexis grinned. "Yes, it is. How do we do this?"

Carlos stroked his goatee again. "That's the tricky part. Homeland Security and Border Patrol are thick. I got a spot just west of Hidalgo where we can cross. He'll meet us there."

Alexis wasn't exactly eager to cross the Rio Grande River and sneak into Mexico to get the Ecstasy, but Carlos insisted. He said he didn't mind getting 'pinched' with cocaine or marijuana, but his 'street cred' as a drug trafficker would take a serious hit if he were caught smuggling Ecstasy without a 'pretty *puta*' to blame it on. Alexis agreed to go.

Alexis took this information in. "What's your guy's name?"

Carlos smiled; his gold grill sparkled in the moonlight. "His name is Juan Escobar, but he goes by *El Lobo*."

"He goes by The Wolf?"

"Yeah," Carlos laughed, "I hear he's one *loco cabrón*."

Alexis started walking back to her car but, upon hearing this, she turned back to Carlos. "You *hear* he's a crazy bastard? You haven't done business with him before?"

Carlos flashed his gold grill again. "It's cool, *chica*. He comes highly recommended."

Alexis shook her head. "I don't know, Carlos. This sounds like a bad idea."

The smile dropped off Carlos' face, which made him look dangerous. "Don't waste my time, *puta*. Ya back out now, fine. I get my dime, regardless. Now…are we gonna do this or are you gonna drive your sweet ass back to SFA broke?"

Against her better judgment, but not wanting to abandon an opportunity to make thirty thousand quick dollars, Alexis nodded.

The gold grill grin instantly reappeared on Carlos' face. "Don't worry, *chica*, these tattoo *pistolas* aren't the only ones I'm packin'. If the big, bad wolf causes trouble, I'll put 'em down."

As Alexis and Carlos walked back to their vehicles, Carlos said, "Follow me into Hidalgo. You can leave your car at the Walmart and ride with me the rest of the way."

Alexis didn't like the idea of leaving her CLS Coupe at a Walmart or of riding with Carlos in his piece of shit truck. She knew he could afford nicer transportation and didn't understand why he continued to drive the rusty old truck.

"I don't wanna leave my car in a Walmart parkin' lot. Some Mexican might steal it. Can't we go together in my car?"

Carlos grinned at the Mexican remark. "I'm not comin' back here afterward; more business elsewhere. Your car'll be safe at the Walmart. Park it under a light. Besides, your car can't drive where we're goin'."

By the time Carlos had finished explaining why Alexis couldn't bring her car all the way into Mexico, they were back at their vehicles.

Reluctantly, Alexis nodded. "Yeah, okay. But if someone steals my fuckin' car, I'm taking your shitty truck back to South Padre."

Carlos smiled, and moonlight sparkled off his gold grill again. "My shitty truck's worth more than your import, but…okay, *chica.* Ya gotta deal."

Alexis found Carlos' statement more than a little odd, considering his truck was an ancient, rusted pile of shit, but she nodded. They got into their vehicles and headed west for Hidalgo.

Chapter One

A full moon hung bloated and low in the cloudless predawn sky. Its silvery light penetrated the thick East Texas woods and illuminated the fog-blanketed forest floor. The woods were alive with the sounds of critters foraging before the morning sun sent them into hiding for the day. A low, hungry growl brought a hush to the forest and sent the critters scurrying for safety. Another growl, a third, and a fourth joined the first. The pack was hunting.

~ * ~

Russ Lomax climbed into his 1966 International Harvester at four thirty a.m. on Monday, May fifth, as he had most mornings since his beloved wife Alma passed away eight years prior. She went quickly. That had been a blessing. Some abdominal pain followed by a diagnosis of pancreatic cancer. Eleven days later, she was gone.

Before Alma's passing, she had breakfast on the table every morning at five a.m. sharp. Since her passing, Russ made the fourteen-mile pilgrimage from his ranch to the Golden Biscuit in Pine View every morning, except Sundays. On Sundays Russ slept in to six a.m., had toast with coffee, and attended the eight a.m. service at Pine View First Baptist Church, the church where they were married in 1946.

Monday through Saturday Russ ate breakfast at the Golden Biscuit. He always ordered the same breakfast. Two sunny side up eggs, toast with real butter, crispy bacon, crispy hash browns, and black coffee. The food wasn't as good as Alma's home cooking, but the Golden Biscuit provided something Russ needed, companionship.

At five a.m. several 'old timers' who, like Russ, had no one at home to cook their breakfast frequented the Golden Biscuit. The cook, cashier, and servers referred to the morning crowed as the 'Widowers Club,' only not to their faces.

The old timers would talk about the usual things, like the weather, crops, livestock, the weather, the price of seed, fuel, feed, the weather, aches, pains, and, of course, the weather, while they mopped up egg yolks with toast between sips of coffee. After the food, coffee, and conversation were exhausted, they would say their goodbyes, which usually comprised something like, "See ya tomorrow, the good Lord willing," pay their bills, they were notoriously bad tippers, climb into their ancient trucks, and head for home before most folks were out of bed.

~ * ~

Russ turned the key and the old IH coughed and sputtered into life. Like the pack that was hunting only a few miles away, the sound of the old IH, which had several holes in the exhaust system, sent critters scurrying away. Russ spied a raccoon scurry under his house and made a mental note to deal with it when he got back from the Golden Biscuit.

He rummaged through the clutter on the seat beside him until his leathery hands closed on a cassette tape, and he plugged it into the under-dash cassette player he'd installed in the early 1980's. Patsy Cline's velvety smooth voice crackled and hissed out of the RadioShack speakers he'd installed the same day he put the player in. Last, but certainly not least, Russ took a Levi Garrett plug of chewing tobacco out of the chest pocket of his bib-overalls and bit off a chew, which had been getting harder to do with each tooth he lost. He put the IH in gear and drove out of his driveway.

The fog blanketing the forest floor also covered County Road Five Seventeen, which was the only road from Russ' ranch house to Pine View. He depressed the foot switch several times, alternating between low and high beams, trying to decide which provided better light to drive by. Neither seemed to help much.

He reached down and grabbed the coffee can he kept on the floorboard, brought it up under his hairy chin, and deposited a stream of tobacco spit into it. The can was about a third of the way filled with sawdust, which helped keep it upright on the floorboard and, in the event, it tipped over, the sawdust absorbed most of the spit to keep it from making a mess.

As usual, a streamer of spit dribbled down his chin, another side effect of losing teeth. He wiped it away with his shirtsleeve. Years of chewing and dribbling created a permanent brownish stain on the chin hairs of his snow-white bread. Alma hated that brownish stain. Russ referred to it as his 'tobacco dye job.' Alma didn't like that either.

As Russ deposited the makeshift spittoon to the floorboard between his feet, he rounded a left-hand turn leading to a steep downgrade in the road. Before his headlights dipped down with the road grade, he spotted a pair of red eyes glowing in the darkness several hundred yards away, where the road graded upward out of the low spot.

Seeing critters' eyeshine in headlights wasn't uncommon in East Texas, but something about those eyes had the hairs on the back of Russ' neck standing on end. He couldn't ever remember seeing red eyeshine. Greenish? Yes. Whitish? Yes. Yellowish? Yes. Red? No. Even if the critter those eyes belonged to had been at the top of the road rise, they seemed to be too high.

What kind of critter would be that tall? Russ thought.

To Russ, it didn't look like the eyes were reflecting light. It looked like they were projecting light. Like they were glowing. As if some inner fire illuminated them. This really prickled his neck hairs.

All these thoughts crossed Russ' mind in the matter of seconds it took to drive the length of the downgrade. As his truck started up the other side, Russ realized he had been holding his breath. The headlights lit up the fog-covered road before him. There was nothing there. He depressed the foot-controlled high beam switch. Still nothing.

Russ exhaled slowly and thought, *Just seein' things, ya old fool.*

County Road Five Seventeen was basically a foliage tunnel at that point in the road. The thick forest closed in on each side and the tree limbs interlinked above, creating a living, green ceiling. Most mornings Russ loved the way his headlights created a halo effect as they illuminated the foliage tunnel. That morning, the tunnel made him feel uncomfortable. It made him feel trapped.

Movement on the right side of the road caught his attention. Something big and black shifted in the shadows.

Russ had time to think, *Bear*?

A pair of red, burning eyes flashed from the shadows.

Too tall, Russ thought.

Movement to the front drew Russ' eyes back to the road. About a hundred feet in front of his truck, something big and black was emerging from the fog. It was standing up, unfolding as it did. Up on two legs.

"What the hell?" Russ whispered to Patsy Cline.

It was big, too big, at least eight feet tall and broad across the shoulders and chest. It had long, muscular arms that hung down below what looked too much like a human waist to be an animal. Its front paws looked more like hands with straight razors for fingernails.

Bigfoot? Russ thought.

He was close now, too close. Any thoughts of it being a Bigfoot were expelled when the beast raised its head and stared down at Russ. There was no doubt it was looking directly at him.

The glowing red eyes chilled Russ' blood and caused his bladder to let go. Its elongated, hairy snout opened, and Russ saw it was full of long, porcelain daggers.

It's a werewolf, and it's smilin' at me, Russ thought.

In that instant, Russ decided his only chance of survival was to run it over. He smashed his foot down on the accelerator and the IH lurched forward. It wasn't fast, but it was built like a tank. If he could just get the beast under the wheels, he might have a chance.

At that moment, he remembered the second one he saw on the right side of the road. Russ looked right just in time to see the beast slam into the side of his truck. The passenger side window exploded into the cab and showered Russ with broken glass. The heavy IH swerved slightly left but continued forward.

"Fuck you, ya fuckin' mutt." Russ shouted triumphantly.

For a fleeting moment, Russ thought he might actually make it. Then another one hit the driver's side of the IH. Glass shattered into the side of his face, inflicting a dozen minor cuts in his wrinkled flesh. The pain was immediate and intense. The IH swerved slightly to the right but continued forward.

Russ was almost on top of the one in front of him. It stood there defiantly and unconcernedly. Just as the bumper with heavy-duty cattle guard hit it, the beast leapt high into the air and came down heavy on the hood, which crumpled under its substantial weight and the engine died.

That was when the fourth creature landed in the truck's bed and smashed through the back window. Russ felt its long claws dig into his shoulders as it started to drag him through the broken back window.

Before it could, the one on the hood let out a guttural growl that shook the truck, and the one trying to drag Russ through the back window released him immediately. In that instant, two things became perfectly clear to Russ. First, the one on the hood was the pack leader, the alpha. Second, it wanted to be the one to kill him.

The inevitable calmed Russ. He missed Alma dearly, and he

realized he was only seconds away from seeing her beautiful face again. He let the trusty IH coast to a stop in the left-side ditch.

The beast on the hood seemed to understand Russ was surrendering because it made no move to attack. Once the IH stopped moving, it climbed down off the hood. It amazed Russ by how gracefully it moved now that the hunt was over, and its prey had been cornered.

The beast walked on its hind legs around to the driver's side, opened the door with its hand-paw, and stepped back to let Russ exit the truck. As Russ stepped out of the truck, he realized how damn quiet the forest was. Not a single bird, insect, or critter to be heard. Even the beasts, Russ could clearly see the four of them, were silent. The only sound was the rapid 'thump-thump' of Russ' heartbeat hammering in his chest.

He knew the beasts could hear his heartbeat, too. He wondered which one would eat it. He knew it would be the pack leader.

As if reading his thoughts, the beast grabbed Russ by the shoulders, not painfully like the one that smashed through his back window, and effortlessly lifted his six-foot, two-hundred-twenty-pound body from the ground until they were face to...snout.

Russ already pissed himself, but he refused to suffer any more indignity at the hands, paws, of this beast. As Russ stared defiantly back at the beast, he realized his initial thoughts about the eyes were correct. The red glow was internal, like the very fires of hell were burning behind them.

The beast let out a snort that bathed Russ' face in its foul, hot breath.

Hellfire in the belly too, Russ thought.

It raised its snout to the bloated moon and released a demonic howl that rattled Russ to his core. The other three joined in, and Russ suffered his last indignity; his bowels let go. Liquid shit ran down his legs and splattered on the road beneath him.

Russ let out a laugh when he thought about the beasts getting a mouthful of shit while they dined on his scrawny legs. The laugh brought the alpha's attention back to Russ. It sniffed the air, as if just catching the shit stench, and wrinkled its snout. This caused Russ to laugh out loud; a hardy, full-belly laugh. The beast snorted in Russ' face again.

"What are ya waitin' for, ya smelly son of a bitch? I hope ya fuckin' choke."

With that, Russ summoned one last act of defiance. He still had a chaw in his cheek. He bit down on the tobacco, sucked all the juice he could muster out of it, and sent the thick stream of brown spit directly into the beast's left eye. Not a drop landed on his beard. Alma would have been proud.

It flinched back, shook its head violently, and let out a yelp.

"Burns, don't it *bitch.*"

The pain Russ felt next was like nothing he'd experienced before. The beast's finger-claws dug into his back and its thumb-claws punctured his chest. It squeezed him together with vice-like strength. Russ heard his old bones crunching and felt his ribs snap as the beast compressed him like a human accordion.

Blood poured out of his mouth. He would have choked, but he couldn't breathe for the pressure in his chest. Just when he thought his heart would explode and put him out of his misery, the beast stopped squeezing him. It was playing with him.

It opened its gaping mouth, turned its head to the side, and slipped its deadly jaws around Russ' neck. When its hot tongue snaked around Russ' neck, he vomited. Blood, bile, and the chaw of tobacco erupted from his mouth.

The beast bit down, but not quickly. Russ felt the long, dagger teeth sink slowly into his flesh. Deeper into his flesh and his larynx collapsed. He struggled to breathe. He felt the long canines scrape against the vertebra in his neck. A severed artery in his neck sent white spots flashing over his vision. He couldn't breathe. The canines crunched into his spine. His body went limp, and he lost all feeling as his spinal cord was severed.

Russ thought, *I'm comin' to see ya, darlin'.*

His body separated from his head, falling to the shit, blood, and vomit-splattered road. He thought no more.

~ * ~

The pack wasn't interested in eating him, except his heart. The alpha woofed down whole. It had been the hunt they craved. Russ hurt the pack leader when he spit in its eye. Pain wasn't something it was used to, especially in wolf form. Russ had to pay for that, pay beyond death.

The pack didn't just shred Russ' body, they eviscerated it. Razor sharp claws tore flesh and underlying shriveled muscles from bones. A brutal swipe across his belly sent Russ' blueish-gray intestines spilling onto the ground in a gush of blood. Organs were ripped from chest cavity. Powerful jaws snapped bones like twigs. Razor sharp clawed hands ripped arms and legs from his torso. Every part of Russ' body was rendered unrecognizable as being human remains, except his head. This had been left on the IH's crumpled hood like a grotesque hood ornament.

When the pack finished destroying their prey, each member urinated on the bloody pile of flesh and bone that had once been Russ Lomax. As a final act of degradation, the pack leader defecated on the remains.

Dawn was coming. The pack let out a last howl and dissolved into the foggy forest. Pine View County would awake to a very different world that morning. A horrifying world and the horrors were just starting.

Chapter Two

A sound pulled Sheriff Garrett Lambert from a deep sleep. It had been one of those times when dreams and reality meld. It is difficult to tell where one ends, and the other begins. In the dream, he heard a train whistle blowing. As he awoke, he thought it sounded more like a howl.

He rolled his head and looked at the clock on the nightstand, four forty-three a.m. glowed blue in his dark bedroom. He had a little over an hour before it was time to get up and go to work. Being sheriff, he worked regular hours. Unless something bad happened. Garrett wouldn't be working regular hours in the foreseeable future.

Garrett closed his eyes to grab that last hour of sleep when the howls, came again. A chill ran up his spine.

Although he tried to go back to sleep, he couldn't shake the chill the howls gave him. They were eerily similar to a howl that haunted him in a recurring nightmare. The first time he had the nightmare happened fourteen years ago. Then, about once a year, it would claw, that was the right word, its way back into his subconscious and he'd be forced to relive the horror all over again.

It had been easy for Garrett to track the time of the nightmares because Paige, his daughter, was always in it and her age in the nightmare changed with her actual age. She had been a year older each time he experienced it. The first nightmare happened shortly after Paige turned two and shortly after she turned fifteen the last time. Garrett shuddered as he realized Paige recently turned sixteen, which meant he could expect a nocturnal visit from his tortured subconscious soon.

Thoughts of the nightmare, as well as the howl that pulled him from a deep sleep, gnawed at his nerves. After several looks at the clock to check how much sleep time he had left, he abandoned the idea of getting a little more sleep.

He sat up and swung his feet onto the carpeted floor. Remembering a line from an old movie, *Die Hard*, he sat there for several seconds making fists with his toes in the carpet.

Garrett chuckled. "That actually feels pretty damn good."

He grabbed the pack of Marlboro Reds, called Cowboy Killers by one of his deputies, and lighter off the nightstand. He pulled a cigarette from the pack, tapped the tobacco end absently against the pack twice, stuck it between his lips, lit it, and took a deep draw. Instant relief coursed through his body. He hated loving smoking.

After a few more deep draws, the jitters brought on by the howls subsided. He stood up, stretched, and made his way to the bathroom. He emptied his bladder and shook twice.

"Shake it more than twice and you're playin' with it," his dad, who was full of colorful sayings, said often.

Garrett flushed, went to the sink, planted his hands on the counter, and looked into the mirror. He needed a shave. He didn't enjoy shaving but drug a razor across his face every other day or three to keep up appearances.

Can't have the sheriff looking like a vagrant, he thought.

He considered his reflection a little longer. His brown hair was thinning, but not to the point of needing to shave his head. Considering his aversion to shaving, it would probably never get thin enough to warrant such drastic measures. He kept it short though, number two setting on his trimmer. His hair was graying around the temples, but, as Paige put it, the gray made him look distinguished. He thought Paige was just being kind, but he'd take it.

After taking in his face in the mirror, his eyes wondered down to his chest and stomach. He was in pretty good shape for a thirty-four-year-old guy with a desk job. He would not win a body-building competition, but his love-handles were manageable, and he hadn't developed the dreaded man-boobs some of his high school buddies were sporting. Garrett was six foot two inches tall and just a smidge, fifteen pounds, over his high school football playing weight of one hundred eighty-five pounds.

Not too bad, Garrett thought.

Considering how events unfolded after he graduated high school, 'not too bad' applied, not only to his reflection, but his life.

~ * ~

In high school, Garrett had been charismatic, sanguine, and personable. Everybody's friend and quite the chick-magnet. He had been athletic, too. Garrett was the starting quarterback for the Pine View High Woodpeckers. The Woodpeckers were 1998, A-1 conference state champions Garrett's senior year.

With eight seconds left, and down by four points, Garrett took a QB option eighty-one yards into the end zone to score the winning touchdown. Coach Shields named Garrett MVP and gave him the game winning all, which was displayed on a shelf in Garrett's office. Folks who knew him then, when visiting his office, would pick up the game-ball and reminisce about the eighty-one-yard scramble that made Pine View High School, A-1 state champs for the first time in school history. Garrett enjoyed the accolades.

Pine View High School was small, but some college recruiters took notice. They offered him a football scholarship to Blinn Junior College. If successful at Blinn, he could transfer to Texas A&M. Garrett couldn't wait to get out of Pine View.

"Small towns breed small dreams," was another of his dad's sayings.

Dreams, even small ones, too often die.

The summer between graduating high school, class of 1999, and leaving for college brought monumental, life-altering changes to Garrett's world. Lacy Little, his girlfriend for all of four months, announced she was pregnant. Everything in him wanted to leave, but he couldn't. He did the 'right' thing and proposed. They got hitched before she was showing and Garrett went to work logging, which was the fallback profession for folks in Pine View who wanted to earn more than minimum wage.

Garrett's folks owned one hundred and eighty-eight wooded acres just south of Pine View. When Garrett told them Lacy was expecting and he intended to marry her, they gifted him a five-acre track on the east side of their property off County Road Five Eighty-Eight. Garrett cleared a pad, secured power, and septic, drilled a water well, and went into debt for the first time in his life when he bought a brand-new, single-wide mobile home. He and Lacy moved into it the night of their wedding. Things were moving fast.

Marriage was great for a couple of months. Lacy looked good, damn good, and they had non-stop sex. They enjoyed sex in the morning, sex when Garrett could come home for lunch, sex when he got home from work, and sex when they went to sleep. Those were good days for Garrett.

As Lacy's belly swelled, she lost interest in sex.

She always had an excuse. "I'm too tired," "I don't feel well," "I'm too fat," "My back hurts." Those were bad days for Garrett.

Garrett knew he didn't love Lacy, and he was pretty sure Lacy didn't love him. They got married because she was expecting, and it was expected. Not a good foundation to build a future on.

When the sex dried up, Garrett joined the Pine View Volunteer Fire Department. Not so much to put out fires, but to have an excuse to be away from Lacy. It was as a volunteer firefighter that Garrett got to know several of the Pine View County Deputy Sheriffs.

Deputy Sheriff Mark Harper and Garrett became friends and, when Mark asked Garrett if he'd like to do a ride-along, Garrett jumped at the chance. Not so much to catch bad guys, but to have another reason to be away from Lacy.

He wasn't with Lacy when Paige came crying and wiggling into the world. He'd been on another ride-along with Mark. Looking back, he knew not being there when Lacy gave birth to Paige was the proverbial straw that broke the camel's back of their marriage. It limped along for another two years, by which time Garrett was a deputy sheriff, but ended when Garrett made an unexpected trip home and found Lacy's legs wrapped around Mark Harper's sweaty back.

They didn't hear him come in because Lacy had been being quite vocal. At first Garrett thought she was in trouble but, as he made his way quickly toward the bedroom, he realized he wasn't hearing panicked screams. He was hearing screams of ecstasy.

Garrett pushed the bedroom door open and stood there, his hand hovering over his nine-millimeter Glock 17 pistol, watching Mark's hairy ass bob up and down as he fucked Lacy.

"Fuck me. Fuck me hard!" Lacy panted and yelled.

She used to yell like that when Garrett fucked her, back during Garrett's good days, but she hadn't done so recently.

A wave of emotions washed over Garrett as he watched his mentor and friend fuck his wife. Anger, betrayal, sadness, and a sense of loss flooded his senses. He realized his hand closed over the grip of his pistol, as if some unknown force, a monster hiding deep inside him, moved it there. This move produced another emotion, fear. Fear that some part of him really wanted to kill Mark, Lacy, or both of them.

He took a couple of deep breaths to steady himself and let go of his pistol. In doing so, symbolically, he let go of his marriage and a final emotion washed over him, relief. The relief had been so complete that, without realizing it, a smile spread across his face. He felt like a strangle grip released and he could breathe again.

Instead of shooting them, Garrett said, “I was wonderin’ what, or *who*, ya did on your nights off, Mark.”

The reaction had been comical, and Garrett fell into a fit of laughter as he watched it play out. At the sound of his voice, Mark screamed like a woman and rolled off Lacy. He did this at a most unfortunate time, just as the fruits of his labor were maturating. His ‘baby juice,’ what Lacy called semen when she thought she was being cute, launched out of his little pecker as he tried desperately, and unsuccessfully, to cover himself in the tangled sheets.

Garrett made a mental note to burn the sheets. Scratch that. He’d burn the whole fucking bed, which he did the next night as he took shots of Jose Cuervo.

Meanwhile, Lacy was lying there with her legs spread and a confused look on her face. Confusion caused by Garrett’s laughing.

Instead of apologizing or making some excuse, Lacy screamed, “What’re ya laughin’ at?”

Garrett put a hand up, showing he needed a moment to respond, and, when he got his laughter under control, said, “You. I’m laughin’ at you. Ya stupid bitch.”

They were harsh words but delivered calmly. The calm retort seemed to unnerve Mark.

He scrambled out of bed, his little pecker now limp and trying to crawl back inside his body and grabbed up his clothes. “I’m sorry, Garrett. Really, bro. It just kind of happened.”

Lacy, now pissed, shouted, “It’s been *happenin’* for over a year.”

At this bit of information, Mark, looking positively traumatized, bolted out the back door, which was in their bedroom and opened on to a deck Mark helped Garrett build about a year ago. With a slam of the door, Mark disappeared into the night.

Garrett shouted, “See ya at work, *bro*.”

Garrett heard Mark’s truck rumble into life and thought, *Smart to park out back.*

There was the sound of gravel spraying the vinyl trailer siding as Mark made a hasty escape.

With Mark gone, Lacy unloaded on Garrett. “This is *your* fault. You’re *always* gone.”

This had been true, and Garrett nodded in agreement.

This seemed to incense her further, and she shouted, "Are ya fuckin' queer now? You don't want *this* anymore?"

She grabbed her crotch and used her fingers to spread her 'sweet spot,' which had been another of her stupid sex nicknames.

"I'm not queer, but I sure as shit don't want *that* anymore?" Garrett responded, pointing at her sweet spot.

Lacy seemed to have a thought. "*You're* fuckin' someone else. You come in here all high and mighty 'cause *ya* caught me fuckin' Mark and *you're* cheatin' too. You piece of shit. I fuckin' *hate* you."

As if to stress the point, she threw a pillow at Garrett, which he easily dodged.

When Garrett didn't respond, Lacy cried. For a second, Garrett felt sorry for her.

Lacy sobbed, "I never loved you, Garrett. This was a mistake. A mistake caused by a mistake. I should'a had a fuckin' abortion."

There it was—out in the open. He agreed with everything she said, except the abortion part. As far as Garrett was concerned, Paige was the only thing in the world that mattered. The only bright spot in the darkness of their marriage.

Paige was his life. He volunteered to work nights so he could spend days with Paige, while Lacy worked noon-to-nine at the Pine View Grocery. He worked the eleven-to-seven shift. After his shift, he would hurry home and sleep until Lacy had to go to work. It wasn't enough sleep, but he and Paige had naptime together from three to five. That sufficed. His time with Paige became the only thing that made it all work, and Lacy expressed the wish Paige had never been born. He felt rage building inside him, but he stayed it.

In a calm voice, Garrett said, "I'll pick up Paige and go to Mom and Dad's when my shift's over. I want ya out by the time I come back here to get ready for work tomorrow night."

Lacy stiffened at this. "You're kickin' *me* out?"

"Not so stupid after all."

He knew this would piss Lacy off, but he didn't care.

Lacy screamed, "You can't kick me out. We're married. Half this shit's mine, you...*dickhole*."

Still calm, Garrett said, "Wrong. My folks had a feelin' this wouldn't last, so they put the deed in my name, only my name, *before* we were married. I bought the trailer-house before we were married, too.

They'll be some shit to split, but not this land and not this fuckin' house."

Lacy seemed to deflate before his eyes again. For another second, Garrett felt sorry for her again.

She stiffened again and screamed, "I'm takin' Paige. You'll *never* fuckin' see her again."

Spit flew out of her mouth as she finished her threatening retort and landed on her still exposed left tit.

Bitch looks crazy, Garrett thought.

He said, "I changed my mind. Get out now."

He thought he might have to remove her with force, which would have been bad if she ended up with bruises she could later point to as indications of abuse, but his concerns were unwarranted. She deflated again, got off the bed, and started to get dressed.

After she pulled her shirt on, she said, "What about Paige?"

"You mean, what about the missed abortion?"

Lacy winced and tried a fresh approach.

"I'm sorry Garrett. Really, *sorry*. Please don't kick me out. We *can* make this work. I'll be the perfect little wife. I promise."

She looked at Garrett, smiled, and added, "I'll swallow and let you do that *other* thing ya want to do."

She opened her arms as if expecting a hug.

Garrett's formal education ended with his high school graduation, but he wasn't a stupid man. He knew what she had planned. She'd play nice so she could stay the night and clean him out when he went back to work.

Garrett opened his arms and Lacy, smiling, wrapped her arms around him. He locked his hands around her lower back, picked her up, and started toward his side of the bed.

Lacy, thinking Garrett wanted to take her up on both offers, swallow and the other thing, said, "Not now, Garrett. Not so soon after…Mark was here. Tomorrow mornin', when ya get home from work. I promise."

She kissed him on the cheek.

Garrett had no intention of putting his pecker in any of Lacy's orifices then or ever again. The back door, through which Mark fled, was on his side of the bed. He intended to put Lacy out the same door.

As he moved passed the bed and continued toward the door, Lacy caught on to his intention. She began struggling to free herself from

Garrett's hold.

"Put me down."

"I will. Once you're outta *my* house."

This put Lacy in a state of panic. She began hammering her fists into Garrett's back and trying to knee him in the crotch. Garrett held her too close for her to rupture his nuts, which he was sure she intended to do.

When Garrett opened the door, Lacy screamed, "Fuck you. Fuck you, Garrett. Mark was a better fuck than you."

Garrett set her down on the deck and, placing his forearm across her chest to minimize the possibility of bruising her, shoved her back, closed, and locked the door.

Lacy began kicking and pounding on the door and screaming vile things, "You *faggot*. You throw me out instead of fuckin' *my* ass? What's the matter, Garrett? My ass isn't good enough for ya? Is it that ya want a *man's* hairy asshole with sweaty balls for you to play with? So, *you* can suck *his* dick and swallow. You fuckin' *faggot*!"

Garrett didn't hang around and listen. He quickly made his way to the front door and locked it, too. Apparently, the idea of getting back in through the front door occurred to Lacy shortly after Garrett left the back door because, within a few seconds of his locking the front door, Lacy was pounding on it and resuming her rant.

Again, Garrett didn't hang around and listen. He headed back to the bedroom, picked up Lacy's keys from the bowl on the coffee table as he passed it, dug her overnight bag out of the closet, and began cramming a couple of every item she would need in the morning; panties, bras, pants, and shirts, into it. When the clothes were stuffed inside, he went to the bathroom, grabbed her toothbrush, her deodorant, and stuffed them into the overnight bag too. She would have to do without makeup in the morning.

After he packed her essentials, Garrett removed the house key and his truck key, leaving only her car key, on her key ring. Still secure knowing she was still at the front door, because he could hear her pounding on it and cussing up a storm, he placed the overnight bag, with her car key on top of it, on the back deck. He locked the door again.

Garrett returned to the front door and said her name loudly to get her attention. It worked. Lacy fell silent and ceased pummeling the door.

Still calm, Garrett said, "I left some clothes, other essentials, and your car key on the back deck. Take 'em and leave."

There were several moments of silence then a defeated Lacy said, "What about Paige?"

"I'll take her to my folks' tonight."

Still sounding defeated, Lacy said, "What about the rest of my stuff?"

"Come back tomorrow afternoon and I'll let ya take everything that belongs to ya."

Even more defeated, Lacy said, "Where am I supposed to go?"

"I don't know. Go to your folks'."

Just to pour a little salt in Lacy's wounded pride, he added, "Go to Mark's. He's a better fuck, right?"

Lacy kicked the door hard enough to put a little dent on the inside and screamed, "I fuckin' *hate* you."

After a moment of silence, Garrett heard her stomp off the front deck. Shortly after this, he heard the sound of her car door opening and slamming shut. Her engine roared into life, and she floored the accelerator. Lacy put her car in gear and Garrett heard the sound of gravel spraying the trailer's vinyl siding and the clink of it hitting his patrol vehicle, as she spun around the drive and shot out on to County Road Five Eighty-Eight.

Garrett opened the front door and watched her taillights grow smaller then disappear. Her folks and Mark lived in the direction she headed. Garrett smiled as he realized he didn't really give a shit whose house she went to.

With Lacy gone, his attention turned to Paige. He peeked into her bedroom and found, thankfully, she was fast asleep.

Baby-sleep is a blessin', he thought.

He picked up the phone and made the call he realized he had been, eventually, always going to make. His mom, Mary, picked up on the second ring.

"Garrett?" she asked in a sleepy voice.

"Hi, Mom," Garrett said in what he hoped was a casual voice.

"Is everything okay?" she asked, not sounding as sleepy.

"Well…" Garrett started to explain, but his mother cut him off.

"Ya finally kicked Lacy out," she interrupted with no sleepiness left in her voice at that point.

"How…" Garrett started but was cut off yet again.

"Oh, honey. Y'all got married for the wrong reason. A baby is a gift from God, but they aren't a magical bonding agent. It was only a matter of time before y'all figured this out. What happened?"

Garrett started to tell her something, not that she'd been fucking Mark Harper, his mentor and friend, ex-friend. Instead, Mary said, "Never mind. Not my business. I suppose ya want us to watch Paige, if Lacy didn't take her. Please tell me Lacy didn't take her."

It amazed Garrett at how perceptive his mother was.

He actually had to suppress a chuckle when he said, "No, she didn't take Paige. Will ya please watch her for me?"

"Of course, I will." Mary said gleefully. "That little booger is the light of my life. Ya wanna bring her here, or should I come to your house? That might be better, so ya don't have to wake her up."

Garrett first thought he'd have his mom come to his house. After sleeping through the shitstorm of an argument, baby-sleep can be deep, he didn't think Paige would wake up if he took her to his folks. Even if she did, she'd zonk right back out, baby-sleep was powerful stuff, when he got her there. That wasn't the clincher. He didn't want his mom and Paige there, if Lacy showed back up with her brothers, Lance and Lane, who were two puffed-up assholes, intent on causing trouble.

He didn't relay these concerns to his mom. He told her he'd bring Paige over and see them in the morning when his shift ended.

His baby-sleep thoughts were right about Paige. She didn't stir as he lifted her from bed, laid her on the front seat of his patrol SUV, and handed her off to his mom, who had been waiting outside when he got to their house.

Mary took Paige and gave Garrett a kiss on the cheek before going back inside with his little bundle of heaven wrapped up in her arms.

As he watched the door shut and the porch lights turn off, Garrett thought, *our lives will never be the same, Paige-Turner*.

Paige-Turner was his nickname for her because, like a good book, he couldn't wait to see what the next page in the story of her life would reveal.

As an afterthought, *Is that good or bad*?

As with most things in life, it would be a mix of the two—but, mostly, good.

The rest of Garrett's shift had been uneventful, which was good because he figured he was in for an eventful day. He wasn't wrong. When his shift ended, he went home and called his mom to check on Paige. She was still sleeping, and that was good, too. Garrett needed time to sort some things out before he heard from Lacy. As long as Paige wasn't awake and looking for him, he had some time. He told his mom to call him as soon as she woke up, hung up, and went to work.

Aside from Lacy's belongings, clothes, books, he knew what she contributed to the marriage, and he wanted it all arranged outside for her when she eventually showed up. Garrett saw enough romantic comedies, Lacy loved them, to know the scorned spouse was supposed to recklessly throw all the offending party's shit out a window or recklessly toss it out on the yard. He had no intention of doing that.

He placed all of her closet clothes in trash bags to keep them clean and placed them on the front deck table. Her shoes went into boxes. Her other clothes, unmentionables, were easier to take care of because they were in her dresser. Garrett dumped his belongings out of the dresser and drug it out onto the front deck. The entire bedroom suite belonged to Lacy before they married, so he did the same with it. He retrieved his personal revolver and other items from the nightstand on his side of her bed before taking it outside. He dismantled the bed and dragged its components outside, except for the mattress and box spring, which were a wedding gift to them from his parents. He had special plans for them later.

He placed trash bags across the top of her dresser to keep it from getting scratched, and placed every knickknack she brought into, and purchased during, the marriage, where she could see them.

When he started removing her things, he thought it might hurt a little. It didn't. It had been therapeutic. He was cutting her, every part of her, out of his life. Like removing a malignant tumor. He put all her makeup in boxes and moved them outside. The coffee table and end tables went next. Followed by her wall art, if you could call it that, six prints of cats playing with yarn and other things, went into trash bags on the front porch. Luckily, the sofa, recliner, kitchen table and chairs were his. They stayed. To make sure Lacy didn't have cause to be a further pain in the ass, he also gave her all the wedding gifts. At least the ones he remembered them receiving. The only room he took nothing from, and he knew this would be a point of contention, had been Paige's room.

She can bitch all she wants, but she's not takin' one fuckin' item from Paige's room, Garrett, with a sense of eagerness to engage in the impending battle, thought.

Within two hours, he was done. Almost three years together came down to a half-empty house and a front deck and yard full of crap. As far as Garrett was concerned, it had been the best two hours of the previous two years of their marriage.

As he was standing there admiring the excised tumor that were Lacy's belongings, his cellphone rang.

Without checking who had been calling, he answered. "Is she awake?"

"I didn't sleep, you *dickhole*," Lacy hissed into his ear.

He heard Lacy's mom, Lynn, in the background say, in a shocked tone, "Lacy."

So, she didn't go to Mark's, Garrett thought, but suppressed the urge to ask her why she hadn't.

He thought it had been because Mark was just in it for the sex, but, six months later, Mark ended up being husband number two out of Lacy's eventual four husbands, so what the hell did he know?

In response, and in a very cheerful voice, Garrett said, "Good mornin', sunshine."

Obviously pissed, which gave Garrett abundant satisfaction, Lacy hissed, "Fuck you, *dickhole*."

There were more gasps and stutters from Lynn in the background, which made Garrett all the happier.

"I want *my* shit. *All* of it," Lacy growled.

"Your shit is waitin' for ya out front. In fact, I'm lookin' at it right now," Garrett replied and, although he tried not to, he laughed.

This sent Lacy into a frenzy, much like the one she'd had outside the front and back doors the night before, which, to Garrett, seemed like a lifetime ago.

She called him a faggot, told him to find a faggot butthole to fuck because he was never fucking hers, hoped his dick got covered in shit, hoped he got AIDS from guzzling faggot cum. The whole time Lynn gasped and stuttered in the background.

Later, when the Visa advertisements came out, Garrett would say to whoever would listen, "Wedding costs? Freedom sucking. Almost three years of marriage? Soul sucking. Hearing Lynn gasp and stutter as Lacy cussed me out? PRICELESS."

After what seemed like several minutes of Lacy wishing him many homosexual calamities, Lynn jerked the phone away from Lacy and, sounding out of breath, said, "Garrett, can we come by and get Lacy's things later today?"

Lacy, then in the background, shouted, "He threw my shit in the dirt."

Before Lynn could say anything, Garrett said, "I didn't throw her stuff in the dirt, Missus Little. I took great care to make sure I didn't damage anything, and it's *all* out front, organized and ready to be loaded. I'll even help y'all load it."

A pause followed in which Garrett could still hear Lacy cussing a blue streak and, sounding appreciative, Lynn said, "Thank you, Garrett. It'll be later this afternoon because Mister Little, Lance, and Lane are gonna help. We need their trucks. Does that work for you?"

Upon hearing this, Lacy screamed, "Don't be polite to that *dickhole*, Mamma."

Garrett heard Lynn cover the phone, but he could still make out a muffled, "Shut up, Lacy. No sense makin' this more difficult."

When the phone had been un-muffled, he heard Lacy sobbing in the background and Lynn said, "I'm sorry, Garrett. Lacy is a bit…emotional. What was I sayin'? Oh yeah, does later this afternoon work for you?"

More like bat shit crazy, Garrett thought.

Instead, he responded, "Yes, ma'am. That'll be fine. Just call me before y'all start over."

"Yes, of course," Lynn continued. "I know ya said you've moved all of Lacy's belongin's out of the house, but would it be okay if we looked inside just to make sure ya didn't miss anything?"

"Yes, ma'am. Not a problem."

There had been a brief pause in the conversation, Garrett thought he knew what was coming, then Lynn said, "Can we see Paige when we come?"

That's exactly what he thought she'd ask.

Garrett considered this a minute and then answered honestly, "I don't think that's a good idea, Missus Little. As ya pointed out, Lacy's a bit…emotional, and I don't think any of us want Paige to witness another of her…emotional outbursts. It's a blessin' she slept through what happened last night."

After another brief pause, in which he could hear Lynn take several deep breaths. He thought she might be about to cry, and he hated that thought. For all of Lacy's faults, of which he was fast discovering, were many, Garrett had been very fond of her folks. Lance and Lane were puffed up dickholes. Lacy's new favorite word, it occurred to him. Larry and Lynn were always nice to him.

When Lynn finally spoke, she said, "Yes, probably best if she weren't there this afternoon."

At this, Lacy screamed, "He can't take *my* baby from me. No matter what I did, he can't take *my* Paige away."

This scream ended in deep sobs and, God help him, Garrett felt sorry for her. Part of his feeling sorry for her stemmed from her accepting some responsibility for what had been happening. "No matter what I did," resonated with Garrett. He had been sure, no matter what she'd told her folks when she showed up in the middle of the night looking haggard and carrying her overnight bag, Lynn heard that too.

He wouldn't be the one who told her folks what he'd walked in on, but once Lynn had some variables, the math wasn't difficult. Even if Lacy didn't admit what she'd done, that simple sentence planted a seed.

Garrett took a deep breath. "Missus Little, I have no desire to take Paige away from Lacy or y'all. No matter what happened between Lacy and me, she's a good mamma to Paige and y'all are great grandparents to her. We just need to sort everything out when…emotions aren't so raw. We will sort this out. I promise. In fact, why don't we settle on y'all havin' Paige this weekend?"

Garrett could sense Lynn's relief before she spoke.

Lynn exhaled. Apparently, she'd been holding her breath. "Thank you, Garrett. We would love to have her this weekend. I'll call ya later, when we start your way. Bye-bye, sweetie."

That last word meant a lot to Garrett. Lynn called him "sweetie" since he and Lacy started dating in high school. That she ended their conversation that way let Garrett know, no matter how things turned out between him and Lacy, they turned out okay, better as divorced friends than as a married couple. He and Lynn would be okay. That mattered.

He said goodbye and felt pretty good about things. Not two minutes after he hung up from Lynn, his mom called and told him Paige-Turner was awake and asking for her daddy. Garrett felt damn good.

Garrett spent the morning with Paige—bath-time, more like splash-time, followed by story-time. Her favorite book had been *Guess How Much I Love You*. She identified with Little Nutbrown Hare. Followed by playtime, they worked a puzzle with sizeable pieces. By noon, lack of sleep was catching up with him.

Paige didn't like it when her daddy slept during the day. She'd prefer he play with her nonstop, but, even at her young age, she knew he wasn't home most nights and needed to sleep sometime. So, when Garrett passed her off to Nana, she didn't put up a fuss. Nana was fun too.

Garrett told his mom to wake him up at four o'clock. She scoffed, telling him he needed over four hours' sleep, but agreed to wake him up at the requested time.

Garrett was tired, but he didn't realize how exhausted he had been until he laid down on his old bed and was out within minutes of his head sinking into the pillow. It had been a deep sleep, but unfortunately, it wasn't a restful sleep. His subconscious mind had been fixated on the events of the previous night and infiltrated his dreams.

In the dream, he came home unexpectedly and heard Lacy screaming in their bedroom. When he opened the bedroom door, instead of seeing Mark's hairy ass bobbing up and down as he violated his wife, he saw a room of horrors.

It was dark. The only light source came from directly above the bed and spotlighted Lacy's naked body. Her wrists and ankles were tied to the bedposts. She was covered in blood, but Garrett couldn't see any wounds. Worse still, Lacy had a grotesquely distended belly, and something was moving beneath the over-stretched skin.

Garrett tried to scream but couldn't. He tried to move but couldn't. He couldn't even close his eyes to shut out the gruesome scene.

The thing moving inside of Lacy pressed up against her skin and Garrett saw a face. A deformed face with a wide mouth. Its teeth, fangs, broke through the skin. Lacy screamed.

Movement from the shadowed corner of the room registered in Garrett's peripheral vision. He couldn't move his eyes to make out who or what it was. It was moving toward Garrett, but staying out of the light, preferring the concealing shadows. It was close, so close that Garrett could smell its dank musk. It smelled like a wet dog. It, he knew it was an it by then, moved in front of Garrett, but with its back to him. It was tall, broad across the shoulders, and covered in coarse black hair. It moved to the other side of the bed, Garrett's side, where the back door was.

Just leave. Garrett's mind screamed.

Only it didn't. Instead, it stepped into the light.

Garrett's dreaming mind was having difficulty registering what he saw before him. It was huge. Its pointy wolf ears, they *were* wolf's ears, brushed against the eight-foot-high ceiling. Its arms were elongated and muscular. They ended in large bony hands that had long, razor-sharp claws.

It looked at Garrett, and his heart froze. As bad as the rest of it had been, its face was truly a thing of horror. It had a long snout, and it drew its lips up in a snarl, which revealed a mouth-full of pearly white, dagger length teeth. Its eyes unnerved Garrett the most. They were red, fire red, and flickered like a flame. To Garrett's ultimate horror, it winked at him, as if saying it would do what Garrett hadn't done the night before. Kill Lacy.

Lacy stared at the werewolf, Garrett's mind finally registered what *it* was—and screamed so loud it hurt Garrett's head. The thing inside Lacy was still trying to chew its way out of her. Its pearly white fangs, much smaller than the big one's but still deadly, were tearing the flesh of Lacy's distended belly as they came together with a vicious snap. Its head pushed through Lacy's belly in a spray of blood and Garrett's mind snapped. The thing eating its way out of Lacy had been a grossly distorted visage of Paige.

It was clearly his little Paige-Turner, but her face had been elongated into a snarling snout. Her dagger teeth snapped at bits of Lacy's flesh that hung from her mouth. Her ears were pointed and covered in light brown, downy hair.

As Garrett watched, still unable to move, the Monster-Paige pulled her tiny hands out of Lacy's womb and began clawing at Lacy's crotch with miniature versions of the big werewolf's claws. Lacy's screams were at a vocal cord shattering pitch as her little girl shredded her 'sweet spot.'

Garrett wanted it, needed it to stop. His mind couldn't take it anymore and the screaming was going to split his head.

As if reading his thoughts, the big werewolf's clawed hand moved with unnatural speed across Lacy's neck and opened a gaping wound that hemorrhaged intermittent streams of blood as Lacy's heart pumped her life away.

Garrett thought the screams were bad, but the gurgling sounds escaping Lacy's shredded throat were far worse.

The spurting blood streams slowed to a trickle then stopped altogether. Garrett watched as Lacy's chest rose, taking in a last breath, and deflated with one last, wet rattle.

As Lacy died, Monster-Paige stopped feasting; she had been

hungrily ripping junks of meat from Lacy's inner thigh in the last seconds of Lacy's life. She held her hands up to the large werewolf.

She holds her hands up like that to me when she wants me to pick her up, Garrett's confused mind thought.

That's exactly what the larger werewolf did.

The gentle care with which the monster picked up Paige amazed Garrett. Its long, sharp claws didn't leave a scratch as it slipped its hands under Monster-Paige's arms and lifted her blood covered, naked body, naked except for the light brown, downy hair that covered her entire body, out of what had been left of Lacy's abdomen. There had been a sickening, wet, slurping sound as Monster-Paige pulled free.

As Monster-Paige came out, Lacy's body heaved upward, as if not wanting to let go, then fell back with a liquid splat that made Garrett need to puke. Garrett could see inside Lacy's body through the gaping hole. Her insides were shredded, as if Monster-Paige had been having a little in-utero snack.

After extracting, delivering, Monster-Page from Lacy's dead body, the big werewolf rested her in the crook of its arm, as Garrett so often did with his Paige-Turner, lifted its head toward the ceiling, its nose touched it, and let out a howl that loosened Garrett's bowls.

He thought it was the most unholy sound he'd ever heard, but he had been wrong. That honor went to Monster-Paige when she turned her little elongated snout upward and joined the bigger werewolf's howls.

When the howls ended, the big werewolf turned and faced Garrett, its fiery red eyes danced in the gloomy room. Garrett thought he was next, desert for his little girl, but he had been wrong, again.

The werewolf reached back with its unnaturally long arm and opened the back door. Monster-Paige opened and closed her tiny, bony, blood covered, clawed hand at him. She was waving bye-bye. Just before the big werewolf turned and disappeared into the night with his little girl, Garrett saw her eyes flare red with the same burning intensity as the big werewolf's eyes. With that, they were gone.

Garrett could feel his body come back to him as he tried to break free of the paralytic hold and go after Paige. He could move again, but something was holding him back. His voice was back too, but very distant.

He was screaming, "Bring her back. You can't have her. Bring my little girl back," at the emptiness behind the opened back door.

His voice was getting louder, getting closer. He could move a little more and the room was getting brighter. His skin felt wet and chilled. He lunged for the door and hit his head on something. It hurt.

Garrett's eyes flew open, all comprehension gone.

He screamed, "Bring her back," in a very real, loud voice that hurt his throat and startled him.

He didn't know where he was. He tried to move, but the bed sheets were so tangled around his body he found it difficult to do so. The sweat-soaked bed sheets made it even harder to disentangle his body. His head crammed against something. The headboard. That's what his head hit.

Whose headboard? Garrett thought.

He realized it was his headboard from when he was a kid. His heart was hammering in his chest, and he was taking in gulps of air.

Just a dream, he thought. *Not a dream. A fuckin' nightmare from hell*, he corrected his thought.

All of this transpired in a matter of seconds. As he came back to reality, he glanced toward the bedroom door, half expecting to see the werewolf and Monster-Page there waving at him but saw his frightened mom instead. She was clinching her fists to her chest and looking at Garrett like she didn't know him.

Finally, in a shaky voice, she said, "Are ya okay, Garrett?"

Garrett, trying to sound casual and failing miserably, said, "Yeah, Mom. Just a bad dream."

He didn't like how he sounded, and he could tell it unnerved his mom, too.

"Who had Paige, Garrett?"

Before he could answer, she followed up with, "What's Monster-Paige?"

Garrett tried to chuckle, but it came out like more of a gurgle. It reminded him of how Lacy gurgled her last breath in the dream and a shiver went up his spine.

Trying to sound a little less crazy, Garrett said, "It was a bad dream, a nightmare, Mom. I'm sorry if I freaked ya out. It's already slippin' from my mind…so I couldn't tell ya who had Paige or what…what did you say…Monster-Paige was, even if I wanted to."

Mary studied her son for a moment, not sure she believed him but willing to let it go. "It's four o'clock and Paige-Turner wants her daddy."

With that, his mom left him alone with his tattered thoughts.

Despite the dream, thinking about Paige brought a smile to his face. He quickly collected himself and went to spend quality time with Paige-Turner until the Littles called. Unfortunately, they called about twenty minutes after he emerged from the horrible dream.

The part about forgetting the dream had been the biggest lie Garrett had ever told his mom. He remembered every surreal moment of it and would for the rest of his life. To his horror, it would become an annual recurring dream. The only difference being Monster-Paige aged with Paige's age and each year the brown downy fur became darker, longer, and coarser.

With each recurring dream, Lacy's poor, stretched abdomen would start out larger than it had been the year before and Monster-Paige, older each year, would chew and rip her way out of Lacy, mutilate her genitals, and snack on her inner thighs. Lacy's end had been always the same, a dead, shredded sack of meat.

The ending changed slightly, too. About the time Paige had been twelve years old, the big werewolf stopped carrying her out the back door. Instead, they would link their clawed hands, almost like lovers, and walk away together. Before they left, Monster-Paige always waved bye-bye, and her eyes always flared red with that inner fire.

Things that didn't change were Garrett waking up in a state of confusion, not knowing where the dream ended and reality began, soaked in sweat, tangled in wet bed sheets, and screaming, "Bring her back," through straining vocal cords. On the bright side, he didn't always bump his head. Thank God for small favors.

~ * ~

Garrett got to the house before Lacy and her family did and parked his truck around back where, he realized, Mark's truck had been parked less than twenty-four hours earlier. The difference being, Garrett was parking out of the way to give Larry, Lance, and Lane room to pull their trucks up next to Lacy's stuff, not so he could bone someone else's wife.

Garrett let himself in and made one last sweep of the house to see if he'd missed anything in his morning haste. A floor lamp in the living room had questionable provenance.

When in doubt, Garrett thought.

He grabbed the lamp and headed out the front door with it when the band of Littles came pulling in the driveway. Garrett could see Lacy sitting between Larry and Lynn in Larry's truck. He waved and started down the deck steps with the lamp. Larry and Lynn waved back. Lacy did not.

He felt sure Lance and Lane would be puffed up dickholes. He liked Lacy's new favorite word, and they didn't disappoint. Garrett liked, and had gotten along with, both of them in high school, even played football with both, Lance, before Lance graduated and Lane before Garrett graduated, but they got overprotective when Garrett started dating Lacy. Just minor threats and warnings mumbled here and there. Nothing big, just guys with a sister tuff-talk.

When Lacy turned up pregnant, they took it up a notch. They caught him out at the Mill Road Barn, a secluded old sawmill where high school kids partied, and tried to 'put a whoopin,' another of his dad's sayings, on him.

Two against one should have been an easy route for them, but Garrett kicked Lance, the bigger of the two, in the nuts hard enough to make him puke, which immobilized him long enough for Garrett to take Lane out with a punch to the throat. Lance limped and Lane wheezed away, cursing him under their breath, with their tails between their legs.

Although they never tried to put a whoopin' on Garrett again, word got around Garrett fought dirty. Like two on one wasn't dirty fighting? They always puffed-up around him; chest out, shoulders squared. That day had been no different. After all, Garrett 'wronged' their sister by kicking her out.

Garrett felt sure they were clueless to the fact their sweet sister had been getting a steady stream of dick from Mark Harper. Hell, they should have been glad Garrett and Lacy were over. Puffed up or not, Garrett thought they were happy to be moving Lacy out of his house. Out of his life.

Garrett thought of the old saying about a frown being an upside-down smile. In that case, Lance and Lane were sporting world-class upside-down smiles. This thought made Garrett laugh out loud, which produced threatening looks from Lacy's puffed-up brothers. This made Garrett laugh all the harder.

He knew he should stop because it looked like he was goading them, but he couldn't. They just looked so damn stupid. When he caught sight of Lynn's disapproving stare, he choked back the laughter.

About thirty minutes after they arrived, all of Lacy's worldly possessions were crammed into the back of three pickup trucks. At that point, Larry and Lynn approached Garrett.

"I'm sorry 'bout laughin' earlier," Garrett explained. "Lance and Lane were givin' me the ol' evil eye and it struck me as funny."

Larry looked back, as if checking to make sure they weren't within earshot. They were sitting on the tailgate of Larry's truck. He turned back. "They can be shits, but they're just bein' protective of Lacy."

Shocked, Lynn said, "Larry. Don't call our boys shits."

She whispered "shits" so that it came out more like a hiss. This tickled Garrett, but he held it back.

Larry looked at Lynn. "Well, it's true. They are actin' like little shits."

Lynn made a face but before she could respond, Larry looked at Garrett and continued, "Son, we don't know what happened last night and it's none of our business, anyway. You're a good kid…good man. You always have been. Ya stepped up when Lacy got pregnant and did the right thing by marryin' her. Lynn tells me you're gonna step up and do right by Lacy, Paige, and us now. Do I have your word that you will?"

Garrett nodded, and they shook hands.

Larry nodded. "That's good enough for me."

It was Lynn's turn to talk. She looked a little nervous, but she said, "I noticed that none of Paige's things are out here."

It was an unasked question, as a statement, Garrett had been ready for. He took a deep breath. "No, all of Paige's stuff is still in her room…where it belongs."

Lynn winced a little, but Garrett continued. "I don't want Paige affected by this any more than necessary. Haulin' half of her belongin's to your house…or wherever Lacy ends up livin' might put stress on her…stress she doesn't deserve. I'm more than happy to go shoppin' with Missus Little, or…hell, even Lacy, to help put together a room Paige can call her own on the other side of wherever she ends up livin' when she ain't here. I'll even pay for her new stuff."

Garrett waited to see how the Littles received his proposal and felt relieved when they both smiled back at him.

Larry stuck out his hand again. "That's damn good enough for me, son."

Lynn interjected, "*Darn* good enough for us, sweetie."

Garrett shook Larry's enthusiastic hand.

With that out of the way, and everyone feeling a little better about things, Lynn reminded Garrett that Lacy wanted to go through the house and double-check for anything he might have missed. Garrett told Lynn that would be fine and made, what the Littles surely thought, given the circumstances, an odd request. He asked if he could go into the house with Lacy. Just the two of them.

Lynn shook her head, but Larry said, "I'll ask her."

When Lynn gave him a doubtful look, Larry said, "Can't hurt to ask," and walked over to the truck's passenger side window.

Garrett couldn't hear the conversation, but he saw Lacy shaking her head in an emphatic "no." Larry kept talking, and after about a minute, Lacy nodded. Larry opened the door and Lacy stepped out. She looked, somehow, smaller, meeker, to Garrett.

Lance and Lane, sensing what was happening, started puffing up again. Larry told them to 'grab tailgate' and they settled back down. They were still grumbling but doing it with their asses on the tailgate. Larry walked Lacy over to Garrett. She wouldn't look at him.

The awkward silence broke when Larry said, "Okay, you two go have a look-see."

As Garrett turned to climb the porch steps, Lynn said, "We're right here…if ya need us, honey."

Apparently, Lynn wasn't so sure Sweetie wouldn't beat the shit out of Honey.

If she knew the restraint I showed last night when I walked in on Honey getting her sweet spot stuffed with another man's pecker, she'd know Honey wasn't in any immediate danger, Garrett thought.

After they entered the house, Garrett closed the door behind them. He knew this might trouble the Littles, but he didn't care. This was his and Lacy's life being divided up, not theirs.

The silent house enveloped them. More silent than Garrett could ever remember it being.

Lacy said nothing as they went through the kitchen. She looked around in some drawers and cabinets but claimed nothing as hers. The living room wasn't difficult to determine what belonged to whom. Garrett gutted it except for the sofa and recliner, which she knew came from his folks. As they went down the hall, she didn't even look in Paige's room, which surprised him. Eventually, they were in their room, which had been completely gutted. Only Garrett's crap strewn on the floor where the bed once stood and his TV from her dresser remained.

Lacy spoke for the first time. "Where are the mattress and box spring? They're yours and they weren't out front."

"They're out back."

Lacy looked at him for the first time. "Why are they out back?"

It was Garrett's turn to look away, and he did as he said, "I'm gonna burn 'em."

"Oh," Lacy responded.

Garrett looked back at her and saw tears filling up her lower eyelids. When they spilled down her cheeks, she turned away and wiped her face with her shirtsleeve.

Garrett knew some feeling of lost love did not bring the tears on, but more a feeling of a lost future. No one gets married thinking it'll be over in a few years. Even people who get married for the wrong reasons hope against hope it'll survive.

It surprised Garrett when he felt tears spilling down his cheeks, too. He didn't wipe them away. Instead, he placed a hand gently on Lacy's shoulder. That simple gesture broke the tension between them. She spun around, and they embraced. Lacy had her head buried in his chest and was crying—sobbing. Garrett put his chin on her head and held her tight as he cried, too.

After several minutes, Lacy took a deep breath and, with her face still pressed into Garrett's chest, said, "I'm sorry, Garrett. I'm *so* sorry. Believe me. *Please* believe me."

As Lacy continued to apologize, the nightmare vision of her mutilated body flooded into Garrett's mind. He held her closer.

When Lacy appeared to be apologized out, Garrett took her by the shoulders and pushed her far enough away so he could look at her. Lacy looked up at him and her jaw fell open.

She stammered a little before saying, "I've never seen ya cry before."

"Not true," Garrett corrected her. "Remember that time, when you were on top, and ya came down hard and smashed my left nut all to puddin'? I cried that day."

Lacy looked at him, as if she didn't know who he was, for several seconds. Then she smiled. The smile turned into a laugh, and, within seconds, they were both laughing so hard the tears came back. It had been a good laugh, a cleansing laugh that went on for at least a minute.

When they'd caught their breath, Lacy smiled. "Yep, ya cried that day."

They looked at each other for several more seconds. Lacy went up on her tiptoes and kissed him on the lips. Nothing too sensual, but she held it for several seconds.

When their lips parted, Lacy smiled. "Thank you for not being a giant *dickhole* to me. You could'a been, and I would'a deserved it."

"No matter what, we got Paige out of this and that makes it worth it to me."

Garrett saw the tears fill her bottom eyelid again, but they didn't spill over.

She smiled and kissed him again. "Yes, we did."

Just like that, things didn't feel so awkward between them. Garrett didn't know what the future held for either of them, but he felt sure they'd get along. More importantly, they'd do the best they could by Paige.

~ * ~

Garrett kept all of his promises, immediate and long-term. The Littles had Paige that first weekend after Garrett and Lacy split and most weekends until the divorce had been completed. Garrett also went shopping with Lacy and Lynn and, true to his word, paid for everything Paige needed in her 'other' room. Those were the immediate promises.

The long-term promises had to do with the divorce, custody, and child-support. Garrett and Lacy hired attorneys but, as the attorneys discovered, it had been an amicable procedure that required little haggling on their part. The possessions were already split, the land and improvements, water well and septic system, were Garrett's before they were married and, even though Lacy had a right to any equity accrued in the house since she began contributing to the household, trailer houses don't appreciate, they depreciate. So, there had been no equity to divide. Lacy wasn't interested in halving the loss. Not that Garrett cared or expected her to do so.

Dealing with Paige had been simple, too. Lacy and Garrett agreed to joint custody. Paige would spend weekdays with Lacy and every weekend with Garrett. They would alternate holidays, and Paige would spend summers with Garrett. Garrett agreed to provide Paige's insurance through his job, cover medical expenses, and all back-to-school expenses, clothes, school supplies. Lacy would cover all other expenses.

Given Garrett's job, nightshift and two weekdays off, Lacy's attorney, Mr. South, complained about Garrett's ability to spend time with Paige when she was in his custody. Garrett had that covered.

Within a few days of their split, it was common knowledge at the sheriff's department Garrett caught Mark fucking his wife and he had kicked Lacy out. Garrett used this information to his advantage.

He approached the sheriff, his predecessor Oliver Henry, and told him the rumors were true. Mark Harper destroyed his loving marriage. Sheriff Henry listened sympathetically and asked if there was anything he could do to help Garrett. Garrett explained the custody deal he and Lacy agreed upon, pointing out, given his current schedule, he wouldn't ever have time with Paige. This was true, but Garrett was laying it on thick.

Sheriff Henry listened and nodded in the right places. When Garrett left Henry's office, he had the seven-to-three dayshift, and his new days were Monday through Friday. The icing on the cake, his ex-buddy, Mark, would have to work Garrett's old nightshift.

Sheriff Henry said, "Serves the homewrecker right."

Sheriff Henry kept his word too and left Garrett on the day shift until he retired in 2012, at which time Garrett ran for, and won, the office of sheriff. His day shifts continued.

~ * ~

After the divorce, the years flew by. Lacy married Mark six months after Garrett caught them in bed and divorced him about a year later. Not one to enjoy being alone, Lacy married husband number three, who it had been rumored she'd been cheating on Mark with, a few months after she and Mark divorced.

Husband number three had been an out-of-towner named David Richmond. Garrett never liked him and was thrilled when he got busted selling prescription drugs, Oxycodone, to be exact, at a bowling alley in Nacogdoches. The shame of it had been too much for Lacy, and she divorced him immediately. After that, Lacy spent a few years alone. Not alone, because she had Paige, but without a man in her life.

About three years after dumping David, AKA the 'drug dealer,' she hitched her wagon to Albert 'Al' Sanders and remained married to him for the prior eight years, a landmark for Lacy. Al owned the Lone Star

Chevrolet, GMC, Buick, and Cadillac dealership in Pine View.

Garrett liked Al a great deal, and not just because he sold Garrett his personal vehicle at dealer price. Garrett purchased all the Pine View County Sheriff's Department vehicles, seven Chevy Tahoe SUVs, from Al, so it evened out. Garrett liked him because Al turned out to be a good husband to Lacy and a caring stepfather to Paige. Garrett and Lacy remained close; he had always been there when she needed him.

Garrett never remarried. He dated off and on. Dating only Mandy Davis for the previous three years. Mandy started her freshman year Garrett's senior year. He didn't remember her when they met again in 2012 under less-than-ideal circumstances. Mandy, of course, idolized Garrett in high school. The eighty-one-yard scramble sealed the deal, and he had been okay with that. She was smart. Mandy owned Good Stuff Thrift Shop in Pine View. She was pretty with blonde hair, sky-blue eyes with white flakes that looked like clouds, and a killer body. Most importantly, Paige liked her.

Even though Paige could understand 'adult' relationships, Mandy never stayed over when Paige stayed with Garrett. That Mandy didn't complain made Garrett like her that much more.

Eight years after Garrett and Lacy divorced, he built a house on his five acres. He and his dad moved the single-wide trailer to the deer lease, which had been a sight better than the leaky barn that served as their camp house for as long as Garrett could remember.

The new house wasn't anything spectacular, twelve hundred square feet, three bedrooms, two baths, ranch. Still, it was home. Paige had her own room. The baby stuff had long since replaced with posters of Taylor Swift and Justin Bieber. Her boyfriend's name was Justin, too. The guest room served as Garrett's home office. Life was good.

~ * ~

As Garrett studied his reflection in the mirror, he thought of Paige, and a smile spread across his unshaven face. It was only Monday, Paige went back to Lacy's house the previous afternoon, but the countdown to Friday had already started.

On Friday, Paige would again be at his house when he came home. Friday was Pizza Night, pepperoni and jalapeños for him and Canadian bacon and pineapple for Paige.

Thinking of Paige, as it always did, brightened Garrett's mood immeasurably.

Feeling better about Monday, Garrett said to his reflection, "On second thought, I think I will shave."

After the shave, he showered, got dressed, poured sweet tea, no coffee for Garrett, in his travel mug, grabbed his keys, and left for work. The nightmare and howls were the furthest things from his mind.

As Garrett started the Pine View County Sheriff's SUV, he thought, *it's gonna be a great day.*

He couldn't have been more wrong. The bad day he was about to have would seem trivial as the next few weeks unfolded.

Chapter Three

The first several hours of Deputy Sheriff Tyrone 'Ty' Jackson's night shift were relatively uneventful. He pulled over two speeders on Highway Sixty-Nine. One was a polite young woman who attended Stephen F. Austin State University in Nacogdoches. The other was a not-so-polite redneck who didn't appear to like the color of Ty's skin. Ty caught the polite young lady doing eighty-three in a seventy-five zone and gave her a warning. He caught the not-so-polite redneck doing eighty in a seventy-five zone and gave him a ticket. Ty enjoyed having discretion in his job. Ty liked his job, period.

Like his boss, Sheriff Garrett Lambert, Ty was a Pine View native, born and raised. Besides sharing a birthplace, Ty had also been athletic in high school. He too played football but, at five feet ten inches tall and weighing in at a very solid two hundred and twenty pounds, he had been the starting running back. Ty broke every single year, A-1 conference running back records his senior year and led the Woodpeckers to the 2006 A-1 conference state championship, which had been the first championship since Garrett's team did it in 1998.

Ty had lots of college offers and, unlike Garrett, several were from prestigious universities—Texas A&M, University of Texas, Texas Tech, and Oklahoma State were the top contenders. Ty surprised everyone. Instead of playing football on the collegiate level, Ty enlisted in the Marines. Ty's dad, Derrick Jackson, had been a Marine and often told Ty how important service to one's country is and how the Marines had made him a better man.

~ * ~

In 1999, when Ty had been ten years old, a hit-and-run driver struck and killed Derrick Jackson. Derrick's truck broke down, and he had been walking back to the sawmill where he worked to call Felicia, Ty's mom, when he had been hit.

The investigation showed it appeared as if the vehicle that struck Derrick Jackson deliberately veered onto the shoulder to do so. The coroner ruled Derrick Jackson's official cause of death as vehicular homicide. Although the investigation did not officially link race to the hit-and-run as a motive, the guilty party had never been apprehended, so their race remained unknown. There were suspicions in the East Texas African American community that race remained a factor. Derrick's murder happened about a year after three white men in nearby Jasper County dragged another black man, James Byrd Jr., to death, behind a pickup truck.

Ty didn't care about the motive. Regardless of the why, his dad was dead. Eight years later, to honor his father, he joined the Marines.

Two weeks after graduating high school, Ty flew to San Diego and reported for basic training at Camp Pendleton. Thirteen long weeks later, one week for processing and twelve weeks of training, he was a Marine. After two weeks leave back in Pine View, which seemed to have changed immeasurably in the thirteen weeks since he left, he had a larger worldview by the time he returned, Ty reported to Camp Lejeune in North Carolina. He spent six months there before being transferred to Afghanistan for the first of his three tours of duty.

For his first two tours he was stationed at combat outpost Terminator in the Maywand District, Kandahar Province. For his last tour, he had been stationed at combat outpost Michigan in the Dara-I-Pech District, Kunar Province. Ty saw a lot of combat and witnessed many depravities during his time in Afghanistan, especially during his second tour in Kandahar, which coincided with President Obama's surge. The suicide bombers, 'Kandahar Crazies' to the Marines, were hard to handle. Not only would they target American troops, but they would also target places where women and children were likely to be. Worse still, they weren't above using children as the delivery method.

On one occasion, Ty, an E-2 at that point, had been on forward patrol with three other E-2s from his unit and his unit E-4, Corporal Dirk Burnett, on a convoy with domestic supplies, food for the locals. About a hundred yards forward of his position were around a dozen local men. From what he could see, none of them carried firearms, but they were advancing. About fifty yards out, Dirk ordered the locals to stop and disperse.

Language always being a barrier, they didn't have a translator, but five Marines pointing guns usually conveyed the message well enough. They stopped and appeared to be dispersing. As they parted, a little girl, who couldn't have been over eight or nine years old, appeared from inside the group. They were concealing her. Once they parted, she started running toward Ty's group. They all raised their guns. Ty had his finger on the trigger of his M4 carbine and resigned to squeezing it if she crossed a blast kill-zone spot he placed at about twenty-five yards out. It didn't come to that.

Whatever hell the men strapped to her tiny body prematurely detonated about thirty-five yards out. They heard a loud explosion and saw a large fireball. The little girl's body disintegrated in a spray of blood and body parts that rained down on the Marines—big bomb. Ironically, she had been much closer to the Afghani men when she detonated. The blast killed four of them outright and injured another six to where they couldn't escape. Once Ty and his fellow Marines secured the injured men. They called in the incident requesting transport and medics.

It was only then, after the adrenaline subsided, that Ty noticed a pain in his right thigh. He saw blood on his pants, but thought it came from the little girl. He felt around and found a hole in his fatigues. There was something stuck in his leg. He tore the pants to get a better look and saw something ragged protruding from his thigh just above the knee. Without thinking, he pulled it out, which caused a little more discomfort, held it up, and studied it. He couldn't get his mind around what he was holding. He thought he knew, but it just didn't seem possible.

Dirk, who watched Ty remove the object, said, "Holy shit, Ty. That's one of the little girl's fingers."

That incident earned Ty the first of his two Purple Hearts. Ty received the second Purple Heart after an improvised explosive device hit the Humvee he rode in.

The patrol started like all of the countless other Kunar patrols Ty had been on. There were six Humvees on the patrol and Ty had been in the fourth back. One second, they were joking about their Afghanistan 'vacation' and the next second, the world went belly up.

The explosion went off directly under the front of Ty's Humvee. Ty sat in the back seat, which, with luck, saved his life. The explosion was deafening and the blast concussion knocked all the air out of Ty's lungs. Breathing would have been difficult because the Humvee was suddenly choked with sand, smoke, and shrapnel.

As Ty's senses came back to him, he realized the Humvee flipped over front to back, not so much flipping over as being tossed over. They were flying. It came to rest on its roof about twenty feet from the detonation point. Ty experienced a brief eerie silence before the chaos of tortured screams filled his senses.

Ty, not realizing he had a compound fracture of the left clavicle, released his seatbelt, and fell onto the Humvee roof. The sand was settling, which cleared his vision. Bobby 'Bulldog' Benson, who sat in the driver's side back seat, no longer had a head. A jagged dashboard fragment blew back and sliced it off. Ty looked down and saw Bulldog's head between his knees. Bulldog had a look of surprise on his face.

Unable to help Bulldog, Ty focused his attention on the screaming coming from the front seat, which came from Dirk Burnett. Dirk rode in the front passenger's seat. The blast had been so concentrated and powerful it broke the engine mounts and pushed the engine into the cab, where it rested on Dirk's and the driver, Clint McDonald's, lap. Clint wasn't screaming and Ty knew why; the steering column punched through Clint's chest, which collapsed the steering wheel, folding it like an umbrella. Clint was beyond Ty's help, too.

Ty scrambled out of the upside-down Humvee and yanked the front passenger door open. Dirk looked at Ty with such despair it unnerved him. Dirk had always been larger than life and tougher than nails.

He can't be too hurt, Ty thought.

When Ty undid Dirk's seatbelt, Dirk fell to the Humvee roof. His legs, from just below his crotch, did not. They remained trapped and crushed beneath the weight of the engine.

Ty dragged Dirk out of the Humvee, which he hadn't realized until they were clear of it, had been on fire. Dirk's stumps left a thick trail of blood in the sand. By this time, other Marines from the patrol were converging on them. At that point, the adrenalin rush wore off, and Ty felt exhausted. After collapsing next to Dirk, he felt the pain from where his clavicle broke the skin. He wiped his face, and his hand came away bloody. He didn't know if the blood came from him or one of his fellow Marines. It had been his blood. His vision went bright white.

Am I dying? Ty thought before he passed out.

Ty woke up a day later in the hospital, and only then realized the extent of his injuries. Besides the clavicle compound fracture, he had twenty-seven stitches above his right ear, a severe concussion, and a shattered left ankle. When he asked about Dirk, the doctor told him Dirk was alive, but he lost both legs and his left arm.

Ty received his second Purple Heart and the Silver Star for heroically pulling Dirk from the burning Humvee despite his injuries. Ty didn't feel like a hero. He helped his Marine brother, as any Marine would do, but he accepted the medal.

After convalescing in the Heathe N. Craig Joint Theater Hospital on Bagram Airfield for three days, Ty was sent state-side where he rehabbed his ankle and served the rest of his four-year enlistment period at Camp Lejeune.

When his enlistment was up, he briefly considered reenlisting, but opted not to. His dad had been right. Ty felt he was a better man for having served, and he felt as though he adequately served his country. Not that his sacrifice measured up to the thousands who died or the many thousands more who, like Dirk, left more than a little blood and terrible memories in Afghanistan, but enough.

When Ty returned to Pine View, it seemed smaller than ever, but he was happy to be home. Continuing in his dad's footsteps, Ty took a job as a logger and settled into civilian life.

Shortly after returning home, Ty ran into his old high school flame, Jasmine Cooke, at a Woodpecker football game, where he had been honored for his service. 'Local Football Star Returns Home a Military Hero' read the headline in the Saturday edition of the *Pine View Post*. He still didn't feel like a hero. Still, he limped out to mid-field during half-time to receive a standing ovation from the crowd and a certificate of appreciation from Pine View Mayor, Mac Peterson.

Ty and Jasmine became inseparable over the next few months. He proposed on Valentine's Day and on May 11, Jasmine Cooke became Jasmine Jackson. Ten months later, they had a son; they named him Derrick Tyrone Jackson after the grandfather he'd never meet and the dad who still walked with a slight limp on chilly mornings.

As far as Ty was concerned, his life was settled. He was married to a woman he loved deeply, and he had a son. He and Jasmine wanted at least two more children, though. Ty had a job that paid well enough that Jasmine could be a full-time mom, which is what she wanted to do, and was an assistant coach for one of Pine View's pee-wee football team, named the Hornets. A drive home from work one day changed his life and not in a bad way; for Ty, at least.

~ * ~

He'd been working a job off Highway Twenty-One, west of Nacogdoches. Fridays were early release and they shut things down at three o'clock. Ty waited at a stop sign for a Toyota Camry coming from the east to go by before he pulled onto Highway Twenty-One and headed west for home. As the sedan went by, Ty saw a man and woman in the front and a child's head barely visible above the window opening in the back seat. It looked like the man who had been driving was looking at his cell phone as they drove by.

Not smart, bro, Ty thought.

After they passed, Ty pulled on to Twenty-One behind them, accelerated to seventy-five, and set his cruise control. He ended up about a hundred yards behind them.

Highway Twenty-One has many curves and different elevations. Not the kind of road someone should play with their phone on. As they rounded a left-hand curve and started up a steep hill, Ty saw a log-truck at the top of the hill.

Log-trucks have bars extending up on either side of the fifth-wheel hookup, bars extending up on either side of the back axels, with a pipe that runs from the fifth-wheel hookup to the back axels that houses break lines for the back wheels and electric wiring for the back lights. Once logs are cut and limbs stripped off, debarking takes place at the sawmill. A crane is used, Ty's job for his logging outfit, to stack the logs between the front and back uprights. Once full, everything is tightly chained down to keep logs from bouncing off the trailer. The end product is a log-filled expanse from fifth wheel to back axels.

The log-truck had been pulling across Twenty-One to head east, which left plenty of time to stop and let the log-truck navigate its left turn. Ty tapped his brakes to disengage the cruise control and started coasting up the hill, letting the grade slow his speed. He also turned on his emergency flashers.

Ty knew from experience log-trucks rarely made a turn onto a main road in one attempt. The log roads they exited were usually only narrow dirt paths cut to allow access to the logged property and cutting a turn too sharply could cause the back wheels to slip off the road resulting in a stuck truck or, worse, an overturned truck. Ty saw this happen several times. So, he always put his emergency flashers on until the log-trucks were securely on hard pavement—all eighteen wheels.

Ty was looking ahead, but his thoughts were on getting home to Jasmine and Derrick. A blast from the log-truck's air horn brought him back to reality and the horror that was about to unfold in front of him. The log-truck's cab had made it into the east-bound lane of Twenty-One, but the back axle was still on the log path side of Twenty-One with the expanse of logs stretching across all lanes. The Camry in front of Ty showed no signs of slowing.

The horn blast must have alerted the man driving the Camry because Ty saw it swerve, as if looking for a way around the log-truck. The brake lights went on.

Ty screamed, "Duck down," to himself. The driver of the Camry certainly couldn't hear him.

It was too late.

As Ty watched in disbelief, the Camry smashed into the log expanse in a spray of shattered glass and crumpled metal. The Camry rode low enough that the bottom half continued under the logs while the car's top half sheared off.

Ty instinctively needed to help, if anyone remained alive to help. He sped up and brought his truck to a stop a few feet from where the Camry hit the logs. The roof of the Camry remained a crumpled mess that momentarily stuck to the logs. He could see what remained of the Camry, then a convertible, in the east side ditch about a hundred feet on the other side of the log-truck.

He thought, *God, please let 'em have ducked.*

No one popped up in the Camry. When the crumpled mess of the Camry's roof dislodged from the logs and fell to the pavement with a crash, Ty understood why no one popped up in the Camry. The bottom log was peppered with bits of glass, steel, and plastic from the Camry's roof. There were two very distinct, head shaped, patches of blood, bone, hair, and gray matter splattered on the bottom log, too.

Ty momentarily felt helpless. An instant later, he remembered the child in the back seat. He bolted from his truck and ducked under the logs.

As he did this, he heard the truck-driver, a guy named Otis Williams, who Ty loaded logs for, log-truck drivers were mostly independent contractors who hauled for many mills and logging companies, many times in the past, say, "They had room to stop, Ty."

Ty wasn't about to stop and chit-chat about what was then a moot point. His mind singularly focused on the kid he saw in the back seat.

Without slowing, Ty hollered, "Call nine, one, one."

He got to the Camry quickly. His 4.4 second, full-padded, forty-yard dash days were behind him, but despite his wounded ankle, he was still quick on his feet and skidded to a stop on the passenger's side of the Camry. He never suffered from PTSD—some bad dreams from his time in Afghanistan, but nothing paralyzing. What he saw then would haunt his dreams for some time to come.

The man and woman in the front seat, as the head sized and shaped blood, bone, hair, and gray matter patches on the bottom log showed, were headless. Not a clean-cut decapitation like Bulldog's. It removed their heads in a crushing, ripping motion that left jagged and torn neck wounds.

Ty looked into the back seat, hoping against hope the child ducked. She had, but what he saw still made Ty choke back bile that crept up his throat like a hot snake.

The little girl, she couldn't have been more than eight or nine years old, had been sitting in the center of the back seat. She had slipped out of the shoulder harness portion of her seatbelt and doubled over at the waist, her head between her knees, and her fingers interlocked over the back of her head. Like she had been assuming the crash position on an airplane.

Ty could see, under the blood and gore covering her back and head, she had blonde hair. Ty hoped like hell she hadn't seen what had been on the back seat on either side of her. Judging by the pile of vomit splattered between her feet, she had.

On either side of the little, blood-splattered, blonde-haired girl had been what was left of her parent's heads. The impact destroyed them. What remained were two piles of blood, brains, teeth, skin, bones, and hair, no more recognizable than a pumpkin dropped from a tall building onto concrete. The pile on the right of the little girl, what had been left of her mother's head, had blonde hair just like hers.

Ty opened the back door. It surprised him how easily it opened, like it hadn't just been in a collision serious enough to decapitate the two front occupants. Ty unlatched the little girl's seatbelt, and gently scooped her into his arms, making very sure to not let one part of her parent's shattered heads touch her. He lifted her from what was left of the Camry and, he suspected, her happy childhood.

As he was removing her, he saw two things, one pissed him off and one unnerved him. What pissed him off was he could see a cellphone still clutched in her father's hand. What unnerved him had been a bloodshot eyeball looking at him from the lump of blood, brains, teeth, bones, and brown hair that belonged to her texting and driving dad.

That eyeball seemed to say, "Take care of my little girl."

As Ty started to turn and take the little girl to his truck, he heard retching behind him. It was Otis. He vomited what looked like several Grand Slam breakfasts from Denny's.

Get your shit together, Otis, Ty thought.

He figured Otis was due for a good puking. After all, he'd had to choke back bile, too.

He took the little girl to his truck. More cars were pulling up behind his truck by then. He laid her down on the bench seat. Ty got a blanket he kept in his truck bed toolbox for chilly mornings when he was waiting for log-trucks to load. He realized the last time he'd used it had been while waiting for Otis to show up the previous February. Ty covered the little girl with it. He knew the signs of shock from his time in Afghanistan and the little girl was in shock. About the time he finished taking care of the little girl, her daddy's eyeball would approve, to the extent he could, he heard a siren coming from the east.

The Pine View County Sheriff's SUV sped west in the east-bound lane and came to a stop by Ty's truck. The deputy, Ty thought he recognized the guy, exited his SUV and ducked under the logs. Ty knew the deputy would eventually want to hear from him, so he waited by his truck, he had no desire to see the gory scene again anyway, while the deputy questioned Otis.

While Ty waited, DPS and an ambulance arrived. DPS came on the west side of the log-truck, the ambulance came on Ty's side of the truck. Ty tried to get them to tend to the little girl, telling them the other occupants were beyond their aid. Ignoring him, they ducked under the logs and disappeared. It was with some satisfaction Ty heard one or both of them lose their lunch, the sound of retching, followed by loud, liquid splats on Highway Twenty-One. When they reemerged from under the logs, they were both sporting ashen complexions and were more eager to tend to the little girl.

As they lifted her out of Ty's truck, she grabbed his hand and squeezed it tight. This was the first sign of awareness he'd seen from her and, although it hurt his heart to let her hand go as they finally loaded her into the ambulance, she refused to let go until then. He considered her grasping at him a good sign.

Surely there are people in her life she can hold on to? Ty thought.

Ty visited her in the hospital with Jasmine and Little D, as they called him, the next day, and met her very appreciative aunt and uncle. Their names were Brooke and Hunter Milbank. Law enforcement told them Ty had been the first 'on scene' and took care, as the eyeball requested, of June, until help arrived.

Because of the trauma she'd endured, Ty wasn't sure if June would remember him, but, to everyone's surprise, she jumped out of the hospital bed and wrapped him in a tight hug. Ty hugged her back and stroked her beautiful blonde hair, the blood and brains since washed away.

He didn't ask, but he was sure June's aunt and her mother were sisters. Brooke sported the same blonde hair as June and the lump of mush on the seat beside her. About an hour after they arrived, Ty and family said their goodbyes and left June with her new family. Brooke and Hunter had twin daughters a year younger than June.

As they left, Ty thought, *she'll be just fine. She's not headed for Rusk State Hospital*, which was a state facility for the insane. He smiled.

~ * ~

About the time the little girl was being loaded into the ambulance, the deputy came up to Ty and introduced himself as Deputy Garrett Lambert. Ty thought he looked familiar and, of course, he knew who he was. Every Woodpecker football player knew about the eighty-one-yard QB scramble that brought Pine View High its first A-1 state championship.

When Ty introduced himself, it surprised him to find Deputy Lambert knew who he was, too. Garrett attended the Homecoming Football Game that honored Ty at halftime. They stood there for several minutes, the accident forgotten, and recited their football stats to one another.

When they got back to discussing the accident, Ty told Garrett everything he witnessed since the Camry passed him before he pulled onto Twenty-One behind it. He left out the part about the little girl's father's eyeball looking at him and telling him to take care of his little girl.

Garrett confirmed Ty's suspicions the male driver had been texting. Garrett powered up the cellphone. He found text exchanges between the driver and the female passenger. Apparently, they had been texting each other 'adult' texts so the little girl would be none the wiser about what her folks were up to. That cleared up the nagging question bouncing around in Ty's head, why had the woman not seen the truck either?

At least the little girl saw it and ducked in time, Ty thought.

When Ty and Garrett parted, Garrett gave Ty his card and told him to call him if he ever wanted to talk football, Woodpecker or otherwise. A week later, Ty called Garrett and invited him to his house for supper. After supper, Ty and Garrett talked while Jasmine and Little D listened. Little D chimed in occasionally.

At ten o'clock, Jasmine excused herself and Little D, who was sound asleep in her arms, saying, "I'll leave you two football studs to your past glory."

Ty jokingly said, "That hurts my man parts, woman."

Jasmine winked at Ty, gave Garrett a wave, and left them to their past glory.

Ty and Garrett continued to talk about football, life, hunting, and many subjects two guys who are becoming friends talk about while they drank beer until almost midnight. By the time Garrett left, they were good friends, and Ty was convinced he wanted to be a Pine View County Deputy Sheriff. Garrett promised to help in any way he could, and, like all his promises, he kept this one.

When Garrett won the election for Pine View County Sheriff in November 2012 and became sheriff in January 2013, Ty became his first new hire.

~ * ~

At four thirteen a.m., on Monday, May fifth, Ty received a disturbance call and, given the name and address of the caller—Carla Weaver, Twenty-One Eighteen, County Road Five Sixty-Nine. Ty, who was only a few miles from the address, rolled his eyes as he reported he would handle the call.

The eye roll had been because he, as well as every other Pine View County Deputy Sheriff, was very familiar with Carla Weaver. She was a seventy-six-year-old widow who called in a disturbance every time she heard a bump in the night, or any time of day. Most deputies referred to Carla as 'The widow who cried wolf'. Not responding wasn't an option.

Ty spun his SUV around and headed her way.

Carla's driveway was little more than a narrow dirt road off County Road Five Sixty-Nine. If it weren't for the dented mailbox atop a leaning post on the side of Five Sixty-Nine, passersby wouldn't know there was a driveway. Carla's house was about a thousand feet back in the woods and not visible from the county road.

As Ty turned into the driveway, he switched on the windshield post mounted spotlight and drove slowly toward her house, sweeping the spotlight from left to right, knowing he was unlikely to see anything but letting her know he was taking her call seriously none the less.

When he got to the end of her driveway, he saw Carla had all her outside lights on, which illuminated her 'yard.' The yard was really nothing more than a dumping ground for lots of crap, broken-down cars, tires, kitchen appliances, furniture. Ty swept the spotlight into the woods surrounding Carla's house a final time, switched it off, killed the SUV engine, radioed dispatch that he was on the premises, and stepped out of his patrol vehicle.

As Ty was closing the SUV door, Carla came out on her front porch carrying a double-barrel shotgun that was almost as long as she was tall. Ty wasn't alarmed. She often greeted deputies brandishing her trusty twelve-gauge.

"Oh, Officer Ty, I'm glad you're here," Carla said excitedly.

She never called him Deputy Jackson, and Ty stopped correcting her on his second or third disturbance call.

Ty climbed the porch steps and said, as he always said, "Howdy, Missus Weaver. Think ya could put that shotgun down for me?"

Carla looked down at the shotgun in her arms, as if she were seeing it for the first time and gave Ty a weak smile as she leaned it against her house by the front door.

"Thank you. Now, what seems to be the problem this mornin'?"

Ty listened as Carla told him about the events that led to her calling the sheriff's department. It started when something hit the side of her house with a loud 'thump' and woke her up a little after four o'clock.

"It sounded big," Carla elaborated.

A scraping sound followed the loud 'thump' under her bedroom window, which was on the back, right-hand side of her house. She told Ty the scraping sound gave her 'shiver's.'

When she heard a commotion in her pigpen out back, she grabbed her shotgun and went out the back door to, "Shoot the critter that was after my pigs."

What she told Ty next unnerved him and he immediately felt foolish for feeling so. She said there were awful sounds coming from the pigpen, deep, loud growls and screamin' pigs.

She shouted, "Get outta my pigpen." and fired a warning shot in the air to "scare off whatever was after my pigs."

Carla looked nervous. "It got quiet after I shot, Officer Ty. Too quiet. Not a sound around. Except…breathin'. I could hear somethin' breathin' out there. More 'n one thing too…I think. I may be a silly ol' woman, but that breathin' scared me…bad. So, I came inside and called the police."

Ty considered Carla and her story for a moment. "Go on back inside, and I'll have a look around."

Carla gave him an appreciative smile. "Thank ya, Officer Ty."

As she was closing the door she added, "Be careful. Whatever was back there was…evil."

Ty assured Cara he would be careful and headed down the porch steps to investigate.

With his trusty Mag flashlight lighting the way, Ty headed around the right side of Carla's house. He wanted to see if there was evidence of the 'scraping" she'd heard under her bedroom window.

Carla's house was pier and beam construction, meaning it was raised instead of on a concrete slab. Ty looked for evidence of the scrapping sound below the bedroom window at about the height where an animal, or person trying to scare an old lady, could reach. The weathered blue wood siding had peeling paint and some rot. Ty saw no sign of recent damage, though.

Ty raised the flashlight beam toward the window and found the source of the scraping sound. There were four deep, ragged gouges cut into the siding from just below Carla's bedroom window, which had to be about seven feet off the ground.

Ty studied the gouges, trying to determine what could have caused them. He put his hand up to the gouges and spread his fingers, trying to judge the size, and spacing. Ty had big hands, but the gouges were wider.

Must've been a rake or pitchfork, Ty thought.

That would certainly explain how high the marks were. He took out his iPhone and took several pictures, one with his hand spread to show size and spacing.

Ty looked at the gouges one more time before heading to the pigpen out back and thought, *they look more like claw marks*.

After navigating through the clutter, junk, which was fast overtaking Carla's back yard too, Ty found the narrow path leading from the house back door to the pigpen that was about a hundred feet away, just before the yard turned into dense forest. Ty advanced on the pigpen slowly, sweeping his flashlight beam from side to side as he did.

So much crap, Ty thought.

The collection of assorted automobiles, appliances, and furniture from the front yard had long ago spilled into the backyard.

So many places to hide, he added as an afterthought.

The pigpen comprised a shelter with its back facing the house, north so the winter wind wouldn't chill the pigs, and a fenced in area. The fence was about four feet high to facilitate Carla being able to dump food in the trough over the fence. The fenced in area was about three-hundred square feet where the feed trough and mud puddles pigs enjoy so much were.

Ty raised pigs in high school while in FFA. He knew they got a bad rap for being stupid, dirty animals. They were smart animals. They always shit in one spot away from their food source, and mud was just a way for them to cool off. Ty's pigs preferred to cool off in the kiddie-pool he put in their pen.

As Ty approached the pigpen, it struck him by how damn quiet everything was. No frogs croaking, no crickets chirping, no nothing. Not even the usual sounds of critters—raccoons, armadillos, opossums, foraging in the very near forest. He pointed his flashlight at the woods. Nothing there.

Ty rounded the shelter and pointed his flashlight inside. He was startled by what he saw. The pigs, from the carnage he couldn't determine how many there *had* been, were ripped to pieces. Hind legs, forelegs, and heads were strewn about. Some torsos were torn in half and displayed jagged claw marks and vicious bite wounds. The shelter's dirt floor was covered with blood and entrails.

There was a sudden grunt from within the pen to Ty's right and it startled him so much he jumped, and his right hand closed around the grip of his pistol. Keeping clear of the pen, Ty pointed the flashlight toward where the sound came from and saw a very large Duroc boar. It must have been Carla's breeder pig. It had been in a smaller pen by itself. Boars will eat piglets if left to their own devices, so separating them from sows and piglets was standard practice. At first Ty thought it laid on the wet ground for an early morning cool down but, as he approached it, he saw differently—the ground was saturated with blood.

The boar had to have weighed in at five hundred pounds. It had a massive head with large tusks, at least eight inches long, protruding from its lower jaw. The tusks were covered in blood and Ty could see a clump of thick, black hair stuck to its right tusk. The boar put up one hell of a fight against whatever wreaked havoc in the pigpen, but his wounds were severe.

In the flashlight's beam, Ty could see several unnaturally large bite marks on its back, like whatever attacked it had jaws large enough to close over the boar's wide back and bite down on both sides at the same time. The boar was also sporting several claw marks on its right side. One of which had opened the boar's side and belly to where its intestines were out and trailing behind it. Seeing this, Ty realized the boar must have crawled from where it had been attacked to where it was then lying.

The boar gave another tortured grunt. Ty shone the flashlight it its face. The boar's eyes were wide with terror. Ty pulled his pistol from its holster to put the beast out of its misery when it gave a tremendous shudder. Its massive head fell to the blood-soaked ground with a sickening 'splat' and 'thud.' Its eyes rolled up, showing only the whites, and it expired with one last grunt.

While Ty felt sorry the boar suffered, he was glad he hadn't needed to discharge his weapon to put it out of its misery. Even something as straightforward as simply ending the boar's suffering would require paperwork and paperwork was Ty's least favorite part of the job. With the boar dead, Ty went about the business of collecting evidence, the hair on the boar's tusk, and documenting the scene, taking pictures with his iPhone.

Ty squatted down beside the pen fence just opposite the boar's head and propped his flashlight against the hog-wire fencing so its beam shone directly on the bloody tusk on which the coarse, black hairs were stuck. He pulled one of the rubber gloves he kept tucked between his utility belt and pants, always be prepared, and snapped it onto his right hand.

Unfortunately, always being prepared didn't apply to having an evidence bag handy. Ty retrieved another rubber glove, blew into it to open it up, and held the opening between his thumb and index finger so it would hang open. He reached through the hog-wire fencing. The opening was large enough to accommodate his hand and he plucked the hairs from the tusk.

With the hairs removed, Ty could get a better look at the specimen. He brought it closer to the flashlight and tilted it to see the base of the hairs. Ty saw skin at the base of the hairs. It was dark, almost as dark as the hairs. Very pleased, because skin would allow for a more in-depth, DNA analysis, Ty deposited the skin and hairs in the rubber glove that was serving as an evidence bag, rolled it up, and placed it in the right breast pocket of his uniform shirt. He removed the other glove, wadded it up, and stuck it in his right back pocket. With the evidence collected, it was time to take pictures.

Ty grabbed the flashlight and stood up, his knees popping as he did. *Just high school ball and my knees are shot*, Ty thought.

As he walked toward the shelter where most of the carnage took place, Ty pulled out his iPhone and tapped the camera app. Before taking pictures of the mutilated pigs, he stepped back toward Carla's house and took a wide-angle shot of the pigpen, shelter, and woods beyond. Then he started snapping pictures from outside the pen.

Going inside the pen to get close-ups of the wounds would have been ideal, but Ty knew that wasn't an option. At least not in the dark. If he did, he'd likely ruin any animal tracks left behind by whatever turned Carla Weaver's pigpen into a late-night buffet. Another deputy would have to return when the sun came up and further document the scene.

With each flash from the camera, the horrific details of the pig's last moments of life were illuminated in stark relief, captured in binary ones and zeros on the iPhone's sixty-four GB hard drive. After each picture, Ty would check it to make sure he captured what he intended to. While studying one picture, Ty realized what he'd initially thought were entrails leaking out of a gash on one large sow were not yet delivered piglets.

"What the fuck happened to y'all?" Ty asked aloud, as if he were questioning a living, human victim.

When he took enough pictures of the dead pigs in the shelter, Ty walked back to the boar and snapped a few pictures of the wounds that were visible on its side facing the shelter. He hadn't yet looked at the side of the boar that faced the thick woods, which started about twenty feet from the south end of the pigpen fence.

Ty made his way around the end of the pen and pointed the flashlight at the boar's other side. It had been ripped open to where he could see the boar's ribcage. The boar's skin and muscle were shredded and hung in flaps from its side.

With his back to the woods, Ty pointed the iPhone at the ragged wound and was about to snap a picture when he got the distinct feeling he was being watched. The hairs on the back of his neck prickled and his arms broke out in goose bumps.

~ * ~

Ty knew everyone could sense danger; it's one thing that helped homo sapiens evolve. Ty refined this sense during his three combat tours in Afghanistan. When he first started having 'hunches' about impending threats, his patrol buddies gave him a hard time. As more and more of his hunches came to fruition, they relied on them.

If Ty suddenly stopped and looked in a particular direction, someone on patrol with him would always say something like, "We gotta Ty hunch happenin' boys." Eventually, "Ty hunch" had been shortened to "tunch" as in, "We gotta tunch happenin' boys." Ty was having a very strong tunch that something was watching him from the woods.

Not wanting to turn around too suddenly and provoke an attack, but needing to turn around before whatever mutilated the pigs, his tunch told him whatever the pig mutilator had been, that's what was watching him from the woods, attacked him from behind, Ty readied himself.

He tucked the iPhone into the left breast pocket of his uniform shirt. The flashlight was in Ty's left hand so he would bring it up under his gun hand to illuminate where to shoot, if it came to that. Ty unsnapped the holster strap that kept his sidearm from bouncing out of the holster if he were ever engaged in a foot pursuit. He'd been on two, one with a tweaking meth-head and one with an ill-tempered drunk. He pulled the pistol from its holster, flipped off the safety, and slowly turned to face the woods.

He pointed the flashlight into the woods directly behind him, where his tunch indicated danger. He saw nothing, but the flashlight beam didn't penetrate more than a few feet into the woods, which were dense with undergrowth. To further hamper visibility, an early morning, low-lying fog was seeping out of the woods and into Carla's cluttered back yard. Ty could feel something was still watching him, something just outside of his sight.

There was a metallic scraping sound to Ty's right. He turned quickly and thought he saw something large move into the woods about thirty feet from where he stood. His head moved quicker than the flashlight and, even though it had been a cloudless, full moon night, he couldn't be sure he'd seen anything more than the pile of tires and the rusted hulk of an old refrigerator the flashlight beam was then resting on.

For a second, Ty felt silly. Then he heard something—it sounded large—crashing through the undergrowth off to his left. As Ty spun and pointed the flashlight in the area from which the crashing came, the crashing suddenly stopped. From directly in front of Ty, out of sight, something took a deep breath and snorted. Then it growled. It was a deep, raspy growl that rumbled through Ty like base from a subwoofer. Another growl joined the first from the right, and then two more from the left.

Ty's tunch told him to get the fuck out of there, but to do so slowly. He took a step backward, and the growling stopped. Somehow, that unnerved him more than the sinister growls. Ty wasn't about to analyze the situation. Instead, he took another step backward and to his right to maneuver around the pigpen. He could hear breathing in the woods, deep breathing, and he understood why it unnerved Carla so badly she called nine-one-one.

Ty took another step backward, then another, and another.

Nothing came after him, but it sounded like the breathing advanced through the woods with each step he took. He was passed the shelter at that point and on the narrow trail that led back to Carla's house. The breathing stopped.

Ty froze, not sure what to expect. Seconds passed like minutes, but nothing happened. Ty took another step backward. His foot hit something, and he fell over backward. His butt landed on something hard that sent a shock through his body. He scrambled to his feet and saw a hubcap half buried in the dirt, that he'd tripped on, and a dented old milk jug, that he'd landed on.

He heard unfamiliar noises from the woods; it sounded like demonic laughter. This laughter, a mix of growls and yips, sent shivers up his spine that unnerved him more than anything, including what he experienced in Afghanistan, ever unnerved him before.

As the laughter subsided, somehow, Ty found the nerve to turn his back on the woods. He had his dignity, and the laughter wounded it. Ty slowly walked back towards Carla's house. The junk in Carla's back yard seemed to close in on him.

So many fuckin' places to hide, Ty thought again.

Although walking forward, Ty still took several apprehensive looks over his shoulder as he neared Carla's house. Nothing came after him. As he rounded the corner of Carla's house, he looked up at the gouges in her siding.

They're fuckin' claw marks, Ty thought.

~ * ~

From about ten yards into the woods and down low in the thick underbrush, four pairs of burning red eyes watched the deputy disappear around the side of the old woman's house. The alpha snorted again, and a thick stream of blood and mucus jetted from its wolf-like snout. It enjoyed watching the deputy squirm. It could smell the fear oozing out of his pores. It could hear his heart hammering in his chest and the rapid, shallow breaths he was taking.

For the alpha, instilling fear in other living creatures was almost as much fun as ripping them to pieces with its claws and teeth. It knew the members of its pack wanted to kill the deputy. They wouldn't start an attack. That was the alpha's prerogative. The alpha wasn't ready to kill the deputy yet. It marked his scent, though, so he would be easy to track if or when it decided to kill him.

The pigs were fun, a bit of bloodlust, but the big boar inflicted a wound on the alpha's lower leg with its tusks as the alpha had 'played' with it. The wound would heal by the time it took human form again, but the boar paid a price. The alpha bit down across the boar's broad back, lifted it off the ground, and used its razor-sharp claws to disembowel it. That had been when the old woman from the house screamed and blasted her gun. The alpha and two of its pack retreated to the woods to watch and wait. The fourth stayed in the yard lurking among the junk, concealed from view.

The alpha enjoyed watching the boar drag its dying carcass across the blood splattered mud with its intestines spilling out behind it. The alpha decided it would kill the old woman for interrupting play time when it heard the approaching vehicle from several miles away. Its hearing was acute in wolf form.

It knew its pack was growing restless, but watching the deputy as he realized he was no longer at the top of the food chain made waiting worth it. The way he jumped when the pack member leapt from behind the refrigerator into the woods, the way his heart quickened when another member rustled the brush, and the way he trembled when they growled. It particularly enjoyed it when the deputy tripped and fell on his ass. It felt good to laugh in wolf form.

It could clearly hear the deputy talking with the old woman at the front of the house. It almost decided to kill both of them when it heard a truck rumbling in the distance. Its large pointy ears twisted back to better hear. By the sound of it, the truck was a couple of miles away. That didn't matter. In wolf form the alpha and its pack could cover that distance quickly.

Its pack was restless. It was time to hunt. The alpha turned and sprinted away on all fours. The pack fell in behind it. Russ Lomax had minutes left to live.

~ * ~

Ty never felt more relieved than he did when he was on Carla Weaver's front porch. The tunch was still there, but somehow, he sensed he was no longer in immediate danger.

Carla opened the door on his first knock. She looked small and worried.

Ty took a deep breath. "I'm sorry, Missus Weaver, but your pigs are dead."

Carla looked surprised. "All of 'em? Even Bingo?"

She saw this didn't register with Office Ty. She clarified, "My big boar. His name is Bingo."

Ty nodded.

Carla looked truly shocked. "What could'a kilt him? He's big as a bear and twice as mean…if'n he don't know ya.

"He's a teddy bear with me. He took after ol' Gentry's bull when he got out once and damn near kilt him. Cost me somethin' like three hundred dollars to patch up that bull. Almost slaughtered Bingo after that…but I just couldn't bring myself to do it. Guess I'll be eatin' pork for a while now, though. Huh?" she finished with a nervous laugh.

Ty didn't have an answer for what killed Bingo and he didn't think eating Bingo was a good idea. He told her as much. He told her he'd gotten some hair and skin that could be analyzed.

"Oh good," she said, "So you'll have some DNA results later today?"

Ty had to stifle a chuckle. He, and most everyone at any level of law enforcement, were familiar with this misconception. They called it the 'CSI Affect' because, on the crime shows, they always secured DNA results in a matter of hours, not the matter of weeks or months it sometimes took. When Ty told her how long it could take, Carla kicked the doorframe in frustration.

Ty said, "I know a professor of zoology and biology at SFA. Her name is Doctor Emily Yost and she's good at identifying critters by their hair. We've used her on cases before. I can take a few hairs to her and get her opinion on what it might be. The DNA results will be more definitive, but it can't hurt to see what she thinks."

Carla liked that idea.

With that out of the way, Ty explained he couldn't get into the pigpen to get better pictures and someone else would be out a little later, when the sun came up, to further document what happened to her pigs. She understood. He also told her to stay inside until the next deputy arrived. She didn't have a problem with that. Finally, he told her she wouldn't want to see the remains of her pigs. On this, she pushed back.

"It's a free county and my property."

Ty told her he didn't think she'd like what she saw, but admitted it was indeed a free county and her property. She could look if she wanted to.

"Not until the deputy arrives," he reiterated.

She conceded.

What Ty didn't tell her about had been the growls and demonic laughing. She'd heard the breathing, and that had been bad enough. No need adding to her distress.

As Ty made his way back to the patrol SUV, he realized the tunch was completely gone. Whatever mutilated the pigs and played, that's what it felt like, with him from within the woods, was gone. He was sure of that.

He opened the back of the SUV and retrieved an evidence bag, into which he placed the rolled-up rubber glove that contained the hair and skin. With a Sharpie, he wrote, Carla Weaver, Twenty-One Eighteen, CR Five Sixty-Nine, 5.05.15, on the evidence bag's white strip, sealed it, and dropped it into the evidence kit.

As Ty shut the back end, a howl shattered the early morning calm. It was like nothing Ty ever heard. Although the tunch was gone, that howl sent shivers down his spine, goosebumps spread across his arms again, and it felt like the bottom fell out of his stomach. When he gathered himself enough to walk again, he headed for the SUV's driver's side door.

Just as he reached it, Carla opened the front door of her house and shouted, "What the fuck was that?"

It's what killed your fuckin' pigs, Ty thought.

He lied and said, "Probably coyotes. Just stay inside, Missus Weaver."

Carla shook her head emphatically. "No fuckin' way that's a coyote."

Then the howl, howls, came again. Carla jumped back inside so quickly she was only a blur and slammed the door hard. Ty, feeling like he'd never be happy again, got into the SUV, belted, started the engine, and drove out of Carla Weaver's driveway.

~ * ~

Ty still had about two hours left in his shift, which ended at seven o'clock, so he decided to cruse some of the nearby county roads to see if there were other mutilated animal carcasses in the vicinity. If he came across something, he'd mark it on GPS so someone could investigate further once the night gave way to daylight. A little voice whispering at the back of his mind told him daylight meant safety. That little voice, a new tunch, had been wise.

After driving the length of County Road Five Sixty-Nine back to where it dead-ended into FM Twenty-Two, Ty turned left, toward the direction the howls came from, drove about a mile to where County Road Five Seventy intersected FM Twenty-Two, and turned left onto CR Five Seventy. As he drove the length of CR Five Seventy, about four miles, to where it dead-ended into Highway Twenty-One, the low-lying fog that seeped out of the woods behind Carla's house completely covered the road, making visibility difficult.

At the end of CR Five Seventy, Ty turned right on Highway Twenty-One, still heading toward the howls, drove about another mile, and turned right on CR Five Seventy-One. Although the fog was still hampering visibility, the eastern sky was turning a deep purple as the sun rose.

About the time Ty convinced himself he was wasting his time looking for mutilated animals, he rounded a left-hand curve and saw headlights glowing in the fog a couple of hundred feet up the road. The odd thing was that the headlights weren't pointed directly at Ty, as they would have been if the vehicle were driving toward him. They were pointing off the side of the road, to Ty's right, and stationary.

Probably stuck, Ty thought as he sped up towards the fog-haloed headlights.

The purple eastern sky turned an angry shade of orange by the time Ty pulled up to the vehicle, which was an International Harvester truck. Even with the better light afforded by the fast-rising sun, Ty's mind struggled to make sense of what he was seeing. It was Russ Lomax's truck. He'd known Russ Lomax for most of his life, and it looked like Russ was popping up out of the IH's crumpled hood.

Ty stopped his SUV just a few feet from the IH and stared at Russ Lomax's face. There was blood and other liquids, brown and green oozing from Russ' mouth and down what used to be his white beard. His eyes were wide but showed only white.

Like Bingo's eyes after he died, Ty thought.

That thought brought Ty back to reality and, for the first time, he saw what he was seeing. Russ Lomax's head wasn't popping out of the IH's crumpled hood, it had been resting *on* the IH's crumpled hood. Like a grotesque hood ornament.

Ty depressed the radio call button. "Code seven on CR Five Seven One. I repeat, code seven on CR Five Seven One. It's Russ Lomax."

Code seven meant 'dead person.'

Ty had considered calling a code five, which was 'murder,' but it was too soon to tell, even though he was damn sure Russ' head hadn't gotten up there on its own.

A second later, his radio chirped, and he heard, "Ty, this is Garrett. I'm on my way. Twenty in three minutes."

Ty was glad Garrett was the one responding.

Chapter Four

The old, dilapidated Wiseman barn stood in a small clearing, deep in the woods, southeast of Pine View County. It had last been in regular use in the late 1960's when Dale Wiseman attempted to capitalize on the peace, love, rock and roll era. He grew marijuana and sold it to a distributer out of Houston. He'd have gotten away with it if the Feds hadn't blindly stumbled into his crop while looking for moonshiners. They did, and that had been that.

After Dale's conviction on drug trafficking charges, the federal government seized his land, forty-four acres, and barn, and he received a sentence of twelve years in federal prison. He served his time in the Federal Correctional Institution in Texarkana, Texas and returned to Pine View after being released. Shortly thereafter, Dale was convicted of raping a fourteen-year-old girl in nearby Jacksonville. For this crime, he received ninety-nine-years in the Texas State Penitentiary at Huntsville. Twenty-seven months into his ninety-nine-year stretch, guards found Dale dead in a pool of blood and shit in the showers with a broken broomstick protruding from his rectum.

When asked his thoughts on Dale's demise by a reporter, the father of the girl whom Dale raped simply said, "Hope it hurt."

Since the days of Dale's arrest and drug trafficking conviction, the Wiseman land, now owned by the federal government, became overgrown and the barn fell into disrepair. A pine tree fell across one end and partially collapsed the roof. Rot ate through many of the bat-and-board side panels. All the windows had long since been broken. A lightning strike started a fire that burned a hole in the front right corner of the roof. If it hadn't been for the deluge of rain that accompanied the lightning, the barn would have been reduced to a pile of smoldering ash. That it still stood was a testament to its construction long ago.

The barn became home to all matters of critters, insects, and reptiles. Occasionally a hunter or teenager would wonder up the twisted and overgrown drive that led to the barn. There had been no reason to stay, and they didn't. On this morning, a 2003, four-wheel drive, four-door Ram pickup was parked behind the structure. It was matte black with tinted windows. A string of Mardi Gras beads dangled from the rearview mirror.

Although the sun was fast rising in the east, turning the morning sky an angry orange, the thick canopy created by the treetops kept the forest around the barn in deep shadows. A commotion in the woods sent nearby birds into startled flight. Four large, hairy beasts emerged from the woods, wisps of fog trailing them, and made their way into the barn. An assortment of growls, snorts, and yips soon developed into moans, cries of pain, and heavy breathing—transformation was painful. The barn fell silent. Several minutes later, four people emerged from the barn. They got into the Ram pickup and disappeared down the overgrown, twisted drive, a woman in the driver's seat.

~ * ~

When Garrett rolled up behind Ty's SUV, he saw Ty used crime tape to section off Lomax's truck and the ditch to the right. Ty sat on the back bumper of his patrol SUV. Ty got up and came toward Garrett's vehicle as he killed the engine and stepped out.

"It's bad, Garrett."

Off duty and when alone on duty, Ty referred to him as Garrett. On duty with others around, he always referred to him as Sheriff Lambert. Garrett could tell what happened had shaken his friend.

"Show me."

Ty stepped aside and swept his left arm toward the taped off area. After you, the gesture implied. Garrett stepped past Ty, who fell in behind him, and started toward Lomax's truck. As Garrett cleared the cab of Ty's SUV, he got a better view of Lomax's truck and the trophy left on its crumpled hood. Garrett stopped suddenly, causing Ty to run into him, and took in a deep breath.

As the breath rushed out, Garrett uttered a hushed, "Holy shit."

Aside from Russ' head being displayed prominently on the hood, the IH had been beat all to hell. The passenger and driver doors were buckled inward as if something large rammed them. He could see the glass on both doors and the back were shattered. The backrest portion of the driver's side seat had blood on it.

As Garrett's eyes were drawn back to the hood, he noticed the crumpled middle, but not as if he'd run into something. In the middle of the hood, on either side of the midline, were two deep depressions. As if someone, something, bipedal, and very heavy, jumped onto the hood.

"Holy shit," Garrett repeated.

To which Ty responded, "That's not the worst of it."

Ty stepped around Garrett and led him around the front of Lomax's truck to the carnage in the ditch. Garrett took it all in without saying a word. What he saw could have been the shredded remains of any large animal. Nothing but blood, torn flesh, organs, cracked bone, and intestines. What distinguished the pile of gore as human were the shredded fragments of bib-overalls intermixed with the remains and two lace-up work boots had, what were unmistakably, human legs sticking out of them. The legs ended in shredded flesh and crushed bones.

After what seemed to Garrett to have been minutes, but had only been seconds, he pointed at the pile of feces on the pile of Russ Lomax. "Is that…?"

"Scat," Ty finished the interrupted question.

Garrett shook his head in disbelief, then he looked back at Russ' head. "What the fuck could do this?"

It was a rhetorical question, because he didn't believe there was a rational answer readily available.

Ty responded, "The same thing that mutilated Carla Weaver's pigs."

Garrett, unaware of the disturbance call from Carla Weaver, looked back at Ty. "Tell me. Tell me everything."

Ty recounted everything that transpired on the call. He even told Garrett about his tunch, which he wouldn't have shared with anyone else, except his old Marine buddies. He left out the part about falling on his ass while backing away, though. Some indignities are personal.

When he finished, Garrett said, "Have ya documented this scene?"

Ty nodded. "I've got pictures of everything. Inside the truck, too. I collected some hair fibers from the back glass and," he crinkled his nose, "I collected some of the scat."

Garrett gave Ty an approving pat of the shoulder. He checked his watch. It was almost seven, which meant the seven-to-three shift deputies would already be at the department.

He took out his cellphone and called the department dispatch. Karen Parker, the eleven-to-seven dispatcher, answered. Garrett told her to send Deputies Billy Hoyt and Connor Perry to his location on County Road Five Seventeen. He also told her to send out the County Coroner,

George Krats, and the county tow-truck driver, Brent Simmons. Last, he asked her to track down Russ Lomax's next of kin. Garrett thought his daughter Margaret might live in Dallas.

As the fog in the forest dissipated, so did the fog in Garrett's head. He was getting his investigative groove back.

When Garrett hung up with Karen, because they had time to kill until Hoyt and Perry showed up, he asked Ty to show him the pictures he'd taken at Weaver's place. Ty took out his iPhone and tapped on the 'Photos' app. He started swiping through the pictures he'd taken of the Lomax scene. There were quite a few, and he stopped when he got to the picture of Bingo's back, which were the last he'd taken at the Weaver scene.

Garrett studied the picture for several seconds. He looked at the bite marks on Bingo's back closely.

After several seconds, Garrett said, "That's a big fuckin' bite."

Ty nodded and wondered aloud, "What in East Texas could do that? Bear?"

Garrett pondered a second. "Grizzly bear, maybe. Only there aren't grizzlies in East Texas."

More silence, then Ty said, "You know how some folks say the New York sewers are full of alligators' people get as pets when they're little and flush 'em when they get bigger?"

Garrett nodded.

"Then," Ty continued, "the alligators get big as shit feedin' on rats, trash, and shit."

"Ya think a fuckin' alligator did this?"

"No, not alligators. What if someone released some grizzlies they couldn't care for anymore?"

Garrett considered this theory for a minute. He didn't think it was likely, but nothing else made sense either.

After looking at the Bingo picture a little longer, Garrett gave a nod and Ty continued swiping through the shots. After studying each briefly, Garrett would give a nod and Ty would swipe to another picture. When Ty got to the wide shot, he took of the shelter, pen, and woods beyond, he swiped past it quickly.

Garrett said, "Whoa, whoa. Go back."

Ty swiped back to the picture. "That's just one I took to show the whole pigpen."

Garrett held out his hand. "May I?"

Ty handed Garrett his phone.

Garrett brought the phone up close to his face and studied the picture for a few seconds.

He positioned the phone to where Ty could see it and pointed at the woods. "What the hell are those?"

Ty studied the picture but didn't see whatever Garrett was pointing at.

"What's what?" Ty asked.

Garrett did a reverse pinch on the picture, which enlarged it, then used his finger to slide the picture to a particular place.

"That," Garrett said, pointing his finger at two red dots burning from within the dark woods.

Ty studied the burning red dots, and a chill went up his spine as he realized those dots would have been directly in line with where he'd been standing when his tunch went off.

"There's two more sets," Garrett said.

He used his finger to move the picture to the left. As he did, two more burning dots came into view, then two more.

When Garrett pinched the picture back to normal size, Ty could clearly see all three pairs of burning red dots hovering in the dark woods.

Ty cleared his throat. "Lightning bugs?"

He was trying to rationalize the irrational.

Garrett shook his head. "No way. Lightening bugs put off a greenish-yellow glow. Not red, and look," Garrett pointed at the dots again, "They're evenly spaced. Like…"

"Eyes," Ty finished Garrett's sentence for him.

They looked at each other, neither wanting to acknowledge what they both understood to be true. The burning red orbs were eyes.

As if saving them from having to confirm this, they heard an approaching vehicle. It was two vehicles, Hoyt and Perry were pulling up behind Garrett's SUV. They walked back to meet them.

Upon viewing Russ Lomax's remains, Hoyt lost his breakfast and Perry let out several tortured gagging sounds, but he didn't spew. Once they regained their composure, Garrett instructed them to stay at the scene and wait for George Krats and Brent Simmons. They nodded their pasty white faces.

Garrett took Ty aside. "I know your shift's over, but do ya mind goin' back out to the Weaver place with me? I'd like to look around; see where those…eyes were."

Ty didn't relish the thought of going back out there, but he nodded.

"Good man," Garrett said.

A few minutes later, Garrett and Ty were coming to a stop in front of Carla's Weaver's house. By the time they exited their vehicles, Carla was out of the front door and heading toward them.

"Officer Ty, Sheriff Garrett. I didn't expect y'all back so soon."

"Well," Garrett answered, "I wanted Deputy Jackson to show me around while his memory's still fresh."

Garrett stressed 'Deputy Jackson' in the hopes Carla would catch on to his proper title. She didn't.

"Officer Ty told me my pigs are dead. All of 'em…even Bingo. What the hell could'a kilt Bingo?"

"That's what we're tryin' to figure out. Mind if we have a look-see?" Garret responded.

Carla threw her arms up in frustration. "Look-see all ya want, Sheriff Garrett. Just catch whatever the hell kilt my pigs."

"How many pigs were back there?" Garrett asked.

Ty felt embarrassed for not having asked Carla that obvious question when he'd been there earlier.

"Three sows, one of 'em was expectin', and Bingo."

Ty shook off his embarrassment and stepped forward. "This way, Sheriff Lambert."

As Ty and Garrett started around the house, Carla fell in behind them.

Ty said, "I don't think ya want to see this, Missus Weaver."

"It's still a free country. That black asshole in the White House hasn't taken our personal property…yet. No offense, Officer Ty."

"None taken," Ty responded with a chuckle.

Ty wasn't a fan of the black asshole in the White House, either. Not because he feared for his personal property, but because he didn't think Obama had been much of a Commander-in-Chief.

When they got to the side of the house, Ty realized he hadn't shown Garrett the picture of the claw marks under Carla's window; they had still been pondering the picture of the burning red eyes when Hoyt and Perry arrived on the Lomax scene.

Ty stopped and pointed out the claw marks. Garrett looked at them for a few seconds, put his spread hand in front of the gouges, just as Ty did a couple of hours earlier, to gauge the size and spacing.

Garrett pulled a foldable ruler from his utility belt, unfolded it, and placed it on top of the claw marks. They were a little wider than the twelve-inch ruler. Without being asked, Ty took a picture of the claw marks with ruler for size reference.

Ty noticed Carla was being quiet, and he looked over at her. Her jaw was slack, and she'd gone an ashen-gray color in the face.

"Tha-that's right under my b-b-bedroom window."

Garrett looked at Carla and saw how frightened she was.

"You sure ya don't wanna go on back inside, Missus Weaver? We'll let ya know when we're done out back," Garrett said.

Carla looked from Garrett to Ty and back to Garrett.

In a small voice, she said, "I think I will."

Garrett and Ty watched her walk away.

As she did, she muttered, "It was tryin' to get into my dad-burn bedroom."

She shuddered and disappeared around the front of the house. A few seconds later, they heard the front door open and close.

Garrett turned back toward the claw marks. "That's gotta be seven feet to the window. The damn things are more than a foot across."

He looked at Ty.

Ty shrugged. "Grizzly could reach that high."

Garrett nodded.

What else could it be? Garrett thought.

After considering the claw marks a little longer, Ty led Garrett around the side of the house and down the narrow path to the pigpen. He saw the hubcap he'd tripped over and gave it a kick as he passed it. All that did was hurt his damn toe.

As they neared the pen, Ty could see Bingo's carcass along the back fence. His wounds looked even more grievous in the daylight, and Bingo had been nothing compared to the carnage under the shelter. To make matters worse, flies had already discovered the pork smorgasbord. Dense swarms of them buzzed around the pen as they dined and laid eggs on the already rotting meat.

As bad as the sight had been for Ty, Garrett was seeing it for the first time and was taken aback by the savagery of the attacks. Garrett surveyed the scene for several moments.

After taking it in, he pointed at the aborted piglets. “Are those…?”

“Unborn piglets,” Ty finished for him.

Finishing Garrett’s thoughts had become a habit that morning.

Garrett looked around for several more moments. “It’s hard to tell with the parts scattered around, but it doesn’t look like, whatever did this, actually ate any parts of the pigs.”

Ty hadn’t considered this, but considering there were three sows, he realized Garrett’s observation had been correct.

“What kind of predator doesn’t eat what they kill?” Garrett wondered aloud.

“Maybe Missus Weaver’s shotgun blast scared ‘em into the woods before they could get to eatin’ ‘em.”

“Maybe,” Garrett responded, but he didn’t sound convinced.

Then Garrett added, “It’s possible it was a thrill-kill.”

That statement hung in the air for several moments.

Garrett broke the silence. “Well…I guess I’ll take a closer look.”

Garrett opened the gate and stepped into the pigpen. He scanned the blood-covered mud for tracks, but there was no sign of any. The violence and chaos of the attacks obscured anything resembling an identifiable animal track. As he scanned what remained of the pigs and pig parts, he noticed claw and bite marks, which he took up-close pictures of with his iPhone.

After thoroughly documenting the remains of the sows, Garrett made his way to Bingo’s pen to study the bite marks on his back. The fang punctures were very clear.

He took the foldable ruler back out and placed it on the bite mark from fang to fang. It measured just under six inches across. He took a picture then repeated the procedure on the reverse side of Bingo’s back. These fang punctures were about a quarter of an inch closer together. Garrett surmised the closer together fang punctures were from the lower jaw. Dr. Yost would confirm this a few hours later.

With the bite marks measured and photographed, Garrett grabbed a sturdy-looking piece of straw from the ground and carefully inserted it into one of the upper-jaw fang punctures. When he could no longer easily insert the straw, Garrett bent it over, extracted it, and measured the canine depth. It was five inches.

Garrett looked at Ty, who had been watching him quietly. “That’s a big, deep fuckin’ bite.”

Ty nodded in agreement.

Garrett exited the pigpen and looked at the woods from which the three sets of burning red eyes were watching Ty.

"Let me see that picture with the eyes again."

Ty, his phone already out because he'd been taking pictures too, swiped through the pictures until he found the one Garrett asked for, and handed him the phone.

Garrett looked from the picture to the woods and back several times. There was a prominent pine tree in front of him and the furthest set of eyes were just to the right of the pine.

He handed the phone back to Ty. "Go back to where you were standin' when ya took this picture. I'm gonna see if I can find where the one on the furthest right was standin'. If I can, and you can see me, I'll adjust my height until ya think my eyes are about the same height as those."

"Roger that," Ty said as he turned and made his way to where he took the picture.

Garrett started making his way into the woods. The underbrush was thick, but he could navigate through it with little trouble. He saw several signs where the underbrush had been disturbed, broken twigs and flattened brush. Anything larger than a raccoon, like a deer, could have flattened the brush that way. He didn't see hair the color of the sample Ty removed from Bingo's tusk or the sample he'd retrieved from the shattered back window of Russ Lomax's truck.

He was just about to give up when he noticed two deep impressions on the pine needle covered forest floor. They were about three feet apart.

Wide stance, Garrett thought.

To not disturb the impressions, Garrett stepped around them and turned to face the way he'd come. He was about thirty feet into the woods, but he could clearly see Ty standing on the far side of the pigpen.

Garrett shouted, "Bingo."

"The pig?" Ty shouted back.

For a moment, Ty's response didn't register. It was then he remembered the boar's name, and he chuckled.

"Not the pig. I found where it was standin'," Garrett clarified.

"Oh," Ty shouted back.

With that clarified, Garrett shouted, "Can ya see me good enough to get a height estimate?"

"Not really."

Garrett considered this problem for a moment and retrieved a penlight flashlight he carried in his utility belt. He twisted it on and positioned it on the side of his face in line with his right eye.

Before he asked if Ty could see the light, Ty shouted, "I see that."

Good deal, Garrett thought.

He shouted, "Higher or lower?"

He could see Ty looking from his phone to the woods.

After several comparisons, Ty shouted, "Lower."

"Okay. I'll start squattin' down slowly. Holler when it looks right."

"Roger that."

Garrett started slowly squatting and, when his head was about four feet off the ground, Ty shouted for him to stop. Garrett's eyes were focused on Ty, but something close in front of him glinted in the flashlight beam and caught his attention. The underbrush directly in front of his face had been sprayed with what looked like bloody mucus. It hung in tendrils from the twigs and leaves.

Garrett took several pictures of the bloody mucus and the depressions, which, because of the blanket of pine needles, didn't provide any detail about what made them. He retrieved rubber gloves and an evidence bag from between his utility belt and pants. After donning the gloves, he snapped off some blood and mucus coated twigs and deposited them in the evidence bag, which he sealed and tucked into his uniform shirt.

About the time Garrett finished collecting the mucus, Ty shouted, "You okay in there?"

"Yep. I found some bloody snot and was baggin' it. Let's see if we can pinpoint where the other two were."

It took a little time, because the reference points weren't as defined, but Garrett, with Ty's instruction, located where the other two 'suspects' were standing, lurking, observing. These locations offered nothing more than the approximately three feet wide depressions in the pine needle covered forest floor. He saw no more mucus, blood, or hair. Garrett took several pictures of the imprints, though.

After finding and documenting the positions of the three sets of burning red eyes, Garrett maneuvered his way out of the woods and joined Ty, who waited for him by the pigpen. Garrett pulled the evidence bag out of his shirt and handed it to Ty.

Ty inspected it for several seconds. “I heard one of ‘em, the one that was directly in front of me where you got this…snort. Reckon this came from that?”

Garrett, not sure what he reckoned about any of this, shrugged his shoulders and started for the narrow path that led to Carla’s house.

Ty fell in behind Garrett and was just about to take another kick at the hubcap, when he remembered the scraping sound and large shadowy hulk, he thought he saw jump into the woods from behind the rusted-out refrigerator.

“There was a fourth.” Ty shouted.

Garrett, whose nerves were already raw from the morning’s events, jumped at Ty’s sudden outburst. By the time he turned around, Ty was already heading back toward the pigpen.

As Garrett caught up, Ty said, “There was a fourth. At least, I think there was. I heard a scrapin’ sound from behind that fridge,” he pointed at the old, rusted refrigerator standing by a pile of old tires, “and, when I looked, I thought I saw somethin’…somethin’ large, jump into the woods.”

By the time Ty finished telling Garrett about what happened, they were standing in front of the refrigerator.

Garrett watched Ty climb over a pile of tires and disappear behind the refrigerator.

No sooner than Ty was out of sight, Garrett heard him say, “Holy shit.”

“What is it?”

After a brief pause, Ty said, “Claw marks.”

Garrett climbed over the tires and joined Ty behind the refrigerator.

There were claw marks all right. They were about the same size as the ones under Carla Weaver’s bedroom window. Only these hadn’t gouged wood; these ripped through the cooling coils and metal beneath. Four long, jagged, horizontal claw marks.

Garrett looked at Ty. “Holy shit is right.”

After taking pictures of the claw marks with his trusty foldable ruler to reference their size, Garrett tromped back into the woods to locate where it settled in to watch Ty. That’s exactly what he thought they were doing. He found the same three-foot-wide depression marks about thirty feet into the woods directly in line with the refrigerator but no other evidence. He took a few pictures and looked back to where his friend was standing in Carla's cluttered back yard.

These fuckin' things are organized, Garrett thought.

A chill ran up his spine as he realized how lucky Ty was to be alive. If they'd wanted to, they could've done to Ty what they did to the pigs and Russ Lomax. Of that, Garrett had been certain.

So why didn't they? Garrett thought as he made his way out of the woods.

He didn't have an answer for that internal question.

His mind, ever the jokester, offered one, *Maybe they don't like dark meat.*

As offensive as the thought had been, Garrett couldn't hold back a hearty laugh.

"What's funny?"

"Nothin'," Garrett said, as he emerged from the woods, "I'm just glad you weren't on their menu."

Ty gave a nervous laugh. He knew he was lucky to be alive. "Me too, brother. Me too."

As they walked back up the narrow path to Carla's house, Ty kicked the hubcap and Garrett called the sheriff's department. Erica Harris, the seven-to-three dispatcher, answered on the second ring. He asked if Karen located Margaret Lomax-Carter before leaving. Erica didn't know, but she'd investigate it and get back with him. He told her to call Earl Wells. Earl was a heavy machinery operator who did work for the county from time to time. His son, Brad, was in Paige's high school sophomore class. He told her to have him come out to Carla Weaver's house with his backhoe and bury her pigs on the county's dime.

Garrett ended the call with Erica as they came around the front side of the house and saw Carla sitting on her front porch.

"Well?" she asked, getting to her feet.

"Well," Garrett said, "I wish we had somethin' concrete to tell ya. We just don't know what got after your pigs."

Carla let out a "harrumph" suggesting, more than any words could, she thought Sheriff Garrett and Officer Ty were about as useful as tits on a boar. Tits on Bingo.

Ty cleared his throat and, because he thought something should be said in their defense, said, "Maybe a bear."

Carla harrumphed again. "There ain't no bears in East Texas."

Ty was surprised when Garrett offered Carla his alligator theory about grizzlies let loose in the area. Carla seemed to consider this for a second.

She shook her head. "Bears don't howl."

She had them on that point. They all heard those God-awful howls.

To change the subject, Garrett told her Earl Wells would come out with his backhoe to bury the pigs. Carla balked until Garrett told her the county would pay the expense. That lightened her mood to where she smiled. A toothless smile, but it took years off her weathered face.

Garrett and Ty said goodbye to Carla and started back toward their vehicles.

"Your shift ended a couple of hours ago. Email me your pictures and give me the evidence you've collected. I'll check it in, send what needs sendin' to Dallas for DNA workup, and take some hairs to Doctor Yost at SFA."

"Ya sure? I don't mind takin' the evidence back to the department. Give ya a head start on gettin' to SFA."

"I'm sure. You're tired, and ya almost got eaten by a pack of howlin' grizzlies. Go get some sleep."

Before Ty could respond, Carla shouted from her front porch, "Werewolves howl like that. My grandpap tolt me East Texas used to be thick with werewolves! If they're back, we're fucked!"

With that, she went inside and shut the door.

Garrett and Ty looked at each other for several seconds, waiting to see which of them would say Carla was a crazy old coot. Neither of them did.

Finally, Garrett said, "Get some rest. You'll need it. You're on again tonight."

Ty nodded in agreement.

~ * ~

Before handing in the evidence collected at both scenes, and instructing Deputy Jennifer Ellington, who checked in and was cataloging evidence in the 'Cage' on the seven-to-three shift, which was to be sent to Dallas for DNA analysis, hair, skin, bloody mucus, and feces, Garrett transferred several hairs from both scenes into separate evidence bags to take to Dr. Yost at SFA. Before leaving, he checked with Erica to see if she'd gotten Margaret Lomax-Carter's contact information, she hadn't, and if she'd contacted Earl Wells about burying Carla Weaver's dead pigs, she had. With no other pressing business at the department, Garrett headed for SFA.

About twenty minutes later, Garrett turned on to Raguet Street and pulled up in front of the Science Building. After he parked, he took a few minutes to email Dr. Yost some, not all, of the pictures he and Ty took of the wounds. He went inside and took the elevator to the second floor.

When he got to Dr. Yost's door, it was closed. He knocked, but no one answered. Her office and class hours were posted on a laminated card next to the door. Garrett scanned it quickly and saw her Monday office hours started at eleven o'clock. When he looked at his watch, he saw it was ten thirty-six a.m.

Just as Garrett sat down on a bench down the hall from Dr. Yost's office to wait for her to arrive, she was in class until ten fifty, his cellphone 'dinged,' meaning he'd received a text. It was from Erica. She tracked down a working cell number for Margaret, which she included in the text.

Garrett sent a quick thank you text and tapped on the number included in the text. He hated making these calls.

A pleasant-sounding woman answered on the second ring. Garrett confirmed the woman who answered was Margaret Lomax-Carter, and she was Russ Lomax's daughter. He told Margaret her father was deceased.

After a brief pause, and in a small voice, Margaret said, "What happened?"

This was the tricky part. Garrett didn't exactly know what happened. Was it murder or an animal attack or both? He certainly wouldn't give her details. She didn't need to know her father's body had been ripped to shreds and shit on.

Garrett took a deep breath. "We haven't determined the cause of death yet. All I can tell ya at this point is that it happened this mornin' while he was drivin' his truck."

There had been another pause and then Margaret said, "Did he suffer?"

I think he suffered his ass off, Garrett thought.

Instead, he said, "I think it was pretty quick."

He didn't enjoy deceiving Margret, but there had been no reason to add to her grief.

Another pause and then Margaret said, "Thank you, Sheriff

Lambert. I'll be there as soon as I can, to make arrangements and see to Dad's things. It might take me a few days to get things in order here before I can come down. Will that be okay?"

Garrett told her that would be fine, offered his condolences, and hung up. It warmed Garrett's heart that her dad's passing saddened Margaret. Not that it made her sad, but because she cared enough to be sad. Many times, uncaring reactions to the news an elderly parent or grandparent passed away shocked him. He blamed it on how greedy and throwaway society became. Greedy in that survivors often seemed more concerned with what the deceased left them than in the fact they were gone, and throwaway in that the elderly were too often shipped off to 'Senior Living Centers' and forgotten. Margaret had been sad, and that was good.

Garrett was pulled from these thoughts when the elevator opened, and Dr. Yost stepped out.

"Sheriff Lambert. To what do I owe the honor of your visit?"

Emily Yost was strikingly beautiful. She was in her early thirties. She had long sandy-blonde hair and big green eyes. Her body, which was always accentuated by the choice of tight-fitting clothes she wore, was tight and curvy in all the right places. She could have been a pinup girl, if she hadn't gone the science route. Not for the first time, Garrett wondered how the young men in her classes concentrated on a single word that passed through her pouty lips.

"Nothin' good."

As she unlocked her office door, she said, "Well, come on in then."

Garrett followed Emily into her office, removing his cowboy hat as he crossed the threshold, and took a seat, one of two, on the 'student' side of the desk. Once Emily was settled in her much nicer chair, she got down to business.

"Let me guess. You've got remains with animal activity and you want me to identify the critter?"

She gave him a little wink when she used the word 'critter,' which was his vernacular.

It wasn't a stretch of a guess. Emily helped Garrett out several times since he'd become sheriff, which had been the same year, after receiving her Ph.D. from Columbia, SFA hired her as a tenure-track assistant professor. They grew in their jobs together and had a good working relationship and professional respect for each other. What Emily didn't know was how different the circumstances of the present visit were.

She consulted in two previous inquiries. One had been a hunting accident unreported for several days because the man in question wasn't supposed to return from the deer lease for several days after he, apparently, accidentally shot himself while cleaning his gun on the front porch of the lease cabin and another was a clear hit and run where the victim had been thrown into a ditch and not discovered until county inmates were picking up trash several days after the victim had been hit. Both bodies were in various states of decomposition, with animal activity present where critters had snacked on the deceased's remains before being found. Garrett never brought Emily a case where the apparent demise of the victim were the paws and jaws of the animal he needed identified.

Garrett shifted in his seat a little. "This one's a little different, Doc."

Emily put her elbows on the desk and leaned forward. "Tell me."

Emily listened with increased interest as Garrett told her about the events with Carla Weaver's pigs and the horrible details of Russ Lomax's death.

When he was finished, Emily leaned back in her chair. It swiveled and tilted as she considered the information.

She absent-mindedly chewed on the inside of her bottom lip, a bad habit her mother said made her look foolish, for a few moments. "You've got pictures?"

"Way ahead of ya, Doc. Check your inbox."

Emily swiveled to her computer, which was on a side desk, woke it up, and clicked on the Outlook icon in the Windows toolbar. The program opened, and several new unread emails loaded into the preview pain. Garrett's email was second from the top, just under a Viagra spam email. Emily double-clicked on the attachment paperclip, which downloaded the picture files into a new folder. She opened the folder, shift highlighted all of them, and double-clicked the files to open them in a picture preview program.

The pictures loaded one by one but so quickly it wasn't easy to make out details until the last picture, first picture taken, of the claw marks under Carla's bedroom window filled the twenty-one inch, flat-screen, iMac, computer monitor.

Emily looked at the claw marks and started to ask Garrett how wide they were, but Garrett expected her question. "They're a little over twelve inches across. There's another picture in there with my ruler overlaid for size reference."

Emily nodded and started going through the pictures, each of which she studied carefully.

When Emily got to the picture of the bite on Bingo's back, Garrett told her there were more pictures of the bite with his ruler for size reference later as well. She nodded again and went to the next picture, which was Lomax's head resting on the truck hood.

Emily took a sudden breath and turned away from the monitor to face Garrett. Her face went ashen white. She tried to speak but placed her hands over her mouth instead.

A few seconds later, her composure regained, she said, "Holy shit. A little warning next time, Sheriff Lambert."

Garrett apologized, but he reminded her he'd told her what happened to Russ Lomax, head and all.

"You did," she admitted, "but hearing about something is a lot different from seeing it."

Garrett noted how she didn't drop her 'g's like native East Texans did. A sure sign she wasn't from East Texas, which she wasn't. She was from Connecticut.

How different this world must be for you, Garrett thought.

What he said was, "You don't need to look at the Lomax pictures, Doc. I'm pretty sure the same critters that chewed up Missus Weaver's pigs did the same to Mister Lomax."

The statement had been sincere, but he was sure it would light a big enough fire under Emily to power her through the remaining pictures. After all, she was the expert. It did.

Emily, sounding a little defensive, which didn't bother Garrett. "Oh, so now *you're* the expert on *critters*? I don't think you're qualified to make that determination, Sheriff Lambert."

With that said, Emily turned back to the monitor and started going through the remaining pictures. Garrett, an East Texas country boy with a high school education, just manipulated Miss Connecticut, Ph.D. into looking at the remaining pictures. He stifled a chuckle, but he couldn't quite suppress the grin. Emily, looking at the computer monitor, didn't notice the shit-eating grin.

As Garrett suspected she would, Emily studied the size referenced bite marks in detail. She jotted a few things down on a notepad beside the monitor and looked at the pictures several more times.

Emily turned her attention to Garrett, the defensive tone now gone. “I don’t suppose you measured from the incisors, or canines, to the back molars?”

It was Emily’s turn to put Garrett in his place. He shook his head and told her he hadn’t.

“I don’t suppose I can look at the boar?”

He didn’t know for sure, but he told her they were probably in the ground already. Truth was, he didn’t want to go back out to Carla Weaver’s place and look at the damn pigs again. Emily shook her head, obviously disappointed.

Garrett remembered the straw he’d stuck in the canine puncture wounds to measure how deep they were and, by extension, how long the fangs were. When Garrett shared this information with Emily, she congratulated him for the excellent idea. He didn’t mind that she talked to him like she probably talked to her dip-shit students when they’d mastered some basic science skill. He felt redeemed.

After Garrett told Emily the puncture wounds were five inches deep, she scribbled a few more lines on the notepad. When she finished, she swiveled back to face Garrett.

“Well, what’s your best guess?” Garrett asked.

Emily picked up the notepad and considered it briefly. “The only animal capable of making these bite marks is a large bear. A grizzly certainly could but, going off the width between the canines, which match nicely to grizzly canine spacing, and extrapolating the distance between the canine punctures to the back molars…since I don’t have the *actual* measurements…the bite is too deep for a grizzly, and the snout is too long. Polar bears have snouts this long. Its bite would probably be the best match.”

When she finished, Garrett looked at her with what he was sure had been a stupid expression. “Your tellin’ me polar bears killed Lomax and the Weaver pigs?”

Emily laughed, but it wasn’t at his expense. “I’m not saying that at all. Neither is indigenous to East Texas. All I can tell you is the bite marks most closely resemble the bite of a polar bear. The claw marks under the window and on the back of the refrigerator match nicely, size wise, with a polar bear, too. Although now that I think about it, clawing through the metal on the back of the fridge would be tough for even a polar bear to do."

Garrett felt frustrated. He and Ty had speculated everything Emily told him earlier. He already knew they weren't indigenous. Feeling stupid, but needing to eliminate all possibilities, Garrett told her about Ty's alligator release scenario.

To Garret's surprise, Emily didn't dismiss the theory outright. Instead, she recounted several incidents where wild animals escaped enclosures, attacked, killed, and consumed humans. When Garrett pointed out none of the pigs or Mr. Lomax appeared to have been consumed, Emily nodded and admitted it was a far-fetched idea.

Just about the time Garrett thought he'd exhausted all avenues of inquiry with Emily, she said, "Did you say you had hair samples?"

Garrett couldn't believe he'd almost forgot about the damn hairs. He pulled the baggies, one from each scene, out of his breast pocket and dangled them in front of Emily's face. Her eyes lit up.

She grabbed a ring of keys from a bowl on her desk and she said, "To the Bat Lab, Sheriff Lambert."

She was striding out the office door before Garrett finished laughing.

Garrett followed Emily down a long hall that went the length of the building and into a large room with island desks in the middle of the room and counters with cabinets, above and below, that lined three of the four walls—the fourth had an instructor's desk in front of it and a whiteboard on the wall behind it. The countertops had sinks placed every few feet and, what Garrett remembered from his high school biology class, gas nozzles between each sink.

Emily walked over to one cabinet, slipped one key from the key ring into the lock, and unlocked it. She pulled a microscope out of the cabinet, used her knee to shut the cabinet, placed the microscope on the counter, plugged it in, and turned it on. She used the keys to open a top cabinet, from which she pulled a tray with glass slides, plastic coverslips, tweezers, and eyedroppers. Finally, she grabbed a box of latex gloves and gloved both hands.

With everything in place, she turned to Garrett and held out her hand.

Garrett handed her one baggy. "This one's from the pig tusk."

Emily unsealed the baggie and used the tweezers to extract the specimen. She placed the hairs on a slide, wet them with a dropper, put the coverslip on, and placed the slide on the microscope stage and secured it in place with the stage clip.

"Time to look," Emily said as she lowered her eyes to the eyepiece.

Garrett watched as Emily twisted the focus knob, raising and lowering the stage, until she settled on a suitable setting. While Emily looked at the slide, she mumbled something under her breath.

"What's that?"

A moment passed and then Emily said, "It's *Canis lupus*."

"Pardon?"

"The genus is *Canis,* and the species is *lupus*. Whether the subspecies is *familiaris*, I can't tell here."

Frustrated, Garrett said, "English, Doc."

Emily turned to face Garrett. "Canine. They're canine hairs. This sample has guard hairs from the outer coat and wool hairs from the inner coat."

Garrett looked at her. "They're dog hairs?"

Talking slowly, like Garrett had been slow, Emily said, "The genus is *Canis,* and the species is *lupus*. This genus and species cover all canines…dogs, wolfs, and dingoes. What I don't know is the subspecies, which would tell us exactly what kind of *Canis lupus* the hairs belong to. DNA analysis will identify the subspecies, though."

When Garrett didn't respond, Emily said, "Let me check the other sample to at least determine if both attacks were made by the same animal."

Garrett handed her the second baggie and watched as Emily repeated the previous steps with the second hairs. After peering into the eyepiece for a much shorter time than she spent on the first sample, Emily confirmed the second sample, though only comprising guard hairs, came from *Canis lupus,* too.

They looked at each other, without speaking, for several seconds.

Garrett broke the awkward silence by saying, "So…I'm lookin' for a pack of *big Canis lupus* runnin' around East Texas killin' pigs and old men?"

Emily studied Garrett for several seconds, as if deciding whether she should say what she was thinking.

"Those odds are about as good as it being grizzly or polar bears," she said.

"Except," Garrett added, "grizzlies and polar bears exist. Giant

Canis lupus' don't."

Emily turned back toward the microscope and said, kind of half-hearted, "What about werewolves?"

Garrett laughed out loud.

Carla Weaver's one thing, but Doctor Yost too? Garrett thought.

Somewhat composed, Garrett said, "You're kiddin', right? I mean…you're a scientist. Ya can't seriously believe in werewolves?"

When Emily turned back to face Garrett, she looked very calm.

She cleared her throat. "That's right, I am a scientist. As a scientist, I know there are many animals and plants that have yet to be identified. It would be arrogant of me to think I have a perfect understanding of the world and all its mysteries. Do I think there's a pack of werewolves terrorizing East Texas? I think it's *extremely* unlikely. I won't close my mind to the possibility. I will follow the evidence. The *Canis lupus* hairs are the only evidence you have now. I'd follow that evidence if I were you."

By the end of Emily's speech, Garrett felt bad for having dismissed the possibility so quickly. He felt stupid for entertaining the idea.

Not knowing what else to say, Garrett, with a hint of frustration clear in his voice, said, "So…I guess I need some silver bullets or somethin'."

Garrett had been more than surprised by Emily's response.

She laughed. "I just identified the hairs…that's my expertise. If you want an expert on werewolves, talk with Doctor James Huff in the English Department."

"There's a werewolf expert workin' in the English Department at SFA?"

"Well, he's an expert on literature…mythology, folklore, and the occult, to be specific. He's a lot of fun at parties."

Admitting to himself talking with Dr. Huff couldn't hurt, Garrett thanked Emily and headed over to Huff's office on the second floor of the Liberal Arts building. He was about to be schooled on all thing's werewolf and, unbelievably, it would prove invaluable information.

~ * ~

Jasmine had been in the living room playing with Little D when she heard Ty shout. At first the shouts were incoherent, but she soon realized Ty was calling her name. She had no reason to be concerned, but something in the way Ty was calling her name unnerved her. She left Little D playing with his blocks and hurried to their bedroom.

As she was reaching for the doorknob, Ty screamed, "I love you."

Rattled, Jasmine quickly twisted the doorknob and stepped into their bedroom. Ty was thrashing about, tangled in the bedsheets. Jasmine rushed to the bed, grabbed Ty by the shoulders, and started shouting his name. His eyes flew open, and, for a moment, Jasmine didn't recognize the man she'd been married to for several years. He looked scared. He looked crazed.

As Ty came out of the nightmare that invaded his peaceful sleep, he had no sense of where the nightmare ended, and reality began. He was looking into Jasmine's big, avocado green eyes and she looked scared. She had been scared in the nightmare, too. Ty tried to push the nightmare away, but it refused to be subdued.

In the nightmare, he'd been behind Carla Weaver's house at the pigpen and looking down at Bingo when the tunch went off. He turned around and looked at the darker than dark woods. A dense fog oozed; it looked almost like a flowing liquid from the woods. As the fog wrapped around Ty's legs, he felt it grab at him and immobilize him. It was as if the fog turned to concrete and hardened around his legs. The woods erupted in guttural, demonic laughter.

Ty scanned the woods, looking for the source of the laughter. One by one, four pairs of burning red eyes opened in the darkness and looked back at Ty. A sound, moaning, came from behind Ty. Although his legs were still immobilized, set in the concrete-fog, some unseen force turned Ty, so he was again facing the pigpen. Bingo's carcass was gone, and a human body replaced it. Ty's eyes strained against the darkness to better see the body. It, like Bingo, was covered in blood. The bite and claw marks that were on Bingo were on the human body. Its intestines were trailing out behind it.

It moaned again and, to Ty's disbelief, the wounds were too grievous for a human to survive, it stood up. Its back was to Ty but there had been something familiar about the long black hair that cascaded down its, her, it was a her, back. It turned to face Ty and his spine turned to jelly. He'd have fallen, but the unseen force that turned him had been, apparently, supporting him.

Jasmine was standing before him. She was naked, but covered in mud, which obscured any details of her body. But Ty could clearly see the ragged gash across her abdomen and intestines spilled out of it onto the mud at her feet. Ty tried to go to her, but the concrete-fog held him fast. He called her name. Her head jerked up violently, her hair flew back and revealed her face. She looked at him.

Her eyes were as white as Bingo's dead eyes. Ty called her name again, and a wicked smile spread across her beautiful face. He called her name again and her dead, white eyes flared red. Then she changed.

Coarse black hair started sprouting all over her body. Pointy ears grew out of her thick, black hair. Her facial features contorted and a long snout pushed out of her face—it had been full of dagger length, white fangs. As she grew taller, her arms elongated, and long claws replaced her manicured fingernails.

In a matter of seconds, his beautiful wife transformed into a hulking werewolf. Ty shouted her name again, and it looked down at him, as if seeing him for the first time. It studied him briefly then raised its horrific snout to the full moon to let out a demonic howl.

The howl was broken off when a voice from the woods, which had been barely distinguishable from a growl, said, "Kill him."

The creature that had been Jasmine looked down at Ty.

"I love you, Jasmine," Ty whispered.

The flame in its eyes dimmed and went out. He was looking at Jasmine's avocado green eyes and he knew she saw him, recognized him. For a moment, he thought she'd come back to him.

The growling voice, somehow, he knew it had been the alpha, commanded, "Kill him."

The red flames immediately ignited in its eyes, and it snarled as it opened its jaws incredibly wide. Ty could hear the beasts in the woods laughing. The creature that had been Jasmine snapped at Ty's head.

He had time to scream, "I love you." before the jaws clamped over his head and crushed it like rotten fruit.

Jasmine was holding his shoulders as he fought against something restraining him.

The fog, I'm stuck in the fog, Ty's mind screamed.

He was covered in sweat and his heart hammered in his chest. Seeing her so close, and not knowing if she was real, startled him. He tried to push her away, but she wouldn't let go. He had to, needed to get away from her before she changed again.

Jasmine was saying something, but he couldn't focus enough to hear her.

Then, "Ty. Ty. You were havin' a dream, Ty," got through.

He steadied himself and looked around. Ty was in his bedroom, and was tangled in the bed sheets. Not fog. He looked at Jasmine. She looked scared, but her eyes were avocado green and full of love for him. Ty grabbed her and wrapped her in a desperate hug.

Jasmine held Ty tight. She could feel his heart beating quickly within his muscular chest. She held him until it slowed to a normal pace and his breathing was slow and deep. Ty was asleep.

She gently lowered his head to the pillow, kissed him on the forehead, and went back to play with Little D.

Ty was dreaming again, but this time he dreamed about his and Jasmine's first date. A smile spread across his sleeping face.

~ * ~

Garrett took the elevator to the second floor of the Liberal Arts building. Upon exiting the elevator, he followed Emily's directions and went down the hall to the left to the last office door on the right. The door was ajar, so Garrett knocked on it.

A high, almost feminine voice said, "Come in."

Garrett pushed the door open and, taking his cowboy hat as he did, entered James Huff's office.

It was the opposite of Emily Yost's office. Where her office had been neat, clean, and organized, Huff's office was messy. Books, bluebooks, and papers were piled on every horizontal surface. It was dirty. A thick layer of dust covered every horizontal surface that hadn't been recently disturbed and disorganized. Nothing seemed to have an actual place, but there was a place for everything. His office was dark, too. There were two big windows behind the desk and florescent lights in the ceiling. The blinds were closed, and the florescent lights were off. The only light in the room came from the computer monitor and a small desk lamp partially obscured by a pile of books. Garrett immediately felt claustrophobic.

What caught Garrett's attention were the books. On the wall beside Huff's desk there were three built-in bookshelves that went from the floor to the nine-foot ceiling. These bookshelves were stuffed past capacity with books. Books were stacked sideways on top of other books to where there had been no space for more books. There were also three stand-alone bookshelves, around seven-feet tall, that were crammed to the bursting point. The particleboard shelves sagged from the weight of the books. Everywhere Garrett looked, there were piles of books on the floor. He stepped over several of these to get to the chair Dr. Huff suggested, with an outstretched hand, he should have a seat in.

Before sitting, Garrett grabbed Dr. Huff's outstretched hand, shook it, and introduced himself. Dr. Huff's pudgy hand limply gripped Garrett's.

Dead fish handshake, Garrett thought.

Dr. Huff seemed startled by Garrett's uninvited greeting, and, upon release, he produced a pump bottle of hand sanitizer from behind a pile of bluebooks, pumped a healthy portion onto his right palm, and worked the thick liquid feverishly over his pudgy hands.

If you're that worried about germs, clean your fuckin' office and let some light in, Garrett thought.

Between the dark, cramped, messy office, the limp handshake, and the hand sanitizer zeal, Garrett decided he didn't like Dr. Huff. From years in law enforcement, he knew first impressions are often wrong, so he reserved final judgment for later. When he left James Huff's office about twenty minutes later, Garrett realized Dr. Huff was eccentric, but very likable. Garrett thought Emily was probably right. Huff would be a hoot at parties.

Garrett sat down in the only student seat available. There wasn't room for another one, which didn't seem to be a problem to Garrett, because he didn't think many students would visit Dr. Huff. Garrett crossed his legs, placed his cowboy hat on his left knee, and took a moment to study Dr. Huff. He'd been too distracted by his office to take in anything more than his pudgy hands at that point.

The pudgy hands belonged to a pudgy man. He had a friendly, round face and little blue eyes. He had a patchy brownish, gray beard and light brown hair ringed his balding head. A pair of reading glasses were perched on the end of his button nose. His little blue eyes were looking over them at Garrett.

James Huff put his pudgy arms on his desk. "So…you want to know about werewolves?"

The frankness of Dr. Huff's statement surprised Garrett.

The surprise must have shown on his face because Dr. Huff laughed, a hearty full body laugh that Garrett liked. “Emily called me and told me you were comin’.”

Garrett noticed he dropped the ‘g’ from ‘coming’ and warmed up to the guy.

Garrett confirmed he was interested in learning about werewolves. He told James about the attacks from the previous night. He didn’t reveal Russ Lomax’s name, or that the pigs belonged to Carla Weaver. He didn’t offer to show him the pictures. Garrett provided Emily the omitted information, pictures, and evidence because she had been consulting on an official matter. Dr. Huff was more of an information source. To Dr. Huff’s credit, he didn’t ask for additional information.

Dr. Huff listened intently as Garrett recounted the events. Every so often, he would give a quick nod, as if something resonated.

When Garrett finished, he said, “That’s it, Doctor Huff. What do ya think? Is there a pack of werewolves roamin’ East Texas?”

Dr. Huff leaned back in his chair, it squeaked in protest, and folded his pudgy arms over his ample belly. “Please, call me James. Can ya do that?”

Garrett nodded.

“Okay then. Shut my office door and I’ll tell ya what I think.”

Garrett could reach the door without leaving his seat. Thinking James wanted privacy to discuss werewolves, Garrett pushed the door shut.

James wanted privacy, but not for the reason Garrett thought. As soon as the door clicked shut, James produced a bottle of Glenfiddich Scotch and two glasses from a desk drawer. He held one glass out to Garrett, but he waved it off.

“Suit yourself,” James said as he poured himself a double.

He brought the glass up to his lips and downed half of it in a single gulp.

“I find it’s best to hit it hard once and savor the rest,” James explained.

As if proving the point, he brought the glass back up to his lips and took a small sip. When he finished, he put the glass on his desk.

James cleared his throat. “Understand everything I’m gonna tell ya is based on myth…folklore.”

Garrett nodded.

James continued, "Myths and folklore are almost always based on some truth…some fact. There are people who believe they're wolves. They suffer from clinical lycanthropy…the delusion they can transform into a wolf. It's rare, but psychiatrists have diagnosed people with this affliction. Interestingly, these folks *transform* when the moon is full."

James saw Garrett's surprised reaction to his last statement.

He chuckled. "They don't grow hair and fangs and claws. Their mannerisms change. They become violent and they growl and howl at the full moon. Their facial features change…a little, though. They snarl and bare their teeth…their human teeth."

"No offense Doc…James," Garrett interrupted, "but this doesn't help me. Whatever perpetrated the attacks last night wasn't some violent, nut-job growling and baring their human teeth. The wounds were grievous."

James nodded his round head and sipped his Scotch. "I'm not suggestin' a violent, nut-job inflicted the wounds you described, Garrett. Just about every culture in history has some version of the werewolf *myth*. The creatures they describe are strikingly similar.

"The creature may have the head of a wolf, jackal, hyena, coyote, or even a dingo, but they are very similar and canine in nature. That those diverse cultures that have never crossed paths share this myth leads me to believe they are built on shared events…not nut-jobs baring human teeth. As I said before, myths and folklore are almost always based on some truth. Some fact."

Garrett considered what James told him for several moments. "So, ya think it's possible?"

James nodded and took another sip of scotch. "Unlikely, but I believe it's possible."

Garrett, recalling the Hollywood horror flicks from his youth, said, "The full moon was last night. So…if it was a werewolf, we're safe for another four weeks. Right?"

James shook his head, his pudgy cheeks wobbled slightly as he did. "That's a myth *within* a myth, Garrett."

"Come again?"

James took a deep breath. "The Hollywood crap is just that…crap. They've perverted the myth for the sake of givin' the good guys time between full moons to track down the werewolf and slay it before it can kill again. Real life, as I'm sure ya know, given your line of work, is rarely that convenient. No, no…it won't be that easy.

"A true werebeing can change at will, day or night, any day of the month they wish. It is believed werewolves get some power from the moon…all cultures share that myth as well. So, it may be the case that they're at their strongest durin' the full moon. I believe that to be true. A true werewolf could come through that door right now and have its way with us. I dare say it would find me the more appetizing of us, though."

He finished with another hearty laugh. First impressions be damned, Garrett liked James.

"Okay, how do I…?"

"Kill it?" James finished for him.

That happened a lot that morning, Garrett realized. He nodded.

"Well, Hollywood gets some things right. A silver bullet will do the trick. Werewolves have been around a *lot* longer than firearms. Anything silver will do it…even a silver butter knife. I don't think ya want to get that close, though. Also, the silver must penetrate and stay in the werewolf until it's dead. If ya take it out before it's dead, it'll heal. The myths agree that fire and decapitation will kill a werewolf, too. It must be the head, though. If ya cut off a limb, it'll grow back."

When James finished telling Garrett how to kill a werewolf, Garrett changed his mind about the scotch. James happily poured Garrett a drink. He stopped the pour at a single and poured himself another double.

James raised his glass. "Good luck and Godspeed, Garrett."

They clinked glasses and Garrett followed James' earlier lead. He hit it hard. It went down warm and smooth.

Given everything that transpired over the last eight or nine hours, Garrett felt pretty good about things. He wasn't sure he believed in werewolves, but he was going to be prepared. When he stood up to leave, James stood up. He was only about five feet tall and held out his hand. Garrett shook it and, this time, James' hand had been a little firmer in his. Not much, but a little.

I caught him off guard earlier, Garrett thought.

As Garrett stepped out of the dark and cramped office, James called to him. When Garrett turned to look at him, he saw James pumping hand sanitizer into his right palm. Garrett felt a smile spread across his face, but what James said next killed it.

"Garrett, Hollywood got something else right, too. Don't get bitten and live. The virus…or curse, is passed from werewolf to victim by its bite. While a mature werewolf can change at will, the first transformation doesn't take place until the first full moon after bein' infected. So, those who are bitten and live will become a werewolf on the next full moon.

"Actually, this might explain why there's suddenly four...a pack roaming East Texas. One werewolf, the alpha, could've bitten three people over the past month and those three matured last night. If this is the case, though, the alpha can spend the next month turnin' more people. By the June full moon, ya could be dealin' with more of 'em."

Garret considered this bit of unexpected theory. "I'll have hospitals and doctor's office in the area report any animal bites that come in."

James shook his head, his cheeks red from the scotch, wobbled. "A werewolf's bite will heal quickly. Anyone bitten would probably not need medical attention within a few hours."

This just keeps gettin' better and better, Garrett thought.

As if reading Garrett's thoughts, and knowing he needed a lifesaver, James said, "Oh yeah, I almost forgot to tell ya somethin' important. Kill the alpha and ya end the pack. Whatever werewolf started this, and there's always an alpha, it's its curse runnin' through the pack. Here, the myths diverge slightly. Some say killin' the alpha kills the pack...as in dead. While others say killin' the alpha releases the pack from the curse."

"Killin' the alpha might *cure* the pack?"

James nodded.

"Which do you believe?"

James thought a moment. "Does it really matter?"

"It does if the pack has innocent victims," Garrett quickly responded.

"True," James agreed, "but maybe they wanted the curse."

This response surprised Garrett, and he shot back, a little too angrily, "Why the hell would anyone *want* this curse?"

James didn't shrink from Garrett's tone.

"Think about it, Garrett. Strength, power, speed, enhanced senses...bein' able to hear and smell things miles away. Seein' in the dark. Bein' the top dog...no pun intended...the apex predator in East Texas, hell...on Earth. People have killed and done unspeakable things for a lot less."

Garrett hated to admit it, but James made a good argument. There were plenty of people who would find those traits very appealing. James said this like he was in awe of the werewolves. Like him or not, it rubbed Garrett the wrong way.

Garrett looked at James. “It sounds like you admire these monsters.”

James smiled a friendly smile. “I do.”

Garrett shook his head, but James continued.

“Think about it, Garrett. They’re the perfect predator. As fast as a big cat, the strength, teeth, and claws of a big bear, the bite force of a crocodile, and the cunnin’ of a human. Like it or not, that’s somethin’ to be admired. More important, though…I respect ‘em. So should you.”

Garrett considered James’ last words. He wasn’t sure he could admire the werewolves, but he would follow James’ advise about respecting them. If they were real, lack of proper respect was likely to get Garrett killed, and he knew that.

“Okay, James, I’ll respect ‘em. I’ll admire it when its head is on my trophy wall.”

James broke into a hearty laugh and, now that he was standing, Garrett could see James’ big belly shaking…like a bowl full of jelly.

When he stopped laughing, James said, “It’ll be a human head on your wall.”

“How’s that?”

“They revert to human form when they’re killed. Otherwise, we’d have proof of their existence.”

Garrett hadn’t considered this, but it made sense. Werewolves had the ultimate protection from detection. No werewolf's body, no proof werewolves exist. He gave James a friendly tip of his cowboy hat and said goodbye.

~ * ~

Garrett had a lot to think about as he drove back to the sheriff's department and prepared to brief the three-to-eleven shift. Should he share the werewolf theory? The voters elected him for his position. How quickly would they recall him if he started talking about werewolves? If more people were slaughtered over the next month and a werewolf army arrived in Pine View County on the June full moon, he’d lose his job as well.

What to do? Garrett thought.

~ * ~

The briefing for the three-to-eleven shift began at two thirty p.m. There were five deputies working the shift, Missy Gonzales, Randy Abbott, Mike Middleton, Jerry Baker, and Foster Timpson. Garrett hired two of them, Missy Gonzales and Jerry Baker, since becoming sheriff. Two, Foster Timpson and Randy Abbott, were hired by the previous sheriff, Oliver Henry, after Garrett became a deputy and Mike Middleton had been a deputy for over twenty years. Garrett liked and got along well with all of them, but Mike Middleton was his 'go-to' deputy on the three-to-eleven shift, much as Ty Jackson on the eleven-to-seven shift and Billy Hoyt on the seven-to-three shift were his 'go to' deputies.

News of Carla Weaver's pigs and Russ Lomax's death had, of course, been conveyed to the five deputies and they were discussing the events when Garrett entered the briefing room. They immediately fell silent.

Garrett walked to the front of the room and plugged a USB drive into the computer. He picked up a remote from the podium and turned on a sixty-inch television connected to the computer.

"Dim the lights, please."

Mike, who sat closest to the switch, got up, dimmed the lights, and sat back down.

"Okay," Garrett started, "I'm sure y'all are aware of what happened last night. I'm gonna run through pictures that were taken by Deputy Jackson and myself at both scenes. Some are *very* disturbin'. If ya need to look away or leave the room, I'll understand. Please hold your questions until after I've finished."

With that said, Garrett, using the computer mouse, scrolled through the pictures, and explained each of them in as much detail as he could. There were some sharp intakes of breath and a few groans, but no one looked away or left the room. Garrett was proud of his deputies.

When Garrett finished the slide show, the questions came fast and simultaneously.

"What did this?" Missy questioned.

"Is there more than one of 'em?" Foster asked.

"Where'd it come from?" Randy added.

"What has red eyes?" Jerry put in.

"How tall would it have to be to claw the house there?" Foster questioned.

Mike was the only deputy who didn't fire off a question. He just sat there calmly as his colleagues inundated Garrett with questions.

After letting his deputies burn off a little nervous energy, by hurling questions at him, Garrett raised his hands and patted the air. The deputies fell silent.

"I'll tell y'all what I know and what's speculated."

Four of the deputies, not Mike, were fidgeting nervously in their seats as Garrett started telling them what he'd learned from Dr. Yost. Garrett omitted Emily's remark about it possibly being a werewolf and his conversation with James. Earlier in his office, while preparing the evidence slideshow, Garrett decided against sharing the werewolf theory. Instead, he went with grizzly bears in East Texas, alligators in the New York sewer, theory initially offered by Ty.

Although Garrett never quite bought into the grizzly bear theory, it amazed him how quickly his deputies, except for Mike, embraced it.

"Ya know," Jerry said, "it wouldn't be hard to get some grizzly bear cubs into East Texas. Eventually, they grow up and get hungry."

"Or," Foster added, "they escaped from a private big game preserve. There are a couple of those in East Texas. People would pay big bucks to shoot a grizzly bear."

Garrett let them speculate for a few more moments then raised his hands. They quieted immediately. Garrett started the speech he planned to give. He hoped his words would keep them vigilant and safe.

"I want y'all to be on the lookout for anything out of the normal…like large dead animals with wounds similar to those on Carla Weaver's pigs. If ya find somethin' like that, mark the location on GPS and call it in. Do *not* get out of your vehicle and investigate. There will be time for that later. Y'all ride solo and I don't want any of ya out in the open…alone, if there are grizzlies about. If, God forbid, ya come across another human victim, call it in, ask for backup, and contact me on my cellphone. Again, do *not* get out of your vehicle alone and investigate."

At this, Missy said, "What if we can see the victims still alive? Are we supposed to stay in our vehicle and watch 'em die?"

Garrett pondered her question for a moment. It was a good question he hadn't considered. After a moment, he said, "Call it in and wait for backup."

They greeted this statement with a murmur of disapproval.

When they quieted down, Garrett said, "These things…grizzlies, can kill quickly. If the victim's still alive, you…most likely…rolled up on an attack in progress and scared 'em away. If that's the case, they could still be nearby. I know it goes against everything y'all believe…everything y'all were trained to do. If ya come across a livin' victim, do *not* get out of your vehicle. Y'all can't help anyone if you're dead, too."

Garrett waited and watched as his words sank in. The murmurs of disapproval from before turned into head nods. He had been relieved to see this.

He glanced at his watch and saw it was two fifty-five p.m.

"Alright guys…and gal, the message of the day is to be alert, be safe. Questions?"

None were forthcoming.

"Dismissed."

All five got up and four left. Mike stayed behind.

Mike approached Garrett. "These…grizzlies didn't eat any part of what they killed…did they?"

Garrett sensed Mike hadn't bought into the grizzly theory as the rest had. He'd been too quiet. Now he was certain Mike hadn't. Garrett confirmed, as far as he could tell, no part of the pigs or Russ Lomax were ingested. The autopsy report would show Lomax's heart had been missing, but Garrett wouldn't receive it until the following day.

Mike looked at Garrett for several long moments. "Ya know…my family's been in East Texas long since before Sam Houston avenged the Alamo at San Jacinto. That's a lot of history. Things get passed down from one generation to the next. Stories mostly. One story comes to mind now. One about the *nahual*."

"What's a…*nahual*?"

"Hold your horses, Garrett. I need to tell ya the complete story."

Garrett nodded.

"It was in the early eighteen hundreds, when Texas was still part of Mexico. My great, great, great…add a few more greats for good measure, Grandpa Milton Middleton's cattle ranch was wiped out in a matter of nights. Well over a hundred head. All tore to hell and back, but nothin' eaten. Well, Grandpa wanted to know just what the hell tore up his herd. So…one night he staked out a couple of goats and climbed a nearby tree. He waited and waited. Nothin' happened. Dawn was comin', and he was just about to climb down when he saw it creepin' out of the woods.

Big hairy fucker...all teeth and claws. It closed on the goats quick as a whip and tore 'em apart, just like it'd done with the cattle. It looked up at Grandpa with burnin' red eyes.

"Grandpa took a shot at it with his musket and hit it square in the chest. Didn't faze the damn thing in the least. It came after Grandpa, and I wouldn't be here today except...the damn thing *couldn't* climb the tree. It tried, but it couldn't do it.

"This makes sense, when ya think about it. Cats can climb trees, but dogs can't. Cats have retractable claws that grab hold of the tree bark to find purchase. This *nahual* had large sharp claws on its hand-like front paws. Too sharp. They shredded the bark and sliced into the tree trunk. Its weight dragged it down, cutting deep slashes in the tree trunk. Its hind feet were just like large wolf paws, and it couldn't find purchase with them. Grandpa waited it out and, once the sun came up full, it disappeared into the woods.

"To answer your question, a *nahual* is the Mexican version of a werewolf. Only, legend has it that a *nahual* is more like a werecoyote. Also, I said things get passed down...mostly stories, but not *just* stories. Somethin' else that was passed down through the generations is a crate full of silver musket balls my great, great, great, throw a few more in, grandpa made to kill the *nahual*, which he did the very next night.

"He only had silver enough to make two musket balls that day...melted down a silver weddin' spoon. To hear it told, my great, great, you know how great, grandma was none too happy about Grandpa meltin' it down, but he did. He staked out a couple more goats that night, climbed the tree, and waited. Sure as shit, it came back just before dawn. Instead of goin' directly for the goats, it went for Grandpa's tree. It was snarlin', growlin', snortin', and howlin' up at Grandpa. Grandpa aimed straight down and put a silver musket ball down its throat in mid-howl.

"It started rippin' at its own neck with its razor-sharp claws, like it was tryin' to dig the silver out. Smoke started comin' out of its mouth...like the silver was burnin' its insides. That was when it fell over, thrashed about a bit, and went still. Grandpa loaded the second silver musket ball and shot it in the chest...for good measure. That hole smoked, too.

"Here's where things get weird, though. When Grandpa climbed down from the tree, he didn't see a dead *nahual* layin' on the ground. It was a fellow cattle rancher, a man named Otis Fletcher, from a few spreads over. He was naked as the day he was born…smoke still leakin' out of his mouth and chest.

"Grandpa didn't reckon anyone would believe his version of the truth…figured he'd be strung up for killin' a fellow rancher, so he buried Otis Fletcher in the woods on his property. After that, he started stockpilin' silver and makin' musket balls…although, from what I heard tell, he never used 'em again.

"My wife's been on my ass to sell those musket balls for the silver for a while. Silver prices were way up about a year ago. I think it's a good thing I held on to 'em…now. 'Course, musket balls ain't much good these days. I can melt 'em down and fit 'em to nine-mil casin's. I've got the equipment. What'a ya think, Garrett?"

Garrett digested every aspect of the story, as Mike told it. Had he heard this story the day before, he'd have dismissed it as a family history that got twisted over the many years and many telling's. Unfortunately, this wasn't the day before and, considering everything that transpired over the last twelve hours, and the conversation with James Huff, Garrett believed the story to be damn accurate.

Garrett looked at Mike. "I think that's a damn fine idea, Mike. If the county balks at reimbursin' ya for the silver, I'll pay ya out of my damn pocket."

Mike gripped Garrett's shoulder. "I appreciate the offer, Garrett. …If this is what we hope it ain't, the silver will be put to use for what my great, great, *fuck* a lot of greats, grandpa intended it to be used for."

Garrett couldn't argue with that logic.

Before Mike left the briefing room, he said, "I'll get on it first thing when I get off Friday night. I know it's only Monday, but the full moon was last night. We should be safe for a bit. I'd do it when I get off tonight, but I need some sleep before I come in tomorrow afternoon and it'll take all night, and the better part of the mornin', to melt the silver down and make the nine-mil rounds. God willin', and with the help of strong coffee, I'll have at least a clip full for every deputy by Saturday afternoon. Will that work?"

Garrett considered telling Mike werewolves could change at will and the full moon passing wasn't a guarantee they'd be 'safe for a bit.' However, Mike had offered to donate his silver and time to equip the department with the tools necessary to kill werewolves. He couldn't very well order Mike to make them that night, and he couldn't afford to give

Mike the next night off. Saturday would have to do.

"That'll be fine, Mike. Thanks again for doin' this."

Mike nodded and left the briefing room.

~ * ~

Tuesday, Wednesday, and Thursday of that week were uneventful. No more werewolf attacks.

Chapter Five

The alarm on Paige's iPhone went off and pulled her from a restful sleep. She grabbed her cell and tapped the annoying alarm off. She looked up at the ceiling and watched the ceiling fan spin lazily above her bed. A smile spread across her face when she remembered it was Friday. Friday meant the end of the school week, Pizza Night with her dad, and, possibly, a date with her boyfriend, Justin Anderson.

Justin was seventeen, a year older than Paige. They'd been going out for about six months and things were getting serious.

Paige was doing her midmorning stretch and yawn when the text 'ting' sounded on her cellphone. The text came from Justin Anderson. He always texted her first thing in the morning. It had been their 'thing.' She quickly entered her four-digit passcode and tapped the Messages app.

The little blue text bubble popped up and she read, 'Woke up thinkin' bout u. Wanna see? 😍'

Paige giggled. The giggle girls do when they want a boy to think they're cute, even though Justin couldn't hear her, and she already knew he thought she was cute.

She wanted to see but wrote back, 'Lol! U know the rules. No sexting!'

Although she had no proof, Paige was convinced her dad monitored her cellphone to make sure she behaved.

The transparent bubble with three little moving dots popped up, which meant Justin was typing a reply.

Seconds later, the transparent bubble turned blue, and she read, 'Dang girl! I was gonna show u the smile on my face. Get ur mind out the gutter! 🤪'

Paige laughed out loud and wrote back, 'Lol! Ur bad! But I luv u, anyway!'

The transparent bubble with moving dots popped up then turned blue with, 'Luv u back! Mrb tonite?'

MRB was short for Mill Road Barn, where there was supposed to be an end of school party that night. Justin bugged her to go all week.

Paige wrote, 'Want to, but it's Friday. Pizza nite with dad.'

Moving bubbles, 'Ditch pizza nite.'

Paige responded, 'I'll ask if I can go after we eat.'

Moving bubbles, 'He'll say no, u know he will. ☹'

Paige wrote, 'U r prob rite. ☹'

Moving bubbles, 'Sneak out?'

Paige considered this request. She wanted to go to the party, but she didn't like the idea of sneaking out. If her dad found out, it would kill the trust he had in her. They enjoyed a great relationship built on mutual respect and trust. Paige never gave him a reason not to trust her. She was a good student, A's and B's. She didn't drink, smoke, or do drugs. She was still 'pure,' as her dad referred to those who hadn't engaged in the 'baby making activity,' another of his phrases.

She had no desire to drink, smoke, or do drugs, but purity was getting a little difficult to maintain. Although Justin wasn't pressuring her to 'go all the way,' they'd done some things that felt good, damn good. If those things felt damn good, Paige figured the other thing would be amazing.

Even though she thought Justin was *probably* the guy she'd eventually give herself to, she wasn't ready to commit…yet. When things got a little steamy, she always put the brakes on. MRB could be the time and place to keep her foot off the brake pedal.

Justin would pout, but Paige had other ways of 'deflating' the situation, so he didn't pout for long. Justin was always eager to address her needs. Feeling good, damn good, Justin never gave Paige the 'big O,' which was her mother's vernacular for orgasm. He tried *hard* to please her, and she appreciated his efforts.

She texted Justin that sneaking out wasn't a good idea, but a little fib would be a lesser transgression of her father-daughter relationship. Instead of asking her dad if she could go to a party at the Mill Road Barn, he knew what went on out there because he partied there when he had been in high school, she'd ask if she could go out with Justin and his younger sister Lindsey, who was Paige's age and her best friend since kindergarten.

It had been Lindsey who talked Paige and Justin into going out. At first, Paige thought the idea gross because, growing up spending so much time at the Anderson's, Justin was the closest thing to a brother she had. After the first kiss, she didn't think of him as a brother again.

The fib would be a little fib of omission in that she'd ask her dad if she could go out with Justin and Lindsey, but not volunteer the destination. If he asked where they were going, the little fib of omission would become an outright fib, because she would tell him they were going to a movie and to the bowling alley after the movie.

She knew this would be a risky move in any father-daughter relationship, but it was especially risky when your dad was the county sheriff. All her dad had to do was ask one of his deputies to drive by the movie theater and bowling alley to see if Justin's truck was in the parking lot. If it wasn't, her dad could mobilize deputies on duty to find her and bring her home. Paige wasn't sure her dad would go to those lengths to catch her fibbing, but she wasn't sure he wouldn't either.

After they made the plan, Justin texted, 'If he says no to movie and bowling too, will u sneak out?'

Paige thought about this for a few seconds and, feeling guilty but wanting to see Justin, texted, 'Yes.'

~ * ~

Later that morning, Paige was sitting in second period biology. She liked biology and the teacher, Mrs. Rogers, but her mind was very troubled. More than anything, she wanted to see Justin that night, but the thought of deceiving her dad didn't sit well with her. If he let it go with the simple request to go out with Justin and Lindsey, she could live with the omission. If she had to lie and tell him they were going to the movies and bowling or, worse still, sneak out, she would cross a line she'd never crossed before.

As if in tune with her thoughts, her cellphone, which she hid from Mrs. Rogers's view on her lap under the table, vibrated. She chanced a glance at her cellphone as Mrs. Rogers turned to the whiteboard to further explain heredity using a two-by-two matrix that contained an assortment of big 'Rs' and little 'rs' with Mendel's Peas written across the top of the matrix.

Paige saw a text from Justin, 'Mrb is gonna rock! Everyone's goin!'

Before she could respond, Mrs. Rogers called on her and asked her to explain eye colors that could result from two brown-eyed, dominant parents who both shared a recessive blue eye gene.

Paige quickly answered, "There would be a one in four probability of having a blue-eyed child. The rest would be brown-eyed…one with two dominant brown-eye genes and two with a dominant brown-eye gene and a recessive blue-eye gene. But their eyes would be brown...like their parent's eyes...because the brown-eye gene is dominant."

Mrs. Rogers gave Paige a big smile. "Very good, Paige."

Good thing I read the chapter, Paige thought.

Mrs. Rogers turned back to the whiteboard and said to the class, "If you look in the lower right-hand corner of the matrix, you'll see two little 'r's. This means..."

Paige's mind left the lecture as she texted Justin, 'Can't wait!'

~ * ~

It was two forty-two p.m. and Paige was in her last class of the day, which was Government. Mr. Pepper had been lecturing about the Bill of Rights and how the Supreme Court selectively, over the years, incorporated several of the first ten amendments of the Constitution to the states.

"Can someone tell me one of the Bill of Rights amendments that hasn't been incorporated?"

Paige was watching the clock, but she listened to Mr. Pepper, too. After several seconds of awkward silence, Paige looked around the classroom and saw there were no excited hands in the air.

Mr. Pepper scanned the room. "Anyone?"

Paige's hand went up and Mr. Pepper quickly called on her.

"The Third Amendment...quartering of soldiers...hasn't been incorporated."

"Very good, Miss Lambert. Very good."

He went on to explain why the Third Amendment had not been incorporated.

Paige's cellphone vibrated in her lap, and she chanced a quick look. The text was from her best friend, and Justin's little sister, Lindsey, who was sitting two seats in front and one row to the right of Paige's seat. They usually sat next to each other in classes they shared but Mr. Pepper separated them after accusing Lindsey of cheating off Paige's test, she had been, earlier in the year.

Lindsey's text was brief and to the point, 'Suck up!'

Paige looked up and saw Lindsey looking back at her, grinning. Mr. Pepper's back was turned, so Paige quickly gave Lindsey the middle finger, which caused Lindsey to laugh.

Mr. Pepper turned around quickly. “Something funny, Miss Anderson?”

Lindsey quit laughing immediately. “No, Mister Pepper. I’m sorry.”

Smugly Mr. Pepper said, “What would be funny, Miss Anderson, is you taking my class again next year.”

With that shot landed, he turned back to the whiteboard and resumed lecturing on the Bill of Rights and incorporation. Lindsey put a finger gun to her head and pulled the imaginary trigger. Paige repressed a laugh.

The next fifteen minutes dragged out for what seemed to Paige an hour or more. When the bell rang at three o’clock, there was a stampede of students eager to start their weekend rushing for the door. Lindsey hung back to wait while Paige stuffed her textbook, notepad, and pen into her backpack. They exited Mr. Pepper’s classroom together.

As they were leaving, Mr. Pepper said, “Enjoy your weekend ladies. Be sure to read chapter ten for Monday…Miss Anderson.”

One last shot for Lindsey.

They wished him a good weekend and disappeared into the crowded hallway.

When they’d walked about ten feet away from Mr. Pepper’s classroom door, Lindsey said, in her best Mr. Pepper impersonation, “What would be funny, Miss Anderson, is you taking my class again next year.”

Paige cracked up and hung onto Lindsey, as if she needed the support.

Lindsey, in her own voice, said, “What would be funny is Mister Pepper biting my ass.”

“Actually, that might hurt a little. To make matters worse, he’d have to see and touch your ass.”

“Ya know what I mean…bitch.”

Paige did, but she cracked up all over again from Lindsey calling her a bitch.

When they rounded a corner that led to their lockers, they literally ran into Justin and Matt Cooke, who was Justin’s best friend.

“What took y’all so long?” Justin asked.

“Yeah,” Matt joined in. “We thought y’all left already. We were headin' out to the parking lot to find y'all."

"Paige was suckin' up to Mister Pepper…again," Lindsey opined.

"Hey," Justin exclaimed, "no suckin' up, down, or around any guys but me."

Paige instantly blushed, and pushed between Justin and Matt. "Shut it, Justin."

Matt, being a typical teenage guy, made some vulgar sucking sounds as Paige continued to her locker.

She heard a 'thud' and Matt said, "Damn, bro."

Justin elbowed Matt in the chest to shut him up. That made Paige smile.

Lindsey's locker was three down from Paige's and, as Paige loaded all the books she'd need to complete the various weekend homework assignments, she couldn't help but notice Lindsey wasn't bothering to collect the needed books from her locker.

Might not be just Mister Pepper's class she retakes next year, Paige thought.

Because Lindsey had been packing light, she joined Justin and Matt at Paige's locker before Paige finished loading up her backpack.

"MRB is gonna be *sick* tonight. The whole damn school's goin'." Matt said.

Before Paige, Lindsey, or Justin could respond, Brad Wells pushed into their group and put an arm around Lindsey, which she immediately shrugged off. Brad had a reputation for being a little strange. "Not the crunchiest chip in the bag," her dad would've said.

"Y'all hear 'bout ol' Missus Weaver's pigs?" Brad asked.

They all shook their heads.

Brad smiled. "Somethin' went to town on those little piggy's Sunday night. Tore 'em up. Even that big-ass boar of hers."

"Bullshit." Matt responded.

"If I'm lyin', I'm dyin'." Brad shot back.

"Where'd ya hear about this?" Justin asked.

"My dad," Brad responded, as if that explained everything.

Seeing they needed more convincing, Brad said, "Her dad," he pointed at Paige, "called my dad and told him to take his backhoe out to Missus Weaver's place and bury her kilt pigs Monday mornin'."

"Monday? Why're ya just tellin' us now?" Matt asked.

Brad grinned. "'Cause he just sent me the pictures he took. Wanna see?"

The boys nodded. Paige and Lindsey did not.

Brad produced his cellphone and started swiping through the pictures. Paige and Lindsey turned away several times—the images made them sick to their stomachs—but Justin and Matt were oohing and aahing. The grosser the picture, the louder the ooh and aah.

When Brad finished going through all the pictures, Matt said, "What the fuck could do that?"

"Daddy thinks it was a bear," Brad offered.

"Ain't no bears in East Texas," Justin chimed in.

"Is so," Brad defended. "Black bears are comin' back."

"A black bear…even if they were comin' back, which they ain't, couldn't do that," Matt added.

Paige finished loading her backpack. She and Lindsey broke away from the boys and started for the parking lot. As far as she was concerned, it didn't matter what killed the pigs. What mattered was her dad knew about it. That meant he was going to be in 'Supper Sheriff' hyper-protection mode when he got home. That meant he would probably say no to her going out with Justin.

Lindsey, not noticing Paige had been miles away in thought, said, "Those pictures were *so* gross. Why do boys like that sort of stuff?"

When Paige didn't respond, Lindsey said, "Earth to Paige. Come in Paige."

Coming out of her inner world, Paige said, "I'm sorry, Lin. I wasn't listenin'. Those pigs. They were *so* gross."

Before Paige could explain why the slaughtered pigs were problematic, Justin and Matt caught up with them.

"What's the matter? Those pictures upset your girly sensibilities?" Matt joked.

"The better question is…why do boys *like* gross crap?" Lindsey shot back.

Paige didn't want to listen to Lindsey and Matt bicker so, when she saw her car ahead and to the left, she broke away from the group. As she was digging the key fob out of her backpack, still hearing Lindsey and Matt arguing in the distance, Justin jogged up.

"What's the matter, Paige-Turner?"

Justin called her Paige-Turner since he overheard her dad use the nickname. At first, she minded because it had been her dad's nickname for her. She grew to enjoy hearing Justin call her that, too.

Paige pushed the 'unlock' symbol on the fob, opened the door, and tossed her backpack into the front passenger seat of her car. It was a 2015, Dragon Green, Chevy Sonic. Her mom and dad gave her the car for her sixteenth birthday present. They'd gotten it at the dealer price from her stepdad Al, who owned a dealership in Pine View, but that didn't take away from how much she appreciated the car. She loved her little Sonic and named it Lil' Dragon.

Paige turned and looked up at Justin. He was tall and handsome. Justin had strawberry blonde hair that had been too long for her dad's liking, which meant it was the perfect length for Paige, and big green eyes. He tried to grow a mustache, which was little more than a few almost transparent blond hairs. Paige thought it was silly, but Justin was proud of it, so she pretended to like it. He had a fair complexion, which made his lips appear very red in contrast. Paige loved his lips. She went up on her tiptoes and kissed his red lips. He kissed her back.

When their lips parted, but they were still close, Justin said, "What's wrong? Is it those pigs?"

Paige nodded.

Justin puffed up. "Don't you worry 'bout the critter that tore up those pigs. I'll protect ya, little lady."

Paige giggled, even though she didn't feel giggly. Being cute was important. "I know ya will. I'm more worried 'bout Daddy lettin' me go out after he saw what happened to those pigs."

Justin looked at her for a few seconds. "Then you'll sneak out. Right?"

Paige nodded again.

After they kissed goodbye, Paige got into Lil' Dragon and headed for her dad's house. She wanted to get her homework done before her dad got home so she could use it as ammo.

"All my homework's done," when she asked if she could go out with Justin and Lindsey.

Please let me go. Paige thought.

She didn't want to lie to him. She certainly didn't want to sneak out, but she committed to both options, if it came to that.

About ten minutes later, Paige pulled up in front of her dad's house. She killed the engine, grabbed her backpack, and headed inside to do her homework. If nothing else, she was looking forward to seeing her dad and Pizza Night. She had been so preoccupied with her thoughts she didn't notice how quiet the woods around her dad's house were.

~ * ~

A single dark form, deep within the woods behind Garrett's house, watched Paige go into the house. The alpha considered attacking her to inflict an infectious bite, but it felt too exposed in the light of day. It marked her scent, though, and could revisit the idea later. It moved on.

~ * ~

Paige finished her homework a little after five o'clock. Knowing her dad would be home soon with the pizzas, she got things ready so they could eat as soon as he arrived. They usually ate at the dining room table but, on Pizza Friday, they ate in the living room so they could watch *Jeopardy*.

~ * ~

Garrett recorded all five episodes of *Jeopardy* during the week so they could watch them together. They usually watched two on Friday, two on Saturday, and one on Sunday before she left for her mom's house but, sometimes, if they didn't watch a movie or two after, they would marathon through all five on Friday night. They would play against each other. Not keeping written score, a more mental tally of who answered more questions correctly. Her dad always won. It amazed Paige how much trivial information her dad possessed. When she asked, often, how he knew so much, he would tell her it's because he reads a lot.

Outside of spending his free time with Paige, reading had been his favorite activity. His favorite genera were non-fiction, historical novels. He'd read all of Bill O'Reilly's *Killing* books; his favorite had been the one on Patton. This was because World War Two was his favorite historical period. His favorite book of all had been Ambrose's *Band of Brothers*, which happened to be his favorite miniseries too. Moore's *We Were Soldier Once...and Young* had been a good read as well. He read fiction, too. He'd read Tolkien's *The Lord of the Rings* and *The Hobbit* several times. He was a fan of Martin's *Song of Ice and Fire* series. Like most avid readers of this series, he was impatiently awaiting the sixth installment, *Winds of Winter*, and was afraid Martin would drop dead before finishing the series. He also enjoyed horror books by authors King, Koontz, Barker, and Nacogdoches native Joe Lansdale. Overall, he considered himself well read.

~ * ~

Paige placed two plates on the coffee table along with salt, pepper, red pepper, and Tabasco sauce, which her dad used to 'doctor' his pizza. Paige didn't think pizza needed 'doctoring.'

About the time she finished setting the coffee table, she heard her dad's SUV pull up in front of the house. Seconds later, he came through the front door carrying two Papa John's pizza boxes. After setting the pizza boxes on the coffee table, Garrett wrapped Paige in a big hug.

The conversation was predictable.

"How's school?" Garrett asked.

"It was school."

"How's work?" Paige asked.

"Better since Monday."

Knowing the pigs were killed on Monday, the answer gave Paige hope her dad might let her go out.

"Load up my plate. I'll be right back," Garrett said.

He went to his bedroom to change out of his uniform while Paige loaded slices of pizza on their plates. When Garrett returned to the living room, he flopped down in his recliner, the same recliner that had been in the old trailer house the day Lacy left. He picked up the remote control, turned on the television, and pulled up the DVR menu. It was empty except for a folder containing five "New" episodes of *Jeopardy*. Garrett selected the episode from the previous Monday and pushed the play button. After fast forwarding through a partial hemorrhoid commercial, Alex Trebek walked on to the *Jeopardy* stage.

"Phone off, Paige," Garrett reminded Paige.

He had a rule about no texting, browsing, or calls during 'family time,' which had been any time they were together.

"Yours, too?"

Garrett chuckled. "Nice try. I'm always on duty."

"I'm always a teenage girl."

They had this exchange every time they ate, but it was fun. Paige put her iPhone on silent and slipped it into her back pocket so she could feel it vibrate if anyone tried to contact her.

Garrett and Paige spent the next twenty-something minutes, Garrett fast forwarded through the commercial, answering clues—providing answers—through pizza filled mouths. Garrett won again.

When the first *Jeopardy* was over and the pizza gone, except for the leftovers they would eat for breakfast the next morning, Paige volunteered to clear the coffee table. Garrett offered to help, but Paige told him to keep his seat. She was sucking up before asking if she could go out.

Paige took the plates into the kitchen, dumped her crust into the trash, Garrett ate his crust, along with one empty pizza box. Finally, she rinsed the plates and put them in the dishwasher. She put the salt, pepper, and red pepper back in the pantry, and took the pizza box that contained both their leftovers along with the Tabasco sauce to the refrigerator.

Before closing the refrigerator, Paige said, "You want a beer, Daddy?"

When Garrett responded with, "Not tonight, sweetheart," Paige knew something was up. Her daddy always drank a few beers on Friday night. She suspected whatever was up would work against her plans to go out with Justin without lying or sneaking out.

She was right.

"Water, then?"

"Yes, please."

Paige grabbed two bottled waters from the refrigerator, closed the door, and returned to the living room to watch Tuesday's *Jeopardy*.

Preoccupied and nervous about asking her dad if she could go out with Justin and Lindsey later, Garrett trounced her in the second Jeopardy.

When it was over, Garrett said, "Up for a movie or two? Or more *Jeopardy*?"

Paige took a deep breath and gathered her courage. "Well…I wanted to ask ya if I can go out with Justin and Lacy tonight."

Without hesitation, Garrett said, "Not tonight, sweetheart."

"Please, Daddy. I did all my homework. I promise we'll be home early."

"Not tonight, sweetheart."

Frustrated, Paige said, "Is this because of those pigs?"

It surprised Garrett to find out Paige knew about the pigs. Pine

View's newspaper, the *Pine View Post*, had access to police reports, but it was a small, bi-weekly paper. The mid-week edition came out on Wednesday, but the paper completed it on Tuesday. The paper hadn't contacted the sheriff's department about the Carla Weaver's pigs or Russ Lomax's death until late Tuesday. They were tipped off when Margaret Lomax-Carter called in the obituary for her father, Russ. The news reached them too late for the Wednesday edition. The next edition wouldn't come out until Saturday.

"How the hell do ya know about the pigs?"

"Brad Wells told us. Even showed us pictures his dad took."

"Of course, he did. Looks like I'm gonna have to have a talk with Earl 'bout how to behave when he's workin' for me," Garrett responded in an irritated tone.

Paige waited a couple of seconds and asked, "What did that to the pigs?"

Garrett quickly considered how much to tell his daughter and decided on very little. He didn't want to scare her or, worse, make her think he was crazy.

"We're not sure, kiddo. Some large animal is about all we know."

Paige took a deep breath and lied to her dad, "We were gonna go to a movie then go bowling. Doubtful a big animal would attack us in town."

That had been true, but Garrett had information Paige didn't. Russ Lomax had been attacked while driving on a county road. The way to Pine View entailed taking County Road Five Eighty-Eight through several miles of dense woods.

He shook his head. "I'm sorry, sweetheart. I want ya to stay in this weekend."

Disappointed by his answer and scared about the prospect of sneaking out later, Paige put a smile on her face. "It's okay, Daddy. I enjoy spending time with you, too."

Garrett smiled back. "All right then, pick out a couple of movies. No horror flicks tonight, though."

Garrett and Paige enjoyed horror movies, but Garrett saw enough real-life horrors earlier that week and preferred something light to watch.

Paige thought it odd her dad ruled out horror movies. They both liked them, but she didn't question it. After some discussion, they decided on the first *Back to the Future*. Garrett thought the sequels were crap, and

The Breakfast Club. Garrett loved 1980's movies and Paige was enjoyed them, too.

After putting *Back to the Future* in the DVD player, Paige told Garrett she needed a quick bathroom break.

As she was making her way to the bathroom, Garrett said, "Onesy or Twosy?"

Paige laughed. "Daddy, that's so inappropriate."

"Okay, don't answer. I'll just time ya."

"You're so bad, Daddy," Paige said as she closed the bathroom door.

She didn't need to pee when she went into the bathroom. She needed privacy to text Justin. Once in the bathroom, she killed two birds with one stone. Paige pulled her cellphone out of her back pocket, 'dropped trou,' as her dad put it, and took a seat. It didn't surprise her to see a text from Justin on the lock screen. She'd felt her cellphone vibrate while eating.

Justin had texted one word, 'Well.'

Paige texted back, 'He said no.'

The transparent bubble with three little moving dots popped up immediately.

Then the blue bubble popped up with, 'What time can u sneak out?'

Paige texted back, '11.'

Moving bubbles, 'I'll park on Five Eighty-Eight to the right of ur dad's driveway about 10:50. Ok?'

Paige's thumbs hovered over the little keyboard.

Am I really gonna do this? She thought.

Without giving it another thought, Paige quickly texted back, 'Ok.'

With both businesses taken care of, peeing and texting, Paige slipped the phone back into her back pocket, washed her hands, and left the bathroom.

When she opened the bathroom door, Garrett yelled, "It was a onesy."

Paige laughed, but she was feeling queasy at the thought of sneaking out later. In her opinion, she'd rather face the animal that tore up the pigs over her dad if he caught her sneaking out.

When the movies were over, Garrett stretched and gave an exaggerated yawn. He was tired but very relieved no one from the three-to-eleven shift called with a problem, at least not yet. It was a little after ten p.m. and Garrett wanted to call Ty.

~ * ~

He'd already filled Ty in on everything he'd learned from Dr. Yost, Dr. Huff, and Mike Middleton on Monday before Ty's shift started at eleven o'clock that night. He wasn't sure how Ty would take the news that a pack of werewolves might be roaming the woods of East Texas, but his friend deserved to hear all the information he'd accumulated through the day. Also, it would be Ty's job to pass on to the eleven-to-seven shift, the instructions Garrett delivered to the three-to-eleven shift. Tell the deputies to stay in their vehicles, call for backup.

To his credit, Ty took the information well, which surprised Garrett a little. Ty didn't tell Garrett about his werewolf dream, though.

~ * ~

That night, Garrett just wanted to remind Ty to convey all the relevant instructions to the other deputies on the eleven-to-seven shift and to call him on his cellphone if anything happened.

When Garrett got up, Paige did, too.

Garrett gave her a big hug. "I'm gonna turn in, Paige-Turner. I'm sorry 'bout not lettin' ya go out tonight. I hope ya understand."

Paige hugged him back and, feeling guilty because of her plans to sneak out and see Justin anyway, said, "It's okay, Daddy. I can make it through a weekend without seein' Justin."

Garrett kissed her on the forehead. "G'night, Paige-Turner. I love ya bunches."

"G'night, Daddy. I love ya bunches more."

Garrett went into his bedroom to call Ty and Paige went into her bedroom to prepare to sneak out and meet Justin.

Within a few hours of Garrett and Paige saying goodnight to each other, one of the four, Garrett, Paige, Ty, and Justin, would be dead, two infected, and one would be desperate for answers.

~ * ~

Headlights sliced through the fog blanketing the overgrown drive that led to the Wiseman barn. A matte black, 2003, four-wheel-drive, four-door, Ram pickup with tinted windows rumbled into the not-so-clear clearing around the old, dilapidated barn and parked behind it—out of sight should anyone, however unlikely, venture up the drive. Four people exited the truck and hurried into the barn.

Once inside, they stripped and placed their clothing neatly on the ground in the back corner of the barn. It was dark inside the barn, but they'd soon be able to see without need of light.

The woman bent over, placed her hands on her knees, and let out a sharp cry of pain—the change was beginning. The men, not yet as accustomed to the agony of transformation, fell to the ground, writhing in pain as their bodies contorted in unnatural ways. Bones broke and reshaped themselves as their human anatomy transformed into what was a blend of human and wolf. As the human cries of pain morphed into snarling growls, the forest outside fell silent.

Moments later, four hulking beasts emerged from the barn. The one that had been a woman absorbed its surroundings with its acute senses. It sniffed the air and detected a familiar scent. One it marked earlier that day. It went down on all fours and disappeared into the forest; its pack close behind. The pack was on the hunt.

~ * ~

Garrett's conversation with Ty was brief. It struck Garrett then, through all the conversations they'd had that week about the possibility of werewolves roaming the woods of East Texas, Ty had not once questioned the veracity of the possibility.

When Garrett questioned Ty's lack of questions, Ty said, "I've never had a tunch like that, Garrett. Nothin' has ever…scared me like that. I'm not sayin' I'm beyond fear. Plenty scared the shit out of me in Afghanistan, but this was…different. Like my soul was screamin' in fear. So, if ya tell me there's a chance, we're up against somethin'…unnatural, I'm open to it."

Before they hung up, Garrett said, "Don't be a hero tonight, soldier-boy. Mike won't have the silver bullets ready until tomorrow afternoon. If some weird shit happens, call me. No Purple Hearts or Silver Stars in civilian service."

"Roger that."

The hero impulse ran deep in Ty, too deep for him to ignore. It would cost him dearly.

After he hung with Ty, Garrett got ready for bed. He thought he'd have trouble falling asleep, but he was out within minutes of his head hitting the pillow. Unfortunately, it wasn't a restful sleep. His old subconscious friend paid him a visit that night. He would be ripped from the dream about an hour later, as Monster-Paige, now sixteen and more wolf-like than ever, lunged toward him by his cellphone ringing.

~ * ~

After dressing in blue jeans, boots, and a tight-fitting top Justin liked, Paige pulled her hair back in a ponytail and put on a Pine View County Sheriff cap her dad gave her, pulling her ponytail through the gap above the Velcro sizing fastener. She'd never been to an MRB party, but her attire seemed appropriate. She used the many pillows from her bed to form a Pillow-Paige under the covers. After several attempts, she was satisfied, if her dad checked on her before she got back, he'd think it had been her body bundled up under the covers.

Once she was dressed and Pillow-Paige had been constructed, she turned off her bedroom lights and sat down on the foot of her bed, careful not to alter the form under her covers. Even with the lights out, her bedroom was bathed in silvery light from the waning, gibbous moon that rose above the trees and pushed its way into her bedroom through the curtain covered windows. She glanced at her bedside clock, ten twenty-eight p.m. She was excited and nervous. She couldn't tell which dominated her emotion more. It was nervousness.

After sitting on the bed for what felt like hours, time seemed to have slowed to a crawl, Paige got up and peeked out the window. She didn't expect to see anything, and she wasn't disappointed in that notion. Paige just didn't know what else to do. She sat back down on the bed and her legs started bouncing with nervous energy. She stood back up, went to her door, and pressed her ear against it. The house was silent. She sat back down and looked at the clock, ten forty-one p.m.

After a couple of minutes, Paige got back up and started pacing nervously around her bed and checking the clock every few seconds. The digital blue numbers told her it was ten forty-eight p.m. She sat back down again when her cellphone vibrated in her back pocket.

It startled her so badly she almost screamed. She calmed herself with a few deep breaths and pulled out her cellphone.

The text from Justin read, 'We're here.'

Paige texted back, 'I'll be right out,' and put her cellphone in her back pocket.

It was time, and Paige's nerves were raw. She listened at the door again—the house was still quiet. She opened her bedroom door slowly and felt relief when it didn't creak. As she started to step from her carpeted bedroom floor to the tiled hall floor, she remembered the sound her boots made on the tile and pulled her foot back.

How stupid can you be, Paige-Turner? Paige thought.

She quickly removed her boots, laced the fingers of her left hand through the pull-straps, and stepped out into the small hall separating her bedroom from her dad's home office.

When she pulled her door shut, there had been a click as the latch slipped into the strike plate. It wasn't loud, but in the silent house, it sounded like a gunshot to Paige. She froze with her hand still on the doorknob and waited for her dad to come investigate. After several long seconds, time slowed again, Paige exhaled. She hadn't noticed she'd been holding her breath until that moment.

Feeling sure her dad hadn't heard the noise, Paige tiptoed across the living room to the front door. She quietly unlocked it and twisted the doorknob. The door cracked open and warm night air pushed past her. She stepped out onto the front porch and pulled the door shut. This time, Paige kept the doorknob twisted so it wouldn't click as it hit the strike plate. She was a quick learner. After she released the doorknob, she gave the door a gentle push to make sure it latched. It was. Paige pulled her keys from her front right pocket and engaged the deadbolt lock. She was out.

Paige quickly put her boots back on and stepped off the porch. The sky had been cloudless and the light from the not quite full moon high above her illuminated the surroundings to where she could see clearly in the silvery moonlight. She walked at a brisk pace past the three vehicles—her dad's personal truck, his Sheriff SUV, and her Lil' Dragon—parked out front. With those cleared, and the house about a hundred feet behind her, Paige took off jogging down the driveway.

Her dad built his house at the back of his five acres, so the driveway had been long and traversed thick woods on either side. As Paige jogged its length, she felt very alive. The night air that rushed past her face had been warm and thick with the scent of pine trees. The woods were alive with the sounds of frogs, crickets, and cicadas, and more than once, something small scurried into the woods as she jogged by. Paige wasn't concerned. Her mind had been far away from Carla Weaver's dead pigs and whatever attacked them.

When she got to County Road Five Eighty-Eight, forgetting what Justin texted her, she looked left for his truck. It wasn't there. Panic threatened to close in, but she looked right and saw him parked a little way up the road. A couple of seconds later, she opened the front passenger door.

Justin and Lindsey, who sat in back seat, were arguing about something but they stopped as Paige climbed in.

"Told ya," Justin said.

"Told ya what?" Paige asked as she shut the door.

"Lindsey thought you'd chicken out."

Paige looked in the back at Lindsey. "Is that so?"

Lindsey shifted uncomfortably. "Well…I mean…your dad *is* the sheriff."

"The sheriff is fast asleep. If he were awake, he'd be pointin' his gun at Justin through his window by now."

Justin jumped and took a quick look out of his side window, as if to check. This sent Paige and Lindsey into fits of laughter.

"Hilarious," Justin said.

He started laughing, too.

Still giggling, Paige said, "It would probably be a good idea to get the hell outta here…just in case he wakes up."

Justin put his truck in drive and pulled onto County Road Five Eighty-Eight.

After about a quarter mile of driving in the moonlight, he turned on his headlights and shouted, "To the MRB."

In unison, Paige and Lindsey shouted, "To the MRB."

As they drove off into the night, Paige thought, *this is gonna be the best night ever*.

She could not have been more wrong.

~ * ~

Many miles away, the alpha picked up on the second scent it marked earlier that day. The scent of the girl it saw going into a house in the woods.

Later, its wolf hybrid human brain thought.

It already had plans for the old woman with the shotgun and the deputy, the first scent it marked, it observed from the woods after playing with the pigs. If its plans worked out, and it had been sure they would, it could take care of the old woman and deputy at the same place. At the old woman's house. Then it would turn its attention to the party it could hear many miles away. It didn't know how it knew, but it had been sure the girl it marked would be at the party.

Werewolves weren't the only animals with a pack mentality. Teenagers liked to gather together, too.

Chapter Six

What Pine View High School students called the Mill Road Barn since the mid-1980's was the empty shell of a two-level, metal building that had once been a privately owned and operated sawmill. The building was a large, fifteen thousand square feet, I-beam framed structure with corrugated metal panels for siding and roof. The roof had corrugated fiberglass panels intermixed with the metal ones to allow natural light in. It had a concrete floor and the windows, like the Wiseman barn windows, had long ago been broken, and were spaced evenly along the two long sides of the building. Each end of the structure had large double doors that could open wide enough to accommodate timber deliveries. The double doors were on tracks on the outside of the building, and, over the years, the tracks fell into disrepair, so that now only one door on one end opened. There were stairs along the inner wall at the end of the structure by the only working door that led to the second level, which comprised a bathroom that no longer worked and an office that looked down on the sawmill operating area.

The teenagers who frequented the MRB referred to the office as the 'Wood Room,' a not-so-clever double entendre and euphemism for the excited, adolescent erections that arose as inexperienced boys tried to have sex with equally inexperienced girls on a musty old couch that Garrett and some friends hauled up the stairs and into the office when he had been the inexperienced boy and Lacy had been the inexperienced girl. It was very possible Paige had been conceived on that couch. There was a chain at the bottom of the stairs that could be hooked across the stair railing. When the chain stretched across the stairs, the Wood Room was in use.

~ * ~

Rufus Redding owned and operated the sawmill. Unfortunately, Rufus liked to gamble and spent most weekends in Shreveport, Louisiana on the gambling boats. To make matters worse, Rufus wasn't a good gambler. When money got tight and he had to choose between paying the loan on his sawmill or paying his gambling debt, he paid the gambling debt.

To Rufus' way of thinking, paying the gambling debts instead of paying on the sawmill loan made perfect sense. After all, if he didn't pay his gambling debt, he wouldn't be allowed to continue to gamble. Rufus figured gambling was the only chance, however remote, he had of keeping the sawmill. It became a viscous cycle. Like most hopeless gamblers, Rufus knew he was just one hand of Texas Hold 'Em, his game of choice, away from being rich. He wasn't.

After not paying the sawmill loan for six months, East-Tex Commercial Bank declared the loan in default and seized the property in September 1983. The property comprised a large metal building, various pieces of sawmill equipment: trimmers, tilt hoists, sorters, edgers, planers, carriage rigs, and ban saws, two forklifts, and ten acres of land.

~ * ~

About a month after declaring the loan in default, the bank sent an appraiser to inventory the property. When the appraiser entered the metal building, he came upon a gruesome scene. Rufus' decomposing head hung in a rope noose attached to the second level railing. Rot and weight separated his body from his head. It looked like his body exploded when it hit the concrete floor. Dried blood, guts, and organs were splattered around the body in a perfect circle about ten feet across, like a bomb went off inside him. Flies were thick in the air and maggots wriggled in and out of the remaining flesh, which made Rufus' body undulate on the floor like part of him lived still.

The appraiser immediately covered his mouth with his hands, but vomit exploded through his fingers and added to the gore on the floor. He stumbled outside, gasping for clean air, and called the sheriff's department. The responding deputy found a note in the office that simply said: You gotta know when to hold them and know when to fold them. Rufus folded.

The coroner confirmed what the appraiser suspected; Rufus' body exploded. Rufus had been a big man, six foot four inches tall and about three hundred and fifty pounds. As the flesh of his neck rotted, decomposition gasses expanded in his abdomen. When what was left of his neck could no longer support the weight of his bloated body, it fell to the concrete below and exploded on impact.

The coroner placed the initial time of death at two to three weeks before discovery. It had been close to accurate. Insect activity analyses and additional tissue examinations later pinpointed time of death to a more accurate twenty to twenty-three days.

~ * ~

Rufus made one last trip to the boats a few days after the bank took his sawmill. He'd lost everything, including a gold pocket watch passed down from father to son. Rufus had a son, but he gambled the pocket watch on a losing hand, which ended the generational father to son passing. Because of his gambling, his wife divorced him. His son and two daughters didn't want to be in his life either. Gambling took everything from him, but he couldn't stop. After one last bad night at the gambling boats, Rufus drove back to what used to be his sawmill, wrote the note he thought had been clever, tied off the rope, and jumped over the rail.

Unfortunately, for Rufus, he had been about as good at hanging himself as he was at gambling. His neck didn't break when the rope snapped tight. The noose wasn't tight, and it pulled up under his jaw, crushing his larynx. He tried to breathe, but no air would pass. He tried to scream, but the rope crushed his voice box and what came out of him had been nothing more than a ragged whisper.

As he wiggled and clawed at the rope, the noose tightened. The pressure in his head was unbearable. He clawed at the rope cutting deeply into his neck, but all he did was gouge his skin. This skin had been found under his fingernails during the autopsy. This evidence, and that Rufus' spine had still been attached to his skull, would lead the coroner to conclude Rufus suffered a slow and painful death. He nailed that one.

Rufus was about to expire. His hands hung limp next to his large body and his legs dangled motionlessly. His vision was going dark, but he could still see around the sawmill as his body slowly spun at the end of the rope. He changed his mind about killing himself as soon as he realized the initial rope snap hadn't killed him, but the pressure in his head became so intense he just wanted it over.

He tried to close his eyes, but his eyelids would no longer come together. Rufus heard two simultaneous 'pops' and he was no longer looking around the sawmill. He was looking at his unshaved chin. His eyeballs popped out of the orbital sockets.

As his vision closed to a pinpoint, Rufus thought, *I should've played the hand a little longer.*

~ * ~

The equipment, always in demand in East Texas, auctioned off quickly. The land and building were not. In 1989, an investor out of nearby Tyler, Texas, purchased the building and land for seventy cents on the dollar of what Rufus owed. There had been some brief activity around the MRB, mostly upkeep repairs that had local teens worried they were going to lose their party spot. As quickly and unexpectedly as the activity began, it ended.

The rumor around Pine View High School was the investor suddenly died and his surviving heirs were fighting over the inheritance. This was accurate. The will had been disputed in probate court for many years. When the affairs were finally settled, the surviving beneficiaries had little interest in the Pine View County property. A pipe, cattle gate had been put across the access road, which had been chained and locked. The geniuses who installed the gate put both hinge bolts pointing up, so access to the MRB could be gained by simply lifting the hinge side of the gate off the hinges and dragging it out of the way, which had been exactly how students since before Garrett's days in high school accessed the MRB for parties.

The Pine View County Sheriff's Department had been aware students frequently held parties at the MRB. Sometimes they would get word of a planned party and a deputy would park in front of the gate to wave off disappointed students as they arrived. Other times, a deputy would make a surprise visit to the MRB, which had comical results. The teens would bolt in all directions with beer cans, liquor bottles, and red solo cups flying in their wake. Eventually, realizing their vehicles were at the barn, they'd come skulking back out of the woods.

These 'busts' were usually handled in a small town, rural, East Texas way. Meaning the teens were forced to pour all remaining alcohol: beers, bottles of assorted liquor, and an occasional keg onto the ground. Sometimes a deputy would 'confiscate' an unopened bottle or a heavy thirty-pack of beer as 'evidence,' which meant they'd drink it later. The teens didn't complain because, outside of the occasional belligerent drunk who would cause trouble and be hauled in to sleep it off in the county

'Drunk Tank' along with a call to their parents, the deputies usually determined which of the partiers were sober. Many teens came for the atmosphere and not the alcohol. The officers would let them drive the intoxicated teens home.

~ * ~

The current partiers arrived at the MRB about nine o'clock. The gate had been removed so cars and trucks, mostly trucks, started flowing in. There were plenty of places to park around the barn and parking was, considering there were no outlined parking spaces or parking attendants directing parking, remarkably organized.

Most of the party attendees were juniors and seniors. Freshmen and sophomores, who could catch a ride like Paige and Lindsey, attended too. On that evening, twenty-six students attended the MRB party, which accounted for a large percentage of the 1-A, Pine View High School student body. By party's end, the 1-A, Pine View High School student body would be substantially smaller.

The first order of business had always been to get a bonfire going in front of the end of the barn with the only working door. Luckily for the generations of MRB partygoers, firewood was a commodity in abundance in East Texas. After stacking the firewood, and soaking it with gasoline, a trail of gasoline leading away from the pile was poured. The honor of lighting the trail of gasoline usually went to whoever brought the gasoline but was often handed off to the nearest pretty girl. That is, if it wasn't a pretty girl who brought the gasoline. With the bonfire lit, the party kicked into high gear.

Although not every partygoer indulged, there had always been an abundance of alcohol on hand. The alcohol was acquired by means underage teenagers employed since the Twenty-first Amendment repealed the Eighteenth Amendment, prohibition of alcohol, in 1920—by stealing it from their parent's liquor cabinet or by paying someone with loose morals a large fee to purchase it for them.

On that evening, there were, as always, an assortment of liquor, mostly vodka, tequila, bourbon, as well as coolers with iced down beer, mostly Miller Lite, Bud Light, and Coors Light. Several seniors pooled their money and secured a pony keg of Miller Lite, which had been set up inside the MRB. Being enterprising young men, they were charging a dollar for each red solo cup of beer they sold. Students who hadn't been able to secure their own libations were happy to pay.

There were several students inside the metal building. Most of them were in proximity of the keg, and someone had secured the chain across the stairway, meaning the Wood Room was in use. One boy who went in on the keg brought a Bluetooth speaker and streamed music to it from his cellphone. Miranda Lambert's *Gunpowder & Lead* blasted out of the little speaker and reverberating off the corrugated metal siding, which amplified it greatly.

Even though the keg had been set up inside the MRB, the party was not contained within. Many students brought lawn chairs and were positioned around the bonfire with their coolers handy. Others were sitting on opened tailgates and still others slipped off into the woods for make-out sessions. The Wood Room hadn't cornered the MRB market on adolescent sexual experimentation. Occasionally, a couple would get a little hot and heavy in a vehicle. These sessions were likely to be interrupted and, since the proliferation of smartphones, could cause embarrassing pictures circulating the student body by the next day. To avoid this, those who wanted a more private party used the Wood Room or the actual woods.

The music outside the metal building was always an overlapping mix from several vehicles competing to be the loudest. While Miranda Lambert was echoing off the walls inside, Lynyrd Skynyrd's *Free Bird*, George Strait's *Amarillo by Morning*, Evanescence's *My Immortal*, and Kenny Chesney's *You Had Me from Hello* were playing over each other outside; *Free Bird* was the loudest.

Justin had The Eagles' *Hotel California* blaring in his truck as they drove past the de-hinged gate and up the drive leading to the MRB. The windows were open, and he soon heard *Free Bird*, along with a few other less recognizable tunes, drifting through the dense trees.

He turned off his radio. "I *love* Free Bird."

When they arrived at the MRB, it was eleven eighteen p.m.

~ * ~

The Pine View County Sheriff Department's eleven-to-seven shift included Deputy Ty Jackson along with three additional deputies, Danny Stutter, Crystal Zimmer, and Austin Turner. Ty began the shift briefing at ten thirty p.m. by conveying Sheriff Lambert's instructions to them.

"Be on the lookout for large dead animals. If ya find one, mark the location on GPS and do not get out of your vehicle. If an injured or deceased citizen is located, call for backup but do not render aid alone."

He delivered the same message every night that week.

Once again, Crystal Zimmer voiced the same objection about not helping an injured civilian. She raised this objection during every briefing that week. Ty explained, again, the animals that attacked the citizen might still be nearby. Ty should have taken his and Garrett's advice.

Once the briefing was over, Ty and the other deputies checked out their patrol SUVs from the motor pool and hit the streets. More accurately, they hit the country roads.

Each of the four deputies had a quadrant of Pine View County that were their primary domain. Ty had the southern quadrant where the previous activities, Carla Weaver's pigs and Russ Lomax's mutilations, took place. Crystal patrolled the east quadrant where the Mill Road Barn was located, Danny patrolled the northern quadrant, and Austin patrolled the western quadrant.

As Ty drove toward County Road Five Sixty-Nine, he wanted to drive by the Weaver place. Karen Parker's voice crackled over the radio, "Emergency call at Twenty-One Eighteen, County Road Five Sixty-Nine."

Ty depressed the call button on his shoulder-mounted microphone. "I'm about two miles out. I'll be there in a jiff."

He slammed his foot down on the accelerator and the big SUV, powered by a fuel-injected 6.2-liter V8 engine, launched forward.

As he slowed down to turn off Highway Twenty-One onto County Road Five Sixty-Nine Karen's voice crackled through the radio again. "Um…Ty, she said to tell ya that they're back."

Ty took the corner with one hand on the wheel so he could depress the call button with the other. "Roger that."

With the turn successfully negotiated, Ty slammed his foot down on the accelerator again.

"I'll get you fuckers," Ty said, but his hand wasn't depressing the call button, so he said it to himself.

He had been about a mile away from Carla's house when he heard the first howl. He didn't need a tunch to know he was about to put his life in danger. The howl, then howls, conveyed that message clearly.

~ * ~

Carla Weaver had a restless, anxious week. On Monday she stayed up from around four that morning, when she heard the thump against her house, the scraping under her bedroom window, the vicious growls, her pigs screaming as they were slaughtered, and, worst of all, that unholy breathing until around midnight that night. The sounds weren't the only things haunting Carla. The things she'd seen put her nerves on edge, too.

She didn't go down to the pigpen, but she watched from the back porch as Earl Wells used his frontend loader to scoop up what had been left of her pigs and dump them in the hole he'd dug with the backhoe attached to the other end of the tractor with the frontend loader. When she saw the big, back wheels of the tractor come up off the ground, she figured Earl had Bingo in the bucket. She was correct.

She couldn't see much, but she saw a stiff, red hair covered leg. Bingo, her only Duroc, had a leg stuck out of the bucket and a long trail of muddy entrails hung from the bucket, too. Earl had to raise the bucket up high to not run over the trailing innards and, when he dumped Bingo into the pit, Carla thought she saw a massive bite across Bingo's broad back.

Every time she tried to lie down and catch some sleep throughout the day, some sound or another would startle her awake. She'd sit quietly and listen to see if the sounds posed a genuine threat or if it were her imagination. None of the sounds were threats. About three o'clock, she gave up on the idea of taking a nap and busied herself with knitting as well as game show watching.

She, like Garrett, was an avid *Jeopardy* watcher. Unlike Garrett, she thought Alex Trebek was a 'damn handsome man.'

Frequently, she said, "If I were a younger woman, I'd rub one out thinkin' about ya Alex Trebek," to her television.

She wasn't younger and the only thing she rubbed was homemade liniment oil on her aching joints. She also liked to watch *Wheel of Fortune*. Not that she had been good at figuring out the puzzles, or providing questions to Alex Trebek's clues, either. She thought Pat Sajak was cute too. Less rub worthy, though.

Around four o'clock that afternoon, with her game shows watched and her arthritis flaring in her hands from knitting, Carla made supper. She loved cooking from scratch. Tonight, her heart and hands weren't into laboring over a home cooked meal, so she opted for one of the microwave dinners she kept on hand for her grandchildren.

She picked a breaded chicken strips, mashed potatoes, and green beans meal. It tasted like crap, but it satisfied Carla's small appetite. With supper out of the way, Carla took a shower. Monday wasn't one of her usual shower days. Shower days were Sunday, Tuesday, and Thursday. After seeing Bingo dumped into the hole, she felt dirty, and the shower soothed her aching bones. It washed away some of her tension, too. After the shower, she dressed in her nightgown, climbed into bed, grabbed the Bible she kept on her nightstand, and started reading.

It shamed her to admit it, but reading the Bible always put her to sleep after a few passages. It was a private shame, though, as she would tell none of the old crones who frequented her church, which happened to be the same church Russ Lomax attended. Pine View First Baptist Church.

Carla repeated this new routine, minus the daily shower and microwave dinners, for the rest of that week. Friday found her still anxious and startling at every creak omitted by her old house, but the demons that killed her pigs hadn't returned. There had been some comfort in that.

On Friday night, reading the Bible wasn't putting her to sleep. The sun slipped down below the horizon. The waning, gibbous moon crested over the woods behind her house as she read.

She had been reading Second Corinthians 6:14, "Do not be yoked together with unbelievers. For what do righteousness and wickedness have in common? Or what fellowship can light have with darkness?" when she realized it had grown dark outside.

She looked at the bedside clock. It was eleven o eight p.m. A chill ran up her spine.

Carla couldn't remember whether she locked the front and back doors. Suddenly frightened, but not sure why, Carla bolted out of bed and ran to the back door.

They're out back, she thought, as she twisted the deadbolt.

With the back door locked, Carla ran to the front door and engaged that deadbolt, too. Carla's heart hammered in her skinny chest so fast and hard she thought it might explode.

She leaned against the front door for several moments, waiting for her heartbeat to slow to a semi normal rate. It slowed and, just when Carla felt silly for almost scaring herself into a cardiac event; that's what her doctor warned her against if she didn't stop frying just about everything she ate, she heard a scraping sound on the front door, which she was still leaning against. She let out a terrified scream and jumped away from the door. Something outside let out a guttural, demonic laugh.

As Carla ran to the corded telephone, which hung on a wall in the kitchen, something heavy hit the back door. She let out another terrified scream as she grabbed for the phone. With phone in hand, she quickly dialed nine-one-one. A window, it sounded to Carla like the one in her bedroom, shattered.

The nine-one-one operator answered on the second ring and, in a calm voice that Carla immediately hated, said, "Nine, one, one. Is this an emergency?"

"Yes, it's a fuckin' emergency."

"Ma'am, if you'll just…" the operator said, but Carla cut her off.

"They're back. They're back. Tell Officer Ty they're fuckin' back." Carla screamed as she heard something crash through the back door.

"Okay ma'am, I'll convey the…"

The phone went dead before the nine-one-one operator could finish the sentence.

Carla dropped the phone and backed into the far corner of the kitchen. She could feel one beast step into her house through the back door. The raised floor shook as its heavy foot came down on it. Just then, the front door crashed in, and she felt the floor shake again as the one at the front door stepped inside.

Although scared beyond anything she'd experienced in her life, Carla's mind screamed inside her head, *Get in the pantry*.

The scared part of Carla's mind had been confused, but then it hit her. There was a trapdoor in the pantry's floor that granted access to the crawlspace beneath the house. Her late husband, Mitch, installed it so he could more easily access the house's plumbing without crawling under from the outside. The pantry was directly behind her.

Carla quickly opened the pantry door and slipped inside. It was dark inside the pantry, but Carla, being a very organized woman; she would have felt compelled to clean and organize Dr. James Huff's office if she'd seen it, knew where everything was. She also knew Mitch, God rest his soul, always told her to keep the trapdoor clear of clutter so he wouldn't have to 'wrestle clutter' out of his way when he needed to use it.

Old habits die hard, and Carla kept the trapdoor clear of clutter since Mitch passed away three years prior.

The beasts at the front and back doors stood silently, like sentries, in place, as if guarding against her escape. Carla could hear their sinister breathing. It echoed throughout the house. As Carla hooked the middle finger of her right hand into the trapdoor metal pull ring that would allow her to open it, she heard something crash in the living room. The crashing sound was followed by a 'thud' that shook the entire house, and one beast let out a quick yelp. Carla, thinking someone, Officer Ty, arrived and hurt one of them, felt a moment of relief. Then she heard something large rapidly advancing on the kitchen and it was growling.

Carla quickly pulled the metal ring. The trapdoor flew open, and Carla jumped into the dark void just as the pantry door exploded over her head. For the briefest of seconds, Carla dared to believe she'd make it. Then a gigantic hand with razor-sharp, long claws closed over the top of her head and jerked her back into the light of the kitchen and the horror looking down at her.

What is a werewolf, Mister Trebek? Carla's mind provided an answer to the unasked *Jeopardy* clue.

She was almost proud of herself for answering correctly earlier when Sheriff Garrett and Office Ty pondered what killed her pigs. Carla felt pain like nothing she'd ever experienced, and she'd given natural birth to all six of her children in that very house, rip through her body. Rubbing one out to Alex Trebek was the last thing on her mind.

~ * ~

Ty pulled into Carla Weaver's drive too fast. His SUV fishtailed and took out her mailbox, but he wasn't concerned with the mailbox or body damage inflicted on his vehicle. He sped up her driveway at breakneck speed and skidded to a stop next to Carla's beat up, 1970's Ford pickup. He quickly surveyed the scene, and he didn't like what he saw.

Carla's front door was broken down and he could clearly see long claw marks on the siding next to the door. He depressed the call button on his shoulder-mounted microphone when he heard an agonizing scream from within the house. It was Carla.

Ty instinctively wanted to rush in the house to Carla. Everything inside him screamed for this action. Ty fought this off for a moment and did two things before letting nature take its course.

First, he depressed the call button. "I need backup at Twenty-One Eighteen, CR Five Six Nine."

Then he called Garrett's cellphone.

~ * ~

Garrett tossed and turned in his bed. He was covered in sweat and tangled in his bed sheets. In the nightmare, sixteen-year-old Monster-Paige, now more werewolf than ever before, just stepped out of Lacy's mangled body and stood next to the larger werewolf. This time, the larger werewolf wasn't that much larger than Monster-Paige. When Monster-Paige lifted her deadly hand, Garrett expected her to wave bye-bye and leave through the back door as they always did in the past. This time, the larger werewolf let out a demonic laugh that filled Garrett's already terrified and petrified dream body with a new level of terror. As if responding to the laugh, Monster-Paige lashed out toward Garrett with her clawed hand. She rushed toward Garrett, snapping her dagger teeth viciously.

Garrett had time to scream, "Paige."

He heard a distant ringing sound just as Monster-Paige's teeth were closing around his neck.

Garrett sat bolt upright in bed. His heart was running a marathon in his chest. He tried to raise his hands to his neck, wanting, needing to make sure Monster-Paige hadn't ripped it open, but his arms were tangled in the sheets. The distant ringing sound he'd heard in his dream no longer seemed distant.

I'm awake, Garrett's mind screamed inside his head.

As that understanding washed over him, he realized the ringing came from his cellphone.

What this might portend washed over him, too. He quickly grabbed his cellphone and tapped the little green circle with a phone receiver in it. "This is Garrett."

It was Ty on the other end.

~ * ~

After the eighth ring, Ty had been about to cancel the call when he heard Garrett say, "This is Garrett."

To Ty, Garrett sounded out of breath and agitated. He didn't have time to inquire why this might be. "I'm at Missus Weaver's house, Garrett. They're back."

Without hesitation, Garrett said, "Stay put. I'm on my way."

Just then, another agonizing scream filled the night air.

Before Ty could respond to Garrett's instructions, Garrett, having heard the scream through the phone, said, "Is that Carla?"

"I'm pretty sure it is."

Garrett, knowing Ty so well, said, "Stay put, Ty. Wait for me and backup."

Ty took a deep breath. "Ya know I can't do that, Garrett."

Garrett screamed, "Stay put."

Another scream came from inside Carla Weaver's house.

"I have a plan," Ty said and ended the call.

~ * ~

Garrett bolted out of bed and dressed quickly. As he left his bedroom, he briefly considered waking Paige to let her know he was leaving. He didn't want to worry her or take any time answering questions she might ask, though. Garrett knew she would likely wake up when he tore out of the driveway, and this might worry her as well. He kept a magnetic sticky-notepad and pen on the refrigerator so he could keep track of what he needed when he went grocery shopping.

He grabbed the pen, wrote, I'll be back later, on the top sheet, and tore it off. Garrett quickly, but quietly, opened Paige's door. He had been relieved to see her sleeping form beneath the covers. Garrett stuck the note to the inside of Paige's door, where she'd have to see it if she got up for any reason, quietly shut her door, and exited the house. Not two minutes after Ty's call, Garrett was speeding away from his driveway on County Road Five Eighty-Eight. He was only a few minutes away from Ty.

Stay put, Ty, Garrett thought.

~ * ~

After he hung up on Garrett, Ty grabbed the dash mounted Remington 1100, twelve-gauge semiautomatic shotgun with pistol grip and collapsible stock. He switched the safety off and stepped out of his SUV. The night had been still and quiet, except for Carla Weaver's occasional screams. Ty's tunch was screaming for him to be cautious. He would be. Ty took something out of his left breast pocket and clutched it in his left hand.

This better fuckin' work, Ty thought as he took a step toward Carla's house.

As Ty's right foot came down on the lowest step of Carla's porch steps, something shifted in the shadows to his left. When he looked in that direction, he saw two burning red eyes glowing at him from the darkness at the corner of the house. Instinct told Ty to shoot it. Caution told him not to. A menacing growl on Ty's right drew his attention—two burning red eyes glowed out of the darkness at him from that side, too.

They're flankin' me, Ty thought.

Each of the beasts took a deliberate step toward Ty. They took another step. The beasts weren't attacking, they were advancing.

They're not flankin' me, they're herdin' me, Ty corrected his earlier thought.

Ty started up the steps, and the beasts closed together at the bottom, blocking his retreat. As he stepped onto the porch, he saw Carla's front door hadn't been broken down. It had been ripped apart. There were large claw marks visible on parts of the door that were still discernible as having been a door. The rest of the door was not much more than splinters. He felt one beast behind him step on to the steps. The pawfall was so heavy it shook the porch. They wanted Ty inside. He stepped across the threshold.

Carla's house was referred to as 'shotgun style,' meaning it was a straight shot from the front of the house to the back of the house. As Ty looked toward the back door, which had been splintered like the front door, he saw a third beast stooping in the doorframe.

This had been the first time Ty got a good look at what he'd been thinking of as beasts. He was looking at a werewolf. For the first time in Ty's life, he was truly terrified.

Garrett told Ty Dr. James Huff described werewolves as the perfect predator. Ty could clearly see why Huff said this. The werewolf stooping in the back doorway was massive. Its broad shoulders were wider than the doorway. Its arms were muscular and long, and its large, bony fingers were capped with long claws. It was clicking them together threateningly. Its hind feet were enormous paws.

This explains their trouble climbin' trees, Ty thought.

If he lived through this, which he thought was unlikely, he'd tell Garrett about their hind paws.

Of all the werewolf's features, its head and face were the most terrifying. It clearly had wolf features, but they were grossly enlarged. Its snout was easily more than a foot long and the porcelain white, dagger length teeth looked too big to fit in its snarling snout.

Just then, it snapped at Ty, and he could see he wasn't mistaken in that assessment. Its large canine teeth protruded on either side of its dangerous snout.

All the better to eat ya with, Ty thought.

Its ears were overly large, pointy, and positioned on either side, but at the top of its wolf skull. They twitched in all directions, taking in sounds Ty's human ears could not detect.

All the better to hear ya with, Ty thought.

Even considering its dangerous snout, Ty thought its eyes were its most terrifying feature. Although thirty-plus feet away, at the back of the house, Ty could clearly see its red eyes flickering from deep within its furrowed brow. It looked as if the very fires of hell were fueling the ungodly creature.

All the better to devour your soul with, Ty thought.

Ty took in all of this within a matter of seconds. He finally knew what he was truly up against. In a strange way, this relaxed him.

"Know your enemy." Sergeant Rex Fuller, Ty's Marine boot camp drill sergeant, used to bellow at them during drills.

Ty raised his shotgun and pointed it at the werewolf in front of him. He knew, if the legends were correct, shooting it with steal buckshot wouldn't kill it, but it might slow it down. If he could blow one of its legs off, all the better. The werewolf didn't even flinch. When Ty lowered his aim to one of the werewolf's legs, it, incredibly, seemed to understand Ty's intent and dove back just as the shot went off. There was a spray of blood and a yelp, but Ty knew his shot hadn't been on target enough to remove one of its legs.

As soon as the shot went off, Ty heard and felt the entire house shaking. The two behind him bounded up the porch steps. He spun around to unload on them, but they were quicker than him.

As Ty spun around, a massive, clawed hand connected with his right shoulder and sent him flying into the wall to his left. As he connected with the wall and continued through it in a crash of plaster and backboard, he pulled the shotgun's trigger. He didn't have time to aim, but he felt elated as he witnessed the left lower leg of the werewolf that hit him dissolve away in a spray of blood, bone, and fur. Its yelp of pain had been even more satisfying.

Ty's Marine training kicked in and he rolled up in a crouching position with the shotgun aimed at the hole in the wall his body created. He could still hear the one-legged werewolf yelping from the living room, but neither tried to follow him through the hole.

"You better be afraid of my black ass." Ty shouted.

Everything went quiet, even the yelping werewolf fell silent. For a moment, Ty dared to hope he'd scared them off. That was the moment he felt the back of the house shudder and he realized the third werewolf was back.

As Ty formulated a plan to deal with the three werewolves, he clutched the object in his left hand even tighter. Its points pierced his palm, but he didn't care. Then it hit him. There were four werewolves the previous Monday, not three.

Just then, as if the fourth could read Ty's thoughts, Carla screamed, "Run, Officer Ty."

The scream came from behind the wall to Ty's right. As he turned to point the shotgun in that direction, the wall exploded in on Ty and the fourth werewolf, Ty knew in his gut was the alpha, crashed in on top of him.

Ty tried to ball up to protect his head, neck, and gut. The massive werewolf grabbed him by the left shoulder. Its long claws stabbed into Ty's flesh, and it, effortlessly, lifted him into the air. The collision knocked the shotgun from his hands, but he managed to clinch it between his knees as he was lifted off the floor. He tried to reach it with his right hand. No such luck. It fell to the floor.

The alpha dangled Ty at arm's length and looked at him. Its fiery red eyes flickered fiercely. Its snout snarled up, revealing more of its deadly teeth as thick, blood tainted drool oozed in long stringers, and it growled at him. That growl shook Ty to his bones.

Ty thought his time was up and was about to deploy the secret weapon still tightly clutched in his left hand, but the alpha turned, keeping Ty at arm's length and out of reach, and stepped back through the hole in the wall it created into Carla's bedroom.

What Ty saw was worse than anything he'd seen in Afghanistan and, unbelievably, worse than what had been left of Russ Lomax. What made it worse than Russ Lomax was one thing missing from that scene. Russ had been dead. Carla was still alive.

Carla laid face up on her bed. If she'd been wearing something earlier, which Ty was certain she would have been, her clothing was gone. Her naked body was covered in blood and deep, ragged claw marks. Ty knew enough from his three combat tours in Afghanistan that none of the claw marks were fatal. Major arteries in her neck, inner upper arms, and inner thighs were avoided in the attack. Carla's wounds were inflicted to incapacitate and cause pain. Ty couldn't see a single bite mark on Carla's shredded body.

For what end? Ty thought.

Then it hit him. She was bait. Bait to lure him to them.

What do they want with me? Ty thought.

Carla's head rolled toward Ty and the alpha. Blood was leaking from her ears, nose, and mouth. Still her eyes were clear. She looked at Ty with her piercing blue eyes, and he realized just how beautiful and kind they were. Tears cut through the plaster and dirt on Ty's face and ran down his cheeks.

"I'm sorry, Missus Weaver," Ty whispered.

Carla took a deep breath that appeared to cause her great pain. Her whole body trembled. "No…I'm sorry, Deputy Jackson. It was you they wanted. Haven't ya reckoned that out yet?"

That Carla Weaver finally addressed him properly, revealing she'd known all along and was just messing with him, hurt Ty's heart more than the alpha's claws digging deep into his shoulder.

.

"I know," Ty whispered.

It was as if the alpha had been waiting for this conversation to take place, like it understood what they were saying to each other. As soon as Ty acknowledged he knew they were after him, the alpha reached out and decapitated Carla with one quick swipe of its massive claws. Her head bounced off the nightstand and landed on the blood-soaked, carpeted floor between the werewolf's pawed feet. When Ty looked down at it, Carla's beautiful, kind, and dead eyes looked up at him.

Something inside Ty snapped, and he began screaming many

curses at the alpha as he trashed around trying to get loose or get close enough to use his secret weapon. All his thrashing and cussing produced more pain in his shoulder as the alpha squeezed tighter, driving its long claws deeper into Ty's body. When Ty ran out of steam, the alpha laughed at him with the same demonic laugh he'd heard when he fell on his ass the previous Monday.

This infuriated Ty even more but, as he gathered strength for another chance of delivering his secret weapon, the alpha flung Ty across the room. He crashed through the bifold closet doors and smashed into the back wall of the house, which was much sturdier than the inner walls. The impact jarred Ty's entire body as all the wind was forced from his lungs and his left hand inadvertently opened.

Ty fell to the closet floor, which had been covered in debris from the demolished bifold doors, shoes, and other items of clothing displaced when he crashed into them, and immediately started digging in the rubble, trying to find the precious item. A reflective glint by his right hand caught his attention. He pushed a wooden slat from the bifold doors aside. He found it. As he reached for it, claws dug into his left shoulder again and pulled him out of the closet and into the air.

The alpha flung Ty onto the bed, onto Carla's headless body, which was still lying there. As Ty came down heavily on top of Carla's body, a loud fart exploded from her backside. It made Ty feel like he needed to puke, but the werewolves, there were three in the suddenly cramped bedroom, the fourth werewolf, the one that lost its left leg wasn't there, broke into their demonic laughing at the fart sound. Ty thought their reaction to the fart had been juvenile.

The alpha broke off the laughter with a sudden, authoritative growl that shook the walls. The other two werewolves immediately fell silent. The alpha reached out and grabbed Ty by his injured left shoulder and lifted him into the air. It grabbed Ty's right shoulder, but not painfully, and pulled him close to its snout.

Ty kicked it in the gut, but his boot bounced back as if he'd kicked a brick wall. The alpha eyes flared a brighter red when Ty's boot connected, but there had been no other sign the kick inflicted damage. The alpha turned its massive head to the side and opened its deadly jaws.

Ty tried to struggle as the alpha's jaws encircled his neck, but he couldn't move. Ty felt the dagger-like canines pierce his skin as they sank into his neck. He thought about his beautiful Jasmine and the son he wouldn't get to watch grow up. Just when Ty thought the alpha would snap its jaws shut and remove his head, it retracted its bite. Ty felt its hot tongue lick the puncture wounds, as if tasting him.

As the alpha released Ty from its deadly bite, its head and ears cocked toward the front of the house. It let out a demanding growl, and the two other werewolves in Carla's bedroom bolted toward the back door. The alpha looked back at Ty, and it winked at him. It hurled Ty back into the closet and bolted from the bedroom.

For a second, Ty thought they were gone, all of them. Then he heard a crash and a frustrated growl from the living room. The werewolf missing its left leg hadn't left with the others. Ty immediately started digging in the debris where he'd seen a metallic glint earlier. As he flung a shoe out of the way, he saw it. He quickly grabbed it and bolted back through the hole in the wall the alpha created when it grabbed him. The floor had been covered in debris but, unlike the small object safely clutched in Ty's left hand again, the shotgun was large, and he easily found it. Ty grabbed the shotgun and climbed through the hole in the wall made when the now one-legged werewolf swatted him through it.

When Ty climbed through the hole back into the living room, he immediately noticed two things. A human lower leg and a trail of blood leading toward the back of the house. Ty bolted out of the back door and found the one-legged werewolf holding onto the porch step railings as it hopped down the steps. Unbelievably, Ty could see its missing left leg was already regenerating—the stump was getting closer to the ground. Ty knew if its leg grew long enough to support its weight, it would be gone. He had to act.

Ty aimed the shotgun at the werewolf's left elbow and pulled the trigger. As its lower left arm separated from its body, the werewolf let out a loud yelp and toppled over on its left side. It hit the ground with a 'thud' that shook the porch. Then it rolled over and lashed out at Ty with its remaining right arm. Ty pulled the trigger. Its reaching right hand evaporated in a red mist. The yelp it let out when its right hand was blown off sounded, to Ty, more like a human cry of pain. That brought Ty satisfaction.

It rolled over on its front and tried to crawl away but, each time it tried to push off with one of its stumps, it would yelp and recoil from the stumped limb in pain.

Ty jumped off the porch, kicked it in its left side as hard as he could, and yelled, “Look at me.”

It lashed out with its teeth, much more quickly than Ty thought possible, given its current state. This time, Ty had been quicker, and he jumped out of reach.

Ty pointed the shotgun at its chest and pulled the trigger. A large, ragged hole appeared in the center of its chest.

It’s now or never, Ty thought, and he jumped on top of the thrashing werewolf.

It tried to snap at Ty, but he smashed it in the lower jaw with the shotgun butt. He plunged his left hand into the gapping chest wound. He pushed his hand up into its chest cavity to ensure it wouldn’t come back out, let go of his secret weapon, and quickly pulled his hand free.

The reaction had been immediate. The werewolf let out a strangled howl as smoke hissed out of the chest wound. It thrashed so violently that Ty got thrown off if it, not that he minded being out of personal contact with it. It thrashed and yelped a few more times, then it went limp, smoke still oozing out of its chest wound. Then it transformed back into a human.

Ty watched in amazement as the werewolf's body shrank in size. The coarse black hair retreated into skin that was turning pinker and more human by the second. The transformation in its head and face intrigued Ty most. Its ears shrunk in size and repositioned themselves on the sides of the almost human head. Its dagger length canines shortened back into its gums as its snout shrank back to form a human face. The face was that of a young man with light brown hair. How normal and unthreatening the young man, who moments ago had been a viscous werewolf, shocked Ty.

Ty remembered the way they had laughed at Carla’s flatulence and when he’d fallen on his ass. He’d thought it had been a juvenile response. He hadn’t been too far off. The one-legged, one-armed, no-handed man with a smoking hole in his chest couldn’t have been more than twenty years old.

The adrenaline rush that fueled Ty’s aggression subsided. He suddenly felt exhausted and the pain from his many wounds, but mostly his ravaged shoulder, returned with vengeance. He felt lightheaded and on the verge of passing out. Ty slumped backward and would have ended up flat on his back, but the porch railing had been behind him and propped him up.

In the distance, he heard an approaching siren. Ty realized the alpha must have heard the siren from many more miles away.

That's why it cocked its head and ears that direction before it and two of its pack fled, Ty thought.

Ty looked back at the fourth pack member. The smoke coming out of the chest wound had been little more than wisps that quickly dispersed in the cool night breeze. The body suddenly, and violently, convulsed, which startled Ty out of the stupor that overtook him.

Ty was on his feet and pointing the shotgun at the convulsing form in seconds. Before he could pull the trigger, the body stilled. In the distance, miles away, Ty heard a howl. It was followed by two more howls.

~ * ~

The alpha and its two remaining pack members were miles away from the old woman's house when it realized something was wrong. The alpha knew the injured werewolf would regenerate its lower leg in a matter of minutes and fall in behind the pack, but its scent remained where they parted.

The alpha slowed and stopped. The other two stopped beside the alpha. The alpha sniffed the cool night air. It smelled of werewolf and human blood, the deputy's and the old woman's. At that moment, the scent changed. The alpha no longer smelled a mixture of werewolf and human blood. It smelled a mixture of three distinct humans, the deputy's, the old woman's, and Seth Daniels' blood. The alpha instantly understood what this meant—the deputy somehow killed the injured werewolf.

It briefly considered returning to the old woman's house and killing the deputy and whoever was arriving with the siren, but it knew that would be counterproductive. The deputy would replace the pack member he killed when the June moon was full, and it planned to turn more humans, who were partying in the woods a few miles away. Especially the girl whose scent it marked earlier that day. The alpha knew she was at the party because her scent was intermixed with twenty-five other scents. It had plans for the girl.

The alpha let its pack mate with her wolf the previous Sunday night after their first turn, but she didn't enjoy it as much as she thought she would. Turning the girl would give her pack a bitch to mate with and, whether she liked it, she wouldn't be able to refuse the alpha's wishes. If she did, the alpha would kill her and turn another bitch.

As these thoughts were going through the alpha's mind, it sensed Seth take his last breath. In human form, Seth had been her boyfriend and the first person she turned after becoming a werewolf. She would grieve for him as a human later, but the werewolf deserved immediate recognition. The alpha turned its snout to the moon and howled. The other two, sensing what the alpha sensed, joined the alpha's howl.

The alpha looked back toward the old woman's house one last time before sprinting away on all fours toward the sounds and smells of the party. The two remaining pack members fell in behind their alpha.

~ * ~

Garrett, much as Ty had done about fifteen minutes earlier, fishtailed into Carla Weaver's driveway and sped up to her house, skidding to a stop next to Ty's SUV. A quick look through the driver's side window of Ty's SUV confirmed what Garrett had suspected—Ty hadn't waited for him or backup.

Garrett grabbed his dash-mounted twelve-gauge shotgun, stepped out of his SUV, and yelled, "Ty! Sound off, Ty!"

From the back of the house, Garrett heard Ty respond, "I'm out back, Garrett."

Garrett's relief at hearing Ty respond almost overwhelmed him. Ty didn't sound great, but he was alive.

Still feeling a sense of urgency, Garrett ran around the side of Carla Weaver's house—he didn't notice the fresh set of claw marks under her bedroom window or that it had been broken. As he rounded the back of the house, he quickly assessed the situation. Garrett saw a young man lying face up with two limbs and a hand missing, and a large hole in his chest that a thin patch of fog or smoke hovered over. He saw Ty, covered in a chalky substance and blood, leaning against the porch rail with his shotgun pointed at the ground.

Ty grinned at Garrett and pointed the shotgun at the body. "I killed the fucker. Not the alpha, though."

"Was it?" Garrett asked, suddenly finding it difficult to say the word werewolf.

Ty nodded. "Oh yeah. Big, hairy fucker…all teeth and claws."

Garrett stepped closer to the body and inspected it. In his expert opinion, the shotgun caused all the wounds. This had been welcomed news to Garrett. If a shotgun killed it, the silver myth was just that. A myth. This would make killing the alpha much easier. Unless killing the alpha would require silver and only its pack members could be killed more easily.

These thoughts were swirling around in Garrett's mind.

He was brought out of them when Ty said, "Missus Weaver's dead."

Garrett looked at Ty and the shattered door behind him. He'd also noted the similarly devastated front door as he skidded to a stop next to Ty's SUV. That they gained access to Carla's house was evident. Sad as the news had been, it wasn't surprising.

Garrett said, "I guess 'the widow who cried wolf' should've cried werewolf."

He immediately regretted how flippant the remark sounded and hoped his friend wouldn't hold it against him.

"She did. Monday mornin'," Ty reminded him.

Garrett felt lower than a snake's belly.

To redirect the conversation, Garrett said, "Did the shotgun kill it?"

Ty shook his head.

Puzzled, Garrett said, "I don't understand. It's dead…right?"

Ty nodded.

"You got some silver shot in your shell?"

Ty shook his head again.

Frustrated, Garrett said, "How the hell did ya kill it?"

Ty grinned. He was having fun at Garrett's expense for making the glib remark about Carla Weaver. "I blew off its left leg by accident…lucky shot as I was being thrown through a wall."

Garrett realized then the chalky substance covering Ty was plaster.

"That hobbled it somewhat, but it still made it from inside the house to the porch steps. I blew off its left arm so it couldn't use it to support itself. When it fell, I blew off its right hand so it couldn't claw me with it. When it was pretty much harmless…except for its teeth, I blew that hole in its chest."

Ty pointed the shotgun at the chest wound.

More frustrated, Garrett said, "Okay, you immobilized it. Good thinkin'…and blew a hole in its chest. What I want to know is how'd ya *kill* it?"

Ty grinned again. "Hold your ponies, Garrett. I'm gettin' to it.

Where was I? Oh yeah, after I blew the hole in its chest, I jumped on top of it. It tried to bite me, but I busted it upside the head with my shotgun. I plunged my fist into its chest wound and deployed my secret weapon."

Ty let that hang in the air just long enough for Garrett to say, "What the fuck is your secret weapon?"

Ty's grin turned into an outright smile, and he said, "The Silver Star commendation I got for rescuing Corporal Dirk Burnett in Afghanistan."

The information took a couple of moments to sink into Garrett's thoughts. His hopes that methods other than silver, fire, or decapitation could kill the werewolves were premature. He accepted this information with disappointment. Mike Middleton had promised silver bullets to kill them. That would help. Ty said he hadn't killed the alpha. That was bad. He took one of the four werewolves out. That meant there were only three left. So many conflicting thoughts. Too many.

Garrett looked down at the naked, bloodied, and dead young man who had been a werewolf.

He wondered aloud to himself, "Why'd they come back to Carla's house?"

Garrett wasn't expecting an answer, but Ty supplied one.

In a certain tone, Ty said, "She was bait."

Garrett turned his attention from the body to Ty. "Bait? Bait for what?"

Again, in a certain tone, Ty said, "Me."

Garrett shook his head, trying to keep Ty's answer from taking hold and staying in his mind.

"You?"

Ty nodded.

The answer was taking hold, and Garrett didn't like what it implied.

Knowing but not wanting to accept it, Garrett said, "What the fuck would they want with you?"

Ty took a deep breath. "A new pack member, I reckon. A chocolate flavored werewolf."

Garrett was afraid to ask, but he mustered the courage. "Did it?"

As the question had been coming out of Garrett's mouth, Ty tilted his head away from Garrett, exposing his neck. Garrett could see two large puncture wounds well clear of Ty's carotid artery, as if on purpose, which, if Ty was to be believed, and Garrett had no reason to believe otherwise, had been the case.

Garrett didn't think things could get much worse. He had been dead wrong. At the exact moment this thought bounced around inside his troubled mind, several Pine View High School students, who started the evening partying at the MRB, were lying in pools of their own blood, their bodies ripped to shreds, and Paige, alone in the woods, was being stalked by the alpha.

~ * ~

The MRB party kicked into high gear. The Wood Room accommodated its third couple of the evening. Inside the metal building, business thrived around the keg and Led Zeppelin's *Stairway to Heaven*, in honor of the blushing girl and eager boy who just climbed the stairs to the Wood Room, was blaring through the Bluetooth speaker. Outside the metal building, the bonfire was roaring and Pink Floyd's *Comfortably Numb*, an apt description of several students, was drowning out two other tunes from stereos with fewer watts flowing through their speakers.

Paige, Justin, and Lindsey were sitting on Justin's tailgate. Brad Wells and Matt Cooke stood in front of them. Brad and Matt chugged sixteen-ounce Bud Lights with abandon. While they were both intoxicated, Matt was the more inebriated of the two. Paige knew Lindsey had a crush on Matt and tried to facilitate a conversation between them, but Matt seemed more interested in drinking with Brad than hooking up with Lindsey.

Off to their right, Paige heard someone puking their supper, and she felt glad she didn't drink.

That'll be Matt soon, Paige thought.

She didn't understand the teenage attraction to drinking. Her dad let her take a drink of his beer once. The taste wasn't bad, but she couldn't imagine drinking several cans of beer. Besides, she was having a good time without altering her mental faculties. Justin's hand was in hers. She loved how big and strong it felt. It comforted her. He comforted her. Paige leaned her head against Justin's strong shoulder, and he gave her a warm kiss on the forehead. She loved his lips, too.

After kissing Paige on the forehead, Justin put his lips close to Paige's ear and whispered, "Ya wanna get outta here?"

Paige smiled and nodded.

Justin slid off the tailgate, placed his hands on Paige's waist, and lowered her smoothly to the ground.

"Excuse me, boys," Justin said as he pushed between Brad and Matt with Paige's hand in his.

"Where're you two goin'?" Brad asked.

"None ya," Justin replied.

As they walked away, Matt and Brad fell into adolescent hoots and hollers about how Justin was going to 'get lucky' and telling him to 'wrap his wiener.' Paige blushed but didn't care what they said. She thought about how good Justin's hand felt in hers.

In the back of her mind, a little voice said, *He might get lucky tonight, if he has somethin' to wrap his wiener with.*

They were by the bonfire, heading for the woods on the far side of the metal building, when Justin suddenly stopped and cocked his head back in the direction they had come.

"What's the matter?" Paige asked.

Justin shushed her and continued to listen.

After several seconds, Justin said, "Did ya hear that?"

"Hear what?"

Justin hesitated a second or two. "I thought I heard…howlin'."

"Howlin'? What kind of howlin'?"

Justin shook his head, as if clearing out old cobwebs. "I don't know. Like nothin' I ever heard before, though. They sounded…sad."

Paige laughed. "If this is your way of tryin' to scare me outta the woods so I'll go in the Wood Room with ya, it won't work. No way I want those idiots knowin' our business."

Justin scowled. "Seriously…I thought I heard somethin'."

Paige grinned. "C'mon Little Red Justin Hood. The only big, bad wolf in those woods will be me. Tonight might just be the night that Granny welcomes ya inside her warm little house."

Justin looked at her and a big grin spread over his face.

"Unless you're afraid," Paige teased him.

"I ain't afraid of no big, bad wolf."

Justin and Paige walked beyond the metal building and disappeared into the dense woods to the north. He had the perfect spot to take her, and he prepared it for a night of fun. Teenage, naked fun.

~ * ~

The pack closed the distance from where it stopped when the alpha sensed Seth's passing, to the woods surrounding the MRB in a matter of minutes. The pack stopped on the west side, just far enough back so the dense woods concealed them from view, should anyone look their direction.

The alpha surveyed the situation. It knew the girl was away from the party, in the woods to its left. It also knew she wasn't alone. That was of little concern. It would kill the boy, it could tell by smell the girl was with a boy, before turning the girl. It could also smell their sexual arousal. That would make what was coming even more enjoyable for the alpha.

The two remaining pack members knew the girl belonged to the alpha, but they also knew everyone else was fair game. They trembled and drooled with anticipation, like excited dogs that hadn't eaten in days. When the alpha broke away and started stealthily moving through the woods to the north, the pack stayed put and waited for the alpha's signal to attack.

~ * ~

Paige and Justin maneuvered through the dense underbrush slowly. They had gone about a hundred feet in at that point.

"Ouch." Paige cried out.

"What happened?"

"Somethin' scratched my arm," Paige responded in an irritated tone.

"Want me to kiss it and make it better?"

"How much further?" Paige whined.

"It's not much further. I promise," Justin assured her.

"It better not be," Paige warned. "The door to Granny's warm little house is startin' to close."

"In that case I'll huff, and I'll puff, and I'll blow the door open," Justin joked.

"Wrong wolf story," Paige told him.

Justin didn't respond to that statement because he didn't want to chance making her angrier. He'd been trying to get Paige to open that door for too long to screw it up with another pun. Instead, he tightened his grip on her hand and moved deeper into the woods. Several moments later, he pushed through a layer of underbrush and saw it—a clearing in the woods with a small pond in the middle.

"We're here." Justin announced.

Paige followed Justin through the last bit of underbrush. When she stepped out from behind Justin to see where he brought her, the picturesque beauty of the landscape took her breath away. The clearing had been about two acres in size, with a small pond in the middle. The surface of the pond had been perfectly still and looked like black glass. The silver, waning gibbous moon floated directly above and reflected off its still surface like a mirror image.

On the far side of the clearing, at the pond's edge, had been a large oak tree. Several of its roots snaked into the tranquil pond and several of its large, low branches stretched out over the water, too. Between the moon and its reflection on the water, there had been enough light for Paige to see a rope swing dangling from one of the tree's outstretched limbs.

When Paige caught her breath, she whispered, "It's beautiful, Justin."

Justin, pleased with himself, smiled. "A pretty place for a pretty girl."

It had been corny, but Paige melted.

Yep, Granny's door's wide open now, Paige thought.

That thought made Paige laugh out loud.

Justin, not privy to her inner thoughts, said, "What's funny?"

"The look on your face."

"What look?"

"The look," Paige teased, "when I tell ya that the door to Granny's little, warm house just opened all the way."

Justin looked confused. "You know I'm not good at English and all those…similes, metaphors, and whatnots. Are ya sayin'…?"

Paige cut him off. "I'm sayin' that you can make love to me under that beautiful tree over there."

Paige pointed toward the large oak tree across the pond.

"Hot damn. Seriously?" Justin yelled.

"Seriously, but only if ya have a…raincoat for your little friend."

Justin grinned so big it threatened to take over his entire face. "I've got three."

A little shocked by Justin's response, Paige said, "Three?"

"Well, ya never know when or how many ya might need."

"The when is now but the how many is one."

"We can use the others later, right?" Justin asked, almost begged.

Anyone who thinks that men have all the power has never been around a horny one, Paige thought.

Paige smiled. "That depends."

"On what?" Justin asked anxiously.

"On whether I like it. Pressure's on, big boy."

Justin grinned again. "Challenge accepted. Prepare to be pleasured, little lady."

Paige laughed at this and blushed. The moonlight didn't reveal the blush.

Justin grabbed Paige by the midriff, flung her over his shoulder, and started walking toward the oak tree. Paige kicked and pounded on his back a little, but she laughed the whole time.

~ * ~

The alpha skirted the MRB, making its way toward where the girl whose scent it marked and the boy were about mate; it knew they were close to mating because their sex pheromones were thick in the cool night breeze, when it saw a lone form stumbling toward the woods. It was Matt Cooke. The stench of alcohol oozing from his pores and being exhaled on his breath offended the alpha's keen sense of smell. It wrinkled its snout and watched as the boy stumbled into the woods about twenty feet in front of where the alpha crouched.

Matt stumbled a few feet into the woods, braced his right hand against a tree, bent over, and expelled a large portion of the beer he'd been drinking in a stream of warm, foamy, amber vomit. He took a few deep breaths, hoping he was finished puking, but his saliva glands were still too active. Drool trickled over his bottom lip and another stream of warm vomit erupted from his mouth adding to the pool of sick between his feet.

"Please God, let that be it. I swear I'll never drink again if ya let that be it," Matt said to the, what he thought, empty forest.

He'd made this promise many times before. That night, either God knew Matt was full of crap, or He wasn't listening.

The alpha, dead silent when it needed to be, crept up behind Matt, which blocked his way back to the MRB, stood up on its hind legs, and looked down at the still doubled over boy making deals with God.

God's not here, the human part of the alpha's mind thought.

Matt felt better after the second eruption of vomit and straightened up. He took a few deep breaths and wiped his mouth on his shirtsleeve.

Already forgetting his deal with God, Matt thought, *I've got room for more beer now*.

Matt turned around to head back to the MRB, but all he saw was darkness.

"What the…?" Matt said, as his mind tried to comprehend why there was blackness where he should have seen the metal building and light from the bonfire.

The darkness rumbled, and Matt's blood went cold.

He looked up and saw two burning red eyes looking down at him.

"Holy fu…" Matt's words were cut off as the alpha's clawed hand ripped his throat open.

Matt's hand flew up to his shredded throat. He felt warm blood gushing from the wound. He tried to scream, but only produced a sickening gurgling sound from his severed trachea. Matt tried to stem the flow of blood but couldn't. He felt suddenly weak and fell to his knees in the puddle of vomit and blood. He looked up at the creature that attacked him. Matt tried to grasp what he was seeing. Its red eyes flickered in the darkness.

Matt could feel the flow of blood between his fingers slowing. His vision grew dark around the edges and quickly narrowing. His trunk muscles could no longer support the weight of his upper body. Matt fell backward onto the forest floor. His head connected hard with a protruding root, but he didn't feel it. He was beyond feeling.

As his vision narrowed to a pinpoint on the creature's burning red eyes, Matt thought, *It's a fuckin' werewolf*.

With that he thought no more.

The alpha squatted over Matt's dead body and emptied its bladder on his ashen colored face. When finished, it moved on through the woods toward the girl and boy.

~ * ~

After Paige and Justin left, Lindsey tried to carry on a conversation with Matt, but he was drunk and more interested in hanging on Brad than he was in hanging with her. When Matt stumbled off into the woods to piss or puke, he hadn't told Brad or Lindsey why he left, Lindsey slid off her brother's tailgate.

"Where're ya goin'?" Brad asked.

Lindsey shrugged. "I'm gonna lay down in the back seat for a while."

"Want some company?" Brad asked with a grin and a wink.

Yeah, but not from you, Lindsey thought.

She said, "Oh, Bradley. Your timin's awful. I got my monthly visitor."

Lindsey didn't have her monthly visitor, but her mom told her saying she did was an easy way to scare eager young men away. It worked.

Brad made a face like he'd suddenly smelled something rotten. "Okay then. I'll just leave you two alone."

As Brad walked toward the bonfire, Lindsey climbed into the back seat of Justin's truck, locked the doors, and stretched out on the back seat.

~ * ~

The alpha made it to the far side of the clearing just in time to see the boy, who had been carrying the girl over his shoulder as she thrashed and giggled, lower her to the ground by an enormous tree. It studied the landscape briefly while it formulated a plan. It decided it would skirt the clearing and take up a position in the woods directly behind the enormous tree. It knew the pack waited for its signal before it wreaked havoc on the other partygoers and it could sense they were getting restless. The pack would wait for the alpha's signal, and it wanted the murder of the boy and the turning of the girl to be perfect. The alpha, keeping concealed in the shadowy woods, crept away.

~ * ~

Justin lowered Paige gently to the ground, so her feet were between his, and wrapped his arms tightly around her waist. Paige put her arms around Justin's neck, went up on her tiptoes, and kissed him softly on the lips.

When their lips parted, Paige said, "How'd ya find this place?"

Justin smiled, clearly pleased with himself. "Daddy used to take me an' Lindsey fishin' here."

Paige studied Justin's face for a moment. "Have ya ever brought another girl out here?"

Justin smiled. "Nope. You're the first."

Clearly skeptical, Paige said, "Not even Maggie Crawford? Y'all dated for like…six months."

Justin shook his head. "Nope. Not even Maggie."

Paige, suddenly curious about Justin and Maggie, said, "If not here, where?"

Justin shifted slightly on his feet. "We never…did it."

Clearly doubtful of Justin's answer, Paige said, "Never?"

Justin shook his head.

"She wouldn't let you?"

Justin laughed. "Oh, no. She was willin'…horny as a toad!"

"But y'all never did?"

"Never."

"Why not?"

Justin kicked at a rock in the dirt. "I wanted my first time to be with someone…special."

It took several moments for Paige to digest Justin's statement.

When it did, she said, "You've never been with a girl?"

Justin shook his head.

Surprised, Paige said, "You're a virgin?"

Justin took a step back. "Well, don't say it like it's a dirty word."

Paige stepped toward Justin, covering the distance he'd put between them when he stepped back, and put her arms around him. "I'm sorry. I didn't mean it like that. I'm just…surprised. I'm happier than anything else."

Justin hugged her close, and they kissed again.

This time when their lips parted, Paige said, "So…I'm first time special?"

Justin smiled. "I love you, Paige-Turner."

Paige smiled back. "I love you, too."

They kissed again, but this was a deep kiss that involved hands pawing at clothing. They parted kissing long enough for Justin to pull Paige's shirt over her head. Paige unbuttoned Justin's shirt and pealed it off his shoulders.

They were about to kiss again when Justin said, "Wait, wait. I forgot to show ya somethin'."

Paige, having waited sixteen years to do what they were going to do, didn't want to wait. She grabbed Justin's belt, undid it, and yanked it free of the belt loops.

As she had been going for the button and zipper, Justin grabbed her hands, and spun her toward the big oak tree. "Look."

Paige didn't know what she was supposed to be looking at or for but, as her eyes scanned the tree, she saw it. There was a tree house about eight feet up in the tree where the many branches reached out from the enormous trunk.

Justin said, "I know ya said ya wanted to make love under the tree, but I thought the tree house might be better. More…private."

Paige loved the idea, but she'd lived in East Texas her whole life and had known all kinds of critters probably infested the structure.

When she told Justin this, he smiled. "I came out here after school and cleaned it up."

Paige was impressed.

She grinned at Justin. "Ya did, did ya?"

Justin grinned and nodded.

Paige collected her shirt from the ground as Justin collected his shirt and belt. They walked up to the tree. There were two-by-four boards nailed to the tree trunk, creating a ladder that went to the bottom of the tree house.

Justin stepped up to the ladder. "I'll go up and get the latch open, then help ya up."

Paige nodded and watched as Justin climbed the makeshift ladder to the bottom of the tree house. She heard a loud screeching sound as the rusty tree house door hinges resisted intrusion when Justin opened the door. That screeching seemed impossibly loud to Paige. She listened closely. She could hear music and an occasional shout from the party drifting through the woods, but the party seemed far away. Something was missing from the night, but Paige couldn't quite put her finger on what. Then it hit her. All the usual deep wood sounds she'd heard when she ran down her dad's driveway to meet with Justin earlier were missing. The woods around the clearing were quiet. Unnaturally quiet.

Paige stood at the base of the big oak tree in her bra and jeans, and she suddenly felt exposed; like someone or something watched her. She clutched her shirt to her chest to cover her bra-covered breasts and looked around quickly. She scanned the woods, looking for the source of the feeling and silence. Nothing there.

Just then, Justin said, “Ya comin’ up?”

His voice sounded so loud in the unnatural silence that it startled Paige and made her jump.

Paige took a deep breath and scolded herself for being a silly girl. “Right behind ya.”

As Paige turned back toward the makeshift ladder, she glanced into the woods directly behind the big oak tree and saw two burning eyes peering out of the shadows at her. It had been a passing glance and when Paige looked back, the burning red eyes were gone.

You’re bein’ a silly girl, Paige-Turner, she thought to herself.

She mounted the ladder and, a few seconds later, the burning eyes were the last thing on her mind.

~ * ~

The alpha got into position quickly and watched as the boy and girl started taking each other’s clothes off. The alpha knew the girl was ready. The girl’s sex musk was the most powerful scent for miles. When they stopped and headed for the enormous tree, the alpha experienced a moment of panic, which had been something it wasn’t used to. For all its power, trees presented a problem. As it started to signal the pack to attack and take out the boy before playing with the girl and turning her, it saw the tree house that was their obvious destination. It could easily reach the tree house. The panic subsided.

It relaxed and watched as the boy climbed up into the tree house. The squeal of the hinges pierced the silent night. It watched as the girl stopped and surveyed the woods. It could tell she suddenly felt anxious because a powerful scent of fear mingled with her sex musk and her already arousal induced, fast heart rate suddenly quickened.

The girl looked directly at the alpha as she turned to climb into the tree house. It had been a quick glance, but the alpha wasn’t ready to terrify her yet. The alpha quickly ducked down in the deep brush and watched as the girl climbed up into the tree house. When it heard the hinges squeal shut, it crawled out of the woods on all fours and crouched under a low-lying limb it could use to propel itself into the tree house, when it was ready.

~ * ~

After Paige climbed into the tree house, Justin shut the trapdoor and twisted a wooden latch that locked the floor door shut. When Justin turned on a battery-powered lantern, Paige saw there was a cot under a window on the backside of the tree house with green, Paige's favorite color, satin sheets that had a matching green satin pillowcase. There were candles everywhere, and Justin started quickly lighting them. When they were all lit, Justin turned off the lantern, and the interior of the tree house became bathed in a soft orange glow. Justin did more than clean up the tree house. He turned it into a romantic hideaway.

"You did all this today?"

"Well, I worked on it for a couple of days. I had to bug-bomb the crap out of it before I could put the stuff in here."

"It's perfect," Paige whispered.

"I'm glad ya like it. This is why I wanted ya to sneak out if your dad didn't let us go."

"I'm glad I did," Paige admitted.

As her eyes adjusted to the softer light, Paige saw there was a shelf in the back corner over the pillow end of the cot that had a Bluetooth speaker on it. Paige was still looking at the speaker when Justin tapped play on a playlist he created on his iPhone and Alabama's *Feels So Right* played softly.

Paige couldn't believe it. Many years ago, when she and Lindsey were eight or nine years old, Paige told Lindsey she wanted *Feels So Right* playing the first time she kissed a boy. It had been just silly girl talk, but they caught Justin spying on them because he laughed when Paige said this. They chased him off while he laughed and made exaggerated kissing noises, but he remembered.

Tears were streaming down Paige's face as she turned to Justin. "You remembered that?"

Justin blushed a deep pink. "Of course, I did. I remember everything 'bout ya, Paige-Turner."

Paige grabbed Justin in a tight hug and buried her face in the crook of his neck.

Justin held her. "I know it's not your first kiss, but I thought it kinda…felt right."

"It's perfect."

After sobbing for several moments, Paige pulled her face back and looked at Justin. It was like she was seeing him for the first time. It was love at first sight. She kissed him and he kissed her back. It had been a deep, hungry kiss. Justin's clumsy fingers tried, unsuccessfully, to unhook Paige's bra. She let him try, not wanting to wound his pride for several seconds, but he was getting nowhere fast. Not breaking the kiss, Paige reached back and unhooked her bra for him. With that obstacle cleared, Justin had no problem removing the garment. With the bra out of the way, Justin's warm, strong hands cupped her breasts and squeezed them gently.

It had been more than Paige could take. She broke the kiss and pushed back from Justin.

Startled by Paige's sudden move away, Justin said, "Did I do somethin' wrong?"

Paige laughed. "Nope. I need room to do this."

Paige kicked off her boots, stood up, undid the button on her jeans, and unzipped them. She hooked her thumbs in the waistband of her jeans and panties. In one fluid movement, she pealed her jeans, along with the panties, down her legs where they crumpled around her feet and ankles. She stepped out of them and stepped toward the satin sheet covered cot.

Justin was still sitting on the floor with a truly stupid look on his face that made Paige want to laugh. He tried to get up, tangled in his legs, and fell face forward onto the trapdoor. Paige laughed at this, but she did so quietly. Preoccupied, Justin didn't notice. When he finally found his feet, he kicked off his boots, and pealed his jeans and boxers off. He tripped on these and fell against the side of the tree house. The crash knocked a candle over, but Justin caught it before it hit the ground and put it back.

By the time Justin was composed enough to make his way to the cot, Paige was already lying on it. She undid her ponytail and her long brown hair cascaded over the pillow. Justin never saw anything more beautiful.

He took a step toward the cot, but Paige held up a finger. "Aren't ya forgettin' somethin'?"

Justin had been clueless, and it showed.

"Raincoat for your…not so little buddy," Paige reminded him as she looked at his stiff member.

Justin spun around, bent over, and started digging through his crumpled jeans for his wallet. Even though Paige knew she loved him, and she thought he was beautiful, she could've done without the current view she had of him, bent over, exposing his hairy ass crack and droopy balls.

When Justin found his wallet, he shouted, "Eureka," as if he'd found gold instead of his condom stash.

Justin kept his back to Paige as he extracted the condom from its wrapper, which had been lubed and ridged for her pleasure, and rolled it onto his excited member.

When he turned back around, he shouted, "Ta-da."

He was proud of himself.

For a second, Paige didn't understand the presentation. She looked at his member and the florescent green condom covering it. Paige started laughing.

Justin laughed. "It's your favorite color, right?"

"Yes, it is. Now get over here and pleasure me like ya promised."

Justin saluted, which looked thoroughly ridiculous with his florescent green gun pointing at Paige. "Yes, ma'am."

Justin hurried to the cot, his florescent green gun bobbing uncontrollably as he did, and laid down on top of Paige.

"Go slow," Paige whispered.

"I would never hurt ya, Paige-Turner," Justin said, and kissed her softly on the lips.

~ * ~

Outside the tree house, under the window, the alpha rose from its crouch. It was time to kill the boy and turn the girl. It was time to signal the pack to attack. It raised its nightmare snout to the moon and howled.

The howl pierced through the night air and drowned out music playing in and around the MRB. Every teen in attendance stopped what they were doing and looked north, in the direction from which the howl came. One by one, the music sources died out as sound systems turned off.

General murmurs of, "What the fuck was that?" and "That sounded fuckin' close," circulated through the groups of teens. Two more howls filled the night from the west—these were much closer.

Lindsey, who had stretched out in the back seat of Justin's truck and dozed off, had been startled awake by the first howl. As she laid there trying to get her mind to grasp the source of such a horrible howl, not knowing if it had been real or dream induced, she heard the party music die out.

Not a dream...they heard it, too, Lindsey thought.

She began to sit up and look around when two more howls sliced through the silent night. These came from in front of Justin's truck and were so close she felt them. They rattled her bones.

As Lindsey laid there, frozen with fear, she saw two large, black shapes pass between Justin's truck and the truck parked next to it on the passenger side. The black shapes frightened her so badly, she found it hard to breathe.

From the vicinity of Justin's tailgate, she heard Brad shout, "What the holy fuck."

Unable to control her actions, like rubbernecking a nasty car accident, Lindsey popped up and looked out the back window just in time to see one creature grab Brad. Brad let out a scream that got the attention of several of the outside partiers, but the scream choked off when the beast clamped its jaws around Brad's neck. With what looked to Lindsey no more effort than it would take to snap a toothpick, the beast quickly twisted its head and Brad's head separated from his body. When it bounced into the bed of Justin's truck with a hollow 'thud,' Lindsey let out an involuntary gasp.

The second creature advanced rapidly on the screaming and scattering partiers. The one that dispatched Brad started after the second one but, hearing the gasp, turned back to Justin's truck.

Lindsey saw it turn and quickly ducked down out of sight. There had been a heavy 'thud' in the truck bed that made the whole truck shake.

Oh God, it's comin' for me, Lindsey's mind screamed.

She held her breath and willed her heart to stop hammering in her chest. The seconds passed like minutes. She expected the hideous beast to drag her from the truck and murder her, but it didn't.

The screams coming from her fellow students and friends intensified to a fever pitch. She felt sure she could hear both beasts snarling and growling from a distance. Not knowing where it came from, Lindsey summoned the courage to take another look. She slowly rose until her eyes had barely cleared the back window and surveyed the situation.

What she saw made her gag uncontrollably. Aside from Brad's head face down in the truck bed and his headless body slumped against the driver's side wheel well, the truck shaking 'thud' had been the beast throwing Brad's body into the truck bed, still leaking blood from his torn neck, Lindsey saw several motionless bodies scattered around the outside of the metal building. Their corpses were contorted in unnatural ways.

Worse still though, she watched as one of the beasts dragged a screaming girl from a car parked close to the bonfire and toss her into the flames. Lindsey recognized the girl as being Justin's ex-girlfriend, Maggie Crawford. As Lindsey watched in dismay, Maggie's long blonde hair burst into flames and swallowed her head in an orange ball of fire. Lindsey didn't think a human could scream with such pain, but Maggie was. As her clothing, a denim mini-skirt and tight-fitting sleeveless top, burned, Maggie crawled out of the fire. Maggie's hair was burned off and Lindsey could see her head and face looked like a black canvas with rivers of blood-red lava bubbling up between cracks. Maggie's arms and legs were an angry red, with large, yellowish blisters boiling up in many places. As Maggie crawled, a softball size blister on her right thigh burst and the yellowish fluid splattered on the ground by her knee.

The beast that threw Maggie into the fire picked her up by the head with its right hand and held her burnt, squirming body at arm's length. The blackened skin on Maggie's head cracked and peeled away as the beast's clawed fingers dug into her skull. Blood gushed over her face. Her shirt had burned away by then and Lindsey could see Maggie's once perky breasts were covered in large, yellowish blisters, too. When the beast rammed its left hand into Maggie's chest, she finally stopped screaming. Lindsey watched as the beast extracted what she had been sure was Maggie's heart from her chest and woofed it down in a single bite. It tossed Maggie's lifeless body into the bonfire and moved toward the building, where Lindsey could hear many agonized and terrorized screams.

Lindsey's mind ran in several directions at once. *What are those things? How many are there? Just two? I need to get outta here. Am I safe now? Did Justin leave the keys in the truck?*

The last thought reminded her Justin and Paige went off together. She knew where he took her. To the pond their dad used to take them to fish. She also knew why Justin took Paige there. She helped him clean it up for the 'special' occasion. Justin swore her to secrecy, and it took every bit of willpower she possessed to not tell her best friend what Justin planned for their first time, but she kept her promise. Now they were alone in the woods.

Lindsey suddenly felt guilty for not thinking of Justin and Paige sooner, but she chalked it up to being traumatized, which she had been. She pulled her cellphone out of her back pocket and checked the reception bars. She only had one. She quickly dialed Justin's number. After a few connection clicks, she heard the first ring in her ear. Then she heard Justin's ringtone, the Angry Birds music, blare into the otherwise silence of the truck cab. He'd left his cellphone in the truck.

The ringtone sounded impossibly loud, and it startled Lindsey so badly she jumped and let out a quick scream. Realizing any sound was likely to bring unwanted attention her way, Lindsey quickly ended the call and cut the Angry Birds off in mid-flight. She held her breath for several seconds and listened. She could still hear screams and growls coming from a distance. Half expecting to see one or both of the nightmare beasts sprinting toward her, Lindsey found the courage to take another look out the back window—they weren't coming for her. All she saw were the same crumpled bodies that had been there before and Maggie's burning body in the bonfire.

Lindsey ducked back down in the back seat and tapped her first speed-dial number, which had been reserved for her BFF Paige. When Paige's phone started ringing it, thankfully, didn't set off a cacophony of Taylor Swift's, *Shake It Off*, which was Paige's current ringtone.

She has her cellphone, Lindsey thought.

~ * ~

As Justin prepared to make Paige feel so right, a nightmarish, ear-piercing howl went off like a siren from just outside the tree house. Justin, who'd propped himself up with his hands on either side of Paige's shoulders so he could watch her face as he entered her, involuntarily brought his hands up and cupped them over his ears to, unsuccessfully, block the unholy sound. Not only did it not help block out the unholy sound, Justin fell onto Paige, and their foreheads connected painfully.

Paige hardly noticed the pain caused by the head-butt from Justin, because the howl felt like it had shredded her brain. She covered her ears too, but to no relief. As the howl subsided, Paige realized the only thing she could hear had been the internal beating of her heart, which was threatening to leap out of her mouth.

She uncovered her ears at the same time Justin uncovered his.

He pushed up and looked at Paige. "What the fuck was that?"

Paige could hear him, but it sounded like she was listening to him through a thick wall. Paige had no idea what it had been and told him—her own voice sounded more internal than external.

Justin rolled off Paige and shook his head back and forth quickly, as if he were trying to dislodge a bug that took up residency in his ear. When Justin said, "It helps," Paige could tell her hearing was coming back, but she shook her head, anyway. She wasn't sure the shaking helped, but her hearing was back to where she could hear heavy breathing from just outside the tree house. It sounded gruff. Justin heard the breathing, too.

He said, "What the fuck is that?"

Before Paige could stop him, because she had a terrible feeling about that breathing, Justin sat up and poked his head out of the tree house window.

Justin said, "Holy shi…" but his words were cut short when a large, clawed paw-like hand grabbed him by the face and, effortlessly, pulled his body through the window that had been too small to accommodate his size—Justin's shoulders were too wide for the window but went through when boards and bones snapped.

Paige screamed and scrambled to the now larger window to see what grabbed Justin. What she saw horrified her. Justin lay on his back on the ground. Blood covered his face, and his shoulders were in the wrong place—much lower than they should have been. Bloody white sticks protruded from Justin's upper chest on either side of his neck. It took Paige a moment to realize the sticks were Justin's collarbones. Worse still, she saw a gaping wound where what Justin referred to as his 'junk' had been.

Thinking he was dead, tears spilled from Paige's eyes.

Then she saw his eyes open wide, white orbs in his bloody face, and he screamed, "Run, Paige."

She wanted to run, but she couldn't leave him. Not if he was still alive. She started to tell him to hold on, when something wet hit her in the face and fell on to the satin green sheets. When she looked down to see what hit her in the face, her mind couldn't comprehend what she saw. She knew what it was but, like Justin's shoulders, it wasn't where it belonged. Her hands felt like they belonged to someone else as she picked up the florescent green object and brought it up for a closer look.

As her mind finally accepted what her eyes were seeing and her hands were holding; Justin's junk, she heard a demonic, growling laugh from just outside the broken window. Her eyes drifted up from florescent green, condom covered, detached penis, and locked on the smoldering red eyes of the alpha werewolf standing next to Justin's body.

It smiled at her, and Paige screamed.

~ * ~

The two werewolves at the MRB successfully herded the remaining, and living, nine partiers into the metal building, where they huddled in the center of the concrete slab. Some were sobbing uncontrollably, some were praying fervently, and some stood stark still, in a catatonic state.

The two werewolves paced back and forth in front of the one working door. Occasionally, they would snap or claw at each other when their paths brought them close together. It was taking every ounce of their self-control to not attack the remaining humans and rip them to shreds, but they knew their alpha had plans to increase the pack and to disobey the alpha was akin to suicide.

A noise from the second floor of the metal building brought the two werewolves to an abrupt stop. One of them leapt up the stairs with lightning speed and crashed through the Wood Room door. The other werewolf remained in front of the door, blocking the only exit.

A girl screamed, and a boy yelled, "Don't fuckin' touch her."

Seconds later, a naked body crashed through a Wood Room window that looked out over the old sawmill floor. It landed on the concrete amid the shattered glass and broken window frame. The boy's head smacked the concrete with a sickening 'thud.' His body went into convulsions as a pool of blood grew around his cracked skull like a red liquid halo. Moments later, his body stilled. Freddy Colburn sold his last red solo cup of keg beer.

Before Freddy's body stopped convulsing, the upstairs werewolf emerged from the Wood Room with Ella Patterson tucked under its right arm. Ella, clad in a large shirt, Freddy's shirt, was kicking and screaming. The werewolf didn't seem to notice. Instead of taking the stairs back down, it leapt over the railing and landed gracefully on its feet twenty feet below.

While the landing hadn't affected the werewolf, the jarring stop broke several of Ella's ribs and knocked the wind out of her. This didn't affect the werewolf, either. It flung Ella toward the huddled group of teens.

She sailed through the air and landed with a 'thud' and a pain-filled scream in front of her fellow students. The landing broke several more ribs and her right wrist.

~ * ~

Once more, Paige's mind couldn't comprehend what her eyes saw. The gibbous moon shone bright enough for her to make out its features clearly. When it took a step toward the tree house, the last tumbler in Paige's mind clicked into place and registered what it was. It was a werewolf. With speed beyond anything Paige saw before, it leapt at the broken window. When it crashed into the tree house, the whole tree shook from the impact.

Paige, with speed she didn't know she possessed, leapt backward, away from the window, and came down hard on her bare butt on the trapdoor. The wooden twist latch cut deeply into her left buttock, but she didn't notice. The werewolf's paw-like hand reached inside the broken window and started ripping boards free to gain access.

Desperate for anything to protect herself with, Paige quickly scanned the contents of the tree house. When the werewolf hit and shook the tree house, several of the candles Justin lit toppled over and onto the floor. It was a long shot, but Paige had to try.

Moving quickly, Paige grabbed up two of the closest candles and, using her feet, pulled the satin sheet from the cot. She balled up the satin sheet and touched the candles to them. When her efforts yielded smoke, but no fire, Paige panicked. The werewolf had almost tore out enough boards to enter the tree house.

C'mon damn it, Paige's mind screamed.

The werewolf's head and shoulders were inside the tree house. The flame finally took, and the satin sheet burst into flames. She tossed the burning sheets onto the werewolf's face.

The werewolf let out a startled yelp and started tearing at the flaming sheets with its clawed hands. It overbalanced and fell backward out of the tree house. Paige knew little about werewolves, but she felt sure a burning sheet wouldn't kill it.

As she turned to exit the tree house through the window on the pond side, *Shake It Off* started playing. Paige forgot about her cellphone. She didn't have time to dress, but she grabbed at the wad of clothes on the floor that were her jeans and panties and pulled her cellphone from the back pocket. She wasn't about to stop and answer it, but she saw it was Lindsey calling. Paige did one more thing before fleeing the tree house. She grabbed two more lit candles and tossed them on the cot that still had a fitted satin sheet on it.

~ * ~

The alpha hadn't expected the girl to fight back. When it thought about turning the girl, it thought she'd probably piss herself and faint. It certainly didn't expect her to be resourceful enough to use fire against it.

The alpha knew fire was one of the few methods that could kill a werewolf. Not that the burning sheet was fire enough to do so, but the burning sheets startled it and injured it. The hair on its ears, snout, neck, and shoulders were burned off in a cloud of burnt hair stink. Worse than being startled and injured, the wounds would heal quickly, the backward fall from the tree house embarrassed it.

As the alpha ripped the last of the burning and melting material from its face and stood up. It considered killing the girl instead of turning her, but it decided against killing her. It would make her suffer as a human that night and make her suffer as a werewolf after her first transformation by making her the pack bitch. The alpha leapt back up toward the hole in the side of the tree house.

~ * ~

Paige scrambled out of the pond side tree house window and on to a large limb that stretched out over the water. Not knowing whether werewolves could swim, she briefly considered diving into the pond. Doing that would destroy her cellphone and she needed it to call her dad.

He's gonna be so pissed, Paige thought.

After that thought, she chuckled. Her dad being pissed about her sneaking out was the least of her problems. She had a werewolf trying to kill her. Paige dropped the eight feet from the limb to the soft pond shore mud and took off running toward the MRB.

Paige had about halved the distance between the tree house and the woods that separated the pond clearing from the MRB when she heard an angry growl coming from the tree house. As she continued running, the woods getting increasingly closer, she heard commotion coming from the tree house. Sounds of wood breaking, things being tossed around, and increasingly louder growls filled the night.

It's lookin' for me and its pissed, Paige thought as she ran into the woods.

~ * ~

When the alpha climbed back through the hole in the side of the tree house, another fireball greeted it as the sheets on the cot ignited. Instead of falling out of the tree house, the alpha dove forward into the middle of the structure.

It didn't see the girl. It sniffed the air, trying to detect the girl's scent, but it couldn't detect her through the acrid smoke. When it realized it lost her scent, it lashed out and smashed the shelf holding the speaker. Either the increasing smoke in the tree house or the burning sheet the girl threw on its face affected its ability to smell. It let out a loud growl and overturned the cot to see if the girl was hiding under it. She wasn't. The alpha, furious at this point, started growling louder and slashing the tree house's wooden walls.

The fire in the tree house was spreading quickly. The alpha knew getting trapped in that burning structure could kill it. With a final menacing growl, the alpha launched itself through the pond side window, creating a large, splintered hole in the wall as it did, and landed in the soft mud directly behind Paige's footprints. The alpha quickly determined the direction of the footprints and looked toward the woods. When it looked at the woods, it saw Paige duck behind a tree. The alpha went down on all fours and sprinted toward the girl.

~ * ~

As Paige entered the woods, she heard a particularly menacing growl erupt from behind her. Paige skidded to a stop and spun around just in time to see the werewolf crash through the pond side of the tree house and land in the mud where seconds before she had been standing. She could see tendrils of smoke rising from the werewolf's hairy body.

Burn you fuck. Paige thought.

She knew it wasn't on fire. The wood side of the tree house became fully engulfed in flames, though. She thought about Justin's body lying on the ground on the burning side of the tree house and realized his body would probably burn. For a moment, she thought she might cry. When she looked back toward the werewolf, its flaming red eyes were looking directly at her. She ducked behind a large pine tree.

~ * ~

There was a lot of activity around Carla Weaver's house after Garrett arrived and found Ty bitten, but alive. With the werewolves gone, he canceled the backup call Ty placed. Austin Turner, who patrolled the western quadrant of Pine View County, had been close when Garrett canceled the backup and came anyway. Garrett didn't mind. With Ty injured, Garrett could use Austin's help, but Garrett felt sure the pack wasn't done spreading mayhem. He didn't want all his deputies in one place if something else happened. Deputy Stutter was still patrolling the northern quadrant and Deputy Zimmer was still patrolling the eastern quadrant.

Aside from Garrett, Ty, and Austin, paramedics were at the scene tending to Ty's injuries. They told Ty he'd need to get a course of rabies shots. They had no way of knowing, given the source of Ty's bite, rabies didn't concern him at all.

Besides the law enforcement and paramedic personnel at the scene, George Krats, the county coroner, and two of his staff were there, too. As delicately as he could, Garrett pulled George aside and had a little talk with him. Garrett told George there was a foreign object in the deceased subject's chest and he was to not remove it until he could be there. To George's credit, he didn't protest Garrett's instruction.

When Garrett finished talking, George folded his arms across his chest. "Are ya gonna tell me what's goin' on?"

Garrett nodded. "I'll tell ya tomorrow when I see ya 'bout what's in the suspect's chest."

Garrett broke away from George and headed toward Austin, who bagged the suspect's left arm and had been carrying it and the suspect's lower right leg, also bagged, to his SUV.

"Good for prints?" Garrett asked Austin as they met.

Austin held up the bag and looked at the fingers. "Should be."

"Great, I want those run ASAP."

"Will do."

With everything in order, Garrett and Austin took pictures of the carnage before the other folks started showing up. Garrett headed toward Ty, who sat on the back bumper of the ambulance. He was holding an icepack to his right shoulder and his neck wound had been cleaned and dressed. A gauzy white bandage encircled his neck like a turtleneck shirt or one of those dickeys Howard Wolowitz always wore on *The Big Bang Theory*.

Garrett sat down on the ambulance bumper next to Ty. "Good shot there, buddy."

"Which one? I fired several."

"Left arm shot. Austin said it looks like we'll get clear prints. Could be a good lead."

"Ya think?"

Garrett nodded. "I do. Wouldn't surprise me none if this pack knows each other in human form."

They sat in silence for a couple of moments and Ty said in a low, discreet voice, "It fuckin' bit me, Garrett. I'm gonna turn into one of those fuckin' things next full moon."

Garrett studied his friend for a moment. The truth of it devastated Garrett when Ty showed him the bite. For Ty's sake, he needed to stay calm.

Garrett took a steadying breath. "We've got until the next full moon to find the alpha. We'll find it, Ty."

"If we don't?"

When Garrett didn't immediately provide an answer, Ty said, "I'll kill myself before I turn into one of those fuckin' things and kill somebody else."

Garrett considered what Ty said for a moment. "Don't go doin' anything stupid…like eatin' one of Mike's silver bullets. We'll find it and kill it."

Ty shrugged. "From what Doctor Huff told ya, that might kill me, too."

This had been true, but James Huff also said it might rid the pack members of the curse, too.

Garrett smiled. "Killin' the alpha gives ya a fifty percent chance. Shootin' yourself in the head with a silver bullet is a hundred percent dead. Play the odds, Ty. Play the fuckin' odds."

Ty nodded. "Okay, I won't eat a silver bullet…yet. What if we can't find the alpha in time?"

Garrett considered Ty's question for a moment. "I'll lock ya up in one of the holdin' cells."

"If it doesn't hold me in?"

Garrett looked Ty square in the eyes. "If it doesn't hold, I'll shoot ya myself."

Garrett's response satisfied Ty. He knew he could trust his friend to keep his word. Ty gave Garrett an appreciative nod.

As Garrett started to get up and check on George's progress with collecting Carla Weaver's remains, his cellphone rang.

Garrett looked at his cellphone and said to Ty, "It's Paige-Turner. She must've got up and saw my note. Wanna say hi to her?"

Ty smiled, he and Paige were close. "Hells yeah."

Garrett tapped the speakerphone option. "Hey, sweetheart. Sorry I had to leave. I'll be home in a bit."

Garrett's blood froze in his veins when he heard Paige say, "Daddy. I'm so sorry, Daddy."

The fear in his little girl's voice bit into Garrett's soul.

Suddenly scared, Garrett said, "What's the matter, Paige?"

Sobbing, Paige said, "I snuck out with Justin and Lindsey. Justin's d-d-dead. It killed him. It's after me, Daddy."

On the thin edge of panic, Garrett said, "Where are ya?"

Paige didn't respond for several seconds, but Garrett could hear her breathing.

Paige whispered, "I hear it, Daddy. It's gettin' close."

"Where are you?" Garrett shouted.

In a whisper so faint Garrett could barely hear her, Paige said, "MRB. I'm scared, Daddy."

Before Garrett could tell her he was coming, a loud growl erupted from the cellphone speaker. Paige screamed, and the phone went dead.

Garrett was in a dead run for his SUV the second the connection died.

He shouted, "MRB. Call it in. Bring every fuckin' body."

A second later, he was in his SUV. He needed out, but he was blocked in. He spun the wheel to the left and hammered the accelerator.

The backend of his SUV fishtailed and slammed into George Krats' coroner van, but he didn't slow down. Several seconds later, he squealed his tires onto County Road Five Sixty-Nine and shot into the night with his siren blaring at breakneck speed.

He heard Ty make the call over the radio. Within seconds, Deputies Stutter, Zimmer, and Turner confirmed they were on route to the MRB.

Ty's voice cracked over the radio. "I'm right behind ya, Sheriff."

Garrett looked in his review mirror and saw Ty's SUV gaining on him.

If he's catchin' me, I'm not goin' fast enough, Garrett thought, and he smashed down even harder on the accelerator, until it was on the floor.

Chapter Seven

After ducking behind the large pine tree, Paige quickly dialed her dad's cellphone number and waited for him to answer. He answered on the second ring and started talking to her before she could say anything. As he talked, Paige could hear the werewolf's growling breaths as it advanced on her position. She quickly, and as quietly as possible, moved deeper into the woods. Underbrush cut into her legs as she did and ducked behind another large pine tree.

When her dad stopped talking, Paige started by apologizing for sneaking out. She knew she should get right to the point but, if she didn't live, and she thought she probably wouldn't, she needed her dad to know she had been sorry for going against his wishes.

Before she finished apologizing, she heard the werewolf crash into the woods. Paige moved deeper into the forest and ducked behind another large pine tree.

Paige took a deep breath. "I hear it, Daddy. It's gettin' close."

Paige looked back and saw the large, shadowy figure of the werewolf advancing toward the tree she hid behind. She darted to a nearby pine tree and pressed her back to it. The ragged edged pine bark cut into the exposed flesh of her back and buttocks, but fear dwarfed the pain the cuts created.

Her dad shouted, "Where are you?"

Paige, close to tears, because she could hear the werewolf's heavy breathing directly behind the tree that she had been using to conceal her body, whispered, "MRB. I'm scared Daddy."

The alpha appeared in front of Paige, like black smoke. It looked down at her with its burning red eyes and let out a growl that rattled the bones in Paige's body.

When she screamed, the werewolf knocked the cellphone from Paige's right hand with a swat from its clawed left hand. Paige felt its razor-sharp claws dig into the flesh of her cheek as it swatted at the cellphone and warm blood began running down her cheek.

The power behind the swat instantly numbed the right side of her face. Paige probed at the inside of her cheek with her tongue, and it slipped all the way through her inner cheek and popped out on the outside of her cheek.

I think it'll be a closed-casket funeral for you, Paige-Turner, Paige thought.

Although scared out of her mind, this thought made Paige chuckle. This, in-turn, made the werewolf take a step back and study her. It knew the girl was scared. It could smell the fear on her like the smell of rot on a corpse and hear her heart hammering in her chest. It didn't expect her to chuckle.

Paige spat a wad of blood on the ground and yelled, "Just do it, bitch."

The werewolf smiled a sinister snarling smile and, by tapping into the smallest part of human ability left in its wolf brain, said, in a voice more growl than human articulation, "Run."

Upon hearing anything remotely human escape from the horribly dangerous werewolf snout, Paige's jaw dropped open. She wasn't sure she'd heard what she thought she'd heard; like her mind had been playing tricks on her. It wasn't attacking, though.

As she pondered this, the werewolf took a deep breath into its massive chest and growled, "Run. Now."

Paige did.

She knew the werewolf was playing with her. It would catch her and kill her when it finished playing with her. She would take any opportunity afforded her to live just a little longer. Perhaps, she thought, there might be strength in numbers, so she ran toward the MRB party.

Paige could hear the werewolf keeping easy pace with her, and only a few yards behind her, as she neared the MRB clearing. She could see the bonfire flickering through the trees and underbrush ahead. Paige abruptly stopped and the werewolf, close behind her, stopped as well.

Paige rethought her initial 'strength in numbers' idea. On one hand, twenty-something people might scare off the pursuing werewolf. On the other hand, she might serve the werewolf twenty-something more victims on a plate.

Paige stood there pondering the outcomes; she excelled in and liked statistics. She heard the werewolf move in close behind her. She registered something else from the MRB or, more precisely, she registered the lack of something from the MRB. No music. The surrounding area and metal building were quiet. Deathly quiet. All Paige could hear was the bonfire crackling and popping, and the werewolf's heavy breathing behind her.

Seconds later, the werewolf's clawed hand pushed hard against Paige's back, its claws raked deep gashes down her back as it did and shoved her out of the woods and into the clearing around the MRB. Paige tried to keep her balance. The shove had been so powerful and unexpected she came down on her chest with enough force to knock the wind out of her. The fall also produced several cuts and scratches on Paige's exposed breasts, stomach, knees, and upper thighs.

As Paige lay there trying to suck air into unaccommodating lungs, she became angry. It wasn't enough for the werewolf to simply kill her and be done with it. It wanted to torture and humiliate her. It wanted to play with her like a cat plays with a mouse by swatting it around before administering a kill bite to its neck. Paige decided she would not play mouse to the werewolf's cat any longer.

Her diaphragm finally contracted, and Paige sucked much needed air into her lungs. She was flat on her face, and she could hear the werewolf stalking toward her. Paige went up on her knees and hands and looked frantically for something, anything, she could use as a weapon. She didn't see anything, but she felt something she landed on stuck to her chest and stomach. She looked between her breasts and saw a piece of two-by-four lumber stuck to her chest. It was long enough so the other end stuck out between her spread legs like a wooden tail.

Paige's mind couldn't comprehend why the two-by-four was sticking to her body, but she found out when she tried to remove it. Several long, rusty nails slipped free of the puncture wounds created when Paige fell on it. It hurt like hell, but Paige detached herself from the piece of lumber.

With the two-by-four free, Paige went up on to her knees and wrapped both her hands tightly around one end of it. The werewolf was close. She could feel its hot breath wash over her head and shoulders when it exhaled. Gathering all the strength and courage she could muster; Paige suddenly swung around and smashed the nail side of the two-by-four into the werewolf's outer left thigh.

She hit the werewolf with enough force to break the two-by-four in half. The part in her hand went flying and landed about thirty feet away. The part she hit the werewolf with remained stuck to its leg by the nails that punctured its tough hide. The werewolf let out a yelp Paige reasoned more from surprise than pain and jumped back a few feet. It let out a threatening growl and ripped the two-by-four from its leg. It raised the shard of lumber over its head, and Paige was certain it would bludgeon her with it. Instead, it flung the piece of two-by-four at the MRB metal building, which was a couple of hundred feet away.

There had been so much force behind the throw, the piece of lumber penetrated the building's metal siding, as if hurled there by a tornado. Paige heard the piece of lumber hit the concrete floor on the inside of the metal building and she heard something else. Shocked responses from people inside the barn. Just as she was getting her hopes up that some of her fellow students were still alive and, somehow, they might fight back against her werewolf tormentor, she heard something else, something more ominous, from inside the metal building. Vicious growls. It was growling, plural, Paige knew. From within the metal building, she heard a girl scream.

~ * ~

Ella Patterson was battered and bruised from the treatment she'd received from the werewolf that broke into the Wood Room where she and Freddy went to have sex. They were engaged in the act when they heard the howls and the chaos that followed the howls. Freddy crept over to one of the Wood Room windows, the one he would eventually be thrown through, and peaked out at the floor below. When he quickly ducked back down and turned toward Ella, she saw his normally ruddy face had turned ashen white.

He crawled back to Ella, who was still lying naked on the moldy couch, and whispered, "Werewolves…two of 'em."

Of course, Ella didn't believe Freddy. She started to tell Freddy how full of shit she thought he was, but he clamped his hand tightly over her mouth. Ella didn't mind a little rough sex, and even tried a little sadomasochism with Freddy before. She had a riding crop she used to train her pigs to walk beside her with when she showed them in the Pine View High School FFA Livestock Show and Rodeo that she let Freddy gently spank her bare bottom with occasionally, but the hand over her mouth would not be tolerated. Ella yanked Freddy's hand away to tell him to finish without her, when she heard angry growls echoing through the metal building.

"Told ya," Freddy whispered.

Ella knew something was in the metal building, but she damn sure didn't believe in werewolves.

When she sat up, Freddy hissed, "Where're ya goin'?"

"To see," Ella hissed back.

Freddy grabbed her by the shoulder, but she shrugged it off. "Fredrick Wayne Colburn. You will *not* touch me again *until* I tell ya that ya *can*."

Freddy retracted his hand as if he'd touched something hot. In a way, he had.

Ella slid off the couch and crawled to the window on her hands and knees. She could picture Freddy getting an eyeful of her exposed girl 'parts,' her mom referred to all sex organs as 'parts,' and the stupid, lustful look that would be on his face when she turned around and crawled back to him. Despite the screams, growls, and Freddy's warning there were werewolves in the building, a grin spread across Ella's face at the thought of him looking at her 'parts.' The grin died when she peaked through the window.

As Ella looked through the window in disbelief at the two werewolves that herded several of her classmates into the building, her blood turned cold inside her body. She quickly dropped back down and returned to Freddy, who sat on the floor with his back against the couch.

"Told ya," Freddy said when Ella scooted up next to him.

Freddy wasn't lying about the werewolves, but Ella despised him for gloating at a moment like that.

Instead of getting into an argument with him, she whispered, "What're we gonna do?"

Freddy shrugged. "Stay hidden up here."

"If they find us?"

Freddy shrugged his shoulders again.

Normally, Ella didn't mind being naked in front of Freddy. She even enjoyed the way her naked body gave her some control over Freddy. He'd do anything she asked him to do, if she threatened to cover some of his eye candy. He enjoyed the things she had him do. Her nakedness suddenly made her feel vulnerable. She put her left arm across her breasts and cupped her right hand over her crotch.

Freddy, likewise, still naked, noticed. "What's wrong?"

Ella whispered, "I feel too…naked."

Freddy looked quickly around the Wood Room for their clothing. It had been scattered over the floor and furnishings. He saw his T-shirt draped over the back of an old office chair. He could reach it.

"Ya want my shirt?"

Ella nodded.

Freddy grabbed the waist end of the T-shirt and started pulling it off the chair. When the pull met resistance, without consideration for the effect, Freddy gave the T-shirt a hard tug. When he did, the chair tipped over and crashed onto the floor.

Freddy hissed, "Fuck. Shit." and tossed the T-shirt to Ella.

As Ella slipped the T-shirt over her head, she heard and felt the upstairs shake, as one werewolf bounded up the stairs. Freddy got up quickly and braced his body against the door, but it did no good. The werewolf busted into the room and sent Freddy flying into the opposite wall. The werewolf turned its hungry, red eyes toward Ella and its long, slobbery tongue lapped at its snout. When it came toward Ella, she screamed.

Freddy yelled, "Don't fuckin' touch her," and lunged at the werewolf.

The werewolf moved impossibly quick. It turned and caught Freddy in mid-flight around the neck. Freddy let out a strangled gagging sound. Ella could see frightened panic in Freddy's eyes. They were wide with fear. The werewolf launched Freddy through one of the Wood Room windows. Ella heard the hollow 'thud' Freddy's body made when he hit the concrete, but she hoped against hope he survived. The werewolf snatched her up and deposited her with the other survivors. Broken ribs, wrist, and all.

All hope Ella had of Freddy surviving the fall evaporated when she got, painfully, to her feet and looked at the blood halo growing around Freddy's head. Ella could see Freddy's eyes were wide open, frozen in his last terrified seconds, but they weren't seeing anymore.

Ella's eyes roamed to the two hideous werewolves corralling them in the building. Then back at Freddy's dead body.

I think you got lucky, sweetheart, Ella thought.

A couple of minutes passed since the werewolf killed Freddy and Ella was put in with her remaining classmates. Unfortunately for Ella, Freddy's shirt wasn't quite long enough to cover her 'parts.' Ella tried holding the hem down in front and back but doing so caused throbbing pain in her ribs and wrist. Crossing her arms in front of her had been the only position that produced the least amount of discomfort. She abandoned modesty for comfort's sake. She wasn't too concerned with anyone getting a look at her parts. Modesty wasn't one of Ella's virtues, even in the best of circumstances; let alone when she had broken ribs, a broken wrist, and werewolves about to eat her.

Besides, of the nine other survivors, three were girls. Ella could not care less if they got an eyeful. They might even pick up some grooming ideas, and Ella slept with three of the six boy survivors. Of the three remaining boys, Ella messed around with two of them. Quincy Wiseman was the only boy who hadn't had the privilege of becoming acquainted with Ella's 'parts.'

When the two werewolves jumped past Freddy's body for the two-by-four, Ella took off for the opened door at a dead run. It had been a foolish attempt at freedom, and she knew it the second she started running. Each step jarred her broken ribs and sent waves of pain throughout her body. Within a few steps, she stopped and doubled over at the waist, in pain. If they were looking her way, they were all getting a good look at her 'parts.' She was well beyond caring about that, though.

The pain in her ribs hurt like hell. That pain seemed far away when one werewolf clamped its razor, claw tipped hand over her head and lifted her off the ground. It flung her across the building to where the second werewolf waited. When she hit the concrete, the pain in her ribs and wrist returned full force. She let out an agonizing scream. The scream cut off when the second werewolf plunged its clawed hand through her chest, ripped out her still beating heart, and woofed it down in one bite.

Ella lived long enough to see her heart disappear down the werewolf's hideous snout. After seeing such a horrifying sight, her vision narrowed to a pinpoint and winked out entirely.

No white light, Ella thought, and she thought no more.

The werewolf gave her dead body a tremendous kick that sent it flying. It landed face up on top of Freddy's body with a sickening 'thud' and blood sprayed up out of the ragged chest wound onto Quincy's, who was still standing next to his dead friend's body, face and covered his glasses.

Quincy looked down at Ella's remains. Through his blood-splattered glasses, he could clearly see Ella's 'parts.' Under different circumstances, he had a crush on Ella, he would have found that sight appealing. There had been nothing appealing about it then. Quincy vomited beer and bile on Freddy and Ella's bodies.

~ * ~

Paige heard someone inside the MRB vomit, but her attention was back on the werewolf standing several feet away. It was seething with rage. Gnashing its teeth and clinching its long, clawed hands into fists. Not knowing where the courage or strength came from, Paige got to her feet and charged the werewolf. Paige didn't know what she would do when she got to it, but she could tell the attack move surprised it because its flaming red eyes went suddenly wide.

In the split second it took her to cover the ground between where she'd been and where the hulking werewolf stood, she remembered watching *The Wolfman* remake starring Benicio del Toro with her dad and that silver could kill a werewolf. She had silver. It wasn't much—a silver necklace with a small silver crucifix on it her dad gave her for First Communion and Confirmation the previous year. Her parents weren't Catholic, they weren't religious at all, but they didn't object to Paige's wishes to become Catholic. Paige converted after spending many Sundays in church with Lindsey and her family. It was around her neck. She never took it off.

As Paige closed the last few feet between herself and the werewolf, she yanked the necklace and crucifix from her neck and balled what she could of it into her right fist. She needed to get close for her plan to work. Paige planned to push the silver crucifix into one of the nail holes on the werewolf's left leg. The werewolf thwarted that plan when it grabbed her quickly and painfully by the shoulders. Its dagger length claws dug into Paige's flesh and hoisted her up, so they were face to snout.

The surprised look from Paige's attack was gone, and all Paige could see in its fiery red eyes were rage and hate. It shook Paige violently, as if scolding her for daring to attack it, and the silver crucifix slipped from her fingers. Paige panicked, but one end of the necklace stuck between two of her fingers. When the werewolf stopped shaking her, she quickly, but carefully, used her fingers to gather the necklace back into her hand. She was very relieved when she felt the crucifix. The crucifix's loop could slip over the male end of the clasps, but not the female end. Blind luck kept the female end of the clasps in her fingers and not the other end.

Divine intervention, Paige thought.

When the werewolf stopped shaking Paige, it huffed a hot breath in her face. It smelled like death. Its grip on Paige's left shoulder intensified to where she thought might pass out from the pain. Paige realized it was doing so to release her right shoulder. Its left clawed hand released her shoulder and grabbed her painfully on her right wrist. It pulled Paige closer in to bite her neck but, when it repositioned its hand, it freed up Paige's right hand that still clutched the silver necklace and crucifix.

Its mouth was close to Paige's neck. So close she felt its hot drool drop onto her right breast.

It's now or never, Paige thought.

She brought her right fist up and punched for the werewolf's open mouth. She punched too far back and caught it in the side of the head. Unconcerned, the werewolf laughed. Paige felt its canines brush against either side of her neck and its hot tongue lapped at her throat.

Summoning every ounce of strength she had, Paige screamed, "NOOO."

She kicked against the werewolf's chest and pushed back as hard as she could. The move didn't buy her much room. Paige felt the werewolf's sharp teeth pull away from her neck for a moment. It looked at Paige with amusement and opened its mouth as a demonic chuckle erupted from within its hellish chest.

Paige saw an opportunity and took it. Prepared to sacrifice her arm, she rammed her fist into the werewolf's gapping maw. It bit down immediately, but not with the force Paige expected. It could have easily taken her arm off at the elbow, but the bite barely broke the skin. With her arm still plunged elbow deep in the werewolf's mouth, it chuckled again. Paige looked into the werewolf's burning eyes. They looked pleased.

Paige didn't understand what was going on. She expected it to bite her arm off and ingest the silver, which, she hoped, would kill it. Instead, the bite barely broke the skin, and it looked pleased with itself. After the chuckle, the werewolf released the bite and started pulling its head back.

"No fuckin' way." Paige screamed.

She pushed her arm back into the werewolf's mouth as far as she could reach and opened her hand.

The reaction had been immediate and violent. The werewolf jerked its head back, its canines ripped fresh wounds down Paige's right forearm as it did and threw Paige to the ground several feet away. Smoke started streaming from its mouth and it let out a mangled howl. As Paige watched, the werewolf's body began to change. It shrank and the thick, black hair retreated into its body. It clawed at its mouth and smoke continued to billow out of it. Its long snout changed too. It receded back to one that looked more human.

Paige heard the commotion from behind her and turned to see what caused it. It was two more werewolves, and they were heading directly toward her. She felt sure they were going to rip her to pieces, but they paid no attention to her. Instead, they ran to the first werewolf that looked more human than ever. Just as the other two werewolves made it to Paige's attacker, she saw her blood covered necklace and crucifix shoot out of her attacker's much more human mouth. It looked at Paige, and it surprised her to see that its blazing red eyes transformed into big, blue human eyes.

Beautiful eyes, Paige thought.

The other two werewolves grabbed the third and disappeared into the woods.

Paige stood up on shaky but satisfied legs and walked over to where her blood covered necklace and crucifix were lying on the ground. They were still smoking.

I hurt it, Paige thought.

That wasn't quite right.

I hurt her; Paige corrected her previous thought.

Paige saw enough of what it was becoming, to know its gender. It had a feminine face and she clearly saw small breasts forming on her ever more human body. Paige didn't think she had been old either. Maybe she wasn't as young as Paige, but she couldn't be more than a few years older, if that. Paige reached down with her mangled arm and picked up her lifesaving necklace and crucifix. It felt unnaturally warm in her hand.

Must be warm from being inside that hellish beast, Paige thought.

She looked at the nasty gashes on her right arm.

I'm gonna need stitches for that, Paige thought.

She had been wrong on both counts. The wounds would be gone within a few hours, and, within a few days, she'd no longer be able to tolerate the burning sensation she felt when wearing the silver necklace and crucifix. She had been cursed.

Paige heard commotion and voices from behind her. When she turned to look, she saw several of her classmates streaming out of the MRB. She and they didn't know it, but Paige saved them from their fate.

The alpha planned to turn them all.

As a few of her classmates ran toward her shouting things like, “Are they gone?” “Where’d they go?” and “I’ll get my gun.” Paige felt suddenly very naked. She covered herself as best she could.

Seconds later, Lindsey broke through the students hovering around Paige and wrapped her in a hug. When she stepped back and realized Paige was naked, Lindsey pulled off her shirt and gave it to Paige, which left Lindsey in her jeans and bra. Paige slipped Lindsey’s shirt over her head and tugged it down. Like Ella, Paige had to tug down the front and back hem to cover her ‘parts.’ Unlike Ella, she didn’t have a broken wrist and ribs to contend with, so she managed. Also, unlike Ella, none of the boys standing around her saw her ‘parts,’ so she would’ve managed even if her ribs and wrist were broken.

Lindsey looked around and back at Paige.

Lindsey opened her mouth but, knowing what she was about to ask, Paige said, “It killed him, Lin. It killed Justin.”

She sobbed. Lindsey wrapped her in a tight hug and sobbed, too. In the distance, Paige heard a siren approaching.

Daddy’s gonna kill me, Paige thought.

~ * ~

The nearly ingested silver badly hurt the alpha and it needed the support of its two betas to escape into the woods. The pain and fear it felt from almost being killed were eclipsed by rage it felt for the little bitch who shoved the silver down its throat. The little bitch ruined its plans to turn several humans and increase its pack. It wanted to go back and rip her little head off, but caught between human and werewolf form, it had been too vulnerable. The alpha wouldn’t kill the little bitch, but it would make her pay in unimaginable ways.

The alpha tried to transform back into a werewolf several times on the way back to the Wiseman barn but unsuccessfully. The silver corrupted the transformation process. It considered trying to transform back into its full human form but had been concerned one of its betas might take advantage of its very weak human body for any manner of reasons. The alpha knew its betas wouldn’t kill it. Doing so would rob them of the power they enjoyed. They might do other things to its human body, though. Things that would be difficult to forget. Things that almost happened the night its human became infected. It stayed in the uncomfortable half transformed condition.

It experienced discomfort for many reasons. Werewolf bones don't conform to a partial human body very well. Besides the agony it felt in its body, its senses kept switching from human to werewolf and back again, which irritated and disorientated it. One moment the alpha could see in the dark. The next, human sight left it almost blind and stumbling over unseen terrain. Similarly, its hearing would go from acute, when it could hear for miles, to human, when all it could hear had been the rustle of the underbrush as they plodded through it and the animalistic grunts of its betas. Worse still had been its sense of smell. In werewolf form, its betas smelled pleasant, even appealing. In human form, they smelled musty and repugnant.

When the pack finally arrived at the Wiseman barn, the alpha dismissed its pack to hunt in the surrounding woods. It staggered inside the barn and fell to the dirt floor with a 'thud.' As it lay in the dirt, coping with the pain and disorientating senses, it thought of ways to make the little bitch pay for what she'd done. She would be the pack bitch for the other betas to use as they pleased. The alpha decided that previously, but she would also suffer immeasurably in other ways, too.

As dawn approached, the betas returned to the barn. The alpha waited until they were well into their transformation to human form before it tried to transform as well. At first, it couldn't trigger the transformation. In the past, all it need do was will the transformation, and it happened. The alpha felt on the edge of panic when it felt the transformation finally kick in. Moments later, she was lying on the floor, naked, and fully human.

Her body ached in places and ways she'd never experienced before. Usually, the transformation back into human form, although painful during the process, left her feeling alert and invigorated. Any wounds she sustained in werewolf form would heal during the process, too.

Not only was she not feeling alert and invigorated after the change, the puncture wounds on her leg where the little bitch hit her with nail laden two-by-four were still present. They were well on the way to being healed, but they hadn't healed completely. Above all else, her throat hurt the most. She could feel blisters on the back of her tongue and throat where the silver burned her.

Her two betas, in human form then, came toward her. She couldn't tell whether they were concerned, scared, or angry about the preceding night's events. She knew she couldn't show any weakness, though. She quickly tucked her injured leg beneath her bottom and sat up.

"Are you okay?" Dillon Albertson asked.

She turned Dillon, who had been one of Seth's best friends since grade school, the same night she turned Seth and Cole. Thinking of Seth, and how the deputy killed him, stung her, and she didn't immediately respond.

This gave Cole Duncan an opportunity to say, "What the fuck happened?"

Cole was the pack wildcard and the hardest for her to control. She only turned him because he had been Seth's fraternity, 'Big Brother,' and Seth wanted him in the pack, but she didn't like him. If trouble came from within the pack, it would come from Cole. This she knew.

She took a deep breath to steady her growing anger. "I'm fine, Dillon. Thanks for askin'. As for what the fuck happened, the little bitch shoved a silver necklace down my throat."

Cole scowled. "Let's fuckin' kill her."

"No," the girl said. "I bit her before she tried to kill me, and we need her."

Cole scoffed. "I say we fuckin' kill her."

The girl's anger rose, but she kept a calm demeanor. "What *you* say doesn't matter. Besides, I thought y'all wanted a fuck-toy bitch."

Dillon nodded, but Cole laughed. "Fuck her? Maybe I'll turn a fuck-toy bitch of my own. Maybe I'll start my own fuckin' pack, so things get done right."

The anger inside her erupted, and she transformed into a werewolf much more quickly, and with less pain, than she ever had before. Within a couple of seconds, she was towering over Dillon and Seth. This frightened Dillon and he backed away quickly, but Cole stood his ground. His eyes flared red, and he started to transform. He was going to challenge the alpha.

Unfortunately for Cole, his transformation took much longer than the alpha's. His snout barely started to elongate when the alpha backhanded him across the barn. He crashed into the side of the barn and fell behind a pile of old tractor parts. The beta closed the distance in two large strides. Cole, still not fully transformed but more werewolf than he had been when the alpha knocked him across the room, leapt from behind the tractor parts at the alpha. The alpha caught him and slammed him to the dirt floor with bone shattering force.

The impact suspended Cole's transformation, and he started to turn back into a human. The alpha locked its jaws on either side of Cole's increasingly human neck and bit down until its canines punctured his skin. Cole stopped struggling and laid perfectly still. He was submitting.

The alpha considered removing his head with a quick bite, but it already lost one of its packs and it didn't want to lose another. Cole's defiance had to be punished, though. The alpha pulled its head back and stood up. Cole, expecting another assault, waited several seconds before getting to his feet. When he did, the alpha swiped its clawed hand across Cole's chest and opened four deep gashes. Cole fell to his knees as blood gushed from his chest. The alpha knew the wound would heal within in a few hours, but it also knew it would hurt like hell until it did.

The alpha quickly transformed back into human form. This transformation had been quick and relatively painless, too. Also, the wounds on her leg and in her throat were completely healed. She felt alert and invigorated.

She looked down at Cole, who looked up at her with a knew-found respect. "We good here?"

Cole averted her gaze and nodded.

Good boy, she thought.

She said, "Let's get dressed and get the fuck outta here."

A few minutes later, the matte black Ram pickup turned on to Highway Twenty-One and headed east toward Nacogdoches. A Pine View County Sheriff's SUV passed them going the other direction. As they passed, the girl driving the Ram pickup raised two fingers off the steering wheel in a friendly 'howdy'" gesture common in rural areas. Sheriff Garrett Lambert returned the gesture and disappeared around a curve in the Ram's review mirror.

~ * ~

Deputy Crystal Zimmer arrived first at the MRB. The carnage quickly overwhelmed her as well as the frantic eyewitness accounts of werewolves attacking the students. As she made her way through the survivors, finding Paige alive relieved her a great deal.

As Crystal keyed her shoulder-mounted radio and told Garrett she'd found Paige, when his SUV skidded to a stop by the bonfire with Ty's close behind him and Austin bringing up the rear. Deputy Danny Stutter, who patrolled the far north side of Pine View County when Ty put out the urgent call to converge on the MRB, arrived a few minutes later.

The full force of the eleven-to-seven shift of the Pine View County Sheriff's Department was at the scene and it wasn't enough personnel to process the carnage and evidence. Garrett called Kay Parker, who was the over-night dispatch, and asked her to contact the Department of Public Safety, the state police, and request their assistance. The DPS would contact the Texas Rangers and request their assistance, too.

Garrett was more than content to hand over the bulk of the investigation to the other law enforcement agencies. This would give him more free time to identify and kill the alpha.

~ * ~

After picking Paige up, nearly crushing her in a bear hug of relief, and sobbing until he felt his knees getting weak, Garrett put her down and stepped back to inspect her. His eyes were immediately drawn to the nasty rake marks on her right arm. The gashes looked more like claw marks than bite marks.

Please let those be claw marks, Garrett thought.

Paige had been using her right hand to hold down the front of a blouse Garrett didn't recognize as hers. Without processing the situation, Garrett grabbed Paige's right arm around the wrist and yanked it up so he could inspect the wounds closer.

"Daddy." Paige yelled, jerked her arm away, and quickly pulled the front of the blouse back down.

It was only then Garrett realized Paige wasn't dressed. He quickly scanned the surrounding teenagers, looking for Justin. He didn't see Justin, but he saw his sister, Lindsey, a few feet away, looking sheepish in her jeans and bra.

Why the hell is Paige wearing Lindsey's blouse? Where the hell are Justin and her clothes? Garrett thought.

It wasn't a hard puzzle to solve, even for a dad who hadn't been in law enforcement for almost fifteen years. He made a mental note to kill Justin later.

As Garrett unbuttoned his uniform shirt, he said to Paige, "We'll talk about this later."

When his shirt was off, he handed it to Paige. "Put this on and give Lindsey her shirt back."

Paige took the shirt. "Where? There are people everywhere."

Garrett quickly surveyed the situation. "Ty and I will block for ya. Change behind us."

Ty nodded in agreement, but Paige said, "Please, Daddy. Not out here. Someone might see."

Garrett turned his back on Paige and Ty did the same, pressing his shoulder against Garrett's. Then he beckoned Lindsey over.

She'd been watching and seemed to understand what was going on. He said to Paige, "Not a request."

When Lindsey joined Paige behind Garrett and Ty, Paige said, "This is so embarrassin'."

A couple of seconds later, Lindsey stepped out from behind Garrett and Ty with her blouse back on.

Garrett started to turn around, but Paige gave his shoulder a shove. "Not buttoned up yet, Daddy."

She sounded irritated, which Garrett took as a good sign. When Paige finally gave the 'all clear,' Garrett and Ty turned back to face her. His uniform shirt hung down to Paige's mid-thighs, which had been good. Garrett was still concerned with the wound on Paige's right forearm, though. He grabbed her wrist again. This time she didn't pull away and inspected the injury.

It didn't look like a bite.

Hopeful, Garrett asked, "Did it claw ya?"

Paige could tell her daddy desperately wanted it to be a claw wound, and she'd seen enough horror flicks to know why. A line from the old black and white, Lon Chaney, Junior *Wolfman* movie had come to her about how even a good man could become a wolf after being bitten by a werewolf.

Paige had a hard time wrapping her mind around the implications of the bite. Too. An hour earlier, she didn't believe werewolves existed. Not only did she now know they existed, she'd been bitten. If the Hollywood movies were correct, the bite infected her and she would become a werewolf, too.

Without answering her dad's question, Paige slowly, but forcefully, pulled her arm from her dad's grasp.

Garrett didn't need Paige's verbal confirmation the werewolf's claws did not cause the wound. He saw it in her face and in the way she pulled her arm away from him. Like it could infect him, too. Despair washed over Garrett like a tidal wave, and his knees went weak again. This time, the weight of the situation won, and he sank to his knees in the red dirt at Paige's feet.

Paige looked from her dad to Ty and back to her dad again. Her mouth opened and closed several times as she tried to find something to say. She looked like a fish out of water gasping for oxygenated water.

After several wordless awkward moments, Paige went to her knees in front of her dad. "This isn't real, Daddy. This can't be real. I can't turn into one of those...things and murder people."

Fresh tears welled in her bottom lids and spilled down her cheeks.

Garrett took Paige's small hand in his and thought about how his nightmare ended since Monster-Paige turned about twelve years old; with her clawed hand in the larger werewolf's hand as they turned and left the blood splattered bedroom of his old trailer house.

You can't have her, Garrett thought.

He said, "I'm not gonna let that happen, Paige-Turner."

"Yeah," Ty said as he squatted down beside Paige and Garrett and pointed to the bandage around his neck, "and you're not alone."

Paige gawked at Ty for several moments and did her fish out of water impression again before finally saying, "You too? It bit ya too?"

Ty nodded, but Paige wasn't finished.

She looked at her dad. "Why didn't it kill me…us? It could've killed me easily. It k-k-killed Justin." Fresh tears ran down her face, but she continued, "It was taunting me…playin' with me. Why, Daddy? Why didn't it kill me?"

Garrett and Ty exchanged a knowing look that irritated Paige.

Angrier than she intended, she said, "What do y'all know? What aren't y'all tellin' me?"

Garrett started to talk, but Ty cut him off. "We don't know for certain, but we're pretty sure it marked me Monday mornin' when I was dealing with Missus Weaver's dead pigs. It used her as bait to get me back out to her house tonight. It could'a killed me, too. It had its jaws wrapped around my neck, but it only bit hard enough to break the skin. Then it left. My guess is…it marked you at some point, too."

"But why?"

Garrett answered with, "To infect ya…to turn ya. To make ya a member of its pack."

Paige looked horrified, and more tears spilled down her cheeks. When she shook uncontrollably, Garrett grabbed her and pulled her onto his lap. Ty put a hand on Paige's shoulder and gave it a reassuring squeeze.

Garrett, holding back tears of his own, said, "I'm not gonna let this happen to ya, Paige."

Through sobs, Paige blubbered, "H-how are ya gonna stop it, Daddy? H-how?"

Garrett held her tight. "I'm gonna find the alpha…the one that bit ya and kill it."

Ty added, "*We're* gonna find it and kill it."

Paige looked at the two men she trusted most in the world. "Will that work? Will that keep us from turnin' into one of those…monsters?"

One way or another, Garrett thought.

He said, "It'll work, Paige-Turner."

"You promise?"

Garrett nodded.

"Pinky promise?"

Paige hadn't asked Garrett to pinky promise on anything since she was eight or nine years old. When she'd first started with the pinky promise thing, she told him pinky promises were for important promises and they couldn't be broken. It hurt Garrett's heart beyond description to hear Paige revert to that childhood comfort.

Garrett smiled, and hooked pinkies with Paige. "I pinky promise."

Garrett couldn't believe the affect the pinky promise had on him—it somehow made everything more real. He fully intended to find the alpha and kill it to save Paige and Ty. Failure wasn't an option and the pinky promise made that even more clear. As a bonus, it seemed to have a calming effect on Paige. When she was composed, all three of them regained their feet.

Garrett saw Lindsey still standing nearby and watching them. The gravity of what Paige said about Justin being killed by the werewolf set in, as he remembered Justin and Lindsey were siblings. He'd always been very fond of Lindsey, who basically lived with him and Paige during the summer months when Paige stayed with him full time, and his heart went out to her.

Even though Garrett thought of Lindsey as being a second

daughter, she couldn't know about Paige getting bitten by the werewolf. Things were going to be bad enough once word got out about what happened at the MRB. Every swinging dick in East Texas had a plethora of guns and they would be out in force hunting for the murdering monsters. If word got out Paige had been bitten, things could get ugly fast. Although he hated thinking it, he hoped Lindsey thought Paige's little breakdown related to the death of her brother, Paige's boyfriend. He needed her to think that. It would be difficult because Paige and Lindsey shared everything, but he had to make Paige understand the importance of not telling Lindsey the werewolf bit her.

Garrett turned to Paige. "Paige, sweetheart. Listen to me. Are ya listenin'?"

Paige nodded.

Garrett continued, "You can't tell *anyone* ya got bit by that thing. I mean *anyone*. Not even Lindsey. Do ya understand?"

Paige protested. "Daddy, I tell Lin *everything*."

Garrett shook his head emphatically. "Not this ya don't. I mean it, Paige. Crazy shit's gonna start happenin' 'round here when folks find out 'bout this. It's gonna scare people…bad. Scared people do things they wouldn't normally do."

Garrett let that sink in for a second or two and added, "Like kill people they think are gonna turn into werewolves. Even a sixteen-year-old girl."

Paige furrowed her brow and it gladdened Garrett to see this bit of information sink in. Then she said, "Daddy, Lin wouldn't tell anyone. Besides, how am I gonna explain this?"

Paige held up her wounded arm.

Garrett shook his head again. "No, not even Lindsey. Ya can tell her it clawed your cheek, that's fine. Tell her ya raked your arm against a broken tree limb when ya were runnin' back here. Better yet, roll my shirtsleeve down and don't mention it again."

Paige, still defiant, said, "I can't hide this. It'll take weeks to heal, and it'll leave a nasty scar."

Garrett looked at Paige's arm. "If you're infected, that'll heal in a few hours and there won't be a hint of a scar."

Paige looked at the ragged wound with disbelief.

"Does it even hurt anymore?"

It amazed Paige to realize it didn't hurt. Not even a dull throb of pain remained.

She looked at her dad and back at her arm several times. Finally, she said, “No, it doesn’t hurt anymore.”

She tongued the inside of her cheek and found the gash had already closed to where her tongue wouldn’t push through it.

With a tone of wonder in her voice, Paige said, “My cheek’s already healin’, too.”

“My bite and claw wounds don’t hurt anymore either,” Ty added.

To Paige, Garrett said, “Folks won’t understand this, Paige. I know Lindsey would never *intentionally* put ya in harm’s way. If you tell her ‘bout this and she tells *anyone* else, even just because she’s worried ‘bout ya, things could get ugly.”

Paige nodded and started rolling her dad’s shirtsleeves down.

Not quite satisfied, Garrett said, “Pinky promise ya won’t tell anyone ‘bout the bite, *even* Lindsey.”

They locked pinkies and Paige said, “I pinky promise I won’t tell anyone about the bite.”

“Even Lindsey?” Garrett added.

“Even Lin,” Paige agreed.

Two pinky promises in one night, Garrett thought.

When they broke the pinky hook, Garrett said, “I need to do my job and have a look-see around here for a few minutes. I want you and Lindsey to go over there with Deputy Zimmer.”

Garrett knew Crystal wasn’t handling the carnage well, and he thought watching over Paige and Lindsey for him would make her feel useful. He didn’t want Paige left unattended, either.

Garrett called Lindsey over, she was at Paige’s side in seconds, and walked them over to Deputy Zimmer who leaned against the side of the MRB metal building, probably for support, and looking in the only direction that didn’t include mutilated bodies.

When Crystal saw Garrett heading in her direction, she stopped leaning against the building. She’d felt lightheaded since seeing several teenagers’ bodies violated so violently. Especially the body in the bonfire. She could tell it had been a girl by her legs, which were partially in the bonfire. She straightened up to meet Garrett.

When they were close, Crystal said, “Sheriff Lambert.”

A simple statement of his name, but Garrett knew she, in her own way, tried to apologize for her lack of professionalism at the crime scene.

Far from being disappointed in Deputy Zimmer, Garret thought her reaction to be very human and he understood. Had she not been affected he would have been worried she was a sociopath.

Not believing, under the circumstances, it was possible, Garrett managed a smile. "I have an important job for ya, Deputy Zimmer."

Crystal immediately looked concerned, like he had been going to ask her to photograph the bodies or something similarly distasteful.

When Garrett said, "I need ya to keep these two young ladies' company while I have a look-see around," tension visibly left Crystal's features.

With obvious relief in her voice, Crystal said, "Yes, sir. I can do that."

As Garrett and Ty headed toward the front of the metal building, Paige, too, felt relief. After the crushing bear hug, when her daddy noticed the state of her undress, he'd told her they were going to talk about 'this,' meaning her lack of clothing, later. While she had been nowhere near happy about being bitten by a werewolf, she hoped the bite, and what to do about it, would drown out all other conversation.

As if reading her mind, Garrett turned, and pointed at her. "When I get back, we're talkin' 'bout what went on with y'all tonight."

Paige, mimicking Deputy Zimmer, said, "Yes, sir."

After Garrett turned and started away again, Paige looked at Lindsey.

Lindsey whispered in Paige's ear so quietly even Deputy Zimmer, standing next to them, couldn't hear, "Did y'all?"

Paige shook her head and new tears leaked out of her puffy, red eyes. She couldn't believe an hour ago, she and Just in were about to make love. It had been perfect. The candles, the green, satin sheets, *Feels So Right* playing on the Bluetooth speaker, and even Justin's florescent green condom. Now Justin was dead, and the werewolf that killed him infected her. Paige didn't think things could get much worse, but she was wrong.

~ * ~

As the days passed and the June full moon got closer, she would feel a connection with the alpha that excited her, and that excitement repulsed her. The connection would include flash visions through the alpha's eyes while it hunted. Killing animals and humans. What would frustrate her most, though, was she couldn't use the connection to locate the alpha. Paige thought the alpha used it to play with her, but from a distance. That wasn't the case at first, but it progressed to that point, eventually.

Chapter Eight

In the time Garrett dealt with Paige, the MRB got crowded with officials involved in many duties. Two DPS officers arrived and were trying to question several of the students. Garrett didn't intervene, but he could tell the DPS officers were having a hard time comprehending the information they were getting. Two ambulances also arrived, and four paramedics were treating some students for shock and checking the bodies for signs of life, but they were clearly dead. No one called them, but several members of the Pine View Volunteer Fire Department arrived and were helping where they could. Garrett knew from his time as a volunteer firefighter, they monitored radio calls and showed up out of boredom even when there wasn't a fire. Garrett appreciated their efforts, but he also knew the volunteers, and the stories they would spread about what happened at the MRB would be the impetus for vigilantism actions that were sure to come. George Krats, the county coroner, arrived and looked extremely overwhelmed.

Garrett saw Deputies Danny Stutter and Austin Turner talking with a small-framed student and he and Ty headed in their direction. As they passed the bonfire, which had been reduced to smoldering embers by the volunteer firefighters, two of George Krats' employees were pulling the body of a young female from the ashes. From the waist up, her body was nothing more than a blackened, vaguely human form with angry red cracks crisscrossing what had been her flesh. Her right arm snagged on a branch on the parameter of the bonfire and the blacked skin peeled off like an arm-length glove. Bubbles appeared on the exposed flesh, as if it had been boiling, and burst with an audible 'popping' sound. The sight turned Garrett's stomach upside down, but he fared better than one of Krats' employees who dropped the girl's legs and vomited. Garrett looked away and continued toward his deputies.

When Garrett and Ty joined Danny, Austin, and the student, Garrett said, "Please tell me y'all documented that victim before they pulled her body out of the fire."

Danny and Austin nodded, and Austin said, "We've documented all the victims we've found."

Garrett nodded. "Who's missin'?"

"Near as we can tell," Austin said, "two are unaccounted for."

Danny referenced a notepad in his hand. "We know Justin Anderson and Matt Cooke were here and are currently unaccounted for. We're just goin' off what the kids have told us, so there could be more."

Garrett nodded. He knew Justin was dead, but he didn't know as to the whereabouts of Matt Cooke.

Garrett looked at the small-framed student. He looked scared and nervous.

Austin noticed Garrett's attention shifted to the student. "This is Quincy Wiseman. He was in the buildin' with most of the other survivors."

Garrett stuck out his hand. "Hey, Quincy. I'm Sheriff Lambert. Ya probably know my daughter, Paige."

Quincy shook Garrett's hand. His hands were little, but the grip was much stronger than Garrett expected. "Yes, sir. I know Paige. She wasn't in the buildin'. Is she okay?"

Garrett broke the shake. "She's fine, Quincy. Thanks for askin'. Can ya tell me what ya saw…what happened here tonight?"

Quincy was silent for several seconds, and he looked even more anxious. Garrett had been sure the boy was worried no one would believe his werewolf story.

Danny said, "It's okay, Quincy. Just tell Sheriff Lambert what ya told us."

Quincy chewed his bottom lip for a moment, but he took a deep breath and spoke. Once Quincy got to talking, he talked a lot. When Quincy finished relaying his eyewitness account of what happened, Garrett thanked him and told him to go over with the other students and wait until they could get them home.

Once Quincy was out of earshot, Garrett turned to Ty. "Well, what'a ya think?"

Ty looked from Garrett to Danny to Austin, and back to Garrett. "I think they were plannin' to turn the kids in the barn to make the pack bigger."

Danny, who hadn't been at Carla Weaver's house earlier and didn't know about Ty's encounter, scoffed. "Hold on here, Sheriff. You're not believin' this werewolf shit…are ya? I mean…this is some kind of mass hysteria or somethin'. They probably took some new designer drug that caused hallucinations. They reacted violently to the werewolf hallucinations and killed each other."

Before Garrett could respond, Ty turned to Danny and, with a stern tone, said, "They're real, Danny. I encountered four of the fuckers earlier at Carla Weaver's place. I'm not on drugs. They shredded her body just like they shredded Russ Lomax's body and the bodies of the kids scattered around here. You saw their injuries. You really think a bunch of hopped-up kids could do that?"

Danny looked at the three of them with obvious disbelief. Garrett knew he had a difficult time believing there were werewolves in East Texas. A few days earlier, Garrett felt like-minded.

Garrett placed a hand on Danny's shoulder. "Look, Danny. I know this is hard to believe. It took me a while to get my head around it, too. This *is* real. Ya need to get your head in the game."

It was clear Danny still wasn't convinced, but he said, "Okay, say I believe werewolves are killin' and turnin' folks. Next, you're gonna tell me we need silver bullets to kill the fuckers."

Garrett nodded. "That's exactly what I'm gonna tell ya."

Danny scoffed. "Well, that's just great. 'Cause I'm fresh outta silver bullets."

Garrett smiled. "Mike Middleton is makin' 'em for us. He thinks he can have at least one clip of 'em for each of us when he comes in for his shift later today."

It pleased Garrett to see that hearing Mike Middleton was making silver bullets seemed to resonate with Danny.

Danny looked at Garrett for several seconds. "You're serious?"

Garrett nodded sternly.

Danny shuffled his feet nervously. "Okay, but…if they're real, how do we know silver actually kills the fuckers?"

"'Cause I killed one of the four fuckers with silver at Carla Weaver's house earlier."

Danny's jaw dropped, and he looked at Ty. "What, you've got silver bullets?"

Ty grinned. "Nope. I blew a hole in the fucker's chest with my shotgun and crammed my Silver Star so deep in the hole I think I felt its backbone."

Danny was silent for several seconds then said, "You're serious. This happened."

Ty nodded. "As serious as a heart attack."

Danny looked at Austin. "What about you? Do you believe this?"

Without hesitation, Austin said, "I haven't seen one, but I saw what was left of Carla Weaver's body and the human body of the one Ty took out. Humans can't do this kind of damage, Danny. So…yeah, I believe."

When Austin finished, Garret said to Danny, "We good here?"

Danny nodded.

To both Danny and Austin, Garrett said, "What's the current count on deceased and survivors?"

Danny referenced his notepad again. "Okay…I told ya about the two missin' kids. Not knowin' their status, we've got eleven survivors and thirteen dead."

Garrett saw many dead bodies, but the thirteen dead count, fourteen counting Justin, had been staggering.

That's a lot of sad house calls, Garrett thought.

Garrett took a deep breath and, thinking about making the house calls, said, "How many have been IDd?"

"All of 'em," Austin responded.

"Even the girl in the fire?" Garrett asked.

"That's Maggie Crawford," Austin responded.

Garrett knew that name because he'd heard Paige talking with Lindsey about how she flirted with Justin. Maggie Crawford had dated Justin before he and Paige got together. He also knew who she was from a previous visit he'd made to tell Maggie's mother her husband died when he wrecked his truck. The thought of visiting Missus Crawford with this news set heavy on his heart.

Garrett took another deep breath. "Okay. Get contact info for the deceased. Check the boy's wallets, the girl's purses, look in the vehicles, and run license plates to do so. When you're done, leave it in my SUV. Then, check with DPS to make sure they're done with the survivors and take 'em home."

Garrett and Ty turned to leave, until Austin said something that stopped them in their tracks.

"One of the…werewolves bit Ty, Sheriff Lambert. If they're real, and the myths are true, doesn't that mean Ty's infected? That he's been turned and will be part of the pack. Those are Ty's words, sir," he said.

It concerned Garrett, once they believed in werewolves, someone would put this together. If Austin hadn't responded to the call at Carla Weaver's place, Garrett might have been able to keep Ty's bite between them, but that wasn't the case. Before turning around to address Austin, Garrett looked to his right at Ty. Ty gave Garrett a brief nod, as if saying, "It was bound to come out." Garrett nodded back and turned around.

Garrett squared off on Austin. "That pretty much sums it up, Austin. I've been doin' some research…talkin' with folks who have degrees beyond your capabilities, and I've been told those who are infected won't turn until the next full moon. Also, I've been told, if we kill the alpha that infected Ty, the curse is broken. All ya need to concern yourself with is helpin' me find and kill the alpha before the next full moon, which is on June second."

"If we can't find and kill the alpha by June second?" Austin asked.

Anger welled inside of Garrett, but he remained outwardly calm. "You let me worry 'bout that, Austin. I don't want either of you startin' any trouble for Deputy Jackson while we work on resolvin' this. Understood?"

Austin and Danny showed they understood with curt nods.

Garrett felt sure everyone in the sheriff's department would know about Ty's bite within the next eighteen hours, time for a full shift rotation, but it was out of his hands. With luck, folks who didn't need to believe in werewolves, staff employees, wouldn't believe and the folks who needed to believe, gun carrying deputies, wouldn't treat Ty differently. At that point, all Garrett could do to protect Ty and Paige was find the alpha. He'd put a silver bullet in its head and end it. He could do his best to make sure no one harassed Ty at work, and no one found out Paige had been bitten, too.

Piece of cake, Garrett thought as he and Ty made their way back to where he'd left Paige with Lindsey and Deputy Zimmer.

~ * ~

After her dad left, the weight of Justin's death hit Paige like a truck. She and Lindsey clung to each other, sobbing for several minutes. When the crying eased, Paige was thankful Lindsey didn't ask for details about what happened. She knew her dad would want details, and she wasn't sure she could handle telling what happened more than once. The events kept bouncing around in her mind like a buzzing bee but telling it would be difficult.

Several minutes passed. Just when Paige was hoping her dad put off talking with her that night, he and Ty came around the side of the building.

Garrett walked up to Deputy Zimmer. "Danny and Austin are trackin' down contact info on the…deceased. Once DPS is through talkin' with the survivors, I want y'all to start takin' the kids home. You can start with Lindsey."

Before Crystal could respond, Paige said, "Can I go with Lin, Daddy?"

Garrett shook his head. "No, sweetheart. I need ya to tell me what happened with you and Justin, and I need ya to do it right now."

Paige looked uncomfortable.

Tears spilled down Lindsey's cheeks. "What am I supposed to tell my folks 'bout Justin, Mister Garrett?"

Garrett mentally scolded himself for forgetting Lindsey's brother was dead. Telling her folks about Justin's death was his responsibility, not hers. He needed to talk with Paige, alone, and he didn't want to leave Lindsey unattended while he did because he didn't know how long the conversation with Paige would take. He had been trying to sort through the problem when Crystal came up with a solution.

Crystal, needing to feel useful, said, "Lindsey can ride with me while I take some of the other kids home. When you and Paige are done, you can take Lindsey home."

Garrett liked the idea and appreciated Crystal for coming up with it.

Garrett looked at Lindsey. "Would that be okay, Lindsey? Ride around with Deputy Zimmer until Paige and I are done talkin'. When we're done, I'll take ya home and talk with your folks."

Lindsey nodded.

One problem solved; only about a million to go, Garrett thought.

Before Lindsey left with Deputy Zimmer, she and Paige hugged out another quick cry. With Lindsey and Crystal gone, Paige, Garrett, and Ty were alone in their own group.

Garrett looked at Paige. "Okay, Paige-Turner. Tell us what happened."

Paige shifted uncomfortably, looked at Ty and then back at her dad. "Daddy, this is embarrassin' enough. Do I have to tell ya this in front of Ty?"

Garrett waved a hand at Paige, pointing out her state of undress.

"We don't care 'bout *that*. We'll talk 'bout *that* later. We want to know what happened when you and Justin were attacked."

Garrett could see the relief of not having to talk about what she and Justin were doing wash over Paige's features.

She straightened up. "Yeah, okay. I can do that."

Garrett and Ty listened closely as Paige relived the ordeal. Tears leaked down her cheeks when she told them about Justin being killed, but she got through it without breaking down completely.

Paige was all too happy to leave out the sexual aspects of the story, but she knew her dad and Ty weren't stupid men. Given her lack of clothing as well as the fact she and Justin were alone in the tree house, they knew they were engaged in something of an adult nature.

Even though her dad told her she didn't have to discuss what went on between her and Justin, Paige blurted out, "We didn't do it, Daddy. I won't lie. We were gonna do it, but…Justin got killed before we did."

As far as confessions went, and Garrett heard hundreds, Paige's had been believable. Part of him had been relieved, but he'd have preferred they had uninterrupted sex over what had happened.

Garrett pulled Paige into a hug. "It's okay, sweetheart. I believe ya."

Ty watched them hug and was glad he had a son instead of a daughter.

After the hug, Paige powered through the rest of the ordeal quickly and more unfazed than Garrett thought possible. Garrett had her repeat several key parts of the event. Specifically, the parts about the werewolf speaking to her and the partial transformation.

Garrett, clearly surprised by this information, said, "It spoke to ya?"

Paige nodded again. "It told me to run."

This information seemed very important to Garrett. He'd assumed the wolf part of their brain consumed the human part while transformed. If they could speak, maybe they could reason. If they could reason, perhaps they didn't have to kill. Perhaps they could control this impulse. If they could, Garrett reasoned, maybe Ty and Paige could restrain themselves as werewolves. Garrett had a feeling it was a long shot, and he intended to discuss it with James Huff later. It felt like a life preserver of hope in a sea of despair. He clung to it.

Garrett found the part about the partial transformation and how

Paige triggered it equally amazing and important. He could barely contain the pride he had in Paige for having the nerve to ram her hand down its throat and deposit the silver crucifix and necklace there. It had been only dumb luck Garrett gave Paige the silver version.

He'd intended to get her a gold crucifix and necklace, but, as he often did, he waited until the last minute to buy the gift and the gold version had been out of stock. The Walmart associate told him they'd have more in gold in the following week, but Garrett wanted Paige wearing it when she converted. When he had given it to Paige before the Mass, he apologized for it not being gold and told her he'd return it and get the gold one the following week, if she wanted him to. Paige, true to her sweet nature, told him she loved it, and she would never take it off.

Thank God Walmart was out of the gold ones, Garrett thought.

After Paige retold the partial transformation events for the third time, Garrett turned to Ty. "I think we can use this. If we can get silver on the alpha…like a chain around its neck…or silver on the teeth of a bear trap, it'll be less dangerous when it turns back into a human. Then we can take him out."

"*Her*, Daddy. Y'all could take *her* out," Paige corrected him.

Garrett and Ty looked at each other and then back at Paige. News the alpha had been female floored Garrett. In fact, he found it difficult to believe.

"Her?" Garrett asked Paige.

Paige nodded.

Still not convinced, Garrett said, "Are ya *sure* about this? Absolutely *sure*?"

"I'm sure."

"How human did it get? How could ya tell?"

Paige was getting frustrated with her dad's unwillingness to believe what she had been telling him. "Human enough for me to see her tits."

Garrett and Ty exchanged shocked looks again.

"Tell me everything you remember 'bout her."

Happy her dad finally believed her, Paige said, "There isn't much more to tell. I saw her breasts, but her face was still kinda stuck between human and wolf. Oh. I'm pretty sure she's white because her skin was gettin' lighter as she lost her wolf hair. I don't think she's much older than me. Maybe a few years…so late teens or early twenties."

"Anything else?"

Paige thought for a moment and then one last detail materialized in her mind.

Excited, but not entirely sure why, Paige blurted out, "Blue eyes. She had big blue eyes!"

Garrett considered this information briefly. "Did ya recognize her? Is she a Pine View High School student? Was anyone who looks remotely like her missin' from the party tonight?"

Paige thought about her dad's questions and tried to attach the blue eyes to anyone she knew and anyone conspicuously missing from the party for several long seconds.

She shook her head. "No, Daddy. I didn't recognize her eyes. I would've if I'd seen 'em before. They were that beautiful and looked so out of place in her half-wolf face."

Garrett pulled Paige into a hug and kissed her forehead. "That's okay, sweetheart. Ya did good, Paige-Turner. Ya did real good."

It wasn't a lot of information, but substantially more than he'd expected. The werewolf Ty killed transformed into a young man who Garrett believed to be in his late teens or early twenties, too. If they weren't Pine View High School students, and they were in their late teens to early twenties, they were most likely students at Stephen F. Austin State University in Nacogdoches. SFA had a substantially larger number of students, around twelve thousand, than Pine View High School, but it was a promising start. Especially if they got a hit on the young man's fingerprints. Garrett thought the initial pack was most likely composed of people the alpha knew. If he could get a hit on the fingerprints, he felt sure he'd be able to narrow the odds of finding the alpha.

Be in the system, you fucker, Garrett thought.

When Garrett released Paige, he looked at her. "Ty and I need to go check where you and Justin were attacked. Go wait in my SUV until we get back."

Paige shook her head. "No way. I'm goin' with y'all."

"Sweetheart, ya don't need to go. Besides, those things might still be out there. You'll be safer here."

In a matter-of-fact tone, Ty said, "They're gone."

Garret looked at Ty. "Is this one of your tunches?"

Ty shook his head. "No…I just know they're gone."

Before Garrett could respond to Ty, Paige said, "Ty's right, Daddy.

They're gone."

That Ty and Paige were certain they were gone, interested, and concerned Garrett. Both emotions were attached to the fact Ty and Paige already appeared to have some kind of connection with the alpha. There was no other reasonable explanation. On the interesting side, he thought they might use their connection to hone in on the alpha. On the concerned side, he thought the alpha might use the connection to hone in on Ty and Paige.

Still not completely convinced they could be sure the werewolves were gone, Garrett said, "How can y'all be so sure they're gone?"

Ty and Paige shared a knowing glance. Paige shrugged her shoulders, which lifted the bottom of Garrett's shirt a couple of inches. It wasn't enough to expose anything, but Paige quickly dropped her shoulders and tugged the bottom of the shirt back down. If they hadn't been discussing the connection between Ty, Paige, and the alpha werewolf, Garrett would have found the gesture comical. There had been nothing funny about their discussion, though.

Ty, oblivious to what Paige did because he stood next to her, not in front of her like Garrett, said, "I…we just know. It's like we're…"

"Connected," Paige broke in.

This had been exactly what Garrett suspected, and he pressed the issue.

"Can y'all tell where they are?" Garrett asked.

Ty and Paige glanced at each other again, as if they were hesitant to share this information with Garrett.

After several awkward moments of silence, Ty said, "No. I just know they're far from here."

"I do know she's mad," Paige added.

Ty nodded in agreement. "Yeah, she's pissed."

This information made the hair on Garrett's neck and arms prickle. He inadvertently rubbed his hands across his forearms, as if he'd caught a sudden chill, like someone had stepped on his eventual grave.

When the feeling of someone stepping on his eventual grave subsided, Garrett said, "Okay, I believe y'all. They're gone. I still don't think it's a good idea for you to go with us, Paige. Ya don't need to see this."

Paige took a deep breath. "I've already seen it, Daddy. I'll never be able to un-see it. I wanna go with y'all."

Garrett studied Paige for a moment. She'd changed in the last couple of hours and not just in the bitten by a werewolf way. Garrett thought an ordeal, such as the one Paige experienced, would have broken her. She seemed stronger of will than ever, though. He decided that wasn't necessarily a bad thing.

Garrett gave Paige a stern look. "Okay, you can come with us. But you're barefoot, so you're ridin' piggyback through the woods."

Paige got a horrified look on her face. "Daddy, no. I'm not wearin'…my butt might hang out."

Garrett laughed. It felt good to laugh again. "Well, I guess some forest critters will be seein' two moons tonight."

Paige's bottom lip protruded in a pouty gesture. "Okay, but Ty walks in front of us."

Ty broke into a full-throated laugh and, in an exaggerated ghetto dialect, said, "Girr, I don' wanna see yo skinny, white ass. I be likin' junk in my brown sugga booties."

At this, they all broke into uncontrolled, full-body laughter. The hysterical laughter was out of place, and several first responders and remaining students look toward the laughing threesome. At one point, Paige bent over at the waist and grabbed her knees to keep from falling over. Quincy Wiseman, who watched them laugh and wondered what the hell could be so damn funny, got his second 'cooter shot' of the night. Hell, it had been the second cooter shot of his life. Death and horror aside, Quincy thought the party ended on a high note.

After the Ty induced laughter ended, Garrett, Ty, and Paige walked over to where the MRB clearing ended and the woods began.

Paige pointed to a blood smear on a tree trunk. "This is where I came outta the woods."

Suddenly, the hysterical laughter they'd shared seemed to have happened in another life for Garrett.

Garrett removed the flashlight that hung on his utility belt and handed it to Paige. "Take this and keep it on Ty's back. I believe they're gone, but I don't want us gettin' separated."

As Paige took the flashlight from her dad, Ty retrieved a flashlight from his utility belt, turned it on, and pointed it into the dense woods.

Once Paige turned on Garrett's flashlight, Garrett said, "Let's do this. Saddle up, Paige."

Garrett squatted down to keep Paige from having to climb onto his back. When Paige wrapped her arms around Garrett's neck, she accidentally whacked him in the temple with the flashlight.

"Oops. Sorry, Daddy."

Garrett wasn't entirely sure it had been an accident. The whack might have been payback for the piggyback ride she didn't want to take. He said, "No harm, Paige-Turner."

He reached back, grabbed the back of her knees, and hoisted her onto his back.

Situation aside, it had been a long time since Garrett gave his little girl a piggyback ride, and it felt good to do it again. Paige seemed less enthused.

She placed her chin on Garrett's right shoulder. "This is *sooo* humiliatin'. I feel *sooo*…exposed."

Garrett, who kept his comments about what Paige and Justin had been doing to a minimum, said, "Well, Paige-Turner, ya should've thought about that before ya took your damn clothes off."

Paige knew her dad was right, she'd put herself in the situation, but she said, "I didn't know it was gonna turn out this way."

"No, ya thought you'd sneak out, have your fun, sneak back in, and that I'd be clueless."

"That was the plan."

"Well, ya know what they say about best laid plans."

Paige was silent for several seconds and then said, "Yeah, they got my boyfriend killed and me infected by a werewolf."

Hearing this response, Garrett let the subject die. He followed Ty into the woods.

As they made their way through the dense woods and thick underbrush, Paige pointed out several places where she'd tried to hide from the stalking werewolf.

At one of the first hiding trees they came to, Paige said, "This is where it knocked the cellphone out of my hand, and clawed my face, while I was talkin' to ya, Daddy."

Ty started sweeping his flashlight beam around the base of the tree and, within seconds, saw something reflecting in the light a couple of feet from the tree.

"Found it," Ty said as he reached down and picked the cellphone up.

When he pushed the 'Home' button, the cellphone instantly lit up.

Ty chuckled. "It still works. There's a new selling point for Apple. 'iPhones can take a werewolf attack and keep on tickin'."

They all laughed at this.

Who knew Ty was such a comedian? Garrett thought.

Paige held the flashlight in her right hand, but she immediately reached out her left hand, opened and closed it like a child reaching for something it desperately wanted. "Gimme, Gimme."

Although Paige couldn't see it, Garrett rolled his eyes. "Seriously, Paige? Ya need your cellphone that bad?"

Unapologetically, Paige said, "I wanna text Lin and make sure she's okay."

"You need to worry 'bout holdin' on to my neck, not textin' Lindsey."

With what sounded like pity for her dinosaur dad, Paige said, "Oh, Daddy. With textin', I can multitask like a pro." Before Garrett could respond, she added, "But never while I'm drivin'."

Paige was lying, but she only texted while driving slow and there were no other cars around.

Garrett wasn't sure he believed Paige, but he would have that conversation with her later, too.

Ty handed Paige her cellphone, and she saw the screen was lit. She had several texts from Lindsey. She quickly, but to the side where her dad couldn't see, tapped in her passcode, and tapped the 'Message' app.

She didn't have time to go through all of Lindsey's texts, but she read the last one quickly, 'I think u probably lost ur cell cause u were naked when I saw u. But I needed to text u. I hope ur ok!'

Paige quickly texted back, 'It was in my buttcrack! Jk! Just found it. I'm ok. I'll text u when we r done.'

Her cellphone dinged immediately with Lindsey's response of, 'Lol! OK.'

It took some maneuvering, but Paige leaned back enough to slip the cellphone in the left breast pocket of her dad's shirt. Even though the situation felt far from normal, clinging to her dad's back with her privates very exposed, having her cellphone back comforted her and made her feel more normal.

From a few feet ahead of Garrett and Paige, Ty said, "I can see a fire. We must be close to the pond, clearin'."

They were. Within a minute, they emerged from the woods into the still picturesque clearing.

The moon had been lower in the sky from when Paige and Justin were there earlier, but it still reflected off the calm, dark water. Paige looked at the moon with wonder. It was so beautiful. She knew if her dad and Ty couldn't kill the alpha in time, it would eventually bring about horrible changes. Paige involuntarily shivered.

Garrett felt her tremble. "You okay?"

Paige lied. "Yeah. I just got a chill."

Again, Garrett wasn't sure he believed her, but he let it go.

As they walked toward the tree house, they could see the fire reduced it to not much more than the decking floor, which still burned in several places. Remarkably, the oak tree, most likely aided by a wetter than usual spring, hadn't caught on fire. Some leaves on branches near the tree house were blackened, but the tree was intact. Garrett figured the old oak tree would, most likely, outlive all three of them.

When they were about a hundred feet away from the tree, Paige squeezed her dad's neck. "I changed my mind, Daddy. I don't want to see Justin again. Not like that."

Garrett and Ty stopped. Garrett said, "This is why I didn't want ya comin' with us, Paige. You want me to carry you back to the MRB?"

Garrett could feel Paige's chin sliding back and forth on his shoulder, which was an obvious sign she didn't want that.

Garrett started to say, "While we document Justin's death," but he thought better and said, "I'm not leavin' ye here by yourself while we…do what we need to do."

Paige loosened her grip on her dad's neck. "I'll be fine, Daddy. They're gone. If ya still don't believe me, listen for yourself."

This seemed like an odd request to Garrett, but he obliged her by listening for whatever he was supposed to hear. All he could hear were the usual woodland night sounds. Frogs croaking, crickets chirping, cicadas buzzing.

After playing along for several moments, Garrett said, "All I hear are the usual nighttime critters doin' their nighttime stuff."

"Exactly."

"Exactly what?"

"When the werewolves are around, the woods go unnaturally quiet." Paige said.

Before Garrett could respond, Ty said, "She's right, Garrett.

Remember, I told ya how unnaturally quiet it was at Carla Weaver's house when I was checkin' her dead pigs? It was quiet like that 'cause they were there…in the woods watchin' me."

Garrett considered this new information briefly and decided he believed them. He still didn't like the idea of leaving Paige unattended.

As if reading his thoughts, Paige said, "They're gone, Daddy. I'll be okay."

Reluctantly, but not wanting to piggyback Paige back to the MRB, or put her in a situation where she might see Justin's body, Garrett relented.

"Okay," Garrett said as he squatted down to let Paige slip off his back, "but let me know if ya hear…nothin' or sense somethin'."

When Paige's feet were back on the ground, she said, "I will. Go take care of Justin."

Garrett brushed her cheek as only a father can. "I will, sweetheart."

Then he and Ty headed for the large oak tree.

Because Paige told them where Justin had been killed, Ty concentrated his flashlight beam on the backside of the tree. The first part of Justin they saw had been his left hand, which had been fisted and splayed away from his body.

Ty took a step forward, looking intently at Justin's fist. "Is that…?"

"Hair," Garrett finished for him.

Coarse black hair jutted out from between Justin's fisted fingers.

Ty exhaled heavily. "The kid must've put up a hell of a fight."

Garrett had the same thought and found new respect for the boy who intended to defile his daughter.

Garrett and Ty took a few steps closer, ducked under a large, low-hanging branch, and got their first look at Justin's body. Like Paige earlier, Garrett had a hard time identifying the blood-covered white sticks protruding from either side of Justin's neck.

Without Garrett asking, Ty, who'd had a similar break in Afghanistan, pointed the flashlight beam at the sticks. "Those are his collarbones."

Garrett, remembering Paige told them the werewolf pulled Justin through the too-small window, figured the broken collarbones resulted from that. Paige telling them the werewolf grabbed Justin by the head and pulled him through the too-small window by it also explained Justin's face, which had four deep gashes going from his chin to forehead and was covered in blood. By Garrett's estimation, these wounds, while certainly painful and debilitating, weren't fatal. The fatal wound had been one Paige hadn't been able to tell them about. Not because it embarrassed her, but because she found it too painful to tell.

Ty's flashlight beam traveled down Justin's body and came to rest on the bloody region that should have contained his genitals. Although they didn't realize they were doing it, both men moved a free hand to their crotches and protectively cupped their junk.

After several silent seconds, Ty said, "It ripped his fuckin' dick off."

"Balls, too," Garrett added.

After several more silent seconds, Ty said, "That was on purpose. It…she…whatever the fuck ya want to call the damn thing, did that for shock value."

Garrett didn't disagree, but he added, "Or to send a message."

Ty looked crosswise at Garrett. "Message? What kind of message?"

Garrett took a deep, steadying breath. "That Paige is hers and it's the only one that can fuck with her."

Ty shook his head. "Uh, uh. That ain't happenin'. Fuckin' with me's one thing, but it can't fuck with Paige. We gotta find and kill this fucker, Garrett."

Garrett moved the hand he didn't realize protectively cupped his junk to his friend's shoulder and gave it a reassuring squeeze. "That's the plan, brother. That's the fuckin' plan."

When Garrett and Ty returned to Paige, she asked, "Was he burned?"

There were some embers close to Justin's feet, but the werewolf pulled him far enough from the tree that the falling debris didn't burn his body.

Leaving out details, Garrett said, "No, sweetheart. He didn't get burned."

Paige's second question was, "Why aren't you and Ty bringin' him back?"

"We still need to document the scene and we need help to bring him back. After I get ya back to the MRB, I'll send some folks to do both things."

Close to tears again, Paige said, "Will they be careful with him?"

Garrett pulled Paige into what might have been the one-hundredth hug of the night, and stroked her small, trembling back. "I'll make sure they are, sweetheart."

Sobbing, Paige said, "He tried to save my life, Daddy. He t-t-told me to run."

Garrett thought about Justin's balled up fist full of werewolf hair and pictured him grabbing at the werewolf to hold it back.

Garrett hugged Paige tighter. "I know he did, sweetheart. Justin's a hero in my book."

~ * ~

Garrett had no way of knowing whether that happened, but, as usual, his instinct had been correct. After seeing Paige's face in the busted-out window of the tree house and screaming for her to run, Justin, with his dying strength, grabbed one of the werewolf's hind legs and tried to keep it from attacking Paige. It had been a futile attempt, but it slowed the werewolf enough to keep it from getting to Paige in the tree house. The outcome would have been the same for Paige, bitten and infected, because the alpha wanted her in its' pack. Without knowing it, Justin's actions, gave Paige time to run and think. Using her silver crucifix and necklace on the pursuing werewolf, saved the seven students who were herded into the MRB from being turned. Justin had been a hero.

~ * ~

When the hugging and crying were over, Paige, without complaint the second time, climbed back onto her dad's back and let him piggyback her back to the MRB. By then, she was mentally and physically exhausted. She needed the support. Having her arms wrapped around her daddy's neck, and feeling his strong back pressed against her front, comforted her in ways she didn't know she needed comforting. She felt safe.

She thought back to when she had been younger, and Daddy piggyback rides were a normal event. Part of her, a big part, wished she could go back to that time. It had been so much easier. Boys, except for her dad, were gross and school had been fun back then. As a bonus, she wasn't a werewolf in waiting back then, either.

Or was I? Paige thought.

~ * ~

A nightmare she'd had when she had been eight or nine years old prickled the depths of Paige's consciousness. She couldn't remember many details; just that her mom had been dead on a bed in a pool of blood. Her dad had been standing by the bedroom door of his old trailer house unable to move, and there had been a large werewolf, that she wasn't afraid of, standing next to her. Paige remembered she felt rage like she'd never experienced. Deep, hateful rage.

The nightmare happened on a night Paige stayed at her dad's house. The dream scared her so badly she ran into his room and crawled into bed with him. She woke him up, and he held her until she fell asleep. Paige wondered how he'd react if she got scared and climbed into bed with him now. Would he think she was silly and tell her to go back to her room? Would he hold her until she fell asleep again?

~ * ~

When they got back to the MRB, Garrett let Paige slide off his back just inside the clearing because, as Paige put it, "I don't want anyone pervin' my backside."

Garrett told Paige to wait in his SUV while he 'buttoned things up.' Paige texted Lin that she was back before she'd taken two steps away from Garrett and Ty.

With Paige taken care of, Garrett and Ty found George Krats, the County Coroner, who made good headway in processing the deceased. Garrett told George about Justin's body and Ty volunteered to take a crew back to the tree house to document the scene and retrieve his remains.

Before Garrett left George, he said, "Take care of Justin's remains, George. He was Paige's boyfriend, and I promised her he'd be treated well."

George looked scandalized. "I *always* treat the dead with respect, Sheriff Lambert."

That George referred to Garrett as "Sheriff Lambert" wasn't lost on him. He offended George.

Garrett grabbed George's shoulder reassuringly. "I know ya do, George. I made a promise to my little girl and I'm passin' it along."

Before George could respond, and it looked like he intended to, Garrett walked away.

I don't have time to stroke your professional ego, Garrett thought.

Having taken care of Justin, Garrett headed for the remaining students. Crystal made good progress on getting the survivors home. There were only three left. Garrett didn't want to question the students about what happened. His deputies got their contact information, and there would be time for that later. He just wanted to check on them. They were, to borrow a term from Ty, 'shell-shocked.' Thankfully, aside from some bad dreams and a little therapy for post-traumatic stress, they would live.

As Garrett turned to leave the students, the small-framed boy who Garrett talked with earlier, Quincy Wiseman, said, "Can ya kill 'em, Sheriff Lambert? Can ya kill werewolves?"

Garrett knew Quincy and the other two frightened students he hadn't been introduced to needed reassuring.

Garrett smiled a friendly, reassuring smile. "Ya bet your ass we can, Quincy."

It surprised Quincy the sheriff remembered his name, but he thought it made him look important in front of his fellow students.

His small chest swelled slightly, and he said, "How? I heard they're harder to kill than cockroaches."

Garrett chuckled. "Silver, Quincy. Silver kills 'em."

"Ya sure 'bout that?"

Garrett bent over at the waist so he could look Quincy directly in the eyes. "I'm damn sure, Quincy. In fact, one of my deputies killed one earlier tonight. That's why there were three here instead of four."

At hearing there would have been four werewolves terrorizing them instead of three, all three students gasped. Garrett wasn't sure he should have shared this information, but he knew they were scared and in need of something positive to end the night on. He wasn't aware Quincy got his positive ending with a 'cooter shot' from his daughter earlier.

Garrett smiled. "We got this under control. Okay?"

They all nodded, and Garrett walked away.

Garrett had one last thing to do before he could take Lindsey and Paige home; check in with the DPS officers. From his years with the Sheriff's Department as a deputy and sheriff, he knew both DPS officers well. Steve Sweeten, a thirty-year veteran of the DPS, had a calm demeanor and a likable personality. Garrett felt thankful to see Steve when he rolled up on an accident or crime scene.

Jon Darling, a small man with small-man issues, was quick to excite and slow to reason. Garrett had a feeling Jon chose law enforcement as a profession because it allowed him to carry a gun and gave him power. Garrett wasn't thankful to see Jon roll up on an accident or crime scene.

Given Garrett's opinions of the two DPS officers, he approached Steve.

Steve saw Garrett coming, and stuck out his hand. "Some mess, huh?"

Garrett didn't disagree.

He shook Steve's hand. "That about sums it up."

Jon, who had been standing nearby and listening, said, "What's this bullshit about monsters…werewolves? I think they're all on crack…or meth. Werewolves my ass. How fuckin' stupid do they think we are?"

Of course, Garrett knew the truth, but was more than happy to let them think otherwise.

Steve ignored Jon. "I heard ya had two more killin's with similar MO's."

Garrett nodded. "Sad, but true. Russ Lomax and Carla Weaver were killed in similar ways. Lomax early this week and Weaver a couple of hours ago."

In a snide tone, Jon said, "Werewolf get 'em. too?"

Garrett chuckled. "One of my deputies, Deputy Jackson, took out one perp who was involved in the Weaver murder. He *is* very human."

Garrett stressed the present tense because, technically, the perp was currently human.

Steve considered this statement for a moment. "Then what the hell's up with these eyewitness accounts? What caused those wounds? I ain't never seen nothin' like it before."

"Drugs," Jon insisted.

Garrett had to be careful here. He had been comfortable with his previous technical statement. While he wanted the DPS officers thrown off the werewolf trail so they wouldn't interfere with his investigation, he wasn't comfortable lying to them outright.

Thankfully, Steve answered his own question when he said, "I guess it could'a been some deranged fuckers dressed in some kind of hairy costume or somethin'."

Jon added, "Yeah, with those Freddy who-the-fuck, from Elm Street, razor gloves on."

To this, Garrett added another factual statement, "Most of these kids were drunk or…" he looked at Jon to feed his theory, "on drugs."

Steve mulled this over for several seconds. "That makes more sense than werewolves runnin' around East Texas."

It relieved Garrett to hear Steve come to this conclusion.

Garrett stuck out his hand, which Steve grasped. "If y'all've got this, I need to get my daughter home."

While still shaking Garrett's hand, Steve said, "I forgot she was out here. We didn't have time to question her. Did she see anything?"

Garrett broke off the handshake and, keeping with his technically correct input, said, "She wasn't here, at the barn, when the others were attacked. She and her boyfriend snuck off for a little…romantic interlude. She's embarrassed and shook up. As a professional courtesy, I'd appreciate it if y'all leave her to me."

Steve had three daughters, all older than Paige, so he understood Garrett's concern.

He smiled. "Of course. You get her home. As a professional courtesy, let us know if she tells ya anything that might help us with our investigation."

Garrett smiled back. "Will do."

As Garrett had been turning to leave, Steve said, "Oh, and let us know what ya find on the perp Deputy Jackson took out. Lomax and Weaver are yours, but there's no reason we can't work together."

Garrett, without turning around, said, "Will do, Steve. And y'all keep me informed on what y'all find out here."

Garrett wasn't stupid enough to think the DPS and the Texas Rangers, when they eventually got involved, would not be baffled by the evidence, hair, saliva, wounds, and start entertaining suspects that weren't in hair suits with razor gloves—they had more advanced resources at their disposal than Garrett did. The longer they sniffed in the wrong direction, the better Garrett's odds were of finding the alpha and disposing of it in a way that helped Paige and Ty. He already had a deadline, June second, which would be the next full moon, and he had a feeling he'd need every minute of that time.

~ * ~

When Garrett finally climbed back into his SUV, he found Paige sitting quietly in the front passenger seat, looking at a sheet of paper. There were fresh tears on her cheeks.

"What ya got there, sweetheart?"

Paige handed him the sheet of paper. Garrett looked at it and saw a list of names with addresses and phone numbers associated with each name. At the top of the paper, Austin had written, Contact info for MRB deceased. At the bottom of the list had been, Justin Anderson, Matt Cooke?

The question mark next to Matt Cooke's name showed his status had been missing and presumed dead. Matt's body would be discovered the following morning by a hound dog named Molly, and the question mark next to his name would be removed. This would bring the official dead-count to fifteen.

~ * ~

When Garrett sent Paige to his SUV, he'd forgotten he'd asked Austin to leave the requested information there. Paige found the list on the driver's seat almost as soon as she got into the SUV and read it. Justin's name hurt the most, but it was a small school, and she knew everyone on the list. Some she cared for less than others, like Justin's ex-girlfriend Maggie Crawford, but none of them deserved to be butchered the way they were. Aside from losing Justin, what hurt her most was the thought she might butcher innocent people in the same manner in less than a month. She decided then, if her dad and Ty couldn't find and kill the alpha before the June full moon, she'd kill herself. She knew exactly how she'd do it. The same way she'd intended to kill her werewolf attacker. She'd swallow her silver crucifix and necklace.

~ * ~

After seeing what Page had been reading, Garrett said, "I'm sorry, Paige-Turner. I forgot I asked Deputy Turner to put this in my SUV. You, okay?"

He immediately realized that had been a stupid question. "Scratch that…I know you're not okay. In time, ya will be. I promise. I'm here for ya, twenty-four seven. If ya need to talk, cry, or just sit quietly."

Paige turned her puffy eyes toward her dad. "I know, Daddy. I love you."

Garrett grabbed Paige's left knee and gave it a reassuring squeeze. When he did this, Paige leaned toward Garrett and gave him a kiss on the cheek.

Kisses on the cheek weren't alien in their relationship. They kissed hello, goodnight, and goodbye. Garrett couldn't remember the last time Paige did so outside of those circumstances. The simple gesture of affection touched him deeply.

Garrett put his arm around her neck and kissed her on the forehead. "We'll get through this, Paige-Turner. Everything's gonna be okay. I promise ya."

"I know, Daddy."

When the tender embrace ended, Garrett said, "I'll radio Deputy Zimmer and find out how close to the MRB she and Lindsey are."

Paige held up her cellphone and flashed a text from Lindsey at him. "They're almost here."

Yours really is a connected generation, Garrett thought.

As that thought ended, Garrett saw headlights coming up the drive behind him in the review mirror. It was Deputy Zimmer's department SUV.

The moment Crystal's SUV stopped on the passenger's side of Garrett's SUV, Lindsey jumped out and quickly made her way to Paige. Similarly, Paige jumped out of Garrett's SUV and met Lindsey mid-way. They embraced like they'd been separated for years, not hours. When they did, the back of Garrett's shirt rose, and Paige's backside fell out.

Garrett quickly turned away and thought, *I've gotta get that girl some damn pants*!

After their embrace, Paige and Lindsey got into the backseat of Garrett's SUV. Garrett navigated the SUV out of the crowded MRB parking area and headed for Lindsey's house, where he would deliver her to her parents. He would have to break the news to them that their son, Justin, was dead. Garrett wasn't looking forward to this and it would be the first of fourteen such stops he would make that horrible night.

A few minutes into the drive, Lindsey said, "Mister Garrett, were those things really werewolves?"

Garrett expected this question and had an answer prepared.

Although he'd been purposefully vague, but technically honest with the DPD officers to keep them from interfering with his investigation, he didn't see the point in trying to mislead someone who had been there. By her own account, Lindsey saw little, because she had been hiding in Justin's truck, but she saw enough.

Garrett calmly said, "Yeah, Lindsey, they were. I don't think it'll help your folks, or anyone else, to tell 'em it was werewolves."

Lindsey didn't immediately respond. Garrett glanced in the review mirror and saw she was chewing on her bottom lip while she thought about what he'd said.

A few seconds later, Lindsey said, "Is it because they might not believe it and it would only make copin' with Justin's death more difficult?"

That response was exactly what Garrett had been hoping for.

Garrett said, "That's right, kiddo. They're gonna have enough to deal with without trying to comprehend what really happened. They don't need to be worryin' 'bout somethin' like this while they grieve."

Lindsey was quiet for a few more seconds then asked the next question Garrett expected. "What're ya gonna tell 'em happened to Justin?"

This question had been a little more complicated to answer. Much like the situation with the DPS officers, Garrett didn't want to be outright dishonest with Lindsey's parents, or any of the other parents he had to have similar conversations with. He had an answer ready, though.

"I'm gonna tell 'em that Justin and the others were murdered by several, yet unidentified, suspects. That the weapon used appears to be somethin' sharp, but we haven't, yet determined the exact nature of the weapon."

Garrett glanced in the review mirror again and saw Lindsey nod her head once, as if agreeing what he would tell her parents was acceptable.

Lindsey said, "They're probably gonna ask me what I saw. Should I lie to 'em?"

Garrett shifted his gaze in the review mirror so he could see Paige more clearly.

She was looking directly at him with an expression that said, "Yeah, Daddy. Should she lie to her parents?"

Garrett gave Paige a wink. "Absolutely not. Don't lie to your folks,

Lindsey. …Tell me what ya *actually* saw."

Lindsey thought about this for a few seconds. "Just big…shadowy forms. I couldn't make out any details, but I saw 'em do horrible things. One bit Brad's head clean off and another one ripped Maggie's heart out of her chest and ate it."

Lindsey told Paige about this while they were waiting with Deputy Zimmer earlier, but she still winced at the retelling.

After letting these details sink in, Garrett said, "You tell your folks what you're comfortable tellin' 'em, Lindsey. But," he added, "I don't think I'd want to hear those details if my child were murdered."

Garrett watched in the review mirror for Lindsey's reaction. When she nodded to herself again, Garrett felt relieved.

Over the next few minutes, Paige and Lindsey held a whispered conversation while Garrett drove.

When Garrett pulled off Highway Seven onto County Road Four Seventy-Six, which was the road Lindsey's house was on, Paige said, "Daddy, can I spend the rest of the night with Lin?"

Garrett expected this question, too. "I don't think that's a good idea, sweetheart. The Andersons are gonna be dealin' with family matters tonight."

Garrett expected Paige to protest, but Lindsey said, "Please, Mister Garrett. Paige is like family to all of us. My folks think of her like a daughter. Justin and I think of her like a sister."

That makes them bein' naked and about to jump each other's bones a little weird, Garrett thought.

Before Garrett could respond, Paige said, "If I can't spend the night there, what're ya gonna do with me? Leave me at your house alone, make me ride with you while ya tell the rest of the parents that their kids are dead, or take me to Mom's house?"

Garrett hadn't considered this. He thought Paige would probably be safe at his house alone. That the pack moved on like Ty and Paige said. He didn't want her to be alone after all she'd been through. He didn't want to take her to Lacy's house, either. If everything he'd learned about werewolves were correct, Paige's injuries would heal soon and he'd prefer to not have to explain them, and the remarkable healing, to Lacy.

Garrett planned to revisit the conversation he'd had with Lindsey, about being vague with her parents, with Paige later, as it related to questions her mom would have. Of course, given Paige's encounter, she would have more difficulty covering the truth without outright lying. If things went well, they would have until Sunday afternoon to work that out. Assuming Lacy didn't hear about the MRB Massacre, as it would be referred to in the Wednesday edition of the *Pine View Post* and come to his house to see Paige. Garrett planned to call Lacy on Saturday afternoon and tell her Paige hadn't been at the MRB when the killings happened, and she was okay. One more deceptive truth. He hoped that would give them until Sunday afternoon, when Paige left, to get her story tight.

With those two options unacceptable, that left having Paige to ride with him or spend the night with Lindsey.

Garrett thought about this for several moments. "I'll make a deal with y'all. Lindsey, after I tell your folks about Justin and answer questions they might ask, you can ask 'em if Paige can spend the night. But only once. If they say no, no beggin'…from either of ya. Deal?"

In unison, Paige and Lindsey said, "Deal."

Garrett remembered something important. "What 'bout clothes, Paige? You need to get some damn pants on."

"Paige and I are about the same size, Mister Garrett. She can wear some of my clothes."

By the time this conversation ended, Garrett was pulling into the Anderson's driveway. Their house was in a small subdivision. Garrett dreaded what he would have to do when they got there.

Their house was dark when he pulled up and parked in front of it.

Garrett, realizing he hadn't asked Lindsey an obvious question, said, "Do your folks know you and Justin were out? Did y'all sneak out too?"

Garrett looked at Paige in the rearview mirror as he asked the second question, and she glanced away.

"They know we were out."

That had been good news to Garrett. If they'd sneaked out to meet Paige, Lindsey's parents might have found some twisted logic in blaming Paige for the whole thing.

Garrett nodded. "Let me do the talkin'."

The girls nodded, and they all got out of the SUV.

As they approached the front door, the porch lights came on. For a moment, Garrett thought the Andersons would meet them at the door. As Lindsey fumbled with her keys, he realized they were motion-activated lights. He'd been planning to install some at his house. Given all that had happened that night, he decided to install motion-activated floodlights around his entire house. They would pick up werewolf movement too and some warning, no matter how little, would be better than none.

When Lindsey unlocked and opened the door, cool, air-conditioned air washed over them. The house was dark, comfortable, and quiet inside. Garrett hated he was about to turn their comfortable world upside-down.

From the years of friendship between Paige and Lindsey, he knew both of Lindsey's parents well. Her dad, Andrew, owned an Allstate Insurance Agency in Pine View and handled Garrett's auto, house, and life insurance policies. Her mom, Gloria, was a stay-home mom and one of the sweetest women Garrett knew. He wasn't looking forward to this.

After they stepped into the living room, Lindsey turned on the light and Garret closed the door. Lindsey started toward her parent's bedroom door, which was at the back of the house on the left.

Before she'd taken more than a few steps, a light went on in the bedroom.

The door had been ajar so Andrew and Gloria could hear their children come home, and Gloria called out, "Justin? Lindsey? Is that y'all?"

Lindsey stopped walking, and the tears started flowing.

She sobbed, "It's just me, Mom."

Garrett heard a commotion from within the bedroom and a couple of seconds later a very concerned looking Gloria emerged from the door. She had been dressed in nothing more than a nightshirt and, although she registered Paige and Garrett standing in her living room with a quick glance, she did not cover herself more.

She went directly to Lindsey. "What's the matter, baby? Where's Justin?"

She looked over at Garrett. "Where's Justin?"

When Paige started sobbing, Gloria shouted, "Andrew, get in here!"

A couple of seconds later, Andrew emerged from the door wearing nothing but his boxers. The situation was confusing. Garrett had to return order.

Once Andrew joined Gloria and Lindsey, Garrett said, with as much compassion as he could, "Gloria…Andrew, please have a seat."

As Garrett witnessed so many times in countless different

situations, people who are close to panic need someone to direct them, and they usually complied. The Andersons were no different. They sat on the couch and held on to each other. Returning order had been the easy part, next came the hard part.

Garrett told them Justin had been killed. Their reaction had been typical, if such a thing can be typical. There had been denial quickly followed by uncontrolled sobbing. Garrett thought Gloria's heart wrenching sobs would haunt his dreams every bit as much as the dreaded werewolf nightmare he'd had for the fourteenth time earlier that night.

When they were in control of their crying enough to speak, the questions Garrett expected came. He answered them in the manner he'd described to Lindsey and Paige on the ride there. They didn't press for more information and Garrett hadn't expected them to. He knew they'd have more questions later, but he'd deal with that when the time came.

When Garrett completed his business, only thirteen more to go, and the Andersons, although grieving beyond anything Garrett could, or wanted to, comprehend, Lindsey asked her parents if Paige could spend the night.

Gloria answered immediately, and Garrett had been glad to hear it.

She said, "Of course, she can. She's family."

Garrett thanked them, told them he'd pick Paige up in the morning, and offered his heartfelt condolences again.

Before leaving, Garrett called Paige to him.

He pulled her into a tight hug. "I love you, Paige-Turner."

"I love you too, Daddy."

In a quieter voice so the Andersons couldn't hear, he said, "Remember, don't tell Lindsey about the bite."

Paige nodded against his shoulder.

"If ya…sense anything…or hear, see anything, anything that concerns you, anything at all, call me."

"I will, Daddy," Paige whispered.

"This is very important, Paige."

"What?"

"Put on some damn pants."

Garrett felt Paige's body shudder as she suppressed a giggle, which, given the situation, would have been widely inappropriate. "I will, Daddy."

Garrett released Paige, gave her a kiss on the forehead, she kissed him on the cheek, said his goodbyes to the Andersons, offered condolences one last time, and left the house. When he got back into the SUV, he looked over the list of deceased to see how many names he knew on at least a semi-personal nature. Of the thirteen remaining names, Garrett knew eight of them.

As far as prioritizing them, one name stood out as needing to be addressed next—Brad Wells. Brad's dad, Earl, was a heavy machinery operator who Garrett hired to do many Pine View County work. Most recently to bury Carla Weaver's pigs. He'd shared pictures of the mutilated pigs with his son, Brad, who had now met the same end. Garrett put his SUV in gear and pulled onto Highway Seven. It was going to be a long night.

~ * ~

Paige sat with the grieving Andersons for several minutes. It felt good to be with people who shared her love for Justin. They understood her loss more than her dad did. Grieving or not, her lack of clothing became increasingly uncomfortable. Especially after Mr. Anderson put his arm around her waist and pulled her into a group hug. Though unintentional, the move caused her dad's shirt to rise, and she had been briefly exposed. Mr. Anderson's head had been down, and he had been crying when it happened. Paige hoped his eyes were closed because, if they weren't, he would've gotten an eyeful of her nakedness. That would have been bad enough, and her state of undress would certainly lead to embarrassing questions later.

After the group hug, Paige politely extracted herself from the Anderson family and stood up. Mr. and Mrs. Anderson didn't seem to notice her absence, but Lin looked up at her.

Paige grabbed the hem of her dad's shirt, lifted it a little, and mouthed, "I need clothes."

Whether Lindsey read her lips or took in the meaning of the hem grab, Paige didn't know which. Lindsey nodded and Paige took that as an affirmation of her intent. Paige made her way quickly to the stairway and ascended them two at a time.

The second floor of the Anderson's house had been Justin and Lindsey's domain. It was configured more like a separate two-bedroom apartment than an extension of the living quarters below. The stairway opened into a large living room area with a couch, recliner, coffee table, and an entertainment center against the right-hand wall that included a forty-five-inch flat-screen TV, Blu-ray player, stereo, and two gaming systems—a PS4 and an Xbox 360. The left side of the large room had a small dining area with a table and four chairs. The kitchenette had a small refrigerator, microwave, and sink. It also had cabinets with drawers containing dishes and silverware. There was a pantry stocked with many goodies to eat. Lindsey's only, and recurring, complaint about her and Justin's living space concerned their not having a dishwasher. Paige, who had a room, a nice room, at both her parent's houses, thought Lin's dishwasher bellyaching silly, but she didn't tell Lin that.

On the far right side of the second floor were Lin and Justin's bedrooms. Lin's on the left and Justin's on the right. A 'Jack and Jill" bathroom, the outer wall of which was the wall the entertainment center was against, joined their bedrooms.

The bathroom configuration resulted in embarrassing situations for the siblings over the years and Paige cracked up each time Lin conveyed one of these 'horrifying' stories. The problem was, to have bathroom privacy, whoever had been in the bathroom needed to remember to lock the other's bathroom access door from inside the bathroom, which is not something they always remembered to do, especially when in desperate need of the facilities. The toilet was in its own private room so they could use the sinks while one or the other had been 'taking care of business,' so to speak, but 'accidents' still happened.

As Paige made her way through Lindsey's bedroom into the bathroom, one 'accident' occurrence flooded over her. She was thirteen years old and spending the night at Lin's house. She and Lin were up late and talking about thirteen-year-old girl stuff and Lin had to pee. Paige stayed sitting on Lin's bed as Lin opened the bathroom door.

When the door opened, Paige heard Justin yell, "Close the door, dipshit."

Lindsey pulled the door shut and came running back to the bed with her hands over her mouth and giggling like a crazy girl.

When the giggling finally subsided, Lindsey lowered her hands, but not her eyebrows. "Justin's playin' with his wiener."

She fell into a laughing fit all over again. Paige joined in the laughter.

Justin avoided both for the rest of Paige's stay.

Remembering this brought a smile to Paige's face. She never told Lin, but she wished she'd been the one who opened the door on Justin that night. Thinking about Justin masturbating when Lin opened the door brought another, much more recent and much less happy, memory to Paige. Her holding Justin's detached, florescent green member in her hand after the werewolf ripped it off. Her knees went rubbery. She'd have fallen, but she grabbed the sink counter for support. The tears came again, too.

After several moments, Paige steadied herself and looked into the bathroom mirror. A stranger looked back. Her long, dark brown hair was a mess, and her eyelids were so red and swollen she was seeing through puffy slits. What she could see of her emerald, green eyes were roadmaps of bloodshot veins. The bandage on her cheek was black with dried blood and coming off. Paige took the bandage between her thumb and forefinger and peeled it off. She expected to see nasty claw marks and grimaced in anticipation as the bandage pulled free. There was dried blood on her cheek, but no sign of the claw marks.

Paige twisted on the cold-water valve and splashed water onto her face. There was no pain. She scrubbed at the dried blood, and it washed away clean. Her cheek had completely healed. Her tongue probed the inside of her check for confirmation. It was fine. She could make out four faint pink lines on her cheek where the claw marks had been, but, other than that, there were no signs the wound had been there. Paige felt sure the faint pink lines would be gone by morning.

Having seen this, Paige was eager to see the state of her other wounds. Lin had a full-length mirror on the back of her bathroom access door. Paige turned and closed the door so she could see herself in it. As she undid the buttons on her dad's shirt, she realized her hands were trembling. But why? The wounds healing before Lindsey, her mother, or anyone else could see them and ask questions had been a good thing. Why the trembling?

A little claw scratched at the back of Paige's mind with the answer. It scratched closer and closer to the surface as Paige undid the last button and her dad's shirt slipped off her shoulders and piled around her feet on the bathroom floor.

Paige studied her naked body in the mirror, and the claw scratched closer to the surface. She was dirty and covered in dried blood from many wounds, but the wounds were gone. The puncture wounds from the two-by-four with nails in it that stuck to her chest were healed and dozens of scratches and scrapes from her run through the woods were healed, too. The claw scratched closer still.

She remembered falling on her butt on the tree house floor door and how much it hurt when the trapdoor latch dug into her flesh. She ran her right hand over the place on her butt where the pain had been. Dried blood flaked away, but the skin beneath it was unbroken. The claw scratched ever closer to the surface of her mind. Finally, Paige stripped the makeshift bandage off her right arm, the arm that the werewolf's dagger-length teeth bit and raked. Most of the dried blood came off with the bandage and Paige swiped what remained away with a brush of her hand. Her arm had healed, too.

Like her cheek, Paige could see faint pink lines where the ragged wounds were. The little claw scratched its way into her conscious mind with the answer, and Paige's entire body trembled. She looked at her reflection and shook her head violently back and forth, which only seemed to increase the trembling.

She cried and sobbed, "No, no, no, no!"

The little claw that had scratched its way into her conscious mind with the answer, had been a werewolf claw—her werewolf claw. She wasn't trembling in fear or revulsion because her wounds healed so quickly—she was trembling with excited anticipation. She liked the fact her new affliction had brought about these miraculous changes. Not only were her wounds healed, she felt stronger and more alive than ever. She liked that, too.

Paige stopped shaking her head and looked at the stranger in the mirror again.

Will I like killing, too? Paige thought.

To Paige's horror, her reflection smiled, exposing fangs, and nodded at her.

Paige grabbed her mouth and felt her teeth—they were normal. She looked back at her reflection. She saw herself looking small and scared.

"I won't kill," Paige whispered to her reflection.

This time, her reflection didn't disagree with her.

When she was sure she could trust her reflection again, Paige took a hot shower that made her feel more normal, normal being subjective. After the shower, she dried off and wrapped a towel around herself. Because she hadn't planned on spending the night at Lindsey's, she didn't have her toothbrush or other bathroom essentials. She used Lindsey's deodorant and Justin's toothbrush. He wouldn't need it again and she'd had his tongue in her mouth, so it wasn't as gross as using Lin's toothbrush would have been.

When Paige finished with bedtime prep, she found herself in Justin's bedroom. She hadn't planned to go in there, but there she was. She looked around at all the stuff Justin would never touch or use again, and fresh, warm tears ran down her cheeks.

Paige took Justin's pillow in her hands, covered her face with it, and inhaled deeply. She smelled his shampoo, soap, and him on the pillow. She used it to muffle fresh sobs. When the sobs subsided, she put his pillow back and started to leave his bedroom, but she detoured to his closet and opened it instead.

Paige hadn't planned on looking through Justin's closet either but, once she had it opened, she knew exactly what she wanted. She moved the T-shirts along the closet rod until she found the one, she had been looking for. That it might be in the dirty clothes hamper never crossed her mind. It had been Justin's favorite T-shirt; a black T-shirt with three Minions on the front. Justin loved the Minions.

Paige dropped her towel and slipped the T-shirt on. Justin had been a big guy, and the shirt hung down to Paige's knees. Without realizing she was going to do it, Paige hugged herself as if she had been hugging Justin.

When she left Justin's bedroom, she looked back. Tears spilled from her eyes again. "I will always love you, Justin."

She turned off his light, shut his bathroom access door, and went back into Lin's bedroom.

Because she'd been commando long enough, Paige opened the top drawer on Lin's dresser and selected the least sexy white cotton panties in Lin's collection. They were cool and comfortable against her skin. Paige climbed onto Lin's bed and covered up on the right side, her side of the bed. She rolled onto her left side and closed her still puffy eyes.

She was tired, and the pillow was soft, but she couldn't fall asleep. When Lin came into her room a while later, Paige pretended to be asleep. She wasn't exactly sure why she pretended to be asleep, other than that she didn't want to talk or cry anymore that night.

Paige heard Lin in the bathroom, performing her own bedtime prep. A few minutes later, she felt the bed shift as Lin crawled in on the left side, Lin's side of the bed. She felt Lin cuddle up behind her. Paige felt safe. A few minutes later, she slipped into a troubled sleep.

Although she would remember the dream in the morning, she never reached REM sleep. What she thought had been a dream about a decrepit barn, anger, and pain had been Alexis' feelings and experiences being transmitted from the alpha to its newest pack member. The connection was still weak, but it would grow stronger as the June full moon got closer. Although it would horrify Paige to admit it, she would grow to enjoy the glimpses into the alpha's mind.

Chapter Nine

Garrett left the thirteenth house he had to visit and climbed into his SUV. After starting it, he glanced at the digital clock on the SUV's stereo. Five forty-eight a.m. glowed from the display. It was too early to pick up Paige from the Anderson's. After receiving the news their oldest child and only son had been murdered, Garrett wasn't sure any of the Andersons, or Paige, got much sleep. He reasoned, if they slept, it would have been late when they finally nodded off. Garrett wasn't about to knock on their door at six in the morning. He put the SUV in drive and pulled out of the Crawford's driveway.

As Garrett drove along empty County Road Five Fourteen, the sun was brightening the eastern horizon. He welcomed the sight. A new day meant additional problems, but at least the horrors of the previous night were behind him. Knocking on thirteen doors in the dead of night to inform sleeping parents their children would never return home drained Garrett. Some, the ones in shock, took it better than others. The visits were sandwiched between the two most brutal, which were the second and last.

The first visit, to the Anderson's, went reasonably well. The second visit had been Earl Wells, the heavy equipment contractor for Pine View County. He took the news his son, Brad Wells, was dead particularly badly.

After Garrett told him, Earl collapsed on his living room floor and cried, "My boy. My boy."

As Garrett tried to console him, he kept thinking of a scene from one of the Harry Potter movies he'd watched with Paige. Voldemort killed one of Harry's classmates, Cedric Diggory, and the boy's father kept crying, "My boy. My boy." Garrett didn't think he could ever watch that movie again. Seeing it in person made it too real.

Garrett visited Arleen Crawford last. Arleen was a widow. Her husband, Ben Crawford, died in a single vehicle accident on Highway Seven in 2010. It was raining, and Ben drinking. Not an ideal combination. To make matters worse, the tires on his 1978 Chevy pickup needed replacing. He had also been speeding. The DPS report put his truck going at least eighty miles per hour when it hit a thin layer of water in a road grove, hydroplaned, over-corrected, slid into a ditch sideways, his tires sunk into the rain-loosened soil, and the truck rolled; according to the DPS report, at least six times. Ben wasn't wearing a seatbelt and, ejected from the truck during one of those rolls. With all that going on, Ben still might have lived if the truck roof hadn't landed on his chest. The autopsy showed cause of death to be internal bleeding caused by a crushed sternum.

Garrett, then a deputy sheriff, worked Ben's accident and delivered the news to Arleen. Arleen had, naturally, been upset but, before Garrett left her, she said, "At least I've still got my Magpie." Maggie "Magpie" Crawford, who had been thrown into the bonfire, was Arleen's only child.

When, five years after telling Arleen her husband died, Garrett told her Maggie was dead, Arleen lost it. She wailed, she thrashed, she broke things, she fell to the living room floor, and cried uncontrollably. Garrett could get enough information out of Arleen to call her sister, Andrea, who lived in nearby Jacksonville. The news shocked Andrea, but she said she'd come right away.

After the call to Andrea, Garrett got Arleen into her bedroom, and into bed. He got her a glass of water from the adjoining bathroom, and Arleen drank it without putting up a fight. Garrett offered to stay with her until Andrea arrived, but Arleen insisted she would be okay.

When Garrett asked again if she was sure she wanted him to leave, Arleen sobbed, "I only see ya when someone I love dies. Please leave."

He did.

As Garrett pulled up to Highway Twenty-One, Karen Parker's, the eleven to seven dispatch, voice crackled over the radio. "Sheriff Lambert. They found Matt Cooke's body."

"Fuck all," Garrett said to the empty SUV.

Karen's voice crackled over the radio again. "Ya there?"

Garrett depressed the button on his shoulder-mounted radio. "I'm here."

"Ya need the address?"

Garrett depressed the microphone button again. "No. I know where they live."

Garrett stopped at the intersection of County Road Six Hundred and Highway Twenty-One. He wasn't far from the Cooke's house and at least it was west of his location toward Paige and home. He turned left onto Highway Twenty-One and quickly got up to speed.

As he rounded a corner, he saw a matte-black Ram pickup headed east on Twenty-One, toward Nacogdoches. When their vehicle passed, a pretty blonde-haired girl with big blue eyes, big enough to see while passing each other at a closing speed of around one-hundred and forty miles per hour, gave him a friendly finger-off-the-steering wheel wave. Garrett returned the wave similarly.

It's nice to see a friendly face after a night like this, Garrett thought as the pickup disappeared in his review mirror.

~ * ~

Paige awoke from a less than restful sleep, but she felt invigorated. Lin's alarm clock was on the other side of the bed from Paige, but she could tell by the purplish-orange light filtering through the slits in the blinds that the sun was just coming up. Lin and Paige were still cuddled close in bed, but they were back-to-back instead of spooning as they'd been when they fell asleep.

Paige listened to her best friend's soft, restful breathing for several minutes, hoping she might be lulled back to sleep by it, but sleep wouldn't come. Slowly, so as not to wake Lin, Paige slipped out from beneath the warm covers. The Andersons kept their air conditioning at sixty-eight degrees overnight and the coolness felt good. Paige silently stretched as the slivers of morning light turned increasingly orange. She walked to the bathroom and quietly closed the door.

With no window in the bathroom, and Justin's bathroom access door closed too, Paige found herself enveloped in cool darkness. It felt comforting. After her eyes slowly adjusted to the lack of light, she noticed a small, rectangular shape on the sink countertop she didn't remember seeing the night before. Paige turned the light on, winced at the sudden brightness, and looked back at the shape—it was her cellphone.

The cellphone had been in the left breast pocket of her dad's shirt she'd left crumpled on the floor, that now hung over the shower rod. Lin retrieved her cellphone, washed the shirt in the sink, and hung it to dry earlier that morning. Without thinking, Paige picked up her cellphone, pushed the 'Home' button, and eagerly looked for the morning text she routinely received from Justin. It wasn't there. As she looked at the screen, blank except for the time, six eleven a.m., the previous night's events engulfed her like a cold, wet blanket. Fresh tears spilled down her cheeks.

A few moments later, there was a soft knock on the door and Lin said, "Are you okay, Paige?"

Paige briefly considered telling her best friend she was fine, and she'd be out in a few minutes, but she didn't. Instead, she opened the door.

Tears were streaming down Lin's cheeks, too. They embraced and held each other while they cried.

After several moments, Lindsey said, "I can't believe he's gone."

Paige sucked in a sobbing breath. "I can't either. He tried to save my life, Lin."

They held on to each other for several more moments and Lin said, "What happened, Paige? What happened to y'all?"

Paige knew Lin would eventually ask this question. She knew her dad wanted her to lie to Lin about her encounter with the werewolf, but Lin was her best friend. Paige hid nothing from Lin before, and she didn't want to do so now. She was about to break a pinky promise.

It had been silly, because *Teen Wolf* was a make-believe television show, but she thought about how Scott McCall, a werewolf, and Stiles Stilinski, not a werewolf, remained best friends after Scott became a werewolf. Of course, those werewolves were nothing like the monsters that clawed their way into real-life. They kept human qualities. Paige felt sure her friendship with Lin could survive the truth, which Paige decided to tell her.

Paige hugged Lindsey tighter. "I'll tell ya. I'll tell ya everything. Ya gotta promise not to tell anyone else."

Paige felt Lindsey nodding against the side of her head then she said, "I promise. You know you can trust me."

They let go of each other, and Paige took a couple of steps back. She pulled Justin's Minion T-shirt off and put it on the countertop. Lin looked at Paige, who wore only a pair of her cotton panties, for several seconds.

Lindsey's eyes drifted over Paige's body, not sure of what she had been trying to show her. Then the mental image of Paige standing naked, trying to conceal herself, and covered in blood at the MRB flashed in her mind.

Was that Justin's blood? Lindsey thought.

Some of the blood might have been Justin's, but not all of it. Lindsey remembered the nasty, jagged wound on Paige's right arm and her eyes locked on it. Paige's arm looked fine. Lindsey's jaw dropped.

She looked into Paige's eyes. "What the fuck, Paige? Your arm.

Last night it was…shredded."

Paige held up her right arm and rotated it so Lin could see there was no trace of the wound left. Even the faint pink lines had vanished. Paige put the Minion T-shirt back on and stepped past the gawking Lin back into her bedroom. Lin followed.

They sat down on the edge of the bed and Paige said, "This is gonna be hard to believe."

Lin, who was sitting on Paige's right, took Paige's right arm in her hands, and scrutinized it. "It already is."

With Lin still looking at her arm in disbelief, Paige told her what happened when she and Justin left the party for the tree house. Paige told Lin everything except the part about being hit in the face with Justin's junk. Lin didn't need to know that. No one needed to know that.

Lindsey only interrupted Paige twice. Once to ask if Paige liked the way she and Justin fixed up the tree house. Paige told her she'd loved every aspect and thanked her for helping Justin do it. And once to ask if Paige and Justin had 'did it' before the attack. Paige told her they hadn't.

When Paige finished, Lindsey sat silent for several moments, digesting the information.

After a few moments, she said, "If those really were werewolves, and you were bitten, doesn't that mean…?"

Paige nodded. "That's why my wounds healed overnight."

Lindsey, without realizing she was doing it, moved away from Paige slightly. Paige noticed the move, though, and it hurt her heart.

Lindsey shifted uncomfortably. "Does this mean you're gonna sprout hair and fangs tonight and kill people?"

Paige wasn't sure how Lin would react to the truth, but she regretted telling her.

Should'a listened to Dad, Paige thought.

"No, not tonight. Not until the next full moon."

Lindsey looked skeptical. "How do ya know that? Some werewolf…insight?"

Things were spiraling away, and Paige needed to gather it together before it was out of reach.

She took a deep, calming breath. "Yeah, somethin' like that. The point is, I know. I also know if Daddy can find the werewolf that bit me and kill it before the next full moon, I won't change. The curse'll be broken."

Lindsey looked shocked. “Your dad knows you’re a werewolf?”

Paige shook her head slightly. “I’m not a werewolf yet. Daddy knows I’ve been infected. He’ll find it and kill it. I know he will.”

“If he doesn’t?”

Paige knew the answer to this question and, without hesitation, said, “I’ll kill myself.”

On hearing this, Lindsey’s doubts and fears evaporated.

She wrapped Paige in an awkward, sideways hug. “Like hell ya will. I’ll help. We’ll find that bitch and pump her full of so much silver she’ll be worth more dead than she was alive.”

Paige smiled, and hugged Lindsey back. “I love you, Lin.”

Lindsey chuckled. “I love your hairy werewolf ass too, PT.”

PT had been Lindsey’s shortened version of Paige-Turner.

Paige laughed. “My ass is *not* hairy.”

“Ya sure ‘bout that? I’ve seen a little ass-crack hair on ya. Like an ass Mohawk.”

Scandalized, but laughing, Paige said, “I do *not* have an ass Mohawk.”

In that moment, Paige knew she and Lin, like Scott and Stiles, would be okay.

With the awkwardness gone, and the friendship secured, Paige excused herself. She needed to pee and went back into the bathroom. Just as she was about to sit and relieve her bloated bladder, her cellphone, which was still on the countertop, dinged.

Again, forgetting Justin wasn’t there to text her, Paige rushed clumsily from the toilet. The white cotton panties were still down around her thighs when she grabbed her cellphone.

She pushed the ‘Home’ button and saw the text had been from her daddy. ‘You up and ready to go home?’

No texting shorthand from her dad. The clock read six thirty-three a.m.

~ * ~

Garrett turned off Highway Twenty-One into the Cooke’s driveway. As he stopped in front of the house, a woman, looking very disheveled and dressed in a fuzzy, pink night coat, came out of the house and rushed toward his SUV. The woman was Matt’s mother, Melissa

Cooke.

Like most of the parents he visited that night, the ones who, like Garrett, were born and raised in the Pine View, he knew the Cooks. They were a few years older than Garrett because Matt hadn't been conceived while they were still in high school, unlike Paige with Garrett and Lacy. He knew them from school functions and from around town.

When Garrett stepped out of the SUV, Melissa said, "Oh thank God. Have ya found him? Have ya found Matt? Darrell's been out lookin' for him since about three o'clock, but I haven't heard from him in about an hour. Where's Matt, Garrett? Where's my Matt?"

Garrett hated this part, and he hated the fact Matt's father, Darrell, wasn't there for Melissa to lean on when he gave her the bad news.

"Why don't we go inside, Melissa?"

When Melissa heard this, her eyes went wide. She clamped her trembling hands over her mouth, and muttered, "No, no, no, no."

Her knees went weak, and she fell. Garrett, having dealt with similar situations too often that night, got an arm around her shoulders and supported her weight.

"Let's go inside and call Darrell."

Melissa nodded and let Garrett lead her toward the house.

About halfway back to the house, Garrett heard a truck pull quickly into the driveway. He looked back in time to see Darrell's late model Toyota Tacoma pickup skid to a stop beside his SUV. Darrell bolted from the truck, leaving the door open in his haste, and rushed toward Garrett and Melissa. When Darrell got to them, Melissa fell against him.

Darrell wrapped her in his arms, and looked at Garrett with tired, worried eyes. "What's goin' on, Garrett? I can't find Matt."

Garrett avoided Darrell's eyes. Along with tiredness and worry, he thought he saw a hint of blame in them, like Garrett should have prevented whatever had happened to his son. "Let's go inside, Darrell."

Darrell hesitated for a few seconds. He and Garrett ushered the already grieving Melissa into the house. Once inside, Garrett helped Darrell get Melissa to the couch and Darrell sat down beside her. Melissa slumped forward with her elbows on her knees and her face in her hands. Darrell put an arm protectively around Melissa's hunched shoulders. Garrett remained standing.

He took a deep breath. "There's really no easy way to say this."

On hearing this, Melissa started sobbing and said into her hands, which muffled her voice and made it sound haunting, "Oh God, no. Not my Matt. Please God, not my Matt."

Garrett took another deep breath. "I'm sorry…but Matt and several other students were killed last night."

The muffled wail Melissa released made Garrett's heart hurt for her. She slumped further forward and would have ended up like a puddle on the living room floor if Darrell hadn't had his arm around her.

Darrell looked up at Garrett. "What happened? Was there a wreck? Was it the train?"

The 'train' question referenced the deaths of four Pine View High School seniors who tried to race a freight train to a crossing and lost in 2010. Several of the grieving parents asked the same question that night.

Garrett responded to that gruesome accident. The students, two boys and two girls, were crushed inside the crumpled pickup cab and it took almost six hours with the Jaws-of-Life and acetylene torches to extract their bodies. Garrett hadn't been the one who informed their parents. That unfortunate duty fell to Sheriff Oliver Henry, but Garrett thought explaining a train collision would be easier than what he had been, and currently was, faced with. It all came down to the tricky razor's edge dance he'd been performing since his discussion with the DPS officers. Don't lie but shroud the truth. He'd had lots of practice that night and launched into his well-rehearsed explanation.

Garrett told them Matt and the other students were attacked by unknown assailants, technically true, since he didn't know who the werewolves were, at an MRB party. He told them the weapon used wasn't a gun, also true, but he couldn't go into more detail; also true, as it was an active investigation. He told them the DPS took over the investigation and the Texas Rangers would most likely be involved. Garrett finished by telling them he would stay abreast of the other agency's investigations, and keep Darrell and Melissa informed. What he left out, and was unwilling to keep them informed on, was his parallel investigation.

While Melissa remained unresponsive, Darrell nodded in all the right places during Garrett's explanation of their son's death and didn't ask additional questions. Garrett expected this outcome. People accepted information coming from an official, especially one they know and trusted.

When Garrett finished, he offered his sincere condolences, shook Darrell's sturdy hand, gave Melissa's trembling shoulder a reassuring squeeze, said goodbye, and showed himself out. Once he was back in his SUV, he checked the clock. Six thirty-two a.m. It was still early, but he chanced a text to Paige to see if she was awake and ready to go home. Garrett clumsily typed the text. He wasn't good with the little electronic keyboard, or any keyboard. He used the 'hunt and peck' method of typing, but he refused to use the shorthand. He considered it lazy that Paige and her generation were so fluent in using it.

Garrett tapped 'Send' and, not really expecting a quick response from Paige, placed his cellphone in the console's cup holder and turned the key. No sooner had the SUV engine started than his cellphone dinged. Surprised, but pleased, Garrett picked up his cellphone, which hadn't gone to sleep yet, and read Paige's response, 'I am daddy. I luv u.'

Garrett smiled and, as quickly as he could, typed, 'I'll be there in a few minutes. I 'love,' that's how it's spelled, you too.'

Before he could put the cellphone down, Paige texted '♥' back to him.

Garrett put the SUV in gear and drove out of the Cooke's driveway.

~ * ~

Ty remained at the MRB crime scene until around six thirty a.m., at which time he climbed into his SUV and headed back to the sheriff's department. While at the MRB, he avoided any direct contact with the two DPS officers, Jon Darling and Steve Sweeten, because he didn't want to answer questions they might ask. There had been plenty to do. He helped collect the bodies and directed the seven tow-trucks. Tow-truck drivers were like vultures when there were vehicles that needed towing, in that they appeared from nowhere and hovered around the dead vehicles ready to take a bite when they could and collecting the personal effects of the dead and living left behind. So, it wasn't like he hid in the woods or shirked responsibilities. Ty made sure he worked in a different location when the DPS officers headed his direction.

Although Ty's shift wasn't over until seven a.m., and he could have stayed busy at the MRB until then, he wanted to get back to the department in time to change clothes. Ty kept most of his uniforms at home but, like most deputies, he kept one uniform in the department's locker room. Garrett kept a change of uniform in his department SUV, but

Ty hadn't learned that lesson yet.

This became 'normal' practice because deputies never knew if, or when, they would need a mid-shift change of clothes. The usual mid-shift clothing change culprit being vomit from a driver way too intoxicated to drive. Considering they routinely worked automobile accidents, assaults, and an occasional homicide, other bodily fluids, fluids that caused a change of clothes, played a role, too. On that morning, Ty wanted to change out of his bloody shirt so as not to upset his wife, Jasmine.

It was six fifty-one a.m. when Ty got back to the department. That had been good timing because shift change was about to take place and people would focus on things other than Ty. He pulled around the back of the department and parked next to 'Perp Parking,' which had been what the deputies called the covered parking space where people in custody were brought to be processed printed, pictured, ankle grab and probed, before being put into holding cells. Either the pink 'Drunk Tank' where overnighters were placed or private cells where those who presented a danger to themselves or others were placed.

Ty let himself in the 'Perp Door' and had been glad to see, while not empty, there were only two 'Jailers,' non-gun carrying deputies whose only job had been dealing with inmates. They were busy and paid no attention, other than quick glances and waves, to him. The locker room was at the back of the department too, and Ty slipped into the musty smelling room, encountering no one else.

Ty stripped his uniform and under shirts off as he made his way to his locker and inspected them. There were bloody holes where the werewolf's dagger sized claws punctured his chest and back. The collar of both shirts were black with dried blood. There was no way Ty was going to let Jasmine see the shirts, even after they were laundered. He removed his badge, a brass six-sided star with his number Two Hundred Fifty-Eight on it and tossed the shirts into a trashcan. The County would replace uniforms damaged in 'job-related' incidents, but he would have to explain the damage. Throwing it in the trash meant Ty would have to pay for the replacement shirt, but he preferred that to the alternative.

After depositing the shirts in the trashcan, Ty reluctantly approached the bank of mirrors that hung over a line of six white sinks. He didn't know what to expect, and he feared either of the outcomes, wounds healed or wounds still there, for different reasons. If the wounds were healed, as he suspected, because he didn't feel pain associated with any of them, that would confirm the legends were true and he'd been infected. If the wounds weren't healed, that wouldn't mean the legends were false and he wasn't infected. He would have to explain the wounds to Jasmine when she saw them.

The reflection that greeted Ty from the mirror didn't show any of his inward turmoil. In fact, Ty thought he looked younger and, although he wasn't in terrible shape, healthier. His neck and chest still had the remnants of dried blood on them, which obscured his view. He turned on the water, grabbed a paper towel from a dispenser that hung to the left of the mirror, wetted it, and scrubbed the dried blood from his neck. The brown skin beneath showed no hint of the teeth marks. After seeing this, Ty quickly scrubbed the dried blood from his chest. Those wounds were healed, too.

Because he couldn't easily deal with the wounds on his back at the sink, Ty quickly stripped down and took a shower. As he watched the dried blood liquefy in the water between his feet and disappear down the drain in swirling red whirlpools, Ty contemplated his future. Even before seeing his wounds were healed, he knew he'd been infected.

Shortly before leaving the MRB, he'd felt the alpha's rage. About what, he did not know, but he'd felt it. They were connected. As the last bit of blood disappeared down the shower drain, Ty made a vow to himself. He would use the mental connection, and the department's resources, to find the alpha bitch and kill her.

"You fucked with the wrong, black man, bitch," Ty said aloud.

His voice reverberated off the tiled walls and gave it an eerie quality.

Once showered and dressed, Ty checked his SUV keys in. Garrett drove his home. The deputies drove their civilian vehicles to and from the department. The seven-to-three shift deputies were abuzz with talk about the MRB and Carla Weaver. A couple of people threw questions at Ty as he tried to leave without calling undue attention to himself.

Both times Ty said, "Long night, bro. I just wanna go home, kiss my wife, hug my son, and get some rest. We'll talk later."

Because they knew Ty attended both scenes, or because there were other people to ask, Ty saw Deputies Stutter, Zimmer, and Turner through the briefing room window—they didn't persist in their questioning. Ty slipped out the 'Perp Door,' darted to the department's civilian parking lot, hopped into his truck, the same one he'd been driving when he witnessed the log-truck wreck that made the little blonde-haired girl, June, an orphan, started it up, and headed for home. Ty felt fantastic, and that concerned him.

~ * ~

True to his word, Deputy Mike Middleton got right to work on making the silver nine-millimeter rounds as soon as he got home that Friday night. His wife, Becks, short for Becky, had been asleep when he got home, which had been good. He didn't want to explain to her why he was using the silver she wanted to sell to make rounds he declined payment for.

The old silver musket balls were in a crate in the garage. Mike collected it, it was damn heavy, and hauled it to the shed in his backyard. The shed, Mike's version of a 'man cave,' was twenty feet by twenty feet, four-hundred square feet. It contained all his hunting gear, which included many guns and bows. Some mounts Becks wouldn't allow in the house. She didn't mind the regular deer mounts, but she hated the European mount, which were the skull and antlers. The shed had a potbelly stove for heat in the winter, a window-mount AC unit for the summer that Mike switched on high when he got inside, a fifty-inch flat screen TV, Becks 'allowed' Mike one football game per Sunday in the living room, the rest he watched in the shed, two over-sized La-Z-Boy recliners in case he had company, which wasn't often, a full-size refrigerator full of Miller Lite and Diet Dr. Pepper, and a coffee maker that Mike switched it on when he got inside too. For the job at hand, Mike had several reload machines with all the material he needed. Casings, shells, primers, wads, different shot sizes, different caliber molds, and gunpowder for bullets. As well as different materials like lead, metal, and brass to reload ammunition.

Mike started reloading his own ammunition while in high school. He started with a shotgun reloader moving up to rifles and pistols later. The sheriff's department supplied his official use of nine-millimeter ammo, but Mike loaded his own for target shooting, too. The biggest benefit of reloading shells, besides the cost, once he recouped the cost of the machinery, was being able to manipulate gunpowder grain beyond manufacturer specifications. Higher grain meant more velocity. Mike intended to pack as much gunpowder into the silver bullets as he could. He intended to cast them hollow point. This would ensure the round fragmented on impact, which would disperse the silver throughout the werewolf's body in the entry's vicinity.

Mike lit the potbelly stove. He didn't welcome the heat it would generate, but he needed to melt the silver musket balls for casting. He downed a Diet Dr. Pepper while he waited for the coffee to brew. Within thirty minutes, he drank two cups of black coffee and was pressing the first silver bullet into its metal casing. He added the primer, the small charge the firing-pin strikes to ignite the gunpowder and held it up to look at it in the light. It shone like a fine piece of jewelry in the harsh florescent light.

"See how y'all like this, you *nahual* motherfuckers," Mike said to the empty shed.

He placed the silver bullet in a nine-millimeter ammo box and started reloading another one.

Once Mike had a rhythm going, melting silver while he reloaded extra rounds, the process went more quickly than he'd hoped. As he worked, he lost all track of time and was surprised when Becks knocked softly on the door and let herself into the shed.

While most law-enforcement wives would panic upon waking and discovering their husband hadn't slept beside them, Becks knew Mike too well to panic. Twenty-five years of partnership marriage had a calming effect. She felt sure they had a connection that would alert her if Mike had been injured or dead. Still, after pulling her robe on and slipping her feet into fuzzy slippers, she peeked out the front door window for his truck. It was there. She shuffled into the kitchen and poured herself a hot cup of coffee. The coffee maker had a timer and started brewing at six thirty a.m., at which time Becks woke up without the use of an alarm clock. When she went out the back door, she saw smoke coming out of the potbelly stovepipe and, immediately, knew what that meant. Mike was reloading. She knocked softly on the door, so as not to startle him by walking in unannounced. She did this once and Mike jumped, spilling hot lead on the reload table. Becks let herself in.

Mike looked up at Becks. "Hey, pretty lady. Is it mornin' already?"

Becks looked around the shed and reload production process. Her eyes found the crate of silver musket balls and she could tell Mike went through quite a few.

Becks looked at Mike and, without a hint of sarcasm, said, "*Nahual* back?"

Mike, who just finished adding the primer to the bullet he worked on, held it up for Becks to see. "I think so."

Becks heard the several Great Grandpa Milton Middleton *nahual* story many times over the years of their marriage, usually when she brought up selling the silver. While she wasn't sure she believed it, she knew Mike did.

Becks nodded. "You be careful, Mike. I mean it."

Mike, happy Becks hadn't pitched a fit about the silver, smiled. "I will, pretty lady. Ya know I will."

Becks nodded again. "Ya want some breakfast?"

Mike nodded and, when Becks closed the door behind her, went back to work with the remaining melted silver.

When Mike finished with the melted silver, he had two one-hundred count boxes full of nine-millimeter silver bullets. He looked into the crate and saw he'd only gone through about a quarter of the musket balls.

That's a good start, Mike thought.

He cleaned up his work area, smothered the fire in the potbelly stove, turned off the lights, coffeemaker, and AC window unit, locked the shed, and headed inside for breakfast.

Mike fully intended to keep his word to Becks about being careful. After over twenty-five years in law enforcement, he knew he couldn't control what came his way. If it was a *nahual*, at least he'd be prepared.

~ * ~

It took Garrett less than three minutes to drive from the Cooke's house to the Anderson's residence. As he drove the distance, he couldn't help but think about how many times Matt and Justin made the same drive, eager to see each other and how they would never do it again.

Given his profession, Garrett knew life was fragile. Deputy Mark Harper, Garrett's mentor, when he joined the Pine View County Sheriff's Department and the guy who had been fucking his wife behind his back used to say, "Bodies are soft and so many things around us are hard."

Garrett saw this dichotomy in gunshot wounds, knife wounds, too many automobile accidents, and countless other incidents. He once responded to a burglary call and found the suspect, who fell through the attic of an abandoned house, impaled on a broken PVC pipe. He never imagined the 'hard' things would be werewolf teeth and claws.

Thinking about this brought Garrett's thoughts back to Paige and her predicament. Anger boiled his blood like lava and his knuckles went white as he strangled the steering wheel. The thought of his little girl turning into one of those savage beasts was incomprehensible. Garrett thought about the reoccurring dream of Monster-Paige, which he thought became a premonition, and wondered what it all meant. As he contemplated this, he turned onto the Anderson's driveway.

When Garrett pulled to a stop, he saw Paige come out of the Anderson's house. She was wearing an enormous T-shirt that had one of those yellow, goggled, cartoon characters on it and carrying her cellphone. She had his uniform shirt draped over her left shoulder.

Paige climbed into the SUV, leaned across the console between the front seats, and kissed Garrett on the cheek. "G'mornin', Daddy."

As she sat back in the seat and buckled her seatbelt, Garrett said, "Mornin', sweetheart." Then he added, "I thought ya were gonna get some pants."

Paige laughed, pulled up the hem of the T-shirt, which revealed shorts underneath. "Shorts are pants, Daddy."

Garrett nodded and backed out of the Anderson's driveway.

Besides the T-shirt and cellphone, Garrett noticed something else about Paige as well. The wounds on her cheek and arm were completely healed. His worst fears were confirmed.

Not wanting to deal with the elephant in the room or, more accurately, the werewolf in the SUV, Garrett said, "How're the Andersons copin'?"

Paige looked straight ahead. "Not good. I heard Missus Gloria crying in her bedroom while I was waitin' for ya to get here."

Garrett reached over and took Paige's hand in his. "How are you doin'?"

He felt Paige stiffen at the question.

After several seconds, Paige said, "Are ya askin' how I'm doin' 'bout losin' Justin…or how I'm doin' with the werewolf thing?"

Garrett considered Paige's questions briefly. "Both."

Paige sighed. "Not good on either."

Garrett squeezed her hand. "I can't do anything to change what happened to Justin, sweetheart. Be assured I'm gonna do everything I can to change the werewolf thing."

Paige finally turned toward Garrett and he saw fresh tears spill down her cheeks.

She took a ragged breath. "I know ya will, Daddy."

Garrett brought her hand up to his lips and kissed the back of it. He didn't let go of her hand until they stopped in front of his house.

Once they were inside the house, Garrett wrapped Paige in a protective hug and held her while she cried. It was the first time they'd been alone since the werewolf killed Justin and attacked her. Paige needed the release.

After several minutes, Paige pulled back. "Thank you, Daddy."

Garrett took her puffy face in his hands, leaned down, and kissed her forehead.

"It's gonna be okay, Paige-Turner. I promise ya. I'll find it...her and kill her before ya turn."

Paige managed a small smile. "I know ya will, Daddy."

Garrett smiled back. "How 'bout some breakfast?"

Paige smiled again and nodded her head.

While Garrett prepared Paige's favorite breakfast, buttermilk pancakes, she went into her bedroom and closed the door. She looked at her bed with the pillows under the covers to mimic her sleeping in it. Then she looked at her bedside alarm clock. It read six fifty a.m. She couldn't believe it had been exactly eight hours since she snuck out to meet Justin. It seemed like a lifetime ago.

Paige pulled the pillows out from under the covers and propped them against the headboard. She removed Lin's shorts and panties and put on her baggiest, most comfortable sweatpants. She pulled the elastic ankle openings up over her calves and rolled the elastic waistband down, so it was just above her waist. Paige tied a knot in the back of Justin's T-shirt, Lin told Paige she could have the T-shirt, but she would always consider it Justin's, so it fit more snuggly around her tummy. Finally, she ran a brush through her long, dark brown hair. There were fewer tangles than she thought there would be. After brushing her hair, she pulled it back into a ponytail she secured with a green scrunchie. Feeling more normal than she would have thought possible a few minutes earlier, Paige turned to leave her room. It was only then she noticed the note her daddy stuck to the inside of her bedroom door when he left to help Ty. Paige pulled the sticky-note from the door and read, I'll be back later.

Despite everything that happened, Paige grinned because she realized Pillow-Paige had fooled her daddy. Given her daddy now knew she used some kind of ruse to sneak out, Paige wasn't sure it would work again, but she thought she might try it again soon. Her daddy wasn't the only one who was going to find the alpha. Paige thought she might try to use the connection she felt with the alpha to find it herself.

Paige crumpled the sticky-note and tossed it, free-throw style, at the trashcan beside her desk in the far corner of the room. She sunk the shot.

Paige said, "Two points," to her empty room.

She went to help her dad fix breakfast.

By the time Paige got back to the kitchen, Garrett had been scooping the last of the pancakes from the griddle. Paige quickly set the table, and they sat down to a delicious and conversation free breakfast. When the last of the syrup had been mopped up with the last of the fluffy buttermilk, pancakes, Paige cleared the table.

Garrett got up to help Paige rinse the dishes, but she said, "I got this, Daddy."

"Ya sure?"

Paige smiled. "I'm sure. You gotta be tired. Get some sleep."

Garrett was exhausted, but he didn't want to leave Paige alone. Not that he thought she'd sneak away, he hoped she'd learned a lesson on that issue. He thought she might spiral into sadness if left alone with only her thoughts. He also knew he couldn't watch her twenty-four hours a day, seven days a week.

Reluctantly, Garrett said, "Are ya sure? I can stay up with ya a little longer, if ya want me to."

Paige nodded, which made her ponytail bob up and down. "I'm sure, Daddy. If I need ya, I'll come get ya."

"Okay. If you need anything…*anything* at all, wake me up."

Paige hugged him. "I will, Daddy."

When the hug broke, Garrett went to his bedroom.

As tired as Garrett was, he didn't think his troubled mind would let him sleep. He was wrong. He set his cellphone alarm for two o'clock, stripped to his boxer briefs, laid down on top of the covers, and immediately fell into a deep, dream free sleep.

Chapter Ten

After dropping off Dillon and Cole at their separate apartments, Alexis drove up picturesque Raguet Street. It was deserted on that early Saturday morning. She turned right onto Bostwick Street. Her house, the house her dad bought for her to live in while attending SFA, was only about a half-mile from the university and nestled at the end of the dead-end street in a thick growth of trees. When she pulled into the driveway, she clicked the garage door opener clipped to the driver's side visor and waited for the garage door to open. After the garage door opened, Alexis drove the Ram pickup inside and parked it next to her silver Mercedes-Benz CLS Coupe. Alexis pushed the garage door opener again, got out of the truck, and ducked under the garage door before it rattled all the way down. With the truck safely out of sight, Alexis went through the backyard fence gate to the back door of her house. Her keys jingled softly as she inserted the house key in the deadbolt, twisted it, and let herself inside.

~ * ~

The house was far from the mansion she'd grown up in, but it was nice and, compared to an average Nacogdoches house, spacious. Twenty-two hundred square feet of living space, which included a large master bedroom and attached bathroom, two guest bedrooms that shared a bathroom, a study, a large living room, formal dining room, island kitchen with granite countertops, and a game room that had a bar, pool table, and half-bath. The back yard had a covered patio and a five-person hot tub Alexis liked to soak in year-round.

To make the house a home, her dad let her splurge on the credit card. She had all new stainless-steel appliances, plush leather furniture, a sofa, loveseat, and recliner, solid oak furniture, a dining, coffee, sofa, and end tables, nightstands, headboard, desk, bookshelves, and file cabinets, a seventy-inch flat screen TV mounted on the living room wall and a fifty-inch flat screen TV mounted on the wall in her bedroom, Bose surround-sound systems for both TVs, and a queen-size Tempur-Pedic bed that, much like the hot tub, Alexis liked to lie on year-round, too.

When the back door opened, cool air bathed Alexis. Cool air that chilled the sweat on her skin. She stepped into the house and shut the door. All the blinds were closed, and the house was cool and dark within. Just how Alexis liked it. After twisting the back door deadbolt into the locked position, Alexis moved into the kitchen and opened the refrigerator door. More cool air rushed over her body. She reached inside and withdrew a twenty-ounce bottle of Dasani water. Alexis didn't think Dasani tasted different from other bottled water, but it sounded fancier. She downed it in several hungry gulps. Turning always made her thirsty and, after the second turn to put Cole in his place, she'd been exceptionally thirsty. Even after downing two sixteen-ounce Dasanis on the ride home, her thirst persisted. Alexis retrieved another twenty-ounce bottle and drank half of it in a few swallows. She held the chilled bottle against her neck and savored its coolness for several moments. She drank the rest of the water, closed the refrigerator, placed the empty plastic bottles in the blue recycle bin under the kitchen sink, saving the world one plastic bottle at a time, and exited the kitchen.

As Alexis walked through the cool, dark house toward her bedroom, she started removing her confining clothing. Alexis had never been modest. She was proud of her body and enjoyed showing it off. Since her first turn in April, she found clothing, all clothing, constricting. She preferred the nakedness of her wolf form to her clothed human form. In fact, she preferred everything about her wolf form, except the sex.

As a human, Alexis felt empowered by sex. She could get men to do anything for an opportunity to get their cocks wet. After her first turn, Alexis wanted to experience wolf sex. The promised animalistic nature of it appealed to her. If she hadn't turned Dillon and Cole before Seth's first change, it might have gone differently, but the four of them changed together in the old barn.

Alexis saw Cole eyeing her naked human body before the change and smelled his lust for her wolf's body after the change. Her wolf brain had given into the animalistic urges and, after she coupled with Seth's wolf, she let Cole's wolf take her, too. Cole's wolf clawed at her back and bit her shoulder as it fucked her. She knew he had been trying to dominate her, but the human part of her wolf brain, so unlike her true human self, liked that she was being fucked like a mutt. She hated that she'd liked it.

After Cole, she let Dillon's wolf take her, too. Dillon's wolf had been timid and, if she hadn't been so disgusted with herself for liking the way Cole's wolf humiliated her, she might have grown to like wolf sex. She fully intended to give Seth another go when they could turn without the others, but Seth was dead, and she'd never give herself to the pack again. Especially since Cole already challenged her alpha status.

That was why the little bitch she'd turned had been so important. Alexis hoped Cole's wolf would take its sexual frustrations and aggressions out on the new pack-bitch, fuck-toy. After all, a satisfied wolf doesn't cause trouble.

Alexis just needed to keep Cole's wolf obedient until the June full moon. After the dominant display she put on in the barn that morning, when she transformed back into a werewolf quickly and without pain and knocked Cole's half-transformed wolf across the barn, she didn't think he'd give her much trouble until then.

~ * ~

These thoughts were whirling around Alexis' mind as she walked toward her bedroom, leaving a trail of clothes on the floor behind her. When she got to her closed bedroom door, she slipped her panties down around her knees and let gravity take them from there. She opened her bedroom door and stepped out of her panties into her cool, dark bedroom. Her bed called to her. She stretched out on top of the covers and felt her naked body sink into the memory-foam mattress.

Alexis thought about the little bitch who hurt her wolf with the silver necklace, and she scowled. She smiled just thinking about the pain and humiliation the future held for the little bitch. The smile slowly slid from Alexis' face as she fell asleep. A short while later, Alexis' conscious mind sunk into the memory-foam of her subconscious mind. She dreamed about the night she and Carlos went to Mexico to buy two thousand Ecstasy pills from *El Lobo*. The night Alexis had been attacked and turned.

~ * ~

The drive from South Padre Island to Hidalgo took longer than Alexis thought it would, about an hour and a half. This gave her time to go over her distribution plans for the eighth or ninth time. The good thing about Ecstasy, with the pills being small, they were easy to conceal. The previous year, she stashed individual cellophane wrapped pills in her bikini top under her breasts and more individually cellophane wrapped, but condom encased, pills in a place that only an intrusive strip-search would locate. Once she exhausted the bikini top supply, she would find a restroom and restock the bikini top, and no one had been the wiser as to the pill's previous location. Alexis thought she could charge her male customers more for the product if they knew they were stashed inside her, but she kept that information to herself. Her trade secret.

The bikini distribution system worked well on the beach during the day, but she moved most of the Ecstasy in the clubs at night. The club distribution system worked much the same, pills stashed in the same locations, but she stuffed the condom with more pills. Unlike the beach, Alexis usually wore a button-up blouse open and tied around her midriff to the clubs. The blouse afforded some extra concealment of her breasts, which allowed Alexis to carry more pills in the bikini top, too.

The beach and clubs always had law enforcement personnel in the vicinity. They were thick on the beach looking for underage drinking, fights, and drugs. Initially, this made Alexis very uncomfortable. She was sure the stuffed condom made her walk funny, and the cops were watching her every move. She wasn't walking funny, and they weren't paying any more attention to her. Except a few horny Beach Patrol officers who watched her upside-down heart-shaped ass walk away from them.

Alexis learned something interesting about herself from the last Spring Break. She had always been good at being the center of attention when she wanted to be, but she had been equally good at blending in and being anonymous when she wanted to be, too. So good, in fact, when she got over her initial concern cops were watching her every move, she sold all two hundred pills by ten p.m. on the first day. This inspired her to go bigger Spring break 2015.

~ * ~

Ahead of Alexis by a couple of car lengths, Carlos exited Highway Two and turned south onto Spur One Fifteen; Alexis followed. About fifteen minutes later, they drove into Hidalgo. Alexis followed Carlos' rust-bucket truck into the Walmart parking lot and parked toward the front, by the store under a bright light, but in the middle. Carlos stopped his truck several rows back and waited for her. Alexis retrieved the Tumi leather tote that contained the fifty-five thousand dollars, locked her car, looked around to see if anyone paid undue attention to her, and walked the fiftyish feet from her CLS Coup to Carlos's shitty truck.

The truck looked even shitter under the harsh, florescent parking lot lights. It was a 1970, long-bed, four-wheel-drive Chevy pickup. At one time, it had been light blue with a white strip down the side and a white roof. The blue and white paint oxidized. There were extensive areas of surface rust on the hood, roof, bed rails, and along the bottom of the truck body. The passenger door and tailgate were primer gray. About the only thing that looked worth a shit, to Alexis, were the wheels and tires. Alexis was familiar with this odd combination; a five-hundred-dollar vehicle with five thousand dollars' worth of wheels and tires. Another aspect of Carlos' truck that caught her attention was the way it shined, even the rusted areas, in the parking lot light, but she didn't give it much thought.

When Alexis pulled on the door handle, which she thought might fall off in her hand, nothing happened. The door had been locked. She started to tell Carlos to unlock the door when she heard the unmistakable 'thunk' of an electric door lock engaging and she saw the lock pop up on the top of the door panel. Alexis thought it odd that an old shitty truck would have working electric locks, but she didn't dwell on it. She pulled the door open, put the tote on the nicely carpeted floorboard, and climbed inside.

Once inside, her opinion of Carlos' shitty truck popped like an oversized soap bubble. The interior of the truck had been immaculate and far from shitty. There were electric lock and window controls on the door panels. The bucket seats were plush, tan leather that cradled Alexis' ass like soft old hands. The dashboard, headliner, console top, and door panels were covered in the same tan leather. The metal parts of the interior were painted satin black and accented where there had been room, glove box, ashtray, and under the steering column, with tastefully done pinstripes that were the same color as the leather. The steering column had an after-market with tilt and a satin black, three-spoke, leather wrapped steering wheel. The dashboard had an all-digital display, which lit up the driver's side of the truck in a soft, orange glow. The stereo had been turned down low, but Alexis could feel the thump of a deep base coming from the subwoofer behind the console and the in-dash radio displayed the bobbing orange lights of a ten-band equalizer with a spectrum display.

Carlos grinned; his gold grill glinted all that much more gold in the orange glow. "You look surprised, *chica*."

Alexis looked around the truck cab again, her mouth slightly opened. "I am. I thought this was a piece of shit."

Carlos' grin widened, and he said, "This in my incognito-mobile."

Alexis didn't understand and said nothing.

Carlos, realizing she wasn't getting it, explained, "When cops see me drivin' this shitty lookin' truck, they don't think drug dealin' gangbanger. They think I'm some poor ranch hand fuck and don't give me a second thought. What they don't know…and you either, is that it's all camouflage. Even the fuckin' rust is fake. It's painted on and clear-coated over, and the goodies don't stop with the interior. I tricked this bitch from the ground up.

"The frame is boxed, and powder coated. I got anti-lock disc brakes on all four wheels. Air ride suspension…I bet this bitch rides better than your Merc. The real magic is in the drivetrain. I got an Edlbrock, Musi five-fifty-five under the hood…six-hundred and seventy-six HPs outta the crate. Hooker headers addin' to the HPs. An on-the-fly, four-wheel-drive transfer case and a turbo four-hundred tranny puttin' the HPs to the tires. This bitch will outrun most cops on the road and everything off the road."

Alexis did not know what anything Carlos just said meant, but she knew enough to be impressed. She no longer doubted his truck was worth as much, or more, than her CLS Coupe. She'd suffered through enough of Seth's custom car TV shows, *Counting Cars* had been Seth's favorite, to know customizations on old trucks could run as much as a hundred thousand dollars, or more. Above all else, Carlos' ruse impressed Alexis. She had been close to the truck frequently and never gave it more of a thought than to wonder why Carlos didn't drive something nicer. She could see how cops, who would see it in passing on the road, wouldn't give it a second thought. Alexis felt better about Carlos' judgment and his *El Lobo* connection.

Satisfied he'd impressed Alexis with his truck, Carlos turned the steering column key and started the truck. The high-performance motor rumbled under the hood like an angry beast. When Carlos shifted the transmission to drive, the back end of the truck sank as the low-end torque fought against the resistance of the disc brakes. Carlos lifted his foot off the brake pedal and the truck, idling, lurched forward quickly. After navigating through the Walmart parking lot, Carlos turned north on Spur One Fifteen and quickly sped up to just under the posted fifty-five miles an hour speed limit. Aside from driving the 'incognito-mobile,' Carlos knew the best way to avoid encounters with law enforcement was to not give them a reason to encounter him. To, literally, stay under the radar.

After driving north on Spur One Fifteen several miles, Carlos turned onto West Military Highway. Although designated a 'Highway,' West Military was little traveled late at night and the road had been empty. Carlos made drug runs in this area for years and relied on the lack of traffic to facilitate them. When West Military curved north, Carlos slowed and looked for his exit. He marked the spot with an empty Budweiser carton earlier that day. He spotted the marker, shifted the transfer case into four-wheel-drive high, and turned south.

To Alexis, it looked like Carlos was turning south into an overgrown field. After the truck, which rode as well as her CLS Coupe, crested a small rise several feet off the paved road, she saw a rutted path cut through the rugged terrain. The truck navigated the rutted path with ease and, several minutes later, they crested another rise. When the headlights dipped down on the other side of the rise, Alexis saw water. It was the Rio Grande River.

Carlos slowed to a crawl and looked for another marker, a cow skull placed atop a rusted t-post on the sandy bank of the river. This marker showed a narrow and shallow spot in the river that mules and coyotes, smuggling drugs for the former and illegal immigrants for the latter, had lined the bottom of with reject concrete. Concrete that is jack-hammered from construction sites and disposed of. This resulted in a crude surface, but Carlos' truck traversed it easily. Carlos spotted the cow skull, which marked the north side of the makeshift, under water passage, shifted the transfer case into four-wheel-drive low, and turned toward the water.

To Alexis, it looked like Carlos was about to drown them.

She gripped the door handle, ready to jump out. "What the fuck, Carlos."

Carlos laughed. "Relax, *chica*. I know what I'm doin'."

As he finished saying this, the front tires sank into the muddy riverbank. They spun briefly and found traction on the reject concrete.

The tricky part was staying on the underwater road. The Rio Grande River, at that point, was mocha colored, running water. This worked well to conceal the reject concrete, underwater road, but it also made seeing it impossible. If you knew what to look for, slight ripples in the water caused by it flowing over the uneven and shallow concrete, it was possible. Carlos, who traversed it many times, knew what to look for.

Alexis was more than a little surprised when the truck started across the river with no difficulty. She lowered the passenger window and look out and down at the muddy water that was about half-way up the big tires and well below the bottom of the truck's body. Although the truck's air-ride suspension, geared for off-road driving, made the ride relatively smooth as they crossed the water, Alexis could feel the truck dip and sway as the terrain of whatever the tires were rolling over changed.

Alexis pulled her head back inside the truck and looked at Carlos. "What the hell are we driving on?"

Carlos grinned. "It's an underwater road."

Then, just to tease Alexis, he added, "As long as none of it has washed away, we'll be fine."

Alexis gripped the door handle again, but it wasn't necessary. A few seconds later, the front tires sank into the riverbank mud on the south side of the river and the truck drove onto the muddy shore—they were in Mexico.

Several questions were bouncing around inside Alexis' mind. Who built it? How did he know Border Patrol wouldn't be watching? Did it wash out often? She settled on, "Where to now?"

Carlos, sitting forward watching the river ripples as they crossed, eased back in his bucket seat. "Get comfy; we still gotta a little way to go."

Alexis, nervously sitting forward too, relaxed into the soft leather bucket seat, and started mentally counting her eventual profits.

I can't believe how easy this has been, Alexis thought.

After leaving the riverbank, Carlos drove up onto another rutted road and turned west. The rutted road ran parallel to the Rio Grande River. Alexis could see lights and cars traveling roads on the American side, but the Mexican side looked dark and deserted.

For reasons Alexis couldn't quite understand, her arms broke out in goose bumps. She knew it was crazy, but she felt like something in the Mexican darkness had been watching them, tracking them. She let out an unsteady breath and tried to relax, but the feeling wouldn't leave. Then she saw what looked like two red eyes, or slits, flicker in the darkness several hundred feet in front and to the left of Carlos' truck.

"What the fuck was that?" Alexis snapped.

Carlos, thinking she might have seen some sign of law enforcement, stopped the truck. "What? Where?"

Alexis pointed out into the darkness. "I saw something…eyes in the darkness."

Carlos relaxed and chuckled. "Mexico is full of critters, *chica.* Eyes reflect light. Do that again…and I'll throw your skinny white ass out for whatever it is to feed on. Not much of a meal, though, *chica.* You skinny white girls need a little more junk in the trunk. I can feast on a big, round *culo* for days."

He took his foot off the brake and drove on into the velvet darkness.

The sexual innuendo wasn't lost on Alexis, but she ignored it. "They weren't like any eyes I've ever seen and your lights weren't on them."

Carlos chuckled. "I bet you saw a lot of wild critters growin' up in Houston. Relax, we're almost there."

The sarcasm wasn't lost on Alexis either but, this time, she didn't ignore it.

"I went on a wild-game safari with my dad in Zimbabwe in twenty-twelve. We saw all kinds of *critters* and spotlighted at night. None of them had red eyes."

When Alexis said 'red eyes,' she saw Carlos tighten his grip on the steering wheel.

"You know something about these red eyes?"

Carlos chuckled again, but it sounded forced to Alexis.

"What aren't you telling me?" Alexis asked.

Carlos relaxed his grip on the steering wheel. "This ain't Africa, *chica.* Don't worry 'bout what ya *think* you saw. It was probably a faraway fire flickerin'. You can see for miles out here."

Alexis still thought Carlos kept something from her. Something he didn't want her to know.

As she started to peruse the conversation further, Carlos pointed over the steering wheel to the front and left, in the same general area where Alexis saw the eyes. "There's where we're goin'."

Alexis peered into the ink black distance and, at first, saw nothing. The truck crested a rise, and she saw the outline of a darker black structure. It looked like a shadow within a shadow. The only thing that gave it any life at all had been a faint orange light that glowed in what must have been a window.

Carlos slowed, then stopped. "I get my dime now."

Alexis bristled. "Not until the deal's done."

Carlos flashed his orange, dashboard lit grill at Alexis. "I ain't playin' with ya, *puta*. Hand over my dime now…or I take it and leave your safari huntin', spoiled, white ass here. Your choice."

Alexis didn't consider it much of a choice and she had no doubt Carlos meant it. His dangerous side showed occasionally, and Alexis knew better than to push her luck. She unzipped the tote, took out two five-thousand-dollar bundles, and, because she thought she needed to show some backbone or risk crying, threw them at Carlos a little harder than necessary.

As Carlos picked up the bundles that landed on the floorboard, Alexis said, "I suppose you want to count it."

Carlos smiled at Alexis, not the evil grin, but still dangerous. "It's all good, *chica*. B'sides…if ya fuck me on the money, I'm gonna fuck that skinny little ass of yours with one of my *pistolas*."

Slipping into his Tex-Mex, gang-banger accent, said, "Jou wouldn't like that, *puta*."

Carlos had been right. She wouldn't like that at all—especially if the climax resulted in Carlos shooting his pistol's load deep in her ass. That would be killer anal sex—literally. To defuse the situation, Alexis took a third five-thousand-dollar bundle, her spending money, from a side pocket of the tote and handed it to Carlos.

Carlos, genuinely surprised, said, "What's this for?"

Alexis smiled the smile that made most men want to fuck her on the spot. "Call it pistol, ass-rape insurance."

Carlos laughed out loud, a real, unforced laugh. "You got it, *puta*. When we're done, I'll trade ya this nickel for a real shot at your ass."

Five thousand dollars to let Carlos in her back door had been a tempting offer. Alexis wasn't a stranger to anal-sex and even enjoyed it, as well as the begging before letting it happen. She knew Carlos would shoot a less lethal, condom protected load within minutes, if not seconds. It would be a pretty good return on her time. Alexis had principles, though. No sex for money. Fucking Seth after he gave her a nice watch was different, in Alexis' mind.

With that same come-fuck-me-smile on her face, Alexis said, "That's not nearly enough. My perfect, tight ass is worth more than this whole deal."

Carlos grinned a friendly grin. "Ya know what, *chica*? I believe ya. Let's go buy some X."

Before Carlos started driving again, he reached behind the console. Alexis heard a 'click' then the whole console pivoted forward, revealing a hidden compartment beneath.

Without Alexis asking, Carlos explained, "Hidden compartment on top of the transfer case. Can't see it from below and it can't be opened from above unless ya know the secret handshake. It's lead-lined and surrounded by burnt motor oil, which makes it hard for the sniffers to zero in on. After the deal, we can put your X in here, too. More insurance."

After depositing the fifteen thousand dollars in the compartment, Carlos pulled the console back. Alexis heard another click, and it had been impossible to tell it ever moved. Once again, Alexis found himself impressed with the detail of Carlos' drug running operation.

Alexis smiled, an eager smile, at Carlos. "Let's go buy some X."

Carlos took his foot off the brake, and they rolled forward—toward the shadowy structure with one orange glowing window.

Several hundred feet later, Carlos turned left onto what, at one time, might have been a driveway. Alexis could see faint, thin tracks between the thick sagebrush that had, long ago, reclaimed the driveway. When it scraped along the undercarriage of Carlos' truck, it made an eerie sound, like fingernails scratching on the inside of a wooden coffin lid. The scraping sound made the fine hairs on the back of Alexis' neck bristle. The shadowy structure that, in the headlights, Alexis could tell was an old barn, loomed in front of them.

Warning sirens were blaring in Alexis' mind. It felt wrong. Alexis thought about the burning red eyes she'd seen. In her gut, she knew whatever belonged to those eyes tracked their progress to the barn. She wanted to drive away, forget the Ecstasy, and drive away.

They were getting close to the old barn. Too close. She started to tell Carlos to drive away, drive away quickly, when the big barn door slid open. Orange light spilled out of the opening and cut across the sagebrush-covered drive like a glowing knife. A shadow, an enormous shadow, broke the orange beam and stepped out of the old barn.

At that point, Alexis realized she'd been holding her breath. Without exhaling, she thought she might need it to scream, Alexis tried to focus her eyes on the back-lit figure. The figure appeared enormous, bigger than most men, and hunched. It lifted a large hand and waved.

Carlos, stopped the truck, put it in park and started to get out.

Alexis grabbed Carlos' arm hard. "Don't get out."

Carlos looked at her like she was *loco*. "He waved…left-hand wave. That's the signal that we're clear for the deal."

Alexis shook her head. "Something's wrong. It doesn't feel right."

Carlos laughed. "You got me on the safari huntin', but I know you ain't never been on a Mexican drug deal. You're nervous. I get it. Give me the bag and I'll make the trade."

Alexis considered what Carlos said for several moments. She felt nervous, but she didn't think the nervousness came from drug-dealing butterflies fluttering in her stomach. When she and her dad went on the Zimbabwe safari, the guides used a live, tethered goat to lure in a large, male lion. From the safety of the safari truck, Alexis watched the large, powerful lion creep through the brush as it readied to ambush the goat. Alexis had that same feeling then, only she felt like the tethered goat about to be ambushed.

Getting irritated, Carlos said, "Come with me or stay in the truck. Your call, *chica*."

Against her better judgment, but not wanting to be left alone in the truck, Alex relented. If anything went wrong, Carlos had pistols. Alexis grabbed the tote, opened the door, and stepped out into the humid, early morning air. Before she followed Carlos into the barn the large man stepped back inside of, Alexis looked to the west. The orange quarter moon looked like a dimmed, partial sun setting on the empty, sagebrush-ridden horizon.

As Alexis stepped through the orange shaft of light into the barn, she thought, *There's an orange theme to the night.*

~ * ~

The soft, orange light that oozed from the barn door was deceptively bright on the inside, and its brightness temporarily blinded Alexis. When her eyes adjusted, she got her first good look at the barn's interior and *El Lobo*. The barn was empty but for a large, rustic, pine table in the middle with six chairs positioned around it: all resting on a rust-red dirt floor. There was a beat-up leather bag in the center of the table. Alexis had been relieved to see there were no guns on the table. She knew not seeing guns didn't mean they weren't somewhere, but in every drug deal movie she'd ever seen, there were always guns. She relaxed a little.

Her newfound relaxation evaporated when *El Lobo* turned and faced them. Her initial impression of him being a big man were correct. He was at least seven feet tall and broad across the shoulders. He wore dirty denim bib overalls, and his feet were bare and crusted in red dirt. It wasn't his height or dress that unnerved Alexis. His face sent shivers down her spine.

His face was angular with very sharp features, pointed chin, nose, and cheekbones, and his eyes were thin slits that turned up unnaturally in the outer corners. His facial features were wolf-like, and Alexis reasoned this to be the source of his chosen name. The wolf-like features weren't the worst of it, though.

El Lobo had a jagged, milky white scar that went from above his right eye, through his bushy black eyebrow, across the bridge of his pointy nose, through the left side of his unkempt mustache, across his thin lips, and down his pointy chin. Whatever cut *El Lobo* did so with force. Where the scar traversed the bridge of his nose, the bone had been crushed and sunk in, which caused his nose to turn up at the pointy tip. Worse still was where the scar went through his upper and lower lips. The cut obviously hadn't been stitched back together because it hadn't mended together. His upper lip split from just under the left side of his nose and the bottom lip split almost to the left side of his chin. There were no teeth visible behind the split lips.

Just when Alexis didn't think the visage could get any worse, *El Lobo* smiled. When he did, the splits in his lips spread apart, which allowed the left corner of his mouth to stretch back almost to his ear. The smile also exposed what teeth he had left, which were black around the gums and yellow on the top.

In a deep, grumbling voice that befit his large stature, *El Lobo* said, "*Cómo estás*?"

Alexis knew what he said, but she looked at Carlos.

Carlos smiled at the big man. "*Muy bien*."

He pointed at Alexis. "*Ella no habla Español*."

Alexis understood this too, but her Spanish was limited, other than ordering a beer and a few cuss words, so she hoped *El Lobo* spoke English.

El Lobo looked at Alexis, and chuckled a deep, guttural chuckle. "*Sí, sí*. I speak English."

His English had a thick Mexican accent, but it was English.

He turned his broad back on them, went to the table, sat in the largest of the six chairs, which had been at the far end of the table, and said, in a friendly voice, "Come, come. Sit, sit."

When they got to the table, Carlos took a seat next to *El Lobo,* but Alexis opted for a chair at the other end of the large table. Alexis knew *El Lobo* might take this as an insult, but she didn't care. The big man made her uneasy. After she sat down, Alexis placed the leather tote on the table in front of her.

El Lobo looked at Alexis and smiled his hideous smile.

He chuckled and looked at Carlos. "*Ella teme al lobo feroz*?"

Carlos smiled back. "*Un poco. Tal vez*."

Alexis, who only understood the word *lobo* in their conversation, said, "English, please."

Both men smiled and *El Lobo* said, "Jes, jes. English from now on."

Alexis, still uneasy with their private conversation, said, "What did y'all say?"

"He asked if you were afraid of the big, bad wolf."

"What did you tell him?"

Carlos flashed his gold grin at her. "I told him you were a little...nervous."

Alexis stiffened and looked from Carlos to *El Lobo*. "I'm fine."

El Lobo studied Alexis; his thin slit eyes fixed on her. She felt as though he was looking through her, but she refused to look away or show any sign of weakness.

After what seemed a long period of silence to Alexis, but only seconds had passed, *El Lobo* smiled his hideous, split lip smile again. "Jou should be scared, little girl. If I wanted to, I could eat jou up and spit jou out. I am the big, bad wolf that haunts jour nightmares."

Carlos, sensing things were about to go bad and wanting to defuse the situation, said, "Okay, okay. No one needs to be eaten and spit out. We're here for a transaction, right? We give you the forty-k and you give us the X. After that, we're gone. Easy-peasy."

Carlos looked at Alexis. "The money, *chica*. Slide me the bag."

Alexis pushed the leather tote to Carlos, which he grabbed. He unzipped it and dumped the bundled cash on the table in front of *El Lobo*.

Although there was a pile of cash in front of *El Lobo*, he never took his thin, slit eyes off Alexis. She tried to project outward calmness but, on the inside, she was panicking. Carlos assumed the Ecstasy was in the beat-up leather bag on the table and reached for it with his left hand. Before Carlos' hand closed on the bag, *El Lobo* grabbed his wrist.

The big man's large hand covered most of Carlos' forearm. *El Lobo* finally broke his intense gaze at Alexis and looked at Carlos. Alexis felt relieved to have his penetrating eyes off her, but the relief didn't last long. When the big man smiled at Carlos, which revealed his black and yellow teeth, Alexis saw his teeth appeared longer. Especially his canines. She thought about the burning red eyes, or slits, she'd seen in the darkness, and alarm bells went off in her mind.

El Lobo, still holding Carlos' wrist, said, "I think…the deal is changed, *cabrón*. I think I will keep the money, keep the pills, kill jou, fuck the girl, and eat her heart."

His voice changed. It was deeper and gruffer. It sounded almost like a growl. *El Lobo* looked back at Alexis and his eye slits flared, burning red. Alexis screamed.

Carlos tried to pull his wrist free from *El Lobo's* powerful grip but, even pulling with all his strength, the big man's grip wouldn't release. His arm didn't move. *El Lobo* twisted his hand and Carlos' left arm snapped like a dry twig with an audible 'crack.' The ulna and radius bones punctured Carlos' brown skin in a spray of blood. Carlos screamed in pain. *El Lobo* flung Carlos from his chair. He landed on his head on the dirt floor about twenty feet away in a crumpled, still heap.

Paralyzed with fear, Alexis couldn't move. She wanted to run, but her muscles wouldn't respond to the message from her brain to do so. She felt warm wetness in her seat and realized she'd pissed herself.

El Lobo, his eyes still glowing red, sniffed the air. He smiled again and there had been no doubt in Alexis' mind his teeth were growing. His canines were protruding beyond his split lips.

In a voice that sounded animalistic, *El Lobo* said, "Jou pissed jourself. That's okay, *puta*. It mixes good with the fear in jour sweat. The Wolf likes it."

He stood up.

The fear Alexis felt when she realized the glowing, slit eyes she'd seen in the darkness belonged to *El Lobo* dwarfed the fear she experienced as she watched him transform.

El Lobo undid the bib overall buttons with fingers that were quickly elongating into deadly claws and the overalls fell from his body. Remembering what he'd said about fucking her before eating her heart, it horrified Alexis to see his long, thick member was already erect. *El Lobo* let out a loud grunt that shook the barn and caused dust to dislodge from the rafters and float down like hazy curtains. *El Lobo* puffed out his chest and Alexis saw his ribs snap and reform into a shape that looked more canine than human.

As Alexis watched in disbelief, the already large man grew even taller. Grew to at least ten feet tall. Coarse, black hair sprouted from his body, covering it completely.

El Lobo, who had been a werewolf for decades and had complete control over the transformation to where he could change individual body parts without fully transforming at will, saved the best, and most horrifying, aspect of the change for last. His head and face.

He looked down at the terrified girl and grunted, "Look at me, *puta*. See the beast that will rape jou and eat jour frightened *corazón*."

Alexis' eyes fixed on *El Lobo's* still angular human face, except for the canines that still protruded beyond his lips. The 'rape' comment drew her eyes back to where his erect human member had been. What she saw there, and the thought of it penetrating her, horrified her more than anything else she saw. *El Lobo's* already large human member transformed into a massive, more than a foot long, erect, wet, pink, canine appendage with a grapefruit sized knot at its base.

El Lobo saw the fresh horror in Alexis' face when she saw what was in store for her and laughed a demonic laugh. He grabbed the sides of the table with his large hands. The claws cut deep, jagged gouges in the wood and he started thrusting his hips, mimicking how he would fuck her.

Alexis watched the large pink appendage stab the air above the table and noticed something bushy swishing back and forth behind *El Lobo*. When she realized it had been his tail and that he wagged it like a happy dog, an unexpected laugh spilled out of her.

El Lobo heard Alexis laugh. He stopped humping, and his claws dug deeper into the top of the table.

He roared, "Jou laugh at *El Lobo, puta*."

El Lobo leapt onto the table and crawled its length on all fours quickly.

He stopped with his horrible face only inches from Alexis' face and, in a ragged whisper, said, "Laugh at this, *coño pequeño*."

Alexis knew several Spanish cuss words, and she knew *El Lobo* called her a 'little cunt.' His rancid breath was more offensive than his words. She tried to turn her head away from the smell, but *El Lobo* grabbed the top of her head with his massive, clawed hand and held it in place.

After seeing *El Lobo* easily snap Carlos' arm, it surprised her his grip didn't crush her skull like a rotten melon. The claws that gouged the wooden tabletop didn't even break her skin.

El Lobo huffed hot, rancid breath in Alexis' face and grunted, "Look at me, *puta*."

She did.

Alexis choked on a scream as *El Lobo's* head and face transformed. The first things that changed were his ears. They elongated into points and moved from the sides of his head to the top; coarse, black hair sprouted and covered them. With 'cracking' and 'popping' sounds as his facial bones reformed, the of his skull flattened and elongated, and coarse, black hair replace *El Lobo's* curly, black hair. Finally, his angular cheeks widened, and his angular nose and chin elongated. As his snout grew, his unkempt mustache turned into long, wiry whiskers and his black and yellow teeth elongated into pearl-white, dagger-length fangs. Bloody drool oozed from its deadly snout.

The human scar was still there but onyx black instead of milky white. The split in its lips lined up perfectly with the upper and lower canines on the left side of its snout. It gnashed its teeth and Alexis heard the exposed fangs snap together with a vicious retort.

When the transformation was complete, in a voice that had been more animal than human, it said, "Laugh now, *puta*."

Its long, hot tongue came out from between its gleaming fangs and licked her face.

The scream choking Alexis erupted from her mouth. This ended badly because the werewolf jammed its long tongue into Alexis' open mouth and snaked it down the back of her throat.

Alexis gagged on the hot, thick intrusion and wanted to scream. Its tongue penetrated so far down her throat it blocked her throat completely, which kept her from breathing or vomiting. Because it was still holding her head, she couldn't move away from the revolting intrusion. She bit down hard, but her mouth had been so full of its tongue she couldn't get much force behind the bite.

About the time Alexis thought it intended to kill her by suffocating her with its repulsive tongue, it pulled its snout back and withdrew its tongue. The blocked vomit erupted from Alexis' mouth and splattered on the tabletop beneath the beast.

It smiled at Alexis and winked one of its burning, red slit eyes. "We fuck now."

It tightened its grip on Alexis' head, leaned back onto its rear haunches, lifted Alexis by the head from her seat, and placed her on her feet on the table in front of it. It kept a firm grip on Alexis' head to keep her from trying to run or collapse. It slipped one of its razor-sharp claws between Alexis' left thigh and her pee-soaked white shorts and started moving it upward. Alexis thought it meant to penetrate her with the deadly claw and her blood went cold.

It didn't penetrate her. It pulled its claw out and up. It cut through the fabric like a sharp knife, but the slit only went to the top of Alexis' leg. It repeated the move, but the second time its claw wiggled under Alexis' panties and cut through them as well. The only thing left holding Alexis' shorts up had been the thick fabric of the waistband. It slipped its claw under the waistband, gave it a quick upward pull, and sliced through it. Alexis' shorts and panties fell from her waist and gathered around her ankles in the vomit.

The paralyzing fear gripping Alexis broke and became replaced with frantic hysteria. She started screaming and lashing out with her fists. She tried kicking with her feet. All in vain, though. The arm holding her was too long to allow Alexis to connect with it, even with her legs.

After several moments of lashing out, her energy and will to live were spent. She knew she had no way to kill, or even injure, the beast. The best she could hope for was a quick death after the pain of being violated by its large canine appendage.

Unfortunately for Alexis, the werewolf, like the werewolf she would become, enjoyed inducing terror and pain in its prey as much, if not more, as it enjoyed the kill. It even developed kill-routines based on prey characteristics. The very old and very young, it killed quickly and without excessive terror. Men, it killed slowly by disemboweling them with its claws and only after inflicting savage bites on strategic areas that would allow them to live long enough to inflict as much pain as it could. After this, it would decapitate them to keep the curse from taking hold. This had been its plan for Carlos.

Unfortunately, for Alexis, again, women were its favorite prey. It relished what lay in store for the pretty, little American *puta* it held before it. If it was careful, and it was, it could play with, rape and torture her for days.

Alexis, still held up by the beast's massive, clawed hand, which put painful pressure on her head and strained her neck, started to cry. This caused the werewolf to chuckle. This pissed Alexis off and stiffened her spine.

Alexis screamed, "Just do it, you *fucker*!"

The werewolf gnashed its deadly teeth inches from Alexis' face and hissed, "Okay."

It spun her around and started to mount her.

It spun Alexis around so quickly that, at first, she wasn't sure what it planned to do. Its long, sharp claws cut through the straps of her black bikini top. It fluttered to the tabletop and landed in the pool of vomit she'd deposited there. She felt its claws, which grabbed her chest, sink into her breasts. Blood joined the bikini top, bottoms, and vomit on the tabletop, Alexis screamed in pain. That scream died in her throat when she felt its warm, wet canine appendage slip between her upper thighs, just below her crotch.

Alexis screamed, "NO," and struggled.

It just dug its claws deeper into her breasts.

It brought its snout down beside Alexis' right ear and whisper-growled, "You won't enjoy this."

Alexis almost laughed out loud when she realized the werewolf spoke better English than *El Lobo* did. It pronounced 'you' perfectly, as opposed to *El Lobo's* 'jou.' Then it bit down on her right shoulder, its dagger length teeth scraped against bone, and white-hot pain chased the laugh away. She screamed instead.

While still holding Alexis firmly in place with its claws and teeth, it shifted its wolf-like hips back and thrust forward with vicious speed. Alexis, anticipating its next move, clamped her teeth together and closed her eyes. She was determined not to scream. She felt it come into contact with her, then two loud, made louder by the enclosed barn, gunshots filled the air.

The werewolf let go of Alexis and she fell to the table with a 'thud,' her face in the blood and vomit. She looked to her right and saw Carlos, propped up against the side of the barn, with a chrome-plated pistol in his right hand. His left arm hung at his side, useless and oddly bent.

Carlos yelled, "*Morir, démon.*"

He unloaded the gun's clip into the werewolf.

Alexis looked up at the werewolf and saw two bullet holes in its side. Many more holes appeared on its chest as Carlos unloaded the clip, but it didn't look wounded. It sucked in a deep breath and roared so loudly that broken glass rattled from several window frames and shattered on the hard dirt floor. Alexis looked back at Carlos in time to see him drop the empty pistol which had turquoise grips that matched the turquoise and silver tips on his boots and pull another pistol from the small of his back.

Carlos looked at Alexis and yelled, "Run, *amiga*."

The werewolf let out another angry roar and leapt from the table toward Carlos. The force of the leap toppled the table over sideways and spilled Alexis, the money and tote, and the beat-up leather bag to the red dirt barn floor.

When Alexis hit the floor, she feared the heavy table might topple on top of her and crush her. She rolled several feet away. The table remained on its side, which created a barrier between her, Carlos, and the werewolf.

Alexis heard a shot and a crash. She heard a second shot. She heard a third shot, and the werewolf let out a yelp.

Kill the fucker, her mind screamed.

She began crawling back to the toppled table and heard a fourth shot. She got to the table and peeked over the top.

~ * ~

Carlos had a plan and, if he had any chance of living, he knew he only had one shot at making it work. The plan would require two well-placed shots.

When Carlos regained consciousness, he wasn't sure where he was, how he got there, or what was going on. All he knew was his left arm was on fire with pain.

He heard a woman scream, "Just do it, you *fucker*."

Everything became clear. That fucker, *El Lobo*, snapped his arm and threw him across the barn.

Rage replaced confusion, and he looked toward the table. What Carlos saw made him think he'd suffered a severe head injury and had been hallucinating. Alexis was naked and a gigantic werewolf had her bent over in front of it. The large, erect canine appendage made its intent perfectly clear.

Carlos shook his head, which hurt terribly, to correct the vision, but it remained the same. Growing up on the Mexican border, Carlos heard folktales of the mythical *nahual* his whole life, but he thought they were just that, folktales and myths. The beast before him was very real.

Carlos reached behind his back with his right hand and grabbed one pistol secured there by a custom-made holster. Once he had the pistol, he stood up. When he stood up, he became light-headed and would have fallen. Luckily, he landed next to the barn wall, and he leaned against it for support. As he raised the gun to shoot, he saw the werewolf thrust forward. He fired two shots into its exposed side.

After the werewolf dropped Alexis, Carlos unloaded the rest of the gun's clip into the werewolf's broad chest and retrieved his second pistol from the holster. He knew, if the myths were true, he needed silver bullets to kill it, which he didn't have. If his aim was true, Carlos thought he might temporarily wound it to where he and Alexis could escape.

The first part of the plan was to get its attention. He succeeded. The second part was to get it close enough to improve his aim. He wasn't prepared for the werewolf's leaping ability, though.

For Carlos, it played out in slow-motion. The werewolf roared then launched at him from the table. Carlos saw the table topple over, and the flying werewolf was increasing in size as it got ever closer. Carlos, who was an excellent shot, raised the pistol, took aim, adjusted for the beast's momentum and projection, and squeezed the trigger. The werewolf's left eye vaporized in a spray of blood.

Although a successful shot for two reasons, the werewolf was half blind and the impact affected its projection, so it crashed into the side of the barn to Carlos' right instead of on top of him, he didn't have time to take a shot at its right eye. Because the werewolf hit the side of the barn to Carlos' right, its remaining eye could see him. Carlos moved quickly to his left and brought the gun up for another shot.

~ * ~

After hitting the side of the barn with enough force to splinter several large support beams, the werewolf saw, with its remaining eye, the man move away and raise his gun. It lashed out with its right hand as the gun fired; the bullet tore through its right hand and into its right shoulder. The pain had been minimal, and it knew it and all the wounds, even its eye, would heal, but the man's defiance enraged the massive werewolf. It roared and lunged at the man.

~ * ~

Carlos expected the werewolf's lunge and reacted. He moved to his left to draw the beast in that direction then quickly darted to his right to put himself in the werewolf's blind spot. The misdirection worked. Carlos raised the gun and shot it in the left side of its snout. Its nose and upper canines exploded in a spray of blood, bone, hair, and teeth.

The werewolf let out a yelp and spun left toward Carlos, but he tracked quickly to his right to stay in its blind spot. He fired again and its bottom jaw disappeared in the same fashion as its upper jaw had.

~ * ~

The werewolf was experiencing pain it had never fathomed. The pain had been severe. The man was quickly limiting its ability to hunt and kill him. The loss of its canines took its most deadly weapon away, but it could easily kill with its claws. It could still put the woman away, wait to heal, and play with her for as long as it wanted to, and it wanted, more than ever, to make her pay for the sins of the man. Its bigger concern had been the loss of its one eye and losing its nose. Its sense of smell was its most important hunting sense. It could hunt blind, as long as its sense of smell worked. If the man successfully took out its remaining eye, it would have only its keen hearing to hunt with. It had exceptional hearing in wolf form, but hunting with its hearing only would be severely limited.

Not able to see the man who kept tracking to its left, the werewolf tapped into its one remaining, uninhibited sense. Its sense of hearing. Its ears quickly rotated toward its back, and it clearly heard the man's boots shuffle in the dirt. It had one good chance to immobilize the troublesome man. With as much force as it could muster, the werewolf launched itself backward. When it felt its broad back come into contact with the man, its traumatized maw curled up in a celebratory sneer. It fell on top of the man and heard his ribs crack beneath its weight.

~ * ~

Alexis peeked over the toppled table just in time to see the werewolf leap backward and land on top of Carlos. It was a crushing blow and Alexis saw the chrome-plated pistol fly out of Carlos' right hand as it contacted the red, dirt barn floor; it landed several feet away from his outstretched hand.

Carlos grimaced in pain, but he opened his eyes and saw an upside down, from his perspective, Alexis peeking over the toppled table.

Carlos yelled in a hoarse voice, "Shoot its right eye out."

The werewolf rolled over and pinned Carlos to the barn floor.

When the werewolf did this, Alexis got a good look at the damage Carlos inflicted on the beast. There were too many bullet holes in its chest to count and the back of its right paw had a large hole in it. These wounds paled compared to the werewolf's snout, which was gone, and the bloody hole where its left eye had been.

Alexis knew nothing about werewolves, myth or otherwise. Still, she understood the implication of Carlos' statement. If she could shoot out its right eye, it would be blind. Alexis bolted from behind the table to retrieve the gun.

~ * ~

The werewolf looked down at the man with evil contempt. Blood and drool oozed out of its shattered snout and pooled on the man's crushed chest. It was so focused on the man it didn't see the woman dart out from behind the table and go for the gun, which was on its blind side. It snapped its shattered jaws in the man's face and one of its teeth dislodged and fell on his forehead.

It saw the tooth fall from its snout with its one remaining eye and became even more enraged. With amazing speed, it punctured the man's bottom jaw with one of its dagger-length claws. It could have killed the man instantly by driving its long claw into his brain, but that wasn't its intent. It wanted the man to suffer. Instead of killing him, it stopped the upward thrust when its claw came into contact with the roof of the man's mouth, which pinned the man's mouth shut.

Blood flowed out of the corners of the man's mouth and nose as he gurgled. The werewolf pulled its claw slowly forward and the man's lower jaw dislocated with an audible 'pop.' The man screamed in pain through his still pinned shut mouth, but the werewolf wasn't finished. It was a firm believer in the 'Eye for an Eye,' or, in the case, 'a jaw for a jaw,' law of retaliation.

The werewolf yanked its claw forward. The man's lower jaw, tongue, and the upper gold grill that contained several of his dislodged teeth tore free. The man tried to scream. Without a tongue and a throat full of blood, he only gurgled.

The werewolf flicked the man's jaw off its claw with the same care as a child flicking a booger from a finger, it landed with a wet 'smack' several feet away. As it was about to slice the man's chest open with the same claw, it registered movement to its right. Before it could look that way, a gunshot went off.

~ * ~

Alexis got to the gun quickly and picked it up—it felt heavier than she expected. When she turned back to the werewolf to shoot, she realized she was on its already missing eye side. She skirted the beast leaving enough space between it and herself so it couldn't easily reach her if it saw her. She got around to the beast's right side and raised the gun to shoot. Just as she lined up the shot, the werewolf pulled Carlos' lower jaw off.

She saw the brown skin on Carlos' cheek turn white as it stretched. The overstretched skin ripped, and blood gushed out. Alexis suppressed a gag and was lining up again for a shot when the werewolf flicked Carlos' lower jaw in her direction. It landed wet with a 'splat' at her feet, and she had to move to her left to avoid being hit with it. When she looked back at the werewolf and Carlos, she saw the werewolf move its deadly claw to Carlos' crumpled chest. Alexis brought the gun up quickly, lined up the shot, and squeezed the trigger.

The shot had been a bullseye or, more accurately, a wolfs-eye. Because it wasn't a direct, frontal shot, like Carlos', but an angled side shot, the bullet entered its skull just behind its right orbital socket and exited in a massive spray of blood, bone, hair, and eyeball parts.

The werewolf reacted immediately and violently. It was blind, but Carlos, who was still pinned beneath it, became an easy target. It roared and swiped its left paw across Carlos's neck. The move decapitated Carlos and sent his head flying toward Alexis. She dodged it easily, but the werewolf launched in her direction the instant Carlos' head separated from his body.

The werewolf came on all fours, its head down, in a literal blind rage. Alexis jumped to her right, and the beast missed her by inches. As it skidded to a stop, its ears flicked in multiple directions, trying to locate the woman. Alexis' first thought was to run for Carlos' truck, but greed overpowered her survival instinct. She bolted back toward the toppled table—where the money and drugs were.

~ * ~

It heard her footsteps on the hard-packed dirt and lunged toward her on all fours again. It would have had her, but it forgot about the overturned table. This, however, would work in the werewolf's favor.

~ * ~

Just as Alexis got behind the toppled table, the werewolf bowled into it with incredible force. The tabletop smashed into Alexis. She fell hard, and painfully, on her bare backside Unfortunately, the ride wasn't over. The momentum of the hit pushed the table across the barn floor. Its top pushed Alexis, the money, and the beat-up leather bag in front of it like a bulldozer's blade.

When it came to a stop in a corner of the barn, which trapped her, Alexis was covered in dirt. It clung to her sweaty body, and she suffered several cuts and scratches from the rough ride. Alexis started to move, but she heard the werewolf growl. It came from the other side of the toppled table. Alexis realized it only had its hearing as way of finding her, and she held her breath. What she didn't know was the werewolf could hear her frantic heartbeats.

Alexis heard the werewolf back away from the table and thought she evaded it. Its deadly claws closed on the tabletop, and it effortlessly threw the large table across the barn. It broke into several pieces when it landed.

The werewolf, knowing it had the woman trapped, stood up to its full ten feet of nightmarish horror in a show of dominance. Alexis looked up at the deadly beast and decided, if she was going to die, she would make the beast's life as miserable as possible. She didn't know then werewolves regenerated.

From Alexis' position on the barn floor, she had an up close, too close for comfort, view of the werewolf's pink appendage. It became obvious, by the engorging taking place, it intended to pick up where Carlos' first shots interrupted their previous encounter. It intended to rape her.

Adding to Alexis' suspicion the monster had more interest in raping her than in killing her, at least at that moment, it hadn't tried to grab her, which it easily could have. Alexis reasoned, correctly, the only horror the werewolf wanted her contemplating at that moment was how its massive member would shred her delicate lady parts. The werewolf, besides forgetting about the table that benefited it, forgot about something else. Alexis still had a gun.

Alexis sat quietly and watched as the werewolf's grotesque, pink appendage grew to its full length and the grapefruit sized knot popped out of its furry sheath. She placed the end of the pistol's barrel within an inch of the knot. When the werewolf reached down for her, Alexis started pulling the gun's trigger as fast as she could.

Bloody back spray and chunks of flesh covered her face and chest, but she didn't care. She kept pulling the trigger until the clip emptied and she heard clicks instead of gunshots.

~ * ~

As the first bullet entered the werewolf's most sensitive area, it froze in pain and confusion. As a second, third, and fourth bullet ripped through its wolf-hood, it reacted and backed away, but the woman kept firing and hitting her target. When the trigger pulls produced clicks, it wanted to attack and kill her, but its hind legs would no longer support its weight. It fell to the barn floor with a massive 'thud' that shook the ground. Its claws went to its crotch, and it felt nothing but wet pulp. The massive werewolf curled into a ball and whimpered like an injured puppy.

~ * ~

When the werewolf fell, Alexis got a good look at the carnage. Its pink appendage had been detached at the knot and was lying on the barn floor a couple of feet in front of her. As she looked at it, it moved. Alexis screamed and backed as far into the corner as she could, but she quickly realized it wasn't animating—it was transforming back into its human form. Alexis looked at the balled-up werewolf and saw it was transforming back into its human form, too.

Alexis did not know what the transformation meant for her chances of escaping, and she had no desire to find out. By lucky chance, when the werewolf shoved Alexis into the corner of the barn with the table, the money and beat-up leather bag she assumed contained the Ecstasy she had been going to purchase went with her. Alexis stuffed the bundled cash back into her Tumi leather tote and grabbed the beat-up leather bag.

By the time Alexis collected the goods and turned to leave, the werewolf had completely returned to its human form. Alexis, not sure whether the man would still be dangerous, skirted his prone form. When she'd made it to the barn door, *El Lobo* let out a strangled laugh.

Alexis turned and faced the big man. His human form hadn't escaped the werewolf's injuries. His eye sockets were empty bloody holes, and his angular nose was gone, and upper and lower jaws looked like raw ground beef with black and yellow teeth stuck in it.

As Alexis looked at its injuries, she saw a bullet slug ooze out of one hole in his chest and fall to the barn floor. The hole it had come out of closed and only a pink scar remained where the bullet hole had been. She looked back at his face and saw his nose had started to grow back.

Alexis turned and ran from the barn.

As she climbed into Carlos' truck, she heard *El Lobo* yell, in a voice much too comprehendible for a man missing a mouth, "Run, *puta.* But jou cannot run from what jou are. Jou are *nahual.* It is a gift, *puta.* A *regalo* from *El Lobo* to jou. I hope jou kill everyone jou love."

Alexis shut the truck door, started it, and drove east as fast as she could. When she got to the underwater, reject-concrete road, the orange quarter moon was setting on the horizon that was turning a deep purple. The sun was coming up.

~ * ~

Alexis awoke from the dream-memory, she didn't consider it a nightmare, in her cool, dark bedroom. She rolled over onto her back, stretched her naked body across the bed, and thought about what had happened after the dream-memory ended.

That night changed her life in so many ways. The beat-up leather bag was full of Ecstasy—more than double what she had gone there to purchase. On reflection, she doubted *El Lobo* had ever planned to let them live, so bringing more Ecstasy had been arrogant hubris on his part. She hadn't been able to retrieve the fifteen thousand dollars Carlos stashed beneath the truck's console. Alexis didn't know the secret handshake, but that had been okay with her. She still had her dad's forty thousand dollars and the extra product ended up netting her, after replacing the fifty-five thousand dollars she'd borrowed from her dad on her way back to Nacogdoches, eighty thousand and change.

After surviving the werewolf attack, the only awkward situation Alexis encountered that morning had been getting herself and the Tumi tote—she put the drugs and cash in it and ditched the beat-up leather bag on the American bank of the Rio Grande River after successfully crossing the underwater bridge—from Carlos' truck to her CLS Coupe in the Walmart parking lot.

The sun had crested the horizon by the time she got to the Walmart and, aside from being naked, Alexis had been covered in blood and sporting some serious wounds on her breasts and right shoulder. She internally chastised herself for parking so close to the store. As luck would have it, the parking space to the immediate left of her car had been vacant. After parking in the space, she used the truck door as cover to get her car door open. She tossed the tote into her Mercedes, quickly climbed into her car, and shut the door.

The Coupe's tinted windows afforded Alexis more concealment, but she still exited the parking lot quickly. She left the door to Carlos' truck open and the key in the ignition. She hoped someone would steal it and, because she hadn't bothered to wipe her existence from the truck's interior, use it well before getting caught.

On the drive back to South Padre, Alexis pulled into a deserted rest area and used her tote as cover, in case someone drove in to get to the public restroom. It had been vile, but it had water. When she washed the blood away from her wounds, it amazed her to see the wounds were quickly healing. After washing all the blood and gore from her naked body, she used paper towels to dry herself. She went into one stall and wrapped the crappy, one-ply toilet paper around her breasts and midsection until she covered her nakedness as best she could.

She looked at herself in the dingy mirror before leaving the restroom. What she saw was far from ideal, but it would have to do. Walking into the hotel lobby wearing toilet paper attire might raise eyebrows under other circumstances, but not during Spring Break on South Padre Island. Alexis saw men and women wearing less bolt through lobbies before. She thought she'd be fine.

Alexis left the restroom, got in her Mercedes, and drove back to South Padre Island. As she expected, none of the hotel employees approached her as she entered the vast lobby. In fact, a girl behind the check-in counter gave Alexis a 'thumbs up' as she got into the elevator. Alexis returned the gesture before the doors closed.

When Alexis was safely back in her hotel room, she tore the uncomfortable toilet paper from her body and took a long, hot shower. Once she was clean, she turned the AC down to sixty-two degrees, stretched out naked on top of the covers, her preferred sleeping arrangement, and fell asleep. As she slept, she experienced some of *El Lobo's* pain and rage.

In his pain, *El Lobo* didn't guard his thoughts from Alexis as well as he should have. The important information she gleaned from his thoughts were he didn't know who she was and crossing into the U.S. had been too dangerous for him. Several U.S. agencies wanted him. She thought she'd seen the last of *El Lobo*.

Alexis awoke several hours later, confident *El Lobo* would not be a problem and, with her wounds completely healed. She took another shower, then wrapped and concealed the Ecstasy she planned to sell. Alexis 'fixed' her face, put on her best 'fuck me' outfit, and left for the bars. The rest of the week went off without a hitch.

~ * ~

As Alexis laid on her bed and thought about the events of that night, she remembered what *El Lobo* yelled from the barn before she left. "Run, *puta*. Remember, jou cannot run from what jou are. Jou are *nahual*. It is a gift, *puta*. A *regalo*. from El Lobo to jou. I hope jou kill everyone jou love."

A big smile spread across Alexis' pretty face. *El Lobo* had been right about one thing. It was a gift. Alexis didn't love anyone but herself. Losing Seth hurt a little, but she was already getting over that. She'd gladly sacrifice everyone she knew to keep her newfound power.

Alexis' right hand slid up her inner thigh and cupped her crotch. She was warm and wet there. She knew she would be. Thinking about the night she received *El Lobo's* gift always made her wet. Alexis closed her eyes and arched her back. As she satisfied herself, like no man she'd ever been with could, she rethought her plan to not turn again for several days, but she would do it alone.

She wanted to investigate the little bitch's home and see how she could fuck with her beyond what was already in her pathetic future. She didn't need the added aggravation of keeping Dillon and Cole in line.

Alexis let out a soft moan as she climaxed, and her body went limp on the bed. She was ready for a different pleasure. The pleasure of changing. She glanced at her bedside clock. The digital blue numbers read one forty-three p.m. Alexis closed her eyes.

Only a few more hours, Alexis thought.

She rolled over and went back to sleep.

Chapter Eleven

The alarm on Garrett's iPhone went off at two o'clock and pulled him from a much-needed sleep. After tapping the alarm off, Garrett laid on his back and stared at the ceiling for several seconds. The house was silent except for the hum of the ceiling fan. He spotted a wisp of a spider web fluttering in the breeze created by the fan in a corner and made a mental note to get rid of it later.

In those brief seconds after waking, Garrett completely forgot about the events of the previous night. As it always did when he wasn't concentrating on some task, his mind turned to Paige and the horrible memories flooded over him with suffocating clarity. Paige and Ty were bitten and infected. Fifteen students, including Paige's boyfriend, and Carla Weaver were savagely murdered. A pack of werewolves were roaming the dense forests of Pine View County. Garrett remembered Paige and Ty's only salvation was finding and killing the alpha before their first transformation on the June full moon.

Panic flooded over Garrett. His heart started hammering in his chest and he realized he wasn't breathing. He made himself suck in a deep breath and slowly exhaled, trying to calm his nerves. After several deep breaths, his heart rate slowed and the rawness in his nerves subsided. When he regained control of his emotions, Garrett slipped out of bed and got dressed. Before leaving his bedroom, he used a hand towel to knock the spider web out of the corner of the room.

One problem solved, Garrett thought as he left his bedroom.

After pouring a glass of sweet tea, Garrett headed for his home office, which was directly across from Paige's bedroom. Not wanting to wake her, but needing to see her, Garrett quietly opened Paige's bedroom door and peeked in. He saw her slight form balled up under the covers and her long brown hair fanned out on the pillow. The previous night, Paige fooled him by stuffing the covers to make it look like she had been in bed.

How could I have been so stupid? Garrett thought.

She wouldn't fool him so easily again.

Secure in the knowledge Paige was in her bed, Garrett quietly closed her bedroom door and went into his home office. Before sitting down at his computer, Garrett pulled out his wallet and retrieved Dr. James Huff's business card. He sat down, wiggled the mouse to wake up the computer, entered his password, and opened Outlook. Thirteen emails loaded and Garrett scanned through the sender and subjects quickly.

Eleven of the thirteen were junk and Garrett deleted them without bothering to read them. The remaining two emails, one from County Coroner George Krats and one from Deputy Billy Hoyt, were of interest. Garrett read them carefully.

Garrett,

We're very busy this morning. Postmortems are going slowly, but I wanted to update you on Russ Lomax from Monday. We've pieced him back together, which wasn't easy. Lots of trauma. Broken bones, ruptured organs, torn flesh. He was in a hell of a lot of pain before he expired. His heart is missing. Not a surgical extraction. It crushed his sternum inward from the outside. The vena cavae, aorta, pulmonary veins and arteries all show signs of tearing, as if it ripped his heart from his chest. Freaky shit, Garrett.

Waiting on you for the perp's postmortem,
George

Garrett reread George's email several times. He didn't attach meaning to the missing heart, but he made a mental note to ask James Huff about it. Garrett clicked on the 'Reply' button. He thanked George for keeping him up to date and told him he'd contact him later about the perp's postmortem. Then he opened the email from Deputy Hoyt.

Sheriff Lambert,

I ran the perp's prints and didn't get any hits. Whoever he is, he's clean. Wish I had better news.

Billy

This news disappointed Garrett, but it didn't surprise him. In his gut, he didn't believe finding out who the werewolves were would be easy. He clicked on the 'Reply' button and told Billy to keep an eye out for missing persons reports for the entire East Texas region.

Somebody somewhere must miss ya eventually, Garrett thought.

After dealing with the incoming emails, Garrett clicked on the

'Compose Email' button and entered James Huff's email address in the 'To:' field and 'They're real' in the 'Subject:' field. That had been the simple part. Now Garrett had to figure out how to explain what happened. His fingers hovered over the keyboard for several seconds, and he started typing.

Dear Dr. Huff:

Werewolves are real and there's a pack in East Texas. I don't know whether news of last night's events has gotten out yet. Even if it has, which I expect, I buried the truth...for now. They murdered fifteen Pine View High School students last night. My daughter Paige and my friend and deputy Ty Jackson got bitten and survived.

Ty killed one werewolf by shoving his Silver Star commendation into its chest. Can the coroner remove it? If he removes it, will it come back to life? Also, Paige shoved her silver crucifix and necklace down the throat of the alpha when she got bitten. Paige said the werewolf changed back into a human while it was choking on the silver. Can silver stop a transformation?

Also, Paige and Ty have already expressed a feeling of being 'connected,' with the alpha. I'm not sure what that means. They could tell she, the alpha's a young woman, was furious with Paige for injuring it. They knew the pack wasn't close to where we were...that it had moved away. Do you think they can use this connection to find the alpha? Can they reason when they're in werewolf form?

Do you know anything about dreams or premonitions? I've had a recurring nightmare for the past fourteen years. I won't go into detail here but, in the dream, Paige is a werewolf. Until all this, I thought it was just a nightmare. Now it seems more like a premonition. What could this mean? Why would I have this recurring nightmare if it didn't have some meaning?

Sorry to throw all these questions your way, but I don't know who else to ask. I'm not sure whether you check your work email on the weekends. When you get this, if you have time, please call me on my cellphone 936-555-0817.

Thanks,
Garrett

Garrett clicked on the 'Send' button and watched the email

disappear. He opened the top desk drawer and retrieved a pack of Marlboro Reds. Paige didn't like him smoking, and he usually abstained from doing so when she stayed with him, while at the house, at least. After all that happened, he figured he deserved at least one. He grabbed a lighter from the drawer got up from the desk and went out onto the back deck to smoke.

After sitting down in one of the deck chairs, Garrett took a cigarette out, tapped the tobacco end against the box a few times, stuck the filter between his lips, lit it, and took a deep draw. As the nicotine coursed through his body, Garrett exhaled and watched the white smoke get carried away by the light breeze like evaporating mist.

The woods around his house were quiet, but not the unnatural quiet Paige and Ty associated with the presence of the werewolves. Squirrels scurried around in the treetops and, somewhere nearby, a dog was barking. As Garrett sat there enjoying the cigarette and the warm May afternoon, it was hard to fathom the horror that visited his little piece of the world.

When Garrett finished the cigarette, he contemplated smoking another. He had one more before getting to the business that needed getting to; dropping by Lowes to pick up some motion activated floodlights.

As Garrett absentmindedly tapped the tobacco end of the second cigarette against the box, his cellphone rang. He didn't recognize the number on the Caller ID, but he tapped the green answer button, and put the phone to his ear. "Garrett here."

In an excited voice, James Huff said, "They're real?"

~ * ~

Paige faked being asleep when her dad looked in on her. Part of her wanted to let him know, but a bigger part of her wanted him to go away. The bigger part won the internal debate, and she feigned being asleep because she couldn't discuss the connection she'd experienced with him. She couldn't discuss it because she didn't understand it.

Paige awoke to odd sensations coursing through her body. Almost as if she'd been pleasuring herself, but she hadn't been. In the first few seconds of confusion, she enjoyed it. Then she realized she must have been sharing a pleasurable sensation with the alpha. She tried to close her mind as well as her body to the unwelcomed intrusion, but it lingered. Worse still, part of Paige, a large part that would trump her wanting to let her dad know she wasn't awake a few moments later, enjoyed the alien sensations. When the alpha climaxed, so did Paige.

In the pleasure's aftermath, Paige tried to connect with the alpha. She wasn't sure how it worked or whether the connection only worked one way. Paige concentrated on where the intrusions seemed to come from, the center of her head. She could still feel the alpha's presences, her emotions. She was happy. Paige pushed back against the unseen trespasser and felt her perspective shift. Although Paige's eyes were closed, she saw a flash of dim light as eyelids that weren't hers closed. Paige felt chilled air and smelled of musk. A thought whisper-echoed through Paige's mind, *only a few more hours*. Her perspective shifted again. Paige was in her room and in her head. The connection was gone.

Still, it was there. I got into her head, Paige thought.

An exhilarating feeling of triumph washed over Paige. This feeling lasted, but only for a couple of seconds. That quickly, Paige considered the obvious problem reversing the intrusion might present. Did the alpha know Paige trespassed into her thoughts?

Paige found this a troubling issue and was contemplating it when her dad opened the bedroom door to check on her. Not knowing where to begin or what to say, Paige pretended to be asleep. After her dad closed her bedroom door, Paige lay in bed, going over how simple reversing the connection had been.

Although she had concerns the alpha might sense her intrusion, Paige tried to connect again. Nothing. That led Paige to the conclusion the alpha had to start the connection. That conclusion led Paige to another question. Did the alpha know she had connected with her? If she did, why would she allow Paige to know how injured and angry the crucifix encounter left her? Why would she allow Ty to know this, too? Given the evidence, Paige believed the alpha unknowingly connected with her pack when her emotions peaked. All Paige had to do was wait for the emotional window to open again and sneak in like a thief.

Paige felt pretty good about the internal, deductive reasoning session she had. She would tell her dad about it later. Feeling mentally exhausted, Paige closed her eyes and snuggled her face into the soft pillow. Paige drifted into the welcoming darkness of sleep when she remembered the thought that whisper-echoed through her brain just before the connection ended—*Only a few more hours*.

A few more hours until what, you bitch? Paige thought as the darkness washed over her.

~ * ~

James Huff couldn't contain his excitement. Although Garrett reached out to James for answers to his questions, James asked questions nonstop, "You saw 'em?" "How many?" "How big are they?" "What are their human qualities?" "Do they have different colored fur?"

After a few more rapid-fire questions, Garrett interrupted James long enough to say, "I didn't see 'em, Doctor Huff. My daughter and deputy did, though, since they got bitten."

James was silent for several seconds and, when he spoke, the disappointment had been apparent in his voice. "I'm sorry, Sheriff Lambert. I'm being very insensitive...considering what you've been through."

James fell silent again.

Just as Garrett started to respond, James said, "Do ya think it'd be possible for me to speak with your daughter or Deputy Jackson later?"

Garrett smiled at his end of the cell connection. Although he had been up to his neck in shit, he liked James Huff's enthusiasm for the subject. Garrett had a feeling James' enthusiasm would prove valuable as he confronted his impending demons. As usual, Garrett's intuition wasn't wrong. Dr. James Huff would become an integral advisor on the current and future cases.

"I can't speak for 'em, but I'll ask. I'm pretty sure they'll share what they know."

Sounding relieved and excited again, James said, "Thank you, Sheriff Garrett. Thank ya for understandin' an old fool's indiscretion."

"No apology needed, Doctor Huff. But...if ya don't start callin' me Garrett, I might forget to ask 'em."

James laughed, and Garrett could picture his enormous belly and jowls jiggling.

When the laughing subsided to a chuckle, James said, "You gotta deal, Garrett. But only if ya call me James."

Garrett chuckled. "Deal, James."

With that out of the way, James said, "Let's talk about your email."

James cleared his throat. "I have your email in front of me. I'll address each point in order. I have a couple of questions, though."

"Shoot."

"How many are in the pack and what happened last night?"

"Well, as near as I can tell, there were four in the pack. Luckily, or things might'a been worse, Deputy Jackson took one out before they got to the MRB."

"MRB?" James interrupted.

"Sorry. You wouldn't know about the MRB unless you grew up in Pine View. MRB is short for the Mill Road Barn. It's an abandoned sawmill facility. High school kids have been usin' it as party central since before I was in high school. Is that important? Do ya think they knew about the party…that they're high school kids?"

James considered Garrett's questions briefly. "They could be high school kids. Anything's possible. It's more likely the noise drew them to it. I'm sorry I interrupted. Please continue."

"Well, the pack showed up and killed several students who were outside of the buildin' right away. They corralled the rest of 'em inside the metal buildin' and kept 'em there. When Paige hurt the alpha, they left."

James was silent for several seconds before asking. "Was Paige with the other students in the buildin'?"

"No. Paige and her boyfriend…weren't there when the attack started."

He could share a lot with James but telling him Paige wasn't at the MRB building because she intended to surrender her virginity to her boyfriend wasn't something he felt like sharing.

"Interestin'," James said, more to himself than Garrett.

"What's interestin'?"

"The alpha separated from its pack and went for Paige," James reasoned to himself.

"I guess. What're ya gettin' at?"

"This is just a guess, but…I think the alpha marked Paige."

Garrett thought about James' statement briefly. "Marked her? How? When? Why?"

"This is just speculation…conjecture, Garrett. If Paige wasn't at the buildin', and the alpha broke from its pack to seek her out, I think it meant to turn her, not kill her, all along. How and when it marked her isn't important. *Why* it marked her is important."

Garrett thought about the way Paige said the werewolf stalked her through the woods, the way it taunted her. It could have killed Paige, but it didn't. A chill ran up Garrett's spine.

What do ya want with my little girl? Garrett thought.

He took an unsteady breath. "Why do ya think it marked her?"

After several seconds of uncomfortable silence, James said, "I don't know, Garrett. But this might be a good thing."

"A *good* thing? How the fuck can this be a *good* thing? My little girl is gonna turn into one of those *fuckers* when the moon is full in June." Garrett exploded.

After Garrett spent his anger, James said, "I'm sorry, Garrett. Not the best choice of words on my part. I only meant…had the werewolf not marked her, she'd probably be dead like the other students who weren't in the buildin'. That the alpha wanted her, specifically her, in its pack might mean somethin'. Somethin' that can help you…us put an end to all of this. To be honest, I think it intended to turn the students trapped inside the buildin' too…to expand its pack. But…again, that it sought Paige out *is* significant. I'm sure of this."

Garrett immediately felt bad about blowing up at James. He knew James hadn't meant what he said the way he took it. The thought of that thing marking Paige for some specific reason knotted his gut, though. Garrett lit the cigarette he'd taken from the pack before James called and took a deep draw.

After exhaling the smoke, Garrett took a smoke-free breath. "I'm sorry for blowin' up on ya, James. My nerves are raw as hell."

"As well they should be, Garrett. No need to apologize. Let's leave the *why* for later and get back to your email."

"I'd like that," Garrett agreed.

"Okay," James started, "You asked whether removin' Deputy Jackson's Silver Star will reanimate the werewolf. The answer to this is a resoundin', no. Werewolves are not undead creatures, like vampires and zombies. Vampires and zombies die and become reanimated, but ya don't have to die before ya become a werewolf. Once a victim gets bitten, they're cursed."

James considered using Paige and Ty as examples. Knowing Garrett's nerves were raw, he didn't.

"Since," James continued, "they were never undead, they will not come back from the dead. Deputy Jackson can have his Silver Star back.

"The incident that you described with Paige, the silver, and the alpha startin' to transform back into human form is very interestin'. This is one of those areas where werewolf lore diverges. Some writings suggest prolonged exposer to silver will kill a werewolf. A slightly larger collection of writings suggests silver *can* regulate the change. Of course, this would be an external treatment. Any silver introduced internally, for more than a few seconds, would poison the blood, travel to the internal organs, and kill it rather quickly. I subscribe to the latter theory.

"The external treatment would be painful, though. I'll wager Paige won't be able to wear her silver necklace and crucifix within a few days. This is my academic windbag way of sayin' I believe silver can keep a transformation from happenin' and it can reverse the transformation.

"Okay," James continued, "the next item in your email is very interestin', too. I'll tell ya, up front there's not a lot of information on this phenomenon in werewolf myth-lore. Vampires? Yes, they have telepathic powers. They can get into another's mind, read it, and manipulate it. It's called mezmery for vampires. Just because it hasn't been explored doesn't mean it doesn't exist with werewolves.

"In fact, it makes intuitive sense that telepathy of some sort would exist. If you've ever seen a flock of Starlings, the ones that look like a dark cloud, synchronized flyin', I believe you've seen a kind of animal telepathy.

"We know wolf packs, regular wolves, take direction from the pack alpha. Some folks think wolf packs use visual cues from the alpha to know when to attack and such, but why not a sort of telepathy?"

Garrett thought that might have been a question for him but, before he could offer a lame response, James continued.

"Yes," James answered his own question. "I believe the sensations that Paige and Ty experienced are real. It stands to reason packs are mentally linked to their alpha. You stated in your email that the alpha is a young woman."

"That's what Paige said. That's what she saw when it transformed back into a human. A youngish woman."

James was silent for a few seconds and then continued, "This is pure speculation, Garrett. Take it that way. If I'm right, it might help ya narrow your search, though.

"I think she, the alpha, is probably inexperienced. With the pack showin' up now, she was probably turned in March, had her first change in April, which is when she would've turned three people…she probably knew ‘em beforehand, and created her initial pack. Last night she wanted to increase her pack. She lost one member and gained two…Paige and Deputy Jackson. That neither of them was killed, when they easily could’ve been, implies, to me, she…it marked ‘em and wanted ‘em.

“I don’t know where her alpha…her creator is. It’s probably far away for her to be out from under its control. This means, if I’m right, she didn’t get to learn the nuances of bein’ a werewolf from her maker.

“She probably knows she can connect with her pack, but she might not know when she’s letting ‘em into her thoughts. Your email said Paige and Deputy Jackson knew she was injured and angry. I don’t think she would want ‘em knowin’ that…knowin’ she was vulnerable.

“That they sensed this might mean the alpha unknowingly opens its mind when its emotions swing. Yes…they might use this unknown connection to find out things about the alpha that help ya find it.

“I must stress caution here, Garrett. This isn’t fantasy Harry Potter and Voldemort occlumency crap. This is the real deal. If the alpha figures out they’re gettin’ peeks into its mind, the ramifications could be severe. It could kill ‘em to stop the intrusions or it could send ‘em false information to get you and others close to you killed.

“As for whether they can reason in werewolf form, the evidence suggests, they can. By evidence, I mean it selected Paige and Deputy Jackson for its pack and had enough control…awareness to bite but not kill ‘em. Also, and this is just speculation again, I believe it knew the first three pack members. It would’ve taken ‘em somewhere remote, transformed, and infected ‘em.

“Don’t mistake this reasonin’ for something human, Garrett. This is basic animal instinct reasonin’. The alpha knew it needed pack members…strength in numbers. This kept it from killin’ its initial three members. It didn’t let ‘em live because they were friends…outta some misguided loyalty. It didn’t kill ‘em ‘cause it needed ‘em. If you’re thinkin’ ya can reason with Paige or Deputy Jackson if, God forbid, they transform, don’t. Werewolves are vicious, demon cursed creatures. Paige and Deputy Jackson will not be in there. At least not to where they can control their wolves. They would kill ya.”

That last bit of advice cut Garrett to the bone. That, if they did change, he could reason with them, had been exactly what he’d hoped to hear. He then remembered to tell James the werewolf talked to Paige, told her to run.

"It talked to Paige."

"It did? The werewolf? It talked to Paige?"

"It told her to run. When it was in the woods stalkin' her. It told her to run."

"That's interestin'. I wasn't aware they had this ability. It must be difficult to vocalize with a wolf's snout. I'll look into this. Now…about your recurrin' dream," James continued, "This isn't my area of expertise. I can convey some cursory dream-lore theory, but nothin' more substantial. Tell me more about the nightmare."

Garrett told him about every aspect of the recurring nightmare. He had never shared this information with anyone. It had been his private little hell for fourteen years. By the time Garrett finished telling James about the dream, and how Monster-Paige grew older every year, whether James could put meaning behind the dream didn't matter as much to Garrett. Sharing the dream felt cathartic in ways Garrett hadn't expected. Like someone lifted a weight from his shoulders.

James listened closely to every detail of Garrett's recurring nightmare.

When Garrett finished, he said, "It sounds like a premonition."

"That's what I was thinkin'. Why do you say that?"

James thought briefly. "Remember, this isn't my area of expertise, not in my wheelhouse, so to speak, but the subject and recurring nature of the dream lead me to believe it's not just a nightmare. I mean…what are the odds you consistently dream about Paige becoming a werewolf then it happens? Especially since ya didn't believe in werewolves earlier this week. No…there's more to this than coincidence."

"What, then?"

Although James felt certain it was a premonition, he did not know what it meant or why Garrett had been having it.

James thought for a moment. "Your ex-wife was dead, correct?"

"By the time Monster-Paige finished with her, yes. Why?"

"Well," James started, "the scene you presented is reminiscent of a birth. A violent birth, but a birth all the same. As if your ex-wife was giving birth to the monster…to the werewolf. Could she be involved? What about the larger werewolf? Is there anything about it that looks familiar to ya?"

Garrett considered James' observation and question. He couldn't believe Lacy had been part of it, and there had been absolutely nothing familiar about the larger werewolf. Garrett shared these feelings with James.

After hearing this, James said, "Do ya mind if I share your dream with a friend of mine? She's not an academic. She's a witch…an elemental seer. Her name is Lola Laveau, and she is a descendent of Marie Laveau. She's a bit of an odd duck, really. I'm not one to dismiss somethin' just 'cause I can't understand it. Can I share your dream with her, Garrett?"

Garrett heard the legends of the voodoo priestess, Marie Laveau. Most folks in East Texas had. He put little stock in voodoo, witches, or the Laveau family name, but he didn't see where James telling his friend could matter.

Garrett took a final drag on his cigarette and tossed it in the outside fireplace. "Sure. Go ahead. But I wouldn't want her puttin' a hex on me."

James chuckled. "Don't be absurd, Garrett. Lola is a good witch."

Because Garrett expected James to say there were no such things as hexes, the 'good witch' line struck Garrett as exceedingly funny, and he started laughing. The laugh became infectious, and before long, James laughed, too. It had been the first genuine laugh Garrett could remember having since his world turned to shit, and it felt good.

As the laughter dwindled, a long silence ensued. It was as if neither man wanted to acknowledge they were back in the world of werewolves, mutilations, and infected loved ones.

Finally, James said, "Well, Garrett, I know you're busy and you've got shit to do. If there's nothin' else, I'll let ya get to it."

Garrett felt like he had something else to ask James, but it danced on the periphery of his catchable thoughts like an untethered balloon.

"I think that's it, James. Thank ya for listenin' and advisin'. I should put ya on retainer, like Doctor Yost."

James chuckled again. "Unnecessary. I assure ya that knowin' they exist is compensation enough."

"All right then," Garrett started, but the untethered balloon was within reach and Garrett grabbed it.

"Sorry, but I have one last question for ya, James."

"Fire away."

Garrett took a deep breath. "The coroner said that the only thing missin' from the first victim was his heart. He said it looked like Mister Lomax's heart was ripped from his chest. Any significance to that?"

Without hesitation, James said, "The significance is symbolic. My guess is the alpha ate it. Not out of hunger or for any nutritional value the heart has."

"Why eat it?"

"Through the ages, many cultures believed the human soul lives in the heart. This makes sense, primitively. It circulates lifeblood. It's in the center of the chest. Where else would a soul live? By eatin' it, the werewolf is symbolically devourin' its victim's soul. Keepin' it from going to heaven."

Another shiver ran up Garrett's spine and he said, "That's a pretty fucked up thing to do."

James chuckled. "They're pretty fucked up creatures."

He added, "You won't be able to reason with 'em, if they change, Garrett."

Garrett sighed. "I'll just have to kill the wolf bitch before they turn."

James chuckled again. "That's the spirit, Garrett. Kill that fuckin' bitch. If I can help, let me know."

"Will do," Garrett responded and ended the call.

~ * ~

Although Ty's shift didn't start for another nine hours, and he felt like he should get some rest, he couldn't sleep. Even though he had little down time since he last slept, he wasn't tired. In fact, he felt better than he had in a long time.

Unable to sleep, Ty slipped out of the empty bed. Jasmine was with Little D away from the bedroom so Ty could sleep. He walked into the bathroom, turned on the light, and looked into the mirror at where his grievous wounds should have been. Smooth brown skin with no hint of the claw and bite marks reflected.

His cellphone was plugged into the socket beside the sink, charging. He checked it. It was charged, and he saw he didn't have any messages or missed calls. Ty tapped in his passcode, tapped on the green 'Phone' app, and tapped on the second name, just below Jasmine's, in the 'Favorites.' Garrett answered on the first ring.

"How ya feelin'?" Garrett asked immediately.

"Good, too good."

Garrett chuckled. "Isn't feelin' too good kinda like havin' too much fun? No such thing."

Ty knew Garrett had tried to lighten the subject, but he needed Garrett to understand.

"Yeah, like the song says, I ain't ever had too much fun. This is different, Garrett. There's no *hint* of the claw and bite marks on my skin. Nothin'. I don't just feel good, I feel *damn* good…like I did when I was in high school and played football. Even my ankle feels better. No limp."

"Well, don't get too used to it, 'cause we're gonna find and kill that bitch."

Ty let out a nervous laugh. "I hope so, Garrett. 'Cause I can already feel the attraction to this. I mean…I understand why some folks would like to feel this way."

"Don't forget that feelin' comes with being a savage werewolf," Garrett pointed out.

Ty let out another nervous laugh. "Believe me, I won't. I want that bitch dead and my old half-ass feelin' good back. Speakin' of that, anything on the perp I took out?"

"I'm afraid not. Billy ran his prints, and he doesn't have an arrest record."

"I kind'a figured as much."

"Don't sweat it. Somebody, somewhere, will miss him eventually and file a missin' person report on him."

Ty sighed. "Unless that somebody, somewhere, is the alpha. She'd know better than to report him missin'."

Garrett considered this, too. He wanted to give Ty some good news, but there wasn't much of that around.

He remembered what James Huff told him about the Silver Star. "On the bright side, ya can have your Silver Star back."

"Ya sure 'bout that? He won't pop back up once it's removed?"

"I'm sure. Doctor Huff told me, because werewolves aren't undead, they don't come back."

"Ya believe him?"

Garrett thought about Ty's question briefly. "I trust him and that's good enough for me. I'll call George at the morgue and let him know you'll be by to pick it up."

"You're the boss."

The conversation had about run its course when Garrett remembered to ask about the mental connection.

"One more thing, Ty. Have ya…felt her again since this mornin', when she was injured and angry? Doctor Huff thinks you and Paige might use this connection to help us find her."

Ty was silent for several seconds and then, in a hushed voice, said, "Yeah, a little while ago."

"What'd ya feel?"

Ty felt a little embarrassed to discuss the 'feeling' but, if it could help them find her, he'd share it with Garrett.

"Well, a little before two o'clock, I felt her feelin' *real* good."

"Real good, how?"

"Real good in a…sexual way," Ty whispered.

Garrett had been honestly confused. "Sexual?"

Ty took a deep, steadying breath. "She was rubbin' one out."

When Garrett didn't reply, Ty said, "She was flickin' the bean…rockin' the boat…checkin' her oil…she was masturbating."

Garrett didn't get the euphemisms, but he understood the directness of Ty's last point. He also understood if Ty felt it, Paige probably did as well. This thought made him more uncomfortable than just about anything else that had happened in the last couple of days.

For clarification, Garrett said, "Are ya sure?"

"I'm *positive*."

"Positive, positive?"

"I messed the inside of my boxers when she came positive."

Ty realized why Garrett had been being so obstinate. "You're worried that Paige felt it, aren't ya?"

"Well…hell yes I am."

Ty chuckled. "You don't think she's figured out how to do this on her own?"

"You're lucky ya have a son, Ty. You'll probably be proud when he starts jackin' off."

"Damn right," Ty said with a laugh.

"Daughters are different, my friend. Daughters don't have lady parts. They're little girls forever," Garrett explained.

Ty chuckled again. "So, I guess Paige and Justin were sneakin' off last night for a little Bible readin'."

This struck Garrett as funny, and he started laughing. Ty joined in and, within a few seconds, they were both in tears.

Still laughing, Garrett said, "Point taken. I still don't like the idea of Paige feelin' it when that bitch…rubs one out."

Ty laughed again. "What about me? Don't ya feel bad that I can feel it, too?"

"Fuck you. It probably makes your lady parts feel all warm and fuzzy."

They laughed again.

Garrett chuckled and said, "Let's drop the whole masturbation conversation. Did ya get anything else from the…connection?"

Ty thought about the connection and remembered her final thought before he lost her—he had tried to connect with the alpha just as Paige had.

"After she was through…diddlin', I felt her think '*only a few more hours'*."

"Only a few more hours until what?"

"I dunno," Ty answered honestly.

"Do ya think she's plannin' to go huntin' again tonight?"

"That'd be my guess," Ty responded.

"Mine, too."

Garrett thought for a minute. "Mike was supposed to make some silver bullets for all of us. I haven't heard from him, but I'm takin' that as a good sign…that he'd let me know if there was a problem. Be careful tonight. If ya see anything strange, call me on my cell. Even with silver bullets, don't engage the pack on your own."

"Roger that."

Garrett continued, "I'm gonna head up to the department to check in, then I'm goin' to the Nac Lowe's to get some motion activated flood lights for my house."

"You should get some of those critter-cams that hunters strap to trees to track wildlife, too," Ty added.

Garrett hadn't thought of getting critter-cameras, but he liked the idea.

"That's an excellent idea, Ty. I will."

"Glad to help."

"Seriously, be careful tonight, Ty," Garrett reiterated.

"I will. I gotta think if she wanted me dead, she'd have killed me last night."

"Maybe, but that doesn't mean she wouldn't kill ya if she thought ya were a threat,"

"I'll be careful…Dad," Ty joked.

After a shared chuckle, they said goodbye and hung up.

When Ty stepped out of the bathroom, Jasmine cracked open the bedroom door. "I thought I heard ya talkin'. Why aren't ya sleepin'?"

"Can't sleep," Ty said as he walked up to Jasmine and wrapped his arms around her.

Jasmine grinned. "Little D's down for his nap. You want Mama to put you down, too?"

Ty knew exactly what that euphuism meant, and he couldn't remember wanting a nap more than he did right then. About two seconds after asking, Jasmine felt Ty's answer pressing against her.

Thirty minutes later, Ty and Jasmine were covered in sweat and lying naked on their backs under the ceiling fan trying to catch their breath.

Jasmine panted, "Where'd that come from?" He knew where it came from, but he wasn't about to tell Jasmine it had been part of the werewolf package. Instead, Ty slipped his arm under Jasmine and rolled her on top of him.

He said, "I just love ya that much."

Jasmine laughed. "You haven't loved me that much in a *long* time."

Ty smiled. "Ya ready to go again?"

Jasmine grinned. "Yeah, right."

She felt Ty wasn't joking.

A big grin spread across her beautiful face, and she said, "Who are you and what have ya done with my husband?"

Before Ty could think of something clever to say, Jasmine said, "Never mind. I'll keep you, whoever ya are."

As they started into round two of what would be four rounds of lovemaking before Ty left for his shift, Ty thought, *you wouldn't want to keep me if ya knew what I am.*

~ * ~

After talking with Ty, Garrett called George Krats. This conversation didn't go quite as well as Garrett hoped it would. George was a stickler for the rules. Under normal circumstances, Garrett appreciated this work ethic in a county coroner, but circumstances were anything but normal. Garrett told George to go ahead with the postmortem without him being there. He told George to remove the item from the perp's chest and to not document it. At this request, the conversation went south. George balked at the break in procedure and protocol.

"I can't hide evidence," George insisted.

Garrett took a deep, calming breath. "Don't think of it as hidin' evidence, George. Think of it as savin' yourself a crap-ton of questions ya can't answer."

After a brief pause, George said, "What's in his chest?"

Garrett knew this was where he'd secure George's help or lose it badly.

"It's Ty's Silver Star commendation from his time in Afghanistan. It's the only thing that would kill the fucker."

Several moments of silence played out before George spoke, and Garrett realized he had been holding his breath in anticipation of his response.

George let out a sigh. "So…it's true. What those kids were sayin' at the MRB is true?"

Garrett felt relieved George hadn't dismissed the werewolf notion outright, but he didn't sound convinced.

"I'm afraid it is."

George was silent for a moment then said, "They were drinkin', Garrett. How can ya be sure they're tellin' the truth?"

"Because," Garrett said, "Ty wasn't drinkin' when he crammed his Silver Star into the thing's chest. It was full-on werewolf when he did."

George let out a heavy breath. "Holly shit, Garrett."

"Holy shit is right."

"So, this killed Mister Lomax, Missus Weaver, and those kids," George reasoned aloud.

"It and three more."

"Holly shit. Ya got a plan on how to take 'em out?"

"I'm workin' on one. I think this goes without sayin', but…"

"Say nothin' 'bout this to anyone," George finished for Garrett.

Relieved, Garrett said, "I'd appreciate your discretion."

George let out a nervous laugh. "Ya got it, Sheriff. I'll clear the morgue before I remove Ty's Silver Star, so as not to draw any unwanted attention. Tell Ty he can come by and pick it up later."

"Will do. Thanks, George."

"Just get those fuckers before I have to pick up more shredded bodies, Garrett."

"I'll do my best," Garrett assured him.

Garrett ended the call.

Garrett stood on his back deck, taking in the peaceful surroundings for several minutes after talking with George. He felt relieved George would cover for him while he worked out how to find and kill the alpha. It surprised him, though, how easily George accepted the notion of a pack of werewolves roaming East Texas, killing at will.

Strange days, Garrett thought.

Before going back inside to wake Paige and leave on his errands, Garrett fired off a quick text to Ty, letting him know George would have his Silver Star ready to pick up later that day. After sending the text, Garrett slipped his cellphone into his shirt pocket and headed for the sliding doors.

As he put his hand on the handle, his cellphone rang. Thinking it was Ty wanting to know how the conversation with George played out, Garrett answered it without checking the caller ID. It wasn't Ty.

It was the call he knew would come, and the one he dreaded. It was Lacy.

~ * ~

After being up all night making the silver bullets, Mike Middleton overslept and had to rush to get to the department for the pre-shift briefing. He was off on Saturdays, but he wanted to deliver the silver bullets and brief the deputies. As the senior Deputy Sheriff, he could brief any shift Sheriff Lambert wasn't briefing. Luck and traffic lights were on his side, and he pulled into the department parking lot with three minutes to spare.

When Mike entered the briefing room carrying two one hundred count boxes of bullets, he found Missy, Randy, Jerry, and Foster engaged in a conversation about the MRB party. Having worked all night loading silver rounds and slept all day, Mike hadn't heard about what happened at the MRB. As Randy filled him in on what he knew, and what the rumors were, Mike's grip on the boxes of bullets tightened until his knuckles were white.

When Randy finished relaying what he heard, Mike dropped the boxes of ammo on the briefing podium with a 'thud.' "Have a seat."

The nervous deputies fell silent, eased uneasily into the student-style chairs with attached desks, and gave Mike their undivided attention.

Mike looked at the nervous deputies and cleared his throat. "I believe the rumors are true."

"C'mon, Mike. Werewolves?" Foster scoffed.

Missy Gonzales shot a disapproving look at Foster. "There's a long history of *nahual* in East Texas, Foster."

Foster threw up his hands. "Is this a fuckin' joke? Are there cameras in here recordin' us for some new blooper show called *Cops on Crack* or some shit?"

Jerry and Randy laughed at Foster's comment, but they fell silent when Mike gave them a stern look.

Foster started to say something else, but Mike overrode him. "I don't give a shit if any of ya believe in *nahuals* or not. Y'all will be careful. Y'all will keep your eyes open for shit ya don't believe in. Y'all will not engage any shit that ya don't believe in without backup. Understood?"

There were some murmurs, but they all nodded.

When Mike had been satisfied that they were taking his instructions seriously, if not the nature of the threat, he picked up one of the ammo boxes. "Before y'all leave, fill a spare clip with this ammo."

Foster chuckled. "Let me guess. Silver bullets."

Mike chuckled back. "Good deduction skills, Deputy Timpson. Keep this up and ya might make detective someday."

Foster erupted in forced laughter. "Are ya fuckin' kiddin' me? Silver fuckin' bullets? Does Sheriff Lambert know you're doin' this shit?"

Mike smiled a cocky smile. "Sheriff Lambert asked me to make the silver fuckin' bullets. Any more questions?"

Foster sat fuming in silence while Missy, Randy, and Jerry shook their heads, showing they had no questions.

Satisfied the discussion was over, Mike said, "Alright. Come, fill a clip, but don't use these unless ya have no other choice."

All four deputies got up. Missy, Randy, and Jerry started toward Mike to get silver bullets. Foster headed for the briefing room door.

"Come get your rounds, Foster," Mike said.

At first, Mike thought Foster would leave without responding.

Foster stopped at the door. He turned to face Mike and the others. "I'm not indulgin' this bullshit. I'm not a fuckin' child who believes in the boogie man. I'm a deputy sheriff. If there're some crazy fuckers out there dressin' up like monsters and killin' folks, I got all I need to take 'em down right here."

Foster patted his service pistol and disappeared through the briefing room door.

Randy, Jerry, and Missy filled their spare clips in silence. When they finished, Randy and Jerry gave Mike a nod before leaving. Missy loaded her clip slowly, and Mike had a feeling she wanted to talk with him in private.

As soon as Randy and Jerry cleared the room, Missy said, "You believe in the *nahual*?"

Mike nodded. "I do."

Missy slipped the last silver bullet that would fit into her clip. "Bad news, Mike. These fuckers are bad news."

"How do ya know about 'em?"

Missy slipped the spare clip into a leather holder on her belt and snapped the flap over it. "I have family in Mexico. My uncle is a police officer in Monterrey, Mexico. He said drug cartels down there use *nahual* like gang bangers use pit bulls here. For intimidation, retribution and shit."

Mike considered what Missy said for a moment. "Do ya think these werewolves are drug related?"

Missy shrugged. "Could be. I don't know. I just know they're bad news."

Mike nodded. "Yes, they are. Be careful tonight and call me direct if ya see anything…strange."

"Will do, Mike. Thanks," she said and left the briefing room.

Mike picked up the box of silver ammo and closed it. It was then he realized he hadn't loaded his spare clip yet.

Stupid is as stupid does, Mike thought.

After loading his clip, Mike loaded a second clip and took it to Eva Martinez, who was the three-to-eleven dispatch operator.

"If Sheriff Lambert comes in, give him this and tell him it's the special load he requested from me."

He locked the remaining silver bullets in his locker and headed back home for more sleep.

~ * ~

"Where is she? Is she okay?" Lacy said as soon as Garrett answered the phone.

"She's fine."

"What was she doin' there? Why the hell did ya let her go?"

Garrett didn't know how much Lacy knew, but she had obviously been told by someone Paige attended the MRB party.

"I didn't *let* her go."

"What then? Did ya leave her alone while you and Mandy were at her house, fuckin'?" Lacy spat.

Garrett never quite understood Lacy's disdain for Mandy, or any of the other women he'd dated since their marriage ended. Lacy was on her fourth husband and Garrett didn't begrudge her moving on. Still, there it was again, contempt for Mandy.

"I was here. She snuck out."

Garrett heard Lacy snort then she said, "What kind of *father* are you? What kind of *sheriff* are you? Ya don't even know where your daughter is when she's at your house."

Garrett felt his anger rising, but he checked it. "She's sixteen, Lacy. She's gonna do shit like this. Just like we did. Instead of getting pissed off at me, be thankful she's okay."

Lacy didn't immediately respond, but Garrett could hear her breathing into the phone. After several moments of silence, her breathing slowed.

In a much calmer voice, Lacy said, "What happened out there, Garrett? I heard more than a dozen kids were killed, includin' Paige's boyfriend, by some wild animal."

Garrett was back to where he'd been with the DPS troupers and the other parents he'd spoken with after the MRB incident. Telling careful half-truths.

"I can't tell ya much because it's an open investigation…"

"Don't give me that bullshit, Garrett. I'm your wife and she's our daughter," Lacy interrupted.

You're my ex-wife, Garrett thought.

He said, "*Because* she's our daughter, I'm gonna tell ya more than I should."

But not everything, he thought.

"I'm sorry. Go ahead," Lacy relented.

Satisfied Lacy would listen, Garrett said, "What happened at the MRB wasn't the first attack. Monday mornin', an elderly man was killed in the same way. This is why I didn't *let* Paige go out last night. She asked if she could go see a movie and go bowlin' with Justin and Lindsey…not go to an MRB party."

Garrett let that sink in then he said, "I collected evidence from that scene and from some pigs that were killed shortly before the elderly victim. The evidence is animal…hair, and bite and claw marks. I took this evidence to a zoologist and biologist named Doctor Yost at SFA who helps us with this kind of stuff. We're gonna get DNA from the hair and skin, which will tell us exactly what it is. DNA extraction can take weeks. From the bite and claw mark evidence, Doctor Yost speculates that it's an enormous bear. Maybe a grizzly."

Lacy was silent for a couple of seconds and then said, "Holy shit, Garrett. How would a grizzly bear get to East Texas?"

Garrett felt relieved to hear Lacy hadn't dismissed the idea outright. He could work with her question of how one would get to East Texas.

"Well, we're not sure. One theory is that a huntin' club might have some for big spenders to trophy hunt without havin' to go to Alaska to do so."

"They escaped?" Lacy asked.

Garrett had Lacy right where he needed her.

To seal the deal, Garrett said, "Exactly. We're lookin' into all the local huntin' clubs and any private game preserve folks, too. Nobody else knows about this, so keep it to yourself. The best thing you can do is stay put until we sort this out."

After a brief pause, Lacy said, "Okay, I will. Thank you for tellin' me what ya know."

Pleased with himself, Garrett said, "You're welcome."

Garrett hoped the conversation would end there, but it didn't surprise him when Lacy said, "Shouldn't Paige come home today? I mean…you're out in the woods. What if it attacks your house?"

Garrett chuckled on purpose, so Lacy would hear it. "First, it's highly unlikely it will. Bears don't track their prey, they're opportunistic. Second, if it did, I've got enough firepower to handle it. Might even get a nice bearskin rug outta the encounter."

Lacy laughed, which had been music to Garrett's ears. "You're right. Can I talk to her?"

Smiling to himself, Garrett said, "She's asleep. Do ya want me to wake her up?"

There was a brief pause, as if Lacy considered it, then she said, "No. Let her sleep. Tell her to call me as soon as she wakes up."

This worked well because it would give Garrett time to tell Paige exactly what he'd told her mom. Get their stories straight.

"First thing. I promise," Garrett lied.

Both satisfied, they ended the call.

~ * ~

The sound of the sliding back door opening pulled Paige from the empty darkness of dreamless sleep. She knew she hadn't been asleep long, but she felt rested. A moment later, there was a soft knock on her bedroom door.

"Come in."

Garrett opened the door and looked down at her. "How ya feelin'?"

"Okay, I guess."

Garrett stepped into Paige's bedroom and took a seat on the edge of her bed. "I just talked with your mom."

Paige sat up and leaned against the headboard. "How'd that go?"

Garrett smiled. "Better than I thought it would."

He filled Paige in on everything he told Lacy.

When he finished, he said, "Look, I don't want ya to lie to your mom, but..."

"I can't tell her the truth," Paige finished for Garrett.

Garrett smiled again. "Exactly. Can ya handle that?"

Paige grinned. "I'm a little better at tellin' y'all half-truths than ya might wanna know."

Garrett thought about how Paige stuffed her bed to make it look like she had been in it before she snuck out and realized he'd have to keep better tabs on her in the future.

Garrett got up. "Yeah, I'm startin' to figure that out. Call your mom, then get dressed. I got some things to do and you're goin' with me."

Garrett started out of the bedroom and Paige asked, "Where we goin'?"

Without stopping, Garrett said, "To the department and then to Lowe's."

"Can we get somethin' to eat?" Paige shouted after him.

It gladdened Garrett's heart to hear Paige was hungry. "A hungry kid is a healthy kid," his dad used to say.

Smiling, Garrett said, "Anything ya want, Paige-Turner."

Just before Garrett shut his bedroom door to get ready, he heard Paige shout, "Dairy Queen, and I want a hot fudge Sunday for dessert!"

"Ya got it," Garrett shouted back.

~ * ~

Dillon sat in the SFA library trying to study for his upcoming Anatomy and Physiology II final exam. He was pre-med and needed to make a good grade on the exam and in the class if he had a shot at medical school. He found it hard to concentrate. Everything he thought he knew about anatomy and physiology changed when Alexis changed him. Although his eyes were looking at an open textbook, his were thoughts lost in a night's memory in early April when he met the beast.

~ * ~

It had been Saturday, April fourth. Like most Saturday nights, Dillon was home and hadn't planned to go out. When Seth called and asked Dillon if he wanted to 'hang' with him and Alexis, he couldn't say no. That had been Dillon and Seth's history for as long as Dillon could remember, which went back to grade school. They were total opposites. Seth was outgoing, tall, handsome, athletic, and affluent. Dillon was introverted, short, nondescript, intellectual, and middle-class. Somehow their friendship worked. They used each other's strengths to improve both their lives.

Because Dillon often helped Seth with coursework, some of Dillon's other friends thought Seth used Dillon. Dillon didn't see it that way. In return, Dillon got to be a part of Seth's world. A world of nice cars, cool parties, and pretty women. Dillon said yes to Seth's invitation to hang with him and Alexis. She was the latest in a long line of Seth's pretty girlfriends.

When Dillon got into the back seat of Alexis' truck and saw Cole, he immediately regretted his decision to hang. Cole was the antithesis of Seth. Outwardly, Seth and Cole were much the same. Both were outgoing, tall, handsome, athletic, and affluent. Dillon considered Cole dangerous, though.

In short, Cole was the amalgam of every bully Dillon ever knew, and he knew many. Rude, loud, and quick to fight best described Cole's limited personality. He usually reserved the fighting for smaller guys. Although Cole didn't pick on Dillon, because Seth wouldn't allow it, Dillon still felt on edge around Cole. That night started with Dillon on edge and ended with him being so terrified he soiled himself.

As Alexis pulled away from Dillon's apartment complex, Dillon said, "Where we going?"

Seth turned in the front seat to look at Dillon and Cole. "Something special tonight, boys."

Seth told Dillon later he knew what Alexis planned.

When Dillon, who, unlike Seth and Cole, wasn't happy with Alexis' 'gift,' asked Seth why he tricked him into going out with them that night, Seth calmly replied, "Because I wanted you to have some power, buddy."

Seth thought he had been doing Dillon a favor.

Dillon sat quietly in the back seat as Alexis drove west out of Nacogdoches and into the dark forest of East Texas. As they drove, the darkness melted away and Dillon's face became bathed in silvery light. He looked out the window and saw the full moon rising above the tall pine trees that passed by as dark, blurred silhouettes. Dillon found the view beautiful and comforting.

Might be a good night after all, Dillon thought.

Not long after the full moon made an appearance, Alexis slowed and turned off the road onto an overgrown path that wound through the dense woods. The silvery moonlight Dillon found comforting winked out, like an invisible hand flipped an unseen switch, as the tree limbs formed a canopy overhead. The sudden darkness unnerved Dillon.

"What's out here?" Dillon asked.

"You'll see," Alexis responded in a husky voice.

It was the first time she addressed Dillon and something in her voice, it sounded deeper, made the hairs on the back of his neck bristle.

Dillon leaned to his left so he could see out the windshield between Seth and Alexis in the front bucket seats. It looked like they were driving into a black hole. The overgrown path turned to the right, and the trees fell away as they entered a clearing with an old, dilapidated barn in the middle of it. The full moon hung above it like an unearthly spotlight, designating their destination.

Alexis drove the truck around the back of the barn, stopped, and killed the engine.

"We're here," Alexis said in a chipper, and deeper to Dillon's ear, voice.

"Where the fuck is here?" Cole barked.

Before Alexis could respond, Cole said, "What the fuck is this, Seth? You said we were gonna do something special."

Seth looked over his shoulder at Cole. "Don't get your panties in a bunch, bro. I promised you something special and I meant it. Hang on for a few more minutes and you'll see."

Cole grumbled something unintelligible under his breath as he took his seatbelt off.

He said, "There better be strippers with blow in there, bro."

Seth laughed. "Better, bro. I promise."

After they exited the truck, Alexis led them to a side door in the barn with only two out of three rusty hinges connecting it to the door frame. The top hinge had been broken and the bottom two let out an unholy screech in protest when Seth forced it open. Dillon noticed the normal night sounds in the surrounding woods fell silent in response to the screech. Seth stood beside the door as Alexis and Cole entered the barn.

Everything inside Dillon told him, screamed at him, to run away and he hesitated entering the barn.

"Come on in," Seth said.

Dillon remained rooted in his spot. "I don't like this, Seth."

Dillon wasn't the kind of guy who could refer to male acquaintances as 'bro.' It felt stupid coming out of his mouth.

Seth smiled in the silvery moonlight. "It's gonna be okay, Dillon. I promise."

Dillon appreciated that Seth rarely referred to him as 'bro' and he took a step toward the leaning door. The normal night sounds scared into silence by the screeching door hinge swelled in the night air again.

Don't be a pussy, Dillon thought as he stepped into the barn.

Seth followed Dillon inside and pulled the screeching door closed behind him. The forest fell silent again and would remain that way when the beast arrived.

Seth walked Dillon over to where Cole stood. Alexis stood by herself several feet away.

"Y'all stay here. I'll be right back," Seth said.

Seth walked over to Alexis, and they began talking with each other in hushed voices.

Dillon tried to eavesdrop on their whispered conversation but Cole, in a loud voice clearly directed at Seth, bellowed, “This is bullshit, bro. If something amazing doesn’t happen real fuckin’ quick, I’m outta here.”

Because they raised their voices to hear each other over Cole, Dillon clearly heard Seth say, “Are ya sure you can control yourself?” as Cole’s voice died away.

Dillon heard Alexis, in her new, deeper voice, say, “I’m sure.”

Seth whispered something else to Alexis. Dillon couldn’t hear clearly because Cole mumbled, “This fuckin’ sucks, bro.”

Seth took the flashlight from Alexis and walked back over to Dillon and Cole.

When Seth joined Dillon and Cole, Cole said, “What the fuck, bro?”

Seth pointed the flashlight at his own face, which cast eerie, recessed shadows across his handsome features, and smiled. “I promised you something special, bro. It’s time.”

Seth pointed the flashlight beam at Alexis, who stood in the middle of the barn.

Dillon looked at Alexis and saw her pupils flare red. It had been brief, but he knew it wasn’t his imagination.

It’s just retinal reflection from the flashlight, Dillon thought.

The thought felt false, like he had been lying to himself. He took a step back.

Seth noticed Dillon’s retreat, grabbed his upper-arm—not roughly but sternly—and pulled him forward. “Just watch, Dillon. This should be amazing.”

That Seth had said “should be” and not “will be” wasn’t lost on Dillon.

He doesn’t know what’s gonna happen, Dillon thought.

Dillon had been too unnerved to move. He watched as Seth instructed.

Alexis reached up, removed the scrunchie holding her blonde hair back in a ponytail, and dropped it to the filthy barn floor. She shook her head and her long blonde hair fell loose across her shoulders and face. Alexis grabbed the bottom of the tight-fitting, light blue top she wore and, in one fluid movement, pulled it over her head and deposited it on the barn floor next to the scrunchie. She wasn't wearing a bra, but her hair obscured a clear view of her breasts.

Excited, Cole said, "Are ya fuckin' kidding me, bro."

Seth, still pointing the flashlight at half-dressed Alexis, said, "Don't lose your shit, bro. It's gonna get better."

"A lot better," Alexis said in a voice that almost sounded like a growl.

"What's happening, Seth?" Dillon squeaked.

Cole laughed. "For a smart guy, you're pretty fuckin' stupid, Dillon."

"What? What am I missing?" Dillon pleaded.

"Dude…there are three of us and she's got three holes to fill. Seth's gonna let us gang bang his bitch!" Cole shouted.

Dillon looked at Seth for a sign whether Cole reasoned correctly, but Seth's focus, like the flashlight beam, remained on Alexis.

Dillon's mouth went dry, and his fear level increased. He remained, by circumstance not choice, a virgin, and the thought of having first time sex with Alexis and two other guys made his balls shrivel.

Dillon looked back at Alexis just in time to see her unbutton her blue jean shorts and slide the waistband over her hips. Gravity took over, and they crumpled around her ankles. She wasn't wearing panties either, and her hair wasn't long enough to obscure this view. Dillon tried unsuccessfully to swallow the knot that formed in his throat.

"Hot, fuckin' damn, bro. What's the order? Are we going all at once? If we're gang banging, I call muddy helmet. Stick dipshit here with the blowjob so he doesn't get in our way. I don't wanna cross swords with him." Cole blurted.

Dillon, feeling sick to his stomach, looked at Seth. "I can't do this, Seth."

Cole looked at Dillon and, with obvious contempt, said, "You fuckin' pussy. Go sit in the truck while we take care of the bitch."

Dillon and Cole were looking at each other with disdain when Alexis let out a growling laugh and, in a deep guttural voice, said, "Nobody's fuckin' this bitch tonight."

They looked back at Alexis in time to see her fall to the barn floor on her hands and knees. Her smooth back arched upward violently as the vertebra elongated and became more pronounced beneath her skin. Alexis let out a scream that turned into a growl as a thick, black hair began sprouting over her back. Spasms ripped through her muscles that appeared to boil under her skin as they found purchase on bones that were elongating and reforming.

Alexis rolled onto her back, her arms and legs flailed and elongating. Her firm breasts flattened against a rounded and bony canine-like ribcage. Her nipples darkened and four more pairs of dark nipples budded along her ribcage and belly as coarse, black hair continued to cover her chest and abdomen. A spray of blood erupted from the tips of her long, bony fingers as black, razor-sharp claws replaced her manicured fingernails. The transformation had completed, except for Alexis' head and face, which looked alien atop the massive werewolf's body.

Alexis rolled onto all fours and then sprang to her feet. She surveyed the three men standing transfixed and terrified before her through her still human eyes. The transformation was more painful than she expected, and tears slid down her human cheeks. Her eyes flared red, and she gnashed her teeth loudly.

Alexis shook her head violently, and her long blonde hair fell away in a golden blur. Her forehead flattened and elongated as her ears migrated to the top of her misshapen skull and stretched into points. Alexis' bottom jaw swelled wider and dislocated with a loud 'crack.' Her upper and lower jaws elongated. Alexis' human teeth were dislodged from her gums in sprays of blood as dagger-length canine fangs filled in the bloody holes. Course, black hair flooded over her face and head and long, thick whiskers sprouted on either side of her viscous snout.

Alexis was a werewolf for the first time, and she loved how it felt. She loved the feeling of power that rippled through her massive and honed muscles. Alexis loved the enhanced vision, she could see everything in stark relief even outside of the flashlight beam, and the enhanced hearing, she could hear the frightened men breathing and their frantic heartbeats. She loved her enhanced sense of smell. She could smell their sweat, their musk, and their fear. She pointed her snout toward the rafters and let out a demonic howl that rattled the old barn, causing decades of dust to dislodge and rain down on them.

Dillon, a man of science, couldn't believe what he saw. He'd heard of werewolves but, like most people, never considered they existed. He couldn't deny what his eyes were seeing. For a moment, the large, rational part of his mind insisted he'd been drugged with a strong hallucinogenic and what he was witnessing had been nothing more than a trick of his impaired consciousness. That consideration quickly evaporated when he realized he introduced nothing foreign to his body since encountering the others. When the werewolf howled a very loud and real howl, Dillon pissed his pants.

After Dillon's ears cleared from the deafening howl, he heard Cole shout, "What the fuck did ya do to us, bro?"

Seth, in a very calm voice, said, "Relax, bro. It'll be over in a minute."

"Fuck you." Cole shouted, and he bolted for the door.

This had been an ill-advised move, because it caused Cole to move past the very large werewolf. As soon as Cole's path moved within reach, the werewolf swiped its claws across his chest and sent him flying across the barn. Cole crashed into the side of the barn and fell to the floor in a heap. He didn't move.

When the werewolf took a step toward the prone Cole, Seth yelled, "Alexis."

The werewolf stopped and looked at Seth as if it didn't understand. Its eyes flared a dangerous red, but it didn't go after Cole. Instead, it charged Seth. It had him in its deadly hands before he or Dillon could react.

It lifted Seth easily from the ground and held him up until they were eye to eye. The werewolf snapped at Seth's face; its teeth slamming shut with a deadly retort less than an inch from Seth's nose. It bit down on Seth's right shoulder. Seth screamed in agony as blood instantly soaked through his shirt. The werewolf released the bite and dropped Seth to the barn floor with a 'thud.' It glanced at Dillon before turning and heading to Cole.

Dillon grabbed Seth, started trying to get him to his feet, and screamed, "Come on. Let's get outta here."

Seth coughed, and blood leaked from the corner of his mouth.

He pulled away from Dillon. "She won't kill us."

Dillon glanced toward the werewolf and saw it lift Cole from the floor with one arm and bite him on the shoulder, too. Like with Seth, it dropped him. The realization of what living through a werewolf's bite would mean seeped into Dillon's mind. He also realized Seth and Alexis had planned this in advance.

He looked at Seth. "What were you thinking?"

Seth smiled. More blood leaked from his mouth. "She needs a

pack."

Dillon looked from Seth to the werewolf, which turned toward them after dropping Cole, and back at Seth in disbelief.

Dillon looked toward the crooked door and Seth said, "She'll catch you. Just take the bite."

Dillon knew Seth had been right about the werewolf being able to catch him, but instinct overpowered reason and he bolted for the door. Amazingly, the werewolf made no move to snatch him as he ran past it to the door. It's burning red eyes tracked his movements.

When Dillon burst through the crooked door, the rusted hinges let out another loud screech. He tripped on the door threshold, which was a two-by-four, and plowed face first into the ground. The impact chipped both top, front teeth and cut his lip. Tasting his own blood only fueled his need to escape. Dillon scrambled awkwardly to his feet and bolted toward the overgrown path they'd driven in on. He chanced a glance over his shoulder, expecting to see the werewolf closing in on him, but it was nowhere to be seen.

As Dillon made it to the path and left the clearing behind him, darkness created by the tree branch canopy overhead engulfed him. Disoriented by the sudden inky blackness, Dillon tripped again and fell into a patch of something spiny that pierced his face and forearms. The pain added more fuel to the adrenalin pumping through his veins. Dillon scrambled to his feet again and, with his eyes adjusting to the darkness, found the path and ran as fast as he could toward the road they'd turned off.

As Dillon ran, all he could hear was the thudding of his feet on the ground, his ragged breathing as he sucked in air like it had been in short supply, and the internal hammering of his heart, which seemed to have moved from his chest to just behind his ears. He saw light ahead and thought it was the full moonlight at the road end of the path. Dillon realized the light had been coming from his right and getting brighter.

Car, Dillon's mind screamed inside his head, briefly drowning out the sound of his heart.

Dillon ran faster, but the truck rumbled by about a hundred feet ahead of him before he cleared the path. He heard something large crashing through the woods on his left. It kept pace with him.

Although Dillon knew in his rapidly beating heart that he couldn't escape the werewolf, he continued to run for the road. It was all he could do. The crashing in the woods stayed with him and Dillon realized it was playing with him.

When he made it to the end of the path and skidded to a stop on the asphalt road, he expected the werewolf to burst out of the woods and attack him, but it didn't. Physically spent, Dillon put his hands on his knees and sucked in gulps of cool night air. As his breathing eased, he realized how deathly quiet the surrounding woods were.

Dillon stood up straight and gazed at the dark woods where he heard the crashing sounds. A pair of fiery red eyes, low to the ground, pierced the shadowy woods and looked back at him.

Dillon summoned what little courage he had and screamed, "I don't wanna be in your pack. Just kill me, Alexis."

Dillon heard the werewolf growl. The growl was bad, but Dillon's knees almost unhinged when the growl turned into a demonic laugh that shook the surrounding underbrush. He watched as the burning red eyes rose. As the eyes reached their apex, Dillon heard a noise to his left. The sound of an approaching vehicle. Headlights crested a hill in the road and briefly bathed Dillon in the yellow light before they dipped back down.

What happened next happened so quickly Dillon barely registered it at all. The werewolf exploded from the woods and closed the distance between Dillon and it in less than one of Dillon's rapid heartbeats. It slammed into Dillon so hard it knocked all the air in his lungs out of him. The werewolf wrapped Dillon in its powerful arms and rolled into the dense woods on the far side of the road. When the rolling stopped, Dillon realized his neck was inside the werewolf's deadly jaws and its hot, wet tongue snaked teasingly around his throat.

Dillon couldn't move or breathe, he could see, though. The vehicle he'd seen, another truck, slowed to a stop in the road where he'd been standing only seconds earlier.

He heard a woman, she sounded elderly, say, "I'm tellin' ya, I saw a man in the road here."

Then a man, who also sounded elderly, said, "Well…Momma, he ain't here now."

"What if he's in trouble?" the woman said.

"Do ya want me to get out and look?" the man responded.

After a brief pause in the conversation, the woman said, "Somethin' don't feel right, Poppa."

"Oh, here we go," the man said.

"Now, don't do me like that. Listen?" the woman responded.

After another brief pause, the man said, "To what? I don't hear nothin'."

"Exactly. It's too quiet. Let's go. Just drive," the woman responded.

"What about the man ya *say* you saw?" the man asked.

"God be with him," the lady said.

The truck rumbled away.

Dillon knew the werewolf had been trying to keep him from attracting the attention of the people in the truck. Even if it hadn't had its jaws wrapped around his neck, Dillon wouldn't have called out to them. To do so would have been like signing their death warrants.

When the truck was safely out of earshot, the werewolf removed its jaws from Dillon's neck. The relief had been fleeting, though, because it immediately bit down on Dillon's shoulder. White flickers of light danced in Dillon's vision as the intense pain filled his body. The flickers quickly multiplied, and Dillon melted into blinding white unconsciousness.

When Dillon came to, he was back in the barn with Seth and Cole. Cole was still unconscious, but Dillon could hear his ragged breathing and reasoned, correctly, several of Cole's ribs were broken when the werewolf threw him across the barn.

Dillon looked at Seth. "Where is she?"

"Hunting," Seth replied calmly.

~ * ~

The vibrating buzz of his cellphone on the desk beside the unread textbook pulled Dillon from the memory of that night. He looked at the caller ID, saw it was Cole, and, briefly, considered not answering it. After several rings, he answered.

"What do you want?" Dillon said in a terse voice.

"Hey, bro. Is that anyway to greet a pack member?" Cole joked.

"I'm trying to study for my A and P final. What do you want?"

"Okay, okay. No need to get your dick up, bro," Cole said with a chuckle.

Frustrated, Dillon said, "I'm not your bro and my dick's not up. Last chance before I hang up. What do you want?"

After a brief pause, Cole said, "I'm thinking about going hunting tonight. Ya wanna go?"

Dillon knew 'hunting' meant changing. He also knew Alexis told them not to change for several days.

"Alexis said not to," Dillon reminded Cole.

With clear disdain in his voice, Cole said, "Bro, fuck that bitch. What she doesn't know won't hurt her. Besides, I'm thinking about taking her down a notch or two. I don't take orders from a bitch, bro."

Unable to resist taking a dig at Cole, and because he was safely away from him on the cellphone, Dillon said, "Like you did this morning? You really took her down a notch or two...*bro*. No, wait. She bitch-slapped your ass across the barn."

Dillon could hear Cole's heavy breathing and knew he'd touched a nerve.

Angrily, Cole said, "You know what...fuck you, you little pussy. I don't know why the fuck Seth kept you around. I guess he had a puppy long before Alexis had a pack."

The remark about Seth hurt Dillon. He hadn't processed the loss of his best friend or the ramifications of it.

With all the force he could muster in a library setting, Dillon said, "Fuck you, Cole."

"Fuck me? Fuck you, little bro. Seth's not here to protect your pussy ass anymore," Cole hissed.

Dillon ended the call.

After the call, Dillon sat motionless for several moments, taking deep, calming breaths. He thought about Cole going hunting against Alexis' wishes. Dillon quickly knew after she turned him that a mental connection opened between the alpha and its pack.

Could Cole be so thick as to not know about the connection? Dillon thought.

Dillon decided quickly someone as self-absorbed as Cole could miss something like that.

Dillon took a deep breath and exhaled slowly. A smile spread across his face. A big smile that caused his cheeks to contact the bottom frame of his glasses and push them upward.

If this goes well, I might not have to worry about Cole Duncan much longer, Dillon thought.

Dillon looked back at the textbook and found he could concentrate again.

Chapter Twelve

By the time Garrett eased his aching body into his recliner, it was a little after seven o'clock and the sun was low in the western sky. It would soon be dark, and that worried him more than it had since he'd been a little boy who needed a nightlight to keep the Closet Monster away. He felt good about the preparations he took, though.

~ * ~

After Paige was up and dressed, they got into Garrett's personal truck and drove to the Sheriff's Department. On the drive there, Garrett asked Paige about the connection and whether she'd felt anything from the alpha since the pain and anger after the incident with the silver crucifix and necklace. Given what Ty told him about feeling the alpha pleasuring herself, Garrett felt a little apprehensive about broaching the subject, but if James had been correct about the alpha's inexperience and possibly using the connection to find her, he felt it was necessary.

When Paige didn't immediately respond, Garrett said, "I don't need details, Paige. I just wanna know if you've sensed her again since this mornin'."

Paige, who tensed when Garrett first asked her whether she'd sensed the alpha, relaxed. "Yeah. I felt her a little before two o'clock. Only this time she was…happy."

Orgasms have that effect, Garrett thought.

He said, "Anything else?"

Paige thought for a moment. "I saw a flash of dim light. It was like…for a second…I was seein' outta her eyes."

This revelation had promise.

"Could ya make anything out?"

After a brief pause, Paige said, "Not really. It might'a been a ceiling…like she was layin' on her back lookin' up."

Given that she'd been 'flickin' the bean,' as Ty put it, that perspective seemed about right to Garrett.

Paige added, "Right before the connection broke, I felt her think

Only a few more hours."

Until what? Garrett thought again.

That Ty and Paige shared the same connection experience confirmed its reality to Garrett. When it happened earlier, Garrett wasn't entirely certain they weren't reinforcing each other's delusions. He'd seen this behavior in witnesses to a crime or accident before. One witness remembers a minute detail and, suddenly, all the other witnesses remember it, too. Therefore, talented investigators isolate witnesses and question them separately. Garrett accomplished this by getting the same account from Ty and Paige separately. This only reinforced Garrett's resolve to prepare. He didn't know what the alpha planned in a few hours, but he would be as ready as he could be.

"Listen," Garrett started, "there's a professor at SFA who studies mythology. He seems to know a lot about this stuff, and he thinks y'all *might* use this connection to get details 'bout the alpha that can help us find her. Since you and Ty told me the same thing 'bout what happened a while ago, I think this might be somethin' worth perusin'. You'll need to be careful, though. Don't push it."

Paige seemed to tense in her seat, and Garrett thought the prospect of trying to connect with the alpha made her uncomfortable.

Paige said, "Ty felt…sensed her, too?"

"Yeah. He told me everything you did, right down to the only a few more hours thought."

Paige shifted uncomfortably in her seat. "Did Ty tell ya anything else?"

Garrett realized it wasn't the thought of initiating contact with the alpha that made Paige uncomfortable. It had been that he knew about the shared sexual experience that had her uncomfortable.

Not wanting to add to Paige's discomfort, Garrett said, "Not really."

Although Paige felt certain Ty told her dad everything, and they probably got a laugh out of it, she appreciated his discretion. Paige also thought, if he knew, he was probably as, if not more, uncomfortable with talking about it than she was.

Paige relaxed a bit. "I tried to connect with her again, but nothin' happened."

It didn't surprise Garrett to hear Paige tried to start contact with the alpha. She was tenacious.

"Okay. Just be careful," Garrett reiterated.

Paige smiled. "I will, Daddy. I promise."

By the time the potentially awkward connection conversation was over, they were at the sheriff's department. Garrett saw several news vans from the larger surrounding cities of Tyler and Longview in the parking lot. He wasn't looking forward to dealing with the press, but he knew he couldn't avoid it.

Garrett pulled into his reserved parking spot. "Wait here. I'll be out in a minute."

"Can I listen to the radio?"

Garrett smiled. "Anything but rap."

Garrett closed the door and, before he'd taken a few steps, heard the distinctive 'thump-thump' of a rap base emanating from his truck. He turned, continued to walk backward, and looked at Paige. She had her hands cupped around her mouth and was beat boxing exaggeratedly. Garrett started laughing, gave Paige a dismissive wave, turned, and walked toward went into the building.

Several members of the press, who waited outside the Station, questioned Garrett for information about the MRB Massacre. It already had a name.

He politely disengaged with standard responses like, "When I know more, you'll know more," "Too early to speculate," "I can't comment on an open investigation," and "We're followin' every lead."

To escape the press, Garrett went inside and had Eva Martinez buzz him.

When the heavy metal door closed behind him, Garrett said, "Has it been like this all day?"

Eva shook her head. "They only started showin' up 'bout an hour ago. Apparently, news travels before the news knows."

Garrett nodded. "Any messages for me?"

Eva laughed. "Only a couple hundred."

Garrett chuckled. "Why am I not surprised? Anything…unusual happenin' today?"

Eva shook her head. "Nope. Just the usual stuff. A cow got lose on Country Road Five-Thirteen, a stray dog killed some chickens off Highway Twenty-One, a…"

"Ya sure it was a dog?" Garrett interrupted.

Eva nodded. "Positive. Deputy Abbott caught it and took it to the shelter."

Garrett heard enough about the mundane calls. The real reason he'd dropped by was to find out if Mike had made the silver bullets.

"Did Deputy Middleton leave anything for me?"

Eva smiled. "Why, he sure did. I'm glad ya said somethin'. It completely slipped my mind."

She opened a draw under the counter, pulled the ten-round clip out, and handed it to Garrett.

Garrett looked at the top bullet in the clip and saw the shiny silver load. Feeling empowered, Garrett stuffed the clip in his back pocket.

He started to say goodbye to Eva when she said, "Those silver bullets?"

Garrett tried to think of a deflecting response, when Eva said, "A *nahual* killed those kids, Lomax, and Weaver, didn't it?"

Garrett's eyes met Eva's, and he knew she knew.

Eva smiled an uneasy smile. "My *abuelo* used to tell me scary stories about the *nahual* of Mexico. He said only a few things could kill a *nahual,* but silver was the best."

Garrett smiled an uneasy smile, too. "Your grandpa was a smart man."

Eva quickly made the sign of the cross. "I always thought they were make believe."

"Until last Monday, so did I?"

A moment of silence passed then Eva said, "You kill the demon, Sheriff Lambert. Kill it with those silver bullets."

"Kill *them*. I plan to."

Eva sucked in a surprised breath. "Them? As in more than one?"

Garrett nodded. "There are at least three we know of. Deputy Jackson killed one of 'em at the Weaver place."

Eva crossed herself again. "The boy in the morgue was one of 'em?"

Garrett nodded again. "Listen, Eva. I trust ya understand not to share this information with anyone. Especially the vultures out front."

Eva, still wide-eyed, nodded.

Garrett forced a reassuring smile on his face. "I'm gonna sneak out the back. Don't let 'em know I'm gone for a while. Call me direct on my cell if anything…unnatural happens."

Eva nodded again. "Will do."

As Garrett headed away, toward the back of the building, Eva said, "Go with God, Sheriff."

I hope so, Garrett thought.

~ * ~

Paige turned off the rap music as soon as her dad went into the department. She didn't care for rap either and turned it on, and up, to mess with him. She knew Channel Forty-Four on SiriusXM was the *Hip Hop Nation* because Justin enjoyed listening to rap sometimes. This, of course, made her think of Justin, and she choked back tears immediately. Paige pushed the preset button for her dad's favorite channel, Channel Fifty-Eight, *Prime Country* from the 1980's and 1990's. Alan Jackson's *Don't Rock the Jukebox* played mid-chorus. Paige sat back and tried to think about something other than Justin.

After the Alan Jackson song ended, Joe Diffie's *Third Rock from the Sun* started playing. Paige didn't know all the words, but she sang along to the chorus. She loved signing and had a pleasant voice, but she only sang while alone. By the time the Joe Diffie song was over, she was feeling better. Then, as luck would have it, "Shit luck is still luck," her grandpa said, Alabama's *Feels So Right* started playing and her tears started flowing.

Paige wanted to turn the song off, but she listened. She felt she owed it to Justin to hear it through. Even though she cried throughout the song, it made her feel better. The pain of losing Justin had been real and raw, but knowing what he'd done at the tree house, what he remembered about her from snippets of conversations he'd heard over the years, to make her first time so special, comforted her more than it saddened her. She'd loved and been loved in return. That notion warmed her heart and strengthened her resolve to connect with the bitch who'd killed Justin. To connect with her, find her, and help her dad kill her.

When the Alabama song was over, Paige turned off the radio and retrieved a box of tissues her dad kept in the console. She flipped up the visor mirror and studied her puffy face.

"You look like shit," Paige told her reflection.

After a couple of minutes and a handful of tissues, she looked pretty good. Her nose and eyes were still a little red, but not excessively so.

Just as Paige flipped the visor back into place, she saw her dad come around the side of the department.

When Garrett got into the truck, he said, “I went out the back to avoid the press in the front.”

Paige nodded. “Where to now?”

“Lowe’s.”

“For what?”

“Motion-activated flood lights and critter-cams.”

“Good thinkin’, Daddy,” Paige said with a single head nod.

Garrett smiled. “That’s why I’m the sheriff.”

~ * ~

At Lowe’s, Paige opted to stay in the truck. Garrett didn’t think Paige would slow him down in a place like Lowe’s, not a chosen destination for most teenage girls, but he knew he’d finish quicker without her. He found the outdoor lighting section quickly, and he even found motion-activated floodlights very similar to the regular floodlights already installed on the four corners of his house. Thinking they would install easily; he grabbed four sets and went to look for the critter-cams.

After looking for several minutes, Garrett found a youngish lady in a Lowe’s vest. Her name tag had Brenda on it—and he asked her where he could find the critter-cams. Brenda was clueless until Garrett explained what he had been looking for.

When it sank in, Brenda said, “Oh, you mean the game cameras?”

Garrett, not thinking ‘critter-cam’ and ‘game camera’ were so far removed from each other to throw Brenda off her game, but not wanting to be rude, said, “Yes. I’m lookin’ for game cameras.”

Brenda smiled a “you’re an idiot customer, so I have to smile at you,” smile. “Yeah, we don’t have those. Check at Wally World.”

Garrett thanked Brenda and checked out.

When Garrett got back into the truck, Paige said, “What took so long?”

“I was lookin’ for critter-cams they don’t have. So, we’re headed to Walmart.”

Paige smiled. “I *will* go into Walmart with ya.”

Garrett muttered, “Of course, ya will.”

If Paige heard the comment, she ignored it.

The Nacogdoches Walmart was only about a quarter mile from the Lowe's and they were there in a matter of minutes. Like always, the Walmart parking lot had few open parking spots. Garrett drove up and down several rows before he spotted a car backing out of a space close to the store in front of the Garden Center. He zipped into the spot before a car driving the wrong way up the row could get to it. The old blue-haired lady behind the steering wheel scowled at Garrett and flicked him a gnarled, arthritic bird.

Paige saw the gesture and burst into laughter. Garrett tried to remain straight-faced and parked the truck before he too was laughing his ass off.

Between giggle fits, Paige said, "I can't believe that old lady gave you the bird."

Garrett, still laughing, said, "It was a mummified bird."

They laughed even harder.

When they stopped laughing about the gnarled, arthritic bird, Garrett said, "Alright, kiddo. Let's get in and get out."

Paige wiped away the tears, happy tears, on her cheeks, and nodded. "The sooner we're done here, the sooner we hit Dairy Queen."

With this thought in both their minds, they got out of the truck and entered Walmart through the Garden Center.

Once inside Walmart, and out of the Garden Center, Sporting Goods was to the left, just past the Toy Department. Garrett considered that a pretty good layout plan. A place nearby for dads who got roped into going to Walmart to hang out while the wife and kids spent money on toys. Garrett and Paige took the back aisle to avoid the throng of shoppers clustered in the main aisle.

When they approached the Sporting Goods counter from behind, Garrett saw a woman was working there. Garrett didn't consider himself a sexist, but he wasn't hopeful she'd be much help. When he got around and faced her, and saw her name was Brenda, just like the ditsy Lowe's girl, he figured the trip would be a total bust. He couldn't have been more wrong. This Brenda knew her shit. She even knew what Garrett meant when he accidentally referred to them as 'critter-cams' instead of 'game cameras.'

Brenda led Garrett and Paige to the aisle containing the game cameras. There were a plethora to choose from. This wasn't a problem for Super Brenda. She answered all of Garrett's questions and offered advice when needed. Garrett just wanted something that would take pictures and video at night and had a range of about fifty feet.

In the end, Garrett purchased four Moultrie Game Spy A-5 Low Glow, night-vision, five megapixels, digital game cameras. This model had a fifty-foot night range, took night-vision pictures and videos, powered by six included rechargeable, double-A batteries. Brenda assured Garrett they would last up to a month with nightly use and stored the images on eight-gigabyte included SD cards. Brenda assured Garrett they would store thousands of pictures or four to eight hours of videos, depending on the resolution. Even better for what Garrett had in mind. No tools needed to attach the camera to trees. They came with long, adjustable straps that held them in place.

The total, with sales tax, came to three hundred ninety-one dollars and eighty-six cents, but Garrett thought the price worth every penny. Garrett and Paige thanked Brenda and left Walmart.

From Walmart, they drove south on North Street to the Dairy Queen. It surprised Garrett how much food Paige inhaled; a Bacon Cheese GrillBurger, onion rings, cheese curds, and a hot fudge sundae, and he wondered if her appetite had anything to do with the bite. Garrett had a Flame Thrower GrillBurger, fries, and a Butterfinger Blizzard. This filled his belly.

By the time they started on dessert, it had been almost four o'clock.

Knowing he had a lot of work ahead of him, Garrett said, "We can eat these on the way home."

Surprised, because her dad never allowed food or drink in his personal truck, Paige said, "Who are you and what have ya done with my dad?"

Garrett chuckled. "I have a lot of work to do, if I'm gonna get the flood lights and critter-cams installed before dark. Just be careful with that."

Paige smiled. "I'll be careful, if I can help ya put the stuff up."

Garrett clinked his Blizzard cup against Paige's sundae tray. "Deal. You can hand me tools."

With that settled, they got in Garrett's truck and headed for home.

~ * ~

The drive home offered Garrett some digestion time, which he needed because the thought of climbing ladders and trees with the Flame Thrower GrillBurger heavy in his stomach wasn't appealing. When they arrived home, Garrett didn't bother going inside the house. He marched around back, with Paige in tow, to the shed where he kept his riding lawnmower, weed whacker, leaf blower, tools, unlocked it, opened the double doors, and stepped inside.

It was dark inside the shed. The place smelled of grass clippings and gasoline. Garrett loved the way it smelled. He flipped the switch that illuminated the florescent lights hung from the ceiling and they bathed the interior in harsh, white light.

Garrett pointed to the workbench. "Grab my tool belt, Paige."

As Paige went for the tool belt, Garrett took a folding, eight-foot ladder off pegs on the wall opposite the workbench and grabbed the smaller of two toolboxes on the floor just inside the double doors on his way out of the shed.

The back right floodlight was closest, so Garrett started there. As Garrett set up the ladder, put the tool belt on, and selected the proper tools, a Phillips-head screwdriver, Paige went to retrieve the Lowe's bag from the truck. Garrett's intuition about the fit of the new lights turned out to be correct. They had the same size base and fit the existing housing perfectly. Within twenty minutes he replaced all four of the old.

With the motion-activated floodlights installed, Garrett turned his attention to the critter-cams. First, he needed to select the trees he wanted to mount them to. He had hundreds to choose from. Garrett and Paige walked around the parameter of the yard, checking the large pine trees. Garrett knew what he had been looking for. Tall pine trees with no limbs lower than thirty feet, at least one hundred feet away from the house. Since he did not know from which direction the werewolves might approach, he wanted to find trees that basically lined up with the four corners of the house.

After about twenty minutes of looking, Garrett settled on the trees he would install the critter-cams on. With the trees selected, he realized there would still be many blind spots from which the werewolves, if they came, could approach. Without time to run back to Walmart and purchase more critter-cams, Garrett hoped for the best.

Garrett looked up at the tree he would install the first critter-cam on. "Okay, now the fun part."

Paige, looking up at the tree too, said, "How are ya gonna get up there?"

Garrett gave her a wink. "You'll see. Go back to the truck and take one critter-cam out of the box. Put the batteries and SD card in it and meet me back here with the cam and installation instructions."

Paige looked from Garrett to the tree, back to Garrett with doubt, and said, "I'll be right back."

As Paige went back to the truck to get the critter-cam, Garrett returned to the shed. What he needed were items he hadn't used since his logging days. He stored them in the back of the shed, and Garrett had what he needed within a few minutes. He gathered the gear and arrived at the tree before Paige returned with the camera.

When Paige returned with the camera, Garrett had started gearing up. He had metal spikes attached to the inside of each of his boots by two thick, leather straps each, a thick, nylon harness around his waist that had large, metal rings attached on each side. A longer, thick, nylon strap attached to one of the metal rings on the belt. A long, nylon rope tied around his waist and slung over his shoulder, and heavy, leather gloves on his hands.

Paige was too young to remember Garrett's logging days and never saw the gear he was donning. "What's all this?"

Garrett smiled. "When you were a baby, before I worked for the county, I used to be a logger. This is the gear I used to climb trees and clear limbs, if they posed a problem for felling a tree where I needed it to fall."

Paige looked concerned. "Can ya still climb trees with that stuff?"

Garrett gave her another wink. "We're about to find out."

Garrett walked up to the tree and slung the loose end of the long nylon support strap around it. It landed on the ground by his left boot. He picked it up and attached the metal clip on the end of the strap to the metal ring on the left side of the harness. Garrett threw the support strap up the tree a couple of feet and leaned back, putting his body weight on it, to test the hold. It held fine. Garrett raised his right foot about two feet off the ground and stabbed the metal spike into the tree, then he did the same with his left foot. He was off the ground.

Only twenty-eight more feet and three other trees to go, Garrett thought.

Before climbing anymore, Garrett turned to Paige. "When I get up about thirty feet, I'll drop the end of this rope down to ya. When I do, tie it to the strap on the critter-cam so I can pull it up."

Paige, looking more concerned than before, said, "Okay. Be careful, Daddy."

Garrett gave Paige a reassuring grin. "I will, sweetheart."

He started climbing.

It wasn't exactly like riding a bike, in that once he mastered the skill it comes back easily, but Garrett had the hang of strap-climbing again in no time. The old muscle-memory of right foot stab, left foot stab, and sling the strap up repetition felt very natural. Although the old movements came back to Garrett, the strength and endurance of his youth did not. By the time Garret climbed, by his estimation, thirty feet up, his legs, shoulders, arms, and back burned with pain.

He looked down at Paige, who looked tiny and worried, and hollered, "Here comes the rope."

Garrett dropped the rope and watched as Paige tied it to the critter-cam. When she tied it off, he hoisted it up.

Set-up appeared straightforward. Using the adjustable strap to secure the camera to the tree Garrett had to get inventive to accommodate for the downward angle he needed the camera to be in. Although he didn't have any tools with him, he always had his lock-blade Buck 110 hunting knife in his pocket. He used it to dislodge chucks of pine bark, which he wedged behind the top portion of the camera to force the angle down. After a few minutes of work, Garrett was satisfied the camera would capture images of anything on the ground approaching his house. He switched the camera on and the faint, red indicator light on the front of the camera lit up. That left climbing down without falling and breaking his neck.

As when he was a younger logger, climbing down was less difficult than climbing up. This time, at least he didn't have a twenty-pound chainsaw strapped to the harness. Within a few minutes, he was safely back on the ground; winded, but on the ground.

The next three set-ups went smoothly but, because of increasing fatigue and aching muscles, each took longer to complete than the previous set-up.

When he got to the ground after setting up the last camera, Paige said, "Do ya think they'll come tonight?"

Garrett considered her question briefly. If James Huff had been correct that the alpha never intended to kill Paige, Garrett didn't know why they would come back. If the alpha intended to kill Paige, but couldn't because of the silver crucifix and necklace, Garrett thought they might come back to finish the job.

Garrett's mind kept going back to the alpha's final thought. Ty and Paige both sensed it—only a few more hours.

Until what? Garrett thought again.

Not wanting to upset Paige with his thoughts, Garrett said, "I don't know. If they do, we'll know."

Garrett pulled the silver bullet filled clip from his back pocket and handed it to Paige. "I've got these now."

Paige looked at the top, shiny bullet. "Are these silver?"

Garrett nodded. "They sure are. If that bitch shows up here tonight, she's gonna wish she died the night she got bit."

Paige, still looking at the silver bullet, said, "Will ya use one of these on me when I turn?"

A lump formed in Garrett's throat that kept him from immediately reassuring his little girl she'd be okay. That she already contemplated her turn and death, broke Garrett's heart.

Garrett grabbed Paige in a tight hug and swallowed the lump in his throat. "It's not gonna come to that, Paige-Turner. I promise ya."

"If it does, you'll kill me, right? Promise me you'll kill me, Daddy. I don't wanna be one of those... monsters. Promise me, Daddy."

Tears spilled down Garrett's face as he said, "I promise, sweetheart. If it comes to that, I'll do it."

The worst part had been Garrett knew if it came to that, he'd have to kill Ty and Paige. Then he'd kill himself.

God, if you're there, help me save my best friend and little girl, Garrett thought.

It had been the closest thing to a prayer Garrett had mustered in many years.

When the hug parted, Garrett looked at his watch—it was almost seven o'clock.

He wiped the tears from his face and looked down at Paige. "Go on inside. I'll lock this crap in the shed and be in directly."

Paige smiled at her daddy. "Okay. Can we watch a movie?"

Garrett smiled back at her. "Absolutely. Just nothin' scary."

"Who needs scary movies when there are real-life werewolves?" Page joked.

She turned and jogged away toward the house.

Garrett locked the gear in the shed and walked back to his house. He paused on the back deck and surveyed the surrounding woods. He could barely see the critter-cams in the trees behind the house. Feeling as well as he could about the situation, he went inside.

Before joining Paige in the living room, Garrett turned on the front and back motion-activated floodlights. He retrieved his service pistol, swapped the regular clip with the silver bullet one, and chambered a round. He stuck the pistol down the back of his pants and went into the living room.

He saw Paige stretched out on the couch with a Sprite in one hand and the universal remote in the other.

"What did ya pick?"

"Super Eight."

"Super Eight? I thought we agreed on nothin' scary?"

Paige rolled her eyes. "Daddy…Super Eight is *not* scary."

"It's got a big, scary alien in it," Garrett disagreed.

"Yeah, but the monster's misunderstood, and it has a happy endin'. I need a happy endin'."

The weight of Paige's last statement fell heavily on Garrett's heart. Paige needed a happy ending, and Garrett was going to make sure she got it. Besides, he loved the movie.

Garrett smiled. "Okay. Super Eight it is."

"Thank you, Daddy," Paige said with a grin and pushed the play button.

It was a little after seven o'clock when Garrett eased his aching body into his recliner to watch *Super 8* with Paige. Although the sun was sinking low in the western sky, and he did not know what the night might bring, he was ready to kill the alpha bitch to give Paige a happy ending.

~ * ~

The front door to a dingy, foam green and white, single-wide mobile home burst open with enough force to make it smash into the exterior vinyl siding with a crash. The spring-loaded chain that attached the doorframe to the door, to keep the door from hitting the siding, broke long ago and hung from the door like a dead snake. It even rattled when the door swung open or closed.

The force of the door hitting the siding sent the door swinging shut again and revealed a perfect circular hole in the siding where the weathered brass doorknob punched through it the day the spring-loaded chain snapped from a similar, violent opening. Before the door completely closed again, a large, tattooed arm emerged from the darkened trailer and shoved the door open again.

Montgomery ‘Mont’ Lee stepped out of the trailer and onto the stacked wooden pallets that served as a front porch. The pallets groaned and sagged under his substantial weight. To say Mont was a large man would be an understatement. He stood six foot eight inches tall and weighed in at three hundred and sixty pounds. His tattoo-covered arms were as thick as tree trunks and his hands were the size of catcher’s mitts. His long, black hair hung in a ponytail that went half-way down his back and a thick, unkempt beard that went half-way down his belly covered his face. He had a large, crooked nose, bushy eyebrows, and small, brown eyes. Mont was an imposing individual.

Mont was wearing a sleeveless, black, leather vest opened in the front, which revealed his barrel size chest. His substantial belly hung over the waistband of his oil-stained Levi blue jeans, which were held up by a black leather belt with galvanized bolts poked through the leather, held in place with nuts every few inches around its length. Mont wasn’t above removing the belt and using it as a weapon, if the situation called for it. He wore size eighteen, triple wide, steel toe Red Wing work boots to cover his enormous feet.

Mont spread his bear-like arms wide and took a deep breath of evening air. As he exhaled, he broke into a raspy smoker’s cough. The cough reminded Mont he was currently without a smoke. He took a pack of Black & Mild cigars out of the breast pocket of his leather vest, tore the plastic tip off, and stuck it between his thin, mustache concealed lips. Mont pulled a Confederate flag embossed, flip-top Zippo lighter from the pocket of his oil-stained, blue jeans and, with a quick flip-flip move against his jeans, struck the lighter and lit the cigar. He inhaled the sweet smoke and blew it out through his nose like an angry bull.

As Mont started down the steps, which were a series of smaller stacks of wooden pallets, he bellowed, “Are ya comin’?”

From within the trailer, a similar sounding voice bellowed, “Right behind ya.”

Jackson ‘Jack’ Lee, Mont’s twin brother, stepped out onto the pallet front porch, which groaned and sagged under his substantial weight as well.

To the unobservant eye, the large men were identical. From their features to their dress, they were identical. There were subtle differences, though. At three hundred and sixty-five pounds, Jack weighed five pounds more than Mont. Being the bigger of the two had been something Jack took pride in. Mont considered the weight difference to be nothing more than a good bowel movement and appropriately didn't give a good shit.

Although both sported full sleeves, the actual difference had been in their preferred ink. They shared some similar tattoos; Confederate flags, Texas flags, skulls, pin-up girls, and each had a Harley-Davidson tattoo. Where bands and patterns were concerned, Mont preferred Celtic designs and Jack preferred tribal designs.

Jack displayed two final differences when he took a pack of Swisher Sweet cigars out of the breast pocket of his leather vest, tore the plastic tip off, and stuck it between his thin, mustache concealed lips. Although he struck his flip-top Zippo lighter exactly as Mont had, a Texas flag embossed Jack's lighter. After lighting his cigar, Jack made his way down the pallet steps and joined Mont in the overgrown mess that passed as a front yard.

~ * ~

Mont and Jack were committed bachelors. Single, not so much by choice, but by the choices in potential brides available to them. Any women willing to spend time with them, or on top of them, weren't the marrying kind. That suited the twin brothers just fine. They did, occasionally, bring a girl or two home from Knucklehead's Icehouse, which had been their preferred drinking hole. That suited the twin brothers just fine, too.

Like so many other folks in the area, Mont and Jack were born and raised in Pine View. They were a year older than Garrett but, having both failed ninth grade, they went through high school and graduated with him. Although they weren't friends with Garrett, they ran in different circles, they were teammates on the Pine View Woodpecker football team.

During their high school football playing days, they tipped the scales at a more athletic three hundred and twenty pounds each. They were both offensive linemen. Mont played left guard and Jack played right guard. They were the largest players in A-1 division and wreaked havoc on the always smaller defensive players who lined up across the line of scrimmage from them. Mont and Jack were instrumental in the A-1 conference championship win.

Because Garrett called a QB option play, initially they had to provide him with the time and protection needed to complete a long pass downfield. When they heard Garrett yell, ‘Keeper’ they surged forward and plowed into the defensive line. Although, given their size and weight, they were much slower than Garrett, he patiently followed their blocks into the defensive secondary, where the receivers started throwing blocks. Eighty-one yards later, Garrett spiked the ball in the end zone.

Although the coaches, Garrett, and their other teammates recognized their contribution to the game-winning touchdown, Garrett got all the glory and accolades. Mont and Jack faded into obscurity.

Many college teams would have loved to have Mont and Jack anchoring their offensive lines, but their grades prevented them from serious consideration. After graduating high school, the twins took jobs in the logging industry operating chainsaws. While they didn’t wish bad things for Garrett, both were more than a little pleased to see Garrett ended up logging, too.

They were good with the groundwork of felling trees, but neither could use the climbing gear with efficiency. They were too big and too slow. Ironically, this led to a promotion of sorts. Instead of working a chainsaw, Mont and Jack started driving the large machines that gathered and loaded logs onto the log-trucks. The same trucks that orphaned June when her sexting parents slammed into the log expanse between the fifth-wheel hookup and back axels, that hauled the logs from the field to the sawmills.

After doing this for almost ten years, Mont and Jack got their Class A commercial driver licenses, pooled their savings, bought two used but decent Peterbilt trucks and log trailers, started their own company called MJ Trucking, Mont’s initial had been first because he was eight minutes older than Jack, and started contracting with logging companies to haul logs. Not only did they stay busy, they quickly built a reputation for being among the best in the business.

Although their trailer house and unkempt yard suggested impoverished conditions, MJ Trucking, and by extension Mont and Jack, did well. They just didn’t see the point in investing in a structure they primarily used for sleeping.

They spent their money on more important things; like the not-so-small arsenal of every manner of firearm available, legal or otherwise, stashed in their hidden underground bunker. Ironically, the bunker had been much nicer than their trailer. Of course, they believed they'd be spending a lot of time in the bunker after society collapsed.

Not only were the twins' ardent supporters of the Second Amendment, they bought into just about every government conspiracy theory propagated on the Internet. These convinced them the Federal Reserve had plans to intentionally crash the dollar. To protect against this, along with the substantial arsenal, Mont and Jack had a large cache of gold stashed in the bunker as well, and a year's worth of MREs and water. They were ready for the endgame.

They didn't invest all their money in the endgame, though. Mont and Jack weren't above enjoying themselves before the shit hit the fan. Beside their run-down trailer house was a large metal building with a concrete floor. Inside the building were Mont and Jack's favorite toys, their motorcycles, and other necessities.

They each had two motorcycles, and all four were American made, Harley-Davidson perfection. None of that 'Jap crap' for Mont and Jack. Each had a S-Series Fat Boy, for around town and local cruising, as well as an Ultra Limited, for their yearly pilgrimage to Sturgis, South Dakota, for the Sturgis Rally. All four had custom suspensions to accommodate their weight. From the tins to the motors, all four bikes were black, but they could tell them apart by custom leather, monogrammed seats.

Besides the bikes, the building housed two John Deere Gator RSX utility vehicles mostly used for hunting. Seasons didn't matter to the twins. In or out of season, everything was fair game. Their shared pickup truck, which Mont and Jack called 'Beast,' resided in the building, too. Off the Chevrolet assembly line in 1986, Beast sold as a normal, extra-cab, all-wheel-drive, one-ton, dually pickup truck.

Mont noticed the old, tan and brown pickup truck in an overgrown pasture next to one sawmill they frequented with loads and asked the sawmill supervisor about it. The truck belonged to the sawmill owner. When Mont expressed an interest in buying the old truck, the supervisor contacted the owner. The owner said Mont could have it, title in hand, if he hauled it off. The next day, Mont and Jack towed the old truck back to their place, and the work began.

From the moment Mont saw the old truck, he had plans for it. With

Jack's help, they created Beast. First, they remove the old bed and replace it with a heavy-duty, steel, black diamond plate, flatbed. The flatbed had a built-in toolbox along the cab, heavy-duty rails down the sides, and a gooseneck trailer hitch over the back axle. It also had a heavy-duty diamond mesh headache rack with four high-power spotlights mounted on it.

Next, they ditched the factory front bumper and replaced it with a heavy-duty bumper constructed of the same black diamond plate. The front bumper had a massive cattle-guard that protected the headlights, grill, and radiator from impact. It housed two more high-power spotlights and a five-ton winch.

The customization didn't stop with the flatbed and bumper. Mont and Jack dropped a big block 454 engine under the hood. They rebuilt the standard transmission and transfer case, too. In four-wheel low first gear, Beast could pull a fully loaded, eighteen-foot, gooseneck trailer up a twenty-degree incline while idling. This feat earned the truck its Beast name.

Unlike Carlos Garza, whose customization extended to the interior of his tricked-out truck, Mont and Jack didn't care about creature comforts. Beast's interior comprised cracked vinyl seats, cracked dashboard, sagging headliner, and a pair of vice grips that served as a window roller on the driver's side. For hunting, they installed directional spotlights, the kind police vehicles have mounted on their windshield posts, on the driver and passenger side windshield posts. Unlike Carlos' truck, the oxidation and rust on Beast were real. They had one minor interior customization, though.

Jack salvaged a windshield wiper pump-motor and window cleaner solution container from a junkyard. After giving the container and pump-motor a good cleaning, and replacing the tubing, Jack mounted the container and pump-motor under the hood and connected the pump-motor to the battery and a toggle switch he mounted in the glove box. He ran tubing from the container through a hole he drilled in the back of the glove box. After Jack installed the rig, he attached a paper cup dispenser to Beast's dashboard next to the radio. Lastly, Jack filled the new container and called Mont out to the shop to see his creation.

Mont looked at the paper cup dispenser attached to the dash. "What the fuck, Jack. That looks fuckin' retarded there."

Jack giggled, which, coming from a man his size, was creepy

rather than funny. "Hold on to your whiskers."

Jack got in the passenger's seat, pulled a paper cup from the dispenser, opened the glove box, put the end of the tube in the paper cup, and flicked the toggle switch. There had been a hum under the hood as the pump-motor started running and, seconds later, amber liquid shot out of the tube and into the paper cup. When it was full, Jack flipped the toggle switch off, raised the cup to his lips, and shot the content.

"What the fuck was that?" Mont asked.

Jack grinned. "That was Old Time Number Seven, brother."

Mont looked from Jack to the tubing and back to Jack. "Jack Daniel's?"

"None other."

When Jack showed Mont the Jack Daniel's delivery system he rigged, Mont didn't think the paper cup dispenser looked retarded at all. In fact, he thought the whole thing funny.

When Jack joined Mont in the mess that passed as a front yard, he said, "Flip it."

Mont dug a quarter out of his pocket. "Call it."

When Mont flipped the quarter in the air, Jack said, "Heads."

Mont grabbed the flipping coin from the air with his right hand and slapped it onto his meaty left forearm.

"Moment of truth," Mont said as he removed his hand and revealed the quarter.

When Jack saw George Washington's profile shining up at him, he let out a hoot and bellowed, "Sucks to be you, DD."

Disgusted, Mont plunged the quarter back in his pocket. "That's three fuckin' times in a row. Next time you're the DD."

Jack shook his head. "Not unless the quarter falls against me, brother. Them's the rules."

Mont turned away from Jack and kicked a clump of weeds. "Stupid fuckin' quarter."

Jack laughed. "It's your fuckin' quarter. Feed it to the jukebox at Knucklehead's or tip it to Dixie. Don't blame the fuckin' quarter."

It did not piss Mont off because he couldn't drink at Knucklehead's Icehouse. Where Mont and Jack were concerned, DD didn't mean designated driver, although the loser would drive them home. For their purpose, DD meant 'drunk driver.' Meaning the loser had to drive home and, if pulled over, would be the one blowing in the breathalyzer. Those were the rules.

Mont kicked another clump of weeds. "Yeah, yeah. Just get in fuckin' Beast."

Jack laughed and got into the passenger seat. Once Mont settled in behind the wheel, Jack pulled a paper cup from the dispenser, opened the glove box, flipped the toggle switch, and filled it with Jack Daniel's.

Jack held it out to Mont. "Ya want one?"

"Well, fuck yeah."

Mont grabbed the cup and quickly downed the amber liquid. Jack refilled Mont's cup before filling one for himself. Jack swallowed the content in one gulp.

As the familiar warmth spread across his barrel chest, Jack said, "Drive on, big brother."

Mont turned the key, and Beast rumbled into life. He depressed the clutch, shifted Beast into first gear, released the clutch, depressed the accelerator, and drove out of the driveway for a night of drinking at Knucklehead's Icehouse.

~ * ~

As Garrett and Paige were settling into watch *Super 8*, and Mont and Jack were pulling out of their driveway heading for Knucklehead's Icehouse, Alexis had been waking up from a restful sleep. She rolled out of bed and walked to the kitchen without bothering to get dressed.

Alexis opened the refrigerator door and let the cooler air wash over her naked body. She grabbed a twenty-ounce bottle of Dasani water and drank half of it in several gulps. Alexis took a pound of raw ground beef from the 'Meat' drawer and sat down at the kitchen table. After removing the plastic wrap from the ground beef, she scooped a healthy portion of it out with her fingers and crammed it into her mouth. Alexis' vegetarian days were behind her. She didn't even bother to chew the pasty meat. She let it slide down her hungry throat. When the meat was gone from the yellow Styrofoam container, Alexis tipped it to her mouth and drank the remaining blood. She licked and sucked her finger clean.

It wasn't a satisfying meal, but Alexis planned to feed her wolf later. Not a human meal. She had been serious about not wanting to stir up anymore shit by killing people for a few days. There were plenty of deer, wild hogs, and other wildlife to feast on in the woods. Alexis downed the rest of her water, deposited the refuse in the receptacle, trash for the meat wrapping and recycle for the water bottle, and went back to her room to shower and dress.

Twenty minutes later, Alexis backed out of her driveway and headed for the Wiseman barn. As she drove west on Highway Twenty-One, the sun slipped beneath the tree line horizon and the waning gibbous moon began its assent in the south-eastern sky, which had been a beautiful shade of purple.

Almost SFA purple, Alexis thought.

She turned off Highway Twenty-One and on to the overgrown path that accessed the old barn.

Mont and Jack pulled off Highway Seven and onto County Road Five Fifty-Five. County Road Five Fifty-Five was gravel and not well maintained, which had been the primary reason they rarely rode their bikes to Knucklehead's Icehouse. Navigating the potholes on the way to Knucklehead's Icehouse while the sun was still up, and they were sober, wasn't near as treacherous as the ride home, when it was dark, and they were drunk. More than once, both dumped their bikes on the ride home. So, Beast became their preferred Knucklehead's Icehouse mode of transportation.

Beast wasn't without its pitfalls, though. The one-ton suspension was stiff as hell and hitting a large pothole could, and often did, bounce Mont and Jack's heads into the truck roof. The twins weren't fans of the 'government' requiring the wearing of seatbelts and never used them.

After bouncing down County Road Five Fifty-Five for about a quarter mile, the trees on the left thinned and Knucklehead's Icehouse came into view. Knucklehead's Icehouse remained one of the few real icehouses left in East Texas or, truth be told, Texas. The open-air design and industrial fans were all the rage before air-conditioning lured patrons inside with controlled environments.

Knucklehead's Icehouse was an icehouse in the truest sense. It was a large metal building with a sawdust covered concrete floor. All four sides comprised industrial grade, roll up, metal doors that were lowered and locked when it was closed. In the middle of each side opening were industrial, six-foot tall box fans that kept air circulating throughout the interior.

The bar was a square island in the middle of the building with bar stools around all four sides. In one corner, there were three pool tables. The humidity in an open-air environment made the house pool cues crooked as hell. Serious players like Mont and Jack brought their own cues. Across from the pool tables was a 1972 Rock-Ola jukebox that spun real vinyl. It had old outlaw country, Johnny Paycheck, Merle Haggard, southern rock, Lynyrd Skynyrd, The Eagles, and classic rock, Led Zeppelin, AC/DC. There was a small area cleared for dancing, which was rarely used. Tables and chairs scattered around, in no detectable pattern, throughout. If nature called, there were two Porta Potties around the backside of the building. Unless it was a squat and drop situation, most of the patrons, including the women, opted for stepping behind a vehicle to relieve themselves. They did not empty the Porta Potties frequently and they smelled like hell.

~ * ~

When Mont and Jack bounced into the crushed limestone-covered ground that served as Knucklehead's parking lot, they recognized several trucks, bikes, a trike, and cars there. As for Knucklehead's patronage, it was a packed house, which meant there were about ten people there. Mont and Jack helped themselves to another glove box shot, got out of Beast, and walked into Knucklehead's through the front opening.

Mont went directly to the jukebox to rid himself of the cursed quarter. A quarter could still buy three songs at Knucklehead's. He selected A-7, which was Lynyrd Skynyrd's *Give Me Three Steps*, B-11, which was AC/DC's *Highway To hell*, and B-13, which was Pink Floyd's *Wish You Were Here*. After, he joined Jack at the bar who had two Lone Star longnecks and two naked, no salt and lime, Jose Cuervo tequila shots waiting for him. This combo was their traditional first drinks.

They toasted William S. Harley and Arthur Davidson, downed the tequila shots, and guzzled the Lone Star beers dry. Jack finished first, but Mont was the first to let out an enormous burp. Jack followed suit seconds later.

Dixie Rains, the bartender, let out a raspy, smoker's laugh. "You two never change."

Mont grinned. "If it ain't broke…"

"Don't fix it," Jack finished for him.

This caused Dixie to break into another raspy laugh that exposed several missing teeth. While she laughed, she poured each of them two fingers of Jack, neat, in a lowball glass and slid the glasses down the bar to them. She knew their routine well.

~ * ~

Dixie tended bar at Knucklehead's since Mont and Jack started frequenting it after high school. It was one of the few places where they didn't get carded and could enjoy some underage drinking. Dixie was about ten years older than Mont and Jack and wasn't hard on the eyes, especially once the beer goggles were in place. If nothing else, she had all her teeth back then.

Dixie fell into the category of one of those committed bachelor choices who accompanied Mont and Jack back to their trailer many times over the years. To Mont and Jack, Dixie seemed to age in dog years; seven years for each trip the Earth made around the sun. In her late twenties, when they met her, she looked her age. Years of hard living hadn't been kind to Dixie. Now, in her early forties, she looked close to sixty, if she looked a day. Her bleach blonde hair had thinned and looked like ragged straw. Even though she was skinny, the muscles in her arms, which were sleeved in colorful tattoos, wiggled when she moved them. Her tits, which were once small and perky, looked like malformed pancakes with squished strawberries for nipples on her bony chest. This didn't keep Mont and Jack from taking her home occasionally.

When Jack balked at bringing her home once, Mont grinned. "Just close your eyes, brother. She ain't much to look at anymore, but her cooch feels the same."

Jack did as Mont suggested and found he could live with that arrangement. Besides, it wasn't like they were some grand prize women threw themselves at.

"Take it where ya can get it," Mont also said.

Although they weren't comfortable tagging her together, Dixie suggested they pull a threesome just about every time they brought her home, but they had no compunctions about sloppy seconds and took turns with Dixie regularly. Although they would never pull a threesome with Dixie, given enough to drink, they'd probably bring her home again.

Jack soured on Dixie a bit. The last time they brought her home, about a month prior to the current Knucklehead's visit, Dixie lost a tooth while giving Jack a blowjob. Not much freaked Jack out but seeing Dixie's bloody mouth bobbing on his blood-covered tool, and her root-blackened tooth perched on top of his pubes like an ugly egg in a fucked-up nest, did. When Jack told Mont about it later, and actually gagged during the telling, Mont laughed so hard he shit his pants. Then it was Jack's turn to laugh at Mont's expense. The result was Dixie hadn't been home with them since; she'd offered several times, though.

~ * ~

Shortly after Dixie slid their drinks to them, Lewis's 'Bear' Campton came up to the bar and climbed onto the barstool next to Jack. Climbed wasn't a poor description of how Bear mounted a bar stool. He stood only five feet, two inches tall. The trike in Knucklehead's parking lot belonged to Bear. He rode a trike, because his legs were too short to stabilize a motorcycle at a red light without it leaning to one side. He was as thick in the neck, shoulders, chest, and arms as Mont and Jack were. In fact, Bear was the only man who ever beat Mont and Jack at arm wrestling. Mont and Jack believed Bear's short arms gave him an advantage. That didn't change the fact they couldn't beat him.

Bear's age made losing to him even more frustrating for the twins. Bear had to be pushing fifty. He was bald on top, but he always wore a black leather captain's hat to cover his scalp. The rest of his hair was gray and trailed down his back in a long ponytail. He sported a long, gray, braided goatee on his face and a leather eye patch Jack thought switched from one eye to the other on different days. Jack had usually been drunk when he made this observation and never thought to document the eye patch location for later reference.

Bear's only tattoo was on his chest and stomach, which was always visible because he wore his faded, sleeveless, blue jean vest open. It was, hands down, one of the coolest tattoos Mont and Jack ever saw. The tattoo was in deference to Bear's nickname, and the tattoo artist who inked it, an artist in the truest sense of the word. On Bear's chest was a vicious grizzly bear's head, all snarling teeth, and it looked like it appeared to be eating its way out of Bear's chest; bloody, ripped skin hung in shreds around the hole the grizzly's teeth were creating. Lower on his stomach, the grizzly's long, black claws were ripping through Bear's skin. With shading and other tricks of the tattoo trade, the tattoo looked three dimensional. Like it came through Bear's skin.

After Bear perched on top of the barstool, he held up his Budweiser longneck. "Dixie, darlin'. When ya get a chance, I need a refill."

Dixie smiled her tooth-missing smile. "Right wicha, Suga-Bear."

Bear turned to Mont and Jack. "Evenin' boys. Care for a little arm wrestlin'?"

When Mont and Jack simultaneously responded with, "Fuck off, Bear," Bear laughed up a storm.

By the time Bear stopped laughing, Dixie was there with his Budweiser.

Dixie put the beer on the bar in front of Bear. "What's so funny, Suga-Bear? Did ya ask 'em if they wanted to arm wrestle again?"

When Mont and Jack simultaneously responded with, "Fuck you too, Dixie," Dixie and Bear laughed up a storm together.

It was infectious, and within a couple of seconds, Mont and Jack were laughing, too.

Dixie, referring to Mont and Jack's "Fuck you too, Dixie" statement, said, "Was that an offer, boys?"

When Mont and Jack didn't respond, Dixie grinned. "I promise I won't lose another tooth on your pecker, Jack."

Mont laughed so hard he damn near fell off his barstool and Bear laughed until his face became so red it looked like it might pop. That Bear was laughing told Jack the blowjob tooth incident was common knowledge at Knucklehead's Icehouse. Dixie just grinned at Jack and pushed the tip of her tongue through the hole where the tooth fell out. This made Jack laugh with his idiot brother and friend.

Just as this ruckus of laughter ended, another Knucklehead's regular stepped to the bar beside Mont. "What's so fuckin' funny? Bear ask 'em to arm wrestle again, or is it the bloody blowjob story?"

Mont and Jack responded simultaneously again but their responses differed slightly. Mont said, "Fuck you," and Jack said, "Fuck y'all."

This had them all laughing again.

When the latest round of laughter ended, Dixie said, "Ya need another, Trowa?"

Trowa downed the remaining Wild Turkey. The ice made a 'tinkling' sound in the glass.

Trowa handed the glass to Dixie. "Trowa like firewater."

This brought on a few chuckles, but they heard the line hundreds of times.

Trowa Raintree was a strange guy. He was a descendent of the Caddo tribe, indigenous to East Texas. Trowa was tall, not as tall as Mont and Jack, about six feet, four inches tall, slim, and regal. He carried himself with an air of confidence, straight-backed and head up. He had long black hair that always flowed free. He didn't wear it in a ponytail or braid. Unless he rode his Indian Chief Dark Horse motorcycle. Then he wrapped his hair around his neck like a scarf. He had no facial hair and no tattoos anyone knew of.

Mont and Jack knew Trowa from work, too. Trowa was one of the best loggers in the business. He could drop a hundred-foot pine tree on a nickel. Indian Head or otherwise. Before the twins bought their tree hauling trucks and went into business for themselves, they'd worked jobs with Trowa. This was where the strange part came in. When the lunch horn blew, Trowa wouldn't eat with the rest of the crew. He would find a section of land that wasn't logged and disappear into the woods to eat alone, as if he preferred nature to humans. Something else struck crew members as strange. Trowa was always smelling things. He smelled dirt, wildlife scat, leaves, pond water.

Once, Mont asked Trowa what the eating alone and smelling was all about.

Trowa grinned. "Nature."

Most impressive of all, Trowa could climb a tree without climbing gear. He couldn't climb trees with thick trunks but, with the right size tree, Trowa would kick off his boots and scamper up a tree like a cat.

Aside from the nature stuff, Trowa was a good guy and a better drinking buddy. So, no one objected to his joining the group at the bar.

Dixie brought Trowa another Wild Turkey on the rocks and refilled Mont and Jack's Jack Daniel's glasses. Then Bear bought Dixie a shot of what she was having, Smirnoff Vodka, which she gladly took.

The five of them, unless Dixie had to fix a drink for one of the other patrons, sat at the bar drinking, telling stories, mostly about logging, telling jokes, mostly the dirty kind, and laughing for about an hour. They decided to move to the pool tables when old Hank Miller moseyed to the bar.

~ * ~

Hank Miller was an obnoxious, toothless, old cuss who had to be pushing eighty, if he was pushing a day. He was a Knucklehead's regular but not someone others associated with, and this seemed to suit Hank just fine. He'd sit at a table all by himself, swilling draft Pabst Blue Ribbon from a big mug he brought with him. Dixie would fill a regular mug then dump it into Hanks big mug so as not to give him more beer than he paid for.

Hank was always watching everyone else, but he rarely spoke. Unless he got a real good drunk on. That was when he'd get 'loud and nasty,' as Dixie put it. Most nights, Hank would stumble away at closing time and walk to his trailer house only a couple of hundred feet up County Road Five Fifty-Five from Knucklehead's. When the weather got nasty, someone, on the promise of a free drink the next time they were there, would give Hank a ride. Mont and Jack carried him home several times over the years. Hank never appreciated the ride, and the vehicle he rode home in usually needed a good airing out the next day. Hank stank.

On the rare occasions Hank wasn't at Knucklehead's, he was simply referred to as Stank. As in, "I wonder if Stank is dead or just too drunk to find his way here tonight?" Frequently, someone slipped up and referred to Hank as Stank when he was there. As in, "Dixie, I think Stank wants another beer." If Hank heard the slip-up, he did not reveal it. Knucklehead's theory was that he was too deaf to hear much, anyway. He heard the slip-ups, but he didn't care. Hank didn't care about much, other than a cold PBR. He'd drink it warm, if it came to it.

Hank preferred to order another beer by pounding his giant mug on the table until he got Dixie's attention. Even though he didn't tip, Dixie always waited on him politely. That was just the blowjob, tooth-losing kind of girl Dixie was.

~ * ~

Given Hank's reputation, and smell, it wasn't surprising that Mont, Jack, Bear, and Trowa continued to take their leave for the pool tables when Hank walked up.

Hank said, “Did y’all hear ‘bout them boys and girls slaughtered out at the MRB last night?”

Dixie, who was moving down the bar away from Hank too, said, “Yeah, I heard somethin’ ‘bout the MRB earlier. Didn’t hear nothin’ ‘bout no slaughter.”

As if on cue, a portly regular named Norm Hoyt, who was sitting at a table on the other side of the bar sipping on a Crown and Coke, said, “That was me, Dixie-Land. I was talkin’ on my cell ‘bout it when ya brought my last drink.”

At that point, everyone looked toward Norm, even two guys who weren’t regulars who were playing pool with the shitty house sticks. No one noticed the young man who was sitting in the back corner beside the jukebox, but he looked, too.

“What ya know, Norm?” Dixie asked.

Norm Hoyt, Deputy Billy Hoyt’s cousin, knew more than the others. What he didn’t know, because the seven-to-three shift hadn’t responded to the calls, was there had been a werewolf hypothesis floating around the sheriff’s department. He knew gory details about Russ Lomax, Carla Weaver, her pigs, and about the fifteen butchered high school students at the MRB. Norm told them everything he knew.

When Norm ended his tale, Knucklehead’s remained as quiet as a church for several moments.

“What could do somethin’ like that?” Dixie wondered aloud.

“Bear,” Bear offered.

Mont sniggered. “No fuckin’ way, Bear. There might be some black bears in these woods. Black bears don’t do shit like that.”

“Grizzly,” Bear insisted.

“No grizzly in these parts,” Trowa told Bear.

“Might’a had one escape from a game preserve,” Norm suggested.

Hank said, “Might be Bigfoot.”

Everyone looked toward Trowa.

Trowa realized the attention was on him. “What? I’m supposed to know ‘bout Bigfoot?”

“Well…you’re an Indian. Don’t y’all know ‘bout Bigfoot and shit?” Jack jokingly asked.

Trowa laughed. “No more than you do, paleface.”

The conversation about what could have slaughtered everyone in the manner Norm described took on a life of its own. Different theories, even killer aliens, came up and dismissed.

After about five minutes of this back and forth, a voice from the back corner of Knucklehead's said, "It was werewolves."

All eyes in the bar turned toward the source of the statement. Cole Duncan got up and stepped toward the bar.

~ * ~

Alexis undressed quickly and placed her folded clothes neatly in a corner of the barn. Instead of turning inside the barn, as she always had, Alexis stepped out into the cool night air. A light breeze washed over her damp skin and caused goose bumps to spring up on her arms and legs. Alexis inhaled deeply, absorbing the natural smells around her. She willed her right hand to change, and it immediately transformed into a deadly werewolf claw.

So much control, Alexis thought.

Alexis raked her right werewolf claw across the side of the barn and left long gouges in the rotting wood. She let out a loud laugh that echoed through the forest. Then she brought on the full change. When she was in wolf form, Alexis took another deep breath and marveled at how much more her wolf could smell. As the myriad scents whirled around its snout, it isolated the one it sought. The little bitch's scent.

The little bitch's scent mixed with another scent it recognized; one always with the little bitch. This time, it presented stronger and distinctly separate from the little bitch's scent.

Must be the little bitch's daddy, the reasoning portion of the werewolf's brain thought.

The alpha's lips drew up in a snarl and it let out a long, low growl. Drool, still bloody from the recent growth of its deadly fangs, dripped from its snout. It dropped to all fours and sprinted toward Garrett's house.

~ * ~

Jack scoffed. "Werewolves. Get the fuck outta here, kid."

Cole didn't flinch. He continued walking toward the bar. "I was there. I saw 'em."

This took everyone by surprise.

Dixie inhaled sharply. "You were there?"

Cole took a seat at the bar. "Yeah, I was there. I watched 'em tear my friends apart."

"How many?" Dixie asked.

"There were three."

"What'd they look like?" Bear asked.

Before Cole could respond, Jack let out a loud laugh. "Y'all aren't believin' this fuckin' punk, are ya?"

Trowa drained his drink and handed it to Dixie for a refill. "Do not dismiss this notion lightly."

Jack looked at Trowa like he was seeing him for the first time. He shook his head. "A minute ago, you didn't believe in Bigfoot, but ya believe in werewolves?"

"I didn't say I didn't believe in Bigfoot. I said I knew no more 'bout Bigfoot than you did," Trowa corrected Jack.

"Ya know about werewolves?" an exasperated Jack asked.

Trowa nodded.

Dixie handed Trowa his refilled Wild Turkey. "What d'ya know?"

Trowa took a seat at the bar and downed half of his fresh drink in two gulps.

He looked around at his bar mates, who were looking at him. "Native American legend speaks of werewolves. The Navajo called it Yee Naaldlooshii, or a skin-walker. The literal translation of Yee Naaldlooshii is…he goes on all fours."

"Like the *Twilight* werewolves," Dixie interrupted.

Trowa chuckled and shook his head. "Nothin' like those pussies, Dixie. Skin-walkers are evil fuckers. According to the Navajo legend, someone can only become a skin-walker if they are initiated into the Witchery Way. The initiation requires killing someone close, like a family member, or engaging in incest, necrophilia, or bestiality."

"That's fucked up," Bear said.

Trowa drained the rest of his drink. "They're fucked up beasts."

Cole, who sat quietly and listened to Trowa, said, "I don't know 'bout the incest or necrophilia stuff. I know what I saw. I saw three werewolves at the MRB last night."

Jack started to object, but Mont cut him off. "Get that kid a drink, Dixie."

Dixie looked at Cole, then at Mont. "He ain't old enough to drink."

Mont laughed. "Neither were me and Jack when we started comin' here. Besides, it ain't that he's too young to drink, he's too young to buy. I'm buyin'. Pour him a drink."

"What ya havin', kid?" Dixie asked.

"Tequila shot."

While Dixie poured the shot and brought it to Cole on the other side of the bar, Mont, Jack, Bear, and Trowa continued talking.

Jack said, "You're not buyin' this shit, are ya, Mont?"

Mont ignored Jack. "What d'ya think, Trowa?"

Trowa thought for a moment. "It ain't no fuckin' bear or Bigfoot."

"That don't mean it's a fuckin' werewolf, Trowa. There ain't no fuckin' werewolves," Jack injected.

"Maybe not. Still somethin' tore all those folks up," Mont said.

"What's your fuckin' point, Mont?" Jack asked.

Mont grinned. "My point…brother, is there's somethin' out there that needs killin'."

A big smile spread across Jack's hairy face, and he said, "Ya wanna go huntin' and kill whatever the fuck it is?"

"I sure as hell do," Mont answered with a grin.

"I'm in," Bear said immediately.

Mont looked at Trowa. "What'a 'bout you, Trowa? Ya up for some huntin'?"

Trowa thought for several seconds. "If they are skin walkers, they won't die easy."

Jack laughed. "Mont and me got everything short of a fuckin' bazooka. We can kill 'em…whatever the fuck they are."

Trowa looked from Jack to Mont to Bear and back to Jack. "Probably a stupid idea, but I'm in."

Mont let out a hoot and hollered, "One more round over here, Dixie! On me."

Dixie, who was still talking with Cole, trying to get more details from him, looked at Mont. "One more round? It's early. What're you boys up to?"

"We're goin' huntin'," Mont replied.

Mont's response took a few seconds to sink in. When it did, Dixie said, "Huntin' for what killed all those folks?"

Mont threw Dixie a wink. "Yep. Werewolves, Bigfoots, bears. We don't give a shit. Whatever the hell they are, we aim to kill 'em."

Dixie came over to the group. “Y’all think that’s smart? Don’t ya need silver bullets or somethin’ to kill werewolves?”

Mont put his empty glass on the bar. “Hell, if I know. If there’re in pieces from a couple hundred rounds and still ain’t dead, we might have a problem. I don’t see nothin’ livin’ through what we can shoot it with.”

Dixie refilled the empty glasses and got Bear another Budweiser longneck from the cooler.

“To killin’ werewolves.” Mont bellowed.

The four of them clinked drinks and downed their preferred alcohol. Bear let out an enormous burp when he slammed the empty longneck on top of the bar. They all laughed.

Mont said to Bear and Trowa, “Leave your bike and trike here. We’ll load into Beast, head to our place to gear up, and go huntin’ those fuckers.”

When they started digging in their pockets to pay Dixie, she said, “Y’all can square up when ya get back. Seems like bad luck to take your money now.”

They nodded and turned to leave.

Cole spoke up again. “I wanna come.”

Jack faced Cole. “Fuck off, kid.”

“They killed my friends,” Cole responded.

“Ever been huntin’?” Mont asked Cole.

“No,” Cole admitted, “I don’t want a gun. I just wanna be there when y’all kill the fuckers.”

Mont, Jack, Bear, and Trowa exchanged looks and huddled up.

Bear said, “He’s seen ‘em.”

Jack scoffed. “So fuckin’ what? It’s not like we won’t see ‘em if we find ‘em. If they’re even fuckin’ real.”

Mont whispered, “He could be bait.”

Jack chuckled. “I don’t like the little fucker either, but that’s fucked up, brother.”

Mont, still whispering, said, “We won’t let anything happen to him. We’ll just have him stomp around in the woods while we lay in wait.”

“If he don’t wanna stomp around in the woods?” Bear asked.

“We don’t give him a choice,” Mont said with a grin.

Trowa said, “If he was there last night, the skin-walkers might recognize his scent and come for him.”

That settled the conversation.

Mont pointed at Cole. "What's your name?"

"Eddie. Eddie Quist," Cole lied.

Cole didn't want anyone at Knucklehead's Icehouse to know his real name if things didn't go as he planned. He picked the name Eddie in honor of Eddie Quist from *The Howling* movie. Since Alexis bit him, he'd watched as many werewolf movies as he could find. He enjoyed seeing what they got right and what they got wrong about werewolves. Mostly wrong. *The Howling* had been his favorite of the ones he'd seen.

"Okay Eddie. If ya get in the way, you'll likely get shot," Mont said.

Cole smiled. "Thanks. I won't get in the way. I promise."

As the five of them headed for the parking lot, Dixie yelled, "Y'all be careful."

~ * ~

When the alpha got close to Garrett's house, it slowed to a walk and stopped. It was still a couple of hundred yards away, but with its wolf's eyes penetrating the darkness, it could see the house clearly. It could hear sounds coming from inside the house and knew the sounds weren't coming from people.

It heard the little bitch say, "I like this part."

A second later, the little bitch and the man were laughing. This angered the alpha.

As it got closer to Garrett's house, the little bitch and the man's scents grew stronger. What the alpha picked up from their scents didn't please it. After it turned Seth, Cole, and Dillon, they reeked of fear for weeks. Dillon reeked of it still, but Cole didn't reek of it enough. Given Cole's low level of fear, it wasn't surprising he'd been problematic. The alpha sensed very little fear in the little bitch's scent, less than twenty-four hours after it killed her pathetic boyfriend, stalked her through the woods, and turned her. The alpha found this unacceptable.

The alpha started circling Garrett's house with each lap, bringing it a little closer to the structure. As it lapped, it listened, smelled, and watched with intensity. It heard laughter, which increased its rage. On a pass around the front of the house, it saw the little bitch, through opened blinds, stand up and walk toward the back of the house. By the time the alpha rounded the back of the house, it could smell popcorn being microwaved. It continued circling the house while it contemplated its actions.

~ * ~

Beast rumbled to a stop outside the Lee's single-wide trailer. Mont looked over his shoulder into the back seat. "Come inside, boys."

Mont and Jack stored their best weapons in the bunker, but they weren't about to disclose its location to the others. That said, they had a plethora of weapons locked away in their trailer and would arm themselves from that collection. They got out of Beast and made their way up the wooden pallet steps.

Mont unlocked the front door, stepped inside, and turned on the living room light. The others followed him inside. The trailer wasn't in better shape on the inside than it was on the outside. There were holes in the panel walls where Mont and Jack let off steam by punching the walls over the years. The carpet was worn through in places and coming up in other places. A threadbare recliner and couch sagged from years of supporting their substantial weight. The coffee table was littered with dirty paper plates, dirty glasses, overflowing ashtrays, and had cigar sized burn marks in many places.

Jack moved past Mont. "Back here."

He headed down a hallway to the left. Jack led the group down the hallway to a door at the end. He opened it, turned on the light, and the five of them moved into what would have been the master bedroom. Mont and Jack had converted it into their game room.

The game room had a regulation size pool table in the middle, a pool cue rack on the wall, and an assortment of wildlife mounts. Several nice bucks, a bobcat, a boar head, several ducks, and a nice size largemouth bass were on the walls. Two large gun safes stood against the back wall. The game room was every bit as filthy as the living room.

Mont went to one gun safe, and Jack went to the other. After unlocking their gun safes, Mont and Jack opened the doors and stepped back to reveal the contents. Smiles spread across Bear and Trowa's faces. Cole looked uninterested. Trowa headed toward Jack's safe, and Bear went to Mont's.

As Bear and Trowa were admiring the assortment of weapons, Jack looked at Mont. "I'm thinkin' shock and awe protocol."

Mont grinned. "Times two."

Mont and Jack nodded in agreement.

"What's shock and awe protocol?" Bear asked.

Jack took a fully automatic, and illegal, AR-15 assault rifle, with Yukon NVRS night vision scope and an under-barrel mounted flashlight, out of his gun safe. "It's an ambush technique Mont and me use to take down the wild pigs. One of us carries an AR and the other carries a shotgun."

Jack shouldered the AR and took a Saiga, semi-automatic, twelve-gauge, assault shotgun, with an under-barrel mounted flashlight, out of his gun safe and handed it to Trowa. He opened a cabinet at the top of the gun safe and retrieved a loaded Colt one hundred round drum magazine and clipped into the AR-15. Next, he grabbed an Alliance Armament, thirty shotgun shell round, drum magazine from the same shelf and handed it to Trowa. Trowa clipped it into the Saiga.

"The shock," Mont took over where Jack left off, "is the shotgun. The drum is loaded with thirty double-ought buckshot shells. They'll knock just about anything off their feet. The awe is the AR. It'll put anything down."

Bear and Trowa grinned and nodded their heads.

After Mont retrieved his matching AR-15, handed Bear his matching Saiga shotgun, and grabbed loaded drum magazines for each, they locked up the gun safes and the house, loaded into Beast, and drove out of the driveway.

Once they were on the main road, Mont said, "We got the guns, we got the plan, but where to?"

Cole, who said nothing for several minutes, said, "How 'bout the MRB?"

"No fuckin' way. The cops'll have that place locked up as tight as a child molester's asshole in super-max. Besides, why would they go back there?" Jack said.

"For water," Trowa responded.

Confused, Jack said, "Water? There ain't no water at the MRB."

"There's a pond through the woods 'bout a hundred yards behind the MRB," Trowa told him.

"How d'ya know?" Jack asked.

"About six months ago, I was on a job on property just south of the MRB. When the lunch horn blew, I went into the woods to eat. When I was a couple hundred yards into the woods, I smelled water. So, I went lookin'. About fifty yards further in, I found a clearin' with a pond. There was a tree house in a big oak tree on the bank of the pond, so other people know about it."

"Okay," Jack said, "but that don't change the fact the MRB will be locked up tighter than a nun's twat."

"We can take the log access road. It's about a mile south of the MRB road, but it angles back. Like I said, it was only a few hundred yards north of where we were loggin'. If your truck can handle the log road, we can get there."

Mont laughed loudly. "Beast don't need roads. Point me in the right direction, and Beast'll get us there."

Mont stomped down on Beast's accelerator and headed toward the MRB.

A few minutes later, Mont slowed down a bit as they drove past the MRB driveway. As they suspected, the gate was in place and secured with several large chains and locks. Yellow crime scene tape had been draped and stretched on and across the gate and fence posts.

From the back seat, Trowa said, "The log road's about a mile up on the left."

Mont stomped down on the accelerator again and they left the MRB drive behind in a cloud of exhaust fumes.

Mont, who logged his entire adult life, saw the log road before Trowa pointed it out. He slowed and turned left into the ditch that separated the log road from the main road. A temporary gate: three strands of barbwire tied to a tree on the left and a fencepost on the right, held to a tree on the right by two loops of barbwire on the top and bottom, blocked the entrance. Mont stopped.

Trowa said, "I'll let ya through, put the gate back in place, and ride the rest of the way in the back."

"I'll get in the back, too," Bear said.

"Take the shotguns. We'll turn on the floodlights when we get away from the road a piece," Jack instructed.

After Trowa and Bear got out, Jack said to Cole, "What 'bout you, Eddie? Ya wanna ride in the back?"

Cole shook his head. "I feel safer in the cab."

Mont chuckled. "Pussy."

After Trowa pulled the gate back, Mont drove in, but he stopped when Trowa was even with his window. "Twist the hubs for me."

No four-wheel-drive shift on the fly for Beast. It had dependable lock-in hubs on each of the front tires. After Trowa locked the hubs, Mont continued through the opening. He stopped while Trowa replaced the gate.

As Trowa passed Mont's window again, he stopped. "The road splits about a mile up. Stay left. I'll thump on the top when we get to where we need to stop."

Mont gave Trowa a thumbs up, his thumbs were the size of breakfast sausages, and waited for Trowa and Bear to jump onto the back of Beast. When they were in the back, Mont switched Beast's transfer case from two-wheel high to four-wheel low, shifted into third gear, which, unless pulling or climbing something, was a good start gear in four-wheel low, and drove into the dense forest.

About a quarter mile into the forest, the trees thinned considerably from the logging at that point. Mont switched on the high-powered floodlights, four on the headache rack and two on the cattle guard, and everything in front of them, for about a hundred yards, became bathed in harsh, white light. Mont and Jack switched on their directional, windshield post mounted spotlights and started scanning the area on the right and left sides that the six high-powered spotlights didn't illuminate. A low fog was settling on the ground and the directional spotlights cut through it like white light knives.

Where loggers harvested the trees, left the landscape looking like a post-apocalyptic disaster area. They'd cut the tops of the pine trees too small to harvest from the tree trunks and left them to rot on the ground. The pine needles, once green and full of life, had long since turned brown and brittle. They clung to the withered branches like dead fingers.

As they drove the first stretch of the log road, Beast scared up several critters; rabbits, raccoons, opossums, an armadillo, and a small herd of deer scurried from the light. They melted into the foggy landscape. Mont and Jack both regretted not being able to poach some out-of-season venison. They did this often, but kept their eyes peeled for the bigger prize.

Mont chuckled. "I think a werewolf's head'll look good on the game room wall."

"Damn good," Jack replied with a similar chuckle.

When Mont came to the road split, he took the left path as instructed. After the split, the log road deteriorated rapidly. Mont could see the large ruts left by the massive, monster truck size tires of the tree gathering vehicles. He knew the log trucks, like he and Jack drove, didn't come down this road. There were massive, water filled ruts, but Beast bumped through them with ease.

The trees were thickening, revealing they were nearing the end of the cut, when Trowa thumped on Beast's roof. Mont stopped Beast, put it in neutral, and let it idle.

"One for the hunt?" Mont asked Jack.

"You're readin' my mind, brother," Jack replied.

Trowa and Bear jumped down from the back of Beast. They came up beside Jack's window as he pulled paper cups from the dash-mounted dispenser.

"What's this about?" Bear asked.

Jack grinned. "One for the hunt."

He opened the glove box, flipped the toggle switch, and filled the first cup, which he handed to Trowa.

Trowa sniffed the contents. "No fuckin' way."

"What is it?" Bear asked.

Trowa handed the cup to Bear. "Whiskey."

"Jack Daniels," Jack clarified.

From the back seat, Cole said, "That's the coolest fuckin' thing I've ever seen."

Jack, feeling good about his invention, smiled with pride as he handed drinks to everyone, even the kid, and filled one for himself.

When they all had a drink, Jack said, "To killin' werewolves. If the fuckers are real."

"To killin' werewolves," Mont, Bear, and Trowa agreed.

They touched paper cups together and took the shots. Mont killed Beast's engine and switched off all the lights. Darkness fell over them like a heavy blanket.

Mont, Jack, and Cole got out of Beast. Mont and Jack grabbed the ARs leaning against the seat between them. As if on cue, they pulled the sidelever back and chambered a round at the same time. Following their lead, Bear and Trowa did the same with the shotguns. They all switched on the under-barrel mounted flashlights. Four white beams of light pierced the fog, which had gotten thicker.

"This way," Trowa said as he started toward the thick woods to the left of Beast.

Jack fell in behind Trowa. "I'm on Trowa. Bear, you cover our ass with Mont. Eddie, you stay in the middle between us."

Grunts of agreement came from the other four.

As they were about to step from the clearing into the woods, Trowa said, "Keep your heads on a swivel, boys. If the Yee Naaldlooshii gets close before we see it, I think we're fucked."

It's already here, you stupid fucks, Cole thought as the group of werewolf hunters stepped into the thick, foggy forest.

~ * ~

The alpha stopped just inside the tree line on the edge of Garrett's front yard, about a hundred feet from the front door. It stood on its hind legs to see over the truck in the driveway. The popcorn smell, although still powerful, diminished since the little bitch and the man finished it. It saw the man stand up and fought the urge to crash through the window and take his head off.

It heard the man say, "No, I don't think so. It's been a long day for both of us."

The little bitch said, "Please, Daddy. Just one more movie. I'll find a short one."

The man said, "Don't give me those eyes, young lady. Not tonight."

The little bitch said, "You're no fun now that you're gettin' old."

The man laughed. "Old? I'm thirty-four. That's hardly old."

The alpha heard enough domestic father-daughter blather from the man and little bitch. It crouched down on all fours and crept forward from the concealing trees, keeping the truck between it and the house.

~ * ~

Not long after entering the thick woods, Trowa emerged into the clearing with Jack close behind him. Trowa pointed the flashlight toward the tree, to show Jack the tree house, but all that remained of the tree house was the burned-out floorboards. There was yellow crime scene tape wrapped around the tree and a spot on the ground directly in front of where Trowa and Jack stood.

"What the fuck happened here?" Jack asked.

"No idea. It wasn't like this the last time I saw it," Trowa said.

Jack pointed the flashlight at the ground that had the crime scene tape around it. He and Trowa saw the blackened pools of dried blood.

"Fuck me. Must'a been some kids kilt here, too," Jack reasoned.

They heard rustling in the trees behind them and Trowa and Jack wheeled around, ready to unload on whatever came out of the woods. It was Mont and Bear. Trowa and Jack relaxed and removed their fingers from the triggers.

Jack blew out an exaggerated breath. "Good way for you fuckers to get shot."

"Ya knew we were comin' up behind y'all," Mont pointed out.

"Yeah, well…fuckin' announce yourselves next time."

Bear walked up to Trowa. "What happened here?"

Trowa shrugged. "Don't know. It looks like someone bled out."

Mont joined Jack, Trowa, and Bear at the crime scene tape. He looked at the ground with the others.

After several seconds, Trowa pointed his flashlight at the closest bloody spot, then at one a little further away. "Neck and chest, maybe. And…crotch, maybe."

Bear's mouth dropped open, and he said, "Did ya use some Indian shit to figure that out?"

In an exaggerated Indian accent, Trowa said, "Trowa read earth."

Bear, clearly in awe, said, "No shit? You can do shit like that?"

Trowa laughed. "No, I can't do shit like that. I'm speculatin' based on anatomy and that wolves like to eat the soft, easy to get to parts first."

Bear inadvertently cupped his free hand over his crotch. "Soft and easy to get like dick and balls?"

"Exactly," Trowa confirmed.

Mont enjoyed Trowa fucking with Bear, but he realized their hunting party was one short. He rotated a full circle, shining his flashlight around, and didn't see Eddie.

Mont turned back toward the woods. "Where's the fuckin' kid?"

Jack looked up. "He was back with y'all."

Bear said, "I thought he was up with y'all."

"Well, if that don't fuckin' beat all. If we get that fuckin' kid killed out here, it's our asses," Mont fumed.

Bear yelled, "Hey, kid. Eddie. Where the fuck ya at?"

Bear started to yell again, but Trowa hushed him and whispered, "Listen."

They stood there in total silence, not breathing, and listened for several seconds. Mont initially thought Trowa heard the kid and was disappointed when he heard nothing.

Mont whispered, “I don’t hear nothin’, Trowa.”

Trowa nodded slowly and whispered, “Exactly. Y’all grew up in the woods, too. Ever heard ‘em this quiet?”

As the unnaturally quiet forest dawned on each of them, a hungry growl seeped out of the foggy forest directly in front of them. Four flashlight beams pointed toward the woods. Two burning red eyes, about eight feet off the ground, flashed back at them.

~ * ~

Garrett got up from the recliner, his muscles ached more than they had earlier, he took the remote from the coffee table and turned off the television. “I’m goin’ to bed.”

Paige looked at Garrett pleadingly. “Can’t we watch TV for a while?”

“Not me, kiddo. You can watch TV in your bedroom, if ya want.”

“Please, Daddy.”

It wasn’t unusual for Paige to try negotiating another movie, but Garrett sensed something different about her behavior.

“What’s goin’ on, kiddo?”

Paige averted Garrett’s eyes. “I…I don’t wanna be alone.”

Garrett felt like an idiot for not realizing why Paige didn’t want him to go to bed. She was scared.

Garrett smiled. “How ‘bout this? You bunk with me tonight.”

Garrett could see Paige’s nervous tension melt away.

Paige smiled. “Okay. I’ll get ready for bed and be right there.”

As Paige got up from the couch and started toward her bedroom, Garrett turned off the living room light and looked out at the darkness through the window in the front door. Just then, the motion-activated floodlights on the front side of the house turned on.

Paige froze in mid-step. “Daddy?”

Garrett pulled the pistol from the back of his pants and put his hand on the doorknob. “Go to your bathroom, Paige.”

It was the only room in his house without a window, and Garrett thought it would be the safest place for Paige.

"Please don't go out there, Daddy."

Garrett turned the doorknob. "It's probably nothin'. Just a little critter that got too close to the house."

With a tremble in her voice, Paige said, "It's her. I can feel her, Daddy. She's angry."

Garrett opened the door.

~ * ~

When the burning red eyes flashed from the woods, Mont, Jack, Bear, and Trowa pulled their triggers. The fully automatic AR-15 rounds cut into the woods and sent leaves, limbs, and tree bark flying like foliage confetti. The semi-automatic shotgun, double-ought buckshot rounds tore chunks out of large trees and obliterated smaller ones.

After several seconds of constant gunfire, Mont released the trigger of his AR-15, held up his hand, and yelled, "Hold up."

The other three immediately stopped shooting. They stood there silently with the gunfire still echoing in their ears, bluish smoke seeping from the ends of their gun barrels. The smell of gunpowder and tree sap hung thick in the air. Their flashlights pointed at the bullet and shot ridden woods. Nothing moved.

"Nothin' could'a survived that," Bear said.

"If we hit it?" Trowa added.

Jack scoffed. "Course we hit it. Nothin' outruns a bullet."

"Well, let's go see," Mont said with a grin and the four men crept toward the woods.

When they got to the wood line, Mont said, "Don't waste shots. I think I went through 'bout half my ammo back there."

"Switch to bursts," Jack suggested.

Burst mode meant the ARs would release three rounds for each trigger pull instead of the continuous stream on automatic. Mont nodded in agreement and he and Jack switched their assault weapons to burst mode.

"Let's do this," said Jack.

They entered the woods side by side, at the spot where they saw the red eyes, and advanced several feet. They saw lots of devastation to the plant life, but no sign of whatever the red eyes belonged to.

"Impossible," Bear said.

Trowa walked ahead of the other three and to the right. He stopped and pointed the gun-mounted flashlight at the ground.

"What ya got?" Jack asked.

Trowa looked back at the other three. "Blood."

"Hot damn. I fuckin' knew we had to hit the bastard." Mont yelled.

Mont, Jack, and Bear crowded around Trowa. They looked at the small pool of blood on the forest floor.

"Can ya track it, Trowa?" Bear asked.

Trowa pointed the flashlight around and spotted a blood smear on a nearby tree limb.

"This way," Trowa said as he walked toward the blood smear.

As they made their way deeper into the woods, Trowa found more evidence of the path taken by the injured beast, broken limbs, coarse black hair, and blood. Mont, Jack, and Bear were following behind Trowa with about five feet between each of them.

Trowa suddenly stopped and held up his left arm. The others stopped immediately.

"What?" Mont asked.

"It doubled back," Trowa said in a hushed voice.

As soon as the words left Trowa's mouth, a loud growl came from the dark woods, followed by the sound of something very large crashing through the underbrush.

Bear, bringing up the rear, saw the nightmare werewolf leaping out of the foggy darkness at him. He tried to raise the shotgun for a shot, but the massive beast was on him before he could pull the trigger. The werewolf clamped its jaws on Bear's right shoulder and, with little effort and a flick of its massive head, flung Bear into the air. Bear slammed into a tree trunk about thirty feet away and fell to the ground with a bone-crunching 'thud.' He didn't move.

~ * ~

Garrett, with his gun up and ready, walked out onto the front porch and surveyed the woods surrounding his house. Nothing moved and everything was dead quiet.

Too quiet, Garrett thought.

He remembered what Ty and Paige told him about how quiet it got when the werewolves were around and the hairs on the back of his neck and arms prickled.

From behind Garrett, Paige said, "Come back inside, Daddy."

Garrett looked over his shoulder at Paige. "I told ya to go to the bathroom."

While he looked at Paige, her face filled with terror and she screamed, "She's here."

Garrett spun around quickly and saw the monstrous werewolf raise up from behind his truck. It seemed to Garrett like it would never stop growing. Worse than its enormous size were the smoldering red eyes that radiated evil.

Garrett's hands were shaking. He tried to steady them but couldn't. He pulled the trigger. The werewolf went down behind the truck, but Garrett knew he'd missed. A shot that hits its mark sounds different from a shot that misses. Hits are 'thuds,' misses are 'zings.' Garrett heard the shot zing high.

Garrett kept his gun pointed where he'd last seen the werewolf, but it bolted from behind the truck to his right on all fours. Garrett swung the gun toward the fast-moving target and squeezed the trigger just before it disappeared into the woods. Another 'zing.'

"Come back inside, Daddy." Paige yelled.

Garrett, gun still up and ready to shoot, backed through the door and, once inside, shut it. After seeing the size of the werewolf, Garrett knew shutting the door would be useless. It could break through it easily, but shut doors have psychological benefits. He even locked it.

When he was back inside, he turned to Paige. "I think it's gone."

Paige shook her head. "No, Daddy. She's playin' with us."

"You can…sense this?"

Paige nodded.

"It's still out there?"

Paige nodded again.

Just then, the front motion-activated floodlights turned off. The sudden lack of outside light made Garrett and Paige jump.

When Garrett realized the significance of the floodlights turning off; no motion, he said, "Are ya sure? The lights just went off."

Paige nodded. "I'm sure."

As if to verify Paige's assertion, the back floodlights turned on. Garrett, who had been facing toward the back of the house, saw a black mass with burning red eyes through the sliding glass doors.

~ * ~

Jack heard the commotion behind him and spun around just in time to see the werewolf toss Bear like a ragdoll into the woods. The werewolf looked at Jack with burning red eyes and advanced toward him, but Jack brought his AR up and squeezed the trigger. He pulled the trigger prematurely and sent three rounds thudding into the ground at the werewolf's hind feet. It leapt away, landing on all fours, and melted into the foggy darkness beyond the flashlight beam's reach.

"It fuckin' got Bear." Jack shouted.

Mont and Trowa came quickly to where Jack stood.

"It got Bear?" Mont asked.

Jack nodded. "It fuckin' threw him in the air like a cat would a mouse. Like he weighed nothin'."

"You saw it?" Trowa asked Jack.

"Fuck yeah, I saw it. Fuckin' huge. Eight, nine feet tall."

"Where'd it toss Bear?" Mont asked.

"That way," Jack answered, and pointed his flashlight toward a tree about thirty feet away.

The flashlight beam reflected off a large patch of blood about ten feet up the tree trunk.

Mont, Jack, and Trowa made their way toward the tree; their flashlight beams cutting into the fog in all directions as they did. Because of the fog, they didn't see Bear's prone form until they were only a few feet from the bloodstained tree. Mont took a knee next to Bear and placed his fingers on Bear's neck.

"Is he alive?" Jack asked.

"I can't tell. His neck's too fuckin' fat to feel anything."

Bear moaned.

~ * ~

About a second before impact, Garrett realized the black mass with burning red eyes was leaping toward the sliding glass doors. Garrett raised the gun, took aim, and squeezed the trigger at the exact instant the werewolf came crashing through the doors in a shower of glass. He heard a semi-thud.

Garrett grabbed Paige and threw her behind him just in time. The momentum of the werewolf's leap sent it barreling into the dining room table, which launched into the air and came crashing into the couch. The couch launched toward Garrett and Paige, bringing the coffee table with it. When the momentum from the werewolf's impact came to a stop, Garrett and Paige were on the floor with their backs to the front door and a pile of overturned furniture between them and the werewolf.

Expecting the werewolf to leap over the furniture and finish them, Garrett pointed the gun above the overturned couch and waited. A loud, furious growl shook the house and rattled Garrett and Paige's bones. The couch moved slightly, and Garrett's finger tightened on the trigger. They heard a burst of motion and something heavy landed on the wooden deck. Then everything was quiet.

After several seconds of silence, Garrett, still pointing the gun above the overturned couch, said, "I hit it. I think it's dead."

Paige brought her left hand up, put it on Garrett's gun hand, and pushed the gun down. "She's not dead. She's gone."

"Are ya sure? I hit it. I know I did."

Paige looked at Garrett. "Ya grazed her. That was enough for her to know it was a silver bullet and the only reason it didn't bite ya, Daddy."

Garrett, amazed Paige could know all of this, but not doubting she did, said, "It wanted to bite me?"

Paige nodded. "She wanted to bite ya, so she could control ya. Control us."

Garrett thought again about James Huff's notion the alpha never intended to kill Paige; it wanted Paige in its pack.

Garrett looked at Paige. "So, it didn't come to kill either of us?"

Paige shook her head. "Nope. She has plans for me."

"Plans? What plans?"

Paige looked away from Garrett. "She…I don't know, Daddy. It's all a blur now."

Garrett thought Paige held something back, but after what they'd been through, he didn't press it.

Garrett squeezed Paige's hand. "Okay. If ya remember anything, let me know."

Paige smiled, but it looked forced to Garrett.

She said, "I will. She's gone now and I don't think she's comin' back. Can I still bunk with you?"

Garrett smiled a genuine smile. “Absolutely. I’m gonna need to board up that hole in the house first, though. Okay?”

Paige nodded. “Okay, Daddy. I’ll try to put the furniture back in place.”

While Garrett boarded up the back door, after hurricanes Rita and Ike tore up East Texas in 2005 and 2008 respectively, Garrett had plywood cut to cover all his windows and doors, which helped make short work of the patch job while Paige righted the furniture. There were four nasty gouges on the bottom of the kitchen table. Like the claw marks under Carla’s window. The couch had four nasty tears in the back fabric, but nothing was broken.

As Paige went about righting the furniture, all she could think about was the connection that opened between her and the alpha after her dad grazed it with the silver bullet. This enraged and scared the beast. Being scared only fed its rage. It wanted desperately to lunge over the couch and rip her dad apart, but it couldn’t chance a direct hit with the silver bullet. All the rage swirled around it and Paige’s heads as it crouched on the other side of the furniture, its prize so close but out of reach.

Just before it retreated into the safety of the forest, Paige sensed a thought from the alpha that made her stomach turn. Paige saw a clear mental image of a female werewolf being ravaged by a pack, the alpha’s pack, of male werewolves. The sexual coupling was degrading and grotesque. The biting and clawing being inflicted on the helpless female werewolf were worse.

The she-wolf yelped and howled in pain as chunks of its flesh and muscle were bitten away and long claws cut deep gashes in its flesh. All this went on while the she-wolf was being savagely raped. Worse still, Paige knew the she-wolf was her future werewolf. This was what the alpha planned for Paige. Paige knew, after each encounter, her body would heal so they could do it again and again. When Paige realized the alpha wanted her dad in the pack to add to the humiliation, her stomach turned upside-down. It had been too much.

Paige couldn’t tell her dad about this. It was bad enough he knew what she and Justin intended to do the previous night. There was no way she could tell him the alpha planned to make her the ‘pack fuck-toy bitch,’ the alpha’s thought for her, and it wanted her dad in the pack abusing her, too. This was too humiliating to share with anyone. The only satisfaction

Paige had was knowing the alpha knew her dad had silver bullets, and this scared the shit out of her. Knowing this, Paige didn't think she would try to bite her dad again. Believing, even in a worst-case scenario, she wouldn't be engaging in incestuous, werewolf sex with her dad satisfied her, too.

~ * ~

The alpha bolted from the man and little bitch's house before the man could fire another shot with his deadly silver bullets, and it didn't stop running until it had traveled several miles. It crouched beneath a tree, catching its breath. Each exhale produced a rumbling growl that reverberated through the dense woods and sent nocturnal critters scurrying for their holes. Even the birds took flight for trees far from the evil below.

The alpha knew it had been lucky. It dodged a bullet, almost literally. It saw the man's gun pointed at it as it leapt for the glass doors, and heard him shoot. Guns were of no concern to it. As it crashed through the glass, intent on biting and turning the man, it saw the gun's muzzle flash. The bullet hit the metal frame of the glass doors dead center in the alpha's face, and ricochet to its left. It wasn't a complete miss, though. The malformed bullet went through the alpha's left ear.

It was a minor wound, but the pain of the silver penetrating its flesh had been intense and distracting. This sent the alpha into an uncontrolled roll into the table, and it landed on its side on the other side of the piled-up furniture. It wanted to jump up and rip the man apart, for daring to injure it, but the prospect of another shot, a well-placed shot, kept it crouching in fear on the floor. It let out a defiant growl and escaped into the safety of the woods instead.

As it crouched beside a tree, it seethed with rage. Its plans to turn the man and add to the little bitch's degradation were, seemingly, thwarted. It couldn't risk another encounter with the man and his deadly silver. If the little bitch was with him, it couldn't fuck with her, either.

The alpha, so lost in its rage that, at first, it didn't register a sensation clawing at its thoughts. As its breathing slowed, the clawing dug deeper. Then it took hold. The alpha's head jerked upward, and it took a deep breath. It smelled another werewolf. One of its pack members. The alpha let out a low, menacing growl that shook the limbs of the surrounding trees and the surrounding underbrush. It bolted on all fours into the forest, letting its nose and incredible sense of smell lead it to its disobedient pup. Lead it to Cole.

~ * ~

"He's alive." Mont shouted.

Jack and Trowa trained their flashlights on Bear's face. It was pale and blood was leaking out of his mouth, nose, and ears, but his left eye fluttered open. The eye patch on his right eye was askew, revealing an empty eye socket behind it.

Guess he wasn't switchin' the patch, Jack thought.

Bear coughed, and blood sprayed the ground by his mouth. "Where is it?" Bear croaked.

"Don't know," Mont told him.

Jack looked around nervously. "We gotta get him to Beast and get the fuck outta here."

"Can ya walk?" Mont asked Bear.

Bear grimaced. "I can try."

Mont and Jack each grabbed Bear under an arm and hoisted him to his feet. It was then they got a good look at the wound on Bear's right shoulder. Bear's faded, sleeveless, blue jean vest was soaked with sticky blood. Mont, who had been supporting Bear's right side, gently pulled the vest back, and Trowa pointed his flashlight at the area. Where the werewolf's dagger length fangs punctured the front of Bear's shoulder, were two large holes that transitioned into ragged tears in Bear's flesh, where they tore loose when it flung him through the air. There were similar wounds on the back of Bear's shoulder.

"You're gonna need stitches," Mont said.

Bear winced. "And new underwear. I think I shit myself."

Jack laughed. "I almost shit myself and I wasn't in the fucker's mouth."

Bear chuckled at this, and more blood oozed from his mouth.

"We gotta get the fuck outta here. Which way to Beast, Trowa?" Mont said.

Trowa looked around, getting his bearings, and pointed to the left. "This way."

"Lead the way," Jack said.

Trowa started away with his shotgun at the ready, sweeping it from side to side so the under-barrel flashlight could light his way. Mont readied his AR in his right arm and Jack, because he was supporting Bear with his right arm, readied his AR in his left arm.

They only traveled a few feet when a menacing growl rumbled from directly behind them. Mont and Jack let go of Bear, who fell to the ground with a grunt. They spun around as the massive beast leapt. It targeted Mont.

The werewolf landed on Mont and knocked him onto his back. Jack brought his AR up to shoot the beast but, because he might hit Mont, he didn't pull the trigger. Instead, Jack dropped his gun, let out a roar that almost equaled the werewolf's growls, and plowed into the side of the werewolf. He wrapped his massive arms around its neck, and used his substantial weight to knock it off Mont.

As Jack and the werewolf rolled off Mont, Mont punched it in the side of its snout. One of the werewolf's upper fangs went flying from its snout.

Jack ended up on his back with the werewolf on top of him. Its immense weight pressed against Jack, making it hard for him to breathe, but he refused to let go. Jack let out a grunt and increased the stranglehold he had on the werewolf's thick neck, while the werewolf thrashed wildly in his grip.

Mont got to his feet and kicked the werewolf in the side of its head, which sent two more of its teeth flying free. Unfortunately, this move brought Mont too close to the beast, and it raked its claws across Mont's left leg, opening large gashes in his calf muscle. Mont let out a yelp and fell to the ground.

The werewolf grabbed Mont by his wounded leg and pulled him closer. Mont grabbed at a nearby tree to hold on to and, hopefully, keep himself from the werewolf's deadly jaws, but missed. When Mont was close enough, the werewolf brought Mont's leg up, put it in its mouth, bit down, and used its remaining teeth to sever Mont's leg just below the knee.

Mont let out a shrill and feminine scream he couldn't believe came from out of his mouth. The pain dwarfed anything he'd experienced, but the sound of his leg bones crunching turned his stomach. Bile filled his throat and a stream of vomit erupted from his mouth. He rolled onto his side and, through eyes filling with white spots, saw Jack struggling to keep the werewolf in a headlock. Adrenaline coursed through Mont, and he surged toward the werewolf. Mont grabbed the only weapon he could find, his severed leg, and started beating the werewolf in the face with it. Unfortunately, this move put Mont even closer to the werewolf.

The werewolf grabbed Mont by the arm and pulled him on top of it. Mont struggled, but the beast's powerful grip proved too strong.

Jack couldn't see what was going on with his face buried in the werewolf's smelly fur. His plan was to hold on to the werewolf long enough to give his brother time to escape. Jack heard a shriek that sounded nothing like Mont, but he knew it came from Mont. They had a twin connection. Jack squeezed harder, hoping to choke the monster out.

Jack thought his plan might work but, suddenly, the weight on his chest increased substantially. He didn't know it, but with the werewolf and Mont were on top of him, he was being crushed by over nine hundred pounds. Jack tried to breathe, but his chest wouldn't expand. His vision narrowed as blackness filled the periphery of his view of werewolf hair. As his vision narrowed to a slight point of sight, Jack felt his grip on the werewolf's neck falter. He lost consciousness and his arms fell free.

~ * ~

When Trowa heard the growl, he spun around just in time to see the werewolf land on top of Mont. He saw Jack dive on the werewolf and knock it off Mont. Trowa ran to his friends, shotgun at the ready, but there was no way he could risk a shot. All he could do was watch the large twin brothers battle the werewolf and hope for a clean shot.

Trowa's chance at a shot came shortly after he saw Jack's enormous arms slip limply from the werewolf's neck. Free from Jack's stranglehold, the werewolf grabbed Mont by his right arm and flung the three-hundred-and-sixty-pound man at least ten feet away. It flipped over and opened its massive jaws to deliver a bite to the unconscious Jack. Trowa pointed the semi-automatic shotgun at the beast's chest, ready to pull the trigger. Before he could, a second werewolf came out of nowhere and slammed into the first werewolf with enough force to send it flying. It landed next to Mont and came up gnashing its remaining teeth.

Before engaging with the first werewolf again, the second werewolf reached down and ripped Jack's throat out with its deadly claws. It looked at Trowa with its burning red eyes. Before it could move on Trowa, the first werewolf got its attention with an angry growl. The second werewolf looked back at the first werewolf and launched at it with incredible speed.

As the two werewolves came together with a crash, Trowa assessed the situation. He knew Jack was dead and Mont would likely bleed out soon. That left Bear to rescue, but Trowa knew he couldn't support Bear's weight by himself, which meant Bear would soon be dead, too.

Trowa had two options. Try to get to Beast and drive out on the slow log road or seek safety in the treetops. Because Trowa believed the fast-moving werewolves would likely catch him long before he made it to the main road, if he opted for using Beast to escape, that left the treetops as his only viable escape.

Trowa looked down at Bear, who was trying to crawl away. "I'm sorry, Bear."

Bear looked up at Trowa with his one good eye and empty eye socket. "Get the fuck outta here, Trowa. Tell 'em where to find our bodies."

Trowa nodded and darted away.

Trowa could hear the epic battle going on between the two werewolves as he frantically searched for a suitable tree. He didn't know why the beasts were fighting each other, but he knew he needed to be out of reach when it ended. Trowa spun to his right, shining the shotgun's flashlight in front of him, and saw a promising tree. It was only about twenty feet from where the werewolves were fighting, though.

"Fuck it," Trowa said, aloud to himself.

He ran toward the tree.

When Trowa got to the tree, he kicked off his boots and jumped up the trunk. It was a large pine tree, but the trunk wasn't too wide for Trowa to lock his long legs around. Like rock wall climbers, Trowa used his fingertips to gain purchase in the rough bark and pull himself up. With each pull, Trowa would hang by his fingers, briefly, move his legs up, and lock them around the trunk again.

Years of practice, adrenaline, and fear worked in Trowa's favor and, before he knew it, he reached the lowest limbs in the pine tree. Trowa looked down to gauge how high he was and judged it to be about forty feet.

Higher. Trowa thought.

The climbing became much easier in the branches and Trowa was about sixty feet high in a matter of seconds. He draped his legs over a large limb and leaned back against the tree trunk. He looked down to see if he could watch the battle still going on sixty feet below. Between the tree branches, distance, fog, and darkness, Trowa couldn't see a thing. He could hear it though, and it sounded like hell opened and released a hoard of demons.

~ * ~

The alpha quickly figured out what the rogue beta planned to do. It intended to turn the men and start a rival pack. This knowledge fed its rage to the boiling point. When the alpha finally saw the beta sitting on top of the man, about to deliver the turning bite, it plowed into the beta with all its force and speed. As they connected, the alpha stabbed its claws from both hands into the beta's side before launching it off the man. To make sure the man didn't live to turn or tell, the alpha ripped his throat out.

The alpha quickly determined the condition of the three remaining men. Two of them were too injured to escape; one was not. The alpha looked at the healthy man, intent on quickly disposing of the potential problem, but the beta's threatening growl changed its mind. The alpha knew it could catch the healthy man quickly after it took care of the beta. The alpha launched at the beta.

The two werewolves came together with bone shattering force and rolled over in a ball of gnashing teeth and slashing claws. The beta, winded and wounded from its altercation with the two large men and the alpha's stabbing claws, fought with determination. It rolled on top of the alpha and raked its claws across the alpha's chest, opening four deep incisions. The alpha reacted with a slash at the beta's throat that, if it hadn't missed, would have been debilitating.

When the beta celebrated the miss by gnashing at the alpha's throat. The alpha stuck its claws into the left side of the beta's face. With blind luck, one of the alpha's claws punctured the beta's left eye. The beta yelped and shook its head violently, sending blood and drool flying. The alpha took advantage of the beta's disorientation and shoved it back, which freed the alpha and it got to its feet.

The beta rolled over and came up on its feet, too. It sprang at the alpha, grabbed it around the waist, lifted it off the ground, and slammed it into an enormous tree trunk. The tree shook under the impact and several branches broke free and rained down on the two werewolves.

Mistakenly, the beta thought, with the alpha pinned against the tree, it had the upper hand. If it secured the alpha's arms, it might have had the upper hand, but it hadn't. The alpha stabbed down into the beta's back with both sets of claws and raked its paws outward, which opened deep gashes.

The beta howled in pain and stumbled back. As the beta stumbled back, the alpha kicked out with a hind paw and sent the beta tumbling onto its back. The alpha sprang and landed on the prone beta. The beta thrashed about trying to dislodge the alpha, but its strength was spent. After several seconds of thrashing, the beta submitted.

The alpha looked down at the submissive beta and considered its punishment. It really wasn't much of a consideration. The pup challenged the alpha twice in one day and, worse still, it planned to start a rival pack. The alpha couldn't risk the beta's threatening behavior, and it certainly couldn't trust it in the future.

In a swift motion that took the beta by surprise, the alpha locked its powerful jaws around the beta's neck and snapped them shut with a viscous bite. Blood sprayed, bones crunched, and the beta's head separated from its body. The alpha stood up and looked down at the decapitated werewolf. As it looked at the werewolf, the beta's body quickly transformed back into its human form. The alpha stepped away from Cole's naked body. It still had to kill the three men.

Knowing the healthy man would need to be tracked and unconcerned that it wouldn't catch him, the alpha took care of the two injured men first. The larger of the two was still unconscious, and the alpha simply ripped his throat out. The other man put up a fight, which amused the alpha.

It found him trying to hide in thick underbrush. The alpha pulled him up from the underbrush by his injured shoulder, which caused the man to scream and the alpha to chuckle. The man swung his left fist and kicked at the alpha, but his limbs were too short to connect. To play with the man, the alpha stuck its snout out, close enough for him to hit, as if daring the man to do it. The man took the bait and punched at the alpha's snout. Quick as spit, the alpha snapped its jaws shut on the man's left arm and severed it below the elbow. The man screamed. The alpha chuckled.

The alpha lowered the man to the ground and gently let go of his shoulder. The man wobbled on his feet a little, but he remained standing.

When the man looked up at the alpha, it lowered its open jaws onto the man's plump head.

Bear felt the alpha's lower canines sink into his flesh just below his chin and its upper canines pierce the skin on the back of his skull. Bear's knees buckled, but the werewolf's powerful jaws held him up. All Bear could see with his one eye was the reddish blackness of the werewolf's gullet and shiny, white teeth. The stench was worse than the view. It smelled like hell's burp.

Bear didn't know it, but he got off easy. Unlike when the alpha killed Russ Lomax, who spat the stinging tobacco juice in its eye, by severing his head with a slow, deliberate bite, the alpha snapped its jaws closed quickly and popped Bear's head like a rotten grape.

Bear looked down the alpha's gullet, then he looked no more.

The alpha spit the crunchy goo of Bear's head out and sniffed the air to find the healthy man's scent. It found it immediately and knew he was still close. Thinking it would find the man quickly and dispatch him with ease, the alpha followed its nose to the tree where his scent ended. The alpha quickly determined the man wasn't hiding around the tree and followed the scent upward.

~ * ~

Although Trowa hadn't been able to see the werewolf battle, he heard it end with a gurgling crunch that led him to believe one werewolf was no longer a threat. Shortly after the werewolf fight ended, Trowa heard Bear scream in pain. A few seconds later, Bear screamed again. After Bear's second scream, the woods fell silent.

Trowa started to climb down to the bottom limbs to get a better look when he saw a werewolf walk up to the tree. It was directly below him. The werewolf sniffed around the base of the tree and looked up at Trowa. Its eyes flared bright red and it let out an angry growl. Then it jumped.

Trowa held his breath as he saw the werewolf launch itself up. Trowa was about sixty feet up and the leap halved the distance between himself and the angry werewolf. When the werewolf crashed into the tree about thirty feet up, the tree shook violently, and Trowa had to clamp his legs tightly around the limb he was sitting on to keep from falling.

Trowa thought the werewolf would scale the tree and finish him, but that didn't happen. The werewolf frantically tried to gain purchase on the tree trunk, but the bark that had aided Trowa's climb shredded beneath its razor-sharp claws and it fell to the ground with a 'thud' that shook the tree again. The werewolf got back on its feet and launched up the tree a second time that ended as the first attempt had, with it on the ground.

After a third unsuccessful attempt at climbing the tree, the werewolf began snapping its jaws around the base of the tree. After trying, unsuccessfully, for several minutes to chew through the tree trunk, the werewolf looked up at Trowa and let out what almost sounded like a human rage filled scream. It dropped to all fours and sprinted away.

Trowa didn't believe the werewolf gave up and left. He thought it, more likely, planned to coax him from the safety of the tree so it could kill him on the ground. Trowa had no intention of finding out if his suspicions were correct. He would stay in the tree for as long as it took to escape alive.

When Trowa logged the nearby woods, cellphone service was spotty and non-existent most of the time. That had been on the ground. Trowa took his cellphone out of his back pocket and depressed the 'Home' button. When the cellphone lit up, he saw one reception bar. Hoping it would be enough, Trowa dialed nine-one-one and put the phone to his ear.

~ * ~

Because Trowa was outside of Pine View city jurisdiction, the nine-one-one call routed to the Pine View County Sheriff's Department.

Eva Martinez, who was the three-to-eleven dispatcher and answered county nine-one-one calls, only had twenty minutes left on an uneventful shift when the emergency line rang.

Eva answered the phone. "Nine, one, one. What is your emergency?"

The man on the other end of the call, in a very calm voice, said, "I know this is gonna sound crazy, but two…werewolves just killed my friends."

Eva's blood ran cold, but she kept her composure. "Are you in danger, sir?"

The man chuckled. "Not immediate danger. I'm up a tree and the fucker can't climb it. I'm sure it's down there waitin' for me to climb down."

"Don't climb down, sir," Eva told the man.

The man laughed. "Not plannin' to, lady."

Eva wiggled her computer mouse to wake up the computer. The computer had a slow night, too. When the screen lit up, she said, "What's your name and location, sir?"

"My name is Trowa Raintree and my location is sixty feet up a pine tree a couple hundred yards southeast of the MRB."

The location surprised Eva, and she said, "MRB? We've got that place locked down. How did you gain access?"

"We came in on a loggin' road 'bout a mile south of the MRB road."

Eva began to put out the call when she remembered another question. "How many people are…were with you?"

"Three…no, four. Mont and Jack Lee, Bear Campton, and some kid we met at Knucklehead's. His name was Eddie…somethin'. Quaid or Quist or somethin' like that,"

"Are they dead?"

"I'm pretty sure they are. We lost the kid before the fuckers attacked, but unless he can fly or climb trees like me, I'm bettin' he's dead, too."

"Okay, Mister Raintree. Stay put. Help'll be there shortly."

Trowa laughed. "I'm not goin' anywhere 'til the posse gets here."

"Very good, sir," Eva said and ended the call.

~ * ~

Not wanting to put this information over the radio, because reporters and other busybodies liked to monitor law enforcement transmissions for interesting calls, Eve quickly filled out the computerized report and sent it to all the patrol vehicles.

To make sure the deputies saw the report quickly, Eva keyed the dispatch microphone. "Check your screens."

Within seconds, all four deputies on duty responded they were in route.

Eva left the dispatch booth and ran down the hall to the briefing room where the eleven-to-seven shift was meeting before going on duty. When Eva burst through the briefing room door, Ty stopped talking and looked at her.

"It's happenin' again," Eva said.

Ty headed for the door. "Where?"

"Behind the MRB. Info's on your screens."

As Ty went past Eva, he said, "Call Garrett."

"On it," Eva called after Ty.

As soon as Danny, Austin, and Crystal cleared the room, Eva went to the phone on the briefing room desk, picked up the receiver, and punched in Garrett's cell number. He answered on the fourth ring.

~ * ~

His ringing cellphone pulled Garrett from a dreamless sleep. Muscle memory directed his left hand to where the cellphone was plugged in and charging on the nightstand. His hand didn't grab the cellphone. It grabbed a handful of carpet.

Confused, Garrett opened his eyes and looked up into the darkened room. He could see the ceiling fan spinning, but it seemed far away. The cellphone rang a second time, and the cobwebs cleared his mind. It became clear. He was on the floor in his sleeping bag because Paige was asleep in his bed. Garrett crawled out of the sleeping bag as the cellphone rang a third time.

On the fourth ring, Garrett tapped the green phone icon. "Garrett here."

On the other end, Eva said, "They're back."

Garrett turned on the bedside lamp and saw Paige, wide-eyed and looking at him. Paige opened her mouth, but Garrett held up a finger, silencing her.

To Eva, Garrett said, "Where?"

Eva quickly filled Garrett in on the nine-one-one call she received from Trowa Raintree and told him the three-to-eleven and eleven-to-seven shifts were in route.

When she finished, Garrett said, "Call Mike. I know he's off tonight, but we need him. Tell him to coordinate with Ty and have two deputies follow him on the loggin' road. Tell Ty to organize the rest at the MRB. Inform both of 'em to wait until I get there."

"Will do," Eva replied.

Garrett looked at Paige. He knew she believed the alpha didn't want to kill her, but he couldn't leave her home alone. Part of him thought the MRB attack might have been a diversion to get him out of the house. He didn't like the idea of taking her back to the MRB, either, but he preferred having her with him.

"Get dressed. We need to go."

"What happened?"

Garrett got to his feet. "I'll tell ya on the way."

A few minutes later, they were in Garrett's patrol SUV and pulling out of the driveway.

~ * ~

The alpha silently circled the tree at a distance that kept it concealed from the man's human eyes. Its inability to get to the man frustrated it. For all its enhanced abilities and senses, the man remained alive.

After several minutes of circling, the alpha's sensitive ears registered sirens approaching. It stopped and concentrated on the sounds. They were far away but approaching quickly. As they got closer, the alpha heard three of the sirens break away from the others and continue south. The remaining sirens were gathering at the metal building where its pack hunted the previous night. It understood they were trying to encircle it, but this didn't concern it. The forest was its domain and there were more paths of escape than the humans could cover.

Curious, the alpha crept through the woods toward the MRB. It stopped just outside of the MRB clearing and crouched down in the thick underbrush to watch. It could see six vehicles with flashing lights and five humans huddled around a sixth man, a man with a scent the alpha knew well. It belonged to the deputy it bit and turned the night before. The alpha's snout crinkled, and a demonic chuckle rattled the brush in front of it.

The alpha started to leave when another vehicle pulled into the MRB area. Before the doors opened, it caught the scent of the little bitch and the man, her father. It watched them get out of the vehicle and approach the other humans. Rage coursed through the alpha, and it fought the urge to spring from the woods and devour all the humans. If not for the silver in the man's gun, it would have. Angry and frustrated, the alpha retreated deeper into the woods.

~ * ~

Trowa heard the approaching sirens and breathed a sigh of relief. Under normal circumstances, Trowa avoided law enforcement to the best of his ability. Not because he was engaged in unlawful activities, aside from smoking pot regularly, but out of a distrust of the system. Native Americans had a history of poor treatment from the white man's 'justice system.'

After several minutes, the sirens gathered toward the MRB fell silent. Trowa heard more sirens approaching from the south. From the logging road. He realized they were trying to flank the werewolf. Trowa didn't believe it would work, but he approved of their plan. Feeling safer than he had since the first werewolf attacked Bear, Trowa relaxed. That was when the tree shook violently, and Trowa fell from the limb he sat perched on.

~ * ~

As the alpha retreated from the MRB it took one last shot at the treed man. About a hundred yards away from the tree, it took off at a full run on all fours and, with all its considerable strength, leapt at the tree. The technique worked. Almost.

The alpha slammed into the tree about forty feet up. It saw one lower limb within reach, and it frantically grabbed at it. Its claws caught and its massive hand-paw wrapped around the limb. It looked up and saw the man fall from the limb he sat on. The man bounced down a limb then another. He was almost within reach. The alpha pulled itself up. If it could reach the next limb, it could use it to reach the man.

Thoughts of throwing the man from the tree then dropping on top of him and tearing his heart out fueled the alpha's movements. It was reaching for the next limb, only inches from it, when a loud crack issued from the limb it hung on. The limb sagged and the limb the alpha reached for became farther away.

The alpha knew the limb it hung onto was breaking under its substantial weight. With a menacing growl, the alpha lunged for the second branch. Its claws scraped at it, but the alpha was falling, the broken limb still in its grip.

The alpha hit the ground on its back with a thunderous 'thud.' It flung the large, broken limb to its side, where it hit another tree and splintered on impact. The alpha sprang to its feet and looked up at the man, who hung by his hands from a lower limb. It smashed its fist into the tree, but knew the impact wasn't enough to dislodge the man. Frustration drove its fist.

The alpha considered making one more running leap at the tree, but it could hear the humans getting closer and see their flashlights through the trees. It couldn't stay, but it had the man's scent and would deal with him later. It looked up at the dangling man, let out a loud growl, and sprinted into the darkness.

~ * ~

The force of the impact knocked Trowa from the limb he'd been sitting on. He fell across the next limb down on his stomach. The impact knocked the air out of him. Trowa tried to hold on. Without breath and terrified, he couldn't secure a grip. When he hit the next limb down, it caught him under his left arm, which slowed his momentum. As his arm slipped off the branch, he grabbed onto it with his right hand then his left.

Trowa could hear the werewolf beneath him. It sounded too close. He looked down and saw the beast's burning red eyes looking up at him from two branches down. It reached for the next branch up. Trowa knew, if it got a grip on that branch, it would reach and kill him. He heard a loud crack from the limb, and the werewolf fell from the tree.

Trowa didn't wait or watch to see what the crazed werewolf did next. As if his life depended on it, and he thought it did, Trowa swung his legs up onto the branch and started climbing higher. He heard the werewolf's angry growl, but when he finally stopped climbing and looked down, it was nowhere to be seen. He saw the approaching flashlights far below, though.

Trowa cupped his hands around his mouth and shouted, "Over here. I'm over here."

~ * ~

When they started into the woods behind the MRB, Garrett instructed Paige to get directly behind him and grab onto his utility belt. He instructed Ty to stay directly behind Paige. Garrett wasn't taking any chances with her safety.

Not long after entering the woods, they came to the clearing with the pond and the burned tree house. Garrett felt Paige's grip on his belt tighten.

"Just look at my back, kiddo," Garrett told Paige.

Ty pointed his flashlight at the trees ahead and to the right. "He should be in that area."

As they neared the woods behind the tree house, they heard a loud crack, followed by a crashing 'thud.' Garrett pointed his flashlight up in the air and everybody stopped. They listened and heard an angry growl echo out of the forest. Garrett's, as well as everyone else's, fingers moved to their triggers. They waited several seconds, as if expecting the beast, or beasts, to spring from the woods and attack. It, they, didn't.

Shortly after hearing the angry growl, they heard a man yelling, "Over here. I'm over here."

Garrett lowered his flashlight, and they entered the woods.

The man Garrett thought to be Trowa Raintree kept yelling, which helped guide them to him. Before getting to him, though, they came across the decapitated body of a young, naked man.

"Just keep lookin' at my back, Paige," Garrett said.

Paige said, "Okay," but she looked anyway.

Only briefly, because she immediately wished she hadn't. The man, who looked a little older than her, was a bloody mess. His head laid on its side several feet from his body. Paige's stomach turned, and she trained her eyes on her daddy's back again.

Seconds later, they were standing at the base of a large pine tree and shining their flashlights up at a man who must have been seventy feet up.

"You can come down now, Mister Raintree," Garrett shouted.

"Be right there. Back away in case some branches break free," Trowa shouted back.

Garrett, Paige, Ty, and the other deputies backed away.

Garrett watched the dexterous man negotiate the tree limbs like a circus performer. That wasn't near as impressive as how he descended the limbless trunk. Garrett felt sure, without climbing gear, the man would fall and land in a broken heap in front of them. Not the case. The man wrapped his legs around the tree trunk and slid down with no more difficulty than if he were sliding down a firehouse pole.

When his feet were on solid ground, Trowa turned to the amazed onlookers. “Fuck, am I glad to see y’all.”

Trowa noticed the young lady standing behind Sheriff Lambert, who Trowa knew only from reputation. “Sorry, little miss. I’m prone to cussin’, but I’ll try to watch it.”

Paige’s smile told Trowa she took no offence, but he still planned to watch his language.

Garrett, who wasn’t as comfortable with the cussing as Paige, said, “I’d appreciate that.”

Trowa nodded.

Garrett said, “Ya mind tellin’ me what the hell y’all were doin’ out here and what the hell happened?”

Trowa told Garrett the whole story, starting at Knucklehead’s Icehouse and ending with his climbing down the tree. By the time he finished, Mike and the deputies who followed him up the logging road arrived. All deputies, except Ty, who was still with Garrett and Paige, were working the crime scene.

When Trowa finished, Garrett considered the information for several seconds. “The kid. Ya said he told y’all he was at the MRB party last night?”

Trowa nodded.

“What was his name again?”

Trowa stroked his hairless chin, as if thinking. “Eddie Quaid or Eddie Quist. Eddie somethin’ startin’ with a Q.”

Garrett turned to Paige. “Does that name sound familiar?”

Paige shook her head. “Nope. Nobody I know.”

The next logical step would be to have Paige look at the dead boy and see if she recognized him. It wasn’t outside of reason to think the boy used a fake name at Knucklehead’s and was one of Paige’s classmates who survived the previous night’s MRB attacks. The thought of having Paige look at his mutilate remains didn’t sit well with Garrett.

As if reading Garrett’s troubled thoughts, Paige said, “It’s okay, Daddy. I saw worse things last night.”

The truth behind Paige’s statement hurt Garrett’s heart. Even if he could find and kill the alpha, if doing so didn’t kill Paige, he could never save her from the things she’d seen and the memories she’d have forever.

Garrett took Paige’s chin in his hand and tilted her head up so he could look her in the eyes.

When their eyes locked, Garrett said, "Ya don't have to, Paige-Turner. We can likely ID him with other methods."

Paige smiled a hopeless smile. "I can do it, Daddy."

Garrett nodded. He, Paige, and Ty walked the short distance to where the boy's body laid on the ground.

Deputy Gonzales was taking pictures of the victim when they got to the body.

Garrett said, "Give us a sec, Missy."

Missy nodded and stepped away.

Paige looked at the boy's bloody body. She saw nothing familiar about it. No scars or birthmarks she might have seen on a shirtless boy in gym class. She walked around the boy's body to where his head laid. It was turned on its side, so Paige had to get down on all fours and lower her face to get a good look at him. A dead, unfamiliar eye gazed back at her. There was a ragged, bloody hole where his left eye had been.

Paige got up and dusted the leaves and dirt from her knees. "I don't recognize him. He's not a student at Pine View High School."

Out of law enforcement habit, Garrett said, "Ya sure?"

Paige nodded.

That satisfied Garrett.

Garrett thought for several seconds. "Sweetheart, why don't ya go over there with Deputy Gonzales while I run some things by Ty?"

Paige shook her head. "No. I wanna hear what y'all think."

It wasn't like Paige to challenge Garrett, especially in front of someone else.

Before Garrett could respond, Paige said, "I'm in this…right in the middle of this. I have a right to know what y'all are thinkin'."

Again, before Garrett could respond, Ty said, "She's right, Garrett. Few folks have more interest in this than me and Paige."

Before either of them spoke up, Garrett knew he would include Paige in their conversation. She had a right to know.

Garrett smiled. "Two against one. Not a fair fight. But…okay. Get over here."

Paige winked at Ty and grinned at Garrett.

"For the record, I was gonna include ya before y'all double-teamed me," Garrett informed his daughter and friend.

"Sure ya were," Paige joked.

Garrett led Paige and Ty away from the commotion of the crime scene documentation.

When they were far enough removed for privacy, Garrett said, "Here's what I think. I think Eddie over there is one of the werewolf pack that's been runnin' around our neck of the woods the past few days. He's not a Pine View High student, right?"

Paige shook her head.

"He looks about the same age as the one ya took out last night, Ty," Garrett continued.

Ty nodded.

Garrett took a breath. "I think they're college students. Probably from SFA. I think Eddie, or whoever he is, brought the Knucklehead's patrons here to turn 'em, not kill 'em."

"What makes ya think that?" Ty interrupted.

"Think about it. Accordin' to Raintree, the first one didn't kill Bear. It could've, but it didn't. It bit Bear the same way you got bit last night, Ty."

Ty considered Garrett's theory for a few seconds and nodded his head.

"So, Eddie brings some bad-ass bikers out here to bite, curse, and start his own pack. The alpha-bitch figures out what he's up to through that...connection thing y'all got goin' on. She isn't happy about it. So, she comes out here...kills Eddie and the rest of 'em," Garrett concluded.

"Except Raintree, 'cause he's up a tree," Ty added.

Garrett smiled. "Exactly. That's the same thing Mike told me 'bout the *nahual* his super great grandpa killed. That the fuckers can't climb trees. Sorry, Paige."

Paige grinned. "It's okay, Daddy. I've heard those words. I even know what they mean."

Ty chuckled. "Like I said, sneakin' off for a little Bible readin'."

Try as he may, Garrett couldn't keep from laughing. Ty joined in and Paige, clueless to the inside joke, couldn't help but laugh, too.

Through giggles, Paige said, "What's that mean? Bible readin'?"

Garrett said, "Inside joke, kiddo."

Ty gave Paige a wink. "I'll fill ya in later, Paige-Turner."

Garrett scowled. "Not unless ya want a new job."

Ty nodded but winked at Paige again.

A loud throat clearing from Garrett brought Paige and Ty's attention back to him.

Garrett looked from Ty to Paige and back to Ty. "Here's what we're gonna do. First, we'll run Eddie through every system available. Hopefully, we'll get a hit. If not, we're gonna canvas SFA with their pictures."

"SFA's almost out for the summer," Ty interjected.

"I know. I'll head that way Monday mornin'. Where was I? Oh yeah, somebody, somewhere, knows the two boys. If we can connect 'em, I bet we can connect 'em to her."

"If we can't?" Ty asked.

Garrett chewed on his inside lip for several seconds. "We'll ambush that bitch from the trees."

"How do we get her to come to us?" Ty asked.

"We'll bait her," Garrett responded.

"With what?" Ty asked.

"With me," Paige answered.

"With us," Ty added.

Chapter Thirteen

A little after six o'clock the next morning, Garrett donned his tree climbing gear and, with aching muscles, set out to retrieve the SD cards from the critter-cams. As he climbed the first tree, he made a mental note to swing by Walmart and pick up four additional SD cards when he went to Lowe's to pick up a new sliding door. The realization he would have to climb the trees again to put the SD cards back into the critter-cams after he downloaded the images made his muscles ache even more. Extra SD cards would cut the climbs in half.

About an hour later, Garrett dumped the tree climbing gear on his front porch and went inside. The house was quiet with Paige still sound asleep in Garrett's bed. He made his way quietly to his office, shut the door, and sat down in his office chair. It was a high-back leather chair and Garrett sank into its soft comfort with a slight groan. After taking a moment to enjoy the relief afforded by the chair, Garrett wiggled the mouse to wake up his iMac. He entered his password and slipped one of the SD cards into the SD drive. He hadn't bothered to label the SD cards for which critter-cam they came out of, but he knew he'd be able to tell by the view.

The first SD card came from the tree on the back left side of Garrett's house. The first image was time-stamped five fifty-one p.m. It captured Garrett climbing down the tree after setting up the critter-cam and turning it on. The second image, time-stamped eight thirteen p.m., captured a fat raccoon heading toward Garrett's back deck.

"So, you're the little fucker gettin' into my trashcan," Garrett said to the image.

The next two images were both time-stamped eight twenty-seven p.m. The first of an armadillo and the second of the raccoon. Both critters were heading away from Garrett's house, and, from the slightly blurred nature of the images, both appeared to be in a hurry. The next image, time stamped eight twenty-nine p.m., explained the armadillo and raccoon's hasty retreat. It captured the werewolf.

Garrett set back in his chair and exhaled harshly, like someone punched him in the gut. He'd seen the werewolf face-to-face, but only quickly. The image allowed Garrett to look at the massive beast. From the camera's orientation, it appeared to be coming from the back right side of the house, heading toward the front left side on all four feet.

There were several more images on the SD card, but Garrett didn't go through them then. Instead, he created a folder named 'WW Pics' on the desktop and moved all the images from the SD card into the new folder. He did the same with the three remaining SD cards. When he finished transferring the images, the WW Pics folder had fifty-one images in it.

Garrett spent the next thirty minutes culling the non-werewolf images. There were thirteen of these. Five of which captured critters scurrying away shortly before the werewolf appeared and eight, two from each critter-cam, captured Garrett climbing down the tree after turning them on and climbing back up the tree to retrieve the SD cards. After he completed culling, using the time stamps of when the cameras captured each image, he put them in chronological order, loaded them into the 'Preview' program, and scrolled through them.

The first image showed the werewolf approaching from the front left side of the house. Garrett made a mental note to investigate the land in that direction, hoping to find something that would lead him to the werewolf's identity or origin. Most of the remaining images showed the werewolf circling the house and moving slightly closer to it with each circuit. Garrett thought the stalking behavior, along with its inability to climb trees, might prove useful for hunting and killing the bitch.

The final few images were the most disturbing and made the hairs on the back of Garrett's neck prickle. The first of these showed the werewolf change direction and head toward the front of the house. It had been time-stamped nine twenty-one p.m. It had circled his house, stalking them, for almost an hour, and corresponded with when the front, motion-activated floodlights turned on the previous night. Garrett inadvertently shuddered as he remembered the monstrous beast rising from behind his truck. The next image showed a black blur and captured the werewolf sprinting around the back left of the house. It even captured the back floodlights turning on. This happened after Garrett missed it with his first shot.

Garrett knew what came next. The werewolf crashing through the sliding glass doors. The critter-cams didn't capture this, because their range didn't reach the house. The next-to-last image from the back, left critter-cam captured another black blur as the werewolf retreated after Garrett shot at it the second time. The last image came from the front, left critter-cam. The werewolf slowed enough that the image cleared.

Garrett leaned forward and studied the image closely. The werewolf walked on its hind legs and its left hand cupped the side of its head. Garrett zoomed in on the image. The five-megapixel image distorted a little as he zoomed in closer, but not too badly. Garrett scrutinized the werewolf's deadly, clawed hand. The image was a grainy, greenish, night vision capture, but Garrett could clearly see blackish, shiny liquid between the werewolf's fingers. It looked like blood. Garrett knew it was blood.

Garrett smiled and whispered, "I hit the bitch."

Garrett wanted to bolt outside, find the blood trail, and track it to the bitch's dead body, but he restrained the impulse. Instead, he compressed the WW Pics folder into a zip file, opened Outlook, clicked on the 'Compose Email' button, entered James Huff's email address in the 'To:' field, typed 'Proof' in the 'Subject:' field, attached the zip file, and typed.

James,

I think you might find these pictures interesting. They're from my house last night. Take a close look at the last picture. I think that's blood between its fingers. I think I hit the bitch! I'm going out to check now. I'll have my cell. Call me if you can. There's more to the story than what's shown here.

Garrett

P.S. Don't go selling these pictures to some tabloid rag. Consider yourself a Pine View County Sheriff Department consultant. This is now official business.

After emailing, Garrett grabbed his cellphone and quietly so as not to wake Paige, went out the front door. The back door would have been quicker, but it was still boarded up. He made his way around back to the deck and scanned the wooden surface for blood. Within seconds, Garrett saw an elongated drop. From his time in law enforcement, and as an avid lifetime hunter, he knew an elongated blood drop indicted movement while bleeding. This was certainly true of the werewolf.

Garrett knew for certain two additional places where he should find blood; the two spots where the critter-cams captured images of the werewolf leaving. He went directly to the first of them.

It was harder to track a blood trail over outdoor terrain, but Garrett tracked enough injured deer to know what to look for. At the first critter-cam, Garrett found a few small drops of blood on the underbrush. He slowly walked the second critter-cam and saw a few more small blood drops at differing intervals. That the blood drops weren't closer together or larger was a bit discouraging. When tracking an injured deer with a mortal wound, the blood trail had larger blood drops, or even pools of blood, and they were closer together.

By the time Garrett got to the second critter-cam, the blood trail almost disappeared. Garret cursed under his breath and kicked a clump of weeds free from the soil in frustration. He took a few more steps in the direction the werewolf had headed, but the blood trail was gone. Just as Garrett was turning to head back to his house, his cellphone rang.

He looked at the caller ID, saw it was James Huff, and tapped the green answer icon. "What took ya so long?"

James, unable to contain his excitement, said, "It's magnificent. Please don't take that the wrong way, Garrett. I know it's brought a world of shit your way. You've gotta understand. I've studied the lore my whole life and…well…here's actual proof. Actual, fuckin' proof. It's amazin'. Tell me what happened. Everything."

As Garrett walked back to the deck, he told James everything. From the attack at home to what happened to the Knucklehead's Icehouse bikers, Garrett didn't leave a single detail out. When he finished recounting the previous night's events and offering his theory of Eddie being one of the alpha's pack, he'd made it back to the deck.

He retrieved a pack of Marlboro Reds he kept stashed in the smoker, lit a cigarette, and took a deep, comforting drag. "Well, what do ya think?"

After several long, silent seconds, James said, "I don't think it wanted to kill ya, Garrett."

"Come again," Garrett skeptically responded.

James cleared his throat. "I don't think it wanted to kill ya. I think it wanted to turn ya."

Garrett said nothing, so James continued, "Think about it, Garrett. What would it gain in killin' ya? Sure, that would further isolate Paige, but to what end? It wanted Paige for a reason. I'm sure of that, given what you've told me about her attack. No…I think it wanted to turn ya. To get more control over Paige…or instill more fear in her…or somethin'."

Garrett considered James' thoughts on the matter. He trusted James, and Paige conveyed the same feeling to him. The thought James and Paige might be right, the alpha wanted him and Paige to be killing machines in its pack, gave Garrett an uneasy feeling. Like someone pissing, not walking, on his future grave.

Garrett shook off the feeling. "Ya may be right. Paige had the same feelin'."

"Great minds think alike," said James with a chuckle.

Garrett didn't feel like chuckling, so he plowed on. "What're your thoughts on whether I shot it? It left a blood trail, and I was usin' silver bullets. Why didn't I find her dead body at the end of its blood trail?"

Without hesitation, James said, "Ya must've nicked it. If you'd hit it anywhere the bullet could've lodged inside it, you *would* have found her dead body. From the way it's holdin' the side of its head, my guess is that you shot it through the ear."

Again, Paige and James were of the same mind.

"Yeah, but it was a silver bullet. I thought that shit stopped 'em dead in their tracks."

"Sure, but think about it, Garrett. If ya shot it through the ear, the actual contact with the silver would'a been what…a millionth of a second. It's got to be inside 'em so the toxin enters their bloodstream to their organs. As quick as that shot through the ear was, I guarantee it knew ya hit it with a silver bullet."

"What makes ya think that?"

James chuckled. "Because you're not dead or turned. If you'd hit it with a lead or steel load, it would'a kept comin', and *kill*ed or turned ya."

This logic made more sense to Garrett, but it disappointed him.

If only I'd been usin' a fuckin' shotgun, Garrett thought.

This thought gave Garrett an idea, and he made another mental note to ask Mike to make some silver shotgun loads.

Moving on, Garrett said, "Well, what d'ya think happened to the Knucklehead biker boys? What about my theory that Eddie, or whatever the fuck his name was, was tryin' to start a rival pack?"

"Yes. I think you're one hundred percent correct on that call."

Even though no one saw it, a big smile cut across Garrett's face. He got something pertaining to werewolves right. It felt good.

"So…how's that work? Can any werewolf start a pack and be an alpha?"

"Well, yeah. Theoretically, I guess they could."

"You *guess*?" Garrett asked with purposeful, exaggerated shock.

James chuckled. "This isn't science with quantitative certainty. But yes. Theoretically, any werewolf can pass on the curse and be an alpha. Just like with wolves, another wolf can challenge an alpha. So…turning', creatin' werewolves doesn't guarantee alpha status forever. My guess is that this Eddie guy wasn't happy with his current alpha. He might've even challenged the alpha and got put in his proper place. As you've theorized, I think he tried to start a rival pack."

"Okay. So, I get why the alpha would take out Eddie. He was a troublemaker, but why'd it kill Eddie's potential turns?"

James was silent for several seconds and then said, "Could be as simple as uncontrolled rage or as calculatin' as not wantin' to leave witnesses. You said it went after Mister Raintree intently and didn't bite him. I wouldn't read too much into it killin' Eddie's potential turns. Killin's what these things do best. Besides, you're missin' the most important aspect of the encounter."

"What's that?"

"That Eddie's infected didn't die when the alpha killed him."

Garrett hadn't considered this and what it might portend for Paige and Ty. Now that he did, more questions than answers came to mind. If James implied because Eddie's victims didn't die when the alpha killed Eddie, that meant Paige and Ty wouldn't die if he killed the alpha. That was good news. What if Eddie didn't turn his victims long enough for his dying to matter? Garrett relayed this concern to James.

Without hesitation, James said, "Length of infection doesn't matter. The werewolf's teeth penetrated their skin. It infected 'em. Think about how quickly Paige and Ty felt connected with the alpha that bit 'em…how quickly their wounds healed. If killin' an alpha killed its betas, I'm certain the ones Eddie bit would've dropped dead when the alpha took him out. That they didn't drop dead tells me Paige and Ty won't either. The curse from the alpha will end."

"I'm still tryin' to get my mind around this bloodline stuff, James. If killin' alphas releases those it's infected, does that mean we can trace all werewolves back to one source? If so, then killin' that one source would cure all werewolves. Hell, if werewolves have been around for thousands of years, that would make the original alpha one old son-of-a-bitch. Also, if Eddie created a rival pack and killed his alpha, wouldn't that release him and those he'd made from the curse? This is confusin'."

James took a deep breath. "Okay, where to start? First, I doubt Eddie wanted to kill his alpha. Even if he didn't understand the potential risk of losing his wolf by killin' her, he probably wanted to dominate her…humiliate her. If he killed her, some folklore suggests he would've inherited…absorbed her power…her essence in doing so. If this lore is correct, a beta or rival alpha can kill an alpha without releasing those cursed by it. The dead alpha's pack would become loyal to their new alpha…and the curse-line, not bloodline, would transfer to the victorious alpha.

"As to the curse-line theory, the folklore diverges here, too. Some lore suggests there is but one curse-line that can be traced back to a prime alpha. The first…born, not made. The Hellhound. It would be as ancient as creation and immortal. So, killin' it and releasin' all werewolves descended from the one curse-line would be impossible. The werewolf population can only be whittled away at the edges by killin' those who turn alpha and create packs.

"Another line of lore theory suggests that a werewolf can be created through witchery or other acts of evil and depravity. Some European cultures believe killin' a newborn and eatin' its heart under a full moon will curse a person into bein' a werewolf. Some Asian cultures believe that bestiality, sex with an actual wolf, under a full moon, will do it. The Navajo in North America believe incest or necrophilia is evil enough to create a werewolf. Romanian gypsy lore suggests that drinkin' rainwater from the paw print of a wolf on a full moon can turn someone into a werewolf. These acts are linked to the full moon or some witchery."

"What do you believe?"

After several silent moments, James said, "I don't think they're mutually exclusive. I don't see why aspects of both can't exist. If the evil existed to create the prime alpha, the Hellhound, I don't see why the evil to create a werewolf from acts of depravity can't exist, too. And vice-versa. What's important now is we know they exist and killin' the immediate creator doesn't kill the ones it infects. Now ya just need to find and kill the alpha that infected Paige and Ty."

Garrett took a final drag on his cigarette, crushed the ash on the side of the smoker, and flicked the butt into the smoker. "Yep. I'm tryin' to figure that out. As always, you've been a great help, James. I'll let ya know more when I know more."

"Please do. If ya get any more pictures, please send me copies. I promise I won't sell 'em to a, how'd you put it, tabloid rag."

Garrett laughed. "Will do, James. If I really thought you'd have sold 'em, I wouldn't have sent 'em."

After bidding each other goodbye, Garrett called another number before going inside. He'd already made three mental notes that morning and he wanted to check one off before they started evaporating into the ether of his inner consciousness.

Becks Middleton answered on the third ring. "Hey there, Garrett. Mike's still snorin' like a buzzsaw. Want me to wake him up?"

Garrett liked Mike's wife and hearing her chipper voice brought a smile to his face. "No, Becks. I just wanna leave him a quick message."

"Hang on, honey. I'll find somethin' to write with and on."

Garrett heard a drawer slide open and clinking sounds as Becks looked for a pen and paper.

While she rummaged through the drawer, Becks said, "When are ya gonna man up and ask Mandy to marry ya, Garrett?"

Becks' question stung Garrett, but not because he didn't expect it. Becks and Mandy Davis, Garrett's girlfriend of three years, were good friends. She asked him this question just about every time they talked. The realization he thought little about Mandy since the werewolf situation developed stung Garrett. Aside from a brief call to cancel their usual Wednesday night date, which had Mandy asking questions Garrett wasn't prepared to answer, he'd shut her out. He cared for Mandy a great deal and immediately felt guilty for not sharing more with her. He replaced the mental note to call Mike about silver loaded shotgun shells with a mental note to call Mandy and fill her in on everything going on.

Garrett shook these thoughts away. "Ya know Mandy can do much better than me. I don't wanna limit her future by tyin' it to mine."

This was Garrett's standard response to Becks' marriage question.

Becks snorted. "Very true, Garrett. Mandy *can* do much better than you. She's content with ya."

Garrett knew Becks would respond with this. It was almost like a game they played. He also knew she'd responded truthfully. Mandy deserved better than him.

Fortunately, that conversation died when Becks said, "Okay,

what's the message, honey?"

Garrett wasn't sure how much Becks knew about the situation, so he tried to couch his message in terms that wouldn't give too much away. "Ask Mike if he can make shotgun shells with the same material he made the nine mil loads. Buckshot, if he's got the equipment."

Becks laughed. "If he's got the equipment? Honey, if it can be projected from a gun barrel, Mike's got the equipment to make it."

Relieved, Garrett said, "Great. Thanks, Becks."

Before Garrett could hang up, Becks said, "Just to be clear, you want silver buckshot shotgun loads to kill the *nahual*."

Of course, she knows, Garrett thought.

Garrett suppressed a laugh. "Yep. That's what I want."

"Silver bullets. Do ya know how much that silver's worth?" Becks responded, but with no real ire in her voice.

"I offered to pay him for the silver but…"

"Yeah, yeah, I know. It's what his great, great, great grandpa intended the silver for. I've heard it a hundred times if I've heard it once," Becks interrupted.

"Sorry," Garrett offered.

Becks chuckled. "That and a quarter will buy ya exactly nothin'. Ya can make it up to me."

"How's that?"

"Dinner date. Me and Mike and you and Mandy. When this mess is behind us."

"Deal," Garrett agreed.

After they hung up, Garrett heard the microwave beeping inside the house. That meant Paige was up. He headed to the front of the house. The boarded up back door wasn't an option, and went inside.

~ * ~

The trip into Nacogdoches went quickly. Neither of the Brenda's were working, which was good at Lowe's and not so good at Walmart. Luckily, Lowe's had a replacement sliding-door in stock and Garrett had it loaded in the back of his truck within ten minutes of pulling into the Lowe's parking lot.

At Walmart, Garrett and Paige headed back to Sporting Goods for the new SD cards. After looking for several minutes, a helpful associate directed them to the Electronics Department. There, a chunky, pimple faced teen with 'Chuck' on his nametag unlocked a case and retrieved four eight gigabyte SD cards. Chuck told Garrett he needed to pay for the SD cards there, but from the way Chuck eyeballed Paige, Garrett thought Chuck just wanted to look at Paige a little longer. Five minutes later, they were on their way back to Garrett's house.

When they got home, Garrett headed to the shed, got his tools, and placed them on the back deck. Paige helped Garrett carry the new sliding door around back. It wasn't heavy, but too large for Garrett to maneuver on his own. Besides, Paige wanted to help.

Removing the old sliding door frame wasn't difficult. With Paige's help, installing the new one went smoothly. She helped Garrett position the sliding door, handed Garrett tools, and held the door in place while Garrett secured it to the two-by-four framework. The new sliding door was installed and sliding freely within an hour. Garrett took the tools back to the shed while Paige went inside to pour two tall glasses of sweet, iced tea.

Several times during the installation, Garrett noticed Paige scratching the back of her neck and upper chest as if in some kind of discomfort. Once Garrett was back inside and sitting at the table with Paige drinking much needed sweet tea, he noticed Paige scratching her neck again.

"You alright?" Garrett asked.

Paige grimaced a little. "Yeah. My neck's a little itchy, though. I might'a got into some poison ivy or oak last night in the woods."

Garrett got up. "Let me have a look."

Paige's hair was in a ponytail, and she pulled it over her right shoulder. Garrett looked down and saw the skin under Paige's silver necklace was puffy and red. It looked like an allergic reaction.

Garrett took a deep breath. "It's your necklace, sweetheart."

"My necklace?" Paige asked, clearly confused.

"It's silver," Garrett reminded her.

"Ya mean…" Paige trailed off as the reality of why her necklace caused discomfort sank in.

"I'm afraid so. Doctor Huff said this would happen."

Paige turned sideways in her chair and looked up at her dad. Tears were forming in her big, green eyes. "I don't wanna take it off, Daddy."

Garrett gently wiped a tear from her cheek. "I know ya don't. I don't think ya have a choice, Paige-Turner. Right now, it's just irritatin' your skin a little, but it'll get worse. It'll get painful. How 'bout this? Take it off now and see if the itchin' goes away. Then we'll know whether it's the silver or somethin' else."

"Okay, but I'm keepin' it with me," Paige said as she located the clasp and removed the necklace and crucifix. She put it in the right front pocket of the cutoff blue jean shorts she was wearing.

By the time they finished drinking their sweet tea, it was almost four o'clock and time for Paige to head back to her mom's house. For all the usual reasons, missing her mainly, Garrett hated to see Paige leave. The werewolf situation amped up his anxiety level considerably, though.

After Paige packed, which, because both her mom's and dad's houses contained everything she needed, there was only a Walmart bag with her dirty clothes, Garrett walked her to her car she'd named Lil' Dragon. Paige opened the driver's door and pitched the bag of dirty clothes onto the passenger's seat. They stood in the open door for several silent moments. Neither wanted to say goodbye.

"You think Mom would let me stay with ya this week?"

Garrett loved the idea, but he shook his head. "Probably not. Especially after what happened at the MRB. She's worried 'bout ya. Hell, I'm surprised she didn't demand ya come home Saturday when I talked with her."

Paige started to say something but stopped and looked down at her feet instead.

"What's on your mind?" Garrett asked.

Still not looking at Garrett, Paige said, "Do ya think it'll be safe at Mom's? I'm not worried 'bout me. But…what if she comes after Mom and Al?"

Garrett considered this. If he thought this a high probability of happening, he would insist Paige stay with him. Garrett took Paige's chin in his hand and lifted her face so he could look her in the eyes.

"If I thought that would happen, I wouldn't let ya go."

Paige smiled an uneasy smile. "How can ya be sure?"

That was the million-dollar question. How could he be sure?

Garrett smiled back at Paige. "I can't be *sure* of anything. Your mom and Al live in a neighborhood in the middle of Pine View. Everything these beasts have done has been in rural areas. I think, like any wild animal, they're more comfortable in the woods."

"Yeah, but wild animals come into neighborhoods sometimes. I've seen bears, coyotes, and even mountain lions go into neighborhoods on the news."

She had him there. Garrett saw the same news reports. "Yes, but only when they're desperate for food or when new construction encroaches on their natural habitat. These things aren't your average wild animals. Somewhere in them is the ability to think. I don't think they'd risk the exposure. Trust me, sweetheart. I think you, your mom, and Al will be safe."

After several seconds of silence, Paige said, "Okay, but I'm comin' to your office after school and not goin' to Mom's until she's home."

Garrett pulled Paige into a tight hug. "Sounds like a good plan."

When the hug broke, Paige looked up at Garrett. "I love you, Daddy."

Garrett kissed Paige on the forehead. "I love you too, Paige-Turner. I promise ya, I'm gonna find that bitch and kill her."

Paige kissed Garrett on the cheek. "I know ya will, Daddy."

Paige got into Lil' Dragon and drove away.

Garrett watched as Paige got to the end of his driveway, turned right onto County Road Five Eighty-Eight, and headed for Lacy's house. He stood there listening until he could no longer hear her car and silence surrounded him. Not the unholy werewolf silence, but the normal forest silence that contained an occasional bird chirping and pesky squirrels skittering about the tree branches.

The squirrels reminded Garrett he still needed to climb the trees and put SD cards in the critter-cams. His muscles ached just thinking about.

"Sooner begun, sooner done," Garrett said to no one.

It was almost six o'clock before Garrett dragged his worn-out body back inside. He had only three thoughts. Food, shower, and sleep. In that order. As he walked past his bedroom, toward the kitchen, he looked into it and saw his inviting, still unmade, bed. It called to him. Garrett kicked off his boots as he made his way toward the bed and flopped face down onto the soft mattress. He could smell Paige on the pillow and smiled.

Before he closed his eyes, he muttered, "Just a twenty-minute nap and I'll be right as rain."

He closed his eyes, and a deep, dreamless sleep swallowed him.

~ * ~

On the drive to her mother's house, Paige dreaded the questions her mother was bound to throw at her. She'd talked with her mom on the phone briefly Saturday afternoon, fielded several questions, but she used the "I'm too tired to talk about it now, Mom" excuse. Paige didn't think that would work when she got home.

As Paige turned onto Willow Lane and saw her mom's house five houses down on the left, in the back of her mind she heard her dad telling her not to outright lie, if she could avoid doing so, but to be vague with the truth. Paige turned into the driveway and her mom was out the front door with Al in her wake before she came to a complete stop.

Before Paige had her seatbelt off, her mom opened the car door and almost dove into the car with Paige as she wrapped her in a tight hug.

"Oh, sweetheart. I was so worried 'bout you. Are ya okay? You're not. How could ya be?" Lacy blubbered.

Paige hugged her mom back. "I'm okay, Mom. But ya might suffocate me."

Al placed a hand on Lacy's shoulder. "Let her get out of the car. Then ya can suffocate her."

Lacy reluctantly released Paige and stepped back. Paige grabbed the bag of dirty clothes and got out of her car.

The first thing Paige noticed was several neighbors outside who stopped what they were doing and looked at her.

Two houses down and across the street, Mr. Zimmerman, who had been carrying a bag of trash to his trashcan, waved, and shouted, "Glad you're okay, Paige."

Paige waved back. "Thank you, Mister Zimmerman."

Several other neighbors shouted well wishes, too. Paige acknowledged them with thanks and waves.

After this ran its course, her mom said, "Everybody knows 'bout the MRB massacre, Paige. They're all glad you're okay, sweetheart."

News travels fast and bad news travels faster, Paige thought.

Lacy put an arm around Paige. "Let's go inside. I have a *lot* of questions for ya."

As Lacy and Al ushered her inside, Paige smiled and waved at a little boy, he was about six years old, named Dalton Pruitt, who lived next door. Dalton stood by the garage doors of his house and stared at Paige as if he were in a trance. When Paige smiled and waved, a look of pure horror came over Dalton's face. He cried, then he turned and ran to his mom, Sarah, who had been weeding her front flowerbeds but had, like the rest of the outdoor neighbors, turned to wave at Paige. Dalton grabbed his mom's legs like a drowning man grabs a life preserver and clung to her.

"What the heck's wrong with Dalton?" Al wondered aloud.

Lacy shot a look at Dalton and whispered, "I don't think he's right in the head. Strange kid. He'll be ridin' the short bus. Mark my words."

Paige knew what was wrong with Dalton. She terrified him. She could smell the fear oozing from his pores and, before the dark spot grew on the front of Dalton's red shorts, Paige smelled urine.

Just before they ushered Paige inside her mom's house, she heard Sarah say, "What's the matter, Dalts?"

She clearly heard Dalton whisper in a tiny, scared voice, "She's a monster, Mommy."

He sees me for what I am, Paige thought, and a chill ran up her spine.

Lacy wasn't lying about having a lot of questions for Paige. After leading Paige to the dining room table and pouring her a glass of OJ, she didn't ask if Paige wanted a drink, Lacy started rattling off question after question. Paige drank the OJ slowly and did her best to tell the truth without telling the whole truth.

After several minutes of interrogation, Al said, "Okay, Lacy. That's enough. Paige needs to come up for air."

Paige appreciated Al's intervention and snuck a smile his direction when Lacy turned to look at him. Paige couldn't see the look her mom gave Al but knew it well. It was the 'Butt out, she's my daughter' look her mom gave Al anytime he stepped over Lacy's line of warranted input. That Al got this look often only made Paige like him more.

Although Lacy's look meant for Al to back off, the results of his unwarranted inputs were usually successful.

When Lacy looked back at Paige, she said, "Okay, sweetheart. That's enough…for now. If ya *wanna* talk, I'm all ears."

Paige drained the last of her OJ. "Thanks, Mom. I will. All I want now is a shower and some sleep."

As Paige got up to leave, Al said, "You're lucky, kiddo. I talked your mom outta waterboardin' ya for information."

"Not funny, Albert," Lacy snapped.

When Paige laughed, Lacy and Al joined in. Paige gave both a hug and headed upstairs to her bedroom.

Entering her bedroom brought with it a wave of emotions Paige wasn't quite prepared for. Unlike her bedroom at her dad's house, this bedroom had pictures of Justin everywhere.

Paige went to her nightstand and picked up the picture she kept there. She kept it there so it would be the last thing she saw before going to sleep at night and the first thing she would see in the morning when she woke up. It was a picture of her and Justin from Spring Break when they, with several of their friends, went to Lake Nacogdoches. Justin's dad let them take his boat. They spent the day water skiing and swimming. In the picture, a shirtless Justin sat in the boat's driver seat. Paige, in her green bikini, sat on his lap. Justin had his sunglasses perched on top of his wet hair. He looked at Paige with, as Lin pointed out, love or lust.

Looking at the picture reminded Paige of, not only the loss of Justin, but of Brad Wells, Matt Cooke, Freddy Colburn, Maggie Crawford, Ella Patterson, and several others who were there that night and dead at the hands of creatures she would become. A creature that, apparently, Dalton Pruitt could already see in Paige. Hiding just beneath her human exterior.

Paige wiped away the tears streaming down her cheeks and put the picture back on the nightstand. She went into her bathroom, got undressed, and stepped into a hot shower. The sound of the shower gave Paige the cover she needed to let her grief flow. What started as hard and fast tears ended with Paige in the fetal position on the floor of the bathtub sobbing uncontrollably. When emotionally spent, Paige got to her feet and showered.

Paige stepped out of the shower and dried off with a fluffy green towel. After drying, she wrapped the towel around herself and went to the sink. She used her hairdryer to remove the condensation from the mirror—wiping it away left streaks and didn't last like the hairdryer method did. She looked into the mirror and saw bloodshot eyes, puffy eyelids, and a red nosed girl looking back at her.

As she studied her reflection, she realized her necklace and crucifix were missing. So was the itchy irritation she'd felt with it on. Paige tilted her head to the left. She studied the skin that had been red and puffy earlier. It was smooth and unblemished. The thought of not being able to wear her dad's First Communion and Confirmation gift hurt Paige deeply and more tears welled in her puffy, bloodshot eyes.

After brushing her teeth and inspecting them closely to make sure they weren't already turning into deadly fangs, Paige went back into her bedroom to get dressed for bed. She knew exactly what she would wear to sleep that night and every night in the future. Justin's number sixty-four junior high school football jersey. Paige had it tacked to her bedroom wall, but she pulled it down and slipped it over her head.

Although Justin wore the jersey in junior high school, it was big to cover pads, and it fell to Paige's mid-thighs. Paige hugged herself tightly, as if hugging Justin, and climbed into bed. It was only a little after eight o'clock. However, she was mentally, physically, and emotionally spent.

Before Paige turned off her bedside lamp, she grabbed her cellphone, opened the 'Text' app, typed 'Daddy' in the 'To:' line, and, in the text's body, wrote, 'U were right about the necklace. The itching is gone, and my skin is clear. Makes me sad. ☹ I luv u, daddy. ♥'

After tapping on the 'return' key and sending the text, Paige snuggled her face into her pillow. She thought she might cry, again, but much like her dad had, she fell into a deep, dreamless sleep.

~ * ~

The buzzing alarm clock pulled Garrett from a deep, dreamless sleep. He lifted his head and studied the alarm clock, confused by its buzzing. When he'd laid down for a twenty-minute nap, it had been almost six o'clock in the evening.

Why the hell is my alarm clock going off in the evenin'? Garrett thought.

As his eyes focused, he clearly saw the time displayed on the clock was six a.m.

Garrett reached over and turned off the alarm. He rolled over on his back and stretched the night's sleep away. His muscles ached, but he felt more rested than he had since the morning the haunting howls woke him and the living nightmare began.

On his back, Garrett felt the cellphone in his back pocket and retrieved it. That it hadn't woken him during the night surprised him, but this encouraged him. No calls meant no trouble. Garrett pushed the 'Home' button and saw he had one text from Paige.

After reading it, Garrett responded with, 'I promise you'll wear it again. I love you back.'

~ * ~

The incoming text 'ding' woke up Paige. In the confused state between sleep and being awake, she thought it was her morning text from Justin. Excited, Paige grabbed her cellphone and looked at the screen. Before it dimmed and went dark, Paige saw the text from her dad and the reality of the previous few days descended on her like a heavy weight.

Paige tapped in her security code and opened the text app but, instead of replying to her dad's text, she opened a text thread with Lin.

She typed, 'U want me to pick u up?' and sent the text.

The three moving dots popped up immediately and seconds later Lindsey's reply appeared, 'Mom and dad are keeping me home today, maybe all week. I'd rather be in school, but they r not dealing well.'

Before Paige could respond, the three moving dots popped up again, followed by, 'Come by after school.'

Paige quickly responded she would. She got out of bed and headed for the bathroom. Paige wasn't looking forward to going to school and the questions that were sure to come.

~ * ~

There were no news vans in the Sheriff Department's parking lot when Garrett pulled in a little after seven that morning. This relieved Garrett. The last thing he wanted to deal with on an otherwise, to that point, good morning, were a gaggle of reporters sticking microphones and digital recorders in his face and shouting questions at him. Garrett parked in a spot, but not his reserved spot. If a buzzard-like reporter saw a patrol SUV in his spot, they would probably be on him like flies on shit. He went into the building.

Karen Parker, the overnight dispatch deputy, was leaving as Garrett stepped into the lobby.

"Good mornin', Sheriff," Karen said as they met.

"It was a good night?"

Karen smiled. "Nothin' out of the ordinary. So, yeah, it was a good night."

As they parted, Garrett said, "Glad to hear it. Get some sleep."

"That's the plan," Karen said and out the door she went.

Erica Harris, who relieved Karen on dispatch, buzzed Garrett out of the lobby and he made his way to his office. The good morning took a slight hit when Garrett saw what was waiting for him on his desk. A 'Special Edition' edition of the *Pine View Post* with **'MRB Massacre'** as the large, bold headline. Garrett sat down in his office chair, grabbed the newspaper, and started reading:

'What started out as an end of the school year celebration for twenty-six Pine View High School students at the Mill Road Barn turned into a living nightmare. Reports are still sketchy, but from what this reporter has learned from several off-the-record sources, fifteen students were massacred by yet to be identified animals. According to these sources, the attacks were savage. One source said several of the victims were 'torn apart' and there were 'severed limbs' and decapitations.' Identities of the victims and survivors are being withheld out of respect for the grieving community and deserved privacy for the grief-stricken families.

To date, Sheriff Garrett Lambert of Pine View County hasn't committed beyond saying he "Can't comment on an open investigation." This reporter has learned there might be another reason for Sheriff Lambert's reluctance to discuss the investigation. His daughter, Paige Lambert. She is a sophomore at Pine View High School, and one of the MRB Massacre survivors. If Sheriff Garrett can shed more light on what happened at the MRB, and since his daughter was an eyewitness to the carnage, he certainly should be able to. He owes it to his constituents to do so…'

The story continued, but Garrett didn't finish reading it. Instead, he cursed under his breath, crumpled the newspaper into a ball, and launched it toward the trashcan in the corner of his office. He missed. It angered Garrett that the article included Paige's name. The reporter obviously wasn't too concerned with Paige's private grief. Just below that anger lurked the suspicion one or more of the 'off-the-record sources' were Pine View County Deputy Sheriffs.

Garrett cursed again and leaned back in his chair. When he looked up, he saw Jailer Paula Stamford standing in his office doorway. Paula was one jailer who tended to the inmates and when the 'Iron Door Inn,' a nickname given to the facility by an inmate many years before Garrett started working there, was at low capacity, helped with some of the clerical duties. Jailers wore sheriff's department uniforms but didn't carry firearms and had no law enforcement authority outside of the county jail. She had a file folder in her right hand.

"If this is a bad time, I can come back later," Paula said in a small voice.

Garrett sat forward in his chair. "No, now's fine. I just read the story in the *Pine View Post,* and it got my hackles up."

Paula started into Garrett's office. "It's awful that they put Paige's name in the story. They left out everyone else's names."

"My thoughts exactly, Paula."

Paula stepped up to Garrett's desk and held the file folder out for him to take.

"What ya got for me?"

"We gotta hit on the Eddie kid killed Saturday night. That's not his real name."

That his name wasn't Eddie didn't surprise Garrett. This news almost erased Garrett's anger with the *Pine View Post* story. Almost.

When Garrett took the folder from Paula, she didn't turn to leave. "Anything else?"

Paula shifted uncomfortably on her feet and, after several awkward silent seconds, said, "Is it true, Sheriff Garrett? What they're sayin' 'bout…werewolves killin' those kids at the MRB? That can't be true. Can it?"

Garrett placed the file folder on his desk. "There are things at work here that defy conventional explanation."

Paula considered Garrett's response for a moment. "That doesn't answer my question."

"No. No, it doesn't. Do ya really want me to answer your question?"

Paula thought for a moment. "No, I guess I don't. Just tell me this. Can ya kill 'em?"

"Yep. I'm sure of that."

"How can ya be sure?"

Garrett smiled. "'Cause Deputy Jackson's already killed one."

Paula's eyes got big and round, like saucers, and she said, "The John Doe from the Carla Weaver murder?"

Garrett nodded.

Paula exhaled loudly. "Okay, then. You kill the fuckers for what they did to those kids." She blushed and added, "Pardon my language, Sheriff."

Garrett grinned. "No pardons needed. Killin' the fuckers is the plan."

Satisfied, Paula left Garrett's office.

Garrett opened the file folder and saw a processing picture, a mug shot, of Eddie. His eyes were bloodshot and drooping. He looked drunk but it was the same face as the one on Eddie's severed head, minus one bloodshot eye. Garrett scanned the arrest record quickly and saw he'd been arrested for public intoxication in March of that year. He saw Eddie's real name. Cole Duncan. Eager to learn more about Cole Duncan, Garrett called the SFA University Police Department.

The UPD receptionist directed Garrett's call to Detective Max Sloan, who picked up on the second ring.

Garrett introduced himself and said, "I gotta body in the county morgue and the prints come back to an SFA student arrested for public intoxication on March 27th of this year. I need next of kin info to let his folks know he won't be comin' home this summer."

Sounding uninterested, Detective Sloan said, "What's the name, Sheriff?"

Garrett gave him the name.

He heard keyboard keys clicking then Detective Sloan said, "Got him. Yeah, I remember this guy. He got trashed after the Lumberjack men's basketball team advanced in March Madness. We had a damn good team this year. He was a real prick…thought his shit didn't stink. Hang on. I'll have next of kin in a few puter taps."

Garrett heard the keys clicking again and then Detective Sloan gave Garrett the information he needed.

"Anything else I can help ya with?" Detective Sloan asked.

"Actually, I gotta John Doe who looks college age in the morgue, too. Maybe…" Garrett started.

"Were these boys' part of that MRB mess?" Detective Sloan interrupted.

Careful not to share too much, Garrett said, "No. Separate incidents. John Doe was killed Friday by one of my deputies in the commission of a homicide before the MRB incident, and Cole Duncan was killed Saturday night with some bikers he fell in with."

"Shit…y'all been busy."

Garrett chuckled. "You could say that. Mind if I send ya John Doe's morgue shot and see if ya recognize him?"

"We got about twelve thousand students and, since ya can't ID him, I'm guessin' he doesn't have a record, but I'll look."

Detective Sloan gave Garrett his email address, and Garrett sent him the morgue shot.

A couple of seconds later, Detective Sloan said, "Got it."

After several seconds of silence, Detective Sloan said, "He looks familiar. I know I've seen him, but where?"

That was a question Garrett couldn't answer, so he waited for Detective Sloan to sort out his memory.

Several more seconds ticked by and, just when Garrett was losing hope of getting John Doe's ID, Detective Sloan said, "Got it. This is the guy who bailed Cole Duncan out on the PI arrest. Hang on, Sheriff. A few more puter taps, and I'll have him for ya."

Garrett could barely contain his excitement. He kept his mouth shut but pumped his left fist several times.

Garrett heard the 'puter taps' clicking and then Detective Sloan said, "His name is Seth Daniels. I'm sendin' ya his student ID pic so ya can confirm."

Seconds later, Garrett's email program 'dinged' and he opened the email. There was his John Doe, smiling back at him. He had been a few years younger, but it was him.

"I need next of kin on Seth Daniels, too."

"Comin' up."

Seconds later, Garrett had the information he needed.

Before Garrett could thank him and hang up, Detective Sloan said, "Mighty strange these two buddies would end up dead…in separate incidents a day apart."

"It is," Garrett agreed, "it's been a mighty strange weekend."

Detective Sloan was silent for several seconds, and Garrett expected him to launch into a barrage of questions, but he finally said, "Okay, Sheriff. Let me know if I can be of further help."

Relieved, Garrett said, "Will do. Thanks for your help, Detective."

Garrett ended the call with Detective Sloan and studied the pictures of the two dead men…werewolves.

A smile spread across Garrett's face, and he whispered, "I got you fuckers."

He picked up the phone and called Cole Duncan's next of kin. His mother picked up on the other end.

Although Garrett disliked this part of his job, and he had sympathy for Cole Duncan's mother. She didn't know her son turned into a murderous monster. He received some satisfaction in informing her that her son was deceased. Rebecca Duncan took the news well, or as well as expected. She only asked a couple of question. How her son died and how could they get him home to bury him? Garrett gave vague details of Cole's death, an unidentified animal attack, and gave her the county morgue phone number and George Krats' name as a contact.

The call to Seth Daniels' next of kin didn't go as well. Given Seth's death, killed after aiding in the murder of a helpless, elderly woman, Garrett expected it to be a tough call. Seth's mother, Samantha Daniels, answered the phone.

The moment Garrett introduced himself, Samantha wailed, "Oh my God. He's dead, isn't he? I've been calling him all weekend, and he hasn't returned my calls. It was that MRB thing, wasn't it?"

Garrett took a deep breath. "I'm sorry, Missus Daniels. Seth wasn't at the MRB party, but he is deceased."

Samantha Daniels began sobbing. After several moments, Samantha said, "How-how did he…I can't believe he's gone. What happened to my boy?"

Satisfaction with the werewolf's death aside, Garrett wanted to be delicate with the details of her son's death. Garrett cleared his throat and, being as honest as the circumstances allowed, said, "I'm sorry to have to inform ya, but Seth attacked one of my deputies at a homicide he was involved in, and he shot him."

All true, and Samantha Daniels sobbed harder. When the new round of sobs subsided, Samantha said, "Are ya sure? Are ya sure it's my Seth?"

It surprised Garrett a little that she didn't ask for more details regarding the homicide involving her son. Considering her questioning whether he was sure her Seth could be involved, he chalked it up to denial.

Garrett said, "Yes ma'am, I'm sure. Because Seth didn't have a record and prints for a definitive ID, you or your husband will have to come to Pine View County to provide a positive ID before his…we can release his body."

More sobbing followed this. After several more moments,

Samantha composed herself. “I don’t think I can do this, and my husband is away on business. Seth’s best friend since grade school goes to SFA, too. Can he identify Seth’s…body?”

This information peeked Garrett’s interest, and he hoped the friend wouldn’t be Cole Duncan. That would be a dead end. No pun intended.

“No ma’am. I’m sorry, but it needs to be a family member. We can keep Seth in our morgue until your husband can make it here, though. What’s Seth’s friend’s name? I’d like to talk with him.”

Samantha took a hitching breath. “Okay, I’ll call my husband and have him do it.”

Garrett gave her the county morgue phone number and George Krats’ name as a contact, too.

“Seth’s best friend. What’s his name?” he reminded her.

Samantha let out a hollow chuckle. “Sorry, I forgot you asked. His name’s Dillon Albertson. Real smart kid…total opposite of Seth. Not that Seth isn’t…wasn’t smart. Dillon’s pre-med. He could’ve gone to better universities but went to SFA to be with Seth. Seth’s death will crush him.”

We’ll see about that, Garrett thought.

He said, “Do ya have Dillon’s phone number?”

After a brief hesitation, Samantha said, “Somewhere…maybe. I can look for it and call you back.”

“That’s unnecessary. I can call SFA and get his contact info.”

Samantha sniffed. “Okay, Sheriff. I’d say thank you for calling, but it would be disingenuous.”

“I understand, and I’m sorry for your loss. If ya think of anything that might shed light on my investigation, please let me know.”

“I don’t know what that might be, but…Seth had a girlfriend, if that helps.”

Since Garrett had been looking for a third werewolf, maybe Dillon, and a female alpha, maybe his girlfriend, he thought it might help a lot.

Masking his excitement, Garrett said, “It might. Do ya know her name?”

“I never met her. Seth went through a lot of girlfriends. He…was very handsome. He called her Alex when talking with me. So…maybe that’s short for Alexandria? Sorry I can’t be more certain. Does that help?”

“Yes ma’am, it does. Thank you. My condolences on your loss.”

Samantha said, “Goodbye,” and hung up before Garrett could say the same.

Garrett clicked the receiver button and quickly dialed SFA's UPD again. After connecting with Detective Sloan, Garrett asked him for information on Dillon Albertson. A few 'puter taps' later, Dillon's student ID picture, along with several contact phone numbers, were in Garrett's email inbox.

Before letting Detective Sloan go, Garrett asked, "Any chance ya can send me Dillon's class schedule? I'd like to talk with him 'bout Seth in person."

"Yep. Hang on a sec."

Garrett heard the keys clicking and then Detective Sloan said, "You're in luck. He has Monday, Wednesday, Friday classes. It's dead week before finals, so he might not have classes. I'm sendin' it to ya now."

"Thank you, Detective Sloan. I appreciate your help."

"Not a problem, Sheriff Lambert. If ya need anything else, give me a shout. And, please, call me Max."

"Will do, Max, if you call me Garrett."

"You got it, Garrett," Max agreed.

After ending the call with Max, Garrett studied Dillon's class schedule. He couldn't believe his luck. Dillon was in Dr. Emily Yost's AP II class at nine o'clock that morning. The computer clock read eight nineteen a.m. He could get to SFA by nine o'clock, but if Emily wasn't holding class, the trip would be a waste of his time. If Emily was holding class, he would have time to do a little social media investigating, creeping into Seth, Cole, and Dillon's Facebook pages, before driving to Nacogdoches. Garrett fired off a quick email to Emily, asking if she was having class at nine that morning.

While waiting for Emily's response, Garrett went to his Facebook page. Because he used it for investigating purposes only, it was mostly blank. Paige was his only Facebook friend. He typed Seth Daniels' name into the search bar. It was a popular name and dozens of results popped up. Garrett narrowed the search by adding SFA and one page loaded into the browser.

By searching Seth's friends, Garrett found Cole and Dillon's pages too, which he opened in separate windows, so he could compare them with information that linked them and, possibly, other potential werewolves. Aside from Seth and Cole being in the Theta Chi fraternity, Dillon was not, not much jumped out as a potential lead. Suspiciously, given what Samantha Daniels said about Seth having a girlfriend, what Garrett didn't find was any reference to Seth having a girlfriend. His relationship status was 'Single.' A search through Seth's pictures produced nothing of use either. No consistent girl in Seth's company.

Just as Garrett had been giving up on the social media aspect of his investigation, Emily responded to his email. The computer clock read eight fifty-eight a.m.

Cuttin' it close, Garrett thought as he opened the email.

As Garrett read the short email reply, a smile spread across his face. She was holding class.

Garrett 'puter tapped' a quick response, "I'm on my way to you. Please don't let class out before I get there. Thanks, Garrett."

Garrett grabbed his keys and was out of his office before Emily could respond.

~ * ~

The news vans that were absent from the Sheriff Department's parking lot now converged on Pine View High School. Paige saw them as she drove into the school parking lot and pulled her car into an empty spot between two pickup trucks for cover. Although she didn't know about the 'Special Edition' *Pine View Post* story that mentioned her, Paige had a feeling the reporters would be interested in interviewing the Sheriff's daughter and she wanted to avoid that. Before getting out and going into the school, Paige grabbed a John Deere baseball cap she kept in her car for sunny after school outings and pulled it down in front.

After maneuvering around the back of several cars to stay out of sight, Paige ducked her head and started toward the school's front doors. She heard reporters talking with several students as she wound her way through the crowd. When Paige emerged from the throng of reporters and students, she relaxed a little and dared to look up. Big mistake.

Quincy Wiseman eagerly engaged with a reporter when he noticed a dark-haired girl with a John Deere baseball cap pulled down over her face, maneuvering through the crowd of students and reporters. He thought it was Paige, who he hadn't stopped thinking about since the amazing 'cooter shot' he got at the MRB, but he couldn't be sure without seeing her face. Quincy broke off the interview and moved toward the dark-haired girl. When she cleared the crowd, she looked up. It was Paige.

"Hey, Paige." Quincy shouted.

Startled, Paige looked toward Quincy. As she did, a murmur went through the reporters, and all eyes fell on her. The horde of reporters descended on Paige like a pack of hungry wolves on a fresh kill. Paige gave Quincy a desperate look.

Quincy, who realized Paige was trying to avoid being recognized, said, "Sorry, Paige," as the reporters closed around her.

The questions came at Paige all at once, "Paige, what happened at the MRB?" "What does your dad plan to do?" "What kind of animal attacked y'all?" "Were you injured?" "Is it true your boyfriend was killed?" "What's this talk about, werewolves?"

Paige ducked her head and tried to escape, but they surrounded her.

She felt trapped and was on the verge of crying when an authoritative voice bellowed, "That's enough. Move on or I'll have all of y'all removed from school property."

Paige looked up and saw Principal Shields pushing through the reporters toward her. He was an older, big man with a commanding presence. Back when Paige's parents were in high school, Principal Shields taught history and coached the football team.

Principal Shields held out his large hand. Paige grasped it and he pulled her out of the circled reporters, who were still shouting questions at her.

When Paige was clear of the reporters, she said, "Thank you, Principal Shields."

Principal Shields gave Paige a reassuring smile. "It's the least I can do for the daughter of the state championship, MVP."

Paige smiled back.

Once inside the school, Paige made her way through the chattering students, all of whom were talking about what happened at the MRB, to her locker and opened it. Singularly focused on retrieving her books for first period, English with Mrs. Steahli, she failed to notice the black ribbons affixed to several lockers.

Paige closed her locker and automatically looked down and across the hall toward Justin's locker, as if expecting to see him there, and saw a black ribbon bow attached to it. Her eyes drifted down the hall past Justin's locker to the other lockers with black ribbons. She counted nine. Paige looked back from the way she'd come and counted six more ribbons.

The gravity of the loss staggered Paige. Her knees went weak, and her head felt light. If not for her locker close behind her, Paige would have fallen to the ground. She leaned against her locker and fought back tears that threatened to flow. She closed her eyes to shut the crazy world of dead boyfriends and werewolves out.

When she opened her eyes again, Quincy was standing in front of her with a big, goofy grin on his face.

"This is crazy, isn't it?" he said.

Paige nodded.

"I was right there when they killed Freddy and Ella. I even got some of their blood on me," Quincy elaborated.

Paige shook her head. "I don't wanna talk about this, Quincy."

Quincy looked momentarily confused, thinking, *who wouldn't want to talk about this*?

He said, "Yeah, okay. I'm sorry. I guess with Justin and all, you're pretty freaked out."

Paige nodded again.

Quincy leaned in close to Paige and whispered, "I ain't said nothin' 'bout the…werewolves. I'm afraid I might get carted off to the nuthouse in Rusk. I don't think anyone else is tellin' about the werewolves, either. It's like we all got a big secret from the rest of the world."

Quincy's proximity made Paige feel trapped.

She stepped away from her locker. "That's probably a good idea."

She hoped to rid herself of Quincy's company, but he fell in beside her. "Ya look good."

Paige shot a disapproving look at Quincy.

Quincy got the jest of the look. "Not good as in…*damn*, you look *good.* It's just that…Friday night, ya had blood all over ya. I thought ya might'a got hurt by one of those…ya know."

Paige saw the girl's restroom and, knowing Quincy wouldn't follow her in, headed toward it. When she got to the door, Paige said, "Thanks for your concern, Quincy. It wasn't my blood."

"Cool. We both got some spray. Was it Justin's blood?"

Paige pushed through the door without responding.

After the door shut, she heard Quincy say, "Okay, Paige. If ya wanna talk, I'm here for ya."

Paige responded by raising her middle finger at the door, at Quincy beyond the door.

The girl's restroom was empty and quiet. Except for the hum from the harsh florescent lights above. It smelled of disinfectant. Paige went to the large handicap stall, there weren't any disabled students at Pine View High School, so Paige didn't feel guilty about using the large stall and sat down on the closed toilet. The tears that threatened to flow since the reporters surrounded her spilled from her eyes. While she was crying, the bell that signified the start of first period rang. Mrs. Steahli was a sweet, understanding teacher, so Paige wasn't too worried about being late to class.

A few more minutes and several wads of toilet paper later, Paige left the stall and studied her reflection in the mirror. Her eyes were bloodshot, and her lids were red and puffy.

You look like shit, Paige thought.

She splashed some water on her face and, when she looked back into the mirror, she screamed and staggered backwards until she collided with the bathroom stalls.

Paige blinked her eyes and looked back at her startled reflection. Her bloodshot, puffy face blinked back at her, but that wasn't the reflection she saw when she looked into the mirror after washing her face. A horrifying, snarling werewolf had looked back at her.

Thinking it might be a dream, Paige pinched her left forearm. It hurt. She wasn't dreaming. Paige blinked several more times, daring her reflection to reveal the monster lurking inside her. The monster her six-year-old neighbor Dalton saw. Nothing happened. Paige steadied her shaking hands and left the girl's restroom.

Outside of the restroom, Paige ran into Mrs. Davis. Mrs. Davis was her Health teacher freshman year. She was as sweet and caring as her other favorite teachers. Mrs. Rogers and Mrs. Steahli and her councilor, Mrs. Burns. Mrs. Davis took one look at Paige and wrapped her in a hug without asking if she needed it.

After several moments, Mrs. Davis said, "I'm so sorry, Paige. All of this is so horrible. I know it doesn't feel like it now, but you'll feel better…eventually."

Paige sniffed. "Thank you, Missus Davis."

Mrs. Davis released the hug. "I'm here if ya need me."

Paige offered a weak smile. "I know. Thank you."

With a wink, Mrs. Davis said, "Off to class. You're late."

Despite everything, Paige managed a genuine smile, turned, and headed for class.

As Paige made her way to first period English, the halls were empty, and the school eerily quiet. Paige was getting the uncomfortable feeling she was living in a waking nightmare. When the intercom buzzed and Principal Shields's booming voice filled the school, it startled Paige, and she jumped.

"I'm gonna forgo with the normal Monday morning announcements. Our school suffered tragic losses last Friday night. Fifteen of our students…your friends, lost their lives. Eleven survived but witnessed unimaginable horror. I hope that we, as a school, can pull together to offer support to the families and friends of our…deceased students and that we give the survivors time to process the events and heal.

"Our school counselor, Missus Burns, will have open one-on-one and group meetings throughout the week. To help with this, the councilors from Pine View Junior High and Pine View Elementary School are on campus, too. To the degree you're comfortable with, talk with any of your teachers, too. My office door is open as well.

"Now, to hell with the Supreme Court, I'm gonna say a prayer for all the families and friends affected by this tragedy. If ya have a problem with this, be respectful and keep your mouths shut. Our Father, who art in heaven, hallowed be Thy name…"

Paige had just gotten to Mrs. Steahli's classroom when Principal Shields started reciting the Lord's Prayer. She quickly made the sign of the cross and whispered the familiar words along with Principal Shields. When she finished, without thinking, her right hand felt her chest for the crucifix she could no longer wear. Brief panic at its absence quickly turned to anger for the alpha that bit her for making it painful to wear her silver crucifix and necklace.

Paige slipped her right hand into the front pocket of her blue jeans, where she placed the crucifix and necklace. She couldn't wear it, but she could have it with her. Her fingertips brushed across the cool silver, but the cool silver warmed instantly. Paige kept her fingers in contact with the silver for as long as she could. When it became too uncomfortable to continue, she pulled her hand out and looked at her fingers—there were little, puffy blisters on the fingertips of the three fingers that touched the silver.

As Paige was looking at the blisters, they melted away. Within a few seconds, the blisters, and the pain, were gone. Paige opened the door to Mrs. Steahli's classroom and stepped inside.

~ * ~

Garrett turned on to Raguet Street and pulled up in front of the Science Building at nine twenty-eight a.m. Twenty-two minutes of class left. He found it hard to believe it had only been a week since his last trip to see Dr. Yost about the attacks on Carla Weaver's pigs and Russ Lomax's murder. A week ago, he had some hair and bite marks for analysis. Since then, there had been eighteen more murders. Fifteen students at the MRB were gone. Three bikers from Knucklehead's Icehouse were lost. Paige and Ty had been bitten and infected. Also, two werewolves no longer posed a threat.

"One fuckin' week," Garrett muttered to himself.

Before getting out of the patrol SUV, Garrett pulled up the picture of Dillon Albertson on his cellphone and studied the image. He didn't want to reference the image to locate Dillon in the classroom. Confident he could pick Dillon out of a crowded class, Garrett slipped the cellphone into his breast pocket, got out of the SUV, and headed inside the building.

According to the schedule Detective Sloan sent Garrett, the classroom was on the second floor. Garrett took the elevator and started down the second-floor hallway, looking for the room number. It was the first room on the right. After walking up to the door, Garrett listened and was glad to hear Emily lecturing about bursa sacs, which he knew nothing about. Garrett knocked on the door.

Seconds later, Emily opened the door and, with a smile, said, "Good morning, Sheriff Garrett."

She'll never drop the g, Garrett thought.

He said, "Good mornin', Doctor Yost. Mind if I borrow one of your students for a few minutes?"

Emily stepped aside to allow Garrett into the classroom. "Not at all. Come on in."

Garrett scanned the interested youthful faces, looking back at him. It was a large classroom with stadium seating and about seventy students. A few seconds into the scan, Garrett spotted Dillon sitting at the back and on the far side of the classroom. He wasn't wearing glasses, as in his student ID picture, but it was Dillon Albertson.

Like all the other students, Dillon looked at Garrett and he didn't look away when Garrett locked his gaze on him. Garrett dealt with a lot of guilty people over the years, and they usually had a common tell. Not making direct eye contact. That Dillon didn't look away was discouraging, but he would still question him.

Garrett pointed at Dillon. "I need to talk with Mister Albertson."

Dillon looked around with what Garrett thought genuine surprise and pointed at himself. "Me?"

Garrett nodded. "Yes, sir. It'll only take a few minutes."

Garrett turned to Emily. "Is there someplace private I can talk with Dillon?"

Without hesitation, Emily said, "Use my office."

Emily pulled a key ring from her pocket, sorted through the keys, found her office key, and handed it to Garrett. "When you're done, if you have time, stick around until I dismiss class."

Garrett took the key. "Okay. I'll see ya in a bit."

Dillon joined Garrett and Emily at the front of the class.

Garrett motioned toward the door. "After you, Mister Albertson."

Dillon put the strap of a large backpack over his right shoulder and started toward the door; Garrett fell in behind him.

In the hallway, and away from the still opened classroom door, Dillon said, "What's this about, Officer?"

"Sheriff, not officer. I'm Sheriff Garrett Lambert from Pine View County. I'll fill ya in when we're in Doctor Yost's office."

Dillon was quiet for several seconds and then said, "Do I need an attorney?"

"If ya want one. But it's unnecessary. I just have a few questions 'bout a friend of yours. You're not a suspect, you're not under arrest, and I'm not detainin' ya. In fact, you can refuse to talk with me and walk away. Nothin' I can do to stop ya, if ya do."

After hearing this, Dillon seemed to relax a little.

Garrett closed Emily's office door and motioned for Dillon to take one of the two seats that faced her desk; Garrett sat down in Emily's office chair.

Garrett took a notebook and pen from his breast pocket and leaned forward. "No glasses. You're wearin' glasses in your school ID picture."

Dillon shifted in his seat. "I had corrective surgery over Spring Break."

That was a lie. Dillon hadn't needed glasses since his first change.

Garrett wrote, 'Check eye surgery story' on the notepad.

"Who did the surgery?"

"How is my eye surgery related to questions about a friend of mine?"

Dillon was smarter than the folks Garrett usually questioned.

"It isn't," Garrett admitted, "Just curious. Comes with the job. Okay then…how well did ya know Seth Daniels?"

"Knew?" Dillon asked with raised eyebrows.

Dillon was a lot smarter than the folks Garrett usually questioned.

"I'm afraid so. Seth died Friday night."

"How?"

Garrett leaned back in Emily's chair. "Let's start over. How well *did* ya know Seth?"

Dillon shifted in his seat again. "We used to be best friends. He's the reason I'm here instead of at a better school."

"*Used* to be best friends? What happened?" Garrett asked.

"His fraternity happened. I rushed Theta Chi too but, apparently, I wasn't *good* enough. We remained friends for a while after that, but as he got more involved with his fraternity brothers, he had less time for me."

"When was the last time y'all talked?"

Dillon put a hand on his hairless chin, as if trying to recall their last encounter and, after several seconds, said, "Right before Spring Break. Seth was going to Powderhorn Mountain to ski with some of his fraternity brothers. He wanted help studying for his accounting mid-term."

"Did ya help him?"

Dillon nodded.

"Ya haven't spoken with him since?"

Dillon shook his head.

"Did Seth have a girlfriend?" Garrett continued with his questions.

Dillon smiled an envious smile. "Seth had lots of girlfriends."

"Anyone steady lately?"

"Not that I'm aware of."

"Does the name Alexandria or Alex sound familiar?" Garrett probed.

At this question, Garrett noticed Dillon stiffen in his seat. It was brief, but it had been a tell the question made Dillon uncomfortable.

Dillon shook his head slowly. "I'm sorry…but it doesn't sound familiar."

"Ya sure about that?"

Dillon nodded. "I'm sure. Like I said, Seth and I hadn't talked since before Spring Break. We weren't that close before Spring Break. So…it's possible he had a steady girlfriend I didn't know about."

Garrett jotted, 'Lying about the girlfriend' in his notepad, and closed it.

"What about Cole Duncan? Did ya know him, too?"

"Knew?" Dillon asked.

He doesn't miss a thing, Garrett thought.

He said, "Cole's dead, too."

"With Seth? Same…what happened to Seth? You didn't tell me what happened to Seth."

"One of my deputies killed Seth Friday night at a homicide he was involved in," Garrett explained.

"A homicide? Seth wouldn't do something like that," Dillon said defensively.

"Well, he did. Ya said y'all weren't that close lately. People change," Garrett said while thinking, *into werewolves*.

Dillon frowned. "Cole? What happened to Cole?"

"Did you know Cole?"

"I knew him. We weren't friends. Far from it. I didn't like Cole. He was one of Seth's frat brothers. He was kind of…a dick. If Seth killed somebody, Cole was probably involved."

Garrett considered this information briefly. "Can ya think of anybody who might'a wanted to kill Cole?" To tweak Dillon, Garrett added, "Besides yourself."

Dillon raised his hands. "That sounds like the type of question I should have an attorney present to tell me not to answer."

Garrett chuckled. "Relax, Dillon. I was just yankin' your chain. I don't think ya killed Cole. Just wonderin' if ya might know someone who would."

Dillon lowered his hands. "I don't. I wasn't around him much, though. He could've had enemies. He was that kind of guy."

"Okay, Mister Albertson. I think we're done…for now. As the sayin' goes, don't leave town without lettin' me know. You're free to go."

Dillon stood up, turned to leave. He stopped and turned back around to face Garrett. "Was Cole with Seth Friday night? Is that how he died, too? Shot by a deputy?"

Garrett considered how to respond to Dillon's question. He wanted to phrase the answer to reveal another tell.

After meeting and talking with Dillon, Garrett didn't think he was part of the pack. The eye surgery answer seemed convenient, not suspicious. Garrett was sure Dillon lied about the girlfriend, though. That was suspicious. Garrett was sure Dillon knew more than what he told him.

Finally, Garrett said, "Nope. Cole was killed in an unrelated incident Saturday night. He wasn't shot. Best we can tell, a large animal attacked him and ripped his head off."

Dillon stiffened a little; the tell. "Like those kids at the MRB?"

Garrett nodded. "Just like the kids at the MRB. My daughter was there when that happened. In fact, one of 'em bit her. Damned if the wound hasn't healed already."

At hearing this, Dillon stiffened again; another tell. "I'm glad she's okay."

Garrett leaned forward in the chair. "Thanks, Dillon. She's okay for now, at least. Now ya know why this investigation's so important to me. I gotta find these…animals and put 'em down before my daughter isn't okay. Do you understand me, son?"

Dillon nodded, swallowed hard. "Yes, sir. I've told you everything I know."

Garrett got up and handed Dillon one of his business cards. "My private cell numbers on the back. Call me if ya think of anything else that might be helpful."

Dillon took the card and turned to leave.

Garrett took hold of Dillon's arm, not forcefully but secure enough to stop him from leaving. "From what I understand, killin' the alpha will release those who it infected."

Dillon turned his face toward Garrett. His mouth was open, and he looked a lot less sure of himself than at any point in their conversation.

"Killing what releases who?"

"You heard me. Think about what ya might know and call me later."

When Garrett let go of Dillon's arm, Dillon stuffed the business card in his back pocket and opened the office door.

Emily, done with class, leaned against the wall across from her office, talking with two students.

"All done?" Emily asked Dillon.

Dillon said, "Yes, ma'am," and headed down the hall toward the elevators.

To the two students, Emily said, "Give me a sec. I need to talk with Sheriff Lambert."

They nodded, and Emily shut her office door behind her.

Garrett took the seat Dillon had just vacated, and Emily sat down in her chair.

"Oh, nice and warm for me," Emily said with a smile.

Garrett shifted in his seat and thought, *Shoe's on the other foot now*.

"Yeah, I hope ya don't mind my sittin' behind your desk."

"Don't be silly. Of course not. Can you tell me what this was about? Is it linked to the samples you brought in last Monday? Are they linked to what happened at that high school MRB party?"

"You're officially part of this investigation. So, ya can't share anything I'm about to tell ya with the press…or anyone else."

Emily gave an exaggerated eye roll. "I'm aware of my responsibilities to the Pine View County Sheriff's Department. Now…spill."

For the next twenty minutes, Garrett spilled almost everything. He left out the part about Paige and Ty being bitten as well as the alpha's attack at his house. He'd shared the part about Paige being bitten with Dillon to stress the personal nature of his investigation. Telling Emily, a zoologist and biologist, seemed like an unnecessary risk. She might want to study them and, even though Garrett trusted her a great deal, scientists had a history of doing unethical things in the name of science. The Tuskegee syphilis experiment, the Milgram experiment on obedience to authority, and the Stanford prison experiment were just a few examples Garrett knew of.

When Garrett finished relaying what he would share, Emily sat back in her chair, pursed out her bottom lip, and exhaled hard enough to flutter her sandy-blonde bangs.

She said, "What I wouldn't give to study one of them. I'd sell my mom to the lowest bidder."

At hearing this, Garrett knew keeping Paige and Ty's bites out of the story a wise decision. She'd certainly want to 'study' them.

"We've got two dead ones in the morgue. Cole'll probably be gone quick, but Seth'll be there until next of kin can come identify him. That could be a couple of days. You're welcome to look him over."

Emily considered the offer for a few seconds. "Yes, I'd like to do that. If death releases them from the…affliction, it's unlikely I'll find anything. But…you never know until you look at it under a microscope."

Garrett stood up. "Good deal. I'll let George Krats know you'll be droppin' by the morgue."

Garrett started for the door and Emily said, "What about Dillon? Do you think he's one of them?"

Garrett turned back to Emily. "I don't think so. I do think he knows somethin' he's not sharin'."

"Like what?"

Garrett shrugged. "Don't rightly know. It's just a hunch. He has a tell…he stiffened just a little when I asked about Seth's girlfriend. I think he might know who she is."

"If he does, why wouldn't he tell you?"

Garrett shrugged again. "I reckon he's scared. If she's the alpha, and he knows her, he should be."

Emily nodded.

As Garrett was opening the door to leave, he said, "Let me know if ya find out anything interestin' at the morgue."

"Will do."

The two young women who were still waiting outside Emily's office crinkled their noses at the mention of the morgue.

Garrett tipped the brim of his cowboy hat at them. "She's all yours, ladies."

The one with strawberry blonde hair said, "Thank you, Sheriff Cutie."

The one with purple streaks in her blonde hair giggled.

Emily said, "Okay ladies. That's going to go straight to Sheriff Lambert's East Texas head, which won't fit in his ten-gallon cowboy hat after this. Get in here if y'all want to talk about the final exam."

Garrett walked toward the elevators feeling good about two things. First, a collage-age girl hadn't called him cute since he had been married to Lacy. Emily was right. It went straight to his East Texas head. Second, Emily said "y'all" when inviting the girls into her office.

There's hope for you yet, Garrett thought as he got in the elevator and pushed the first-floor button.

~ * ~

After being questioned by Sheriff Lambert, instead of going to chemistry class, Dillon went to the parking garage—looking over his shoulder often as he walked—and got into his car. He sat behind the wheel for several moments, weighing his options. Part of him wanted to drive away from SFA, from Nacogdoches, from Texas, and leave everything behind. He couldn't escape who or what he was, though. The wolf would be with him wherever he ended up.

"He knows too much," Dillon said aloud, and the unsteady nature of his voice unnerved him more.

His mind, always rational and reliable in the past, struggled to make sense of the conversation with Sheriff Lambert. Dillon knew Seth was dead, but not that Cole was dead, too. The way Cole died, decapitated by Alexis, made Dillon very uneasy. The knowledge Alexis could always recruit new pack members only reinforced his dispensability.

This realization reminded Dillon of another nugget of information Sheriff Lambert shared with him. Alexis had infected the sheriff's daughter. Dillon liked the idea of having a pack bitch to use for the animalistic urges common to all mammals. The only sex he'd ever had was when his wolf coupled with Alexis' wolf, and he'd enjoyed it. Infecting the sheriff's daughter seemed unnecessarily reckless. This made it a personal investigation, not a professional investigation, for the sheriff, and Dillon got the impression constitutional limits on law enforcement wouldn't constrain Sheriff Lambert. The sheriff would do whatever was necessary to release his daughter from the curse.

Dillon pondered this possibility. Studying was in his blood. It was what he did best. For any problem he ever encountered, he could always find a solution through research, but he never considered researching werewolf lore. The sheriff had been operating under the belief killing the alpha would release his daughter from the curse. If this were true, Dillon would be released, too.

Can killing Alexis really release me from this curse? Dillon thought.

As soon as that thought entered Dillon's mind, he regretted it. He had been aware of Alexis' mental connection, intrusion, with her betas and it wouldn't be prudent to give her a reason to kill him, too.

Dillon quickly flooded his mind with random thoughts, *I hate Mondays; I need to study for finals; I want some ice-cream; I wish I was taller*, hoping to cover his mental transgression. Then he waited to see if he felt Alexis probing his mind.

When, after several tense moments, Dillon didn't detect Alexis' intrusion, he started his car. Dillon drove out of the parking garage with no idea where he was going.

~ * ~

Garrett exited the elevator on the second floor of the Liberal Arts Building and turned left toward James Huff's office. He did not know if James would be in his office, but since he was already on campus, he thought he'd drop by.

James' office door was ajar.

Garrett knocked on it and heard James' high, almost feminine voice say, "Come in."

Again, the slow passage of time struck Garrett. One week ago, Garrett knocked on James' office door for the first time and now he considered James a good friend.

Garrett pushed the door open. "Hey there, James."

James was delighted to see Garrett. He stood up and stuck out his pudgy hand. "Garrett. Great to see ya. What brings ya to SFA world this mornin'?"

Garrett shut the door behind him.

He grabbed James' limp, pudgy hand, and shook it. "Got an ID on the two dead werewolves. They were students at SFA."

James withdrew his hand after the shake and used the hand sanitizer solution to rid himself of any lingering germs. When he finished, he looked up and saw Garrett looking at his hands.

James chuckled, which made his ample belly jiggle. "It's not you, my friend. I'm a bit of a germaphobe."

He sat down and motioned for Garrett to have a seat. "Tell me what ya know."

Garrett, feeling claustrophobic in James' cluttered, dark office again, but not unsure of his feelings for James, sat down and told him everything that happened that morning.

When Garrett finished relaying the events, he said, "Do ya know any of these boys? Seth, Cole, or Dillon?"

James locked his pudgy fingers under his ample chin. "Their names don't ring a bell, but I teach a couple of hundred students a year.

I'll check my old rosters and let ya know later."

Garrett nodded.

"Do ya think the Dillon kid is the third beta?" asked James.

Garrett considered the question briefly. He'd been considering this possibility since meeting with Dillon. "I'm not sure. He seemed genuinely surprised to find out Seth and Cole were dead. Added to that, the story of how he and Seth drifted apart seems plausible."

"Ya think he knows more than he's lettin' on?"

Garrett nodded. "Yeah. I'm sure he knows somethin' 'bout Seth's girlfriend. The eye surgery too…maybe? If he knows who the girlfriend is, and what she is, why the hell wouldn't he tell me?"

James leaned back in his chair, which caused it to screech in protest. "He's probably scared. Ya basically told him the alpha killed Cole. If he *is* the third beta in the pack, he's powerless against the alpha. If he's not a beta, but knows who the alpha is, he's an easy target. Or…he's tellin' the truth."

Certain of Dillon's tell, Garrett shook his head. "He's hidin' somethin'. I'm sure of that."

James leaned forward, issuing another screech from his chair. "Well? What're ya gonna do? Put him under surveillance?"

"He's out of my jurisdiction, and I can't pull in UPD, Nac PD, the Nacogdoches County Sheriff's Department, or the DPS on it. What would I tell 'em? Be on the lookout for Dillon Albertson gettin' hairy and growin' fangs. No…this'll have to be off the books," Garrett explained.

"I'll do it," James offered.

This surprised Garrett and, while he appreciated the offer, he couldn't impose on James in this way.

Garrett smiled. "I appreciate the offer, but I can't ask ya to do that."

James chuckled. "Ya didn't. I offered."

Garrett shook his head politely. "I can't put ya in this kind of danger, James. If somethin' happened to ya, who would be my expert on the supernatural?"

James let out a full, belly-shaking burst of laughter. "Are ya expectin' more supernatural trouble? Vampires…or maybe zombies? They're all the rage now."

"I didn't expect werewolves, and here they are."

The smile slipped from James' face, and he said, "Actually, once somethin' like this happens somewhere, other supernatural events are more likely to follow. At least that's what the folklore suggests. Listen, Garrett. I *want* to do this. I've studied lore my whole adult life, and it's fascinated me since I was a kid. Let me be a part of this. I'll be careful…keep my distance. I promise."

Garrett found it difficult to deny James a part in the events. A nightmare for Garrett was a dream come true for James.

Against his better judgment, Garrett said, "Okay. If ya see anything…I mean *anything* suspicious or out of sorts, back off and call me."

James' chubby cheeks flushed red with excitement, and he said, "Thank ya, Garrett. You've made an old professor extremely happy. Are ya gonna deputize me…or somethin'?"

"Can't. This isn't my jurisdiction. If I deputized ya, ya couldn't follow Dillon. You're just a concerned citizen helpin' me out."

James nodded. "Of course. I understand. I won't let ya down."

Garrett smiled. "You couldn't if ya tried."

Garrett gave James the address the school had on file for Dillon Albertson and the information he secured through the sheriff's department. Car registration, orange, 1998 Honda Civic, and plate number. After shaking hands, James left to teach class and Garrett headed back to Pine View County. Neither man knew what awaited them in the future, but they would face it together.

~ * ~

Alone in her bedroom, having just awakened from a nap she didn't need, Alexis sensed Dillon's proximity long before he knocked on her door. After killing Cole, Alexis hadn't bothered to connect with Dillon. She hadn't given thought to Dillon at all. He wasn't the problem; that had been Cole. Dillon would never challenge her, but she sensed something troubling from Dillon. She sensed fear on Dillon. Scared people did stupid things.

Alexis slid out of her comfy bed and walked to the front door to welcome Dillon. She was naked and didn't bother to cover herself. She knew her nakedness would catch Dillon off guard and a confused mind was a mind without barriers.

As Dillon approached her door, Alexis could smell the fear radiating from his pores. She loved that smell on victims but, in one of her pack, it made her angry.

Just before Dillon knocked on the door, Alexis opened it. “I’ve been expecting you.”

Dillon’s eyes widened as he took in Alexis’ near perfect body. He’d seen her naked before they turned, but that she would answer her door naked, in the middle of the day, surprised him. Cognition evaporated, and he felt her inside his head.

The look on Dillon’s face when he saw her naked was all Alexis needed to know her plan worked. She pushed into Dillon’s thoughts. From Dillon’s point of view, she saw the sheriff and heard the questions he asked. A fleeting glimpse of what happened, but more than enough to explain Dillon’s fear.

Somehow, Dillon found the courage and independent thought to say, “The sheriff’s daughter? What the fuck were you thinking?”

Alexis’ eyes flared red, and a demonic growl erupted from her full, human lips. She grabbed Dillon by the shirt and, with inhuman strength, yanked him from his feet and launched him fifteen feet into the living room, where he landed with a ‘thud’ and a yelp. Alexis slammed the door and advanced on the still prone Dillon.

Dillon looked up, and he saw what was left of Alexis’ human form. Her head, arms, and legs transformed, her torso had not. Dillon found this oddly attractive, but she was coming for him.

Dillon cowered on the floor and shouted, “I’m sorry, Alexis. I’m sorry.”

He was submitting.

The partially transformed werewolf grabbed Dillon by the shoulders, making sure its claws penetrated deep into his human flesh, and lifted the squirming man from the floor so they were face to face. It snapped at Dillon’s face and bit off the tip of his nose. Dillon yelped again.

“Give me a reason, Dillon,” it growled in Dillon’s bleeding face.

The wolf part of Alexis hoped Dillon would transform and challenge it. It felt on the verge of killing him anyway, and a challenge would seal the deal. Then it smelled urine as Dillon pissed himself and it knew he wouldn’t challenge.

“You’re fuckin’ pathetic,” it growled.

It dropped Dillon to the floor in his piss puddle and growled, “Clean up your pathetic stench.”

Dillon felt sure Alexis was going to kill him like she’d killed Cole.

Even after she dropped him, he expected to feel her dagger teeth on the back of his neck. He rolled into a ball and whimpered like a whipped puppy.

It wasn't until he heard Alexis' human voice say, "Get up Dillon. I'm not going to kill you…now," Dillon dared to look up.

He saw Alexis standing a few feet away, human naked and looking down at him with utter disgust.

While Dillon was getting to his unsteady feet, Alexis walked into the kitchen, opened the refrigerator, and retrieved a bottle of Dasani water. She didn't offer one to Dillon.

After taking several large gulps of water, changing got her thirst up, she said, "So the sheriff came to see you today."

Dillon shied away. "I didn't tell him anything. I promise, Alexis."

Alexis rubbed the cold bottle between her perky breasts and smiled. "I know. If you had, or if you'd challenged me a minute ago, you'd be as dead as Cole."

Dillon put his hand to his tip-less nose, which had already stopped bleeding. "Did Cole challenge you again? Is that why you killed him?"

Alexis took a step toward Dillon, which caused him to take a step back.

She laughed. "Worse. He tried to create a rival pack."

Dillon's mouth fell open. He did not know that was even possible.

Reading his face, not his mind, Alexis said, "Don't get any ideas, Dillon. I'd snap you like a twig."

The 'snap' double entendre wasn't lost on Dillon. He swallowed hard and shook his head so quickly his nose started bleeding again.

"Good boy," Alexis whispered.

After several seconds of silence, Dillon somehow found the nerve to say, "Did you know the girl was the sheriff's daughter?"

Alexis' eyes flared red, and Dillon took several startled, backward steps, but she didn't change or advance on him.

Her eyes flamed out, and she said, "No. That was…oversight on my part."

Dillon took a tentative step toward Alexis. "He's trouble. He knows too much. We should take him out."

Alexis looked away from Dillon. "I tried to…change him. It didn't work out."

This news hit Dillon like a punch to the gut. That Alexis tried to change him had been risky but, that she failed, alarmed him.

"Wh-Why would you change him instead of killing him? Wh-why didn't it work out?" Dillon stuttered.

Alexis turned back to face Dillon and, although her eyes weren't flared, the look was deadly. "Are you questioning my decisions, Dillon? If you are, I'd take that as a challenge."

Dillon backed away again. "No. No. Of course not. I just…"

"I wanted to change him to humiliate the little bitch who shoved the silver down my fuckin' throat."

Dillon's blank expression told Alexis he wasn't following her thinking.

For a smart guy, you're pretty fuckin' stupid sometimes, Alexis thought.

"Explain it to me," Dillon responded to her thought.

This surprised Alexis.

She advanced on Dillon. "Can you get inside my fuckin' head, too?"

Dillon retreated until his legs hit the couch and he sat down without meaning to. Alexis was almost on top of him, and her eyes were burning red.

"Sometimes. Sometimes I get a flash from you. Only when you're mad or hurt or feeling…good. I can't start it. It just...happens," Dillon explained.

"For how long? How long have you been getting these…flashes into my mind?" Alexis growled.

"Since you turned me. I swear I can't get into your head. It's only flashes," Dillon whimpered.

"So, you've tried to get into my head?" Alexis hissed.

Caught, and knowing she'd know if he lied, Dillon said, "I did. Twice, that's all."

Alexis leaned in close to Dillon's face. "Why?"

Dillon could feel Alexis in his head.

He used this to his advantage. "I was curious. That's all. I swear. You know I'm telling you the truth."

Alexis peered into Dillon's mind and saw he had been telling her the truth. The revelation startled her, but it was good she'd discovered it. She realized she might use this reverse connection to her advantage.

She leaned in closer to Dillon, so close her nose touched his tip-less nose. "You want to know why I tried to change the sheriff? Have a look."

Dillon felt his perspective shift, and he was looking back at his own bloodied, startled face. Alexis closed her eyes and Dillon dissolved into her inner thoughts. What he saw played out like a fantasy and he realized that's what it was. The fantasy she envisioned after turning the girl and her dad.

Alexis, Dillon, the girl, the sheriff, and the deputy Alexis changed at the pig lady's house, were in the barn. Alexis, Dillon, the sheriff, and the deputy were naked. The girl was not. She cried and cowered in a filthy corner of the barn. Alexis, Dillon, the sheriff, and the deputy transformed. The girl started screaming and clawing at the barn siding. Her fingernails ripped off and claws started growing from her bloody fingertips. The wolf deputy grabbed the crying girl, digging its claws into her flesh as it did, and threw her toward the center of the barn. The wolf dad caught her and raked its claws across her chest, shredding her shirt and skin beneath.

The girl cried out, "Please stop, Daddy." The girl's snout elongated, and fangs pushed her human teeth out in a spray of blood. She screamed again, but it turned into a gargled growl as her human mouth lost form. The wolf dad dropped her partially transformed body to the dirt floor. The girl's body continued to elongate and grow. Her shorts split and a bushy tail sprang free when they fell off. The wolf dad grabbed the tail of the wolf daughter and pulled its hind end toward its crotch.

Dillon closed his eyes, but to no avail. He felt the eyelids of his corporal body shut, but he wasn't seeing through his eyes. Mental claws still trapped him in Alexis' fantasy. He was powerless to not watch the coupling. When the wolf dad finished, the wolf deputy took his turn. Then it was wolf Dillon's turn. Just as he began to couple with the new pack-bitch, Alexis pushed him out of her head.

The perspective shift back into his body left him lightheaded. He thought he might pass out or vomit. He heard ragged, panting breathing before he realized it came from him. Dillon looked at Alexis and saw a truly evil grin on her otherwise beautiful face.

Without considering the ramifications, Dillon said, "You're sick."

The evil grin on Alexis' face spread inhumanly, and Dillon saw elongated canines protruding from her upper and lower jaws.

Alexis giggled-growled. "You enjoyed it, Dillon."

"I need to puke," Dillon shot back.

Alexis pointed at Dillon's crotch. Her fingernails were long claws. She said, "Puke on that."

When Dillon looked down, it horrified him to see an erection bulging in his loose-fitting slacks.

Alexis let out a laugh that morphed into a howl. "You want me to help you with that? You're basically all I have left…until the next full moon. I promise I won't bite."

She gnashed her fangs loud enough to produce loud snapping sounds.

Dillon leaned forward and vomited between his feet.

Alexis wrinkled her nose. "Clean that shit up when you clean up the piss and blood. You'll find what you need under the kitchen sink."

Then she disappeared down the hall toward her bedroom.

Dillon was almost finished cleaning the multiple bodily fluids he'd deposited on Alexis' living room floor. The blood had partially dried and was the most stubborn to remove, when Alexis strolled back into the living room. She was still naked, and Dillon thought she was purposefully trying to distract him.

Knowing he was on dangerous ground, but wanting answers, Dillon said, "You said you *tried* to change him, but it didn't work out. Why didn't it work out? What happened?"

Alexis squatted down in front of Dillon, legs spread, giving him an intimate view of her womanhood, and pulled her long, blonde hair over her left ear. "This happened."

Dillon's gaze drifted from Alexis' lower exposed parts to her exposed ear and saw a small hole in the top of it. The skin around the hole was puffy and an angry red. Dillon didn't need to be pre-med to know it looked infected.

Surprised, Dillon said, "What happened? Why isn't that healing?"

"It is healing. Slowly. It was a lot worse Saturday when I regained my human form."

"Why? Why is it healing slowly?"

Alexis let her hair fall back down, covering the wound. "Because the sheriff shot me through the ear with a silver bullet."

Dillon's mouth dropped open, and he felt the urge to vomit again.

When he regained enough composure to speak, Dillon said, "We can't stay here. It's too dangerous. We need to leave."

Alexis stood up and held her hand out to Dillon. The claws were gone, so Dillon took Alexis' hand and let her help him to his feet. His legs still felt weak, but he remained standing.

Alexis turned and walked to the kitchen counter, where she'd placed the water bottle on the granite counter. She took several large drinks, emptying the bottle.

She turned to Dillon. "I'm not going anywhere, and neither are you. I'll handle the sheriff. If he doesn't know who I am, I have the upper hand."

This reminded Dillon of Sheriff Lambert's questions about Seth's girlfriend. "He asked me if Seth had a girlfriend named Alex or Alexandria. I told him I didn't know because Seth and I weren't friends anymore."

Calmly, Alexis said, "I know. I saw it when I mind raped you."

"You're not worried? Other people know you and Seth were dating. What about social media? Facebook or Twitter?"

"I took care of it."

"How?"

Alexis smiled. "At some point or another, Seth accessed all his social media accounts. You left out Instagram, Snapchat, WhatsApp, and Kik from inside my house over my Wi-Fi. I captured his login information. After that fuckin' deputy killed him, I accessed all Seth's social media accounts and deleted evidence of our relationship. If someone leads the sheriff my way, I'll say Seth and I went out once last fall, but we didn't click, and I haven't had contact with him since."

"Why would ya capture Seth's login information? Did you plan on him dying and needing to cover up the relationship?"

Alexis laughed. "Of course not. I captured Seth's info long before the gift."

Dillon didn't consider being a werewolf a gift; he considered it a curse.

"Why then?" Dillon persisted.

"For…insurance."

"Insurance?"

Alexis smiled. "I have some…compromising pictures of Seth. Let's just say they involve a strap-on and leave it at that. If Seth ever humiliated me by dumping me, I was going to flood his social media with the pictures. So, I deleted myself from Seth's social media life. It all worked out."

Except for Seth, Dillon thought.

Dillon shook his head. "You really are an evil bitch, Alexis."

Taking this as a compliment, Alexis said, "Thank you, Dillon. You've only seen the evil bitch I let you see. I assure you that, like an iceberg, there's an eviler bitch that you haven't seen. Cross me and you'll find out."

Dillon didn't doubt Alexis' description or threat. He wanted to be away from her. "I should go."

Alexis nodded. "You should. Don't come back here. Bitch's daddy might watch you. When I need you, I'll contact you."

To emphasize the nature of the contact, Alexis tapped the side of her head. Not with her fingernail, but with a deadly claw.

Dillon, frightened by the seemingly effortless control Alexis had over transforming, swallowed hard and nodded.

After Dillon left, Alexis climbed back into bed. She transformed into her wolf. Alexis enjoyed her wolf form more than her human form and curled up for a nap. She had unfinished business with the treed biker and needed rest.

Chapter Fourteen

After the incident behind the Mill Road Barn with Trowa, Bear, Jack, Mont, and the young man who claimed to be Eddie on Saturday night, Garrett tasked Deputy Foster Timpson with taking Trowa home.

Trowa asked Deputy Timpson to take him to Knucklehead's so he could get his bike, but he curtly refused, saying, "Sheriff said to take ya home and that's what I'm doin'."

Trowa pulled into the Knucklehead Icehouse parking lot in his beat up, 1972, Ford F-150 pickup on Monday evening, a little after eight o'clock. The Icehouse closed on Sundays. He came to get his bike. He wasn't worried about his Indian motorcycle. Knucklehead's Icehouse had a policy of locking abandoned bikes, due to drunk patrons getting rides home from slightly less drunk patrons, inside the metal building at closing time.

Trowa parked his truck next to his motorcycle, which someone had moved back outside the building when Knucklehead's opened. It was parked next to the trike Bear would never ride again. He got out of his truck. Because the Icehouse opened on all four sides, patrons inside saw him. News travels fast in small communities, so everyone knew what had happened to them. Several patrons and Dixie came out to meet him.

The questions started immediately and all at once. Trowa let the questions fly for several seconds.

He held up his hand to silence them. "I'll tell y'all what happened after I load my bike into my truck. Thanks for takin' care of it for me, Dixie."

Dixie smiled, revealing her missing teeth. "You're welcome, sugar. I guess someone'll come for Bear's trike…eventually. There's a Wild Turkey waitin' for ya at the bar. On the house."

Norm and a couple of Knucklehead's regulars, using a folding ramp Trowa kept in the bed of his truck, helped Trowa load his bike and tie it down. After they loaded it, they went into Knucklehead's where a crowd waited at the bar.

No sooner had Trowa taken his first sip of Wild Turkey, Hank grumbled, "So, Cochise, was that young buck, right? Was it werewolves?"

Trowa drained his glass, which Dixie promptly refilled, on the house again. “Yeah. Two of ‘em.”

This news brought a collective gasp from the patrons surrounding Trowa.

A man who Trowa didn’t know, the news about Bear, Mont, and Jack brought new, curious patrons to Knucklehead’s, said, “Horseshit. No such thing as werewolves.”

Norm, who sat next to Trowa, said, “My cousin Billy, he’s a Pine View County deputy, is tight-lipped ‘bout what’s goin’ on, but I know this…they’ve carryin’ silver bullets with ‘em.”

This news brought more gasps and a few more comments of disbelief.

Trowa sat quietly while several patrons argued about the possibility of werewolves roaming the woods of East Texas. After several minutes of arguing, which got heated, Dixie rang the antique firehouse bell mounted next to the register several times. The loud ringing brought a hush to the arguing patrons.

When the Icehouse quieted, except for the humming of the four large box fans that cooled the interior, Dixie said, “Everybody just shut the fuck up. Let Trowa tell what happened to Bear, Mont, Jack, and that kid Saturday night. If ya can’t keep your traps shut, there’s four big fuckin’ exits. Take ‘em.”

Nobody spoke and nobody left.

Trowa drained his second drink and Dixie refilled it. Norm picked up the tab on Trowa’s third Wild Turkey. He started talking. There were occasional gasps and a few derisions but, otherwise, the patrons crowded around Trowa were quiet throughout the hour-long telling. Every time Trowa’s drink was empty, someone volunteered to refill it.

When Trowa finished, the Icehouse remained silent for several moments.

Norm held up his glass. “To Bear, Mont, Jack, and the kid.”

Trowa and Dixie, who were enjoying Smirnoff Vodka on ice, clinked glasses with Norm, while others clinked glasses and beer bottles around them. After the toast, the patrons who were surrounding Trowa dispersed. Some to the pool tables. Others migrated to drinking tables or elsewhere at the bar. Dixie got calls from six different directions with drink requests. This left Trowa, Norm, and Hank together at the bar.

Hank took a big drink of PBR from his oversized mug.

Foam stuck in his unkempt, wiry, white mustache. "Never doubted that young buck. My pappy…"

"Bullshit, old man," Norm scoffed and interrupted.

"Let him speak," Trowa responded.

Hank took another big drink, burped, which caused some of the foam in his mustache to dislodge and fall on the bar like wet snow. "My pap said there were werewolves in these parts in the eighteen hundreds. He called 'em somethin' else…started with an N, some Mexican word, I think. He said they were around. I guess it was only a matter o' time 'fore they came back."

Norm, who looked at Hank with veiled disgust, turned to Trowa. "Ya goin' after 'em? If ya are, I can get a couple of silver bullets from Billy. Even if he doesn't know. If ya get my meanin'."

Trowa got Norm's meaning clearly. He would steal the silver bullets.

He shook his head slowly. "No thanks. I don't want no part of those…fuckers again."

"They killed our friends," Norm implored.

Trowa downed his drink. "You didn't see 'em, paleface. These things are fuckin' huge. They're powerful, quick, and agile. They're made for only one thing…killin'. Let me tell ya, they're damn good at it."

"So…we do nothin'?" Norm asked.

Trowa chuckled. "I'm doin' somethin'. I'm gettin' the fuck outta East Texas. There're trees in Arkansas that need cuttin', too. I think I'll mosey that way 'till things here…sort out."

"If things here don't…sort out?" Norm asked.

Trowa shrugged. "Then, hopefully, we'll meet again on the other side…if there is another side."

Trowa raised his glass to get Dixie's attention.

"Another refill?" Dixie asked when she was in front of Trowa.

"Nope, I'm tappin' out. Just wanna make sure I don't have an unpaid tab."

Dixie smiled a friendly smile that almost made her look pretty. "Nope. You're covered, hun."

Trowa stood up, leaned his lanky body across the bar and kissed Dixie on the forehead, which brought a warm blush to her cheeks and made her look prettier still.

"I'll see ya, Dixie," Trowa said.

He turned and left Knucklehead's Icehouse, his second home, not knowing when or if he'd ever be back.

~ * ~

When Alexis awoke from the post-Dillon encounter nap, she was still in werewolf form, which she became increasingly more comfortable in than in her human form. She slid onto the floor on all fours, arched her back, and stretched. Her claws dug into the carpet and ripped deep gashes through it and the thick padding and into the concrete slab beneath. Her wolf brain didn't care about the damage.

The werewolf stood up and walked through the house, ducking its massive head through each doorway to keep from hitting it. At the back door, it put its deadly clawed hand on the doorknob and paused. It knew going outside in the city limits was a risky venture, but it needed to be clear of distracting scents of soap, shampoo, makeup, toothpaste, perfumes, cleaning products, from within the house, to hone in on the scent it wanted.

It stood at the door, listening with its enhanced hearing for any trace of problem-causing sounds. Nothing out of the ordinary registered. The human part of its brain knew the house was at the end of a cul-de-sac with nothing behind it but woods for several hundred feet, but it didn't trust the inferior human reasoning. Satisfied emerging from the house was safe, it twisted the doorknob and stepped out into the dark backyard.

When it stepped outside, dogs in nearby yards for at least a city block started barking. It issued a low, menacing growl that wouldn't register to human ears and the dogs, after a yelp or two, fell silent. The skin of its long snout snarled up in what was the closest thing to a smile a werewolf could produce.

It sniffed the air, taking in a myriad of scents. Its werewolf brain sorted through them with supernatural speed until it isolated the scent it sought. That of the treed man. The treed man was moving away from the werewolf, but it was unconcerned. It snarl-smiled again and transformed back into human form.

After going back inside her house, Alexis grabbed a T-shirt Seth left there and slipped it over her head. It was big enough to cover her 'parts' if she had to interact with anyone before returning to her wolf form, so she didn't bother putting anything else on. She grabbed two litre size bottles of Dasani and her keys before getting in her truck and heading for the old barn she considered her wolf's den.

~ * ~

Trowa's 'house' was a 1966 Airstream Globetrotter travel trailer. It was small, only nineteen feet from bumper hitch to license plate, but Trowa needed little space. He parked the Airstream at the back of the CP Sawmill. The owner, Charles Preston, let Trowa park his travel trailer on his property. He even provided Trowa with free electricity and water, in exchange for Trowa providing a semblance of security when the sawmill closed. Trowa didn't walk the grounds at night with a flashlight, but his presence offered some deterrence.

Trowa parked next to the Airstream and got out of the truck. He checked the tie-downs to make sure the trip home from Knucklehead's hadn't loosened them. They were still tight. He didn't bother with unloading the bike, which would have been next to impossible to do by himself. Trowa planned to hook up the Airstream in the morning and head to Arkansas, so the bike was where it needed to be.

Before going inside, Trowa retrieved a joint stashed under the motorcycle's saddle. He sat down on the wooden crate that served as the Airstream's step, lit the joint, and took a deep drag, holding the smoke in his lungs for several seconds to let it work its magic. After exhaling, Trowa looked up at the clear night sky and marveled at its beauty. The last quarter moon was a perfect half sphere, but still bright in the ink black sky.

As Trowa raised the joint to his lips to take another drag, a sound from somewhere on the sawmill grounds penetrated the quiet night. Trowa scanned the grounds. There were large stacks of logs and shadows everywhere, which meant there were many places for someone or something to hide. Another sound, much closer and like claws scraping on wood, came from behind a stack of logs to Trowa's left.

Trowa stood up, ready to put his escape plan in action, if needed. After the attack, Trowa fully expected the werewolf to come for him, which motivated his plan to move to Arkansas. Because he knew he'd be in Pine View for a few more days, Trowa scoped out the trees close to his travel trailer and found the perfect candidate to escape to. It stood close, only about ten feet behind the Airstream, and the lowest limbs were a good fifty feet up. He'd even stashed some provisions in the upper branches, in case he was stuck there for the night.

~ * ~

To expedite the climb; Trowa was a quick climber, but he knew he only escaped with his life the last time because the werewolves were busy with each other and other prey, Trowa installed a pulley and counterweight system. He attached a pulley to the tree trunk about seventy feet up. The rope running through the pulley had a loop on one end for Trowa's foot, and he tied it to a large log, about five hundred pounds, on the other end, which acted as the counterweight. Trowa had to use his truck to pull the counterweight up into the treetop. Trowa secured the loop end to the tree by a second loop secured to a railroad spike. Trowa drove it into the tree trunk with a sledgehammer. Once his foot was secure in the bottom loop, all Trowa had to do was cut the second loop and up he'd go.

Escaping created another issue. From inside the Airstream, Trowa had three practical ways out. The door, the ceiling skylight, and the trapdoor in the floor. The door seemed an unlikely avenue of escape. Too exposed. That left the skylight and the trapdoor. Which one Trowa took would depend on how the werewolf, or werewolves, attacked, if they did.

~ * ~

The scraping, clawing sounds continued. As if whatever made them was climbing the stack of logs. Trowa kept his eyes trained in the sound's direction and took a step toward the front of the Airstream. A small, dark shape crested the top log and Trowa let the breath he wasn't aware he had been holding escape with a chuckle. It was a fat raccoon digging for insects in the pine bark. A fat raccoon Trowa was familiar with and named Roscoe.

Trowa raised his arms menacingly and shouted, "Get the fuck outta here, Roscoe."

Roscoe raised his scruffy head, looked at Trowa, and went back to digging for insects. Trowa started to take another drag on the joint, then, deciding being stoned if the werewolf came for him wasn't a good idea, pinched the ember off, stuck the joint behind his right ear, and went inside the Airstream.

~ * ~

Headlights pierced the darkness, and a startled rabbit bolted from the overgrown, winding drive that led to the deteriorating Wiseman barn. As the truck stopped behind the barn, the driver's side door opened, and a werewolf's hind foot touched the ground. Alexis, partially transformed, stepped out of the truck, and shut the door with her still human hand that transformed into a deadly clawed weapon after the door closed with a 'thump.'

In her haste to transform and track the man who escaped in the tree, Alexis forgot to remove the T-shirt she'd been wearing. As the massive werewolf's body took shape, it stretched, ripped, and fell to the ground.

The werewolf took in a deep breath to pick up the treed man's scent. It couldn't detect him. Frustrated, it took in another deep breath and sorted the many odors that flooded its heightened olfactory senses. It picked up the treed man's scent. It was weak and masked in a cloud of pungent marijuana smoke, but it was stationary.

A satisfied, rumbling growl broke the unnatural silence. The werewolf dropped to all fours and sprinted into the dark woods toward the treed man's scent.

~ * ~

It was cramped inside the Airstream. As far as amenities went, at the back end of the trailer, there was an upholstered bench with a small table in front of it. The table post mounted in a flange on the floor and could be removed to unfold the bench into a small bed. There was a small kitchenette beside the door that comprised a sink hooked up to an exterior water source, compact refrigerator, a propane fueled Coleman stove, and a two-door cabinet above the sink for storing dishes and other essentials. Across from the kitchenette was a floor to curved ceiling, Airstreams have rounded tops, pantry and closet that contained groceries and Trowa's clothes. At the front of the Airstream, there was a small bathroom with a chemical toilet and shower, also hooked to an exterior water source.

The only modern amenity in the Airstream was a fifty-inch, Panasonic, flat-screen plasma TV mounted to the ceiling on a folding rack that Trowa welded out of one-inch square tubing. When not in use, or while moving the trailer, he could fold the TV flat, and out of the way, against the Airstream's ceiling. A DirecTV receiver and satellite dish on the roof of the trailer connected the TV to cable.

After trying to scare Roscoe away, and coming inside, Trowa lit the Coleman stove and heated a can of Wolf Brand Chili in a cast-iron pot. Once he heated the chili, Trowa grabbed a reasonably clean spoon from the dirty dishes that collected in the sink's bottom, ran it under the water, grabbed a Budweiser from the fridge, and retreated to the bench to eat the chili from the cast-iron pot.

While he ate, Trowa clicked on the TV and pulled up the guide to find something interesting to watch. Without premium or local channels, Trowa had limited choices. With the guide clock showing it was ten thirteen p.m., he missed the prime-time lineup.

Because he couldn't find anything more to his taste, Trowa settled on watching the ten-p.m. re-broadcast of *Street Outlaw*s on the Discovery Channel. It was usually good for a laugh when they fucked up and wrecked one of their rides.

When *Street Outlaws* broke for commercials, Trowa took the cast-iron pot and spoon to the sink, where he gave them a cursory rinse, and deposited them in the bottom with the other semi-dirty dishes. After crushing the Budweiser can in his hand and dropping it into an overflowing trashcan, Trowa grabbed another beer from the fridge and started back toward the bench. At that moment, something large crashed into the side of the Airstream and knocked Trowa off his feet.

~ * ~

The treed man's scent, stronger mixed with chili and beer, led the werewolf to a vast sawmill filled with towering stacks of logs. It listened and heard motors revving and tires screeching on pavement, but these sounds had a mechanical buzz to them. The human part of its brain knew the sounds were coming from a television. The werewolf moved forward stealthily, using the stacks of logs and shadows to keep it concealed.

As it moved closer to the metallic structure, it smelled the treed man inside. A fat raccoon, engaged in its nightly scavenge for insects, startled when it sensed the dangerous predator so close. The raccoon jumped up, lost its footing, and tumbled from its perch atop the stacked logs. The raccoon bounced down the side of the pyramid of logs and landed with a 'thud' on its side. It raised its scruffy head and looked into the burning red eyes of the werewolf. With a quick, snake-like strike, the werewolf bit the raccoon in half. It swallowed the midsection whole before Roscoe's head and tail sections thudded into the dirt at the werewolf's feet.

Ears forward, listening intently, the werewolf heard a mechanical screech of tires, followed by a crashing sound. It heard mechanical music and the man's footsteps within the trailer. The man was on his feet. The perfect time to attack and knock him over. The werewolf leapt over the stack of logs and launched itself on all fours toward the door side of the metal structure. Just before impact, the werewolf tucked its head and led with its left shoulder.

The impact ripped rivets that held the panels of the stainless-steel structure together loose and opened a large split on the side of the Airstream. The door flew open and every window in the trailer exploded in a shower of glass that sparkled in the moonlight as it scattered. Its momentum of the impact rocked the trailer upward, past the tipping-point, and it crashed onto its side with a metal bending and screeching 'thud.'

The werewolf peered through the opening in the trailer's side and saw the man on his back looking back at it from the other side of the trailer, which was now on the ground. It had him at last. The werewolf growled, exerting its dominance and imparting fear in its prey. The werewolf didn't sense fear coming from the man. It startled him. His heart was hammering in his chest, but with adrenaline, not fear. This infuriated the werewolf, and it reached its arm through the opening in the siding to grab him.

~ * ~

The initial impact knocked Trowa off his feet and sent him sprawling to the floor. He saw the side of the Airstream split open from the force of the collision and the dark, coarse hair of the werewolf filled the opening. The windows exploded and showered Trowa in pointed, jagged shards of glass. The Airstream's construction predated the mandated safety glass. He quickly covered his face. Not before receiving several cuts to his scalp, hands, and arms. None of which were serious.

After the initial shock of the brazen and forceful attack wore off, which had been quick, Trowa remembered his escape plan. He put it in motion. The door and the skylight were out. Accessing those would take him too close to the deadly werewolf.

Trapdoor, Trowa thought.

As he reached for it, the trailer tipped over. When the Airstream crashed onto its side, Trowa found the roof replaced with the side of the trailer and a furious werewolf was peering through the split at him. Its red eyes flared like the fires of hell, and it issued a growl that rattled everything inside the trailer. Including Trowa.

Trowa looked at the trapdoor, which no longer provided access to the ground but to the side of the trailer where the door had, seconds earlier, been. The impact and roll bounced the trapdoor opened and Trowa had quick, unobstructed access to it.

Trowa did not know if he could make it through the trapdoor and to the tree before the werewolf caught him, but it would kill him if he did nothing. He looked up at the werewolf and grinned. Trowa saw its eyes flash an angrier red, and he jumped for the trapdoor. Just as Trowa jumped, he saw the werewolf's long arm reach into the Airstream.

Trowa's head and torso made it through the trapdoor, but the werewolf's powerful, clawed hand grabbed his right ankle before he could wiggle completely through. Pain erupted in Trowa's ankle as the werewolf sank its razor-sharp claws into his flesh. Trowa tried to kick free, but the werewolf had too strong of a grip. It pulled Trowa back into the trailer.

When Trowa was back inside the trailer, he hung upside down by his ankle in the werewolf's powerful grip. It used its other hand to rip the slit in the trailer's side wider and stuck its head through the opening and opened its bear trap like mouth wide. Hot drool dripped from between its dagger length teeth onto Trowa's upturned face. It pulled Trowa's foot toward its opened mouth.

For the first time since the attack began, Trowa felt panicked. His hands and forearms were resting on the other side of the overturned trailer as he looked down quickly. He needed a weapon. Trowa knew he couldn't kill it, but if he could hurt it, he might still live to see another sunrise. He saw a large butcher knife in the sink on his left within reach. As Trowa's left hand closed around the knife's handle, he felt the werewolf's hot, wet tongue wrap around his right foot. Its pointed teeth sank into his flesh and white-hot pain radiated throughout Trowa's body.

With adrenaline induced strength and quickness, Trowa used his core muscles to bend upward, and he sank the six-inch butcher knife hilt deep in the werewolf's right eye.

Although the movement was quick and fluid, the visual played out in slow-motion from Trowa's perspective. He saw the shiny tip of the butcher's knife plunging toward the werewolf's fiery red eye and, just before the tip punctured it, he saw the werewolf's eye widen in surprise. He heard an audible 'pop' when the pointed tip penetrated its hellish orb and a satisfying scraping sound as the blade dug into the bones of its orbital socket. Blood and other fluids gushed from the werewolf's deflated eye.

The werewolf's reaction did not play out in slow-motion. It yelped so loud that Trowa heard nearby glass shatter. Trowa thought the shattering glass came from his truck. The werewolf flung him into the side, now the roof of the trailer, hard enough to knock the wind from his lungs. The werewolf shook its head violently, sending blood and drool throughout the Airstream's interior, and reached for the knife handle still protruding from its eye socket.

Though gasping for breath, Trowa knew he needed to take advantage of the distracted werewolf's attempt to remove the knife. He lunged for the trapdoor again, but his shredded right foot betrayed him. He landed with another wind stealing 'thud' on his chest across the trapdoor opening.

It took every bit of strength Trowa had left, but he wiggled through the trapdoor landing on his back. When he looked up from the prone position, he could see the werewolf standing on the top, then the side of the Airstream, still convulsing its head. Trowa got to his feet and, as quickly as his injured right foot would allow, made his way to the escape tree.

When he got to the tree, he put his left foot in the bottom loop and looked back at the werewolf just in time to see it yank the knife from its eye and sling it to the side. He heard a 'pop' and a 'hiss' when the knife ended its flight. Trowa looked in the direction it threw the knife and saw it sticking out of the back tire of his Indian.

This shit just gets better and better, Trowa thought.

A menacing growl and the sound of his Airstream being shredded brought Trowa's attention back to the werewolf. Its head and shoulders were inside the overturned trailer. Trowa realized the beast didn't know he'd escaped. He reached into his pocket for the lock-blade, Buck 110 knife he always carried, but the pocket was empty.

Thinking the knife might have fallen from his pocket while the werewolf dangled him upside down, Trowa panicked. He checked his other pockets. No knife. The werewolf pulled its head from the trailer and looked around. It sniffed the air and then it's one burning eye landed on

Trowa. Resigned to the fact he was about to travel far beyond Arkansas, Trowa leaned his head against the tree. He felt cold steel behind his head.

At the feel of the cold steel, his thoughts cleared, and he remembered he'd left the Buck knife sticking in the tree trunk by the loop fastened around the railroad spike. Without taking his eyes off the werewolf, Trowa grabbed the knife and sliced through the second loop. Trowa ascended quickly. The werewolf lunged toward him.

I'm not fuckin' high enough. Trowa thought.

~ * ~

Paige lay in bed with the lights off, trapped in the gray area between sleep and being awake. She felt exhausted, emotionally as well as physically, but she couldn't turn her mind off. She kept replaying the day's events over and over.

She spent her time at school being asked questions about the 'MRB Massacre' she didn't want to answer. Thanks to her heightened senses, overhearing whispered conversations, many of which were about what she and Justin were doing away from the barn, the rumor mill ran on all cylinders.

After school let out, as promised, Paige dropped by Lindsey's house. This went about as well as school. Lindsey's parents were emotional wrecks. Mrs. Anderson sat quietly on the couch staring at her hands, which were clasped in her lap, sobbing on and off the entire time Paige stayed there. She let out an occasional moan that hurt Paige's heart.

Mr. Anderson was in the backyard drinking beer and, from the plethora of beer cans scattered around his lawn chair, he'd been at it for a while. Between complaining about being stuck at home, intermittent tears for her deceased brother and her deceased crush, Matt, Lin confirmed her dad had been drinking steadily since the previous morning.

When Paige finally left the Anderson's house, after promising Lin she'd come back the next day after school, she felt worse than she had since the werewolf killed Justin. After spending so much time at Lin's, Paige didn't go to see her dad as she'd planned and told him she'd do. She sent him a quick text that she was going to her mom's and drove to her weekday home.

At her mother's house, Paige turned down dinner, saying she wasn't feeling well, which was true. She went upstairs, did her homework, and turned in early. Only to find sleep just out of reach.

Hoping a position change might help her relax and fall asleep, Paige rolled onto her back and looked up at the ceiling. The ceiling fan, on low speed, rotated slowly. Paige followed a single blade with her eyes, hoping to be lulled to sleep by its rhythmic motion. Her eyelids drooped. It was working.

Just as Paige's eyelids closed and she began sinking into comfortable darkness, a stabbing pain erupted in her right eye. Paige cried out in pain and cupped her hands over the assaulted eye. It had only been then she realized the pain wasn't hers. It belonged to the alpha. So did the rage Paige felt radiating from within her head.

With her wits returned, and confident her eye wasn't damaged, Paige grabbed her cellphone from the nightstand and fired off a text to her dad, 'She's hurt and angry! I think she's gonna kill someone!'

The transparent text bubble with little moving dots popped up immediately.

A few seconds later, Paige read, 'Who? Where? Can you see?'

Paige concentrated and tried to connect with the alpha, but its rage was like an impenetrable red wall. She pushed again and felt her perspective shift. Suddenly, Paige was looking out through the alpha's eyes. Not eyes. Eye. The right side of its vision was dark. Paige saw a man she recognized standing next to a tree with his foot in a rope loop. The man cut another loop and ascended the tree quickly. Paige felt the alpha lunge toward the man. She knew the man wasn't high enough to escape the powerful werewolf's leap and, because she did not want to witness, or partake in his death, Paige pushed away from the mental link. Just before Paige's perspective shifted back to her bedroom, she saw the alpha's deadly clawed hand reaching for the man's foot. His bitten foot.

The perspective shift back into her existence, coupled with the sick feeling she got from knowing the man by the tree with his foot in a rope loop was probably dead, made Paige retch. Having not eaten, it was a dry heave.

Glad I didn't eat, or I'd be seein' it again, Paige thought.

Paige looked down at her cellphone. Through blurry eyes, the retch made her eyes water, she saw her dad texted her while she had been…away.

He's texted, 'Anything?'

Paige's thumbs moved with lightning speed, and she texted, 'It's

Mr. raintree! She's there! I think she killed him!'

The little moving dots appeared then, 'I'm on it. Stay put. I'll text you when I know something.'

Paige quickly texted back, 'B careful!'

Then, remembering something important, Paige texted, 'If he's still alive when u get there, she bit him.'

No moving dots; no reply.

~ * ~

Deputy Foster Timpson parked along a stretch of Highway Sixty-Nine with his radar on, and no intention of writing a ticket. Unless someone blew by at a hundred miles an hour or more. His shift was almost over, and he didn't need the hassle. Besides, he found it entertaining enough watching the vehicles break hard when they saw his patrol SUV. Then crawl by at five or ten miles an hour below the posted seventy-five speed limit.

Needing a little jolt to get through the rest of his shift, Foster plucked a can of Skoal from his breast pocket and pinched a large dip into his bottom lip. His girlfriend hated the dipping and spitting, so he partook often while on duty.

As he reached for the spit cup, a Sonic cup, left over from supper, with a napkin in the bottom to absorb the spit in case of a spill, Eva Martinez's voice cracked over the radio. "Reported disturbance at the CP Sawmill."

Because Foster dropped Trowa Raintree there on Saturday night, end of shift or not, he was interested. Foster keyed the shoulder-mounted microphone. "Did ya say the disturbance call came from the CP Sawmill?"

"Negative. The call came from a Miss Tracy Beck who lives across the street from the CP Sawmill," Eva's voice cracked over the radio.

"Nature of disturbance?"

"Loud crashing noises and…possibly dog fightin'."

Dog fightin'? Foster thought.

He keyed the microphone. "I'm only a few minutes away, and I was there Saturday night. I got it."

"Ten-four," Eva's voice cracked back.

Foster switched on the lights and siren. His favorite part of the job was rolling in 'loud and proud.' He kicked up dirt as he floored the accelerator and sped toward the CP Sawmill.

~ * ~

The counterweight worked, but not fast enough. Trowa was only about twenty feet up the tree when the angry werewolf lunged toward him. Given what he saw the werewolf do Saturday night, leap about thirty feet into the air, that when it started the leap from an elevated position atop the overturned Airstream, Trowa felt sure he was seconds away from a brutal death. It didn't play out that way, though.

When the werewolf kicked off the Airstream with all its considerable strength, its hind feet, unable to find purchase on the smooth stainless-steel siding, slipped backward and robbed it of much needed momentum. Its powerful front claws ripped jagged gashes in the stainless-steel siding, which helped propel it up and forward, though. It reached out for Trowa's wounded foot. The counterweight kept pulling him up and the claws missed his foot by only an inch, maybe two.

The werewolf crashed into the tree trunk with enough force to shake a couple of dozen pinecones loose, which rained down on Trowa. It hit the ground on its back with another tree rattling 'thud' where it stayed looking up at Trowa with its one fiery, red eye.

The ascending Trowa watched with amusement as the five-hundred-pound counterweight log descended toward the prone werewolf. Trowa knew it was falling directly on the creature and he fully expected it to avoid the log. Whether disoriented by the collision with the tree, the subsequent fall, lacking depth perception with only one working eye, the counterweight being in its missing eye blind spot, that it had tunnel vision for Trowa only, or all four possibilities, it didn't move out of the way. The counterweight smashed down on the werewolf's midsection with a sickening 'thud.'

When the counterweight smashed down on the werewolf. It let out a pain-filled howl that made the hairs on Trowa's neck prickle and sent wildlife scattering for a five-mile radius.

The counterweight did its job and then some. Trowa hadn't counted on the bonus of squashing the werewolf. Trowa looked down at the werewolf fifty feet below and saw its massive, clawed hands grab the ends of the log. Trowa was safe amid the lowest limbs. He removed his foot from the loop and straddled a large limb just in time.

Trowa watched with respect for the werewolf's inconceivable strength as it lifted the five-hundred-pound log from its midsection and tossed it aside like a paper-mâché log. Unlike paper-mâché, the log crashed into the already destroyed Airstream, took out the satellite dish, and crushed the weakened stainless-steel body beneath its weight.

The rope tied to the counterweight stretched past its breaking point and snapped. The loose rope slid through the pulley and fell to the ground beside the werewolf that was getting slowly to its feet. If Trowa had still been standing in the rope loop, he would have plummeted to the ground to be killed by the fall or the angry werewolf. At this realization, and that he removed his foot from the rope loop only seconds before the werewolf tossed the log, which severed the rope, cold chills ran through Trowa's nervous system.

Although he was safely in the tree, Trowa still had some climbing to do to get to his stash. He put weight on his right foot, and it surprised him to feel the pain subsided. He accredited the pain relief to adrenaline. He started climbing.

After climbing about thirty feet, Trowa found the safety belt he'd installed the day before. The safety belt was just a loop of rope tied around the trunk. Trowa stuck his head and arms through the loop. He dropped his arms so the rope was secure across his chest and under his armpits. It wasn't much, but it would keep the werewolf from shaking him from the tree or keep him from toppling out if he fell asleep. Trowa didn't think either scenario likely, especially falling asleep, but better safe than sorry.

By the time Trowa was securely in his spot, the werewolf regained its feet, and it was looking up at him like a treed cat. Trowa couldn't be sure, but he thought he saw a faint red glow, like a dying ember, in the werewolf's empty eye socket.

A flash of light caught Trowa's attention, and he looked south from where it came. He couldn't hear the siren yet but, from seventy feet up, he could see the unmistakable red and blue law enforcement lights headed in his direction. Trowa looked down at the werewolf and saw its enormous head tracking the advancing vehicle's movement. Since the werewolf couldn't see the lights from the base of the tree, Trowa reasoned the werewolf tracked the vehicle's approach with its keen hearing.

As the advancing vehicle cleared a small hill about a mile away, Trowa finally heard the sirens. When it pulled into the CP Sawmill's drive, Trowa looked down at the werewolf. Part of Trowa expected the werewolf to be gone. It wasn't gone. It looked up at Trowa and he clearly saw a faint, red glow, brighter than before, burning in its once empty eye socket.

Trowa could only take what the werewolf did next one way. Its whiskered upper snout pulled up and back, revealing its porcelain white dagger teeth in a demonic smile. It growled and leapt behind the stack of logs Trowa saw Roscoe digging for dinner on earlier. The werewolf planned an ambush.

Trowa quickly checked his pockets for his cellphone so he could call in a warning. It wasn't on him. Trowa didn't know, but his cellphone slipped from his back pocket when the werewolf dangled him by his feet and was with all the other dislocated items on the bottom, side, of the Airstream.

As the patrol SUV entered the yard, Trowa saw the windshield post mounted spotlight flare into life. Helpless to do anything more than shout a warning to whoever drove the SUV when it was close enough, Trowa watched the SUV maneuver slowly through the stacks of logs toward the back of the yard. He glanced toward where the werewolf was hiding in the shadows. Two burning orbs looked back at Trowa. It was toying with him.

~ * ~

After arriving at the CP Sawmill, Foster turned off the siren and emergency lights. The gate leading into the sawmill was ajar. Foster used the bumper guard on the front of the SUV to push it the rest of the way open and drove into the sawmill grounds. He lowered the window to listen for the sounds that prompted the disturbance call. Crashing noises and dog fighting. The grounds were eerily silent.

The solitary light on the grounds came from a 'Dusk 'Til Dawn' light mounted on a pole by the sawmill structure that only illuminated a small area beneath it. Foster turned on the windshield post mounted spotlight, started scanning the areas to the sides of the SUV, and beyond the reach of the headlight beams in front as he slowly drove deeper into the sawmill grounds.

Having dropped Trowa Raintree off at his travel trailer the previous Saturday night, Foster knew where to find it and he maneuvered between the large stacks of logs in that direction.

As he neared the back of the sawmill grounds, he heard a voice yell, "Go back."

The travel trailer was still out of sight, but Foster scanned the log stacks, searching for the source of the voice. He couldn't see anyone. He continued forward.

The voice, a little louder, closer than before, yelled, "Go back. It's here."

Foster stopped the SUV, stuck his head out of the window, and shouted, "Show yourself."

The voice yelled, "Up here, Deputy. In the trees."

Foster pointed the spotlight upward and scanned the trees at the back of the sawmill grounds. After lighting up several empty treetops, the spotlight beam revealed Trowa Raintree waving his arms from atop a large pine tree.

Foster chuckled and said to himself, "Crazy fuckin' Indian."

Foster drove toward the back of the sawmill grounds while Trowa continued to shout, "Go back."

As Foster rounded a final stack of logs, the SUV headlights fell on what remained of Trowa's travel trailer.

"What the fuck?" Foster muttered before stopping the SUV.

Trowa shouted, "It's here. Go back. Get the fuck outta here."

Foster, still not believing in the werewolf nonsense that infiltrated the sheriff's department, trained the spotlight on Trowa, and stepped out of the SUV.

Trowa pointed to a stack of logs to Foster's right and shouted, "It's behind those logs, Deputy. Get the fuck outta here."

Foster looked toward the stack of logs. He saw nothing.

He looked back up at Trowa. "What happened here, Mister Raintree?"

"It's right fuckin' there. Leave. NOW."

Foster looked back at the stack of logs about thirty feet away. A low, menacing growl rumbled from behind it.

"*LEAVE.*" Trowa screamed.

Foster grabbed the spotlight and quickly positioned its beam on the stack of logs.

He drew his service pistol, trained it on the stack of logs, and shouted, "Show yourself."

Another menacing growl, louder than the first one, cut through the unnaturally quiet night.

Foster moved his finger from the trigger guard to the trigger and, again, shouted, "Show yourself."

It did.

The first thing Foster saw were two pointed ears as they crested the top log. Then its glowing red eyes and elongated, viscous snout emerged. Foster's gun hand started shaking, but he didn't shoot. Law enforcement training stressed double tap center mass when shooting someone. Foster wanted a larger target. Two enormous, deadly, clawed hands gripped the top log and sank into the log's bark. Then, in one fluid movement, the monstrous werewolf leapt onto the top log and looked down at Foster.

Foster looked up at the living nightmare.

Part of Foster's tortured mind heard Trowa scream, "*RUN*."

His legs felt too heavy to move—like he was waist deep in concrete. As the werewolf lunged for him, Foster started firing.

Fuck the double tap, Forster's mind screamed.

In the short time it took for the werewolf to travel the distance between the stacked logs and Foster, he emptied the clip. Although every shot had been a hit, he saw the rounds penetrate its flesh. It did not affect the beast in the least.

The werewolf landed on Foster with bone crushing, the femurs, tibias, fibulas in both legs, and his pelvis shattered, force. Foster cried out as the white, hot pain of so many broken bones erupted throughout his body like a white-hot heat. The werewolf stood over Foster's crumpled body and growled down at him. Foster pissed and shit himself. It grabbed Foster by the neck, lifted him like a rag doll, and body slammed him onto the SUV's hood, which knocked the air from his lungs, crushed several ribs, shattered vertebra in his back, and crumpled the hood under the impact.

Foster, unable to breathe, gasped for breath. As if trying to help Foster get air to his lungs, the werewolf raked its claws across his chest. The razor-sharp claws easily ripped through Foster's Kevlar vest and dug deep into his chest. A coppery taste touched Foster's tongue, and blood erupted from his mouth.

The werewolf grabbed the top of Foster's head with one of its hands, the claws sliced into his scalp, and lifted him from the SUV.

Foster's vision was fading, and the pain subsided. He knew he was dying. The werewolf bent Foster's neck painfully to one side, opened its massive jaws, and wrapped them around his neck.

As the werewolf bit down, Foster thought, *I should'a took the silver bullets*.

No pain. Just the internal sound of crunching neck vertebrae. Foster's vision went dark, and he was no more.

~ * ~

From his safe perch in the pine tree, Trowa watched the werewolf attack and decapitate the deputy who, once he got out of the SUV, he recognized as the deputy who brought him home after the Saturday night attack. Deputy Timpson.

On the ride home that night, Timpson clarified he wasn't buying into the werewolf hysteria.

"No such fuckin' things," Timpson told Trowa.

Do you believe now? Trowa thought.

After biting the deputy's head off, the werewolf looked up at Trowa as if to say, "You're next."

It let out a growl Trowa felt in his bones and hurled the deputy's severed head at him. It had the range and height. Thankfully for Trowa, its aim was off, and the head sailed through the branches to Trowa's right, disappearing into the dark forest beyond.

Under normal circumstances, taunting a werewolf wouldn't be wise. Trowa felt relatively safe in the tree and couldn't help himself.

He looked down at the werewolf and shouted, "Ya missed me, bitch."

In response, the werewolf bolted toward the tree, leapt up on the crumpled Airstream, and launched itself up the tree. It had been a better effort than the first attempt when its hind feet slipped on the stainless-steel Airstream skin, but it still only leaped about thirty feet up, well below the lowest tree limbs. It landed with a 'thud' and a frustrated growl.

The werewolf looked up at Trowa, its eyes burning bright red. Suddenly, it jerked its head in the direction the deputy came. It sniffed the air.

Trowa looked in the direction and saw red and blue flashing lights headed his direction.

Not again, Trowa thought.

A loud growl brought Trowa's attention back to the werewolf. It looked up at him and howled. The unholy sound of fingernails on the chalkboard of Trowa's soul. Trowa's hair prickled, goose bumps broke out on his flesh, and he broke out in a cold sweat.

The werewolf took a viscous swipe at the tree, which shook it and sent bark flying. Trowa felt the werewolf's rage deep inside his mind. Like a tiny claw scratching his brain. It looked up at Trowa, its eyes flared bright red, and it leapt the nine-foot, chain-link with six strands of barbed wire on top fence before disappearing into the dark forest as the siren drew near.

When Trowa looked up, the Pine View County Sheriff Department SUV pulled into the CP Sawmill yard.

"It's fuckin' hidin' again," Trowa muttered.

~ * ~

Garrett pulled into the CP Sawmill yard, lowered the window, turned off the lights and siren, and turned on the windshield post mounted spotlight. Unlike Foster, Garrett didn't know where Trowa's travel trailer was on the property, but he could see another spotlight beam illuminating a stack of logs toward the back of the grounds. Garrett headed for the light.

As Garrett got closer to the light source, he heard Trowa yelling, "Go back. It's here. Go back."

Garrett knew it was there and continued toward the light. When Garrett pulled around the last stack of logs that separated his SUV from the light source, his fears were confirmed. Foster's body was lying on the ground next to his patrol SUV. Garrett pulled up next to Foster's SUV and got out of his.

Trowa was frantically yelling, "It's hidin' in the woods. Get the fuck outta here, Sheriff."

Garrett could tell, from Trowa's voice, he'd climbed a tree again. He scanned the treetops with the spotlight and found Trowa waving his arms and still shouting for him to leave.

"It's gone, Mister Raintree. You can come down now."

Trowa pointed at the dark forest behind him. "The fuck it is. It's hidin' in the woods to ambush ya the way it ambushed your deputy."

Garrett looked at Foster's body. He was close enough to see Foster's head missing from his body. He thought, *Fuck. You should'a took the silver bullets, Foster.*

Ignoring Trowa's continued protests, Garrett keyed the shoulder mounted microphone. "Deputy down at the CP Sawmill."

After a brief pause, Karen Parker, sounding shocked, said, "Down?"

Garrett keyed the microphone. "Down. I need Ty and George Krats on sight."

"Ten-four, Sheriff."

Garrett looked back up at Trowa. "It's gone, Mister Raintree. Come down and tell me what happened."

Trowa shook his head quickly, causing his long black hair to fly around his face. "No fuckin' way, Sheriff. Not until the fuckin' Marines show up and blast that fuckin' thing back to hell."

"It's gone." Garrett shouted.

"How do ya know it's fuckin' gone? You can't know that. You might be pretty sure it's gone. Pretty sure, like close, only works with horseshoes and grenades. If ya got a grenade, I'll think 'bout comin' down. If you're bettin' on a lucky horseshoe, you're on your own, paleface."

Despite the dead deputy at his feet, Garrett chuckled at this. "Listen. What do ya hear?"

Trowa cocked his head and then said, "Nothin'."

"Yeah, but it's the normal nothin'. Crickets, frogs, and other critters. What did ya hear when it was here?"

Even from eighty feet down and a good twenty feet away from the base of the tree, Garrett could see understanding flood over Trowa's face.

Trowa looked down at Garrett. "It was really fuckin' quiet when that fucker was here. Unnaturally quiet."

Garrett nodded. "Ya know it's gone on another level, too."

"What level?" Trowa asked, but he could sense, deep in his mind, it was gone.

"Ya got bit. That…connects ya to it."

Trowa looked shocked Garrett would know this. "How do ya know it bit me? You can't see that from there."

"Come on down and I'll tell ya what I know."

Trowa started climbing down the tree.

When Trowa was back on the ground, Garrett told him everything he knew about the werewolves. Trowa listened in silence and only interrupted when Garrett referred to the alpha as 'she.'

"That's a fuckin' girl?" Trowa asked in disbelief.

Garrett nodded.

When Garrett told him about the sped-up healing. Trowa stomped his right foot on the ground, then looked at it. "I thought it was just the adrenaline maskin' the pain. It's fuckin' healin', ain't it?"

Garrett nodded again and continued with the unbelievable information.

After Garrett finished, Trowa said, "So why'd it run off when you got here, but not the deputy?"

Garrett ejected the clip from his gun and thumbed two silver bullets into the palm of his hand. "'Cause I have these, and it knows I have 'em from when I shot it through the ear. It probably smelled me comin' and got the fuck outta Dodge."

At hearing this, Trowa remembered the way the werewolf sniffed the air, when the sheriff's SUV approached, before jumping the fence and disappearing into the forest.

Trowa looked at the bullets. "So, silver really works on the fuckers?"

Garrett nodded. "You got a gun?"

Trowa looked at Garrett suspiciously.

Garrett read the look correctly. "I don't give a shit how ya got it or if it's even fuckin' legal. Do ya have a gun?"

Trowa nodded. "Yeah, I got a Beretta nine mil."

Garrett handed the two silver bullets to Trowa. "That's all I can spare for now. I'll get ya more later."

Trowa took the bullets. "I was thinkin' 'bout blowin' East Texas and headin' for Arkansas tomorrow."

He looked at what remained of his Airstream. "I guess things have changed. If what ya said is true 'bout me turnin' into one of those fuckin' things on the next full moon, I don't wanna start killin' people in Arkansas…or start another fuckin' pack. I think I best stay and help ya kill that bitch before it happens."

Garrett smiled. "We could use the help."

Trowa smiled back. "So…ya gonna deputize me?"

"Why the fuck not? Raise your right hand."

After deputizing Trowa, they heard an approaching siren in the distance.

"That'll be Deputy Jackson," Garrett said.

"He got bit, too. Him and your daughter?"

Garrett nodded.

"He killed one fucker, too?"

Garrett nodded again.

Before Ty arrived, Garrett excused himself from Trowa's company, walked back to his SUV, and took out his cellphone.

He accessed the text thread from the earlier texting with Paige and typed, 'Trowa was bit and he's alive. I told him everything. He wants to help us kill it.'

Almost immediately after Garrett sent the text, the little blue dots popped up and seconds later Paige responded, 'I think he can help. Luv u!'

Garrett typed, 'I love you, too.'

Thinking the conversation ended, Garrett put the cellphone back in his chest pocket and started back toward Trowa, who was looking at Foster's headless body. Ty's siren was close. His cellphone dinged.

Garrett took it back out and read, 'The werewolf is gone but she's not, daddy. I got a flash. She's in the woods with someone's head. I think its deputy Fosters. She's happy. And disgusting!'

~ * ~

After leaping the fence, the werewolf followed its nose to the deputy's head it hurled at the frustrating treed man. To bring the nighttime forest back to life and mask its presence, it transformed back into its human form.

Alexis picked up the head and looked into its startled, dead eyes. She brought it close to her face and kissed its lips. Alexis bit the lower lip hard. He would not complain and ripped off a piece of flesh, which she swallowed.

The sheriff and the treed man were shouting at each other in the distance. Without wolf's ears, Alexis couldn't quite make out what they were saying, but she didn't care. That she failed to kill the treed man for a second time disturbed Alexis. At least he was hers now or would be when the June moon was full. That brought her some satisfaction.

Alexis took another bite out of Deputy Foster's bottom lip. The coppery taste of blood on her human tongue tasted alluring. She placed Deputy Foster's head on the ground, face up, squatted, and started grinding on it. She had to hold the head in place with fistfuls of its hair. He would not complain about that either, to keep it from squirting away.

The method worked. Alexis climaxed and pulled the head from between her legs. She kissed its lips again and relished the cocktail blend of the head's blood and her juices.

Alexis dropped the head and thought, *Did you enjoy that, little bitch? You did, didn't you? I know you're here, you little bitch. Now that I know, I will fuck your mind every chance I get. After your turn, you're going to get wolf fucked...raped by my entire pack. Even your sweet daddy will wolf rape you, if I turn him. He won't be able to resist your wolf's tight snatch. Or I might kill him instead. Which would you prefer? Dead Daddy or wolf rape Daddy?*

~ * ~

The flash into the alpha's came to Paige quickly. She could see through its…her eyes and feel and taste what she felt and tasted. The head she recognized as one of her dad's deputies. Foster Timpson. The coppery flavor of blood from the bitten lip tasted good to Paige, and that made her feel sick to her stomach. What she did with the head felt good to Paige, and that disgusted her beyond description. When she spoke to Paige inside her head, Paige experienced fear and pure evil on an incomprehensible level. The fear came from the alpha starting the connection on purpose and how she might use this to her advantage. The pure evil came from the plans she had for Paige.

After she asked the last question though, Paige's mind shouted, *I'd prefer your fuckin' head on the wall, you fucked up bitch.*

She ended the connection before Paige could send it, though.

She texted her dad to let him know she was in the woods.

~ * ~

Pleased with herself and knowing the little bitch would text her daddy about their mental conversation, not what she conveyed, but that it happened, Alexis changed back into her werewolf.

Before it sprinted away, it heard the sheriff shout, "She's still in the woods."

It howled and disappeared into the thick, dark forest.

~ * ~

Ty's patrol SUV pulled up next to Garrett's, and he got out.

Garrett shouted, "She's still in the woods."

He took off running toward the back fence. Ty and Trowa followed. Before they got to the fence, the werewolf let out a howl that stopped them in their tracks.

Garrett looked at Trowa. "Is there a hole in the fence we can get through?"

Trowa nodded and pointed to Garrett's left. "Yeah. There's a hole I've been meanin' to fix about thirty yards up the fence line. We'll never catch it."

"We have to try," Garrett responded.

Ty, the voice of reason, said, "He's right, Garrett. We'll never catch it. That's its domain. That howl was just to fuck with us."

Garrett knew they were right, but he needed to kill the bitch for Paige. He realized both men with him had a similar incentive for killing the bitch and they knew it was hopeless. That night.

"We'll get her, Garrett. Not tonight, but we'll get her," Ty said.

Garrett nodded. "Yeah, okay. Y'all are right."

To Trowa, Ty said, "Fill me in on what happened tonight. I know she bit ya, but the rest is…fuzzy."

Trowa finished filling Ty in as the coroner's van pulled up.

George stepped out of the van and stretched his back. "This shit has got to stop. I need my fuckin' eight hours."

"It's one of ours, George. Deputy Timpson," Garrett told him.

George shook his head. "Well, crap on a cracker. Sorry to hear that. He was a nice guy."

Garrett nodded in agreement and pointed toward the farthest of the three SUVs. "His body's over there. Ty and I are gonna look for his head."

"His fuckin' head's missin'?"

Garrett nodded.

"It's gonna be another long fuckin' night, Garrett," George said as Garrett turned and walked away with Ty.

Chapter Fifteen

Tuesday through Friday of that week were a blur of one funeral service after another. Twenty-one in all. Starting with Russ Lomax's funeral Tuesday morning, delayed because his daughter, Margaret Lomax-Carter, needed time to get her affairs in order before she could attend to her dad's affairs, and ending with Deputy Foster Timpson's funeral Friday afternoon. The morgue shipped Carla Weaver's cremated remains to her daughter without a service.

~ * ~

Seth Daniels and Cole Duncan's services were not two of the twenty-one funerals. The morgue shipped their remains home. Cole, identified from fingerprints, departed the Pine View County Morgue on Tuesday and Seth got his ride home on Wednesday after his father, Spencer Daniels, drove down from Dallas to identify his son's remains. Garrett met with Spencer, but the man had been too grief stricken to answer many questions. This suited Garrett just fine.

Before they departed, Emily Yost, after speaking with George Krats, paid a visit to the Pine View County Morgue on Tuesday morning and inspected their bodies. Aside from their grievous wounds, she didn't detect any anomalies in their physiology. She took samples of their blood, epidermis, and hair to inspect later, but these were normal, too. All traces of their having been werewolves evaporated with their deaths. A live subject would have been ideal, but Garrett kept Ty, Paige, and Trowa's condition from her.

~ * ~

Garrett attended all twenty-one funerals in both an official capacity and as a support for Paige where her classmates were concerned. Especially Justin's funeral on Thursday afternoon. The only thing that made Garrett's attending all the services possible had been several services included more than one deceased. Services for students who shared a religious denomination were conducted together. The parents agreed to the multiple services and the extra support seemed to help. This covered twelve of the fifteen student funeral services in three services on three successive days, from Tuesday through Thursday. The largest of services had been the Pine View First Baptist Church service, which included five students, on Wednesday afternoon.

Mont and Jack Lee and Lewis 'Bear' Campton's services were held together too and took place at Knucklehead's Icehouse on Friday morning. It took eight big, burly bikers to lift each of the Lee brother's caskets and six to lift Bear's.

Trowa attended his friend's funerals, but he avoided Garrett. Garrett assumed Trowa needed to keep his distance to keep 'street cred' with his fellow bikers and didn't take the slight personally. He had an important, albeit brief, conversation with him before leaving. After the services, the deceased received a twenty-one-rev salute. Twenty-one revving motorcycles' engines. It sounded like a tractor pull. Garrett left shortly thereafter when the alcohol started flowing. He had two more funerals to attend.

The only student funeral held on Friday had been for Maggie Crawford. The sudden influx of clientele overwhelmed the Pine View Funeral Parlor, the only such establishment in Pine View. Twenty-one funerals were about the number of deceased it dealt with in an average year, not a week. Doug 'Digger,' an appropriate nickname for a man who buried people for a living, Stephens, the owner, and only licensed mortician on staff, had to borrow four morticians and four beauticians from neighboring cities to help with the workload.

The issue where Maggie Crawford had been concerned was Arleen, Maggie's mother, who wanted an open casket service. Normally, this wasn't an issue. Mortician's wax could fill lacerations and be seamlessly covered by a skilled beautician and makeup artist, which Digger's wife, Josephine Stephens, was. Even decapitations, of which there were several that week, could be presentable with some wax, makeup, and a high neck shirt. Maggie's remains were burned badly when she had been thrown into the MRB bonfire, though.

Josephine and the additional beauticians tried for several days, between attending to the other clients, to make Maggie's remains presentable. A wig, wax, and makeup weren't enough to cover the damage. Unfortunately, and against Digger's sound advice, Arleen insisted on seeing Maggie's remains before agreeing to a closed casket service. When Arleen saw her daughter's burned and patched remains, she screamed, vomited on Maggie's body, and fainted. This delayed Maggie's funeral until Friday afternoon, shortly before Deputy Foster Timpson's funeral.

Through it all, Garrett fielded hundreds of questions from frightened citizens, and grieving family members. He received quite a few scornful looks and barbed insults, too. Garrett took these with a grain of salt. He didn't blame them for blaming him. Garrett received a face slap as well. Garrett answered the questions as best he could with half-truths and deflections. He got pretty good at being evasive. Garrett told them he and his department were following up on every lead. True. That they were sorting through all the evidence. Also, true.

Aside from the pain Garrett experienced watching Paige deal with the loss of her friends and Justin, the most taxing service was Deputy Foster Timpson's. Foster's stubbornness, as evidenced by his refusal to take the silver bullets, had led to his death. He had been a good deputy and a better man. Foster started at the Pine View County Sheriff Department as a full-time deputy shortly after Garrett's hire. They learned law enforcement work together and shared more than a few beers over the years. At the end of the graveside service, Garrett presented Foster's grieving parents with the folded flag from their son's casket. A twenty-one-gun salute followed the flag presentation. Three successive shots from seven department issued rifles.

There was a recurring theme to the close of the last funeral. Twenty-one funerals, a twenty-one-rev salute, and a twenty-one-gun salute.

Saint Joseph's Catholic Church held funeral services for Justin Anderson, Paige's boyfriend, Brad Wells, and Matt Cooke on Thursday afternoon. Garrett dreaded this service more than the others for an obvious reason. It would be the most painful for Paige, and he hated it wasn't within his power to take the hurt away. There was going to be one bright spot in the otherwise dreadful day. Mandy Davis was going to the service with him and, better still, coming home with him afterward.

~ * ~

The circumstances of their meeting were less than ideal. Garrett, still a Deputy Sheriff but running for Sheriff, parked on the side of Highway Twenty-One on the north side of a small hill with his radar pointed at the southbound lane. The small hill made it a good speed trap because southbound vehicles couldn't see his patrol SUV until they crested the hill. By that time, it was too late to slow down.

As far as catching speeders went, Garrett had written no tickets. He knew northbound drivers were flashing their headlights to warn oncoming drivers of his presence, but that was out of his control. After an unusually long run of no northbound drivers, a late model Ford Explorer crested the hill in the southbound lane and Garrett's radar flashed '88 MPH' in bright red lights. Garrett switched on the light-bar and siren, pulled a U-turn through the grassy median, and sped up quickly to catch the speeder. The driver was already slowing down and pulling onto the shoulder.

After parking behind the Ford Explorer, Garrett called in the license plate number and waited for the results. The plates came back registered to a 2011, blue Ford Explorer owned by Amanda Lee Davis who was a thirty-one-year-old resident of Pine View, with no priors. Garrett grabbed his ticket book, checked his mirrors for approaching vehicles. There were none. He got out of the SUV and approached the driver's side of the Ford Explorer.

Before Garrett got to the driver's window, it lowered and a pleasant-sounding woman said, "I'm sorry, officer. I know I was speedin'. I was in Tyler at an auction, and I was in a hurry to get home. No excuse...but there it is."

Garrett stepped up to the window and looked into the prettiest blue eyes he'd ever seen. They were sky blue with white flakes in the irises that looked like tiny clouds in a clear blue sky. It wasn't love at first sight, but Garrett couldn't deny an instant attraction.

He cleared his throat. "Actually, it's deputy, not officer."

Amanda smiled, not a fake get out of a ticket smile, but a warm, genuine smile. "I know you. You're Garrett Lambert. You were three years ahead of me in high school. I still remember your touchdown run that won the state championship."

Garrett blushed. He couldn't help himself. "I thought your name sounded familiar when I called in your license plate."

It hadn't, but he couldn't very well say he did not know who she was. That would be impolite. Then Mandy blushed.

Without being asked, Mandy handed Garrett her driver's license and insurance card. Garrett took them, looked them over quickly to make sure Mandy didn't have any driving restrictions and her liability insurance, required by law in Texas, hadn't expired. Everything checked out and he handed them back to her.

Garrett tucked the ticket book under his right arm. "Okay, Amanda. I'm gonna let ya off with a verbal warnin'. The speed limit here is seventy-five. So, try to keep it under eighty."

Mandy laughed. "Thank you, Deputy Lambert. I will. But ya must not remember me too well."

"How's that?"

"My name's Amanda, but I've always gone by Mandy."

"Sorry. I went with the name on your license. Of course, you go by Mandy."

Mandy smiled a smile that made Garrett's heart flutter. "Okay, Deputy Lambert."

Garrett tipped his cowboy hat and started to walk back to his SUV. Then he did something he'd never done before.

He turned around, and walked back to the window, which had still been down. "I hope this isn't too forward of me…it's damned unprofessional, but…would ya like to go out to dinner with me some night?"

Mandy smiled, her cheeks blushed a soft, rose pink, and she said, "I would like that a lot."

They'd been dating since that day.

~ * ~

The triple service, including Justin, started at three o'clock. Garrett left work at one-thirty, went home, and changed from his uniform shirt into a white button-down shirt and a brown sport coat, no tie. These funerals were more about Paige than his official duties. Besides, it wasn't like folks didn't know who he was. There would still be questions to answer.

A few minutes past two o'clock, Mandy pulled into Garrett's

driveway in the same 2011, blue Ford Explorer that happened their first encounter. Garrett opened the front door as she approached and wrapped her in a tight hug. He inhaled deeply, taking in all the wonderful scents. Her shampoo, conditioner, soap, perfume, lotion, deodorant, makeup, and her natural intoxicating scent that was Mandy. He didn't realize how much he'd missed her until he was holding her again.

After the long, tight hug, Mandy pulled her head back, went up on the tips of her toes, and planted a soft, warm kiss on Garrett's lips.

When their lip parted, Mandy said, "I've missed you."

It had only been the previous Wednesday since they'd seen each other, but it seemed like much longer.

Garrett kissed the tip of her nose. "I've missed you, too."

The hug broke, and Mandy took a step back and eyeballed Garrett.

"Look at you, all spiffed up in a sport coat," Mandy cooed.

Garrett, who wasn't comfortable in the sport coat, tugged at the sleeves that felt too short and too tight under his arms. "I feel stupid in this thing."

Mandy grinned. "Ya look so handsome. That's a look that'll get a girl outta her panties in a hurry."

This statement brought a grin to Garrett's face.

He looked at his watch. "We've got about three minutes. That should be long enough."

Mandy laughed. "Slow down, cowboy. I need ya in the saddle for more than eight seconds. We've got all night."

"That's true," Garrett said, "but that doesn't mean the first ride will make the eight second buzzer."

Mandy buttoned the second button down on Garrett's shirt. "Then you'll have to saddle up and ride again and again."

All the rodeo sex euphemisms were causing a noticeable reaction in Garrett—the crotch of his starched Wranglers got uncomfortably tighter.

Mandy noticed. "Okay. Let's put this on hold until after the funerals."

Garrett laughed. "That's hard…pun intended, with you lookin' and smellin' so damn good."

Mandy looked good. Damn good. She wore a black dress that fit her perfectly in all the right places. Not immodest. It went down below her knees and no cleavage showed. It gathered around the waist and accentuated her ample breasts as well as curvaceous hips in a modest, sexy way.

Garrett shook his head to jar loose the thoughts taking root. All of which ended with Mandy's modest, sexy dress gathered around her ankles.

He looked at his watch again. "Yeah, with three funerals, that little church'll be packed. We should head on over there."

Mandy agreed. They got into Garrett's personal truck and pulled out of his driveway.

~ * ~

On the drive to the church, Mandy was uncharacteristically quiet for several minutes.

Just as Garrett started to ask Mandy what was on her mind, she said, "Is there any truth to the rumors goin' 'round town 'bout what happened at the MRB?"

Garrett expected Mandy to broach the subject eventually. He'd gone from the previous Wednesday until Tuesday without calling her. Garrett was thankful Mandy let him bring aspects of his job into their relationship on his terms, and she never pressed him for information. Still, he could hear the relief in her voice when she answered his Tuesday call.

After answering, she said, "I knew you were okay 'cause I've seen ya on TV, but ya could've called sooner."

She was right, and Garrett knew it. He said, "I know. I'm sorry. It's just been so crazy."

In a calmer voice, Mandy said, "I know you've been busy, sweetie. I've just been worried. When can I see ya?"

In response, Garrett asked her to accompany him to Justin's and Foster's funerals.

"Of course, I will. I love you, Garrett."

"I love you, too," Garrett told her, and he meant it.

After mind-chewing Mandy's current question for several seconds, Garrett said, "I guess that depends on what you've heard."

Mandy, still seat buckled, twisted in her seat toward Garrett. "I heard some kind of monster killed those kids and the other folks."

Garrett sucked in a deep breath and exhaled. He'd been less than truthful with so many people, but he'd never lied to Mandy. He'd already decided he would not start lying to her about the werewolf attacks.

"It's true."

Mandy opened her mouth to say something, but Garrett cut her off. "Later. I'll tell ya 'bout it later. Okay?"

"Ya can't just affirm somethin' like that and not elaborate, Garrett."

Garrett wagged a playful finger at Mandy. "Listen to me, Mandy Lee Davis. I could'a made sweet, pleasurable, memorable love to you in about thirteen seconds flat back at the house. I respected your request to save all that hot goodness for later tonight. You can do the same for me on this."

Mandy burst into snort accompanied laughter. Garrett loved that cute snort After the laughing fit she, said, "I don't know how sweet, pleasurable, and memorable it would'a been, but, okay. I want all thirteen seconds and the story tonight."

Garrett agreed.

~ * ~

It turned out leaving a bit early was the right call. Garrett and Mandy pulled into the packed church parking lot at a quarter to three. Garrett parked at the back of the lot, by the cemetery, and he and Mandy got out and started walking toward the church. As they neared the church, Garrett saw Al's balding head in a cluster of people just outside the church doors.

Garrett, thinking Paige would be with Al, put his hand up and shouted, "Al. Al."

Al's head turned toward Garrett. He smiled, waved back, and started moving toward Garrett and Mandy.

When they came together, it disappointed Garrett to see Paige wasn't with him. Lacy was, though. Garrett gave Lacy a hug and shook Al's hand. Al gave Mandy a hug, but Mandy and Lacy just gave each other a cursory nod of recognition that they were sharing proximate space. Mandy tried since they started dating to be nice to Lacy. Lacy refused to reciprocate.

Greetings completed, Garrett said, "Where's Paige?"

Lacy's lips remained tight, thin slits, but Al said, "She came with Lindsey and Justin's folks. She's gonna sit with 'em during the service."

This disappointed Garrett too, but he understood. The four of them squeezed into the small church together, but they sat on opposite sides. That suited Garrett just fine.

Once everyone took a seat and quieted, Garrett could see Paige sitting with the Anderson's in the front pew on the opposite side of the church. He could also see the three closed caskets situated side by side in front of the steps that led to the altar. A piano started playing and everyone stood as the priest, Father Mike, entered the chapel and walked to the altar.

As a non-Catholic, Garrett did not know what to do during the service. He stood when everyone else stood, sat when everyone else sat, and kneeled when everyone else kneeled. Mandy, who was Catholic, kept track of the readings in the Missalette and Garrett read along as the lectors read from the podium. The homily was especially touching. Father Mike knew all three young men through church activities, and he relayed funny stories about each of them. These anecdotes brought much needed laughter to the otherwise somber affair.

When the Mass portion of the services ended, Father Mike walked up the center aisle followed by the pallbearers carrying the three caskets and the family members. Garrett, who sat on the aisle seat in the back pew, saw Paige before she saw him. Her eyelids were an angry, puffy red, her beautiful green eyes looked like bloodshot roadmaps, and her cheeks were shiny rivers of tears. Her silver crucifix and necklace were noticeably absent from her slender neck.

Overwhelming sorrow for his daughter and unadulterated rage for the bitch who caused all this heartache waged an internal battle for dominance in Garrett's soul. Then Paige looked up at him. Her eyes twinkled a little, and a smile touched the corners of her mouth.

She mouthed, "I love you," as she passed by Garrett.

Sorrow and love for Paige beat back the rage. Garrett knew there would be time for rage later.

Once the family members exited the church, the rest of the mourners filtered out. Garrett took Mandy's hand and moved into the bustle of people moving slowly toward the church's double-doors. Someone moved between Garrett and Mandy, and he lost his grip on her hand. Garrett turned to grab Mandy's hand again and looked down into two big, blue eyes set in the beautiful face of a girl with long, blonde hair.

"Sorry," Garrett said, "I thought you were…someone else."

Garrett looked over the blue-eyed girl's head and spotted Mandy a couple of people back. They'd separated quickly.

"It's okay. We're all heading in the same direction," the blue-eyed girl said.

She was right, but Garrett really wanted Mandy's hand in his again. He tried to push back to her, but the blue-eyed girl remained in his way. The other people were trying to push past him.

To Mandy, Garrett said, "I'll meet ya outside."

Mandy nodded.

"Busy week, huh, Sheriff?" the blue-eyed girl said.

Garrett looked down into her big blue eyes again. She looked familiar. Garrett knew he'd seen her before. He couldn't place where, or when.

"Do I know you?" Garrett asked the blue-eyed girl.

The blue-eyed girl smiled. When she did, her full, red lips drew back, exposing a set of perfect, pearly white teeth. Too perfect.

"We haven't met, but I've seen you around."

The throng of people pushed Garrett toward the double doors as he walked backward, having the odd conversation with the blue-eyed girl, who looked familiar. Garrett's right boot heel struck the door threshold, and he toppled over backward. Before he could fall, the blue-eyed girl grabbed his jacket collar and easily righted him.

Surprised, but appreciative, Garrett said, "Thank ya."

When the blue-eyed girl let go of Garrett's jacket, it flapped open and revealed the shoulder holster and pistol.

The blue-eyed girl eyed the gun and smiled her unnaturally white-toothed smile again. "You carry a gun to church?"

Garrett closed his jacket. "I always carry my gun."

"Always?"

"Always." Garrett confirmed.

"Good to know."

Garrett and the blue-eyed girl were outside the church. The crowd thinned as many headed to the cemetery for the graveside service and others went for their cars to leave. Garrett looked back into the church interior, which looked dark compared to the bright May afternoon, and saw Mandy emerge.

She came to Garrett. "Who was that girl?"

Garrett glanced around, trying to spot her, to place her face again, but she was nowhere to be seen.

He looked back at Mandy. "I don't know. She looked familiar. I just can't place when or where I've seen her before."

Mandy smoothed the crumpled lapels from where the girl grabbed Garrett when he tripped. "Well, at least she kept ya from fallin' on your backside."

Garrett nodded, but as they walked toward the cemetery, his brain was still trying to place her face in some context that might help him remember.

The family plots for the three boys were in different areas of the cemetery. Garrett could see three Astroturf covered mounds of dirt that would cover them forever, scattered throughout the grounds. To accommodate all three caskets, they erected a large, green, opened tent in the middle of the primary drive in the center of the cemetery. The tent design, opened on all four sides, wasn't too different from Knucklehead's Icehouse design, where he would attend three more funerals the next day. Several rows of white, wooden, folding chairs were placed on three sides of the three caskets that were placed close together in the middle of the tent. The families, including Paige with the Andersons, were sitting in the chairs. The remaining mourners were standing behind the seats. Father Mike stood at the head of the caskets.

Garrett's gaze went from Father Mike to Paige and back throughout the service. He watched as Father Mike submerged a silver tube with a hole filled bulb on the end in a vat of water and sprinkled the caskets. The family members who were hit with the droplets made the sign of the cross. As some of the water fell on Paige, Garrett found he was holding his breath.

Will that burn her? he thought.

If it did, Paige showed no outward sign of it. She crossed herself and placed her hands back in her lap.

After about twenty minutes, Father Mike said, "This concludes the graveside service. Family members are welcome to accompany the pallbearers to their loved one's last resting place. The rest of you can go to the recreation center for the after-service reception. The Knights of Columbus have graciously supplied barbecue, beans, corn on the cob, mustard potato salad, and drinks."

Garrett looked at Paige and saw she was looking at him.

She mouthed, "Please wait."

Garrett smiled and nodded. Paige got up with the Andersons following a group of young students and older teachers who were pallbearers toward the back of the cemetery.

Some of the remaining crowd headed for the parking lot to leave, while Garrett, Mandy, Al, and Lacy fell in with the crowd heading for the recreation center, which was, as far as Garrett could tell, a fancy name for a metal building behind the church. Upon entering the recreation center, Garrett had to admit he'd misjudged the accommodations.

The interior had painted sheetrock walls, and a tile floor. There were about two dozen tables with four chairs each placed around the opened space. The back wall had a large stage where the Knights had set up with a lot of good smelling food. Bathrooms marked for each sex were at either end of the stage area. The left side wall had a large kitchen. It was a nice setup.

Garrett and Mandy got into the serving line and made their way along the buffet of food. It wasn't just barbecue. It was an assortment of barbecue and plenty of it. There was pork sausage, beef brisket, and chicken to pick from. Garrett grabbed an extra plate for Paige and hoped he wouldn't look like a greedy pig as he loaded both plates. Several of the serving Knights addressed him by name and happily heaped mounds of food on both plates.

With the food and drinks secured, Garrett and Mandy headed for a table close to the door so he could get Paige's attention when she came in. Lacy and Al had the same idea and sat down at the table next to where Garrett and Mandy were sitting. Al offered them a tired smile, but Lacy's eyes looked at the door. Garrett smiled back. He liked Al. He just didn't know why Lacy didn't like Mandy.

A couple of minutes later, the door opened, and Andrew and Gloria Anderson walked in, followed by Lindsey and Paige.

Garrett and Lacy got to their feet and said, "Paige," at the same time.

If it hadn't been so sad and desperate on both their parts, it would have been comical.

Paige looked from her dad to her mom. She clearly understood the implications of whom she went to first, and Garrett felt bad for putting her in that situation.

Garrett started to say, "Go see your mom," but Paige broke his direction.

The joy he felt at being 'picked' first evaporated when he saw Lacy sit back down in her chair and cover her eyes. When he wrapped Paige in a tight hug, overwhelming love for his daughter replaced the guilt.

Garrett lifted Paige off the ground and held her tight for several long seconds. He inhaled her scents too but enjoyed them in a very different context than he enjoyed Mandy's.

When he put her down, he said, "Go see your mom. We can talk in a bit."

Paige looked over at her mom and waved. "I'll be right there, Mom."

To Garrett she said, "She's bein' melodramatic."

This made Garrett smile.

Mandy approached Paige cautiously. She and Paige got along great, but she could feel Lacy burning holes in her back with contentious eyes and didn't want to provoke her further. Paige showed no such compunction. She grabbed Mandy and hugged her tight.

Paige said, "I'm glad you're here. Thanks for takin' care of Daddy."

Mandy choked up, but she said, "Oh, sweetheart. Of course. I love ya both."

As the hug parted, Paige said, "I love ya too, Mandy."

To Garrett's knowledge, Paige had never told Mandy that before.

Paige turned to Garrett. "I'm gonna sleep at Lin's house tonight and go back to Mom's in the mornin'. Will ya pick me up tomorrow at Mom's and take me to Maggie's funeral? Since it'll be Friday, I thought we could get an early start on our weekend afterward."

Garrett smiled. "Of course, I will. I need to go to Deputy Foster's funeral tomorrow afternoon after Maggie's funeral. You up for that?"

"Absolutely. We can grab two pizzas on the way home."

Garrett cleared his throat. "Um, Mandy's goin' to Foster's funeral with me, too."

Paige looked from her dad to Mandy and back at her dad. "So, we'll get three pizzas. The more the merrier."

This was a first, too. Paige liked Mandy just fine, but she'd always been protective of her time with Garrett, which was why he never had Mandy out to his house on the weekends.

"Ya sure?" Garrett asked.

Paige offered a sweet smile. "Absolutely. It'll be fun."

She looked at Lacy. "I better go see Mom before she has an aneurism."

Paige hugged Mandy, then hugged and gave Garrett a kiss. "Two o'clock tomorrow at Mom's."

Garrett nodded and handed her the plate of food he'd gotten for her. "I fixed ya a plate. Take it with ya."

"Thank you, Daddy," Paige said and took the plate.

As Paige turned to leave, she said, "I love you, Daddy."

Garrett smiled. "I love you too, Paige-Turner."

~ * ~

On the ride back to Garrett's house, the conversation naturally turned to Paige. Mandy confirmed Garrett's reckoning Paige never told her she loved her before. Paige never invited Mandy to Pizza Night needed no confirmation—that had been a fact they both had knew.

"I think it's 'cause of all she's been through this past week. She lost her boyfriend and several friends. She wants to hold tight to the people left in her life," Mandy reasoned.

Garrett didn't disagree.

With the Paige discussion exhausted, the next course of conversation turned to what happened at the MRB and other places the previous week.

"Okay. It's later. What's all this about a monster in East Texas?" Mandy asked.

Garrett's grip on the steering wheel tightened, and he said, "I'll tell ya when we get back to my place."

"Then you'll have another reason to put off tellin' me."

"No. I promise I'll tell ya all about it. You will want some wine and I need a beer. I can show ya the pictures of 'em. A picture's worth a thousand words, I've heard tell."

Mandy sucked in a harsh breath. "You've got pictures of it?"

"I've got pictures of one of *them*," Garrett corrected.

"One of *them*? How many are there? How did ya get a picture of it?" Mandy asked in quick succession.

Garrett reached over and took Mandy's hand in his. "I'll tell and show ya everything when we get back to my place."

Mandy squeezed Garrett's hand and nodded.

~ * ~

Promised story and pictures had to wait until Garrett changed clothes. He changed out of the starched Wranglers into sweatpants and from the button-down shirt to a loose-fitting T-shirt. He put the sport coat in the closet.

Before he finished changing, Mandy came into the bedroom with her overnight bag.

"I'm gonna slip into somethin' more comfortable, too."

"Ya could just slip outta that dress and we can get to the fun stuff right now."

Mandy giggled. "Nice try. I get my story before you get your thirteen seconds."

Garrett shrugged. "Okay. But the longer you prolong this, the shorter that thirteen seconds of sweet, pleasurable, memorable love makin' gets."

"I'll take my chances," Mandy said as she unzipped her dress and let it fall around her ankles.

Garrett looked at her standing there wearing a lacy, black bra, silk, black panties, and lacy, black garters holding up sheer, black nylons. "Yeah, I'll be lucky to make eight now."

Mandy giggled. "Pour me some wine, you nut."

"Yes ma'am," Garrett replied with a salute and left the room.

By the time Mandy changed, which also included removing makeup, Garrett was on the back deck half finished with his first Miller Lite longneck. Mandy came out wearing worn, cutoff shorts, a tight, white, spaghetti strap top, and no shoes. She had her blonde hair pulled back in a ponytail with bangs and loose, longer hairs framing her face. Garrett thought she never looked more beautiful than when she tried not to.

She took a seat across from Garrett and picked up the already poured glass of red wine. A bottle of Messina Hof merlot, her favorite Texas wine, was on the table for future refills.

"Okay, Sheriff, tell me what's goin' on."

Garrett told her everything, only pausing to light three cigarettes. Mandy didn't like that Garrett smoked, but she secretly liked the taste of beer and smoke on his tongue when they kissed, of which she was sure they'd be doing a lot of later, so she didn't complain. He drank two more beers and refilled Mandy's wine glass twice.

When the tale had been told, Mandy sat quietly for several seconds, her mouth slightly agape.

She looked at the sliding door, and back at Garrett. "It was here? It crashed through your slidin' doors and tried to get ya?"

Garrett nodded and saw Mandy's body visibly shudder. Whether in fear or disgust, Garrett didn't know.

"Ya wanna see it? The pictures?"

Mandy's response was comical.

She shook her head 'no' but said, "Yes."

Garrett dropped his cigarette into an empty longneck. It hissed when it hit the residue on the bottom of the bottle.

He got up and held out his hand. "Come on."

Mandy took Garrett's hand in one of hers and held the bottle of Messina Hof and her empty wineglass in the other.

She shook the bottle. "I think I might need another bottle for the pictures."

Garrett laughed. "Not unless ya want one hell of a headache in the mornin'."

Mandy let out an uneasy laugh. "I might want to forget all of this."

Before going to his office, Garrett detoured to the refrigerator and got another beer. When they got to his office, Garrett refilled Mandy's wineglass, which emptied the bottle. He typed in his password. He didn't care if Mandy saw it, clicked on the 'WW Pics' folder, loaded them into the 'Preview' program, and clicked on the Slideshow option. The pictures enlarged to fill the screen and displayed each at five-second intervals.

On seeing the first picture of the large, nightmare werewolf, Mandy grabbed Garrett's upper right arm and squeezed it. Her grip increased with each successive image to where Garrett's arm was going numb.

When the slideshow got to the last image, Garrett paused it, and pointed at the beast's left ear. "That's where I shot it. See the blood oozin' from its left ear?"

Mandy released her grip a bit. "That thing bit Paige and Ty and that Trowa guy?"

Garrett nodded.

"Oh, Garrett. Kill it before they turn into one of those things," Mandy whispered.

"That's the idea. Listen, I'm gonna have Paige this weekend. I'm also gonna invite Ty, Trowa, and James Huff out Saturday afternoon to talk 'bout how we can get that bitch. You wanna come?"

Mandy smiled. "Am I part of the group?"

"Ya are if ya wanna be. Paige, Ty, and Trowa have a vested interest in puttin' that bitch down. You, James Huff, George Krats, and me are the only unbitten folks who know the whole truth of it. Emily Yost doesn't know 'bout the folks who're bitten, and I'd like to keep it that way. The werewolves know…of course. Since Paige has warmed up to ya bein' here when she is, that shouldn't be a problem."

Mandy smiled a warm, wine aided smile. "If it's okay with Paige, I'll be here for the secret werewolf meetin'."

She went up on her tiptoes and planted a kiss on Garrett's lips.

Garrett felt her tongue probing his lips and opened his mouth to accommodate the intrusion. Her mouth tasted like sweet red wine.

Mandy felt Garrett's appendage probing her lower stomach. Garrett was a good bit taller than Mandy. She broke the kiss, stepped back, and looked at the tent pitched in Garrett's sweatpants.

She grinned. "Okay, cowboy. Time to ride."

Garrett grinned back. "Yes, ma'am."

Garrett grabbed Mandy, hoisted her into his arms, and started for the bedroom.

Before they were out of the office, Mandy said, "Hold on a sec."

"What?"

Mandy pointed at his desk. "Bring those."

Garrett looked at where Mandy pointed and saw his handcuffs. Surprised, Garrett said, "You want me to bring the handcuffs?"

Mandy grinned. "I've been a *bad* girl, Sheriff Lambert."

Garrett grabbed the handcuffs and set a land speed record for carrying a woman from point A to point B.

Whether Mandy's kinky request came from the wine, the werewolves, the funerals, or a combination of all those things, Garrett couldn't say. What he could say was that it was the most amazing night of sex he'd ever experienced.

The jokes about his staying ability weren't too far off the mark. He qualified as a Minute Man their first go. They did other things, amazing things, while waiting for Garrett's little buddy to rejoin the party, and Garrett lasted substantially longer the second and third time they coupled.

After midnight, Garrett and Mandy, exhausted from the sexathon, fell asleep naked on top of the covers with the ceiling fan washing their sweaty bodies in a cool breeze.

Garrett slept on his left side, facing the front window in his bedroom. He dreamed about a camping trip he took with his dad when he was nine years old. Nighttime had fallen, and they were sitting by a fire roasting marshmallows. Suddenly, someone shone a flashlight in his eyes. Even in his dream, Garrett knew that didn't happen on the camping trip. He came out of the dream and saw a faint light source penetrating through his closed eyelids and registering with his sleeping mind. Garrett opened his eyes.

The motion-activated floodlight just outside the bedroom front window was on. Garrett grabbed his gun from the nightstand and looked at the bedside clock. It was two eighteen a.m.

Mandy, still fast asleep, spooned Garrett with her right arm draped across his waist. Garrett wanted to get out of bed and look outside, but doing so would likely wake Mandy and worry her. So, he laid there and watched for movement outside the window. Nothing stirred from what Garrett could see, but the floodlight remained on for thirteen minutes, which meant something had been moving out there to keep it on. When the floodlight went off at two thirty-one a.m., Garrett held vigil for more than an hour before he drifted off to sleep again. This time, his sleep was dreamless and undisturbed.

~ * ~

A warm, firm grip on a sensitive appendage woke Garrett early the next morning. Mandy was in the mood for more loving and, thanks to the warm, firm grip, Garrett was in the mood in short order. After they made love in the bed, they showered together. One thing, Mandy soaping up Garrett's junk, led to another, Garrett soaping up Mandy's junk, and they had sex again in the shower.

Garrett hadn't had that much sex since the early days of his marriage with Lacy. He wasn't complaining, but he wasn't eighteen anymore, and it took a while to complete the act. This had Garrett and Mandy running late for work and hurrying out the door with travel mugs in hand—sweet tea for Garrett and instant coffee for Mandy. They kissed a little too long, and Mandy made sure she had the correct time and place for Foster Timpson's funeral. She did, and they planned to meet there shortly before the service started. They got into their vehicles and parted company.

Every other morning that week, before showering, Garrett donned his tree climbing gear, swapped out the critter-cam SD cards, and viewed the captured videos. He changed the settings from ‘Image’ to ‘Video’ after the Saturday night attack. The previous night’s captures would have to wait.

~ * ~

Doctor James Huff woke up that Friday morning, as he had every other morning since Monday, tired and disappointed his nocturnal activities hadn’t yielded results, or anything of interest. Since meeting with Garrett on Monday and getting Dillon Albertson’s address, James spent his evenings and most of the nights parked across from the apartment building Dillon lived in. He brought a thermos of black coffee, sandwiches, snacks, and his iPad Air II filled with lots of reading material. He was currently rereading Truman Capote’s *In Cold Blood* for, perhaps, the tenth time. Reading helped keep him awake, comfortable, and entertained while on stakeout.

Also, after meeting with Garrett, James used the university resources to look into Dillon’s academic history. Dillon’s unofficial transcript showed he was an impressive student. He was finishing his second year at SFA, which meant most of the completed coursework dealt with core requirements. English, History, Political Science. He came with thirty hours, which meant he started as a sophomore, so he took quite a few upper-level courses in Biology, Chemistry, and Mathematics, too. To date, Dillon was sporting a perfect 4.0 GPA. This impressed James.

The highlight of James’ week came Thursday night, a little after midnight. Tired, James debated whether to start Part Four, ‘The Corner’ of *In Cold Blood,* or call it a night and go home. He reread the first line several times because he kept nodding off mid-sentence.

Going home won the internal debate. He bookmarked the page and closed the iPad’s cover, which put the contraption to sleep. As he reached for the key to start his truck, movement in the apartment parking lot registered in his peripheral vision. James looked in that direction and saw Dillon getting into his older model, orange, Honda Civic. James started his truck, but not to go home.

When Dillon pulled out of the apartment parking lot, he turned north on Pearl Street, which meant his headlights illuminated James' truck parked across the street and pointed south. James panicked and fell sideways across the front seat of his blue on silver 1985 Chevy Silverado pickup. It was a big truck and James knew he looked out of place behind its wheel, but he enjoyed being able to look down on most other vehicles. He was short in stature and spent most of his interpersonal encounters looking up at others.

Once Dillon passed him, James popped up in the seat, made a quick, not so inconspicuous U-turn on Pearl, and fell in about a block behind Dillon's car. A few blocks up, Dillon turned right on MacKechney Street toward North Street. James picked up speed to catch up before he lost him in North Street traffic.

On any other night, North Street in Nacogdoches would be mostly deserted at that hour. Because many students commuted home to Dallas and Houston on the weekends, Thursday night was 'Party Night' for SFA students. 'Big-Ass Glass Night' at the Flashback bar factored, too.

James turned right onto MacKechney Street just in time to see Dillon break and turn right before reaching North Street. Because James knew the area Dillon turned into, anticipation of discovering the wolf's den died immediately. Dillon pulled into a parking lot that serviced two fast-food establishments. Pizza Hut and Whataburger. The only unknown at that point depended on which Dillon had a taste for?

Deductive reasoning led James to believe young Dillon Albertson had a hankering for a juicy Whataburger. He could've had a pizza delivered. Dillon drove behind the Pizza Hut and parked in the Whataburger parking lot.

Sherlock Holmes would have been proud, James thought as he parked on the side of Pizza Hut, so he faced Whataburger.

Students in search of sustenance to sedate alcohol, and other illegal substances induced munchies crowded both eateries. James opened his iPad and started reading again. The thrill of the chase, albeit a short one, provided him a second wind.

About thirty minutes later, James watched Dillon exit Whataburger, get into his Civic, and head back the way he came. James followed at a safe distance. When Dillon pulled back into the apartment parking lot, James pulled over on Pearl close enough so he could see what Dillon did next, but not so close as to draw unwanted attention to himself. Dillon got out of his car and went inside his apartment. Disappointed,

James went home to get some much-needed sleep.

~ * ~

In his apartment that Thursday night, Dillon crammed for three finals. AP II, Chemistry II, and Statistics and Probability. His grades exempted him from two other core requirements, final exams. Music Appreciation and Introduction to Sociology. Even without the two additional final exams, Dillon felt stressed…and concerned.

On Monday night, he spotted a blue and silver pickup, with a round-faced man behind the wheel, parked across the street from his apartment building. Dillon had a feeling the man wasn't affiliated with any branch of law enforcement, but he also had a feeling the man took an interest in him.

Dillon marked the man's scent that Monday night. The scent, the truck, and the man were gone the next morning. When Dillon got to SFA for class later that morning, the scent was back. Dillon slowly traced it to the Liberal Arts building. He would be late for class, which he never was, but he had to know who had been watching him.

Once in the building, the myriad of scents being jumbled together by throngs of students making their way to class slowed his tracking.

They won't be late, Dillon thought angrily.

In wolf form, because of the much-heightened senses, tracking the round-faced man would have been easy. That wasn't an option. At least not without the uncontrollable urge to rip out the throats of every person he encountered. So, Dillon relied on the lesser, but still more acute than before being bitten, senses of his human form, which led him to the second floor.

When Dillon exited the elevator, the round-faced man's scent was strong and to his left. Knowing, if the round-faced man saw him, he would be on to the fact Dillon was on to him, Dillon peeked around the corner of the left side hallway. The elevators were recessed to keep waiting students and faculty from blocking hallway traffic. On the left, he saw two closed doors, one fully opened door, and one office door, the last one, slightly ajar.

Dillon waited until the hallway was empty. Dillon's nose told him the round-faced man was in the office with the slightly ajar door. He started cautiously down the hall, ready to spin around and break for the elevators if anyone came out of the targeted door. No one did. Dillon edged up to the door and read the nameplate: 'Dr. James Huff.' With that knowledge, he hurried to class.

At home, later that day, Dillon accessed SFA's faculty website and found Dr. Huff's entry, complete with biography and teaching interests. It even had his picture, which confirmed what his nose told him. Dillon read through the biography and saw Huff had an interest in mythology, the occult, and folklore.

He could be dangerous, Dillon thought.

Later that Tuesday night, Dillon caught Huff's scent again. A quick peek through the blinds in his living room confirmed he was back. He returned the next two nights as well.

A stressed and distracted Dillon tried to study Thursday night. To make matters worse, a little before midnight, Dillon 'sensed' Alexis transformed and was out prowling, or something else. He knew he'd only received the flash because she'd wanted him to receive it. This, of course, concerned Dillon, because Alexis' carelessness had pointed Sheriff Lambert in his direction. These thoughts fluttered through Dillon's mind, but he never let them land and take root for fear Alexis might pick up on them.

Dillon felt hungry, which added to the stress. He went through the refrigerator. Sliced cheese, a jar of pickles, and some mustard. Dillon went through the pantry. A box of old Girl Scout cookies and a stale half-loaf of bread. He considered a not too appetizing cheese, mustard, and pickle sandwich with old cookies for dessert.

Another thought entered his mind. Lead Huff out to the old barn, transform, and eat him. That wasn't appetizing either. He enjoyed the thrill of the hunt and the kill while in wolf form, but he didn't relish it the way Alexis did. He surely would not lure the man, nuisance or not, to his death. Besides, Alexis might not be pleased with him if he acted on his own, and he knew what Alexis did to pack members when they pissed her off.

With all considered, Dillon opted for a quick trip to Whataburger. He could really sink his human teeth into Monterey Melt with extra onions and French fries. As a bonus, making a food run would let him know if Huff had really been following him. Dillon felt sure he was, but this would confirm it.

Huff pulled a U-turn and fell in behind Dillon on Pearl Street.

You're not very inconspicuous, Dillon thought as he watched the truck pursue him in the review mirror.

The U-turn confirmed Dillon's concerns. He decided he would try to contact Alexis the next day and fill her in on the meddling Dr. Huff.

The food helped and Dillon felt better as he drove back to his apartment, with Huff following about a block behind him. Shortly after entering his apartment, Dillon lost Huff's scent. A quick peek outside confirmed he was gone. He studied a little longer, but the full belly took its toll and Dillon started nodding off.

A little before two o'clock, Dillon succumbed and fell asleep on his couch with a chemistry text in his lap. Mentally and emotionally exhausted and a Monterey Melt and French fries heavy in his gut, Dillon would have slept the rest of the night.

Alexis woke him with a mental intrusion, *Meet me tomorrow evenin' at the barn.*

The intrusion had been sudden and powerful. She was getting stronger. Dillon sat up quickly, upending the chemistry book. His head reeled. His stomach turned.

I'm going to be sick, Dillon's mind screamed.

He leaned over the side of the couch, retched, and his stomach was no longer burdened with the weight of the Monterey Melt and french fries. What remained of these culinary delights was a brown and orange goop that landed on his chemistry book.

"Fuck," Dillon hissed.

Dillon cleaned up the mess and wondered how he would lose Huff to meet Alexis at the barn. It turned out losing Huff wasn't an issue. He didn't show up Friday night.

~ * ~

That Friday promised to be a busy day for Garrett. He needed to go into the office to check on the investigations, attend the Lee brother's and Bear's funerals, pick up Paige at her mom's, attend Maggie's funeral, then meet Mandy to attend Foster's funeral. Running late because of the extracurricular activities that morning compacted an already full day.

Garrett recovered a few minutes by using his lights and siren to justify speeding for part of the drive from home to the sheriff's department. Outside of an emergency, this was something he had never done before. Extraordinary times, murderous werewolves, called for extraordinary measures. He was behind his desk by eight fifteen a.m. instead of eight a.m.

Nothing waited for him on his desk, which meant no new information on the investigations. At least not on paper. Garrett typed in his computer password, opened Outlook, and waited for the new emails to load. Several seconds later, eighteen new emails popped up in the inbox.

Garrett scanned the senders quickly and deleted the spam. Viagra and investment offers. Several of the remaining emails would need his attention, but they weren't pressing. Two looked promising. One, from James Huff, sent that morning, and one from George Krats, sent the previous afternoon after Garrett left work to attend Justin's funeral. Garrett clicked on the email from James.

Good morning, Garrett,

I have been shadowing Dillon all week. Sadly, I have nothing of importance to report. I thought he was on the move last night, but it was just a run to Whataburger for a late-night snack. I'm willing to keep up the surveillance, if you want me to. Your thoughts?

Best,

James

Garrett reread James' email a second time. It didn't surprise him James' surveillance hadn't turned up anything of use. He knew Dillon Albertson was a smart kid and if he was involved, he'd be cautious. He hoped that Dillon might reveal something. Garrett clicked on the 'Reply' button and wrote:

James,

Thanks for doing this. I know you have better things to do with your time. I doubt he's going to reveal anything of importance. He's too smart for that. Spend your free time doing something more enjoyable.

Speaking of free time, though. If you're free tomorrow afternoon, I'd like to have you out to my house around two o'clock. I'm inviting Ty and Trowa, too. Paige will already be there, and I told my girlfriend, Mandy, about everything that's going on. She'll be there, too. I'll grill some steaks and I thought we might discuss plans to deal with this problem. Let me know if you're interested and I'll send you directions.

Garrett

After sending the reply to James, Garrett opened the email from George Krats, the county coroner. It was curious.

Garrett,

While conducting Foster's autopsy, I noticed a dried substance on his facial region. Specifically, his mouth and nose. I swabbed it, along with all the other swabs, to check for foreign substances. The results came back today. It's vaginal fluid. Unless Foster was engaged in amorous activities before responding to the disturbance call at the CP Sawmill, the vaginal fluid was transferred post-mortem. This is a first in all my years of doing this. I've already sent a sample for DNA testing. Fingers crossed.

George

Garrett reread Georg's email several times. From what he knew about Ty and Paige's pleasurable connection with the alpha, Garrett had a feeling the bitch received sexual gratification from her animalistic power, but this was brazen.

He thought about the text he'd received from Paige while at the CP Sawmill. Page texted the girl wolf had been in the woods with someone's head and 'happy.' Paige also texted the girl wolf was 'disgusting.'

She was humpin' his fuckin' head, Garrett thought.

A chill ran up his spine.

He thought, *and my little girl saw...*felt *that*.

Anger replaced the chill.

After digesting George's email, Garrett responded and told him to let him know if they got a DNA match on the vaginal fluid. He felt sure they wouldn't get a match, but, at least, it was something tangible. Everything else evaporated like smoke in the wind.

With a couple of hours left before departing for the biker's funerals, Garrett started reviewing the remaining emails. Seven required detailed responses. The remaining three only required his stamp of approval for various requests concerning the running of the jail and inmate needs. He finished with fifteen minutes to spare.

Garrett smiled and thought, *Mandy and I have time for one more poke.*

'Poke' had been the term used for sex in Larry McMurtry's *Lonesome Dove*. On his father's recommendation, Garrett read *Lonesome*

Dove in high school and loved it. He loved the mini-series, too.

Garrett began getting up to leave his office when a ding from his computer announced a new email. It was from James, who had been eager to attend the meeting of 'Dumblegarrett's Army.' Garrett knew, from the movies and books, James was making a reference to *Harry Potter and the Order of the Phoenix,* and a smile crept across his face. James also insisted on bringing some homemade muscadine wine to the meeting. Garrett typed out a quick response that relayed his eagerness to taste the muscadine wine and included directions from SFA to his house. By the time he finished, he was running late again.

~ * ~

After the twenty-one-rev salute, but before the drinking started, Garrett approached Trowa, who stood with several big biker guys. An old man who smelled of bad breath and sweaty armpits stood with them. Hank.

"If ya don't mind, I have a couple of quick follow-up questions concernin' what happened to your friends, Mister Raintree."

Trowa nodded and the two of them walked toward Garrett's patrol SUV.

When they were out of earshot of the others, Garrett said, "I'd like for ya to come out to my house tomorrow afternoon around two o'clock. I'm havin' some other folks out who know what's goin' on, and I thought we'd try to plan to take out that bitch before you and the others turn into one of those monsters."

Trowa nodded. "I'll be there."

Garrett reached into his front right pocket, closed his fist around the object there, and removed his hand.

"As promised, I have more of these for ya, too."

Trowa opened his hand and Garrett dropped seven nine-mil silver bullets into it.

"Sorry I couldn't get ya more. That'll have to do…for now."

Trowa closed his fist around the shiny bullets. "This is good. Thanks, Sheriff."

Garrett started to give Trowa directions to his house, but he waved him off. "I know where your crib is, Sheriff."

Garrett found that information a little disconcerting.

The look on his face must have shown it because Trowa chuckled. "Relax, Sheriff. I cut trees down the road from your place about a year ago. I saw ya comin' and goin' while I was there."

Relieved the biker element wasn't keeping tabs on where he lived, Garrett said, "Come hungry. I'm grillin' steaks."

~ * ~

From Knucklehead's Icehouse, Garrett drove to Lacy's house to pick up Paige for Maggie's funeral. He saw her waiting for him on the front porch as he pulled up. It was a twenty-minute drive from Lacy's house to the Pine View Presbyterian Church. During the drive, Paige was uncharacteristically quiet.

"You, okay?" Garrett asked after a few minutes.

Paige offered a weak smile. "I'm fine. I just haven't been gettin' much sleep lately."

Garrett, who engaged in a sexathon the previous night and slept like a baby, until the floodlights woke him briefly, felt guilty. Because he wouldn't tell Paige about his sex induced restful night's sleep, he told her he'd filled Mandy in on everything that happened. Paige didn't mind that he'd told Mandy. He told her about having the people out the next day to plan and how James dubbed their group Dumblegarrett's Army. Paige thought the meeting was a good idea, and she loved the group's unofficial nickname. Finally, he told her about the twenty-one-rev salute at the biker funeral. Paige thought that had been cool.

The church was, unsurprisingly, packed. The Pine View community showed up in full support for all the students' funerals. Garrett and Paige squeezed into the last pew with Garrett on the aisle. When the service finished, the pallbearers, six high school boys, carried Maggie's casket up the center aisle and out of the church.

Following closely behind the casket had been Maggie's mom, Arleen Crawford. Garrett couldn't believe she was the same women he'd spoken with the previous Saturday, after the MRB incident. Being widowed in 2010 and losing her only child took a serious toll on Arleen.

Garrett remembered the last thing Arleen said to him after he delivered the news her husband, Ben, died in a single vehicle, drunk driving, accident. "At least I've still got my Magpie."

Not anymore, Garrett thought sadly.

Arleen was a healthy woman with shiny blonde hair in her early forties. The Arleen being aided up the aisle by a woman who shared familial traits, Arleen's sister, Andrea from Jacksonville, was a shadow of her former self.

Her blonde hair was dull and hung in strings around her shoulders. Her skin was pale and there were angry red blotches and scratch marks on her arms. She also appeared to have lost an unnatural amount of weight in one week. Her cheeks sunk in. Her lips cracked and stretched too tightly across teeth. The outlines of which were visible through her thin lips. The worst part of her appearance was her eyes.

As Arleen and Andrea neared the last pew, Arleen looked up and directly at Garrett. Her sclerae were red pools of bloodshot mayhem. Arleen's pupils looked like black pinpricks in the middle of cloudy gray irises. Her eyes sunk into deep, bony sockets. She looked skeletal.

Arleen stepped toward Garrett. Garrett opened his mouth to offer condolences but, before he could speak, Arleen slapped his face. A hard slap made even more painful by Arleen's fingernails that left scratches on his cheek. The coppery taste of blood swirled on Garrett's tongue. A loud slap, too. The sound amplified inside the small church and seemed to reverberate for several seconds. The reverberation could have been in Garrett's head, which was still reeling.

A collective gasp from everyone in the vicinity followed the slap and the church went deathly silent. They were waiting to see what happened next.

"Damn you, Sheriff Lambert. I see ya twice in five years. First, ya tell me my Ben's dead and now ya tell me my Magpie's dead. Did ya *see* what *they* did to my little girl? I couldn't even have an open casket funeral," Arleen hissed.

She let out a soul-crushing sob and collapsed. Garrett caught her before she hit the ground and helped her stand up.

Arleen looked up at Garrett after he righted her. The anger was gone, and incomprehensible sorrow replaced the anger in her dead eyes.

Arleen reached up with her bony hand, gently stroked the red welt and scratches left from its previous contact, and offered a weak smile that made her look even sadder. "I'm sorry, Sheriff. I know it's not your fault."

"It's okay, Missus Crawford."

He put his arm around her and helped her from the church to the adjoining cemetery, where Maggie would rest next to her father.

After the graveside service, when Garrett and Paige were back in the patrol SUV, Paige said, "I can't believe Missus Crawford slapped you in a church."

"It's okay. Folks are hurtin'. They need someone to blame or hold accountable. I'm the sheriff, so that falls on me."

"It's *not* your fault. You're doin' everything you can to make those…*fuckers* pay for all of this."

Paige's choice of words took Garrett aback. She'd never uttered a curse word beyond damn or hell in his presence before, then only occasionally. Under the circumstance, though, he chose not to address it.

"We know that. They don't. It'll get worse."

"Why? If ya kill her, everything will be okay."

It didn't slip Garrett's attention Paige said 'if' instead of 'when' about killing the alpha.

He took a deep breath. "*When* I kill it, not *if* I kill it."

"Okay, *when* ya kill her. Why won't things get better?"

"Because, sweetheart, they don't know what did these killin's. I'll kill the alpha and end this. They won't know because I can hardly present a young woman to the public as the perp behind the MRB massacre. They wouldn't believe it. So, as far as the public's concerned, this'll go down as an unsolved case. No answers and no one to hold accountable but me," Garrett explained.

Several moments of silence slipped by then Paige said, "That's not fair. What about your re-election?"

Garrett hadn't considered the ramifications of his political future. It was May 2015, and the election would be in November 2016. It was too far in the future to be of concern.

"I'm not worried 'bout my next election, Paige-Turner. All I care about now is findin' the alpha and killin' it."

Paige smiled. "I'd vote for ya if I was old enough to vote."

Garrett smiled back. "Thank ya, sweetheart. If ya could vote…and, if I voted for myself, that would be a solid two votes."

~ * ~

Law enforcement vehicles, cars, trucks, SUVs, and motorcycles from Pine View County, the City of Pine View, DPS, and every other neighboring city and county in East Texas packed the First Lutheran

Church parking lot. Law enforcement was a brotherhood, and it supported its fallen colleagues. Luckily, being the sheriff of the fallen hero, Garrett had a reserved spot near the church. When he pulled into the spot, he saw Mandy standing there, looking as beautiful as ever.

Mandy greeted Paige with a hug and a kiss on the cheek. Garrett with a hug and a kiss on the lips. Only a brief kiss, but it warmed Garrett's heart. When their lips parted, Garrett looked over at Paige, who raised and lowered her eyebrows in a quick sequence like a goofball. It made him smile. Garrett and the two most important women in the world to him went inside the church.

The service was a somber affair and the most personal for Garrett but, unlike the face slap at Maggie's funeral, had been uneventful. After Garrett presented the flag from Foster's casket to his grieving parents and after the twenty-one-gun salute sent birds in nearby trees fluttering into the air, the crowd dispersed.

With the week of funerals behind him, and none in the foreseeable future, the stress of the week slipped from Garrett's shoulders like a tangible weight.

As they neared the parking lot, Garrett said, "If you two wanna go on to the house, I'll grab the pizzas and meet y'all there in a bit."

Paige nodded. "Okay with me."

Mandy smiled. "Sounds good. You remember what kind'a pizza I like, right?"

"I do, but it's not real pizza," Garrett responded with a grin.

To Mandy, Paige said, "What kind of pizza do ya like?"

Before Mandy could answer, Garrett screwed up his face. "Veggie lovers. It ain't pizza without meat."

Mandy and Paige laughed at Garrett's contorted face.

After parting from Mandy and Paige, Garrett had one more thing to do before leaving. Talk with Ty about the Saturday gathering. Finding Ty was easy. Getting him away from Jasmine wasn't.

Jasmine gave Garrett a big hug and started questioning him about why he hadn't been to visit lately, when he was going to propose to Mandy, and about the murders.

"Ty won't tell me a thing," Jasmine said with a huff.

"I told ya, baby. I can't discuss this with ya," Ty responded. He added, "Give me a minute with Garrett."

Jasmine didn't look pleased, but she walked away.

"What's up?" Ty asked once they were alone.

Garrett told him about the Saturday gathering. He left out the Dumblegarrett's Army part, and Ty agreed to come.

Because he had been feeling guilty for telling Mandy what happened while Ty left Jasmine in the dark, Garrett said, "You can tell Jasmine what's goin' on. I told Mandy."

Ty shook his head. "It's different for me. I think I'll keep her out of it."

"How so? Y'all are married. Mandy and me are just dating. Shouldn't ya be more open with your wife?"

Ty laughed. "First, if the womenfolk around ya have any say in the matter, you'll get hitched to Mandy soon enough. As your friend, I'm tellin' ya that you won't find a better woman. Second, it's different 'cause I got bit. Jasmine doesn't need that worry."

In sharing what had happened, Ty's being bitten hadn't occurred to Garrett. He could see how that would change things.

"Okay, my friend. I get where you're comin' from. I'll see ya tomorrow."

They shook hands and parted company.

~ * ~

When Garrett opened the front door to his house about an hour later, he expected to see plates on the coffee table and *Jeopardy,* ready to watch on the television, but the living room was empty. Mandy had parked her car in the driveway, so he knew they'd gotten home. There were no signs of a struggle, but the empty house set his nerves on end. He heard laughter from the back deck and his nerves relaxed.

Holding the three pizza boxes over his head, like a server might hold a tray of food, Garrett stepped out on the back deck and found Mandy and Paige sitting at the table engaged in light-hearted conversation.

Paige looked up and smiled. "'Bout time, Daddy."

"Yeah. We thought you ate all three pizzas on the way home," Mandy added.

Garrett put the pizzas on the table. "What about Jeopardy?"

Mandy, having not taken part in Pizza Friday before, looked confused.

"It's so nice outside this evenin'. We thought it'd be fun to eat out here. We can watch Jeopardy after we eat," Paige responded.

Garrett couldn't argue with her logic. It was a nice evening.

He sat down, loaded his plate with five slices, sprinkled them with the salt, black pepper, red pepper, and Tabasco Sauce Paige put on the table.

When Garrett finished perfecting his pizza, Paige looked at Mandy. "Told ya he put all that on his pizza."

Mandy smiled, shook her head disapprovingly, and took a bite of her Veggie Lover's pizza.

As they ate, they talked, laughed and had an all-around good time. No one mentioned the funerals or werewolves. Things almost seemed normal.

After they'd eaten their fill of pizza, five slices for Garrett and three slices each for Paige and Mandy, the conversation dropped off. Garrett's dad referred to this part of dinner as 'digestion time.' An apt description.

Paige broke the silence. "Anything on the SD cards this week, Daddy?"

Garrett shifted in his seat. He wanted to unbutton his britches but resisted the urge. "Nothin' Monday through Wednesday. I haven't swapped out the ones from yesterday yet."

"I thought ya swapped 'em out every mornin'. Why not this mornin'?" Paige asked.

Garrett's eyes flicked from Paige to Mandy, who was blushing, and said, "I was runnin' late this mornin'."

Paige, having not caught on, said, "That's not like you. Why were ya runnin' late?"

Garrett looked at Paige, cleared his throat, and looked back at Mandy. "Umm…I was…busy."

Paige followed Garrett's gaze to Mandy, who was grinning and blushing, too. "Do you know what he's talkin' about?"

Paige's jaw went slack when she caught on.

She looked back at Garrett. "Never mind. I don't wanna know. You're excused for runnin' late."

Awkwardness aside, Garrett couldn't help but laugh.

In short order, Mandy joined in the laughter. Paige said, "Not funny, y'all."

Then Paige started laughing, too.

After the laughter at her expense ended, Paige said, "Are ya gonna swap 'em out before we go in?"

"Now? After eatin' all that pizza?" Garrett balked.

"I'd like to see how ya climb those trees," Mandy said, taking Paige's side.

Garrett stuck his thumbs into the waistband of his Wranglers. "I'm fuller than a tick on a pug-nosed dog's ass."

Paige burst out laughing at the comment.

Mandy tried, unsuccessfully, to repress a smile. "Oh my, Garrett. You have a way with words."

"Well…it's true," Garrett said with a grin.

He sat up in his chair. "I'll gear up. Go grab the replacement cards, Paige-Turner."

Paige jumped up and went inside, while Mandy followed Garrett to the shed. The often-used gear was just inside the shed doors. Mandy watched as Garrett stepped into the harness and strapped the spikes to his boots.

When Garrett geared up, Paige walked up and handed the four SD cards to him. They were in individual plastic cases that snapped shut. Garrett used a Sharpie to number each SD card one through four. The first tree was the back left tree; closest to the shed. Tree two was the front left tree, tree three was the front right tree, and tree four was the back right tree.

Garrett put the SD cards in his left chest pocket and walked to the first tree with his 'girls' following him.

As he flung the nylon strap around the tree trunk, which he caught on the first try, Paige said, "This could take a while, Mandy. He's not as young as he thinks he is."

Mandy laughed.

Garrett didn't. "Prepare to be amazed, little girl. For that comment, you get to clean up the supper mess on your own."

Paige murmured something derogatory under her breath, but Garrett wasn't listening. He'd gotten much faster at climbing the trees since Paige watched him do it the first time and, full as a tick or not, he wanted to impress Mandy. Garrett stabbed his right foot spike, then the left, flung the strap up, and started climbing. Within a few seconds, he was a good thirty feet up the tree.

"Okay. I'm impressed. You're a quick climber. Do I still have to clean up by myself?" Paige hollered up at Garrett.

Garrett paused for a second. It was best to concentrate on climbing when climbing. "Yep. Unless Mandy, out of the goodness of her heart, wants to help ya."

"I guess if you've seen your boyfriend climb one tree, there's not much more to see. I'll help Paige clean up. You be careful, Garrett," Mandy responded.

With the girls gone, Garrett slowed his climbing to a more comfortable, full belly pace. The first two trees went off without a hitch. At the third tree, he threw the strap around, hooked it to the harness, right foot stabbed the spike, left foot stab, and started climbing. After throwing the strap up the tree the second time, and stepping up, Garrett came to something that hadn't been on the third tree the previous morning when he swapped the SD cards. Something troubling.

There, in front of Garrett's face, were four deep gouges. It had swiped away the rough pine bark and the four gashes were deep enough into the tree that sap oozed from them like amber blood. The slashes were higher on the right side and angled down and to the left. Garrett looked down at the ground and judged the damage to be ten to twelve feet up the tree.

He'd had a visitor. Whether the werewolf lashed out, or just left its mark, Garrett didn't know. He knew the critter cam captured it and might answer the question.

As part of the SD card swap procedure, Garrett checked the battery meter on each camera. The first two were fine, about two-thirds power left. The third camera's battery had been much lower. It only had a third of its battery life left.

"What the hell did you capture last night?" Garrett asked the inanimate object.

It didn't answer, but it would tell. Garrett decided he'd review the SD cards the next morning before Paige woke up.

Replacing the fourth tree's SD card went like the first two. No claw marks and plenty of battery power left. After climbing down, Garrett put his gear in the shed and went inside.

The air-conditioning felt good after climbing the trees in the muggy late evening. Mandy and Paige were on the couch talking, but they stopped and looked back at Garrett when he slid the back door closed.

"Can we check out the SD cards before watchin' *Jeopardy*?" Paige asked.

Garrett exaggerated a stretch. "I'm a bit tuckered out from the climbin'. As ya pointed out, I'm not as young as I think I am. I just wanna flop down in my recliner and beat y'all at *Jeopardy*."

"Okay, but sit on the couch with us," Mandy replied.

She patted the couch cushion beside her to show exactly where he should sit.

If it had just been Mandy there, the ruse might have worked, but Paige wasn't buying the load Garrett was selling.

She looked at Garrett. "What's wrong? Somethin' happened. What is it?"

Because Garrett knew Paige wouldn't give until she badgered the truth out of him, she was like a bulldog with a bone when she latched on to something, he said, "It's just claw marks on a tree. Nothin' major. We can look tomorrow."

"Which tree?" Paige asked.

Garrett didn't want to tell which tree had the claw marks. At least not with Mandy there.

Paige still had that bulldog look in her eyes and he said, "Tree three."

"Which tree's that?" Mandy asked.

"It doesn't…" Garrett started to say.

Paige cut him off. "Front right. Closest to Daddy's bedroom."

Garrett wished like hell Paige hadn't expanded on the tree's location. Mandy didn't know the tree numbering system. He looked at Mandy and waited for it to sink in. Mandy's jaw went slack.

She looked at Garrett. "This was last night?"

Garrett nodded.

"We're lookin' at the SD cards," Mandy declared.

Defeated, Garrett headed for his home office. Mandy and Paige followed him.

Garrett pulled the SD cards from his right chest pocket. Replacements went in the left pocket and used went in the right pocket. He lined them up in numerical order on his desk.

When he went to put the one marked '1' in the SD card reader, Mandy said, "I thought it was tree three?"

"It is, but I have a system," Garrett responded.

Mandy exhaled loudly, but she said nothing else.

The SD card opened in Finder and showed five short videos—nothing over five megabytes.

Garrett highlighted the first and fifth videos and dragged them to the iMac's trash container, but Mandy said, "Why aren't ya lookin' at those?"

Garrett stopped the drag, which deposited the videos on the desktop. "The first and last videos are me. The first is me climbin' down the tree after swappin' the cards out and the last is me climbin' up the tree to swap 'em out again."

Garrett double-clicked on the fifth video. "Look."

The video opened in QuickTime and showed all three of them walking up to the tree and Garrett climbing it. With Mandy satisfied, Garrett closed QuickTime and moved the two videos to the Trash container.

Garrett highlighted the three remaining videos. "These are the ones we're interested in. Since this is tree one, and they're all small files, this is probably the fat raccoon that visits my back deck every night."

Garrett double-clicked on the highlighted videos and QuickTime opened again.

The first and second videos were the fat raccoon. The first one showed him waddling toward the house at ten eighteen p.m. and the second one showed him scurrying away at eleven o three p.m. Garrett and Paige knew what the scurrying meant; a werewolf appeared, but neither said anything. The third video had been nothing more than a flutter of greenish white at four thirty-six a.m.

Before Mandy could ask what the flutter was, Garrett said, "Probably a bug flyin' in front of the critter-cam. I get those every so often."

The SD card from the second tree only had two videos on it. Garrett put them in the Trash container and swapped out the second card for the third. It had four videos on it. The second video stood out immediately to Garrett. It had been almost four gigabytes in size. The hair on the back of his neck prickled.

As usual, Paige didn't miss a thing.

She pointed at the second video. "Holy crap, Daddy. Look how big that file is."

Mandy leaned close to the monitor. "What does that mean?"

Garrett took a deep breath. "It means whatever was there was there for a long time."

He looked from Paige to Mandy. "Are y'all sure y'all wanna watch this?"

They both nodded.

Garrett double-clicked the video file.

QuickTime opened and revealed the back of the massive werewolf as it walked on all fours into the critter-cam range. Mandy gasped. She wasn't as used to the things as Garrett and Paige were. The time stamp started at eleven of four p.m., which coordinated with the time the raccoon made a hasty retreat. The end timestamp wouldn't be visible until the end of the video, but Garrett could see the video was three hours and fourteen minutes long. He knew that would put the werewolf leaving the camera's field of vision about two eighteen a.m., which had been when the motion-activated floodlights woke him up. The hair on the back of his neck prickled again.

After walking into the frame, the werewolf sat down on its hind haunches, like a dog, and stared toward Garrett's house—Garrett's bedroom. If it had stayed still, the camera would have stopped recording and started again when it next moved. Its tail kept swishing back and forth, like a cheerful dog's tail does.

It wants to keep the camera goin', Garrett thought.

Aside from its tail swishing back and forth, its ears constantly twitched as if it were monitoring far away sounds. It periodically sniffed at the air, too. Garrett didn't like that because he knew there was only one fresh scent to mark. Mandy's.

Several minutes into the video, Garrett moved the mouse cursor over the fast-forward button to advance the video more quickly.

Before he did, Paige said, "Wait. Pause it."

Garrett moved the mouse pointer slightly to the left and clicked the pause button.

Paige pointed at the monitor. "Look. Look at her left ear."

Garrett studied the paused image, not sure what he was supposed to see. Then he saw it. A small hole in its left ear.

"It's not healin'," Garrett said.

"Or it's healin' slowly," Paige added.

"That's a good thing?" Mandy asked.

"That's where I shot it with a silver bullet a week ago. These things usually heal in minutes, hours at the outside. That its ear still has a hole in it…with such a minor wound, is evidence of the power of silver to inflict lastin' damage. So, yeah. It's a good thing."

With the ear damage identified and discussed, Garrett fast-forwarded through the rest of the video. Its tail kept swishing, its ears kept twitching, and it kept periodically sniffing the night air.

Even though Garrett had been certain of what the beast would do at the end of the video, he slowed the video to actual speed with about a minute left. Fifteen seconds before the video ended, the werewolf got up on all fours, arched its massive back, stretched like a dog stretches, and walked out of the frame toward Garrett's bedroom. With two seconds left, the foreground of the forest floor turned a brighter, whiter green. The camera captured the motion-activated floodlights switching on. The timestamp had been two eighteen a.m.

Mandy swallowed so hard it was audible. "Oh crap, Garrett. Was it headin' for your bedroom?"

Garrett nodded. "It was two eighteen when the floodlights woke me up."

With no one else saying a word, Garrett double-clicked on the last video.

QuickTime opened with the werewolf walking up to the tree on its hind legs at two thirty-one a.m. The floodlights went out, and the image switched to darker greens and whites. The werewolf looked directly, and deliberately, up at the critter-cam. Its eyes were orbs of white-hot light. It opened its mouth wide, revealing its dagger-length fangs that glowed a slightly less intense white than its eyes. It swiped its right-hand claws across the tree trunk. The impact was so violent the image shook as bark went flying into the night. It turned its head back toward Garrett's house and raised its head twice in exaggerated motions. Garrett understood the message it sent. It was showing it marked the fresh scent. It dropped to all fours and sprinted away.

When it was over, Paige, who also knew what message the werewolf sent, said, "Ya have to tell her, Daddy."

"Tell me what?" Mandy asked, while unsuccessfully trying to keep panic out of her too shrill voice.

Garrett pulled Mandy into a hug. "I think it was markin' your scent."

"She was," Paige insisted.

"What does that mean?" Mandy pleaded as tears spilled down her cheeks.

"It means it can find ya whenever it wants to," Garrett told her and hugged her tighter.

"It means ya need to move in with Daddy," Paige added.

~ * ~

The sun was sinking below the tallest pine trees as Dillon turned onto the overgrown, winding drive that led to the old barn they used to transform in. The barn Alexis considered her den. Meeting Alexis at the barn was a first. She'd picked them up and drove all of them together to the barn in her truck the previous times. Dillon thought Alexis didn't want to be seen in Dillon's company since he was being watched. He wasn't being watched that day. Huff's scent and truck were gone when Dillon left his apartment.

Dillon parked his Civic next to Alexis' truck on the backside of the barn. She wasn't waiting for him outside, but he could smell her pungent musk coming from within the barn. He got out of his car, locked it, which, he realized, was foolish given where they were, and walked toward the side door. The partially hung door screeched in protest as Dillon pulled it open and stepped inside the darkened barn.

As his eyes adjusted to the darkness, Dillon sensed Alexis was behind him. He spun around and saw burning red orbs peering at him from a darkened corner of the barn. She leapt toward him with incredible speed. Dillon saw teeth and claws coming for him. He screamed and threw his arms over his face and head protectively. Dillon braced for impact. It didn't happen. Instead, he heard Alexis laughing hysterically.

When Dillon lowered his arms, he saw Alexis standing in front of him, naked, and doubled over laughing. He wasn't sure what unnerved him more. The joke of attacking him or the speed with which Alexis transformed back into human form in mid-leap.

After the laughing fit passed, Alexis straightened up. "For a werewolf, you're a real pussy. You shouldn't be afraid of anything."

"Say's the girl who killed Cole," Dillon retorted.

Alexis smiled a wicked smile. "Touché."

She walked past Dillon and sat on a rusted piece of farm equipment Dillon couldn't identify.

"What're we doing here?"

Alexis grinned. "The sheriff has a girlfriend. I marked her scent last night, and she's at his place again. So is his daughter, the little bitch."

"So," Dillon said defiantly.

"So…I wanna have a little fun with them tonight," Alexis responded lightheartedly.

Dillon scoffed. "The sheriff also has silver bullets."

Alexis inadvertently touched her left ear where the hole healed slowly.

"We're not gonna get close enough for them to even know we're there."

"What's the point, then?"

Alexis stood up and approached Dillon. In the dying, deep orange light that filtered through the broken windows, rotted siding, and siding gaps, Dillon could see a fine sheen of sweat glistening on her perfect breasts.

Alexis followed Dillon's gaze to her breasts. She took his left hand in her right and pressed it against her left breast. It was a small price to pay to manipulate Dillon into doing what she needed to do. Manipulating men with her body was still more natural to Alexis than bending them to her will as a werewolf. She'd been using her human body for a much longer time.

"He has motion-activated cameras in the woods around his house. I just want him to know we're still strong and we're not scared of him," Alexis explained.

"I *am* scared of him, Alexis. You should be, too. He has silver, fuckin' bullets." Dillon shot back.

Alexis slid Dillon's hand off her breast, down her stomach, between her legs, and cupped it firmly against her crotch. "He won't even know we're there."

Before Dillon answered verbally, Alexis felt his answer growing in his pants.

Men are so fuckin' easy, Alexis thought.

Alexis did something she hadn't planned on doing and it surprised her. She kissed Dillon. A few seconds later, Dillon was undressed, and they were fucking on the dirty barn floor. Dillon finished before Alexis got started, but he enjoyed it.

Dillon rolled off Alexis onto his back and looked up at the partially collapsed barn roof. Tiny particles of dust danced in the shafts of purpling light. He was panting; Alexis wasn't.

After a few seconds passed, Dillon said, "Why'd we do that? You can make me go with you without fuckin' me."

Alexis stood up quickly and looked down at Dillon. "I was horny. You've got what some girls might consider a functioning dick. I used it. Not for long, though. That was less a fuck than it was a spasm."

In his place and humiliated, Dillon got to his feet.

They transformed, Dillon slowly, Alexis quickly, and sprinted into the darkening woods.

~ * ~

"Who is Martin Van Buren?" Paige shouted in response to Alex Trebek's clue of, "The first natural-born President of the United States."

When Alex agreed with her question, Paige jumped up, and pointed at Garrett. "I'm beatin' ya! I can't believe I'm beatin' ya."

Somehow, after the shock of Mandy's being marked dissipated, Paige talked her into the marathon watching of five *Jeopardy* episodes Garrett DVR'd during the week. Initially, Mandy wanted to go home. Over several minutes of discussion, Garrett and Paige convinced her staying there was the more prudent choice.

They didn't mention Paige's idea that Mandy move in with Garrett again, which suited Garrett just fine. Mandy was welcome to stay with him for the duration of the current situation, and beyond if they both thought it a good idea to do so, but living together wasn't a decision to make under the duress of a werewolf attack.

Mandy agreed to spend that weekend with Garrett and Paige and discuss where she'd sleep after that on Sunday. That suited Garrett just fine, too.

By the time Paige started taunting Garrett about beating him, they were on the fifth and last episode of the week. Garrett hadn't known who the first natural-born president had been. He was losing because the werewolf's actions continued to distract him. The thought he put Mandy's life in danger by bringing her to his house gnawed at his brain like a tiny claw in his head. A tiny werewolf claw.

The Final Jeopardy category was 'CELEBRITY MEMOIRS.'

As Garrett started fast-forwarding through the commercials, Paige shouted, "I'm bettin' it all. All five shows."

There was nothing to bet, real or imagined. They didn't keep score with pen and paper.

Garrett smiled. "I'm bettin' all but a dollar. What about you, Mandy?"

Mandy smiled, but it still looked forced to Garrett. "I'll hold back two dollars."

"Y'all are toast. I know celebrities." Page boasted.

When *Jeopardy* came back on, Garrett pushed the play button.

Paige read the clue aloud, "Memoirs by Righteous Brothers singer Bill Medley and this late actor share the same title 'The Time of My Life.'"

As the *Jeopardy* theme music started playing, Paige screwed up her face. "Righteous Brothers? Who the heck are they?"

"A singin' group. They were before my time, kiddo," Garrett responded.

Mandy grinned. "The actor wasn't before your time, Garrett."

"If ya know it, say it before a contestant gets it right, or it doesn't count," Garrett told Mandy.

Like it was common knowledge, Mandy said, "Patrick Swayze." Then she added, "I had such a crush on him when I was younger. I've seen Dirty Dancin' at least a dozen times."

Mandy was correct.

"You won," a dejected Paige said.

Garrett turned off the TV and stood up. "If we're goin' to Mandy's and fetchin' her stuff for the weekend, we best get gone."

As Paige and Mandy were getting up from the couch, Garrett opened the front door and waited for them to exit first.

"Always open the door for women and be the last one through it," Garrett's dad told him more times than he could count.

Mandy went out first, followed closely by Paige. Garrett stepped out and ran into Paige's back. She was rooted to the front porch as still as a statue.

Paige said, "Daddy."

She didn't need to say anything more. Garrett heard it, or heard the lack of it, too. The woods around his house were deathly silent.

Drawing his pistol as he did, Garrett moved quickly past Paige, grabbed Mandy's shoulder, and pulled her behind him. Mandy lost her footing and would have gone down if not for Paige catching her and righting her.

"Get inside." Garrett shouted.

"What's wrong?" a startled Mandy blurted.

"They're here," Paige whispered, but it carried in the unnaturally quiet night.

At that point, a ruckus erupted in the woods to Garrett's right front. Garish growls shattered the silence. A loud, pain-filled yelp that sounded like a dog being tortured followed the growls. The motion-activated floodlights on the front left of the house came on and Garrett could see the underbrush at the edge of his yard moving violently in all directions. He aimed the pistol in that direction and moved his finger from the trigger guard to the trigger. That was when the werewolf came flying out of the underbrush toward Garrett.

It was as if the world slowed down. The massive werewolf came flying out of the underbrush headfirst, as if it took a running leap. Garrett heard Mandy scream behind him, but it sounded like she was screaming under water.

The beast landed about twenty feet in front of Garrett, head down and shoulders squared. Its left shoulder was bloody.

It was huge, but its orientation created a small target. Garrett steadied his finger and waited for a better shot. Double tap, center mass. The werewolf raised its head and looked at Garrett. Its eyes were a dim, dying red. Not the intense flaming orbs he'd seen before. The werewolf clawed feebly at the ground and Garrett saw its right arm broken above the wrist and hung by tendons and meat.

Then, somehow, it stood up on shaky hind feet and faced Garrett, as if it wanted him to shoot it. It looked over its damaged shoulder toward the woods it came from and howled a mournful howl.

Fuck double-tap, Garrett thought.

He squeezed the trigger four times and saw four tightly clustered holes open in the center of the werewolf's broad chest.

The werewolf clutched at the four smoking holes in its chest. Its deadly claws cut slashes in its flesh when it did, as if trying to dig the deadly silver bullets out. It fell to its knees, and then fell face down in Garrett's yard. The impact shook the ground under Garrett's feet from twenty feet away.

Not knowing if the werewolf came alone, and believing it hadn't, Garrett raised the gun and trained it toward the woods again.

Paige said, "She's gone, Daddy."

Garrett's heart thumped so loudly in his ears he couldn't hear anything but the 'thud-thump' of his fast-beating heart. As his heart rate slowed, the familiar night sounds of crickets, frogs, and other critters filled his ears. Garrett looked down at where the werewolf fell and saw a naked young man face down in the grass.

After holstering his gun, Garrett walked up to the body, squatted down, and turned the head sideways, so he could see the face. It did not entirely surprise him to see Dillon Albertson's dead eyes looking back at him. He knew why Dillon was dead. He was the only link to the alpha. Dillon had been the bitch's weak link, and she made Garrett do her dirty work for her, so he'd know how close he was.

"Y'all go on back inside. I've got work to do," Garrett told Paige and Mandy.

Paige had to help Mandy navigate the short distance from the front porch to the front door; Mandy still looked frightened and unsteady on her feet. Garrett called Ty as well as George Krats and started processing the scene.

~ * ~

Ty arrived before George, so Garrett had time to fill him in on what happened and why Garrett thought it happened. Ty agreed with Garrett's theory about the alpha severing the last tie to its human life.

"It's alone now," Ty said.

Garrett nodded. "Let's make sure we keep it that way."

Ty agreed with that, too.

When the County Coroner van pulled into Garrett's driveway, it relieved him to see George behind the wheel. George wasn't completely in the loop on the recent activities; he didn't know about Paige, Ty, and Trowa being bitten. He knew the recent string of murders and deaths resulted from werewolves. The first clue being the removal of Ty's Silver Star from Seth Daniels' chest. He wasn't asking Garrett tough questions, either.

Upon exiting the van, George walked up to Garrett and Ty, who were standing next to Dillon Albertsons' body. "Well?"

"He attacked me when I came outside and I had to shoot him," Garrett explained.

George nodded. "Was he…?"

Garrett nodded.

"Works for me. I came alone…easier to not have questions I can't answer to answer. If y'all will help me bag him, I'll get him to the morgue and do the post-mortem tonight to avoid more questions."

Garrett clapped George on the shoulder. "Thanks, George. I owe ya."

"I like scotch," George said with a wink.

After they collected Dillon's body and processed the scene, an exhausted Garrett climbed into his bed. Mandy and Paige were already in it, so it was a tight fit. Even so, he slept well.

~ * ~

The werewolf made its way back to the old barn slowly, taking time to enjoy the sensations of being the apex predator in the woods. It could hear other animals scurrying away from its presence. Something larger than the plentiful raccoons, opossums, and armadillos moved slowly away to the alpha's right. It sniffed the air. Venison filled its nostrils. The alpha sprinted toward the slow-moving deer.

Seconds later, the alpha caught up with the fat doe. When the doe saw the werewolf, its eyes went wide with fear. The doe tried to leap away, but it's bloated belly prevented a successful leap. The alpha clamped its jaws around the doe's neck and flung it to the ground. The doe let out an almost human scream before the alpha bit down with more force and crushed its windpipe. The alpha listened to the three heartbeats, one strong and frantic, two weak and steady, coming from the dying doe. First, the doe's heartbeat stopped. Without oxygenated blood from the doe, the two weak heartbeats beat irregularly.

The alpha released the doe's neck from its jaws and raked its claws across the doe's bloated belly. Intestines and two fully formed fawns slid out in a rush of blood. The alpha snatched up one fawn and easily bit it in half. It savored the tender, unborn meat, bones, and organs. Two bites later, all that remained of the first fawn was its small, wet head. The alpha tossed it carelessly into the woods and devoured the second fawn. Its hunger placated; the alpha sprinted away.

The werewolf emerged from the woods by the Wiseman barn and walked up behind Dillon's Civic. It put its hands on the trunk and pushed the car toward woods on the far side of the barn clearing. Its claws dug into the trunk lid and left deep scratches in the orange paint. The emergency break was on, but this didn't hamper the powerful werewolf's efforts. Seconds later, Dillon's Civic was thirty feet into the dense woods. The alpha only stopped pushing when the car slammed into a large tree that collapsed the front bumper and crumpled the hood. It looked more like the car had been going thirty miles an hour when it hit the tree, not from being slow pushed on tires that weren't turning. The werewolf's strength and mass made up for the difference in speed. Satisfied it sufficiently concealed the car, the alpha went inside the barn.

Moments later, Alexis emerged from the barn dressed and carrying Dillon's clothes in a tight bundle. She went back to the car and used Dillon's key to open the Civic's trunk. She dropped Dillon's clothes and the keys in the trunk and shut the lid.

As Alexis walked back to her truck, she inhaled deeply and took in the wonderful, wooded night air. She looked up at the silver moon' beauty and only three nights away from the new moon phase.

On June second, seventeen nights from that night, the moon would be full again and she would have a new pack. The little bitch would be hers to torment. First by being the pack fuck-bitch. Then she would have the little bitch turn her father, so he could partake of the little bitch in the future.

Could you shoot your precious daughter with silver bullets if she was coming for you, Sheriff? Alexis thought.

She didn't think he would.

The memory of how *El Lobo* had planned to rape her, while she had been still a human, with his massive werewolf's cock, came back to Alexis.

She grinned, revealing blood still stuck between her perfect, white teeth. "That's what I'm gonna have your daddy do to you on the July fool moon, you little bitch."

There was no one to hear Alexis, but her voice carried on the still night. The nighttime critters hadn't resumed their buzzing, chirping, and croaking chorus. Even in human form, they sensed the werewolf lurking just beneath the beautiful young woman's façade.

Alexis got into her truck and started the engine. As she pulled away from the barn, she resigned herself to lying low until the next full moon. No more trips to the sheriff's house and no more human kills. She would confine her wolf to the deep woods and dine on wildlife until then.

Thinking about dining on wildlife reminded Alexis of the succulent, unborn fawns her wolf consumed. They were so tasty and tender. Alexis' tongue inadvertently slipped from between her lips and licked at some drying fawn blood still on her human face. The coppery taste exploded on her tongue and made her mouth water.

~ * ~

Early the next morning, before Paige and Mandy were awake, Garrett swapped out the SD cards. When he watched the video from tree two, his suspicions were confirmed.

The werewolves were crouched by the tree for over an hour. They stood up at the same time Garrett, Paige, and Mandy were leaving. The alpha clamped its jaws on the beta's shoulder and shook the massive beast like a ragdoll. While biting the beta's shoulder, it raked its claws across the beta's back and opened four deep gashes. The beta lifted its head and yelped. Then the beta clawed at the alpha's chest. The alpha reacted to this assault by letting go of the beta's shoulder and biting down on its right arm. Black blood in the greenish image erupted around the alpha's teeth as it bit almost through the beta's arm. The alpha grabbed the defeated beta by the damaged shoulder and tail and hurled it out of the video frame. What Garrett thought had been a running leap had been a sacrificial offering. After offering the beta to Garrett's silver bullets, the alpha looked up at the camera with its white-hot orbs and winked. It dropped to all fours and sprinted away.

~ * ~

The house was full of commotion as Garrett, Paige, and Mandy prepared for the guests, who would arrive at two o'clock. Paige cleaned the grill, her least favorite thing to do, while Garrett prepped the rib eye steaks and Mandy prepared the vegetables.

The steak prep was simple but tasty. A sprinkling of Worcestershire sauce, salt, black pepper, onion salt, and garlic salt. After applying these, Garrett took a fork and poked holes in the meat. This tenderized and pushed the flavorings into the meat. Then, for added flavor, while grilling the steaks over charcoal and water-soaked wood chips, Garrett put a pad of butter on the steaks after each flip. The result was tender, juicy, flavorful steaks.

Mandy sliced up an assortment of vegetables. Squash, onions, mushrooms, bell peppers, and zucchini. She put them in a zip lock baggie. To the baggie, she added black pepper and Italian dressing. When the charcoal was ready, she dumped the vegetables into a wire basket to be cooked on the grill with the meat.

At about a quarter to two, Ty came strolling around the back left side of the house with a six-pack of Bud Light in one hand and two bouquets of flowers in the other. At the grill, spreading the gray-hot coals around the bottom of the grill with a stick, Garrett saw Ty first.

Noticing the flowers, Garrett said, "Suck up."

Ty grinned. "To pretty girls, always."

Hearing Ty caused Paige to look up and see him. She ran up to him and wrapped him in a tight hug. Ty, with hands full, made a feeble attempt at returning the hug. By the time Paige released Ty, Mandy wrapped him in another tight hug. Ty looked at Garrett and rolled his eyes, as if to suggest the hugs were an inconvenience. Garrett knew he loved every second of the attention, though.

After the hugs, Ty handed each of them a bouquet, which they "Ooh'd" and "Aah'd" over.

Paige said, "Let's put 'em in water and place 'em on the table."

"That's a great idea," Mandy said.

To Ty, Mandy said, "Gimme those and I'll put 'em in the fridge for ya."

Ty handed her the six-pack and walked over to Garrett at the grill.

"You are makin' me look bad, buddy," Garrett told Ty when he was next to him.

Ty grinned. "Not that hard to do."

Garrett started to tell Ty to 'Fuck off,' but the rumble of a motorcycle engine filled the air and diverted his attention. The rumbling died and there was a knock on the front door.

From within the house, Paige yelled, "I got it."

Mandy came out with the flowers stuck in two mason jars, Garrett didn't have a vase, and placed them on the table. A few seconds later, Paige came out with Trowa following her.

Trowa dressed much more conservatively than Garrett saw him dress before. At the biker funerals Trowa had been wearing a black leather vest with no shirt beneath. He had on a turquoise-colored button-down shirt with the cuffs rolled up mid-forearm, new-ish blue jeans, boots, and he was carrying a bottle of Wild Turkey in one hand.

Garrett left the grill and stuck out his hand. "Glad ya could make it. I've got Coke, Sprite, and ice in the house, if ya want mixers."

Trowa took Garrett's hand, but before he could reply, Mandy cleared her throat loudly.

Garrett caught on. "I'm sorry. Trowa, ya know Ty and my daughter, Paige. This is my girlfriend, Mandy Davis. Mandy, this is Trowa Raintree."

Mandy stuck out her hand. "Pleased to meet ya, Trowa."

Trowa took Mandy's hand. "Pleasure's all mine, Mandy."

After the introductions, Garrett said, "Well, I better get these steaks on the grill."

Ty went to the grill with Garrett, and Trowa took a seat at the table with Paige and Mandy. The three of them fell into a discussion about the flowers. Trowa told them the Caddo Indian words for some of them.

There was another knock at the door. The last member of Dumblegarrett's Army arrived. Ty went to let him in.

Garrett, attending the grill, had his back to the sliding door, when he heard James say, "I hope ya don't mind, but I brought a friend."

Garrett minded. He already regretted telling Mandy about what had been going on. It had put her in danger. Now James brought someone else into their group.

Garrett heard Paige squeal, "He's *soooo* adorable."

Garrett turned around and saw the fattest English Bulldog he'd ever seen. It was all white, except for a brindle dot in the middle of his wrinkled head. It was broader across the chest than it was tall, and its long, pink tongue hung out of the right side of its mouth, dripping drool onto the wooden deck. It was panting like it just ran a marathon instead of walking from the front to the back doors.

"This is Winston," James announced.

In a flash, Paige was on her knees in front of Winston.

She grabbed his floppy cheeks. "Look at this face. He is *soooo* cute."

Winston loved the attention. He waddled closer to Paige and licked her face. Paige laughed. To Garrett's surprise, because Mandy wasn't much of a dog person, she got down on her knees and started loving on Winston, too. Trowa even reached down with a long arm and patted the dog's wrinkled head. Winston panted and licked the two giggling girls.

The dog was cool, but Garrett's attention went to what James was carrying in his right hand. A clear, glass, one-gallon jug of amber colored liquid.

James approached Garrett and lifted the jug. "As promised. Some of my homemade muscadine wine. Want a pre-dinner nip?"

Before Garrett could respond in the affirmative, Ty said, "I'll get the glasses. Who's in?"

All hands went up, including Paige's.

Garrett gave Paige a stern look, but she stuck out her bottom lip. "Please, Daddy? Just a little taste."

Garrett looked from Paige to Mandy to Ty to James to discern their thoughts. In return, he got a smile from Mandy, a shrug from James, and a nod from Ty.

Trowa, who he hadn't looked at, said, "The girl's a werewolf. I think she can handle a taste of muscadine wine."

This was unsolicited advice but welcomed. It had also been the first time Paige's, and by extension Ty's and Trowa's, condition came up in a group of people. Tension seemed to melt away. This was the point of their meeting. Everyone, including Garrett, laughed.

Garrett said, "Okay, but just a little."

Paige grinned. "Thank you, Daddy."

When Ty left to get the glasses, Garrett introduced James to the other members of their secret group. He introduced Ty to James when he got back with the glasses, but they'd introduced themselves to each other when Ty welcomed James in at the front door.

James poured a healthy portion of the amber muscadine wine into five glasses and about a shot's worth into the sixth.

When everyone had a glass, James said, "I think a toast is in order. The honor is yours, Garrett."

Garrett hadn't expected making a toast and, for a moment, he couldn't think of anything to say.

He raised his glass. "To killin' that bitch before she kills again."

"Or turns someone else," Ty added.

The glasses came together with 'clinks' and went to eager lips.

Garrett never tasted muscadine wine before and didn't know what to expect. It pleasantly surprised him. The amber liquid tasted sweet on his tongue but carried decisive warmth on the way down. He liked it. He liked it a lot.

After savoring the first tastes, compliments followed. James took them with humility, but Garrett could tell it pleased James to please them. After draining the first round, everyone but Paige got a refill. She protested and even pouted, but Garrett held fast to his prior agreement of a taste. Paige didn't pout long. She was back on the deck, loving on Winston before everyone else's glasses were refilled. After Mandy's glass had been refilled, she joined Paige on the deck with Winston.

Ty and Trowa fell into a discussion about the muscadine wine and James joined Garrett at the grill. Garrett noticed James' left-hand ring-finger didn't have a wedding band on it when he first met him. Law enforcement folks often took in little details without thinking about it.

"Not to be too forward, or pry, but I noticed you're not wearin' a weddin' ring."

James held up his left hand, as if studying it. "Confirmed bachelor, I'm afraid."

Garrett motioned over his shoulder at Paige and Mandy playing with Winston. "That dog's your ticket to pickin' up a lady friend, James. I've never seen those two act like that. I'm a little jealous of Winston."

James chuckled. "If that were my goal, I know your assessment is correct."

"Like I said, I don't mean to pry, but is there a special lady in your life?"

James took a sip of muscadine wine and cleared his throat. "No, no. There's not a special lady in my life. Nor has there ever been."

This information surprised Garrett. James wasn't what most people would consider strikingly handsome, but he had to be someone's type.

"Ever?"

James looked around, as if making sure the coast was clear. "I'm gay, Garrett."

This information surprised Garrett even more.

The look of utter surprise must have been plainly clear on Garrett's face, because James chuckled. "It's not like we have it tattooed on our foreheads, or wear terraria's."

Garrett felt foolish and ashamed for reacting to the information the way he did.

He composed himself. "Of course not. I'm sorry, James. I just assumed…I'm an idiot. Leave it at that."

James smiled. "In East Texas, that is the assumption I'm goin' for." He lifted his glass. "To assumptions."

Garrett clinked James' glass. "And idiots."

They laughed and drained their glasses.

It was only after this interaction with James Garrett realized he knew little about James beyond his academic knowledge of the supernatural. Garrett decided, to whatever degree James was comfortable sharing his personal life, he wanted to know more about his new friend.

When the steaks were charred on the outside and pink on the inside, and the vegetables were soft but still had an internal crunch, Garrett pulled the food from the grill and loaded everyone's plates. As they ate and drank, Garrett, Paige, Mandy, and Ty filled James and Trowa in on what happened the previous night. The two men took in every word without interrupting.

With the tale told, James said, "I think you're right 'bout the alpha killin' off the only link to her human identity. I can't believe I didn't stake out Dillon last night. If I had, he would've led me right to her."

"Or," Garrett said, "he would've led ya to your death."

"Or turn ya," Ty added.

Garrett saw James physically tremble at Ty's suggestion. "I'm glad as hell ya weren't watchin' him last night. We couldn't do this without ya. Or compromised, if she'd bitten ya."

James nodded in appreciation of Garrett's assessment, but he still thought he'd missed an opportunity to find the alpha and possibly end the nightmare.

"Speakin' of compromised," Ty said.

Garrett looked at Ty and saw he and Paige share a quick look.

"What?"

Paige nodded at Ty. "Paige and I have been talkin' 'bout ya makin' plans on how to take out the alpha."

"And?" Garrett asked skeptically.

Paige took up where Ty left off. "We don't think it's a good idea for us to be included in the plans…or even know what they are. We haven't talked with Trowa 'bout this, but he shouldn't know either."

Dumblegarrett's Army just lost half its troops, Garrett thought.

Garrett looked from Ty to Paige to Trowa.

Trowa shrugged. "Don't look at me. I was outta the loop too, brother."

"Why do y'all want out of the plannin'?"

"You just said it 'bout me. They want out, 'cause knowin' might compromise the plan," James answered for them.

Feeling thick, Garrett turned to James.

James gave Garrett a patient smile, like Garrett was sure he had given his students when explaining something complex to them. "It's the connection, Garrett. The alpha knows about it now. Judgin' by what Paige said, 'bout the alpha…pushin' thoughts into her mind, it's learnin' how to use the connection."

"There's a…mental connection with the werewolf and the folks it…turns?" Trowa asked.

Everyone except Mandy nodded.

"Well, shit. Someone could'a told me. I've been thinkin' up ways to kill that bitch all week."

To Paige, Trowa said, "Sorry for the cussin', little miss."

Paige smiled. "Not a problem. I've heard worse."

"I told ya 'bout the connection the night ya got bit," Garrett reminded Trowa.

"Uh, yeah. I'd been drinkin' and had a couple a toots that night. Not exactly conducive for rememberin' stuff," Trowa admitted.

James ignored Trowa's confession and continued, "For a while, Ty and Paige were getting peeks into the alpha's mind without it knowin'. Are y'all still gettin' these peeks?"

Ty and Paige shook their heads. Trowa shrugged his lean shoulders.

"Who's to say it can't do the same to 'em now? If it can get peeks into their minds, anything they know, it could know. Includin' how we plan to take it out," James concluded.

Garrett sat silent for several seconds, digesting the new information. He felt foolish for not considering the connection, and he couldn't deny the logic of the offered theory.

Finally, he said, "Okay, you three are out of the plannin'. I need to know this. Paige has her silver necklace and crucifix, and Ty has his Silver Star. Do you own anything silver, Trowa?"

"Do I own anything silver?" Trowa repeated Garrett's question, "I'm Native American. You ever see a Native American without somethin' made of silver and turquoise? I have a silver wrist band I always wear."

He held up his right wrist, which was bare.

"Damn thing burns my skin now. So, I quit wearin' it."

"Yeah, silver burns werewolves. I can't wear my necklace and crucifix anymore either," Paige explained.

"Well, shit. Sorry, little miss. Someone could'a told me that, too. I tried to wear that damn thing until yesterday. It was burnin' the crap outta my skin.

"Native American culture speaks of the Yee Naaldlooshii, the skin-walker. They're evil beasts, to be sure, but this…connection and silver shit, sorry, little miss, isn't part of the stories. Is there a handbook…or somethin' I can get on werewolves?"

James said, "Actually, I think I have somethin' in my truck you can borrow."

Trowa nodded. "Much appreciated, Doc."

To Garrett, Trowa said, "If ya don't mind my askin', I know ya want us outta the plannin', why do ya wanna know if I have anything silver?"

Garrett looked at James, as if needing permission to share the information.

James gave a quick head nod. "Paige and Ty know this already and the alpha knows it, too. Tellin' Trowa won't compromise anything…even if it pries into his head."

Garrett took another drink of James' muscadine wine. It was his third glass. "When Paige was bit, she crammed her silver necklace and crucifix down the werewolf's throat. This caused it to change back into its human form. It only stopped changin' when it spit the silver out. Paige saw enough of its human form to know it was female. That's how we know this.

"I shared this information with James. He thinks, and I'm inclined to agree that, not only will silver revert the werewolf to human form, it can keep y'all from transformin'."

"Won't that hurt like a bitch? Sorry, little miss," Trowa responded.

Garrett nodded. "It will. Unless we can find it and kill it before the June full moon, silver might be the only thing that'll keep y'all from turnin' into one of those things."

"I don't care how much it hurts. If it works, it'll be worth it," Paige added.

Ty nodded in agreement.

Trowa mulled the information for several seconds. “I can’t be a part of the disharmony these…monsters bring to nature. No matter how much the silver hurts me, they hurt the natural order of nature more. I’m in.”

“What now?” Paige asked.

Garrett drained the last of the muscadine wine in his glass. “I’m gonna drink some more, maybe have a smoke, and enjoy the rest of this beautiful afternoon and good company. Monday, I’ll try to use good old-fashion law enforcement techniques to find her before the next full moon. If all that fails, James and I’ll come up with a solid plan.”

“Do ya have any leads?” Mandy asked.

This was the first time Mandy joined in the conversation and it didn’t surprise Garrett she felt more comfortable interjecting on the human, non-werewolf aspect of the conversation. Even after seeing the video clips and a live werewolf the night before, Garrett knew Mandy was still having a hard time accepting the reality of the situation. That was why something that should have been easy, talking Mandy into staying with Garrett until the nightmare was over, wasn’t.

Garrett knew part of Mandy’s reluctance to move in, even temporarily, had to do with their not being married. She’d told him many times over the course of their three-year relationship she wouldn’t give up her independence without a ring on her finger. Not that Garrett ever asked her to move in. Mandy felt compelled to share this information from time to time. Given the circumstances, Mandy’s continued reluctance was irrational. Irrational in the face of the irrational. With Paige’s help, they talked Mandy into staying at Garrett’s for the duration of the crisis.

Garrett considered Mandy’s question. He had one lead. The vaginal fluid submitted for DNA analysis. After being schooled by James on how those bitten could be compromised, Garrett wasn’t willing to share this with the group, though.

“Nothin’ concrete, but I’m followin’ up on everything I can,” Garrett finally said.

“Well, I’m still willin’ to be bait for her,” Paige offered.

“Me too,” Ty added.

Mandy’s face took on a look of horror and she said, “That’s a horrible idea. Tell me you’re not really considerin’ usin’ ‘em as bait, Garrett.”

Garrett, who was helping himself to another glass of muscadine wine, said, "Let's not get ahead of ourselves. Paige and Ty made that offer the night it killed Trowa's buddies. There's no plan to use 'em, or anyone else as bait."

"I should hope not," Mandy shot back.

"Best put that thought outta your heads, Paige, and Ty. If the alpha picked up on that, it might do somethin'…drastic before the next full moon," James told them.

"It might throw the alpha off," Ty offered.

"Yeah. If we all thought somethin' different, she might get confused," Paige added.

Garrett looked to James, who shook his head. "I can't stop y'all from thinkin' 'bout how to find it, trap it, or…whatever. I think it's best that y'all don't. Don't give it a reason to pay any more attention to y'all than it already is. Let sleepin'…werewolves lie."

The three of them shared quick glances.

Ty said, "I'll refrain. I don't want that thing sniffin' 'round my family."

"Like I said before, I'm new to this. I'll do whatever y'all think's best, Garrett," Trowa added.

Paige was silent.

"Paige?" Garrett prodded.

After a few more moments of silence, Paige said, "Okay. if she lets me in…I'm gonna try to pick at her. Find out stuff about her."

"That could be a trap, Paige," James warned.

Paige smiled. "Maybe. I think I'm smarter than that bitch."

To Trowa, Paige said, "Sorry, big guy."

They all laughed. Trowa laughed so hard tears streamed down his copper-colored cheeks.

With the werewolf discussion exhausted, conversations turned to more pleasant topics. Paige spent most of the remaining time disengaged from the adults and playing with Winston, who only tried to hump her a few times.

Each time Winston did, James would shout, "Winston, no," and apologize profusely.

Paige ignored Winston's amorous intent and continued to rub his coat. No matter where she started rubbing on him, Winston always maneuvered his butt to her hand. James explained the skin folds around

Winston's stubby tail was his favorite 'rub zone,' so Paige obliged and rubbed Winston's butt vigorously. Winston panted and drooled, with his long, pink tongue hanging out of the right side of his mouth.

Around six o'clock, James grabbed the empty muscadine wine jug. "This has been fantastic fun. It was an immense pleasure to meet all of you. Although I felt like I knew y'all before today. Anyway, finals start Monday, and I should get home and go over my exam material."

They met this news with handshakes from Ty and Trowa. Followed by hugs from Mandy and Paige.

When Paige let go of James' neck, she said, "Thanks for helpin' my daddy with all this."

James looked at Paige affectionately, and tucked a wayward strand of her long, brown hair behind her left ear. "It's my pleasure, Paige."

He looked toward Ty and Trowa. "I'll do everything within my power to make sure we break this curse before it can afflict y'all in its full form."

Garrett put his hand on James' shoulder. "We know ya will. C'mon, I'll walk ya out."

Out front, beside James' truck, Garrett shook his limp hand. "With them out of the plannin', I'm gonna need ya more than I thought. Ya up for that?"

James smiled, and tightened his grip, which surprised Garrett. "I'm already kickin' some things around in my head. I'll fill ya in when they're more…concrete."

James lifted Winston, who was too fat to jump, into the truck, and climbed in beside the still drooling bulldog. "I almost forgot. Give this book to Trowa for me."

Garrett took the book and looked at it. It wasn't big, maybe two hundred pages, but the cover caught his attention. The title of the book was *Werewolves: The horrific truth behind the legend*, by Zachary Graves.

Garrett tucked the book under his arm. "Will do."

They parted company.

When Garrett handed the book to Trowa, he looked at it. "The horrific truth behind the legend. I guess I'll find out even if I don't read it."

He announced he was leaving too. Two handshakes and two hugs later, Trowa's Indian motorcycle rumbled to life and he left. That left the three people Garrett cared the most for, excluding his parents, in the world.

The four of them sat on the back deck for another thirty minutes talking about things other than werewolves. Talk turned to their high school football careers, and who had been the better player. Paige asked if she could have a bulldog. Twice. Garrett shot each request down before it could take root, which he knew already happened. Although he got a disapproving look from Mandy and Paige, Garrett smoked two cigarettes.

Mandy was still nursing a glass of muscadine wine. Garrett and Ty finished drinking for the afternoon. Ty had to drive home, and Garrett had to take Paige home and swing by Mandy's house, so she could gather the things she needed for the prolonged stay at his house.

They walked out together. Ty got a hug from all three of them. Garrett's had been of the manly bent arm grasp and one-handed shoulder hug variety. Garrett, Mandy, and Paige followed Ty out of the driveway and turned different directions on County Road Five Eighty-Eight. An hour later, Garrett and Mandy were back at his house, settling into their new, shared domestic lives.

~ * ~

Over the next two weeks, hopes evidence would lead to a good, old-fashioned, law enforcement resolution on the whereabouts of the alpha were not forthcoming. The DNA report on the initial hair collected from the Weaver pig slaughter came back as contaminated. Contaminated because the DNA included *Canis lupus* and human DNA markers. What the lab considered contaminated simply verified what Garrett had since found to be true. The sample had *Canis lupus* and human markers because it had been both human and wolf.

The DNA sample from the vaginal swab came back as belonging to a Caucasian female. There were other hereditary markers, but they were not of use or interest. The only thing that mattered was whether there had been a DNA match in the system. Given they usually take DNA samples from sex offenders, and women rarely commit sex crimes, Garrett wasn't confident in finding a match. So, it didn't surprise him when he didn't find a match.

In a stroke of what Garrett considered pure genius, and to exonerate his department from contaminating the *Canis lupus* hair sample, he ordered the hair and vaginal sample DNA to be compared for similar markers. He felt sure they would find a match there, but those results would not be back before the June full moon. It would simply confirm what Garrett knew in his gut.

Garrett didn't realize he had neglected to follow up on some less than promising leads. This was about to change.

Chapter Sixteen

Over the previous two weeks, Garrett became increasingly frustrated by the lack of progress in locating the alpha or coming up with a solid plan of attack. It was Friday, May 29 and the next full moon, the full moon that would transform Paige, Ty, and Trowa into viscous killing machines, was on Tuesday, June second. Four nights away.

~ * ~

Sitting in his office at the sheriff's department, Garrett looked over the werewolf images and videos from the critter-cams trying, for perhaps the hundredth time, to see if he'd missed anything important. He studied the last image from the night the werewolf smashed through the back door and the blackish blood running through its fingers cupping its left ear. This image came from tree two on the front left of Garrett's house. From its orientation, Garrett could see it headed northeast, and first appeared at that spot, too.

It dawned on Garrett he had never investigated the area in that direction for clues to where the werewolf came from. He'd planned to, in the early days of the investigation, but too much happened in that time to get to it. Since things slowed down, doing so slipped his mind.

The area in question could easily cover a hundred square miles of forest or more. Conventional methods of searching this area of the forest would take days, if not weeks. It was 2015 and technological advancements were making law enforcement much easier. Garrett opened Google Earth on his computer and typed in his home address. The space view of planet Earth with the continental United States of America outlined in yellow zoomed in at dizzying speed. First to Texas, then to East Texas, finally to his house.

From this vantage point, maybe a thousand feet above his house, Garrett could see nothing but woods in the northeast direction. He pulled back the view a little and his parent's house appeared. A chill ran up Garrett's spine as he realized how close the werewolf came to his parent's house. He'd spoken with them several times since the nightmare began.

They came to his house the previous weekend to visit with Paige and Mandy. They ate supper with them, so he knew they were okay. The proximity of the werewolf's path, if it came from that direction, still unnerved him.

Pulling the view back much more would make structures too small to identify, though. Garrett used the mouse to grab the map image and move it. The compass in the top right of the program kept his direction true. This process revealed several more houses, all of which were familiar to Garrett, and one active sawmill, none of which interested him. He was looking for something remote and unused. Two map image moves later revealed something interesting.

A small clearing opened in the dense, green forest and there was a small structure in the middle of the clearing. Garrett grabbed the structure with the mouse, drug it to the middle of the screen, and zoomed in on it. As the structure got closer, Garrett could make out more detail.

It was a barn, and it was clear it hadn't been in use for quite some time. A dead pine tree laid across one end of the structure, which had partially collapsed the roof. There was a large, charred hole in one corner of the roof as well.

"This looks promisin'," Garrett told the computer image.

There seemed no visible access to the barn from the only road, County Road Five Ninety-Eight, that cut through the expanse of dense, green forest surrounding it. Garrett knew trees concealed drives into seldom used structures. He zoomed in on County Road Five Ninety-Eight to where he thought an access road might be and switched to Road View. Instantly, it was as if Garrett stood on the road and looked up the road toward the north.

Using the mouse, Garrett turned to the right and waited for the image to load. When it did, he saw an opening in the trees with nothing but dark shadows beyond a few feet. It looked like a large green mouth eager to swallow anything that dared to get too close. There wasn't a mailbox with an address next to the overgrown drive. Garrett exited Road View, zoomed out, and found another structure, a house, about a half mile south, and on the west side of the barn's location. He could get an address from this structure.

With this information, and Pine View County resources, Garrett could find information on the property and on the individual who owned the property. The forty-four acres belonged to Dale Wiseman. A shady individual who did time in the Federal Correctional Institution in Texarkana, Texas for trafficking marijuana and met an untimely, painful, ass-rape death with a broken broomstick, demise while serving ninety-nine years in the Texas State Penitentiary at Huntsville for raping a twelve-year-old girl in Jacksonville, Texas. Since Dale's conviction on trafficking charges, the property belonged to the federal government.

After learning this, Garrett went back to the Google Earth image and studied it closely. County Road Five Ninety-Eight continued north until it intersected Highway Twenty-One, east of Pine View. Garrett moved the map to the east a little and saw another road intersecting with Highway Twenty-One about two miles east of where County Road Five Ninety-Eight intersected it. This was County Road Six Hundred.

Something about that intersection seemed familiar to Garrett. Having lived his whole life in Pine View County, serving as a reserve deputy, deputy, and sheriff for sixteen years, there weren't many intersections unfamiliar to him. The intersection of County Road Six Hundred and Highway Twenty-One was familiar in the werewolf's context investigation. He couldn't place it.

Several moments passed before it finally registered. That was the intersection he stopped at the morning after the Mill Road Barn attacks when Karen Parker radioed him they found Matt Cooke's body in the woods surrounding the Mill Road Barn. He'd just left Arleen Crawford's house after telling her that her daughter, Maggie, was dead.

When the memory came back, it came back with crystal clarity. He remembered turning left, west, onto Highway Twenty-One to go to the Cooke's house to let them know their son would never come home again. Garrett remembered rounding a curve and seeing a matte-black Ram pickup heading east on Twenty-One toward Nacogdoches. He remembered a pretty blonde-haired girl with big blue eyes giving him a friendly finger-off-the-steering wheel wave as he passed the truck. Garrett remembered thinking it was nice to see a friendly face after such a horrific night.

I've seen her since then, Garrett thought.

Another several moments passed before it finally registered. When it did, Garrett felt like he'd been sucker-punched in the nuts. His nuts crawled up inside his pelvis. The blonde-haired girl with big blue eyes in the truck that morning, the truck coming from County Road Five Ninety-Eight's direction and the Wiseman barn, was the same blonde-haired girl with big blue eyes who grabbed Garrett's jacket lapels when he tripped backing out of the church after Justin's funeral.

This memory came back with crystal clarity, too. He remembered his boot heel hitting the threshold of the church's doors and tripping while walking backward and having an odd conversation with the blue-eyed girl. Garrett remembered how she'd grabbed his lapels and easily, too easily, righted him before he fell. He remembered her eying the gun under his sport jacket and asking if he always carried a gun. Garrett remembered her saying, "Good to know," when he confirmed he always carried a gun.

The Google Earth image zoomed in on the intersection of County Road Six Hundred and Highway Twenty-One. Garrett expanded the view, so it included County Road Five Ninety-Eight and the dilapidated barn. He expanded it several more times until his house came into the image. The image took in a large area, and the structures were little more than dots in tree clearings, but it revealed a clear picture. A straight northeast shot from tree two at Garrett's house to the barn and an exit path from the barn to County Road Five Ninety-Eight to Highway Twenty-One to Nacogdoches where the three dead werewolves attended Stephen F. Austin State University.

It came together with crystal clarity.

Elated, Garrett said, "I've got your fuckin' den, bitch."

A throat clearing brought Garrett's attention from the computer screen to his office door where Jailer Paula Stamford stood holding a paper and a small box. "Sorry 'bout that, Paula. I didn't know you were there."

Paula approached. "No worries, Sheriff. Good news?"

Feeling protective of the information he learned, Garrett quickly minimized the Google Earth program to hide the map. "Maybe. Somethin' to investigate, at least. What ya got for me there?"

Paula handed the paper and box to Garrett. "I need your signature on the kosher meal request for Inmate Goldman, and Deputy Middleton asked me to give ya this."

Garrett took the paper and box from Paula. The box was heavy for its size and, considering it was from Mike Middleton, Garrett hoped it contained the shotgun shells he'd requested a couple of weeks earlier. He quickly signed the kosher meal request and handed it back to Paula.

Paula took the signed request form and left, but she hesitated at the door.

"The full moon's next Tuesday, Sheriff," Paula said.

Remembering their previous conversation on this subject the morning Paula delivered Cole Duncan's real name, Garrett smiled. "I know, Paula. I'm workin' on it."

"Did ya find the wolf's den, Sheriff?"

"Maybe."

Paula smiled a nervous smile and left Garrett's office.

The box contained a full clip of nine-millimeter bullets and five shotgun shells. Garrett hoped for more shotgun shells. A handwritten note from Mike was in the box, too. The note said:

Sorry, there aren't more shotgun shells. These are double-ought buckshot. Each pellet contains about as much silver as a nine-mil round and there are eight pellets in each shell. Do the math. I made ten shotgun shells. Five for me and five for you. I also made enough nine-mil rounds for another full clip for every deputy. The silver is gone. Aim true.

Mike

Fewer shotgun shells than expected or not, Garrett appreciated Mike's rounds. He put the clip of silver bullets in an empty holder on his utility belt, grabbed his cowboy hat, and left the department carrying the box of shotgun shells.

~ * ~

Tempted to use the siren and lights, "Loud and proud," as Deputy Timpson would have said, to get to the Wiseman barn quickly, Garrett did not want to draw unwanted attention to his mission, and he made the drive cold. Cold but not slow. He drove between five and ten miles over the speed limit.

Twenty minutes later, Garrett was at the Wiseman barn drive. In person, it still looked like a large green mouth eager to swallow anything that got too close. A light breeze blew the leaves that only seemed to animate the gapping mouth. The hairs on the back of Garrett's neck prickled as he turned off County Road Five Ninety-Eight and drove into the shadowy orifice.

It became immediately clear to Garrett that, although the winding, overgrown path wasn't in regular use, someone had recently used it. The weeds growing between the two dirt grooves where tires traveled were shorter than the weeds on either side of the path. Not from being cut. They were broken or bent from being hit by the undercarriage of vehicles, a matte-black Ram truck to Garrett's reasoning, as they traveled the path.

Several twists and turns later, the path opened into a clearing and the dilapidated barn loomed in front of Garrett like a dead hulk. The Google Earth image didn't do justice to the overall disrepair of the barn. What windows Garrett could see from that vantage point were broken, and the bat-and-board siding had rotted holes in many places. The damage from the felled pine tree collapsed one corner of the structure, too. Garrett pulled up on the left side of the barn, where he saw a partially hung door, and stopped. Before exiting the SUV, Garrett pulled his pistol.

It wasn't yet noon, but the late May heat was already pushing ninety degrees and the humidity was pushing eighty percent. The sun beat down relentlessly in the clear blue sky. Garrett stood in the bright, humid heat and listened to the forest. Although daytime woods were much less noisy than nighttime woods, he could clearly hear birds chirping and squirrels scurrying in the tree branches around the barn. He relaxed, but just a little. His finger remained on the trigger guard.

Before going inside the barn, Garrett investigated the outer parameter first. From his truck, he walked back toward the path leading to the barn and around the side facing the path. On the side opposite his truck, the downed tree laid on the barn roof. The tree had caused extensive damage to the roof, but it hadn't collapsed the side completely.

This thing's built like a brick shithouse, Garrett thought as he moved to the last side of the barn.

The east side of the barn did not differ from the other sides. More rotting wood and broken windows. Something caught Garrett's attention, though. Something on the ground. There were two somethings. The first was flattened weeds in a distinctive pattern of a vehicle parking in that area several times over many visits. The second was several patches of dead grass between the flattened weeds made by tires and one fresh patch that was brownish, but not yet dead.

Garrett moved to the spot, hunkered down on his haunches, and stuck his finger in the brownish spot. It came away wet. He rubbed the viscous fluid between his thumb and forefinger. It felt slick. He brought it up to his nose and sniffed it. Motor oil.

"Ya gotta leak in your oil pan, bitch," Garrett told no one.

As Garrett stood back up, something in the woods directly in front of him glinted in the sunlight.

He raised his gun, moved his finger from the trigger guard to the trigger, and shouted, “Come out with your hands where I can see ‘em.”

A few nearby birds took flight at the sound of his shout, but nothing in the woods stirred. Slowly, with the gun raised and ready to shoot, Garrett advanced on where he’d seen the glint.

The ground around the barn wasn’t level and, as Garrett walked past his SUV, it dipped about two feet lower. He saw the glint again, and more clearly than the first time. It was a reflection. Still cautious, but less worried than he’d been before, Garrett advanced on the woods.

At the edge of the clearing, Garrett peered into the shadowy darkness of the forest and saw a car about thirty feet in. It was an orange Honda Civic. Without checking the license plate number, which Garrett memorized, he knew who the car belonged to. It was Dillon Albertson’s.

~ * ~

The car disappeared the night Garrett did the alpha’s dirty work and killed Dillon. The missing car became a source of contention for Dillon’s parents. They were told Dillon attacked Garrett who shot and killed him, which had been true. To explain this break from their son’s normal, law-abiding behavior, George Krats told them it might have been drug induced. They balked at the idea, but there had been no other logical reason for their son’s sudden break with reality.

The missing Civic had them speculating someone carjacked Dillon and dosed him. Meaning someone else drugged their son. Garrett didn’t care what they believed, as long as they believed it in Dallas and not in Pine View County. Returning the car might open a new line of communication with the Albertsons, but fingerprint analysis would rule out the carjacking theory, and some planted meth might even convince them of the drug theory. George already told Garrett he would doctor the autopsy report to include trace elements of methamphetamine. Planting drugs and doctoring autopsy reports weren’t Garrett’s preferred method of law enforcement, but desperate time called for desperate measures. These were desperate times.

~ * ~

Not wanting to, but needing to, Garrett holstered his pistol and retrieved a latex glove from his breast pocket and put it on his right hand.

He walked into the woods.

To be thorough, Garrett checked the car's plate. It was Dillon's car. He tried the trunk and both doors. Dillon's car had been locked up tighter than a virgin's knees on prom night, but Garrett noticed something on the trunk that wasn't normal. There were deep scratches in the paint that looked, suspiciously, like claw marks. Discouraged by not being able to access the car's interior, but not surprised, Garrett exited the woods.

Back in the sunlight, Garrett depressed the shoulder-mounted radio microphone. "Erica, this is Garrett. Come back."

Immediately, Erica's voice cracked over the radio, "Yeah, Sheriff. What ya need?"

"I need Brent Simmons to tow a car for me and send Deputy Hoyt, too," Garrett said before giving her the address and brief directions, since the drive had no marker.

Satisfied the needed personnel would soon be there, Garrett turned his attention to the barn. The inside of the barn.

As Garrett walked back toward the barn, he noticed something he'd missed on the structure's front side, beside the leaning door, when he pulled beside it and parked. There were four deep gouges in the barn siding. The height and spacing of the gouges were, by then, all too familiar to Garrett. They were werewolf claw marks. Their claw mark's presence provided further evidence of what Garrett already knew. He'd found the alpha's den.

The door on the north side of the barn hung by the middle and bottom hinge. The top hinge had snapped and, by the look of it, some time ago. An important clue came from the hinges. The top, broken hinge, was thick with deep, crusty, dark red rust on the door and the hinge post. Rust covered the middle and bottom hinges, but the thick rust had flaked off, leaving the hinges crust free and a light, powdery red.

Openin' and closin' the door would knock the thick rust off the connected hinges, Garrett thought.

To test the theory, Garrett grabbed the door and pulled it open. It was stubborn, and it squealed like a pig stuck in mud. It opened and, when it did, a fine haze of rust dust erupted from the middle and bottom hinges. Garrett, pleased with his deductive reasoning, nodded and stepped into the barn. Immediately, he wished he hadn't.

For all the holes in the bat-and-board siding, holes in the roof from the tree and the fire, and broken windows, the barn's interior had been deceptively dark and stuffy. There was old farm equipment that cast dark shadows into the already darkened interior. These shadows obscured much of the floor so that it looked more like a gaping hole than solid ground. It wasn't a cool darkness either. The interior felt warmer than the blazing sun outside. Those discomforts paled compared to the smell.

After inhaling once, Garrett brought his left arm up and buried his nose in the inside crook of his elbow. The uniform shirt smelled of detergent and starch, but it wasn't enough to mask the dank stench of rotting wood, the overpowering stench of urine, moist soil, and, worst of all, the all-encompassing canine musk.

This is her fuckin' den, Garrett thought as his eyes watered from the stench.

Even though the urge to leave the repulsive stench was powerful, Garrett knew he needed to get a better look at the barn's interior. Keeping his nose in the crook of his arm, he holstered his gun and retrieved the Mag flashlight from his utility belt. He turned it on, and the powerful beam of light illuminated the thick dust inside the barn and made the white beam look like a tangible force.

A quick scan of the walls and items in the barn revealed nothing of importance. When Garrett pointed the flashlight at the ground, the light chased the shadows away and turned the hole into a dirt floor. There had been interest there. The light revealed a myriad of footprints. Some were on top of others, while some prints blinded over each other to the point of being useless. There were three distinct varieties of footprints—shoe prints, barefoot prints, and very large paw prints.

Not wanting to breathe the air without the filter of his shirtsleeve, but needing both hands, Garrett reluctantly retrieved his cellphone with his left hand and started taking pictures of the undamaged prints. There were twelve, and Garrett used his own foot next to the targeted footprint as a size reference.

As Garrett turned to leave the stifling barn, his flashlight fell on another set of prints that were behind him and closer to the corner behind the door. They weren't footprints, but it was clear from the two large, rounded imprints that came together, the smooth V-shaped outline about two feet above the large, rounded prints, two smaller, rounded prints close together about two feet below the two large, rounded prints, and two handprints above the smooth V-shaped outline. The large, rounded prints were someone's butt, the V-shaped print had been someone's upper back and shoulders, and the two small prints were knees.

"They're fuckin' in here," Garrett whispered to the barn.

The thought of fucking in that dirty stench made Garrett's stomach turn. He lurched for the door and pushed it open so forcefully the middle hinge snapped with an audible 'crack' and the door fell away from the barn, secured only by the bottom hinge. He placed his hands on his knees and sucked in warm, but wonderfully clean, air. His eyes watered, but the clean air soothed his senses and his breakfast remained where it belonged—in his stomach.

There was still some sweet tea in the travel mug in the SUV. Garrett opened the driver's side door, grabbed the travel mug, and emptied it in two big gulps. He turned around and leaned his backside against the driver's seat. He could stand but needed support.

The outside air was clean, but the smell of the barn was still around him. He sniffed his shirt—it reeked of the barn smells.

Never knowing what might happen when on patrol, or what substance might end up on a uniform—blood, vomit, soot, gasoline, etcetera. Garrett learned early on to carry a change of clothes in his patrol vehicle. He patrolled no more, but old habits die hard, and Garrett was glad they did. He was changing his shirt when he heard the rumble of Brent's tow-truck navigating the twisted path to the barn clearing.

Seconds later, Brent's tilt-bed tow-truck emerged from the path with Deputy Hoyt's SUV was right behind it. Garrett pointed toward the trees north of his location. Brent took the direction and drove that way. Billy Hoyt pulled up next to Garrett's SUV and got out.

"What's up, Sheriff?"

Garrett pointed at the trees Brent drove toward. "I found Dillon Albertson's car in the woods over there."

Billy's mouth went slightly agape for a second. When recovered, he said, "How'd ya know to look out here, Sheriff?"

How did I know? Garrett thought.

"Good, old-fashion law enforcement work."

It was a thin response, anorexic thin, but it would have to do.

Billy just grinned. "I guess that's why you're the sheriff, Sheriff."

I'm the sheriff 'cause I got elected and I probably won't get reelected, Garrett thought.

He smiled back at Billy, accepting his praise, and started walking toward Brent's tow-truck. Billy fell in beside Garrett.

As Garrett and Billy neared the large tow-truck, Brent opened the door, and stepped onto the metal step under the door. "I thought ya needed a tow. Where's the car?"

Garrett regarded Brent. He was a large man, at least six-foot, two-inches tall and pushing two-hundred and fifty pounds. Brent had a bushy, red beard, a long ponytail, and wore grease-stained overalls with no shirt on under it. He had a Confederate flag tattoo on his large, meaty right bicep.

Garrett pointed at the trees. "It's about thirty feet in there."

Shielding his eyes with a large hand, Brent peered into the dense woods for several seconds. "I see it. I'll have to winch it out before I can load it on the tilt-bed."

"Deputy Hoyt needs to take some pictures before ya winch it out. It's locked. Can ya get into it?"

Brent grinned, reached into the tow-truck, grabbed something off the dashboard, and held it up for Garrett to see. "Got my master key right here."

The 'master key' was a Slim Jim. A thin metal tool used to unlock car doors by inserting it between the door glass and hooking one of its notches on the locking mechanism. All the Pine View County patrol SUVs had one, but Garrett had never been good at using them. He could rarely hook the locking mechanism and, when he hooked it, he usually pulled the wrong direction first.

"Okay. Billy needs to take some picture before ya unlock it," Garrett told the big man.

Brent nodded, jumped off the tow-truck step, and landed with a grunt. "I ain't in no hurry, Sheriff."

The three of them walked into the woods.

At the car, Garrett and Brent hung back a few feet, while Billy took several pictures of the car's exterior.

When Billy got to the front of the car, he said, "Looks like he was drivin' fast when he hit the tree. There's a good bit of damage to the front end."

Brent leaned toward the car and looked through the driver's side window. "Airbag didn't deploy."

"What's that tell ya?" Garrett asked.

Brent stroked his long beard, as if thinking. "Could be a faulty airbag. Unlikely, but it happens. It's possible it wasn't bein' driven."

"Then how the hell'd it get in the woods and damaged like this?" Billy scoffed.

Brent considered this for a few seconds. "Someone could'a pushed it with another car or truck."

Although Garrett believed Brent and Billy thought another vehicle pushed the Civic into the woods, knew better. He saw the scratches on the trunk. The amount of strength and body mass needed to damage the front end by pushing it into the tree was clear to Garrett. Both were substantial, and the alpha had been capable. Of that, Garrett was clear, too.

Billy made his way around the passenger's side of the Civic and took more pictures.

He went to the back of the car and paused. "Trunk's scratched up, Sheriff."

Not wanting to engage in a conversation about the scratches in font of Brent, Garrett said, dismissively, "Yeah, I saw that. Just take some pics, so we can open this thing up and get a look at the interior."

Billy obliged. Then it was Brent's turn to deal with the car.

As Brent was walked to the car, Slim Jim in hand, Garrett said, "Don't touch anything."

Without turning around, Brent chuckled. "This ain't my first rodeo, Sheriff."

At the car, Brent slipped the Slim Jim between the glass and door and pushed it deep into the door.

He wiggled it around for only a few seconds. "Got it."

He gave the Slim Jim a quick upward and forward yank. There was an audible 'thunk' and Garrett saw the lock pop up on the inside of the car.

Brent pulled the Slim Jim free and stepped back. "Do your thing, Sheriff."

Before approaching the car, Garrett and Billy donned latex gloves. Garrett opened the driver's side door and peered inside. It smelled of a closed car in the heat but, otherwise, there was nothing of importance initially visible.

When Billy opened the passenger's side door, Garrett said, "Pop the trunk."

Billy opened the glove compartment, where most internal trunk releases were. Dillon's plastic sleeved insurance card fell out. Billy pushed the button, and the trunk popped open a few inches.

To further avoid discussing the scratches, Garrett got to the trunk and opened it before Billy got there. The trunk contained a spare tire, a jack, and a clump of wadded up clothes. Garrett waited for Billy to take several pictures of the trunk's content and before pulled the clothes out. There was a pair of size nine Nike sneakers, a green, polo-style shirt, boxer underwear, faded Levi blue jeans, and a brown leather belt. No socks.

After inventorying the clothing, Garrett went through the pants. This process produced a set of car keys and a smaller key that probably fit a bicycle lock from the right front pocket. Garrett found a wallet in the back, right pocket. The wallet contained Dillon's driver's license, his student ID card, a Chase Visa card in his dad's name, and twenty-seven dollars. Two tens, a five, and two ones.

When Garrett finished, he turned to Billy. "Bag all this evidence. When Brent gets it back to the Department, I want it thoroughly processed; prints inside and out, DNA swabs on anything that looks promisin', and all content cataloged. I want it vacuumed, and that content sifted for trace evidence. Got it?"

Billy nodded. "Got it."

To Brent, Garrett said, "Alright. Let's get this thing loaded."

Garrett wasn't confident the processing labor would produce evidence, but it might. That the blue-eyed, blonde-haired girl's vaginal fluid didn't hit in the DNA database for sex crime offenders didn't mean she hadn't been arrested and printed for lesser crimes. It had been a public intoxication arrest that led to identifying Cole Duncan. Garrett held out some hope. Small but some.

Because Brent's hands were too big for the latex gloves, they kept splitting when he forced them onto his catcher mitt sized hands, Billy got the job of hooking the winch cable to the back axle on Dillon's orange Civic. He wasn't happy about crawling around on the forest floor, he had a thing about spiders, but he did it with minimal complaint.

Once hooked, Garrett and Billy joined Brent at the truck, and he started the winch. Within a minute, the orange Civic was free of the woods. Brent lowered the tilt-bed and continued winching the car.

"I like it when the front tires are straight. This can be a real bitch when they're turned," Brent said, more to himself than to Garrett and Billy.

When the Civic was on the tilt-bed, Brent pulled a hydraulic lever near the cab of the truck and the tilt-bed leveled out.

"I just need to tie it down and we'll be ready to go," Brent announced.

Garrett started to respond, but his cellphone rang before he could.

He looked at the iPhone screen for the caller ID, but it registered as 'Blocked.'

The only time Garrett dealt with a blocked number before had been with a psychiatrist who evaluated a teenage suspect who got caught skinning neighborhood cats.

When Garrett asked why he blocked his number, the psychiatrist said, "I'm available for my patients twenty-four seven. If they need me, they call my service and I call them back. I don't want a bunch of crazy fucks having my cell number."

That made perfect sense to Garrett.

Curious who would call him with a blocked number, Garrett tapped the green answer icon. "This is Garrett."

The voice that responded was smooth and sweet, like warm honey. There had been a lot of Texan in the accent and a hint of Louisiana Cajun in it, too.

"Hello, Garrett. My name's Lola Laveau. James tol' me 'bout your…*experience*. I apologize for not contactin' ya sooner. I was in Louisiana takin' care of some…family business. We should talk now that I'm back."

Two things about the brief introduction stood out to Garrett. The first had been the familiarity. Garrett didn't mind being addressed by his first name, but he'd discovered, over his sixteen years in law enforcement, most folks deferred to his position of authority and addressed him as Deputy in his early years and as Sheriff since his election in 2012. It was possible James hadn't mentioned he was the sheriff, but unlikely. The second had been she referred to his nightmare as an *experience*. This intrigued Garret and he liked Lola's warm, honey voice.

Garrett stepped away from Billy and Brent. "Yes, Miss Laveau. Thank ya for callin'. If ya could tell me what ya think is behind my…nightmare, I'd appreciate it greatly."

A chuckle that sounded like living smoke came from the other end of the call and Lola said, "We're gonna be close, Garrett. Best ya call me Lola. Now, 'bout your…*experience*, I need to *see* ya…in person to be certain. I think I have a pretty good sense 'bout what's goin' on."

Garrett's hope Lola might provide answers and his trust in James' judgment on Lola sank.

She's nothin' more than a sideshow palm-reader, Garrett thought.

Building on that thought, Garrett said, "Let me guess. You're gonna read my palm…or some such nonsense."

Lola greeted this statement with several seconds of silence.

When Lola finally responded, she didn't sound angry or upset, but replaced the warm honey tone with a cold honey one. Instead of the words flowing smoothly off her tongue, they were thick and deliberate.

"I don't read palms, Garrett. I *see* 'em. There's a difference between readin' and *seein'*. Readin' implies there're words to interpret. There aren't words. Only history and deeds.

"James spoke highly of you, Garrett. I tol' him ya might not be ready to be *seen*. He tol' me ya were. You let me know when you're ready for some answers regardin' your *experience*. It's not a nightmare or a premonition. I stake my reputation on that. I think I can help ya, Garrett. I can't do that without *seein'* ya.

"As you saw, my number's blocked. I don't want a bunch of crazy fucks havin' my cell number. Contact James, if ya want me to *see* ya."

Lola used the exact words the psychiatrist used when explaining why he blocked his number. The statement took Garrett momentarily aback.

Just before the call ended, Garrett said, "Wait, wait. Don't hang up."

Lola said nothing, but Garrett heard her exhale, so he knew she was still there.

"I'm sorry, Lola. I'm new to all this. I didn't know…werewolves were real until one bit my daughter. By nature, I'm a skeptic. Comes with my job, but that's no excuse for bein' rude to someone who's tryin' to help. Please accept my apology. I want ya to *see* me and tell me what the…*experience* is about."

There was a brief pause and then Lola, warm honey again like nothing cross happened, said, "Accepted and forgotten, Garrett. The next full moon is only four nights away. I think it's best I *see* ya right away. This is important information, if your palm confirms what I believe, and I'm seldom wrong, Garrett. Can ya come now?"

It wasn't the best time for Garrett to cut out for a little palm seeing from a witch, but he'd been waiting for answers to the recurring nightmare for fourteen years. He still wasn't entirely sure Lola could provide an answer, but he would hear her out. Also, he desperately wanted to see the person who the warm honey voice belonged to. If Lola's visage was half as attractive as her voice, Garrett felt sure she'd be a beautiful woman.

"I can come now. Thank ya for givin' me a second chance."

Lola chuckled her living smoke chuckle again. "Second chances come with second lives, Garrett. This life is just a journey. Folks take wrong turns and stumble all the time. It's up to them to right their path. You were quick to right yours. Good thing, too. It's an important path, Garrett."

Lola gave Garrett her address. He was familiar with the area, but not the exact location.

"I can be there in about thirty minutes."

"That'll be just fine. Look for the bright pink mailbox. That's my drive."

As soon as Lola mentioned the bright pink mailbox, Garrett knew exactly where she lived. He'd driven past it and wondered what kind of person would have a mailbox of that color. Now he knew. A witch would.

"I've seen your mailbox many times while drivin' the county on patrol. I never knew who it belonged to."

"Most folks don't, Garrett. I'll *see* ya shortly."

After ending the call with Lola, Garrett quickly went over what Billy was supposed to do with Dillon's car when it was at the Department. Satisfied things were in order, Garrett got into his SUV and headed north to Lola's bright pink mailbox and, hopefully, answers.

~ * ~

The bright pink mailbox came into view on the right as Garrett rounded a curve in County Road Six Seventy-One. He slowed and turned onto the crushed limestone driveway. Large, hardwood trees on either side blocked the sun's rays and pitched it in shadow, canopied the driveway. Several hundred feet later, the driveway emerged from the foliage tunnel into a clearing.

In the clearing there was a small, well-kept, white pier and beam house with a green metal roof and a detached white garage with matching green metal roof. The garage door was open, and Garrett could see a late 1950's pink Cadillac parked inside. He'd seen the car in and around the city of Pine View and on the roads in Pine View County many times, but he'd never gotten a good look at its driver.

There was a large, covered porch that spanned the length of the front of the house and a porch swing hung to the left of the front door. A woman dressed in a long white dress sat on the porch swing. She waved as Garrett pulled to a stop in front of the house.

As Garrett got out of the SUV, Lola stood up and started toward the steps. The long, white dress flowed all the way to the ground, and it looked to Garrett as if Lola glided, not walked. She glided down the steps and approached Garrett. Garrett took her in.

The woman the warm honey voice belonged to was, as Garrett suspected, stunningly beautiful. Her skin was a shade of soft mocha, and flawless. She had her long, black hair braided into dozens of cornrows with pink and white beads adorning the tip of each braid. The beads clicked together as she walked. The long, white dress hugged Lola's curvaceous body seductively, like a lover. The fabric was sheer and her milk chocolate areolas and perky nipples were clearly visible. Her face was her most stunning feature. Especially her exotic eyes.

Lola's face was diamond shaped with high, wide, prominent cheekbones and a slightly rounded chin. She had full lips that were covered in soft pink lipstick. Her nose was thin across the bridge and button shaped at the tip. Her eyes were enormous and almond-shaped, but that wasn't what made her eyes so exotic. What made them exotic was they were different colors.

The iris in Lola's left eye was a soft shade of brown, almost the same shade of mocha as her skin. Garrett thought it would be easy to get lost in that eye forever. Her right eye was a different story. Although it was beautiful, it projected a dangerous beauty. The iris in her right eye was a deep shade of emerald, green. It was so green, the surrounding woods, grass, and roof appeared to come from a different color pallet altogether. The pupil was a thin, vertical slit. It looked like a cat's eye.

Garrett took all of this in over the couple of seconds it took to close the distance between them.

As they came together, Lola stuck out her right hand. Her fingernails were long and painted bright pink. "Good to *see* you, Garrett."

Garrett got the feeling Lola's right cat eye was seeing more than he felt comfortable showing.

He took her hand in his. Her skin was warm and soft. He said, "It's nice to…*see* you too, Lola."

When in Rome, Garrett thought.

Lola had a considerably firmer grip than James' and she held his hand for longer than a normal handshake. She continued to hold Garrett's hand tightly. Garrett resisted the urge to pull his hand away because he enjoyed how it felt in hers.

Several seconds later, Lola smiled, revealing bright, white, perfect teeth. "You have a good aura 'bout ya, Garrett."

She released his hand, turned, and started gliding back toward the house.

Dumbfounded by the encounter, and unsure what she expected of him, Garrett stood where he was.

Lola turned her head, causing the pink and white beads in her hair to click together. "Come inside, Garrett. We need to talk 'bout your *experience*."

Garrett followed Lola up the steps to the front door.

The interior of the house stood in stark contrast to the exterior, which was light and inviting. It smelled of cinnamon and clove incense. The walls in the room just inside the front door, a living room in most houses, were painted a dark, almost black, shade of red. An assortment of totems made from sticks, twigs, and tree limbs hung on the dark red walls.

The totems were different shapes and sizes. Some were circular, some were triangular, some were square or rectangular. Some were diamond shaped. Some were hollow in the middle. Some had geometric patterns of twigs and leaves weaved in the middle. They ranged in size from large, half the size of Garrett, to small, no bigger than Garrett's iPhone. While some might consider the totems art, they hung on the wall, Garrett thought they served some other purpose.

The room was sparsely furnished. There was a small, round table made of dark hardwood in the middle of the room. Surrounding the table were four chairs made of the same dark wood. The chair on the far side of the table had a high back, the other three had low backs.

Against the left wall was a large, ornate curio cabinet, made of the same dark wood, with glass doors. On the shelves inside the curio cabinet were a myriad of glass jars, ceramic canisters, and small wooden boxes. In the shadowy interior, Garrett could see there were things submerged in a cloudy liquid in some of the glass jars. He didn't want to know what they were.

Lola stepped around the table, sat down in the high-back chair, and motioned for Garrett to sit across from her.

After Garrett sat, Lola reached out her right hand. "Give me your right hand, Garrett."

He put his right hand in the center of the table. Lola took it, flipped it over so it was palm side up, closed her left eye, and studied his palm with her cat eye. Garrett felt foolish, but he allowed Lola to *see* his hand.

After several seconds, Lola smiled a knowing smile and, without taking her cat eye off Garrett's palm, said, "James tol' me 'bout your *experience*, but I need to hear it from you. Leave nothin' out. I need every detail."

Over the next thirty minutes, Garrett told Lola every detail of the nightmare from the first occurrence when Monster-Paige was two years old to the last occurrence after she turned sixteen and how Monster-Paige aged each year.

When he finished detailing the nightmare, Lola said, "Is Paige afraid of the larger werewolf?"

Garrett shook his head.

"Why do you think that is?"

"I don't know."

"Does Paige or the larger werewolf try to attack you?"

"In the last dream, the one I just had, she lunged at me. I woke up before she got to me. I don't know if it was an attack…or somethin' else."

"It was somethin' else."

"What?"

"In due time. What does Paige do before she leaves with the larger werewolf?"

"She waves goodbye to me."

"Why do you think she does that?"

"I don't know. That's why I'm here."

"I know the answers to these questions," Lola told him.

She was silent for several uncomfortable moments.

Frustrated, Garrett said, "Are ya gonna tell me?"

Lola smiled. Her white teeth looked even brighter in the dark room. "Look at your palm and tell me what you *see*, Garrett."

To Garrett, his palm looked like it always had. A jumble of crisscrossing lines.

After several seconds of looking, Garrett said, "I don't *see* anything."

In a tone reminiscent of James explaining why Paige, Ty, and

Trowa needed to be left out of the planning like Garrett was slow, Lola said, "Let me help ya *see*."

Lola placed the long, pink fingernail of her right index finger on Garrett's palm just below his pinky finger and traced a prominent line horizontally across his palm to just above his thumb.

"Do ya *see* that line?"

Garrett nodded.

Lola moved her finger to the bottom pinky side of his palm, near his wrist, and traced another prominent line diagonally to where it ended just below his middle finger.

"Do ya *see* that line?"

Garrett nodded again.

Without lifting her finger, Lola traced another prominent line from just under his middle finger diagonally to under his thumb by his wrist.

"Do ya *see* that line, Garrett?"

Garrett nodded a third time. "Yeah, it's like an arrowhead with a line through the top. I've seen that my whole life. What's it mean?"

"You haven't *seen* all of it, Garrett. Those three lines are strong, stronger than I thought they would be. The other lines are weaker, but they are there. When ya *see* those, you'll see the whole of it and understand the *experience*."

"What other lines?"

Lola still had her long, pink fingernail at the spot where the prominent line ended below his thumb by his wrist.

"It's faint, but it's here," Lola said as she moved her finger diagonally from that spot to where the prominent horizontal line started at his pinky.

"Do ya *see* that line?"

He did; he nodded.

"Okay, last line, Garrett," Lola said as she lifted her finger and placed it on the thumb side of the horizontal line.

She traced a faint line diagonally down to where the first prominent line angled from the pinky side of his wrist to his middle finger. "Do ya *see* this line, Garrett?"

Garrett pulled his hand back, not rudely, and looked at his palm. He saw it. Now that he had, he couldn't un-see it. It was so obvious.

"It's a star."

Lola smiled and chuckled her living smoke chuckle. "Not a star,

Garrett. It's a pentagram."

Garrett looked at his hand again. "What? Like devil worship?"

Lola's smile faltered a little, and she said, "No. Those…blasphemers have corrupted the pentagram. They put it upside down to make it into the head of a cloven, horned goat. Satan's agent. The five points of a pentagram represent the elements: Earth, Wind, Fire, Water, and Spirituality. Not evil. A werewolf is an affront to nature's balance. So, they are marked as cursed with the pentagram."

After considering what Lola said for several moments, Garrett said, "I'm confused. I wasn't bitten. Paige was. I'm not a werewolf. Why am I marked with a pentagram?"

Lola leaned forward and took Garrett's hand in both of hers. "It is *in* ya, Garrett."

"In me? In me how? What does that mean?"

"Someone in your family, your lineage, was a werewolf. While cursed, they produced an offspring," Lola explained.

"What? Like werewolf rape?"

Lola grinned, as if she found the question funny. "No. That wouldn't work."

"Why not?"

"Have you ever seen a dog's cock? They're rather large for their size and they have a bulbous knot. A werewolf's cock would be an altogether different beast, literally.

"I've heard tales of male werewolves rapin' human females for sport and torture, but there'd be nothin' left of the woman's womb to support life. So, the answer to your werewolf rape question is no.

"Someone in your family tree, someone cursed, had sex and that sex resulted in a pregnancy. Could'a been a cursed man who lay with a woman or a cursed woman who lay with a man. Whatever the combination, the sex took place while one or both of 'em were cursed, but in human form. Not as a werewolf."

Garrett shook his head. "So, your tellin' me that my mom or dad has a pentagram in their palm and Paige does too?"

Lola nodded. "Yes. It may be faint…it surprised me you had three strong lines, but it *will* be in Paige's palm and either your mom's or dad's palm."

"What does this mean and how does it relate to my recurring…experience? That Paige became a werewolf makes me think, more than ever, it was a premonition."

Lola got up, walked around the small round table, pulled one of the smaller chairs next to Garrett, and sat down.

She took Garrett's right hand, placed it between her breasts, pressed it against her chest. "What do ya feel, Garrett?"

Garrett could feel her heart beating strongly from within her chest.

Confused, Garrett said, "Your heartbeat."

Lola smiled. "Yes. It is more than *my* heartbeat. We are made of all of those who came before us. My heartbeat's a continuation all the heartbeats of my ancestors. Today we talk of science and genetics, which might make this easier for you to understand. We have always known we are the sum of our past.

"What science and genetics can't explain is that life *experience* is passed from one generation to the next, too. Not only are we a genetic amalgam of our ancestors, but we are also a living amalgam of their lives.

"I didn't become a witch because it's trendy these days to run around naked in the woods and commune with nature. I was born a witch with the ability to *see* because I come from a long line of witches. My mama had the *sight*, and her mama before her, and her mama before her. When I commune, I commune with my ancestors *and* nature, current and past. When I *see*, I *see* through their eye. too.

"It is not different with the werewolf. The werewolf in your past is and has been with you, Garrett. It's buried deep within your being, though. Deeper with every generation removed from its origin. It cannot hide from your subconscious mind. When is our subconscious mind most free to roam, Garrett?"

"When we're asleep."

Lola smiled a big, proud smile. "Exactly. When we're in a deep sleep, those *experiences* are passed on as living memories come out to play. Now…who is the larger werewolf?"

Garrett looked into Lola's mismatched eyes, as if the answer hid in them.

There wasn't much light, but Lola's cat eye seemed to generate its own internal light and Garrett could see his face reflected in it almost as clearly as if he were looking in a rounded funhouse mirror. As he watched, his human reflection transformed. His ears slid up the side of his head and turned into hairy points. His upper and lower jaw elongated, and deadly fangs replaced his human teeth. When his eyes flared red, Garrett looked away quickly.

"Who is the larger werewolf?" Lola asked again.

"It's me," Garrett whispered.

"Yes. It is that part of you that carries the werewolf from your past."

"Why then? Why didn't I experience this before?" Garrett asked in a shaky voice.

Lola was silent for a moment and then said, "Was there murder in your heart? The first time ya had the *experience*? Was there murder in your heart?"

Garrett's head snapped back toward Lola. He hadn't told her about Lacy cheating on him with his then friend and mentor, Mark Harper. He remembered how his hand had gone reflexively to his gun when he first saw Lacy's legs wrapped around Mark's sweaty back. For an instant, before he realized Lacy's infidelity gave him a get-out-of-crappy-marriage-free-card, he wanted to kill both of them. His hand reached for his gun without conscious thought.

Garrett told Lola about what happened the night before the first experience.

When he finished, Lola smiled. "Ya didn't kill 'em. You tamed your ancestral werewolf."

This struck Garrett as an interesting response and he said, "Was it my ancestral werewolf that made me think 'bout killin' 'em? Had I killed 'em, would it have been because of the werewolf in my past?"

Lola smiled. "Many things can drive someone to kill. Some are evil, some are insane, and some, who no one would ever consider capable of killin', are pushed into the act for unknown reasons. Like an ancestral werewolf.

"I tol' ya when we met outside that you had a good aura. I meant it. You're a good man, Garrett Lambert. That is why ya didn't act on the urge to kill Lacy and Mark. That is why ya could keep the killin' ancestral werewolf at bay."

Garrett blushed at the compliment. "Thank you, Lola. Why did Paige…lunge at me in the last dream? If she wasn't attacking me, what was that?"

"It's no accident that your *experience* changed after a werewolf bit Paige. The bite awoke her ancestral werewolf. It made it…real."

"So…, it was an attack?"

"No. More like an…announcement."

"But…if the bite awoke *her* ancestral werewolf, why did this happen in *my* dream?"

As if disappointed in Garrett, Lola sighed. "You haven't been listenin', Garrett. You, Paige, and the other members of your lineage who share the ancestral werewolf are connected. Paige's behavior in your last *experience* changed because the wolf inside of you knows her wolf is awake."

Garrett was silent for several moments as his mind digested the information. To the new, werewolves are an actual part of his brain, it all made perfect sense. If what Lola said were true, he had someone to visit, and he wanted to get gone.

"I really appreciate ya takin' time to explain the experience to me. My mom got into genealogy a few years ago. I think I'll call her and see if I can drop by, shake some family tree branches, and see if a werewolf falls out. They're not good with trees. How much do I owe ya?"

"You don't owe me anything, Garrett. But we're not finished."

Confused, because she explained the experience, Garrett said, "We're not?"

Lola leaned toward Garrett, so close he felt her warm breath on his face, and she said, "We need to talk 'bout Paige and what this ancestral werewolf means for her. Now that a werewolf bit her."

Garrett felt a knot form in his gut.

This doesn't sound good, Garrett thought and slumped in his chair.

As if reading Garrett's thoughts, which didn't surprise him at that point, Lola said, "No, it doesn't sound good, but that's not necessarily the case."

Garrett sat up straight again. "How so?"

"Like you, Paige has the *experience* of the ancestral werewolf deep inside her. It's not as deep as yours is anymore. The bite awakened it. This will make her an exceptionally strong werewolf…if she transforms on the first full moon after being bitten," Lola explained.

"Strong, how?" Garrett interrupted.

"To make this easier to understand, think of it in terms of genetics, and think of the ancestral werewolf as a recessive gene. Dark-haired parents can have a blonde-haired child, if they both have a recessive blonde hair gene. The weaker, less prominent genes, when paired, prevail. It…becomes stronger. This has happened to Paige. The ancestral werewolf is now paired with the current werewolf. Paige's werewolf will be stronger for this."

"Stronger, how? Bigger? Faster? Fiercer?"

"Yes. All of those things. And stronger of will."

"Stronger of will? What does *that* mean?"

"Is your daughter a *good* person?"

"Yes. I'm not just sayin' that because I'm her dad. She has a pure heart."

"This is good. If she is pure of heart, she may tame her werewolf."

Confused, Garrett said, "Tame her werewolf? What does *that* mean?"

"The ancestral werewolf has been with her…inside her…part of her for her entire life. Whether she knew it, she, like you, *has* been controllin' it. If she hadn't been controllin' it, it would've manifested in destructive behavior…killin' animals for fun, enjoyin' the pain and discomfort of others, actin' out violently."

"Like serial killers do," Garrett added.

Lola smiled. "Exactly. Some are evil, some are insane, and some are an enigma. They are the ones who are not strong enough to tame whatever it is inside 'em that drives 'em to kill. That Paige *is* a good person leads me to believe she *has* tamed the wildness inside her. Otherwise, she would act out."

Garrett considered this information for several moments. "So…if she transforms, she *might* control herself?"

"Yes, if she has the will to do so. She's not truly cursed unless, or until, she takes the life of an innocent. If she does that, she will succumb to the beast completely. There are people, strong-willed people with an ancestral connection, who live their entire lives as werewolves and never harm a livin' soul."

"Should I tell Paige about this? Would it help if she knew?"

Without hesitation, Lola said, "No. If Paige knows, her maker might find out. If her maker learns Paige could be a powerful werewolf…one that could challenge its authority, it might decide to kill her before she transforms as the best course of action. Paige is still a frail human until her first transformation. Tell her, if she transforms, to fight the desire to kill."

Garrett nodded.

Several seconds passed then Garrett said, "Why hasn't James told me 'bout this?"

Lola smiled a genuinely warm smile. "James is a sweet man and a dear friend. He is also very knowledgeable about folklore, mythology, and the occult. But his knowledge comes from books…not *experience.* One cannot learn all from books. One must *experience* these things to understand them truly. My people have been *experiencin'* 'em for millennia. What they *experience*, I *experience.* Trust me, Garrett Lambert. I know of what I speak."

Garrett trusted her. For the first time since the werewolf bit Paige, he had hope, even if he didn't kill the alpha in time, Paige would be okay. He had faith she could tame the beast.

That didn't lessen the need to kill the alpha. He still had Ty and Trowa's fate in his hands. If he couldn't kill the alpha in time, he would have to kill them. That wasn't an option.

Garrett pushed back the seat and stood up. "Thank ya, Lola. Thank ya for everything."

When Lola stood up, Garrett stuck out his hand, but she pushed past it and wrapped him in a tight, warm hug. Her body, like her hand, seemed unnaturally warm. She planted a warm kiss square on his lips. It wasn't a romantic kiss, but it lingered longer than a peck.

When their lips parted, Lola smiled. "I have somethin' for ya."

Lola walked over to the wall across from the curio cabinet and removed a small, cellphone sized, round twig totem from it.

She handed it to Garrett. "Keep this with ya on the full moon."

Garrett took it and studied it. The twigs that made the outer shape were pine and, although the twigs were brittle, the pine needles attached to them were flexible and green when they too should have been dead. In the interior of the round exterior was a mesh of very green pine needles woven tightly together with a hollow vertical slit in the middle. After taking it in, Garrett realized it looked suspiciously like Lola's cat eye.

"Will this ward off werewolves?"

Lola living smoke chuckled. "No. It will not. If ya have that with you, I will be with ya."

Not knowing exactly what that meant, and not wanting to get into another lengthy discussion, he was eager to talk with his mom about their family tree, Garrett smiled. "Thank you. I'll have it with me Tuesday night."

Lola opened the front door, and they stepped outside. The bright sunlight momentarily blinded Garrett. Lola didn't appear bothered by the dark to light transition in the least.

At the patrol SUV, Garrett looked back at Lola, who still stood on the porch. "Regardless of Paige's circumstance, there are two other lives at stake. Wish me luck."

"There is no luck. Only fate. I believe your fate is true, Garrett. There are three other lives at stake, not two."

Three other lives? Garrett thought.

Again, as if reading his mind, Lola said, "Yes, three lives. Paige's maker has a maker, too. I see another monster in this. A mountain of a monster. It is the origin of Paige's origin. You can save two girls, Garrett Lambert."

"Save the life of the girl who bit Paige?"

Lola nodded.

"Is she worth savin'?"

Lola shrugged. "All human life matters. She may not be yours to save, though. The mountain monster may control that one's fate."

Garrett realized he hadn't mentioned Paige's maker was a girl to Lola.

He wondered if James had. "Did James tell ya the werewolf that bit Paige was a girl?"

Lola shook her head and pointed at her cat-like eye. "I *see* things, Garrett."

Garrett believed her. He waved goodbye, got in the SUV, and drove out of Lola's driveway. By the time he was back on County Road Six Seventy-One, much of what happened in Lola's house seemed like a faraway dream, but one he'd never forget. He pulled out his cellphone and called his parent's house. He had a family tree to shake.

~ * ~

Garrett's dad, Ray, answered the phone on the third ring. "Hello, son. Everything okay?"

"Hey, Dad. Everything's fine. I was wonderin' if Mom's still doin' the genealogy stuff?"

Ray laughed. "Is she? You should see the home office. It's so packed with boxes and file folders full of genealogy crap that it's hard to close the door."

In the background, away from the phone, Garrett heard his mom, Mary, say, "Who're ya talkin' with 'bout my genealogy work?"

Ray laughed again. "Work? More like an obsession. It's Garrett askin'."

Still in the background, but moving closer, Garrett heard Mary say, "Give me the phone and butt out, ya old coot."

Before she snatched away the phone, Ray said, "Hang up, son. You don't wanna open this box of crazy."

Mary was on the phone, and, in the background, Ray said, "I warned ya, son."

To Ray, Mary said, "Oh…go do somethin' useful."

To Garrett, she said, "Are ya finally interested in our family history?"

"I have *some* interest," Garrett admitted.

In a light, cheerful voice, Mary said, "I'm so happy to hear this, Garrett. It's really fascinatin', when ya get into it. When would ya like to come by?"

"Now, if that's okay?"

"Now's perfect. Have ya eaten lunch yet?"

Garrett hadn't, and he felt it. His stomach was restless. "I haven't eaten yet, Mom."

In a voice Garrett knew meant his mom was smiling, Mary said, "I'll fix ya up a BLTJC. It'll only take a few minutes. How far off are ya?"

The JC in BLTJC stood for jalapeño and cheese. Garrett's rendition on the classic sandwich. Just thinking about it set Garrett's mouth to watering.

"I'm about forty minutes out. So, no rush."

"Perfect. I'll have it ready when ya get here."

They said goodbye and ended the call.

~ * ~

Forty minutes later, Garrett pulled up in front of his parent's house. His dad, sitting on the front porch swing, gave Garrett a friendly wave. Something in his right hand reflected the sun, but the wave was quick, and Garrett couldn't make out what it was.

Garrett got out of the patrol SUV and walked onto the porch, where his dad was working on something between his knees. "What ya doin',

Dad?"

Ray held up a pocketknife in his right hand and a small block of wood that was starting to look like a horse in his left hand. "Just whittlin'. Makin' a horse for Paige. Not much yet, but it's takin' shape. I know she's gettin' older and probably likes makeup and boys more than somethin' like this from her Pap. Do ya think she'll like it?"

"She'll love it, Dad," Garrett told him, and he meant it.

When Garrett started for the front door, Ray said, "You really interested in that genealogy crap, Garrett?"

Garrett hadn't been until an hour previously, but that had changed. "Yeah. I am little. I guess. You're not?"

Ray chuckled. "Past my great grandpap, they're just a bunch of dead folks I never knew and don't care to know about now. I give your mom a hard time 'bout it, but it makes her happy. Her bein' happy makes me happy. That and whittlin'. You wantin' to know 'bout it had her singin' in the kitchen while she made your sandwich. She wouldn't make me one. But I snatched a hunk of your bacon when she wasn't lookin'. Go on in, Son. She waitin' for ya."

Hearing his dad talk about his mom that way warmed Garrett's heart. He tossed his dad a wink and stepped inside the cool, dark house.

The smell of bacon hit him like a living thing and started his mouth to watering again.

"Where ya at, Mom?" Garrett said in a loud voice.

From the back of the house, Mary shouted, "I'm back here. In the home office."

There wasn't an office elsewhere that warranted the distinction, but Garrett didn't care what his mom called it. All he cared about was finding the ancestral werewolf. With a hopeful heart, Garrett headed back to his mom's home office.

The office was a small room to start with and his dad wasn't kidding about the boxes and file folders. They were everywhere. She'd stacked file boxes on top of each other along the wall opposite the computer desk and beside the file cabinet. There were file folders on top of the file cabinet, desk, and some on the floor. The overall effect made an already cramped room claustrophobic. In a strange way, it reminded Garrett of James' cluttered office.

Mary sat in an office chair in front of the desk and there was a folding chair set up next to hers. For Garrett's concerns, there was a plate with a BLTJC, potato chips, a large dill pickle on it, and a large glass of sweet tea on the desk.

Mary looked up at Garrett and smiled. "Come. Sit. Eat."

She patted the seat of the folding chair.

After Garrett sat down, he grabbed the sandwich and took a big bite. The bacon was perfect—not too crispy.

With a full mouth, Garrett said, "So good. Thanks, Mom."

Mary slapped Garrett's knee lightly. "Don't talk with your mouth full, son."

Garrett swallowed and took several gulps of tea. "Sorry, Mom. It's so good. Thank you."

He took another large bite.

Mary waited for Garrett to finish the second bite. "Okay, so what do ya wanna know? Somethin' specific or just general information?"

"Do we have to go through these boxes and folders?" Garrett asked as he looked around the office.

"Don't be silly. The boxes and file folders have printouts of everything, but I've put all the names in an Excel spreadsheet."

Surprised his mom knew what Excel was, and could use it, Garrett said, "Excel? When did ya learn to use that?"

Mary smiled. "I took a class at the junior college in Lufkin. I learned how to use Word, Excel, and PowerPoint."

"I'm impressed, Mom," Garrett admitted.

"Your ol' mom *can* learn new tricks. Now, what do ya wanna know?"

"How far back have ya gone?"

Mary smiled, obviously proud of herself. "On Dad's side, I'm back to eighteen, thirty-three. On my side, I'm back to seventeen, fifty-one. That's when each of our families came to America. Findin' information beyond that gets a little more difficult. I've just been fillin' in gaps for the past six months."

Impressed, Garrett said, "Wow. I didn't know you'd found that much. That's cool, Mom."

Smiling, Mary said, "Thank you, dear. It's been a very rewardin' process. Now…what is it you're lookin' for?"

That's a good question, Garrett thought.

What had he been looking for, and how would he go about telling his mom what he had been looking for? He couldn't ask her if there were any werewolves in the family tree.

After giving it some thought, Garrett said, "Have there been any…strange folks in our history?"

Mary laughed. "That's not information that's easy to find. There've been some…odd ducks in the family. A few folks ended up in Rusk. Prior to that mental facility, there aren't records. What else?"

Rethinking his approach, Garrett said, "Have there been any strange deaths?"

"Oh, heavens yes. They hanged one of your dad's ancestors for bein' a cattle thief. He wasn't happy when I told him 'bout that. There have been at least a dozen murders. Some pretty grizzly. A distant cousin on my side had her privates cut out. Three people died in duals. Some went missin' never to be seen again, and there have been several suicides. Four on my side and twelve on your dad's. He wasn't happy 'bout that, either.

"Beyond that, just normal stuff. This is kind of neat, though. My side has lost at least one person in the Cherokee War, American Revolution, War of Eighteen-Twelve, War of Texas Independence, Mexican American War, Civil War, Spanish-American War, World War One, World War Two, and the Korean War," Mary said proudly.

While Garrett thought that history interesting, it didn't help him narrow the search. Then he remembered the pentagram connection. Knowing whether it was his mom or dad who had the pentagram in their palm would narrow the search to one side.

A bit apprehensively, Garrett said, "Can I see your right hand, Mom?"

"My hand?"

"Yes, please. I just wanna see somethin'."

Mary held out her right hand. "Okay."

Garrett took his mom's hand, flipped it palm up, and looked for the pentagram. Her palm was a roadmap of normal lines and added wrinkles. The skin was milky white and tissue thin. He could see light blue veins under the thin skin, which only added to the confusion.

After several moments of looking, and not seeing the pentagram, Garrett had been to the point of concluding the ancestral werewolf came from his dad's side of the family. Then he saw it. The lines were weak, perhaps from age, but they were there. Like with his own palm, once he saw it, he couldn't un-see it.

Excited, Garrett said, "Have you ever seen this, Mom?"

He quickly traced the pentagram outline in her palm.

Mary pulled her hand back and looked at it. "My pentagram? I've seen it. It used to be easier to see. I'm afraid my wrinkles are obscurin' it a bit. You have one and so does Paige."

Garrett's jaw dropped open. He was dumbfounded she knew about the pentagram in her, his, and Paige's hands.

Does she know what it means? Garrett thought.

After he recovered, he said, "Do ya know what that means?"

Mary smiled a reassuring, knowing smile and calmly said, "It means that there was a werewolf in our family history."

That his mom knew about the ancestral werewolf shocked Garrett.

He felt like everything he thought he knew about his mom had been wrong. "You knew?"

Mary patted Garrett on the knee reassuringly. "Of course, I knew. This got me into genealogy."

"Why didn't ya tell me?"

Mary chuckled. "That's not the kind of thing you tell your kid. I didn't find out from my parents. My Great-Grandma told me just before she died. I was…seventeen. She said she didn't want the...werewolf to die with her.

"I collected what information I could early on but, before the Internet and these genealogy websites, it wasn't easy to do. Just handed down stories.

"Your dad doesn't have the mark but, once I got into genealogy, I liked it and did his side, too. It's good information to have, regardless of whether there's a werewolf in your family tree."

It was time for the important question.

Garrett swallowed hard. "Did ya find it? Do ya know who it is?"

With a big smile, Mary said, "I did, and I do."

Mary turned to the computer and wiggled the mouse to wake it up. When the monitor winked on, the screen showed an Excel spreadsheet with two tabs at the bottom. One labeled 'Lambert' and the other labeled 'Campbell,' which had been Mary's maiden name.

Mary clicked on the Campbell tab. The spreadsheet was full of names and some cells were filled with different colors, yellow, light blue, light green, and light purple.

Mary started scrolling down and to the right. As she did this, Garrett saw a pattern in some of the yellow filled cells. She'd connected them from parent to children and the pattern got narrower as Mary scrolled. A cell filled in red came into view.

Mary stopped scrolling, and highlighted the red filled cell. "This is him."

Making out the black letters in the red filled cell was difficult. Garrett leaned in for a closer look. When the name became clear, Garrett felt a bolt of electricity course through his nerves like hot lightning. He knew the name and from whom he'd heard it.

The red filled cell had the name Otis Fletcher in it. He'd heard the name from Deputy Mike Middleton. Otis Fletcher had been the *nahual* Mike's great, great, great...add a few more greats for good measure, Grandpa Milton Middleton shot with a silver musket ball when Texas was still part of Mexico.

"Holy crap," Garrett whispered.

"Ya know who he is?"

Garrett shook his head, as if clearing cobwebs. "One of my deputies, Mike Middleton, told me that his great, great, great grandpa killed a *nahual* that turned into Otis Fletcher when it died."

"Did he say what happened to him? He's one relative who went missin' never to be heard from again."

"Yeah. He said his grandpa didn't think anyone would believe him, so he buried him on his property."

Mary sorted through a few file folders on the desk, selected one, opened it, took a pen from the desk draw, and wrote, Buried in unmarked grave, across a sheet of paper with Otis Fletcher's name on it.

"Well, that answers an unanswered question for me," Mary said to herself.

To Garrett she said, "Does this help you?"

Garrett considered his mom's question. It didn't help, in that it changed nothing, but it, at least, lent support to the ancestral werewolf theory. Two independent sources identified the same individual as a werewolf, and the werewolf had been a distant relative. That would be considered firm evidence in any law enforcement context.

Garrett took a bite of the pickle and swallowed. "It does. Thanks, Mom."

With the genealogy investigation completed, Garrett concentrated on the remaining BLTJC, chips, and pickle.

When he finished eating, Mary said, "Does this have anything to do with what happened to those kids at the Mill Road Barn?"

Garrett, taking a drink of sweet tea when she asked, nodded to answer his mom's question.

Mary shuddered. "I was afraid of that. You be careful, Garrett. These are nasty creatures."

After finishing the sweet tea, Garrett said, "I know they are, Mom. I'll be careful. Mike melted down the silver musket balls his great grandpa stockpiled and made nine-mil rounds and double-ought buckshot shotgun shells. I'm talkin' with a professor from SFA who knows a lot about this stuff, too."

He purposefully left out meeting with the witch Lola Laveau. His mom was more open to the supernatural than he suspected she'd be, but she might balk at taking advice from a witch.

When Garrett got up, his mom did too.

He gave her a hug. "Sorry to eat and run, Mom. I need to go pick up Mandy."

He regretted saying that immediately. His mom, like Jasmine Jackson and Becks Middleton, believed Garrett should marry Mandy.

On cue, Mary said, "When are ya gonna marry her, Garrett? I love ya and I think you're wonderful, but ya won't find better."

Garrett smiled. "*Et tu*, Mom?"

Mary smiled. "She's wonderful, Garrett."

"I know. I'm thinkin' 'bout it."

This news brought an even bigger smile to Mary's face.

As they were walking out of the cramped office, Mary said, "You, Mandy, and Paige are welcome for Sunday supper. I'm makin' fried chicken."

"Thanks, Mom. Paige isn't spendin' this weekend with me."

Surprised, Mary said, "Why not? Did y'all get in an argument?"

They hadn't argued. They agreed Paige should steer clear of Garrett the weekend before the June full moon. James was coming to visit on Sunday to go over a final plan and they didn't want to give the alpha insight into their planning. Neither enjoyed spending the weekend apart, but both thought it the prudent course of action.

"No. No disagreement. She's spendin' the weekend with Lindsey."

"I understand. They share a loss. Well, you and Mandy are still welcome to join us."

"Thanks, but we already have plans."

They walked out onto the front porch where Ray still whittled on the horse for Paige.

He looked up. "That was quick. I figured the file boxes might avalanche on y'all and I'd have to call spelunkers to dig y'all out."

Mary scoffed. "You're a funny ol' man. Watch that ya don't cut a finger off."

Garrett laughed at the crotchety, love filled interaction between his parents.

They said their goodbyes.

Garrett got into the patrol SUV and headed into Pine View to pick up Mandy. He took to chauffeuring her to and from work since the weekend she, temporarily, moved in. He didn't think Mandy would be in danger while driving, alone, to and from Pine View, but the extra miles were a small price to pay for peace of mind. He had a lot to tell Mandy.

~ * ~

Friday night through Sunday afternoon, when James came to visit, passed quickly. Time might be infinite, but there wasn't enough of it for Garrett. The June moon grew larger each night, like a celestial pregnant belly. Garrett wasn't looking forward to what it would deliver. Three new werewolves, if their plan didn't work.

Keeping with tradition, even without Paige, Garrett and Mandy had Pizza Friday and watched the week's *Jeopardy* shows. Mandy won. Building on a new tradition, Garrett and Mandy enjoyed each other's adult oriented company several times. Without Paige, they enjoyed it on the couch in the living room, on the dining room table, and outside on the back deck in broad daylight. Garrett loved the new tradition.

When not coupled, Garrett stayed busy trying to sort out a plan of action for the alpha. He came up with a basic plan but wanted James' feedback. He felt certain James could identify any flaws and provide additional support. Purposefully, because he didn't think it changed things in the broad scope, Garrett hadn't told James about the eventful Friday. All he told James when they spoke on Saturday afternoon was he'd had a productive day on Friday and promised to fill him in when they met on Sunday. They talked, briefly, about what to do with Mandy Tuesday night, too.

To say Friday had been a productive day was a bit of an

understatement. The first, almost four weeks, of the investigation had yielded very little. They had three identified dead werewolves. That had been good, but not much else. After the alpha realized its pack members were getting peaks into its mind, the connections they knew of ended. On Friday, Garrett had put a face to the alpha, discovered the werewolves' den, discovered the ancestral werewolf connection and what that could mean for Paige, and discovered the ancestral werewolf's name. Not a bad day.

~ * ~

James arrived promptly at two o'clock on Sunday with another gallon jug of muscadine wine. Instead of steaks, Garrett grilled chicken. His mom planted a chicken seed for Sunday dinner. After the food was gone, and they were each on their second glass of muscadine wine, the conversation turned to the full moon just two nights away.

As Garrett shared what he'd learned on Friday with James, he'd already told Mandy everything, he listened carefully and without interruption. He nodded his head a few times, though.

When he finished, Garrett leaned back in his chair, and took a sip of muscadine wine. "We'll, what d'ya think?"

James pondered for a moment. "The ancestral werewolf angle is fascinatin'. I told ya Lola knew her shit. Pardon my vulgarity, Mandy."

Mandy smiled. "I've been livin' with Garrett for two weeks. Trust me, you're not offensive in the least."

Garrett thought about protesting but didn't.

"Lola thinks…because of this ancestral werewolf that has been a part of Paige…a part of you too, that she might tame her wolf?" James asked.

"Yeah, but we can't let it get to that point. If it does, Ty and Trowa might do somethin' they can't undo," Garrett said.

"Of course not. It's just…fascinatin' to ponder the possibilities. Lola said there were people…people with the ancestral werewolf connection…who control themselves and never take an innocent life?"

Garrett nodded.

After a few moments of silence, James said, "Whatever course of action we decide on, it can't be at the alpha's den. That's its turf and it'll have the home-field advantage there. If it doesn't already know you've been there, it will the second it gets close to that barn. Your havin' been there might force it to change its routine. That could work to our advantage."

"I figured the same thing. That spot's out. I have a spot in mind, though.

"When I was a kid, Dad and I used to deer hunt on Trent Stuckey's land southwest of Pine View. There was a nice, little clearin' where we planted oats in the off-season to keep deer interested in it. The clearin' was surrounded by tall pine trees we put foldin' tree stands in. With my tree climbin' gear, and a chainsaw, I think I can put a foldin' tree stand a good fifty feet up one of those pines. The foldin' stand would be a lot more stable a platform to shoot from than straddlin' a pine limb."

"Do ya really need to use Paige, Ty, and Trowa as bait, Garrett?" Mandy asked. She didn't care for this aspect of the plan Garrett ran by her.

Before Garrett could respond, James said, "Yes. The alpha will want its new pack. It knows they'll turn on the first full moon. It'll also know they haven't turned, and it'll come for 'em to find out why they haven't."

"That's what the silver's for?" Mandy asked.

This time Garrett beat James to the punch. "I'll need to blindfold 'em, drive 'em around a bit to disorient 'em, and then, right before the moon comes up, handcuff 'em and put the silver on 'em and climb the tree to my foldin' tree blind."

Full of questions, Mandy said, "Won't it smell ya? I thought they had real good sniffers."

"Yeah, that's a potential problem. I'm gonna no-soap shower Tuesday mornin'. No deodorant, aftershave, or anything like that. I'll rinse wash my clothes with no detergent. Then, after I climb the tree, I'm gonna douse myself in coyote urine. It stinks to high hell, but it should mask my natural pleasant smell pretty good," Garrett said with a grin.

Mandy pinched up her face. "After livin' with him for two weeks, I can tell ya that none of his *natural* smells are pleasant, James."

Garrett said, "What do ya think? Will it work?"

James took a sip of muscadine wine. "It should get the alpha there. If the human part of its brain is workin' at all, it'll know it's a trap. Rage and confusion over the loss of its den and its betas not turnin' will be enough to draw it in. How are ya at shootin' in the dark?"

"I borrowed a night vision scope from work and I'm gonna buy a laser sight for my pistol when I pick up the foldin' tree stand at Walmart tomorrow. I should be fine."

James nodded.

They sat in silence for several minutes, sipping muscadine wine and listening to a woodpecker pecking wood on a nearby tree.

Garrett interrupted the silence. "That just leaves Mandy to worry about."

"I'll be fine here, Garrett," Mandy assured Garrett.

"I won't be here, and I don't like the idea of you bein' here alone."

Mandy opened her mouth to reply, but James cut her off. "Come to my house Tuesday night."

Mandy smiled. "I don't want to impose, James."

James waved a dismissive hand. "Pish. You wouldn't be imposin' at all. I have some very nice first edition books. *The Adventures of Tom Sawyer*, *To Kill a Mockingbird*, and *Lord of the Flies,* to name a few. I've no one to share 'em with. Please let me share 'em with ya."

Mandy couldn't resist James' charm. She couldn't deny she craved culture deeper than *The Big Bang Theory*, which was Garrett's idea of deep thinking. Not that she didn't enjoy the show, but there was more to life.

"Okay. I would love to spend Tuesday night in your company, James," Mandy relented.

James clapped his hands together. "It's a date. I'll pick ya up at your shop in Pine View at five o'clock. Garrett can come get ya at my place after this mess is behind us and he has saved the day."

A smile spread across Garrett's face. Not because of what James said about him saving the day. Their plan to get Mandy to James' house on Tuesday night had gone exactly as James told him it would when they spoke on Saturday.

Garrett expressed reservations about Mandy agreeing to be babysat by James.

James said, "All women want a cultured, gay friend. By East Texas standards, I'm cultured, and I'm gay. She won't be able to refuse. You just watch."

Garrett thought it funny that he never told Mandy James was gay. She told him.

They didn't empty the gallon jug of muscadine wine, but they came close. After James passed Garrett's impromptu sobriety test, head back, eyes closed, touch your nose with the tips of your index fingers and balance on one leg for thirty seconds, James shook Garrett's hand, gave Mandy a big hug, hopped into his too big truck, and drove away.

Back on the deck after James left, Mandy and Garrett got into a playful argument over cigarettes. Garrett wanted one, Mandy didn't want him to have one. Mandy won the argument when she promised to blow something other than smoke if Garrett didn't light up. This led to sex on the porch outside again. Aside from some forest critters, no one witnessed the X-rated show.

~ * ~

The next morning, Garrett called in and took a personal day from work to free up his time. He dropped Mandy off at the Good Stuff Thrift Shop and headed from Pine View to the Walmart in Nacogdoches. Luckily, the Brenda who helped Garrett select the right critter-cams was working again. She remembered Garrett and happily helped him select a folding tree stand. They decided on one with a ladder, but she showed him how he could secure it to a tree without the ladder, which was for access and wasn't load bearing, anyway. She sold him an AimSHOT red laser sight for his pistol, too.

From Walmart, Garrett headed back to his house and collected his tree climbing gear, extra rope, and his chainsaw. Then he was off to Trent Stuckey's land.

The clearing was still there, but it wasn't as clear as it had been twenty-five years ago. The chainsaw made quick work of the small trees that had cropped up in the clearing. Then he had to find the perfect tree. That wasn't difficult. He saw a massive pine tree on the south end of the clearing. Garrett got to work.

It proved to be a slow going, hardworking task. Limbs started jutting out of the pine tree about thirty feet up. Garrett tied the folding tree stand to the harness belt with a long rope and the chainsaw with a shorter rope. He started climbing. When he encountered a limb, he pulled the chainsaw up, started it, and cut the limb.

By the time he'd climbed about fifty feet up, he was soaked in sweat and had sawdust covering his body. His arms and shoulders were on fire with pain, too. After a brief break to catch his breath, Garrett started pulling the folding tree stand up the tree by the long rope. His arms and shoulders were on fire with pain when he finally had the blind in his hands. Garrett swapped out the ropes. He tied the stand to the short rope that dangled from the harness and tied the chainsaw to the long rope and lowered to the forest floor below.

Installing the folding tree stand turned out to be anything but easy. Garrett almost dropped it twice and got the pinky finger on his right hand pinched so hard a large blood blister popped up immediately. An hour later, he secured the blind to the tree. Garrett tied off a safety rope and climbed onto the blind seat. It settled a little, but it held.

From that vantage point, Garrett had a good view of the clearing and the surrounding woods. Satisfied with his work and plan, Garrett climbed slowly and gingerly down the tree. From the ground, the camouflaged painted tree blind was difficult to see. Even knowing it was there, Garrett found it difficult to see. Garrett knew the werewolf had enhanced vision, though. He could only hope it would concentrate on the bait.

Before leaving, Garrett pulled all the cut limbs and downed small trees from the clearing deep into the woods. The prep work took longer than Garrett thought it would. Exhausted, he got into his truck and headed for Pine View to pick up Mandy.

That night, after they showered, Mandy gave Garrett a massage to relieve his aching muscles. Under normal circumstances, that message would've turned into more amorous activities, but Garrett fell asleep mid-massage. Mandy covered his naked body and climbed into bed beside him. Outside, the moon was twenty-four hours from being full.

~ * ~

About the time Garrett fell asleep under the almost full moon, a Monterrey Produce box truck crossed from Matamoros, Mexico, into Brownsville, Texas. The Monterrey Produce trucks made regular trips from Mexico to Texas to deliver fresh Mexican produce to wholesale Mexican food stores that supplied Mexican restaurants with authentic Mexican produce for their recipes. It was a respected company and there had been little scrutiny of their cargo.

The border agent on the Texas side of the border waved the truck through with his flashlight and waved at the driver as he passed. The driver, a mountain of a man with a nasty scar that started over his right eye, crossed his nose, and sliced through his lips, waved back, and disappeared into the Texas night.

Chapter Seventeen

Tuesday morning found Garrett rested but sore. The previous day's activities of cutting, climbing, and setting up the folding tree stand took a toll on his back, shoulders, arms, and abdominal muscles. He rolled out of bed and grimaced as a spasm locked up his lower back.

Thinking of Danny Glover's character, Murdock, in every *Lethal Weapon* movie, Garrett mumbled, "I'm gettin' too old for this shit."

From the bathroom, Mandy said, "What?"

Grinning despite the pain, Garrett said, "Nothin'. I was just talkin' to myself," and got to his feet.

He stretched, which chased away the lower back spasm, but set the remaining sore muscles on fire.

Choking back a moan, so as not to alarm Mandy, he thought, *How the hell am I gonna do this half-crippled up*?

He had no choice. He would power through the pain and do what he had to do to save Paige, Ty, and Trowa from their beastly curse.

When Mandy left the bathroom, Garrett hopped into the shower. Not to soap up and clean off. To rinse away any remaining deodorant, soap, shampoo, and cologne from the previous day. After the shower, Garrett drip-dried to not transfer detergent from a towel to his body and he skipped putting on deodorant and brushing his teeth. He dressed in underwear, socks, blue jeans, and a shirt that went through two rinse cycles in the washing machine with no detergent and dried overnight on the back deck rail. The blue jeans were still a little damp, but not unbearable.

An hour later, Garrett dropped Mandy off at her store, where he received a kiss on the cheek, and headed to the sheriff's department to wrap up any work that needed to be done before going back to the Stuckey land and double-checking the setup.

~ * ~

Unable to awake rested because she hadn't slept, Paige got out of bed and drug her feet across the carpet as she walked into the bathroom. She stood in front of the mirror and looked at her reflection. Her eyes were red, and her lids were puffy from lack of sleep. She bent down and splashed some cold water on her face. It felt good and helped to chase the sleepiness away. When she stood back up and looked in the mirror, it wasn't her reflection looking back at her. It was a naked and attractive young woman with long blonde hair and big blue eyes.

Under normal circumstances, a stranger looking back at her in the mirror would have unnerved Paige. She understood what was happening. It was a flash from the alpha. A crystal-clear flash, Paige didn't think the girl knew it happened. As if the alpha let her guard down for a few seconds. Paige sensed longing from the girl in the mirror.

The night she bit Paige and she shoved her silver crucifix and necklace down the alpha's throat, it transformed back into human form. Paige saw enough of its human form to know it was female, young, and had blue eyes. It hadn't transformed enough to see its human face, though. Now that she could see her face, Paige realized she'd seen the girl since. At Justin's funeral.

The funeral Mass had ended, and the pallbearers carried away Justin's casket, along with Brad and Matt's. Paige and the Andersons were exiting the pew to follow Justin to the cemetery when she sensed someone looking at her. She looked up and saw the blonde-haired girl looking directly at her from the other side of the church. Her big blue eyes were penetrating. Before Paige looked away, the girl smiled at her.

The realization the werewolf that killed Justin dared to attend his funeral filled Paige with a sudden rage. A rage like nothing she'd ever experienced in her life. A raw, hot, tangible rage coursed through Paige. The reflection in the mirror rippled like a stone dropped into still water and the blonde-haired girl's big blue eyes flashed fiery red.

For a moment, Paige thought the blonde-haired girl would transform into a werewolf in front of her. Instead of transforming, the blonde-haired girl said, in Paige's mind, "*That's not possible.*" and her reflection disappeared. When it did, Paige looked at her own reflection again and her green eyes were fiery red.

Thinking it had been a trick of her mind, Paige blinked several times, but her eyes remained burning embers. It wasn't until the all-consuming rage inside her subsided that her eyes returned to their normal green.

Confused, but thinking whatever happened was out of her control, Paige showered, got dressed, and left her mom's house for, perhaps, the last time.

~ * ~

After spending the previous night in her wolf, hunting in the deep East Texas woods and feasting on a large buck that tried, futilely, to impale her wolf with its antlers, Alexis rested and looked forward to the coming night when its new pack would transform for the first time. The first item on Alexis' pack agenda had been to pit the little bitch against her troublesome dad. From Alexis' reasoning, this action would cause one of three outcomes. Dead little bitch, dead troublesome dad, or cursed troublesome dad. Alexis had a preference, cursed troublesome dad, but she could live with any of the possibilities.

Wanting to brush her teeth, she disliked the aftertaste of her wolf's culinary preferences, Alexis made her way to the bathroom. She arrived in the bathroom naked and looked at her reflection in the mirror.

As Alexis looked at herself in the mirror, her mind drifted to a time before the werewolf gift. A time before Seth died. She missed his face, his voice, his touch, his smell, his taste; she missed him. Without the consolation of her wolf, Alexis would have mourned Seth's passing in a more traditional manner. Instead, her wolf comforted her and filled the void of Seth's absence in her life.

When the memory faded, it surprised Alexis to see the little bitch looking back at her through the mirror. She could feel the little bitch's rage. The little bitch surprised her more when her eyes flared a fiery red.

That's not possible, Alexis thought, a second before she closed her mind to the intrusion.

The experience unnerved Alexis to a degree she hadn't felt since the night the troublesome dad shot her wolf through the left ear with a silver bullet. That wound still hadn't completely healed. It looked more like a botched piercing than a bullet hole at that point, though.

Although Alexis had been a complete novice on werewolf lore when she received the gift, she'd seen a few movies and didn't believe they were real, she'd done extensive research on them since that time. There were inconsistencies across the lore. Ways to become a werewolf, ways to kill a werewolf. One consistent, aside from silver being the weapon of choice, consisted in the lore. Those who received the gift wouldn't transform until the first full moon after being bitten.

In Alexis' case, that happened on Saturday, April fourth. She'd found the old barn a week before the April full moon and talked Seth into joining her pack. Seth recruited Dillon and Cole, although they were unaware of what they were being recruited for. Alexis knew Seth thought she'd been delusional, but he humored her anyway. Alexis had no clue she was going to change until it happened. The little bitch's eyes flared werewolf red the morning of the full moon.

"What the fuck does this mean?" Alexis asked her reflection in the mirror.

It means you need to kill the little bitch before she transforms, her reflection replied in her mind.

This fourth option wasn't appealing. The little bitch caused Alexis so much trouble. From the silver in her throat, to trespassing in her mind, to the troublesome dad with his silver bullets. Killing her before she transformed would let her off too easy. Alexis wanted to dominate her, humiliate her, and torture her. Then she would kill her like she killed Cole.

The thought of sinking her wolf's fangs into the little bitch's wolf's neck made her mouth water. When Alexis came out of the fantasy and looked at her reflection in the mirror, her eyes were burning embers. She let the transformation overtake her. Then the werewolf curled up on the bed and fell asleep.

Alexis never got around to brushing her teeth. That was just fine with her wolf. It enjoyed the aftertaste of its culinary preferences. Which, that morning, included the buck's succulent flesh and its heart, lungs, liver, brain, eyes, intestines, and freshly emptied, when the werewolf locked its jaws around the buck's neck, bladder and bowel.

~ * ~

A laughing Little D woke Ty. Ty had a deep, dreamless sleep and, for a moment, he forgot about the curse and what day it was. When it finally registered, Ty moaned and looked at the bedside alarm clock. It was eleven thirty-two a.m. This was much earlier than he usually got up after working the eleven-to-seven shift but knowing it might be his last day with Jasmine and Little D, he rolled out of bed and followed the sound of his laughing son.

When Ty appeared in the kitchen, Jasmine looked up. "I'm sorry, babe. Little D's in a laughin' mood this mornin'. Go on back to sleep.

We'll keep it down."

Ty smiled, lifted Little D from his highchair, and hugged him close, which transferred mashed peas from Little D's chin to Ty's bare chest. "I'd rather spend time with y'all than sleepin'."

"You'll be tired tonight."

Being tired was the least of Ty's concerns for the coming night.

"It's just one night, and it's worth it to spend some time with y'all. Besides, it looks like this little man could use a bath."

Jasmine smiled and pointed at the mashed peas on Ty's chest. "Looks like the big man could use a bath, too."

After giving Little D a bath and putting him down in his crib for a nap, warm baths always made Little D sleepy, Ty and Jasmine took a shower together. The shower activities spilled over into the bedroom. An hour later, Ty and Jasmine were basking in the afterglow. Ty savored every moment as if it were the last time he'd enjoy the earthly pleasures, which, he knew, was a possibility.

~ * ~

Like Paige, Trowa hadn't slept the previous night. He replaced the Airstream with an old, cheap truck bed, camper shell. It had been all he could afford. The camper shell was cramped. Trowa slept in the top part that jutted out over the truck cab and didn't accommodate his long, lanky frame. It also lacked the amenities, stove, and refrigerator of the Airstream. The cramped quarters weren't what kept Trowa from sleeping, though. The sliver and turquoise wristband he put on the previous evening kept him from sleeping.

To Trowa, the wristband had been salvation. It could keep him from transforming into an abomination of nature. It burned his flesh and grated on his every nerve.

Trowa removed the wristband. The pain subsided immediately. He looked at his wrist. The coppery skin in contact with the silver was an angry red, and puffy. It looked like a second-degree burn.

Although the pain was intense, Trowa powered through it. Satisfied he could endure the discomfort that night, Trowa got dressed. He had to stoop his shoulders and lower his head to do so in the camper shell. He exited the camper.

The morning sun felt warm on his face and the pine scented air fresh in his lungs.

As Trowa geared up to head out to the current log cutting job, he thought, *I hope the pain isn't more intense when my body's trying to transform.*

~ * ~

The Monterrey Produce box truck had a maximum speed limit of sixty miles per hour, which made the almost five-hundred-mile drive from Matamoros, Mexico, to Pine View County time consuming. As the sun was coming up, the box truck was nearing Victoria, Texas, which was almost the half point.

El Lobo grinned, which stretched the scar across his lip and revealed his blackened teeth. He said, "*Voy a por ti, puta*," which translated to, "I'm coming for you, bitch," to the empty truck.

~ * ~

There were only a couple of issues that needed Garrett's immediate attention at work, which, considering how ripe the early morning heat made his pits, was good. Garrett made it back out at the Stuckey land by one o'clock. Even though his muscles protested, Garrett donned the tree climbing gear, tied several items to the harness belt, and started climbing the tree.

It had been a slow process, but Garrett made it to the folding tree stand within twenty minutes. After tying off a safety rope, he climbed onto the stand and spent several minutes catching his breath.

Rested, Garrett pulled the Remington 870, twelve-gauge shotgun onto the stand. He preferred the pump-action 870 over the semi-automatic 1100 because 1100's had a reputation of jamming, which was a problem he couldn't risk. His trusty pump-action didn't have that problem. He removed the plug from the 870, which had a silver packed, double-ought shotgun shell in the chamber and four more in the tube. Garrett used a bungee cord to secure the shotgun to the tree just above the stand.

After securing the shotgun to the tree, Garrett pulled the night-vision scope onto the platform and adjusted it to fit his head. With it properly fitted, Garrett secured it to the tree stand with a Velcro loop. Finally, he took the bottle of coyote urine from his left breast pocket and secured it to the platform with a strip of duct tape.

Satisfied he had the needed gear in place, the pistol with silver loads would stay with him, Garrett took his cellphone out and checked it for reception bars. It had two. Not great, but better than one or none. It was time to inform the bait of what time to meet and where.

He unlocked the phone, tapped on the 'Message' icon, and entered Paige, Ty, and Trowa's names in the 'To:' field, and typed, 'Come to my house this evening at six pm. Bring the silver item you need.' He waited for each to respond.

He didn't have to wait long. Ty's, 'Will do' response came first.

Within a minute. Trowa's reply of, 'See you then' came.

That just left Paige. Garrett looked at his watch. It was almost three o'clock. He knew teachers frowned on students texting in class, but he also knew students found ways of texting, anyway.

Just as Garrett started to send a follow-up text, Paige responded. Only not in the group message. She sent a private text.

Garrett tapped on the new text and read, 'Saw her this morning. I saw something else too. Can I come to ur house early?'

Garrett quickly typed, 'Of course you can. I'm about to head home now. Come whenever you want. Are you okay?'

The bubble with three moving dots popped up and, several seconds later, Garrett read, 'I'm fine, Daddy. Something weird happened tho. I'll tell u when I get there. I luv u!'

Garrett typed back, 'I'll see you in a bit. I love you too, Paige-Turner.'

'♥,' Paige responded.

After pocketing his cellphone, Garrett climbed down the tree as quickly as his sore muscles and safety allowed, got in his patrol SUV, and headed for home.

~ * ~

The late afternoon heat dissipated slightly to a balmy eighty-five degrees. Garrett was on the back deck, which was bathed in shadows from the surrounding trees, resisting the urge to smoke a cigarette. He wanted one but knew it would cover his body with the smell of cigarette smoke.

Paige opened the front door. "Where ya at, Daddy?"

"Out back, sweetheart."

Several seconds later, Paige emerged from the sliding doors wearing faded blue jeans that had a large hole in the left knee, scuffed cowboy boots, and a green spaghetti strap top that was too tight for Garrett's liking. She was wearing a Pine View County Sheriff Department cap he gave her with her long, brown ponytail pulled through the adjustment band hole in the back. She spread her arms and walked toward Garrett for a hug.

Garrett held up his right hand. "No hugs today, sweetheart."

Paige stopped and looked confused.

"I can't get your scent on me. I'm doin' everything I can to rid myself of all scents. I took a soap free shower, no deodorant, no detergent on my clothes. I didn't even brush my teeth this mornin'," Garrett explained.

Paige sniffed the air and wrinkled her nose. "No offense, Daddy. I think ya smell more like you than ya ever have."

That removing all the superficial odors associated with being a hygienic human would only heighten his natural scent hadn't occurred to Garrett. He'd hunted enough to know removing the odors associate with civilized living ideal, but he'd never hunted a werewolf before.

The coyote urine will help, Garrett thought.

"I have one more trick up my smelly sleeve. I think it'll help."

"What's that?"

"Coyote urine. I'm gonna douse myself in it later."

Paige crinkled her nose. "That sounds…lovely."

"Tell me what happened this mornin'."

Paige took a seat across the table from her dad.

He listened as Paige told him about seeing the girl in the mirror, remembering her being at Justin's funeral, how her eyes flared red, and what she heard the girl think before the connection broke.

With the tale told, Garrett said, "I saw her at Justin's funeral, too. After you were out of the church, she and I talked."

"You knew? Why didn't ya tell me?" Paige demanded.

Garrett leaned forward to take Paige's hand in his, but he pulled back before they touched.

Not touching her is hard, Garrett thought.

"I couldn't tell ya, sweetheart. What you know, she might know. I don't know who she is. If I did, I'd have paid her a visit and ended this by now. If I'd done my damn job, I might know who she is," Garrett admitted.

In a calmer, forgiving tone, Paige said, "What could ya have done?"

Garrett exhaled heavily. He really wanted a cigarette. "Murder Investigation one-o-one, sweetheart. Always assume the perp will inject themselves into the investigation. Attendin' the victims' funerals is one way they can do that. I should'a had a deputy takin' down the license plates of every vehicle at every funeral."

Paige reached across the table for Garrett's hand. He knew he shouldn't, but he let her take it.

Paige squeezed his fingers. "It's okay, Daddy. This wasn't a normal murder investigation."

He'd never heard a truer statement. Garrett couldn't help but laugh and Paige joined in.

"What about my eyes? Was that a trick my mind played on me?"

"Not if she saw it, too," Garrett reasoned.

"What's it mean?"

Garrett thought long and hard about how to respond. He knew telling her too much of what he'd learned from Lola would be risky. James told him to tell Paige to resist the animal urge.

Finally, he said, "It means you're special, Paige."

Paige smiled. "You always tell me that, because I'm your daughter."

Garrett tightened his grip on Paige's fingers. "It's more than that, Paige. I've talked with two people I trust 'bout this and they agree you're special. I can't tell ya anymore about it. Other than to say…if, God forbid, you transform tonight, fight the beast within you. Fight it like you've fought nothin' before, Paige-Turner. Do you understand what I'm tellin' ya?"

After several seconds of awkward silence, Paige said, "Of course I will, Daddy."

That would have to suffice.

Garrett smiled. "I know ya will, Paige-Turner."

Just then, Garrett's cellphone chimed with a text. He pulled his hand free of Paige's and looked at the screen.

The text was from James and read, 'I have secured Ladyhawk and am in route to my fortified castle. Good luck and Godspeed, my friend.'

Garrett laughed and showed the text to Paige.

"What's that mean?" she asked after reading it.

"Mandy is stayin' with James tonight. I guess that's his code for havin' picked her up."

Paige laughed when she was in on the meaning.

Garrett typed back, 'Thank you, Good Sir. I will send a raven with news when the deed is done.'

Shortly after sending the text, Garrett heard a truck pull into his driveway with a rumbling motorcycle following closely behind. Several moments later, Ty and Trowa emerged from the side of the house.

Ty grinned. "I thought I might find y'all out back."

"Good thing too. I don't know if it's a werewolf thing or if you're just that potent. You reek, paleface," Trowa added.

They all cracked up laughing to where tears were streaming down their cheeks. They needed laughter; it put everyone at more ease than expected, given their evening task. They were together, and they were ready.

"Everyone got their silver?" Garrett asked.

Ty and Paige nodded. Trowa held up his wrist to display the silver wristband.

"Doesn't that burn?" Ty asked.

"Like a bitch. Sorry, little miss," Trowa replied.

They all laughed again.

It was time to go.

~ * ~

The sun was slipping toward the western horizon as Alexis pulled out of her driveway and headed to the barn. It was slightly earlier in the evening than her usual trips to transform, but she wanted more time with her wolf in the woods to locate her new pack member's positions and prepare for the night's activities.

If they knew what they would become and were smart, Alexis thought they would isolate themselves from friends and family in the woods. She would know when they transformed, and a simple howl from their alpha would bring them to her. Then the fun could begin.

~ * ~

Paige, Ty, and Trowa followed Garrett from the back deck to his private pickup truck. Garrett opened the front passenger door and grabbed three pillowcases lying on the seat.

He turned to the three of them. "As a precaution, I'd like y'all to wear these while I drive to our destination."

"She'll smell us and know where we are the second she transforms, Daddy," Paige told him.

"I'm countin' on that, sweetheart. I'm hopin' she doesn't transform until it's dark. By then, we'll be in place. I just don't want her gettin' a head's up flash from y'all before then," Garrett explained as he held out the pillowcases.

Reluctantly, they each took a pillowcase from Garrett.

After loading into the pickup, Paige in the front and Ty and Trowa in the back seat, they slipped the pillowcases over their heads.

"I feel stupid," Paige said.

Garrett looked around the cab at his pillowcase-wearing passengers, and chuckled. "Y'all look pretty stupid."

"Thanks," Ty responded flatly.

"Just think of it as a tiny teepee," Trowa chimed in.

They all laughed again.

Garrett started his truck and drove out of the driveway.

The direct route from Garrett's house to the Stuckey property took about twenty minutes. Since Garrett wanted to disorient his passengers, and potentially the alpha, by traipsing their scent in several places, he took several back roads and purposefully drove in the wrong direction several times on the way.

The sun was sinking below the tallest trees when, forty-five minutes later, Garrett pulled to a stop in front of the gate to Stuckey's property.

"Are we there yet?" Paige asked sarcastically when the truck stopped.

"Yeah, smart ass, we are," Garrett replied.

Paige reached up to pull the pillowcase off, but Garrett grabbed her hand and said to all of them, "Leave the pillowcases on. I wanna walk y'all in blindfolded."

Paige huffed, but she didn't remove the pillowcase.

"Wait here while I get the gate," Garrett told them, before exiting the truck.

After unlatching the chain that secured the gate to a fencepost,

Garrett swung the gate open. He went back to the driver's side back door and guided Trowa around to the passenger side. He helped Ty out of the back seat and Paige from the front.

When they were all out of the truck, Garrett took Paige's right hand in his. "Grab hands and I'll walk y'all in. It's not far, and the ground is pretty level. I'll walk slow, though."

Paige grabbed Ty's hand in her free one and Ty grabbed Trowa's hand in his free one. Garrett led them slowly and carefully through the woods to the small clearing. The walk took about ten minutes and the sun continued to sink in the west.

Once they were in the middle of the clearing, Garrett stopped, and let go of Paige's hand. "Okay. Y'all can lose the pillowcases."

One by one, Paige, then Ty, then Trowa, they pulled the pillowcases off their heads and looked around at their surroundings.

Trowa spotted the folding tree stand high in the pine tree on the south edge of the clearing.

He pointed at it. "You'll be up there ready to shoot the bitch when she shows up? Sorry, little miss."

"That's the plan," Garrett responded.

Ty looked at the tree stand. "We're down here as bait."

Garrett nodded and looked at the sky. The easterly dark purple sky was pushing the westerly burnt orange sky out of existence. It was time for the hardest part of the plan to be put in place.

"Okay boys and girl, I need your silver."

Trowa held up his wrist where the silver wristband was still in place. The surrounding skin was an angry red. Ty reached into the breast pocket of his shirt and pulled the Silver Star from it. Garrett couldn't be certain, but he thought he heard a slight sizzling sound coming from Ty's hand. Paige was the last to hand over her silver, and it pained Garrett to watch her wince as she pulled the crucifix and necklace from the right front pocket of her blue jeans. It would pain him even more to drape it around her neck and leave it there, but it had to be done.

After Garrett collected the silver from Paige and Ty, he retrieved a pair of handcuffs from his back pocket. He needed the handcuffs in case the need to transform overpowered their rational need to remain human. Without handcuffs, they could simply remove the silver obstacle to transforming.

"I need y'all to put your hands behind your back. Who's first?"

None of them appeared to be surprised by the request.

Trowa clasped his hands behind his back and spun around so that his back faced Garrett. "I've probably spent the most time in handcuffs out of the three of us. Slap 'em on, Garrett."

Garrett clicked the handcuffs firmly onto Trowa left wrist first and then the right one that had the silver wristband on it. Trowa's skin was unnaturally warm, bordering on hot. He locked them so, if they hit the ground riving in pain, the cuffs wouldn't click tighter.

Ty volunteered to go next. Garrett took another pair of handcuffs from the other back pocket and locked them in place on Ty's thick wrists. Then it was Paige's turn.

The last pair of handcuffs, the first pair Garrett owned, came from the leather holder on his utility belt. Garrett had to fight back tears as he locked the handcuffs around his little girl's small, delicate wrists. The worst part was yet to come.

With everyone handcuffed, Garrett turned to Ty. "I'm sorry I have to do this, Ty."

Ty grinned. "If it needs doin', best get it done."

Garrett pondered how best to apply Ty's Silver Star so that it would be in constant contact with his skin. Trowa and Paige's applications were obvious. Luckily, Ty was a muscular man with tight fitting shirts. Garrett unbuttoned the second button on Ty's shirt, slipped the Silver Star inside it, and pinned it to the inside of the shirt in front of his bulging right pectoral muscle. Ty winced as the Silver Star pressed against his skin, but Garrett buttoned both buttons to pull the shirt even tighter.

Garrett moved in front of Paige and looked down at her upturned face. Her green eyes sparkled in the dying light.

"It's okay, Daddy."

This time, tears flowed from Garrett's eyes.

He kissed her on the forehead. "I'm so sorry, Paige-Turner. I wish I could tell ya more. If it happens, fight it, sweetheart."

Paige smiled a sweet, reassuring smile. "I will, Daddy."

Garrett carefully slipped the silver crucifix and necklace over Paige's head. He went to great effort, with his fingers spread wide, to make sure none of the silver touched her skin until necessary. When the time came, he gently lowered it onto her skin.

Paige's face contorted, and she sucked in a quick breath, but she didn't cry out. Garrett's heart cried out for her.

As Garrett stepped back from Paige, she said, "Can I kiss the crucifix, Daddy?"

Garrett nodded and held it up to Paige's lips.

There was a distinct sizzle sound as Paige's lips touched the silver crucifix and, when Garrett removed it, he saw blisters on her upper and lower lips where they contacted it. He lowered the crucifix to the outside of Paige's shirt.

"Put it inside my shirt, Daddy."

"Are ya sure? I think the necklace is enough and this'll just increase the pain."

Paige nodded. "I'm sure. I want Him close to my heart."

Garrett did as she requested.

Paige winced again, but she managed a weak smile.

Everything was in order. All Garrett had to do was climb the tree and wait.

Before walking away, Garrett said, "I'm guessin' y'all will know it's comin' before I do. When that happens, hit the ground. I don't want to hit one of y'all with crossfire. I've got a night vision scope in the tree, so I'll be able to see y'all in this tall grass from up there. It might take the alpha a little longer to locate y'all if you're not standin' up in the middle of this clearin'. Okay?"

Everyone nodded.

Garrett headed toward the tall pine tree on the south end of the clearing.

Twenty minutes later, Garrett tied off the safety strap and sat on the blind platform. The shotgun was across his lap, with the butt tied to the platform by a loose rope, so Garrett could retrieve it if he accidentally dropped it. Before putting the night vision scope on his head, he pulled the duct tape loose that secured the coyote urine in place, opened the bottle, and poured a healthy portion of the liquid on both shoulders and both thighs.

From far below and in the middle of the clearing, Garrett heard Paige say, "What is that stink?"

"Coyote urine. Your dad's using it to mask his scent," Trowa explained.

In a disgusted voice, Paige said, "Oh yeah. Well…it's workin'."

Garrett smiled and slipped the night vision scope onto his head.

The western sky still showed a slight orange glow, but the eastern sky was black, and the remaining sky was becoming darker by the second. Garrett looked through the scope and saw everything in clear shades of green. He looked east toward the darkest part of the sky. He saw a light green, almost white, glow emanating just above the treetops.

As Garrett watched, the white, rounded outline of the June full moon rose above the treetops. A chill ran up his spine.

He patted his left breast pocket, which contained the stick totem Lola gave him. "I hope you were right about all this, Lola."

A voice, Lola's warm, honey voice, spoke from inside his head. *I am. She's comin'. So is the other.*

Other? What other? Garrett thought.

Lola's presence was gone.

~ * ~

As Alexis turned onto the overgrown drive that led to the deserted barn, she sensed someone had been there. The closer she got to the barn, the stronger the feeling got. When the truck emerged from the drive into the clearing, the troublesome dad's scent became clear.

Fearing an ambush, Alexis stomped on the brakes and brought the truck to a skidding stop. She inhaled deeply, trying to determine how old the scent was. Being in human form made it hard to tell, but she thought he'd been there several days ago.

That the troublesome dad wasn't currently there relieved Alexis; that he found her den enraged her. Even if he wasn't currently there, his having been there compromised the place. He could come back. This situation hampered her plans to get an early start.

Enraged, she slammed her fist down on the top of the steering wheel, which dented from the impact, and screamed, "I want you fuckin' dead."

After the outburst, she sat there breathing heavily for several moments as she considered her options.

There was only one other place Alexis thought might serve as a safe place to park her truck and transform in private. Because of recent events, she thought it would be deserted. Alexis took her foot off the brake and hammered the accelerator. The truck spun in a tight circle, spraying dirt in a high arc from the outside tires, and sped back down the overgrown path. Alexis headed to the Mill Road Barn.

~ * ~

Highway Sixty-Nine traffic, south of Pine View, had been light that evening. Deputy Mike Middleton drove with his radar gun pointed at the southbound oncoming vehicles when he spotted a box truck on the northbound highway shoulder.

Commercial trucks on the side of the highway weren't uncommon. They got flat tires, had engine and brake problems to name a few. Sometimes truckers just needed a quick catnap. Mike saw and heard it all during his time in law enforcement. His policy had always been to stop and check on roadside trucks.

Even without the personal policy, Mike would have stopped for this truck. It was getting dark, and the truck's flashers weren't on. Nor had the trucker bothered to put out reflective warning triangles.

Mike pulled to a stop behind the truck, put on the emergency lights to alert passing traffic of his presence, and stepped out of the SUV. He approached the truck on the passenger side to keep it between himself and the seventy-five mile per hour drivers. He'd seen dash-cam footage of too many law enforcement personnel hit by careless drivers, especially at twilight, to risk approaching the truck cab on the driver's side, emergency lights or not.

Because the sun slipped behind the treetops, Mike pulled his Mag flashlight and trained it on the passenger side of the box truck. He recognized the Monterrey Produce name immediately. Their trucks were regularly on the roads in East Texas.

Swinging the flashlight at his side, he walked toward the truck's cab. Before he cleared the box end, the truck shook violently and a low, menacing growl emanated from within the enclosed box.

Fuck me, Mike thought as he backed away from the truck and pulled his pistol.

A massive werewolf exploded from the side of the box truck in a shower of wood, sheet metal, and avocados. Mike brought his pistol up for a shot. The werewolf leapt toward him with alarming speed. He had the shot. As he moved his finger from the trigger guard to the trigger, he back stepped into a rut and fell backward. He squeezed the trigger quickly, but the shot had been high. The last thing Deputy Mike Middleton saw were the werewolf's dagger length fangs closing around his face.

After biting Mike's face off with one vicious snap, the massive werewolf bounded into the woods that blanket either side of Highway Sixty-Nine and stopped. It sniffed the air several times. It grinned, which accentuated the split in its upper lip, and sprinted away on all fours.

~ * ~

Several miles away, in the modest, three-bedroom ranch that Mike Middleton called home, Becks loaded the dishwasher after preparing and eating supper alone. Because Mike worked the three-to-eleven shift, Becks became used to eating alone.

That night, she'd prepared a chicken, rice, cheese, and broccoli casserole. One of Mike's favorite meals. Mike's portion was on a tinfoil-covered plate in the refrigerator.

Becks just rinsed the casserole dish under hot water in the sink and was moving it to the dishwasher when she sensed Mike was in trouble.

Being a deputy's wife for as long as she had, Becks knew any shift could be 'the' shift, but she'd never experienced such a strong feeling. The sensation intensified, and she *felt* Mike's life end. Like a switch in her very soul flipped off.

The casserole dish slipped from her hand, hit the ceramic tiled floor, and shattered into dozens of pieces. Becks sank to the floor among the shards of CorningWare, cutting her knees as she did, and sobbed uncontrollably.

~ * ~

The gate to the Mill Road Barn remained closed and remnants of yellow crime scene tape hung from the gate's top bar. Alexis didn't bother with getting out and opening the gate; she plowed through it with the truck's bumper and sped up the road. She skidded to a stop behind the metal building.

Not bothering to remove her clothes, Alexis transformed before she was out of the truck. As her wolf took form, her clothes stretched, ripped, and fell to the ground at her wolf's feet. It sniffed the air several times.

It expected three distinct scents in three distinct, and different, places. The blending of all three scents in the same place momentarily confused it.

They're together, the small, human part of its brain reasoned.

It dropped to all fours and sprinted toward the jumbled scents.

~ * ~

The silvery, full moon cleared the treetops and hung in the cloudless night sky like a spotlight on their location. Garrett's nerves were on edge. He thought the alpha would have made an appearance by now.

From down below, as the full moon climbed higher in the sky, Garrett could hear the moans of pain coming from Paige, Ty, and, to a lesser degree, Trowa. Paige's muffled moans distressed Garrett, which added to his raw nerves. He scanned the woods surrounding the clearing. Nothing moved.

"Show yourself, you fuckin' bitch," Garrett hissed through gritted teeth.

In his head, Lola said, *she's gettin' close.*

Garrett shouldered the shotgun.

~ * ~

The searing pain from the silver crucifix and necklace was becoming unbearable. The higher the full moon got in the sky, the more it burned. Paige could feel the beast inside her wanting, needing, to break free. It surged inside her like a living thing, which, she understood, it was.

Her senses wavered from acute to normal sporadically. One moment she could hear the surrounding insects, frogs, and nighttime critters singing their nocturnal chorus like she always had, then she would hear a faraway television in someone's living room or the clinking of dishes as someone cleared the table after supper. In that instant, she could smell the food they'd been eating. Her vision shifted from normal moonlight darkness and shadows to an almost black and white clarity that chased the shadows away and revealed her surroundings as clearly as if it had been the sun, instead of the moon, above her.

Paige shuddered when she realized how appealing the heightened senses were.

"I don't want this," she hissed quietly.

In her mind, a small part of it that wanted to dominate the whole of it hissed back, *Yes, you do. Set me free.*

~ * ~

When the alpha got closer to the jumble of scents that comprised its new pack, it slowed to a walk and stopped. It searched for the troublesome man's scent, it expected to find it in proximity to the little bitch's scent. It sniffed the air again. It picked up the powerful stench of coyote piss, but no trace of him in the night air.

The alpha killed its share of coyotes over the past two months, and it relished the thought of devouring the one that stank up the night air after it united with its pack.

It advanced toward its pack's scent. It paused and looked up at the bloated moon hovering overhead. It cocked its head and listened.

It heard the little bitch hiss, "I don't want this."

It looked back up at the full moon.

The werewolf that could change at will felt the pull of the full moon. Something was wrong; something the werewolf couldn't quite comprehend. It knew the pull of the full moon should have transformed its pack by then, but the little bitch was still speaking with her human voice.

The werewolf dropped to all fours and advanced toward the jumbled scents more slowly and cautiously.

~ * ~

In the clearing, fighting back the burning silver pain, Paige sensed the alpha approaching before the others did. As if on command, her sporadic senses locked into high gear all at once. She smelled the alpha's musky fragrance at the same time she heard its claws scrape lightly across a tree trunk. She looked in the direction from which the stench and sound came.

In something she could only comprehend as reminiscent of a television or movie special effect when the camera zooms in on a faraway object quickly, her vision zoomed through the dense forest and locked on the alpha. Its fiery red eyes locked on Paige's fiery red eyes. It smiled a demonic smile, dropped to all fours, and sprinted toward her.

"She's here. In the woods to my right, Daddy." Paige screamed.

~ * ~

Garrett, who had been scanning the woods to the left of Paige when she screamed, looked back just in time to see Paige, Ty, and Trowa fall into the tall weeds. He hadn't seen which way Paige faced before she fell, so he did not know which way to her right was when she screamed. An instant later, the surrounding woods fell deathly silent.

When the woods went silent, Garrett heard crashing in the underbrush as the alpha tore toward its unchanged pack. He pointed the shotgun toward the sound and waited for a shot.

The distance between the tree blind and the other side of the clearing where the werewolf came from wasn't optimal for a shotgun kill of a large animal. Double-ought shot would penetrate from that distance, and, according to James, penetration was key. That's why Garrett opted for the scatter pattern of the shotgun blast over the velocity of a single nine-millimeter bullet.

An instant later, the werewolf broke through the tree line into the clearing. Garrett's assumption where it would emerge was spot on. He squeezed the trigger. As he did, the tree he sat in was jolted with a blow that rocked the tree and sent the shot high into the night sky. Garrett saw the wad sail away against the full moon.

Worse still, the massive impact broke one of the metal bands that secured the folding tree stand to the tree. Without the band, weight distribution was the only thing to keep the stand from moving. The impact knocked Garrett to one side of the stand. The stand tilted to that side and slipped down the tree.

Garrett had a decision to make, and he had to make it quickly. If he left the safety rope intact, he would end up hanging from the tree by the safety harness when the blind slid away beneath him. Hanging in the tree would keep the werewolf from reaching him but, without a stable platform to shoot from, it would hamper his aim. In that situation, he might miss the alpha or accidentally hit Paige, Ty, or Trowa.

The other option was to cut the safety rope and ride the blind down. The manufacturer designed the tree blind in a way that prevented it from collapsing and falling from the tree. Instead, it would stutter-step down the length of the tree. He knew he wouldn't be able to get a clear shot while riding the blind down but, once he was on the ground, he could unload on the alpha, end its miserable life, and save Paige, Ty, and Trowa from the curse.

When it came down to it, it wasn't a hard decision for Garrett to make. He quickly slipped the knot on the safety rope from the harness and started sliding down the tree with the folding tree blind.

The bumpy ride made it difficult to see things clearly through the night vision scope. To gauge his distance from the ground, Garrett looked down the tree just in time to see an enormous werewolf, one that dwarfed the alpha by at least two feet, emerge from the woods directly below the tree he'd been sitting in.

~ * ~

After dispatching the deputy by eating his face, the massive werewolf picked up the scent of the *puta,* who caused it so much pain and stole its Ecstasy. It waited to exact revenge, and the wait was almost over.

It shadowed the *puta* from the time of her transformation and marveled at the stupidity of her single-minded wolf. Single-minded to where her wolf didn't register his wolf's scent. Before the *puta* picked up on the fact her fledgling pack members weren't transforming, his wolf knew they weren't, and it knew why. They were using silver to keep it from happening. His wolf could smell the silver burns on their flesh. His wolf could smell the man masquerading his scent with coyote piss, too. The *puta* knew so little about being a werewolf. This pleased the massive werewolf.

Before the *puta* moved toward her pack, the massive werewolf sprinted ahead to get an idea of what the *puta* had been getting into. It saw the fledgling pack members standing in the middle of a small clearing, defying their wolf with the cursed silver. The two men didn't interest it, but the young girl was another story. It felt its wolf-hood stir at the thought of the things it could do to the girl-pup.

It knew the *puta's* pack would become its pack after it devoured the *puta*. The vanquished alpha's pack always submitted, eventually, to the victorious alpha. Some more readily than others. The massive werewolf dispatched many alphas over the course of its life. The *puta's* pack was of his curse-line and would automatically submit. It would decide the man-pups' fate after the *puta* was a pile of meat, blood, and bones.

After finding the fledgling pack, the massive werewolf set its attention on the man masquerading as coyote piss. It followed its nose upward and saw the man high in a tree. Having lived a long time, and surviving its fair share of close calls, it immediately understood what was happening. The *puta* was being drawn into an ambush.

The coyote piss man in the tree was of little interest to the massive werewolf. Other than the silver bullets he planned to kill the *puta* with. The massive werewolf couldn't allow the coyote piss man to kill the *puta*. That pleasure belonged to it.

It quickly came up with a plan that would solve both problems. Kill the coyote piss man and stop him from killing the *puta*. It crept around the back of the coyote piss man's tree and waited to time its move perfectly. When the *puta* charged, the massive werewolf did, too. As the *puta* broke into the clearing, the massive werewolf slammed into the base of the tree with all its strength and speed.

It heard the shotgun go off and knew it went high because it didn't hear any of the pellets thunk into trees, flesh, or dirt. It also heard a metal band 'snap' and the sound of the tree blind falling. Satisfied its plan worked on both problems, the massive werewolf stepped into the clearing.

~ * ~

When the alpha saw the little bitch's burning red eyes looking directly into its eyes, pure rage coursed through its body. All the degrading plans it had for the little bitch flew from its mind. It wanted to kill her where she stood. Right where she stood, defying the glorious gift it gave her. It dropped to all fours and charged the little bitch.

As it charged, it saw the little bitch and the two gift defying men fall into the tall grass, but that didn't matter. It knew where they were. As it broke from the trees into the clearing, it decided to kill all three of them. It had done fine without a pack, and it didn't need the problems keeping a pack in line created. Then it heard the loud boom of a gun.

The alpha dove into the tall grass to conceal itself. It waited for the burn a hit would bring; it didn't come. The troublesome man missed, but he had still been a threat and the alpha didn't know where he was. It was only then, hiding in tall grass like a common animal, the alpha picked up on the man's scent under the stench of coyote piss. That he tricked it only fueled its rage.

The alpha picked up another scent. An old, musky scent the human part of its brain remembered. It was the stench of *El Lobo*. The stench that filled its human nose while *El Lobo* threatened to rape her human with its grotesquely enormous member.

At that moment, the alpha realized it had been demoted to beta status. It also realized, unless it could gain an advantage, it was about to die.

~ * ~

After dropping into the tall grass, Paige, Ty, and Trowa remained still and silent. They heard the crashing of the alpha as it charged toward them. They heard the impact on the tree and the shotgun blast. They heard the alpha hit the ground hard several feet away from where they were lying. They heard Garrett's folding tree blind sliding down the tree. Through it all, they realized nothing changed. The silver still burnt their flesh, which meant the alpha wasn't dead.

~ * ~

The last sound, the sound of her dad's tree blind sliding down the tree, put Paige in motion. If her daddy lied dead on the ground, she would avenge him. If he was on the ground alive, she would protect him.

Using her shoulder to push up, Paige got to her knees and looked in the direction from where she heard the alpha fall. There was a large hole in the knee-high grass, but she couldn't see the alpha from her vantage point.

The sound of the tree blind still sliding down the tree pulled her attention from the hole in the grass. Paige turned toward her daddy's tree and looked up to where the tree blind should have been. A massive werewolf with a badly scared muzzle blocked the view of the tree.

Paige's bladder failed, and warm piss soaked her crotch and ran down her legs. The massive werewolf sniffed the air and smiled a wicked smile down at her. Rumbling laughter erupted from its barrel chest and shook the ground.

~ * ~

The rumbling laughter caused Ty and Trowa to pop up and look for the source. When they saw the mountain-sized werewolf, the smell of their piss joined Paige's.

The three of them might have stayed there like statues rooted in concrete, but Garrett yelled, "Run."

When he did, the massive werewolf looked back at Garrett, who was safely on the ground at the base of the tree.

~ * ~

The ride down the tree on the dislodged stand was harrowing. A couple of seconds into the fall, the stand platform pitched dangerously to the right. Garrett was trying to line up a shot on the new hulk of a werewolf when it did. Had he not dropped the shotgun and grabbed the platform at that instant, he would have fallen the remaining forty feet to the forest floor. He tied the shotgun to the stand, but the rope had been long enough that it ended up dangling under the descending platform.

With about twenty feet still left between the stand platform and the forest floor, Garrett saw Paige pop up in the grass and with the massive werewolf right behind her. Risking a fall from twenty feet, Garrett let go of the platform, grabbed his service pistol, and lined up for a killing shot.

At that point, the massive werewolf's back blocked everything in front of it, so Garrett wasn't concerned a stray bullet would hit Paige, Ty, or Trowa. As Garrett's finger squeezed the trigger, the rounded bar wrapped around the tree that supported the platform weight snapped. Garrett and the blind fell the remaining fifteen feet, and the shot 'zinged.' Another miss.

Impacting the ground jarred Garrett's body and knocked the wind from his lungs. The pistol flew out of his hand and landed in the tall grass several feet away. Panicked, Garrett looked for the shotgun. It was less than a foot away from him, but its immediate use was questionable.

The shotgun hung under the platform when it fell. It hit the ground barrel down. The weight of the blind and Garrett coming down on top of it drove the barrel about a foot into the soil. Garrett knew firing a shotgun with a clogged barrel could cause the chamber to explode in his face.

He sucked air into his burning lungs and yelled, "Run."

When the massive werewolf turned to look at Garrett, he dove into the high grass where he thought his pistol landed. The lost pistol was his only hope.

~ * ~

When the newly demoted alpha heard the troublesome man yell, it chanced a quick look above the high grass. It saw the three gift defying humans looking up at the larger werewolf and it saw the larger werewolf's back turned. That was just the advantage it hoped for. It sprang from the grass and launched itself at the larger werewolf's back.

~ * ~

Her dad's yell hadn't had time to resonate yet, when Paige noticed an enormous, full moon induced, shadow growing over her. Thinking the alpha's attack came for her, Paige ducked just as the smaller werewolf sailed over her. A split second later, it landed on the larger werewolf's back and clamped its jaws around the back of its neck. The roar from the larger werewolf shook the ground and rattled the branches of the surrounding trees.

Taking advantage of the werewolves' preoccupation with each other, Paige ran to the tree with the crumpled folding tree stand at its base. She couldn't see her daddy in the high grass but, when her foot kicked into something and she tripped, she heard him grunt.

Quick reflexes kept Paige from falling on her face. She spun and landed with a 'thud' on her left shoulder next to him.

"Are you okay?" Garrett asked quickly.

"I think so," Paige responded.

Frustrated, Garrett said, "I can't find my gun."

Another loud roar shook their surroundings.

"They're fightin'," Paige whispered.

She sat up in the tall grass to look.

Garrett sat up, too.

The scene looked like something out of a macabre gladiator battle. The smaller werewolf still clung to the larger werewolf's back with its deadly mouth clamped around its thick neck. Blood ran down the larger werewolf's chest in rivers as it tried desperately to grab the smaller werewolf with its razor-sharp claws by reaching over its shoulders. Its massive shoulders were too wide for it to reach the smaller werewolf. Unsuccessful, it changed tactics.

The larger werewolf dropped its right hand down, reached around the small of its back, and grabbed the smaller werewolf's right foot. When it yanked the foot around to the front of its body, the smaller werewolf's teeth pulled free with a large chunk of the larger werewolf's thick neck in its mouth. A spray of blood erupted from the deep wound, but it was free of the smaller werewolf's bite.

The larger werewolf pulled the smaller one up in the air and easily dangled it there with one hand. The smaller werewolf lashed out with its claws and opened eight deep cuts in the larger werewolf's abdomen.

The claw attack was the smaller werewolf's only option, but it was a mistake. The larger werewolf swung the smaller one out to its side, up over its head, and slammed the smaller one into the ground. The force of the impact shook the ground and the smaller werewolf let out a pain filled yelp as several of its bones snapped.

The larger werewolf reached down into the tall grass with both hands and hoisted the smaller one up in front of its deadly muzzle. Its right hand was around the smaller one's neck and its left hand had the smaller one's right thigh in its grip. It opened its mouth impossibly wide and closed it around the smaller one's midsection. It bit down with all its force.

As the larger werewolf's teeth sank deeply into the smaller one's flesh. The smaller one let out a mournful yelp that resonated for miles. The bigger werewolf kept closing its jaws. A couple of seconds later, the larger werewolf's teeth came together with a viscous, bone crunching snap that bit the smaller one in half. It still had the smaller werewolf's two halves held in its powerful grip.

Almost immediately, the lower half of the smaller werewolf regained its human form. Transforming from the large, hairy lower half of a werewolf to the shapely lower half of a young woman. The smaller werewolf's top half, however, remained in its wolf form continuing to snap its teeth and lash out with its claws.

The larger werewolf tossed Alexis' lower half to the left and almost hit Ty and Trowa, who were watching the epic battle from that direction, with it. They ducked just in time, and Alexis' curvaceous butt and legs sailed into the woods.

The larger werewolf squeezed the smaller werewolf's neck with its powerful hand. The fight in the smaller werewolf slowed. It still lashed out with its claws and gnashed its teeth. Its reach got shorter, and its snapping got less frequent as the will to fight left it.

The larger werewolf twisted its hand quickly. An audible 'snap' echoed through the woods, and the smaller werewolf's arms fell limply at its side.

The larger werewolf looked toward Paige and Garrett and grinned a ghastly grin at them. It tossed the smaller werewolf's top half playfully at them. When it landed in the tall grass directly in front of them, Alexis' big, blue, dead eyes looked up at them. The massive werewolf let out a howl that pierced the still night, and it looked toward Ty and Trowa.

~ * ~

Miles away, Lola sat at the dark, hardwood table holding a totem identical to the one she gave Garrett and told him to keep with him as they battled the alpha. The only light in the room came from a single white candle in the middle of the table, but Lola didn't need light to *see*. Her left eye was closed, but the right cat-like eye focused on the totem.

With her cat-like eye and the totem, Lola saw everything that happened through Garrett's eyes, and confirmed her fears concerning the mountain-sized werewolf. It made Paige's alpha and, upon killing Paige, Ty, and Trowa's maker, they now belonged to it.

In the darkened room, Lola whispered, "Remove Paige's silver."

~ * ~

As soon as Alexis' dead body, the upper half, landed in front of Paige, she knew the curse was still on her. The silver still burned her flesh.

"It didn't work, Daddy."

"What didn't work?"

"The silver still burns. Killin' her didn't remove the curse."

Garrett thought back to the conversation he had with James after the alpha killed Cole and the bikers he cursed with his bite. He knew then Paige, Ty, and Trowa belonged to the new, massive werewolf. Their only chance relied on him finding his pistol and taking out the massive werewolf. He started feeling around in the tall grass for it.

Lola's warm, honey voice echoed, *Remove Paige's silver*, in his head.

As Paige looked up from the dead girl to the large werewolf, it took a menacing step toward Ty and Trowa, who stood frozen in place with fear.

It's playin' with 'em, she thought.

A voice inside her head, one she'd never heard and didn't belong to her, whispered, *Remove the silver, and set me free.*

Who are you? Paige asked the inner voice.

I am you, and I am more. Trust me, or that beast will kill your friends, the inner voice replied.

Paige didn't know why, but she trusted the strange voice.

After hearing Lola's voice, Garrett looked at Paige and found her looking at him.

Garrett started to tell her he was going to remove her silver, but Paige beat him to it.

"Ya have to take my silver, Daddy."

Garrett nodded. "I was just gonna suggest that. You can control it, Paige."

Paige smiled a confident smile. "I know, Daddy. Hurry. It's gonna kill Ty and Trowa,"

Garrett chanced a quick glance toward his old and new friends. The massive werewolf was only a few feet away from them. He reached out quickly, grabbed the necklace, and yanked it. The necklace snapped, and he pulled it free. Not knowing what would happen, he crab crawled backward several feet. It happened quickly.

As he watched, Paige grew and sprouted hair, but not the coarse, black hair the other werewolves had. The hair sprouting from Paige's skin looked like spun silver and flowed in soft waves down her arms.

Garrett remembered Paige still had handcuffs on, and he briefly worried they might injure her. As Paige continued to grow, he heard the handcuffs 'snap' and Paige's longer and hairier arms came free. As she continued to grow, her clothes got tighter. They shredded and fell to the ground. There wasn't enough of Paige's body left at that point to make Garrett uncomfortable looking at her, but he couldn't have looked away if he tried. What Paige was becoming wasn't monstrous. Her werewolf was beautiful.

The transformation completed in a matter of seconds. Paige's silver wolf wasn't as large as the massive werewolf. It was taller and wider than the former alpha's wolf, though. Its claws were long and jet black, which contrasted with its silver coat spectacularly. Paige's wolf was lean and muscular.

Garrett looked up at the silver werewolf. "Paige?"

When it turned its head and looked down at him, Garrett saw one final, and very distinct, difference between Paige's wolf and the others. Her eyes were intense and lit from within, but they weren't red. They were green, and minus the inner fire, not unlike her human eyes. The silver werewolf smiled down at Garrett and he wasn't afraid.

~ * ~

From Paige's perspective, the transformation felt more like a change of clothes than a restructuring of her bones, muscles, and internal organs. The moment her daddy removed the silver, Paige felt a surge of energy course through her body. Then she was growing up and out. The only sign Paige had that her body changed happened when she witnessed her nose elongate from her face. The transformation caused Paige no pain.

Within a matter of seconds, all of Paige's senses intensified to a degree the earlier flashes only hinted at. The world was alive in a way she never dreamed possible. More than anything else, Paige felt in control.

You are in control, but I am your guide, the inner voice whispered.

While Paige marveled at her new surroundings, she heard her daddy say, "Paige?"

She looked down at him. He looked so small. She tried to speak, but her tongue wouldn't work to produce sound.

It will come, the inner voice told her.

Paige smiled down at her dad to the best of her ability and could tell by his steady heartbeat he wasn't afraid of her. That made her feel relieved.

The inner voice said, *Your friends need our help*.

Paige looked from her dad to the massive werewolf reaching out for Ty's throat, and a low menacing growl rumbled from her elongated snout. When the larger werewolf turned and saw her, Paige saw surprise in its face and heard the beat of its enlarged heart quicken.

Is it afraid of me? Paige asked the inner voice.

Not afraid, confused. It is an old wolf, but it has never seen the likes of you, the inner voice responded.

What am I? Paige asked.

Evolved, the inner voice told her.

The larger werewolf let out a warning growl and took a threatening step toward Paige. Paige took a step toward it. It growled again but louder, warning Paige to back down. Paige growled back. The larger werewolf's eyes flared bright red. It dropped to all fours and charged her.

The inner voice, Paige's guide, said, *May I*?

Yes, Paige answered.

Then Paige became a passenger and experienced what happened like a spectator wearing virtual reality goggles.

Paige's silver wolf darted right to keep the larger werewolf away from her dad. It changed direction and kept charging. Right before it collided with her, Paige's silver wolf sprang into the air, rotated to her right, and sank her long claws into the larger werewolf's back. Its momentum carried it forward, and Paige's werewolf's claws ripped deep gashes down the length of its broad back.

As the larger werewolf skidded to an awkward stop and fell onto its side, Paige's werewolf landed lightly on her feet and squared off for another charge. After getting back on all fours, the larger werewolf obliged and charged back toward her. This time, at the last second, the larger werewolf, anticipating another leap from Paige's silver wolf, launched into the air. Paige's wolf dropped into the high grass, reached up with both hands, and ripped deep gashes down the length of its chest and abdomen.

The larger werewolf let out a yelp and crashed into the tall grass in an uncontrolled tumble. Before it could regain its feet, Paige's wolf sprang out of the tall grass and landed on top of the face up, prone larger werewolf. It snapped its viscous teeth in Paige's wolf's face, but she easily batted the bite away with a swipe of her right hand. Her claws cut the end of its snout off when she did. The larger werewolf yelped, but blood flowing back into its throat garbled it.

It tried to claw at her, but Paige's wolf caught its arm and effortlessly snapped the bones of its forearm. It yelped again. When it did, Paige's wolf grabbed what remained of its upper snout in her left hand and its lower jaw in her right hand. She flexed and started pulling its jaws apart. The larger werewolf struggled, but its fight was gone. Paige heard the larger werewolf's heartbeat increase and she could smell its fear. Satisfied, Paige's wolf ripped the larger werewolf's upper jaw and head from its lower jaw. A spray of blood erupted as they separated. She looked into its eyes and watched as the glowing embers extinguished. She tossed its upper human head into the high grass.

~ * ~

Ty and Trowa watched the one-sided battle in awe of the strength, cunning, and agility of the silver werewolf that was Paige. As soon as the silver werewolf tore the massive werewolf's head apart, the silver on their skin ceased to burn.

"It worked." Ty shouted.

Trowa nudged Ty. "Not for all of us."

Ty followed Trowa's gaze into the clearing and saw the silver werewolf getting to its feet. Motion to his left caught Ty's attention. He looked in that direction and saw Garrett walking toward the silver werewolf with his pistol in hand.

~ * ~

As Garrett approached the silver werewolf that was Paige, it showed no sign of aggression toward him. It just stood there, watching him approach. Garrett had his gun in his hand, but his finger wasn't on the trigger or trigger guard. It held it by the grip.

He'd found his pistol after the larger werewolf's first charge, but he didn't dare shoot for fear of hitting Paige. After the silver werewolf dispatched the larger one, Garrett waited and hoped, with the curse broken, it would transform back into Paige. When it didn't, Garrett decided to offer himself to the silver werewolf. If it attacked him, he would shoot it then kill himself. With Paige gone, he would have nothing to live for. Killing himself had been a simple decision to make.

When Garrett was close enough that the silver werewolf could grab him, if it wanted to, he stopped and looked up at it. It looked down at him.

"Are ya in there, Paige?"

The silver werewolf nodded.

Ask her to come back to you, Lola's voice echoed in his head.

Garrett looked up into the radiant green eyes. "Come back to me, Paige-Turner."

~ * ~

Immediately after killing the large werewolf that became their new pack alpha, Paige realized her curse hadn't broken. She could tell Ty and

Trowa were released. They were not beholden to her, but she was still a werewolf. She also realized she felt no rage or desire to attack, kill, any of them.

As if answering an unasked question, the inner voice said, *Your wolf is tamed.*

What does that mean? Paige asked her guide.

It means you are not a threat to anyone, her guide responded.

I'm still a werewolf, Paige stated, more than asked.

You always were and always will be. You are in control, not your wolf, her guide responded.

Paige's silver werewolf looked down at her dad. When he asked if she was inside the wolf, she nodded. Then he asked her to come back to him.

How do I do that? Paige asked her guide.

Will it, her guide replied.

She did.

Instantly, Paige's perception shifted. Her senses dulled and the view of her dad went from one where she looked down at him to one where she looked up at him in a matter of seconds. No pain came with the transformation. Again, it felt more like changing clothes than changing bodies.

~ * ~

Garrett watched in amazement as the large silver werewolf transformed back into his daughter. The process looked more like the werewolf melted into Paige than the jerky, painful process he'd seen in movies like *The Howling* and *An American Werewolf in London*.

The transformation happened quickly and was amazing to watch. Unlike when Paige transformed into the silver werewolf and grew out of her clothes, the transformation back resulted in an awkward moment. Paige was naked. She tried to cover the essentials with her left forearm and right hand. She, somewhat, succeeded, but still revealed more daughter skin than Garrett cared to see. He quickly removed his shirt, handed it to Paige, and turned around. Garrett remembered Ty and Trowa were there. He turned to tell them to turn around too, but the gentlemen already had their backs to Paige.

A couple of seconds later, Paige said, "You can turn around,

Daddy."

Garrett turned around quickly, grabbed Paige, and hugged her tight. He wasn't entirely sure he'd ever let her go again.

After a good thirty to forty seconds, Paige said, "Okay, Daddy. I survived a werewolf, but ya might squeeze me to death."

Garrett released her and stepped back to look at her. He couldn't believe she was back and okay. A moment later, Ty and Trowa joined them in the middle of the clearing.

"You're one bad-ass, silver werewolf, little miss," Trowa exclaimed.

"Silver?"

Garrett nodded. "And your eyes were green, not red."

"How'd ya do it, Paige? How'd ya keep from killin' or keepin' us?" Ty asked.

Paige shrugged. "I had a guide."

The three men, clearly confused, just looked at her.

"I can't explain it. I…tamed my wolf."

Garrett put his arm around Paige's shoulders and smiled. "I think I know someone who can. For now, let's go home."

Agreement met this suggestion, and they walked out of the clearing.

Paige stopped suddenly. "My crucifix and necklace. I need to find it."

Garrett patted his front pocket. "I have it, sweetheart. I broke the necklace when I took it off you, though."

Paige held out her hand. "May I have it back?"

Garrett studied Paige for a second. "Ya sure this is a good idea?"

Paige nodded. "I have to know."

Garrett pulled the crucifix and necklace from his pocket and dangled it over his daughter's outstretched hand.

"Ya sure?"

Paige nodded.

Paige could tell the three men were worried. She wasn't. She'd tamed her wolf. Her dad lowered the crucifix onto her palm slowly. It was cool on her skin. Paige smiled so big she felt her ears move and closed her fingers around the crucifix.

"It's okay?" Garrett asked.

Paige, still smiling, said, "It's more than okay. It's perfect."

Garrett dropped the necklace onto Paige's palm. "Let's go home."

Chapter Eighteen

After leaving the Stuckey property where *El Lobo* and Alexis' bodies would remain undiscovered for several months, Garrett and Ty agreed not having to explain what happened there the most prudent course of action. Garrett drove everyone back to his house. When they arrived at Garrett's house, Ty and Trowa departed. Not before Garrett invited them to a Sunday celebration at his house. Garrett waited while Paige changed out of his shirt and into her clothes. While Garrett waited, he sent Mandy a text telling her everything was okay, and they were coming to pick her up.

The drive from Garrett's to James' house took about forty-five minutes and was spent mostly in silence. Unanswered questions still loomed, and the ultimate outcome of the night's events were still uncertain.

Finally, Paige said, "I have to know if I'll always have control."

Garrett, who thought the same thing, said, "I know."

"So…what'll we do?"

After considering the important question for several moments, Garrett said, "We'll find out. Just you and me. We'll go to her…den on Saturday afternoon. It's secluded. That's why she was usin' it. You can…change and we'll see what happens."

"If I attack you?"

"You won't."

"If I do, though?" Paige pressed.

Garrett reached over and took Paige's hand in his. "You won't."

Paige squeezed his hand and left the question unanswered.

When they arrived at James' house, Mandy went to Paige first and wrapped her in a smothering hug. James had many questions. Garrett answered most of them.

He said, "We're still figurin' a few things out, James. We'll know more after Saturday. Come out to the house on Sunday afternoon. Ty and Trowa will be there. We'll fill ya in on the rest then."

It disappointed James that he'd have to wait for the rest of the story, but he understood.

Before Garrett left, he said, "Invite Lola, James. She's a part of this, and I'd like Paige to meet her."

"Will do."

They shook hands, and Garrett left with his girls.

~ * ~

On the ride home from James' house, Garrett received a call about Deputy Mike Middleton's murder. The news hit Garrett especially hard. Aside from Ty, Mike was the only deputy who Garrett associated with outside of work after becoming Sheriff. Double dates with Mike and Becks as well as triple dates when Ty and Jasmine joined them, happed often.

Garrett promised Becks he and Mandy would go on a double date with them after they took care of the werewolf problem. He made this promise when Garrett called to ask Mike to make silver loaded shotgun shells and left the cryptic message Becks saw through immediately. That the date would never happen drove home the finality of Mike's death. That, and Mike's face being bitten off.

Mike's funeral was held on Thursday, June 4th. Like Deputy Foster Timpson's funeral several weeks earlier, law enforcement personnel from the East Texas area packed the service.

Becks remained strong throughout. As did Beck's and Mike's son, Mike Middleton, Junior, who dressed in his Marine Dress Blues. Her and Mike's daughter, Michelle Middleton, were inconsolable. When Garrett presented Becks with the flag from Mike's casket, Michelle fainted and slumped from her white folding chair. If not for Mike Junior's quick reflexes, she would have ended up on the ground.

After the services, Becks approached Garrett and asked to speak with him in private. When they separated from the other mourners, Garrett offered his condolences for, perhaps, the hundredth time.

Becks smiled a sad, but warm smile. "Did ya get 'em? Are those fuckers dead?"

Garrett nodded. "They are. Their bodies are bein' picked clean by buzzards and other critters."

"Good. Was that *missin'* girl one of 'em?"

The 'missing girl' Becks referred to was none other than Alexis Jordan. Her blonde haired, big, blue eyed, picture appeared on the local news on Monday of that week. Her dad, Alex Jordan, reported her missing when she failed to appear in Houston on Monday for a scuba diving trip to Barbados. Apparently, Alexis needed a little R&R after M&M. Murder and mayhem.

The Nacogdoches Police Department, with the help of the Nacogdoches County Sheriffs Department and the Department of Public Safety, headed the search. Garrett wasn't sharing what he knew, nor had he volunteered many labor hours from his department to help search. It didn't surprise him that search volunteers were scarce. Apparently, Alexis Jordan didn't have many, or any, close friends. The ones she had were in her pack and already dead.

Garrett nodded again. "She was."

"What about the other one?"

The only clue Garrett had to the identity of the 'other one' was the Monterrey Produce truck, parked next to Mike's faceless body. They found the truck's actual driver remains, what it left of him after being partially eaten, in the cargo box. The culprit disappeared.

"Near as I can tell, he turned the Alexis girl and came to East Texas to find her."

Becks sighed. "Well, I'm glad ya had the silver bullets to kill the fuckers."

Garrett didn't have the heart to tell her that, aside from Dillon's sacrificial shooting, Mike's silver loads weren't used to kill the other werewolves.

"We couldn't have done it without him, Becks."

Considering Mike's *nahual* story led to the use of trees to escape the reach of the cursed beasts, it wasn't a dishonest response.

Garrett and Becks hugged and promised to stay close in Mike's absence. A promise Garrett intended to keep.

~ * ~

The drive from Garrett's house to the Wiseman barn that sunny Saturday afternoon remained mostly in silence, too. The significance of the trip's outcome hung heavy, like a tangible weight, on both of them. If the taming of Paige's wolf went beyond the immediate need posed to it the night of the June full moon, all would be fine. If not, Garrett would have to put the werewolf, his daughter, down.

As they drove, Garrett noticed Paige periodically ran her finger over the silver crucifix hung around her neck. He'd gotten the chain fixed on Friday. That the silver no longer caused her discomfort comforted Garrett.

When they pulled off County Road Five Ninety-Eight onto the overgrown drive, Paige said, "I sense her…and the others."

Garrett patted Paige's leg. "We're almost there."

Several moments later, they drove into the clearing. Garrett pulled up next to the barn and stopped.

They sat there for several more moments in silence.

Paige smiled. "I guess we'll know in a few minutes, huh?"

"You're gonna be fine, sweetheart."

"You can't know that, Daddy."

"I do."

"How can ya know that?"

Garrett squeezed her leg. "I know because I saw your wolf. It wasn't a nightmare creature like the others. It was…beautiful, and it had kind eyes. Your eyes. Your wolf isn't a monster, Paige."

Considering Garrett always referred to the nightmare, or *experience*, Paige as Monster-Paige, the fact he'd just told Paige her wolf wasn't a monster struck him as funny and he chuckled despite the seriousness of their mission.

"What's funny?"

"Nothin', sweetheart. You'll be fine."

Paige took a deep breath. "I hope you're right. If I'm not…fine, have your gun ready, Garrett nodded. They got out of the truck.

Before Paige went into the barn, Garrett wrapped her in a tight hug, picked her up, and whispered, "I love you," in her ear.

"I love you too, Daddy," Paige whispered back.

He put her down. "You're in control. Remember that."

Paige nodded, removed her silver necklace and crucifix. She handed them to her dad and stepped inside the dilapidated barn.

Paige's senses, acute even in human form, overwhelmed her. Where her father smelled damp dirt, wood decay, and canine musk, Paige smelled so much more. She knew so much more, because she could smell the past. Paige smelled the human blood spilled when her former alpha created its pack. She smelled the sex between the werewolves and the human coupling her dad deduced from the prints on the dirt floor. Paige smelled the conflict between the alpha and one of its betas from the night the alpha bit her.

Paige shook her head to clear her thoughts. She needed a rational mind for what was coming. She walked over to a rusted hulk of farm equipment she didn't recognize and undressed. Concluding the rusty surface was a better option than the damp dirt floor, Paige folded each article of clothing and placed them neatly on the rusted hulk.

When she undressed, she moved to the center of the barn. She didn't know what to do, how to trigger the transformation.

The little voice in her head, her guide, said, *Will me and I will come.*

She did.

The transformation was immediate, swift, and painless. Paige felt as if she was being lifted into the air as her wolf grew to its full nine feet in height. Again, the only sign, from Paige's point of view, her body transformed into something not human, was the view of her long silver-haired snout protruding from her face.

Paige stood there for several seconds, getting the feel of her new body. She felt powerful. She felt invisible, and she felt calm. She felt completely in control. Paige's wolf inhaled deeply, sucking massive amounts of air into her large lungs. The barn smells didn't overwhelm or offend her senses any longer. Her wolf had adapted to the acute senses. She could smell her dad outside the barn. He wasn't afraid.

Her hearing was every bit as acute as her sense of smell. She could hear critters large and small scurrying through the surrounding woods, vehicles driving on distant roads, faraway dogs barking, and the wind blowing through the trees. As if to confirm what she smelled on her dad, she heard his calm heartbeat thumping in his chest. He really wasn't afraid.

Paige walked to the door.

~ * ~

Outside, standing at the back of his truck, Garrett waited for Paige's werewolf to emerge from the barn. Not only did he have his pistol in the holster, Garrett hadn't even unsnapped the safety strap that kept the gun from bouncing out of the holster while chasing suspects. He remained confident Paige's werewolf wasn't a threat. Given the secured pistol, he was, literally, betting his life on it.

The first thing he saw were four long, black claws on the doorframe of the partially hung door. Then a massive, silver-haired werewolf's head emerged. It looked directly at Garrett with its penetrating green eyes. Garrett saw no threat in its eyes.

The silver-haired werewolf had to stoop to clear the top of the seven-foot-high doorframe and, when it cleared the doorframe, it unfolded to its full height. Garrett had to look up at the enormous creature. Paige's silver werewolf stood taller than the alpha and its pack of werewolves by at least a foot and slightly shorter than the alpha's maker. He put her overall height at about nine feet.

The silver-haired werewolf stood just outside the barn door, looking down at Garrett. It made no move toward him. Garrett took a step toward it. "You okay, Paige?"

The werewolf nodded.

Garrett nodded. "I told ya it'd be okay. Can I…touch you?"

The werewolf nodded again and held out its long arm.

Its long arm halved the distance between them. Garrett took a couple of steps to close the gap and put his hand on the werewolf's furry forearm. Its hair was long and soft, like a golden retriever's coat. Garrett stroked it then felt silly for petting his daughter.

He looked up at the werewolf. "Ya wanna take this…new body for a spin? Run around the forest for a bit?"

Garrett saw the sparkle in its penetrating green eyes right before its massive head nodded emphatically.

"Go ahead, then. Just stay away from roads and people."

The silver-haired werewolf dropped to all fours and sprinted into the woods to the east of the barn.

~ * ~

For Paige, the experience of running her wolf felt nothing short of amazing. She felt like a passenger on a virtual reality ride at Universal Studios. The trees flashed by in a blur as her wolf dodged them at full speed. Suddenly, a ravine appeared in front of her. Her first impulse was to stop, but her guide pushed on. Her wolf cleared the forty-foot gap with ease, landing dexterously on the other side without slowing.

Her senses were always ahead of her swift moving body, and they navigated her away from roads and people in the area. When she finally stopped running, she knew intuitively she traveled at least ten miles from her dad.

As she stood there under the canopy of trees, she heard the scratching of small claws on tree bark. To her wolf's ears, everything sounded close, but this was exceptionally close. She turned toward the direction of the sound and saw something that, given the experiences she'd had with the other werewolves, she didn't expect to see. A squirrel. It had its head oriented down on a tree right behind her. Close enough for her to grab and devour, if she'd wanted to. She didn't.

The squirrel cocked its curious head toward her. Its big brown eyes locked with hers. After several seconds, the squirrel blinked and continued down the tree. Paige could hear its little heart beating, but not frantically. The squirrel wasn't afraid of her. Although Paige was still learning the intricacies of her canine facial muscles, she made her wolf smile. She dropped to all fours and headed back to her dad.

~ * ~

Garrett was sitting on the truck's tailgate when, about fifteen minutes after Paige left, the silver-haired werewolf galloped out of the forest. It skidded to a playful stop, throwing up dirt and weeds as it did. It stood up and its mouth moved as if trying to say something. Only grunts and growls came out. Its arms and hands were moving, too. This didn't surprise Garrett because Paige, when frustrated, talked with her hands and her mouth. The silver-haired werewolf was getting frustrated.

Garrett chuckled. "Change back and tell me."

Paige must have thought it important, because the werewolf transformed into her human body right there.

It happed quickly, but Garrett turned away and said, "In the barn, Paige. You're not dressed."

Paige laughed. "Sorry, Daddy. I forgot."

Paige went into the barn.

A second or two later, from within the barn, Paige said, "Sorry 'bout that, Daddy. Clothes aren't important to werewolves, and I was lost in mine."

"No harm, no foul. I turned away before any of your...girly parts popped out."

Paige laughed. "Girly parts? Really, Daddy?"

"Well, you're my daughter, so you'll never have lady parts. What'd ya wanna tell me that was so damn important ya got naked in front of me…again?"

Paige stepped out of the barn, dressed. She ran up to her daddy and gave him a big hug.

While still hugging him, she said, "The animals aren't afraid of my wolf, Daddy. A squirrel climbed down a tree right next to me. I could smell and hear that it wasn't afraid, Daddy."

Earlier, Garrett noticed the woods surrounding the Wiseman barn hadn't gone silent when Paige transformed. He'd taken that as a good sign Paige's silver werewolf wasn't a harbinger of evil, like the others were. Paige's experience with the squirrel provided more proof.

He hugged her back. "I told ya everything would be okay."

On the ride back to Garrett's house, Paige told him all about her run through the woods. Garrett found himself a little envious of his daughter's new abilities. The happiness and relief he felt with the realization she'd tamed her wolf swallowed the little green monster.

~ * ~

By two o'clock that Sunday afternoon, everyone arrived at Garrett's house except James and Lola. Ty worked the grill, giving Garrett a break from cooking, and flipped hamburger patties. Mandy and Paige set out the 'fixins' that included condiments, ketchup, mustard, mayonnaise, and barbecue sauce. Lettuce, tomato, onion, sliced cheese, sliced, dill pickle, and sliced jalapeño were set out, too. Garrett and Trowa were out front where Trowa showed him the new leather saddlebags on his Indian motorcycle. While they were looking over Trowa's bike, James pulled into the driveway with Lola in the passenger seat and Winston's enormous head bobbing between them.

As the truck stopped, Garrett walked up and opened the passenger door for Lola. She slid out of the truck and embraced Garrett in a tight hug.

She stepped back. "You did good, Garrett."

Garrett looked at the stunningly beautiful woman with the magical eye. She dressed exactly as she had when last, he saw her. She wore the white dress that flowed to the ground and gave her movements the illusion of gliding instead of walking. As before, the chocolate brown tips of her ample breasts were clearly visible through the sheer white fabric of her dress.

Garrett smiled. "With your help."

For a moment, while Garrett looked at Lola, everything around him faded from existence. She had that effect on him. Trowa cleared his throat and brought Garrett out of the Lola-induced trance.

Garrett stepped back. "Lola, this is Trowa Raintree. Trowa, meet Lola Laveau."

Lola eyed Trowa briefly. "Caddo Tribe, yes?"

Trowa, who appeared sucked into a Lola-induced trance too, or maybe just fixated on her breasts, Garrett couldn't tell which, nodded. "Yes, ma'am."

Lola laughed. It sounded like velvet come to life. "No ma'ams here, Trowa."

She stuck out her arm. "Garrett's taken and James has other tastes. Will you walk me to the others?"

Trowa hooked her arm. "Yes ma'…I mean Lola."

James came around the front of his truck holding a gallon jug of muscadine wine, with Winston panting and slobbering on his heels.

He stuck out his hand. "So, do I get to hear all the details of what happened Tuesday night now?"

Garrett shook James' limp hand. "After we eat."

James cussed under his breath, and they fell in behind Trowa and Lola.

When Trowa and Lola disappeared into the house, James said, "Lola's strikin', isn't she?"

Garrett nodded.

"How old do ya think she is?"

Garrett considered James' question briefly. That he'd asked led Garrett to believe she might be younger or older than her looks implied.

"She looks to be in her mid-thirties."

James chuckled. "That she does. You'd be closer to her actual age if you doubled that number."

Garrett's jaw dropped.

James laughed.

Trowa was introducing Lola to the others when Garrett and James stepped onto the back deck.

When Trowa got to Paige, Lola held up her hand, cutting off his introduction. “Come here, chil.’”

Paige didn’t hesitate. She walked up to Lola. When Lola opened her arms, Paige fell into them and embraced her.

The embrace went on for several seconds. Everyone had been quiet, as if they expected something magical to happen.

When the embrace ended, Lola didn’t let go of Paige. She moved her hands to Paige’s shoulders, held her at arm’s length, and looked at her with her cat eye.

A big smile spread across Lola’s face, revealing her impossibly white teeth, and she said, “You have the most beautiful aura, Paige-Turner.”

This surprised Garrett because he didn’t remember telling Lola his nickname for Paige. He knew he hadn't.

Paige blushed. “Thank you, Miss Laveau.”

“You call me Lola, chil.’”

Paige cut her eyes toward Garrett. He didn’t allow her to address most adults by their first name. Ty, Mandy, and Trowa were excluded. He preferred Paige to use Miss, Missus, or Mister before their first name.

Garrett, who knew just how old Lola was, smiled. “How ‘bout Miss Lola.”

Lola, never taking her eye off Paige, said, “Miss Lola is fine, if that’s what your daddy’s comfortable with.”

Still blushing, Paige said, “Thank you, Miss Lola.”

Lola said, “Your aura is radiant silver, chil.’ I’ve never seen one quite like it, at least not one this…strong. Do you know what silver signifies?”

Paige shook her head.

“Purity. Your essence is pure.”

Lola slipped one of her long, pink fingernails under the crucifix lying against Paige’s chest and pulled it out about an inch.

“That’s why this doesn’t burn you anymore. Your silver essence is as pure as the silver in this crucifix. That’s beyond rare, chil.’”

“What would the aura of a regular werewolf look like?” Paige asked.

Still looking at her with her cat eye, Lola said, “Fire and brimstone. Coal black and tinged with fiery red. Black signifies evil and red signifies rage. Nasty combination. Nasty creatures, but not you. You are the opposite of all that…nastiness.”

Lola let the crucifix fall back against Paige's chest. She hugged her tight again.

When the second hug ended, Lola released Paige, look around at everyone else like she was seeing them for the first time, and smiled. "I'm hungry. Those burgers smell delicious, but I'm a vegetarian?"

Embarrassed, Mandy said, "Oh, Lola. I'm so sorry. Garrett didn't tell me. If he had, I would've gotten you a veggie burger."

"I didn't know. I'm sure we can fix ya up with a salad," Garrett said.

Lola smiled. "I can make do with these fixins."

"I'm so sorry," Mandy said again.

"No apology needed," Lola said as she started piling lettuce, tomatoes, onions, cheese, pickles, and jalapeños on a plate.

"The burgers are ready. The rest of y'all line up and I'll hook ya up," Ty announced.

James waited patiently until everyone finished eating and everyone, including Paige, had a glass of muscadine wine.

He said, "I have waited long enough. Tell me what happened Tuesday night."

Garrett told most of the story and Paige, Ty, and Trowa broke in with personal details when needed. James listened intently to every detail without interrupting.

With the tale told, Garrett said, "That's it. That's what happened."

"Tell 'em 'bout yesterday, Daddy," Paige said.

Excited, James said, "What? What happened yesterday?"

Garrett took a sip of muscadine wine. "Paige and I were concerned her ability to control her werewolf Tuesday night was a product of the situation. So, we went out yesterday and let her run her wolf."

James' mouth fell open.

He looked at Paige. "How was it? What was it like?"

Paige grinned. "It was amazin'. I ran her for a good twenty miles."

"In about fifteen minutes," Garrett added.

"She's so fast and strong. I jumped a forty-foot ravine like it was nothin'. Best of all, the other animals aren't afraid of my wolf. A squirrel climbed down a tree right next to my wolf and just looked at me like I belonged there."

"You belong there, chil.' Animals can sense evil. They have a kind of *sight* like mine. You're not a threat and they know that," Lola explained.

James moved to the edge of his seat and looked at Paige. Garrett saw James' hands were trembling. He knew what James would ask before he opened his mouth.

"Can I see it, Paige? Can I see your wolf?" James asked nervously.

Paige looked at Garrett, as if needing his permission or approval.

Garrett shrugged. "It's up to you, kiddo. I wouldn't suggest doin' it at school or in public, unless you're on a date and the guy gets handsy, but you're safe here, surrounded by people you can trust. People who love ya."

When Paige looked back at James, he said, "Please, Paige. I've studied werewolf lore my entire adult life. I can die a happy man, if ya let me see your wolf."

Paige smiled at James. "Well…since ya put it that way, Doctor James. Okay."

James was beside himself with giddiness. He clasped his hands to his face. "Oh my. Now I'll probably die tomorrow. It'll be worth it."

Everyone laughed.

Paige got up, unclasped her necklace. She handed it to her daddy and started walking off the deck toward Garrett's shed.

"Where're ya goin'?" James shouted.

Paige, who was wearing white shorts and a white with green stripes T-shirt, looked over her shoulder. "I like these clothes and I'm not gettin' naked in front of those guys again."

Ty and Trowa, who were watching Paige walk away, suddenly started looking at their feet.

"The human body is beautiful, Paige. It's nothin' to be ashamed of," Lola said in her warm, honey voice that seemed, somehow, amplified and filled the area.

Garrett chuckled. "It is while she's sixteen."

Garrett watched as Paige headed around the side of the shed. "The critter-cams are still out there, Paige," Garrett reminded her.

He hadn't checked them since Tuesday morning. They were still up and recording.

"The shed's unlocked, though."

Paige opened the shed door, went inside, and pulled the door partially closed behind her.

"How long does it take?" James asked.

"It's quick. As soon as she gets her clothes off, she'll change,"

Garrett answered.

Just then, as if answering James' question, there came a groan from the shed. Not human or wolf, wood. Followed by a loud 'snap' sound. Garrett immediately knew the weight of Paige's wolf snapped some floorboards in the shed.

Everyone's eyes were glued to the shed when long, black claws wrapped around the partially closed shed door and pushed it open. When the silver-haired werewolf emerged stooped, Mandy and James gasped. It was their first time seeing a werewolf. Lola did not.

Whether Lola didn't gasp because she'd seen a werewolf before, or because she had been more accustomed to the supernatural, Garrett didn't know. All he knew was the sight of Paige's wolf didn't surprise Lola.

They gasped again when it stood up to its full nine feet. James got to his feet and walked toward Paige's wolf as fast as his short legs would carry him.

He stopped directly in front of her and almost toppled over backward as he looked up.

"Magnificent," James whispered.

Lola joined James and looked at the silver-haired werewolf with her cat eye.

She smiled. "You are the most beautiful creature I have ever seen. And I've seen my share of amazin' creatures, Paige."

Although Mandy needed a little coaxing, she, Garrett, Ty, and Trowa joined Lola and James a few seconds later. Winston came, too.

"Come on down, so we can see ya better," Garrett said.

Paige dropped to all fours. She was still taller than James and Mandy.

James lifted a trembling hand. "May I?"

Paige's wolf nodded.

James reached up and stroked her muzzle.

"Magnificent. Simply magnificent."

To Lola, Garrett said, "Why's her coat silver and her eyes green? The others were black with red eyes."

Without asking, Lola scratched the werewolf behind its right ear. "It's her aura…her essence. The others were vile, evil beasts…black and red auras. Paige had the ancestral connection and could tame her wolf. So, even now, Paige is the dominant force within her wolf. Her wolf's aura is sliver, too."

The silver-haired werewolf nodded emphatically. James burst into giddy laughter.

"Is this why Paige's curse wasn't lifted when the alpha and its maker died? Because of the ancestral werewolf?" Garrett asked.

Lola continued scratching behind the werewolf's ear. "Paige isn't cursed, so there was no curse to lift. The alpha's bite awakened the ancestral werewolf that was inside her. Paige tamed it. She has complete control over it. She could go the rest of her life without transformin'. Even on the full moon when all other cursed werewolves *must* transform, Paige will not have to, but I think Paige will take her wolf out to play occasionally."

The silver-haired werewolf nodded again. James laughed again.

The most comical moment came when Winston started humping the silver-haired werewolf's left arm. It looked down at the busy bulldog and let out a low growl. Winston yelped and ran back to the deck as quickly as his pudgy legs would carry him. He hid under the table and looked back at the werewolf as if longing the unrequited love.

After a couple of more minutes of looking at, and touching Paige's wolf, Mandy even stroked her muzzle, Garrett said, "If ya wanna run a bit, go ahead. Just be careful."

Paige enjoyed the fawning attention and compliments, but she also felt a little like the major attraction in a petting zoo. Her dad's suggestion called on her wolf's instinct to run. She spun around and ran into the woods.

When she left, Trowa said, "She's right. The animals didn't scurry away the way they did when the others were around."

"They have nothin' to fear from Paige's wolf," Lola said again.

"Simply magnificent," James said again.

The group of friends went back to deck to drink more muscadine wine and talk.

After a few sips, Garrett said to Lola, "In my *experience*, Paige's werewolf was black and had red eyes. Why didn't I *experience* her as she is now…silver with green eyes?"

"You *saw* only the ancestral werewolf in your *experience*. You didn't *see* Paige's influence on it. Paige is what keeps the blackness in check."

Not wanting to ask, but needing to know, Garrett said, "Could the blackness ever overtake her?"

"Yes, but not likely. Paige has a pure silver aura. The purest I've ever *seen*. She would have to do somethin' totally out of character for the blackness to overtake her. She'll be fine, Garrett."

After that, the conversation turned to other subjects.

Now and then, James would interject with, "Simply magnificent."

About an hour after Paige ran off, she came back in spectacular fashion. Garrett, who faced the back, right side of his house, saw her first. The silver-haired werewolf broke from the underbrush of the surrounding trees at full speed and rushing at the deck. For a split second, Garrett thought something was wrong, that she was being chased. Then she dug into the grass with her hands, sprang into the air, and sailed over them about twenty feet in the air. She landed lightly by the shed and spun around to face them.

James started clapping and yelled, "Magnificent. Magnificent."

Garrett wondered if the experience left James with only one word in his vocabulary.

As if to avail Garrett's concern, James said, "All those years readin' books, and this has been more educational by far."

"Speakin' of books. I have the one ya loaned me in my saddlebags, James," Trowa said.

James waved a dismissive hand. "Keep it. I can come straight to the source now."

When the silver-haired werewolf entered the shed, Garrett heard more floorboards snap and decided, if the shed was to be Paige's den, he'd pour a concrete floor as soon as possible.

A minute later, Paige walked out of the shed. James clapped again.

"Did ya have fun?" Garrett asked when Paige took a seat at the table.

Paige grinned. "Oh yeah. I love runnin' her. If I could get me some stretchy pants, somethin' like the Hulk wears that don't rip off when he transforms, I could save a lot on gas in my car. I'd just run my wolf everywhere."

Ty chuckled. "Yeah, but you'd need a hole in the back of your britches for your tail. When you transformed back, people could see your backside."

Paige thought for a second. "Maybe I could tuck my tail down into a pant leg?"

Ty shook his head. “Not with those claws. You’d shred your britches and be stuck naked again.”

Paige gave up on the idea.

After another hour passed, James poured the last of the muscadine wine into their glasses.

Garrett stood up. “I wanna make a toast.”

When the others were standing, Garrett said, “To good friends and puttin’ the trouble behind us.”

Five of the seven glasses came together with clinks. James and Lola held their glasses back and shared a brief glance at Garrett that the others picked up on.

“What’s the matter? Why aren’t y’all toastin’?” Garrett asked.

James and Lola shared another brief glance.

“What aren’t y’all tellin’ us? The big werewolf took out the alpha and Paige took out the big werewolf. The curse-line is severed. Ty and Trowa are free from the curse. The trouble’s behind us…right?”

James shifted uncomfortably on his feet. “Yes, this trouble is. But…”

“But what?” Garrett asked.

“Trouble begets trouble, Garrett,” Lola responded.

Garrett looked at Lola. “I don’t even know what that means.”

“It means that trouble follows trouble. Folklore is full of these tales. A town falls victim to werewolves. After the werewolves are vanquished, more trouble follows. I mentioned this to ya before, Garrett,” James said.

“What kind of trouble follows?” Garrett asked.

“Unnatural…supernatural trouble. Vampires, ghouls, witches…present company excluded, of course,” James said.

Garrett laughed. “Y’all are kiddin’, right? Vampires? Ghouls? Seriously?”

“After what happened here with the werewolves, with Paige, don’t tell me ya don’t believe these other horrors exist, Garrett,” James implored.

Garrett shook his head. “Okay, I’ll accept they exist. I’d be stupid to deny the possibility. What does what happened here…with the werewolves, have to do with future trouble?”

Lola took over. “Evil, supernatural evil is a beacon for their kind. The werewolves left a… *stain* on Pine View County. These other creatures may be drawn to it.

"James has read about it. I've *seen* it. There are parts of Louisiana so black that few go there. Those who do never come back…not as themselves. These…black areas are created with dark powers. Trouble follows," Lola explained.

"All we're sayin', Garrett, is that we need to be vigilant. We...you need to be open to…other explanations, if somethin' happens," James added.

Garrett looked from Lola to James to Lola again. The others were looking at Lola and James too, in abject silence.

Garrett managed a smile. "For now, the trouble's behind us, right?"

Lola and James nodded.

Garrett raised his glass. "To good friends and puttin' the current trouble behind us."

All seven glasses came together and clinked loudly.

They were trouble free.

For a while…

Epilogue

Garrett looked into the mirror hung above his bathroom sink and studied his reflection. He had a few more gray hairs around his temples but, considering all that transpired the previous summer, he thought more gray hair a small price to pay. Especially since Paige, Ty, and Trowa's very existence were at stake. As always, Paige said the gray hairs made him look more distinguished. Garrett smiled at his distinguished reflection.

The additional gray hairs weren't the only difference displayed in the mirror. Garret was clean-shaven and had a fresh haircut. The combination of these two things made him look several years younger, despite the advanced graying. The biggest difference was Garrett's attire. Instead of the usual uniform or casual dress, Garrett wore a crisp, white, button-down shirt and a deep blue, with small, yellow polka dots, tie. Garrett straightened the tie for, perhaps, the tenth time and looked at his watch. It was almost eleven p.m.

Looking at his watch drew Garrett's attention to another big change in his life. The toothbrush holder now contained two permanent toothbrushes. Mandy's temporary move into Garrett's house during the werewolf scare turned into a permanent living arrangement. So permanent that, one evening in October, at dinner with Paige, Ty, Jasmine, and Becks, he kept the promise to stay close to Becks in Mike's absence, Garrett proposed to Mandy.

Not only did Paige approve of the proposal, Garrett got her blessing before asking. She helped him pick out the engagement ring. They set the wedding date for Saturday, April 30th, 2016.

Garrett looked into the mirror a final time, switched off the light, and left the bathroom.

Mandy wasn't ready to leave. Her current dilemma revolved around which shoes to wear. She was on her knees in front of the closet holding two different colored shoes, one red and one black, against her blue dress.

"Which ones, Garrett? Black goes better, but red is festive. Should I change my dress? Maybe a green dress? Green and red are appropriate colors. I know Paige is wearin' a green dress and we shouldn't match. I could wear my red dress."

"Don't change your dress. No time. Wear the red shoes."

"Black it is," Mandy said with a smile.

Garrett chuckled. "Why'd ya even ask?"

"'Cause I knew you'd tell me the wrong ones."

Garrett laughed. "Whatever ya do, do it quick. We're leavin' in a few minutes. I'll be in the livin' room waitin' for y'all."

When he walked into the living room, it didn't surprise him to find Paige wasn't there, ready to go either. As Paige got older, she took longer and longer to get ready. Garrett assumed this was something women did on purpose. It had happened to Garrett his whole life. Girlfriends who weren't ready when he showed to take them out, his wife, Lacy, who had never been ready on time when they went somewhere, and Mandy, who he resorted to telling deceptively early departure times, so she would be ready to go in time to get where they were going. Why should Paige be any different?

Garrett thought about the Brad Paisley song *Waitin' on a Woman* and chuckled.

That song summed up Garrett's experience with women in five-minutes.

Garrett sat down on the couch and waited for Paige and Mandy.

After a few more minutes, Garrett looked at his watch. It was eleven o five p.m.

He got up. "Time to go, ladies."

"Almost ready, Daddy," Paige replied through her closed bedroom door.

"I'm comin'," Mandy said from their bedroom.

Another minute slipped by and, just as Garrett started to call for them again, Paige came out of her bedroom.

"How do I look, Daddy?"

As far as Garrett was concerned, Paige would always be the most beautiful girl in the world. He was more than a little biased, but the girl he saw standing before him radiated beauty in spectrums beyond the visible. Her long, brown hair was off her shoulders in a loose bun, with several strands falling around her face and neck. It appeared to have been done quickly, but Garrett thought Paige worked on that look for quite a while. She was wearing an emerald, green dress that matched her eyes and made them 'pop.' Around Paige's neck hung the silver necklace and crucifix that seemed to cling to her chest.

Garrett stared at the little silver crucifix and thought about its significance.

Paige noticed her daddy looking at the crucifix and knew he was thinking about the horrible things that happened. She inadvertently ran her finger down the front of the crucifix. Paige did this often without realizing she was doing it. Feeling the small sculpture of Christ on the cross brought her comfort. He was with her, always.

When Paige ran her finger over the crucifix, something Garrett noticed her doing frequently, he came out of his thoughts. "Ya look beautiful."

Paige blushed. "You always say that, Daddy."

Garrett smiled. "That's 'cause it's always true, sweetheart."

Paige walked up to her daddy and straightened his tie. It had still been a little crooked. "Look at you. All dressed up and lookin' handsome."

Garrett grinned. "Yeah, right. I look and feel stupid. This isn't about me. This is your night. Ya ready to go?"

Paige nodded.

As Garrett opened his mouth to call for Mandy, she came out of the bedroom. It didn't surprise Garrett to see Mandy changed her dress. She wore the red dress and black shoes. She looked beautiful, too.

"Well?" Mandy asked.

"I'm the luckiest guy on the planet."

"You look beautiful," Paige added.

"Thank you, Paige. You do, too," Mandy repaid the compliment.

Garrett looked at his watch again. "Time to go, pretty ladies."

They grabbed their winter coats off the hat rack beside the front door, bundled up, and stepped out into the chilly night.

As they stepped off the front porch, Paige looked up into the extremely clear night. Directly above them, as if there to light their way and no one else's, a silvery-white, full moon with a radiant halo around it shone down.

Paige tugged on Garrett's coat sleeve. "Look up, Daddy."

Garrett looked up at the beautiful glowing orb and came to a stop. Paige and Mandy stopped, too.

After several seconds of silence, Paige said, "It's hard to believe somethin' that beautiful can bring somethin' so ugly. I'm glad my wolf doesn't have to transform when there's a full moon like other werewolves."

Garrett nodded in agreement but said nothing.

Paige added, "Do ya think werewolves will ever come here again? That somethin' else might come, like Doctor James and Miss Lola said."

Garrett considered this question many times since his recurring nightmare experience became reality.

He didn't have an answer for Paige, but he said, "I don't know, but I doubt they will."

"Why?" Paige asked.

Garrett sensed Paige's gaze shift from the moon to him. He looked down at her and, sure enough, she looked at him.

Garrett smiled. "Because they know we know how to kill the bastards."

"Beside they'd have you to contend with," Mandy added.

Paige laughed and a vapor cloud of her warm breath erupted into the near freezing night air.

When Paige stopped laughing, Garrett said, "Let's get gone or we're gonna be late."

"Can I drive?" Paige asked as they walked toward the truck.

"You can drive your car, but I'm takin' my truck and I'm drivin' it," Garrett responded in a joking tone.

Paige said, "Fine, you drive. Get all the drivin' in ya can before you're too old to drive and they take your license."

"That's a long way off, kiddo," Garret reminded her.

Paige grinned. "I don't know 'bout that, Daddy. You're gettin' awful gray these days. Folks might think you're older than ya are."

Garrett scoffed. "I thought ya said the gray hair made me look distinguished?"

"Old and distinguished, Daddy. *Old* and distinguished."

"I think your gray hairs makes ya look handsome," Mandy chimed in.

"Thank you, Mandy. For that, ya get to sit up front."

"It makes ya look older, though," Mandy added with a giggle.

Garrett opened the driver's side door. "Well, I hope my old ass doesn't forget where we're goin'."

Paige laughed. "All the more reason I should drive."

Garrett shook his head. "Nice try. Jump in or I'm leavin' without y'all."

Paige and Mandy shared a giggled and got into the truck.

Garrett started the engine and cranked the heat to high. It would be several minutes before the engine was hot enough to pump warm air into the cab, but they couldn't wait. A blue eleven thirteen glowed from the in-dash clock.

Mandy and Paige were already putting their seatbelt on, but, out of habit, Garrett said, "Buckle up."

After putting his seatbelt on, Garrett put the truck in drive, circled around in the front yard, and headed down the driveway. He took a left on County Road Five Eighty-Eight and headed south.

~ * ~

Saint Joseph's Catholic Church served a small, rural parish south of Pine View. At any given Mass, there might be fifteen to twenty parishioners in the pews and their average age would be north of sixty. This Mass was different. The gravel parking lot was filled to capacity and parishioners were streaming into the small church by the dozens. All the excited children in attendance lowered the average age significantly.

Father Mike Young stood outside the church's front doors, in the cold, and welcomed the faithful, and the part-time faithful, with enthusiasm. Hardy handshakes and hugs for everyone. They were his parishioners. He felt thankful for each one of them, regardless of when or why they attended Mass.

~ * ~

Father Mike, which he preferred to be addressed as, was a bit of an oddity in the modern Catholic priesthood. He was young, twenty nine years old, and from Orlando, Florida. He knew from a very young age he wanted to be a priest and devoted his life to that calling. After attending Saint John Vianney College Seminary in Miami, Florida and taking his vows, he spent two years under the guidance of Father Juan Martinez at Blessed Sacrament Catholic Church in Havana, Florida, which served the Cuban American population.

Between his formal foreign language education in Spanish, and the two years he spent with Father Martinez, Father Mike became fluent in

Spanish, which helped him when Saint Joseph's Catholic Church in Pine View, Texas, needed a new priest. Saint Joseph's Catholic Church served the Hispanic population in the Pine View area with daily Spanish only Masses and two weekend, one on Saturday evening and one on Sunday morning, Spanish only Masses. Father Mike accepted the parish appointment and hadn't regretted the decision once in the two years he'd been there.

~ * ~

As the crowd of parishioners thinned, Father Mike looked at his watch. It was eleven fifty-five p.m. Christmas Eve Midnight Mass, which explained the influx of part-time faithful and children, started in five minutes and Paige hadn't arrived yet.

Father Mike got to know Paige well over the previous few months and took a special interest in her growing faith. Whenever they talked, he noticed how Paige constantly traced her finger over the crucifix that hung around her neck. He knew something troubled her from the events related to the horrible murders of fifteen high school students at the Mill Road Barn, one of whom had been her boyfriend. Father Mike presided over three of the funerals. Paige hadn't volunteered to reveal her troubles, in confession or informal conversations. Father Mike didn't press her to. He felt sure she'd talk with him when she was ready.

Father Mike started to step inside the church and close the doors to the chilly night when a truck pulled up in front of the church. Paige jumped out of the truck's back seat and hurried toward Father Michel.

Garrett lowered the driver's door window. "Wasn't me, Father. I was ready on time."

Before Father Mike could respond, Paige said, "I'm sorry, Father Mike."

Father Mike smiled. "I'm just glad you made it. We *need* you. Now get in there and get ready. We're about to start."

As Paige hurried into the church, Garrett said, "I'll park, and we'll be in directly."

Father Mike gave Garrett a 'thumbs up' and followed Paige into the church.

By the time Garrett found a place to park and made it inside the church, Father Mike had started Mass. Although he wasn't Catholic,

Garrett appreciated the beauty and majesty of the Catholic Mass.

Since the werewolf ordeal, Paige became more devoted to her adopted religion. Garrett and Mandy accompanied her to Mass regularly. He hadn't told Paige, because he wasn't sure yet, but he had been considering converting, too. Not just for Paige, though. Mandy, being Catholic, wanted to be married in the Church. The Church allowed non-Catholics to marry Catholics, but Garrett thought it would be a nice surprise for Mandy.

Garrett and Mandy found a space on a pew in the last row. They sat down quietly. Garrett scanned the front of the church for Paige. She wasn't hard to spot in the emerald, green dress. She stood to the right of the altar with the rest of the choir.

When Paige told him she wanted to join the church choir, it came as a bit of a surprise. She'd never showed an interest in singing that Garrett knew of, but he endorsed her decision whole-heartedly. Since then, Garrett saw her with the choir frequently, but she'd told him she had a surprise for him during the Midnight Mass. Garrett settled in and waited.

The wait took longer than Garrett expected. The Mass took particularly long because Father Mike celebrated it in English and Spanish. After saying something in English, he would repeat it in Spanish. It was worth the wait.

As Communion started, Garrett saw Paige step forward and stand in front of a single microphone. The piano player started playing *Silent Night* softly while the full choir hummed along behind Paige. As Paige opened her mouth to sing, Garrett, on his knees like the Catholic parishioners, realized he'd squeezed the back of the pew in front of him so tightly his knuckles were white. He did not know what to expect.

Paige's nerves were so bad her hands shook. She clasped them together in front of her stomach, took a deep breath, and started singing. She had a beautiful voice, but it came out soft and timid. She looked toward the choir director. He raised his chin and made hand motions, instructing her to project her full voice. She did and the next words came out louder and stronger. The choir director smiled and gave her a wink.

Paige's confidence grew, and with it, her voice grew. She forgot about the people in the church, except for her daddy. She could see him and Mandy kneeling in the back pew. The solo was the surprise she'd told him about and she sang for him.

Her singing stunned Garrett. He did not know Paige could carry a note, let alone produce something as beautiful as her version of *Silent Night*, which differed from the normal version he'd heard his whole life. Within a few seconds of Paige's singing, amazed and happy tears ran down Garrett's face freely.

When Paige finished singing, something Garrett never witnessed in any church before happened. The parishioners applauded. Father Mike stopped delivering Communion and clapped.

Paige's cheeks flushed red, but she managed a timid, "Thank you."

She stepped back and joined the rest of the choir. They welcomed her with hugs and high-fives.

When Mass ended, Garrett kept his seat. He knew from previous attendance the choir helped put things back in order. They put missalettes, songbooks, and prayer cards back in the wooden pockets on the backs of the pews and made sure all the knee pads were flipped up, so as not to create a tripping hazard when folks arrived for the next Mass. This took longer than usual, too. Partly because of the influx of the part-time faithful, but mostly because they all wanted to congratulate Paige on her beautiful rendition of *Silent Night*.

Garrett watched the precession of congratulatory parishioners with beaming, fatherly pride for several minutes. When the crowd thinned to a few remaining people, Garrett got up and started working his way toward the altar, putting the assorted materials in the pew-back pockets, and flipping up knee pads as he went. Mandy did the same.

By the time they got to the front first pew, there were only a few people left around Paige, and they were mostly choir members. Garrett maneuvered between them, wrapped Paige in a tight hug, and lifted her from the ground.

Paige giggled. "Did ya like it?"

Garrett hugged her tighter. "I *loved* it. You're *amazin'*, Paige-Turner."

Paige kissed Garrett's cheek. "Thank you, Daddy. You can put me down now."

Although he didn't want the hug to end, Garrett lowered Paige to the floor.

It was Mandy's turn to wrap Paige in a warm embrace.

"That was beautiful, Paige. I didn't know ya could sing like that," Mandy said.

Blushing, Paige said, "Thank you, Mandy."

The other choir members dispersed and started putting the side of the church Garrett and Mandy hadn't done back in order.

Father Mike stepped up to Paige and took her right hand in both of his. "That was wonderful, Paige."

Paige blushed again, or maybe she never stopped blushing. "Thank you, Father Mike."

Father Mike turned to Garrett and Mandy. "Paige must fill your home with beautiful singing."

Garrett shifted his gaze from Father Mike to Paige. "Actually, it isn't. Until tonight, I didn't know Paige could sing like that."

Father Mike's gaze shifted to Paige as well, and he said, "Paige…this is a gift from God. Don't keep it to yourself. Share it. Celebrate it often."

Paige looked at the two men in front of her, her two fathers. One her hero and the other her spiritual advisor. She ran her finger across the crucifix and added her heavenly Father to the list of men who watched over her. At that moment, all her worries melted away.

Paige smiled. "I will…Fathers."

The plural 'Fathers' wasn't lost on either man, and smiles spread across their faces.

Father Mike made a quick walk-through of the church to make sure everything was in order. Finding it in order, he wished everyone a "Blessed Christmas" and dismissed them.

By the time Garrett, Mandy, and Paige exited the church, the parking lot had nearly emptied and, because they arrived late, Garrett's truck was the farthest away.

As they made their way across the parking lot, gravel crunching under their feet, Paige saw one of her fellow choir members about to get into her car. Her name was Melanie Zane, and she was a senior at Pine View High School.

Like Paige, Melanie survived the MRB Massacre, as they referred to it afterward. Because of their shared experience, faith, and signing, Paige became close friends with Melanie in the recent months.

Paige tugged on Garrett's coat sleeve. "I'll be right back."

Before Garrett could ask where, Paige trotted off toward Melanie.

Garrett hollered, "We'll get the truck and come get ya."

Paige waved an 'OK' sign above her head and kept heading toward Melanie.

Garrett, with Mandy's hand in his, crunched his way across the gravel parking lot, climbed into his truck, and started it. He had to drive through a small ditch to gain access to the parking lot, but it was dry, and the truck traversed the ditch easily. By the time he pulled up next to Melanie's car, it was the last one in the parking lot.

He heard Paige say something to Melanie but, through the closed door and engine noise, he couldn't make out what she said. Whatever she said, Melanie found funny, because she laughed loudly. Paige turned and opened the truck door to get inside.

When the door opened, Melanie said, "Merry Christmas, Mister Garrett. You too, Miss Mandy."

Garrett waved and, together, he and Mandy said, "Merry Christmas to you, Melanie."

A big smile spread across Melanie's pretty face, and she said, "I think it will be. Now that…ya know."

Garrett knew. The werewolves were gone.

Garrett gave Melanie a reassuring smile. "I think you're right." Then he added, "Want me to wait until ya get in and get started?"

Melanie shook her head. "No, sir. Thank you, though. I like to sit in my car and reflect a little after Mass."

Garrett briefly considered Melanie's statement. His instinct compelled him to wait, but the horrors of last summer were behind them. Pine View County had one of the lowest violent crime rates in Texas. In the country.

"Ya sure?" Garrett asked.

Melanie nodded. "I'm sure. Thank you, though."

Paige chimed in with, "She'll be okay, Daddy."

Somewhat reluctantly, Garrett nodded and gave Melanie a wave.

Paige said, "I'll call ya tomorrow," and shut the truck door.

Garrett put the truck in drive and started idling away at a snail's pace. He watched in the review mirror as Melanie got into her car. Garrett saw a puff of heated exhaust escape the tailpipe and knew the car started. He pressed down on the accelerator a little and turned left onto the gravel road that led to County Road Five Eighty-Eight. The turn brought Garrett's truck along the side of the church parking lot on his left.

Garrett kept at a slow speed and monitored Melanie's car. She'd parked it on the far side of the parking lot facing the small church cemetery and close to the woods on the right. He didn't feel good about leaving her there alone.

Paige could sense her dad's unease. She reached between the seats and squeezed Garrett's coat sleeve.

When Garrett looked at her, Paige said, "She'll be okay, Daddy."

Garrett smiled, but it felt forced. "How can ya be sure?"

Paige smiled. "Because all the monsters are dead."

As Paige's words sank in, the smile became less forced. He looked at Melanie's car in the review mirror one last time. He pushed down on the accelerator and left Saint Joseph's Catholic Church behind.

Pine View and Pine View County are safe again, Garrett thought.

~ * ~

A shadow, blacker than the surrounding darkness, drifted soundlessly through the dense East Texas forest south of Pine View County. The sound of a woman laughing penetrated the otherwise silent night. The shadow shifted and turned in the direction from which the laughter came. Narrow, silver eyes flashed in the blacker darkness, and, with the faint flutter of leathery wings, the shadow dissolved into the mist and disappeared.

About the Author

leewpayne@me.com

Lee W. Payne has a BS, MA, and Ph.D. in Political Science. He is a Professor of Political Science at Stephen F. Austin State University, where he has taught since 2006. Lee is well published in peer-reviewed academic journals and textbooks but has always enjoyed storytelling. The Pack is his first novel and the first of three novels in the subtitled Pine View County Trilogy. Lee lives in Nacogdoches, Texas with his English Bulldog, Tank.

Made in the USA
Middletown, DE
04 June 2024